TRAITOR'S SUN

A Novel of Darkover

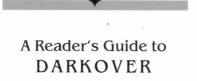

A Reader's Guide to
DARKOVER

THE FOUNDING

A "lost ship" of Terran origin, in the pre-Empire colonizing days, lands on a planet with a dim red star, later to be called Darkover.
DARKOVER LANDFALL

THE AGES OF CHAOS

1,000 years after the original landfall settlement, society has returned to the feudal level. The Darkovans, their Terran technology renounced or forgotten, have turned instead to free-wheeling, out-of-control matrix technology, psi powers and terrible psi weapons. The populace lives under the domination of the Towers and a tyrannical breeding program to staff the Towers with unnaturally powerful, inbred gifts of *laran*.
STORMQUEEN!
HAWKMISTRESS!

THE HUNDRED KINGDOMS

An age of war and strife retaining many of the decimating and disastrous effects of the Ages of Chaos. The lands which are later to become the Seven Domains are divided by continuous border conflicts into a multitude of small, belligerent kingdoms, named for convenience "The Hundred Kingdoms." The close of this era is heralded by the adoption of the Compact, instituted by Varzil the Good. A landmark and turning point in the history of Darkover, the Compact bans all distance weapons, making it a matter of honor that one who seeks to kill must himself face equal risk of death.
TWO TO CONQUER
THE HEIRS OF HAMMERFELL

THE RENUNCIATES

During the Ages of Chaos and the time of the Hundred Kingdoms, there were two orders of women who set themselves apart from the patriarchal nature of Darkovan feudal society: the priestesses of Avarra, and the warriors of the Sisterhood of the Sword. Eventually these two independent groups merged to form the powerful and legally chartered Order of Renunciates or Free Amazons, a guild of women bound only by oath as a sisterhood of mutual responsibility. Their primary allegiance is to each other rather than to family, clan, caste or any man save a temporary employer. Alone among Darkovan women, they are exempt from the usual legal restrictions and protections. Their reason for existence is to provide the women of Darkover an alternative to their socially restrictive lives.

THE SHATTERED CHAIN
THENDARA HOUSE
CITY OF SORCERY

AGAINST THE TERRANS
—THE FIRST AGE (Recontact)

After the Hastur Wars, the Hundred Kingdoms are consolidated into the Seven Domains, and ruled by a hereditary aristocracy of seven families, called the Comyn, allegedly descended from the legendary Hastur, Lord of Light. It is during this era that the Terran Empire, really a form of confederacy, rediscovers Darkover, which they know as the fourth planet of the Cottman star system. The fact that Darkover is a lost colony of the Empire is not easily or readily acknowledged by Darkovans and their Comyn overlords.

REDISCOVERY *(with Mercedes Lackey)*
THE SPELL SWORD
THE FORBIDDEN TOWER
STAR OF DANGER
WINDS OF DARKOVER

AGAINST THE TERRANS
—THE SECOND AGE (After the Comyn)

With the initial shock of recontact beginning to wear off, and the Terran spaceport a permanent establishment on the outskirts of the city of Thendara, the younger and less traditional elements of Darkovan society begin the first real exchange of knowledge with the Terrans—learning Terran science and technology and teaching Darkovan matrix technology in turn. Eventually Regis Hastur, the young Comyn lord most active in these exchanges, becomes Regent in a provisional government allied to the Terrans. Darkover is once again reunited with its founding Empire.

THE BLOODY SUN
HERITAGE OF HASTUR
THE PLANET SAVERS
SHARRA'S EXILE
WORLD WRECKERS
EXILE'S SONG
THE SHADOW MATRIX
TRAITOR'S SUN

THE DARKOVER ANTHOLOGIES

These volumes of stories, edited by Marion Zimmer Bradley, strive to "fill in the blanks" of Darkovan history and elaborate on the eras, tales and characters which have captured readers' imaginations.

THE KEEPER'S PRICE
SWORD OF CHAOS
FREE AMAZONS OF DARKOVER
THE OTHER SIDE OF THE MIRROR
RED SUN OF DARKOVER
FOUR MOONS OF DARKOVER
DOMAINS OF DARKOVER
RENUNCIATES OF DARKOVER
LERONI OF DARKOVER
TOWERS OF DARKOVER
MARION ZIMMER BRADLEY'S DARKOVER
SNOWS OF DARKOVER

TRAITOR'S SUN

A Novel of Darkover

MARION ZIMMER BRADLEY

DAW BOOKS, INC.

DONALD A. WOLLHEIM, FOUNDER
375 Hudson Street, New York, NY 10014

ELIZABETH R. WOLLHEIM
SHEILA E. GILBERT
PUBLISHERS
http://www.dawbooks.com

First Printing, January 1999
1   2   3   4   5   6   7   8   9

DAW TRADEMARK REGISTERED
U.S. PAT. OFF. AND FOREIGN COUNTRIES
—MARCA REGISTRADA
HECHO EN U.S.A.

PRINTED IN THE U.S.A.

For Susan M. Shwartz,
Scholar, Historian and Friend

PROLOGUE

Herm Aldaran snapped awake, his heart pounding and sweat streaming down his chest. He gasped for air and struggled to push aside the bed-clothes, his head throbbing. He sat there, blinking in the faint light that came from the common room of the small apartment, and swallowed hard. His dry mouth tasted like iron filings and his feet felt alien and disconnected from his body. Though his nightrobe was almost drenched around his broad chest, part of the sleeve was still dry enough to use to wipe the moisture off his face. As Herm stood up, the room spun, and he nearly sat down again.

At last his body stopped shaking, and his heart slowed to a more normal rhythm. He glanced at Katherine, his wife of more than a decade, still undisturbed by his movements. In the dim light Herm could see her dark hair spread across the pillow, and the sweep of her brow below it, the curve of her mouth beneath the strong nose. Not for the first time he wondered why such a beautiful woman had consented to marry a plain fellow like himself. It was a puzzle, but he knew it was not because he was wealthy—he was not—or had the ambiguous honor of being the Senator from Cottman IV, as the Terran Federation designated Darkover,

1

the world of his birth. He gazed at her, letting his mind wander a bit, and felt himself settle into relative calm.

Herm realized he would not be able to go back to sleep anytime soon, so he rose and left the bedroom as quietly as possible, careful not to rouse Katherine. He peeped around the thin partition that separated their sleeping quarters from those of their two children and found them undisturbed. Then he padded across the dingy tiles in the small food preparation station and opened the cool cabinet. The carafe of juice was cold in his fingers, and he had a desire to drink right out of the lip of it. Until he held it, he had not realized he was still trembling slightly. He forced himself to find a glass, and poured some of the yellow liquid into it. Then he gulped down half the glass, letting the tart flavor of the juice wash away the nasty taste on his tongue. The cold liquid hit his belly like a blow, and for a moment he felt as if he had swallowed acid. Then the dreadful sensation vanished, although his stomach continued to protest for several seconds. He knew it was only an illusion, but he had the feeling that he could sense the sugar in the juice entering his bloodstream. His breathing deepened, and he shivered all over, chilled where he had been burning only a few moments earlier.

Herm sank down onto one of the stools that stood beside the long counter which served as the eating area, put the glass down before he dropped it, and forced himself to empty his mind. A sense of utter *wrongness* played along his nerves, fretting like the discordant notes of some classic industrial symphony. That style of music had enjoyed a resurgence during his first years in the Chamber of Deputies of the Federation legislature, and he had been dragged to a few concerts. It had stuck in his mind, much to his disgust, for it was not music as he had thought of it, but more like noise, and rather unpleasant noise at that. He hated it, as he hated the stool, the smallness of the room in which he sat, and the cramped quarters assigned him as Darkover's Federation Senator.

When Lew Alton had still been Senator, he had had somewhat larger quarters, and a home on Thetis as well. But those days were gone now, and few if any members of the legislature had off-world places unless they were inherited ones. The Office of Finance had imposed strict travel limitations a few years earlier, which restricted the movements of the members. They could go to their home worlds for elections every five Terran years, but Herm never had returned to Darkover. He had not been elected, but instead had been appointed by Regis Hastur, a man he had never actually met, twenty-three years before. He had worked for eight years in the Chamber of Deputies, and when Lew Alton had vacated the Senate seat, he had taken his place.

Policy changes imposed by the Office of Finance, and numerous other dictates over the years, had ultimately left the legislature prisoner to the whims of Premier Sandra Nagy and her Expansionist cronies. Despite its name, the Expansionists were an austere bunch of autocrats, and each year had seen more and more restrictions imposed on everyone except the most favored members of the Party. As he had told his wife once, on a rare occasion when he was moderately certain there were no listening devices nearby, "The Expansionists say there are limited resources in the Federation—and all of them are the rightful property of the Expansionists!" She had not even laughed.

The three-room apartment was a better domicile than most ordinary Terrans possessed, but Herm had grown up in Aldaran Castle, with stone walls around him, and great, roaring hearths sending out gusts of scent-laden sooty, heated air. An odd thing to miss, after more than two decades. But the scentless, stifling atmosphere of the apartment, which was warm all the year round because of the central controls of the building, still made him feel like a trapped animal. There were eight billion people on the planet, and more every year. He had a great longing for space, for stretches of conifers and the smell of mountain balsam, for the cry of the Hellers' hawks, their russet plumage bright against a sky illuminated by a ruddy sun.

It was not simply a nostalgia for unsullied expanses of gleaming snow that stirred him. Even after two decades, he remained uncomfortable with his situation—felt alien. Herm had never felt entirely clean after using a sonic shower, although it removed all the dead skin and oil from his body. Water, like everything else, was rationed and taxed, and he had a deep longing for a great wallow in a tub of steaming water, scented with oil of lavender. A thick towel of Dry Town cotton to dry with, and a robe of felted wool over his body completed the pleasant fantasy. No clammy synthetic on his skin. . . .

It made his heart ache to think of those things, and he wondered at himself. He had spent almost half his life off Darkover, and felt he should have accustomed himself to it by now. But if anything, his homesickness grew worse and worse. For a moment he remembered his younger self, a yokel by Federation standards, arriving to represent his world in the lower chamber. He had been awed by the huge buildings, the hives and sky-scrapers, the presence of technologies unimaginable on his far-distant world. Despite having grown up with various Terrans who were welcomed at Aldaran Castle, and having a mother who claimed Terra as the planet of her birth, he had quickly realized he was incredibly ignorant. He did not remember much about his mother, for she had died when he was three. And certainly nothing he remembered her saying prepared him for the reality he experienced during his first year in the Chamber of Deputies. She had granted him a strange, unDarkovan name which he understood now was ancient and unusual even by Terran standards, a predisposition toward baldness, and beyond that only distant fragmented memories. *Dom* Damon Aldaran's wives, all three of them, had perished—his father had been tragically unlucky.

It had been fortunate that Lew was there to help him through those first few years. He had learned how to use the technology, how to access newsfeeds on a computer and communicate with people almost instantly. More importantly, Lew Alton had set him to studying the literature and philosophy of a hundred planets, and the complex history of the Federation itself. At first he had been unsure of the purpose of these efforts, and had only read the texts in order to please the older man. But slowly he had come to understand how uneducated he was for the task he had been chosen to perform. With great difficulty he had started to understand the thinking of the Federation, how it was founded on ancient ideas that had never taken root on Darkover—some of them very good ideas.

But now he knew that these ideals were being abandoned, and that the Federation was moving into an area of military dominance and oppression. It had happened before, in the history of humans, but he wished it was not occurring during his own lifetime. And it was not something he could discuss openly, as had been possible when he first came from Darkover. Like every other person on the planet, he was subject to constant observation. And there was nothing he could do about it, since disabling the spy eyes that watched and listened was a serious offense. He wondered what the average person thought about it or if they thought at all. Likely they did not, hypnotized as they were with mediafeeds and vidrams.

But Herm knew that the situation was bad and getting worse all the time. Trillions of credits were disbursed every year to create new technologies. At the same time, very little was spent on the day-to-day existence of ordinary people, whose lives became ever more difficult. He had tried to understand this phenomenon, but it still made no sense to him, and, like most of his fellow legislators, he was virtually powerless to change it.

He was being morbid. It must just be the strain of recent days. Regis Hastur had never filled his original place in the Chamber of Deputies after Herm had vacated it, and he had not encountered another native of his planet in sixteen years. This rarely weighed on him, but he was so tired now that it seemed a heavy burden.

Of late, sleep had become a rare commodity, as the meetings, both public and private, in the two chambers of the Federation legislature had gone far into what passed for night in this dreadful place. Any of Zandru's frozen hells seemed preferable at that moment. The Senate, his labor of almost sixteen years now, was a hornet's nest stirred with an Expansionist stick, and the Chamber of Deputies was little better. But he had dealt with political crises before without waking up in the middle of the night with his heart trying to hammer its way through his chest.

As much as Herm hated living in the Federation, he actually enjoyed the constant turmoil of political life. Or he had until a few months before, when the Expansionist party had finally achieved a slim majority in both houses, and begun to implement policies he opposed. New taxes had been passed for all member planets of the Federation, to build a fleet of dreadnaughts, great fighting ships, when there was no foe to defend against. Some worlds had protested, and even tried to rebel, and combat troops had been sent in to "keep order." It had gone from being a game at which he excelled, with his natural talent for verbal interplay, and the cunning which had always been his mainstay, to a daily nightmare from which he feared he would never awaken.

Recently the flow of events had disturbed a few of the more moderate Senators in the Expansionist Party itself. With what Herm regarded as enormous courage, these men and women had voted against their own majority on a critical defense bill, effectively destroying it, and bringing both the Senate and the Chamber to an impasse. Pressure had been brought, persuasion had been used, but to no avail. Except for endless conferences, meetings, and some lengthy speeches on the floor, no actual business had been conducted for nearly six weeks now, and it did not appear that any would be in the near future. The leaders of the Expansionists were becoming more and more desperate, and the only good that had come out of the mess was that no more new taxes had been passed in the interim. But no benefit could ultimately come from a paralyzed parliament. A government unable to act could inadvertently do more harm than good.

Herm tried to shake away the dour mood that enveloped his mind, and found himself remembering one of the last conversations he had had with Lew Alton, just before Lew had resigned his office and returned to Darkover. Lucky man. He wasn't balancing his bottom on a stingy stool, trying to make sense out of a hysteria that had grown and grown over the past decade. What had he said? Ah, yes. "There may come a time when the Federation loses its collective mind, Hermes, and when that happens, if it does, I cannot really advise you what to do. But when that day arrives, you will know it in your bones. And then you must decide whether to stay and fight, or run from the fracas. Believe me, it will be evident to your intelligence. Trust your instincts then, young man."

Good advice, and still sound. But things were different now than when Lew had still been Darkover's Senator. Then Herm had not been married—what a singularly foolish thing to have done, to wed a widow from Renney with a small son, Amaury. But he had been hopelessly in love! Now they had their own child, his daughter Terése, a delightful girl of nearly ten. They were the light of his life, and he knew that without the anchor of Kate and the children he would have been even more miserable than he was. He realized he had not thought the matter through thoroughly when he met her, fell totally in love, and married her a month afterward. Certainly he had not considered the problems of a half-Darkovan child reaching an age where threshold sickness and the onset of *laran* were real concerns. And he had never told Katherine about the peculiar inbred paranormal talents of his people, although he had always intended to . . . someday. The moment just had never seemed right. And what, after all, would he say? "Oh, by the way, Kate, I've been meaning to tell you that I can read the minds of other people."

Herm shuddered at the imagined scene that would certainly follow. No, he had not told her the truth, not clever Herm. He had just gone on, wheeling and dealing, keeping Darkover safe from Federation predators, and put the matter off until another day. A wave of regret and guilt swept through him, and his stomach felt full of angry insects.

After his mother's death, he had became a private child and had grown into a secretive adult, a habit which had stood him in good stead during his years in the Federation. The very walls had ears and eyes, even those in this miserable excuse for a kitchen—the so called FP Station. Well, two counters, a tiny sink, a cool box and heating compartment were nothing like a vast stone chamber with a beehive-shaped oven in one corner, one or two large fireplaces, and a long table where the servants could sit and eat and gossip. The old cook at Aldaran Castle—she was probably dead now—had had a way of fixing water fowl with vegetables that was wonderful, and his mouth watered at the thought of it. He had not tasted fresh meat since he and Katherine had gone to Renney nine years before. Vat-grown protein had no flavor, even if it did nourish his body.

He forced the delightful vision of a plump fowl running with fat and pinkish juices out of his mind and tried to focus on his abrupt arousal. What had brought him out of his desperately needed rest? He had no sense of a dream, so it must have been something else. Herm shivered all over, in spite of the warmth of the room, and watched the flesh crinkle along his forearms. He had not been dreaming at all. No, it was almost certainly an occurrence of the Aldaran Gift, a foresight he would probably wish to avoid, once he remembered what it was. His *laran* was decent, good enough to catch the occasional thoughts of the men and women he dealt with every day, an advantage he was careful not to display or abuse. He relied much more on his native cunning than on his telepathy—it was a more dependable talent, and less ethically dubious.

Besides, he was a diplomat, not a spy, and just because the Federation kept a watchful eye and ear on his every movement did not seem sufficient reason to imitate them. But he did wonder what the unseen auditors made of his love trysts with Kate. Nothing, most likely, since they must record millions of such incidents every night. Still, the lack of real privacy rankled, the more so because he was sure he was being observed even now. The things that human beings would do in the name of order never failed to astound him.

Now, all he had to do was remember what had awakened him, and get back to sleep. Something was most assuredly up, but it had felt that way for weeks. He had caught the occasional thoughts in the minds of his fellow legislators, and they were deeply perturbed. This was not limited to the opposition either, for he had noticed more than a few Expansionist Senators mentally squirming, their thoughts giving lie to the words issuing from their mouths. Lacking the Alton Gift of forced rapport, which had given his predecessor such an advantage, Herm made do with scraps of unguarded thought, and what he mostly heard was more banal or self-serving than useful.

The halls and conference rooms of the Senate Building were permeated with fear these days, and Herm had observed long-time allies eyeing one another suspiciously. There was good reason to be afraid. Opposition to Expansionist strategies was dangerous, and more than a few Senators had had unexplained accidents or sudden illnesses in the last few years. Trust and the capacity for reasonable compromise, the foundation stones of representative government, had vanished almost completely, replaced by a wariness and paranoia that was chilling to glimpse in the unguarded minds of his fellows. It made the actions of people like Senator Ilmurit appear impossibly brave. She had crossed the aisle with seven other moderates and unwound the tenuously held majority the Expansionists had achieved with such enormous effort, and not a little treachery as well.

His eyes itched furiously, and his muscles twitched. It was infuriating, too, for he knew that he would not have had a vision for any trivial matter. He did not have the Aldaran Gift very strongly, but when it manifested itself, it was always important. Twice in the years he had served as Darkover's Senator it had helped him avoid political traps and betrayals.

He closed his eyes, feeling the tug of exhaustion, and tried to recall the warning that had awakened him. It was muddled, a collection of voices, shouts of distress and words he could barely make out. It took him several minutes of intense concentration to realize that it was not one thing, but two separate events, shuffled together so it was difficult to distinguish between them.

Two women? Yes, that was right. Who? Neither was his Kate, nor the voices of any of the female Senators or Deputies he knew. Then he recognized one, the very familiar voice of Sandra Nagy, the current Premier of the Federation. He had not known it at first because he was accustomed to her usually pleasant alto, the one in which she gave addresses which were broadcast throughout the reaches of the Terran Federation, explaining why taxes would be raised again, or why combat troops had been used against civilian populations.

Herm suddenly realized that he had had no vision, and no dream either, but instead the experience of clairaudience, which was the rarest manifestation of the Aldaran Gift. He had heard the future—if only he could remember the bedamned words! He tensed, knitting his brow fiercely, willing his mind to cough up some clarity and sense. Concentrate on Nagy, he told himself, and ignore the other sounds.

"I cannot permit the functioning of the Federation government to remain at a halt any longer," Herm heard at last. *"Since it is clear that the opposition is determined to hold the legislature hostage to their own inexplicable and selfish goals, I have no choice but to dissolve both the Senate and the Chamber of Deputies until such time as new elections can be held and order restored."*

Herm sat stunned for a moment. When was this going to occur? The Aldaran foresight was never exact, and it rarely offered such useful things as dates or times. He did not doubt the forehearing, however, but could only try to think what it would mean for Darkover.

It was not a complete surprise, for it had always been a possibility, under the constitution of the Federation. No Premier had disbanded the government in more than a century, since before the Terrans had come to Darkover, but he had read the history of such events. What he knew did not reassure him. As often as not, it was a first move to tyranny, oppression, and suffering. And the Federation had already gone a good way in that direction, with their spy eyes in even the meanest domicile, all in the name of security. There was an ever present fear of rebellion which had grown over the past decade until it colored everything. Even those Senators who were reasonable men and women seemed to have caught the contagion. As for the Expansionist members, they drank in their imagined responses to such revolts like fine wine, getting tipsy on vintage visions of retaliation. Sometimes he almost thought they enjoyed their fever dreams of a galaxy-wide apocalypse.

Lew Alton had been right all those years before—the Federation was going to hell in a handcart. The miracle was that it had taken this long. But what should he do now? And what of the other voice, the less distinct one, the unknown woman who had cried in his mind?

Run!

The single word in his mind rang like a great bell, blotting out all other considerations for a moment. Hermes-Gabriel Aldaran was afraid, and he felt no shame in confessing it to himself. He half rose off the uncomfortable stool, then sank back again. There were eyes watching him, and while it might be days or even weeks before any human eyes studied the record of this particular moment, he must be careful not to behave in a manner that would draw attention to his actions. He had Kate and the children to think of.

He went over the remembered words again, feeling more and more frustrated. When was she going to make this devastating announcement? What good did it do him to have foreknowledge if he lacked any clue as to whether the foreseen events would occur tomorrow or next week! Herm made himself consider the immediate situation as calmly and objectively as he was able. A handful of worlds were simmering on the edge of rebellion, and when the Premier disbanded the legislature, at least one of them would use it as an excuse to try to break with the Federation. He understood that, but he could not be sure that Nagy did. Her advisory council was made up almost entirely of the more extreme voices in the Party, those who sincerely believed that they knew better how to run the lives of everyone on Federation planets than their native peoples did themselves.

And what would the dissolution of the legislature mean for the governors, kings, and other ruling bodies of the member planets? Without representation, they would lose their voices completely. Would she suspend the Federation Constitution and institute martial law? Herm rubbed the short beard around his mouth reflectively. No, she would not go that far—at least not immediately. Instead, she and her cronies would wait for some planet to rebel, and use that as an excuse to declare a state of emergency. This was the logical course.

Had troops already been deployed to those planets regarded as either dangerous or potentially disloyal? Herm did not know, and there was no way he could gain access to the files where such information might exist without arousing immediate suspicion. He had better assume that portions of the Fleet were in place or on their way, just to be safe. Hadn't there been something about some war games in the Castor sector? He scratched his head and flogged his weary brain to remember. Yes, it was Castor. There were two worlds there which he would focus on, if he were some Expansionist strategist looking for trouble.

Satisfied for the instant that he had theorized as well as he could without any real information, Herm tried to analyze his own situation. Where did he stand? He was the unaligned Senator of a Protected Planet, and not an overt threat to anyone. He had been careful to cultivate an unthreatening personality, and this had served him well enough during his years. But Herm knew the tenor of the Expansionist mind well enough to realize that if you were not their ally, you were regarded as an enemy. He had seen some of his friends in the Senate destroyed by scandals that he knew were trumped up, and he did not want to wait around to find out if he would become the latest victim. That was unlikely, because Darkover was not an important world. But he had Kate and the children to consider, not just his own Aldaran hide. And once the Senate was disbanded, he would no longer have the immunity of his office to protect him and his family. He could be arrested then, or worse. If only he were not so weary and was able to think with a clear head. Instead, he was just plain scared, and was attempting to resist the impulse to flee.

Herm decided that he had to try to discover when Sandra Nagy was actually going to drop her political bomb, before he did anything more. He rose from the stool and padded across to the household terminal, knowing that at least this action would not arouse much attention from the spy eyes in the walls. He was in the habit of accessing the newsfeeds several times a day, and even at night if he couldn't sleep, as he was now. Indeed, it was such a typical thing that it might allay suspicion rather than otherwise.

He pressed his hand against the glassy surface of the comlink and waited. For several seconds nothing happened and his heart began to beat a bit faster, fearing that he was too late, and that events had rushed beyond his control, that he would be denied access and a goon squad of Expansionist bully boys would come knocking at the door. Then he scolded himself silently. The system had been sluggish for weeks now, due to power blackouts that occasionally blinded half a continent for hours at a time.

Everything on the planet—from voting to food ordering—was dependent on these electronic links. But the shortsightedness of the Expansionists had blocked the funds for improvements, and now the system was beginning to fall apart. It was, Herm knew, symptomatic of all that was wrong in the Federation. Infrastructures were decaying, and no one was able to get a bill through the legislature to do anything about it. The population kept increasing, but the services that supported the people were deteriorating, because the funds needed were being spent on armaments, on the construction of military ships and the training of troops. It was folly, and he knew that he was not the only one who was aware of it. Unfortunately, no one wanted to hear his voice, or those of others who suggested that spending on defense over basic needs was unsupportable.

He thought about his studies of history. However reluctantly they had begun, they were now almost an obsession. His love of history was one of the few pleasures outside his family that he had, an escape from the dreadful present he was living through. For some reason he found himself remembering the tale of a great empire which had existed on Terra just before the age of space travel, a nation that covered most of what had been called Asia and Europe. For half a century it had devoted itself to preparations for a war that never came, and finally it had collapsed into bits and pieces, bankrupted by its own fear. Perhaps the Expansionist movement would run the same course. This thought gave him cold comfort while he waited.

At last the terminal blinked into life. He scrolled the most recent newsfeeds, scanning the words rapidly, looking for any clues that might tell him how much time he had. He ignored reports of food shortages, yet another water riot in the Indonesian islands, the arrival of the Governor of Tau Ceti III for a state visit, and several other items. Ah, here it was, a terse tidbit buried at the end of the most recent feed. The Premier had announced a major speech before the combined houses three days hence. So, that was how much time he had to get as far away as he could. Not much, but enough. It felt right, down in his bones, just as Lew had said it would. And clever as he was, he had always kept a means of escape open.

For an instant all he could think of was that he was, at last, going to go back to Darkover—immediately. A wave of relief made him grin at the flashing screen. But, in all likelihood, he was not coming back, and that presented a fresh set of problems. He must take Kate and the children with him. That was simple enough, except that she would have questions about why they were abandoning their home. And he could hardly tell her the truth, for that would alert the monitors in the walls.

Hernes sighed. Life as a bachelor had been much simpler, but less satisfactory. Kate was an intelligent woman; she would just have to trust him because she would know he was thinking of their best interests. He spent a futile moment worrying over uprooting the children, and then forced it out of his mind. They were young and adaptable, and it was more important to keep them from harm than to worry about anything else. Later, out of reach of constant surveillance, he would explain things. It was not something he looked forward to. She would tear a strip off his hide for not finding some way of telling her earlier and it was probably less than he deserved.

With a grunt, he keyed a program into the comlink, one that had been placed there years before. A message popped up on the screen, with all the correct codes, telling him to return to Darkover immediately. He suppressed a grin, knowing it for a clever fraud, and hoping that the information ferrets had never discovered its existence. It certainly looked official, and if no one examined it too closely, it should allow him to remove himself and his family from danger.

Herm looked at it, tried to appear startled, scratching his head fretfully and muttered. Then, with a pleasure he had difficulty concealing, he keyed in another program. There was a further delay, and sweat puddled under his arms and ran down his sides. Then, almost magically, he found an open passage across Federation space booked on the first departing ship, in perfect order. It allowed him to use his privileged position to usurp the first available cabin, in the first class section of a Big Ship.

He derived a grim pleasure from using his trapdoor. These days, with the Expansionist restrictions, it sometimes took months to book passage, unless one had friends in the right places. But as a Senator he could still pull rank, even though he knew it meant that he would almost certainly disrupt some complete stranger's travel plans. He calmed his conscience by remembering it would likely discomfort some Expansionist party loyalist, since these were the people permitted travel for the most part.

The link scrolled and made a faint and not unpleasant humming noise as it worked. After several minutes a display came up, a routing with a transfer to Vainwal. The system accepted it without query, and he had the booking arranged. They had six hours to get their things together and go to the port. It was not a great deal of time, and he prayed that Katherine would not argue too much.

He allowed his shoulders to slump a little, exhausted from the tension of his efforts. As he relaxed, he heard the voices in his dream return, and realized that he still had not thought about the second one, the unknown voice, fainter than Nagy's. Frustrated, he struggled to hear it. Herm forced himself to take several deep breaths, to create some patience when what he most desired was action. He had only deciphered half the puzzle, and the second voice was likely as important as the first. He must not be hasty. It was hard. Focus, particularly when he was tired, was a difficult discipline. He shut his eyes and balled his fists, willing his mind to bring back the faint, distant words. There was nothing for a moment, and then a flood of images danced across his eyelids. He saw sheets of paper with neat lines on them, and then a bottle of ink fell over, spreading across the pages. *Something has happened to Regis!*

The words made him tremble. Herm forced himself to remain seated for a minute, calming his mind as well as he could. Perhaps his false message from Darkover was truer than he had imagined. He had no idea whose voice it was, reaching through time and space, across untold light-years, to find him in dream and rouse him to action. He was chilled to the bone, and the sweat on his chest was cold on his skin.

Inertia seemed to paralyze him briefly, as his mind spun in tangles of fruitless speculation. Then he made himself stand up, noticing that his knees protested a little, and cross the common room. He poured himself another half glass of juice, then put the container back into the cool box. He placed his empty glass in the rack for the sterilizer, took a deep breath, and prepared to go wake up Katherine. He would have to rush her, not give her time to think, to ask questions—or else abandon her and the children, and that was unthinkable. If only he was not so weary!

Marguerida Alton-Hastur sat at her desk and stared out the narrow window, unsettled for no reason she could put a name to. A glorious early autumn sky, with several interesting cloud shapes in it, filled the opening. She decided one resembled a camel, an animal that had never existed on Darkover and was now alive only in a few wildlife refuges, and remembered how much fun she had had when the children were little, trying to decide what clouds looked like. Once, several clouds had seemed to her gaze to be a pod of delfins frolicking in the seas of Thetis, the planet on which she had grown up. Marguerida had been unable to explain her sudden flood of tears, nor the nature of the images. Her children had never seen the sea, let alone bathed in it, and they could not understand her aching desire for warm oceans and balmy breezes. Funny—she had not thought of that day in ages. She must be getting old, wallowing in memories.

The children were all much too grown up for cloud-gazing now, even Yllana, the youngest, at eleven, and she rather missed the innocent game. Last Midsummer, Domenic, her eldest, had been declared his father's heir designate, despite the very vocal protects of Javanne Hastur, her difficult mother-in-law. It hardly seemed possible—the time had passed so quickly. Before long she might become a mother-in-law herself, and then a grandmother! She hoped that she would like her yet undiscovered daughter-in-law more than Javanne liked her, that she would be kinder, or at least more polite. *But not too soon,* she whispered to herself. As difficult as being a parent had turned out to be, she was in no hurry to have her children leave her.

She looked around the small office she kept in her suite of rooms in Comyn Castle. The hearth was ablaze, and the cozy room was fragrant with the smell of burning balsam. The paneled walls shone, reflecting the dancing light from the fire, and the colors in the pattern of the rug on the stone floor pleased her. The tang of fall penetrated even through the thick walls of Comyn Castle, a fresh smell that never failed to liven her mind. It had taken a long while to get used to the weather on Darkover, for Thetis was almost an endless summer. But now she actually looked forward to changing seasons and the festivals which punctuated them.

From the next room, she could hear the delightful tinkle of a clavier, where Ida Davidson was giving Yllana her music lessons. She smiled at the sound. It was not a syntheclavier of the sort which Ida had used when Marguerida had lived in her house during her years at the University. Such a device was prohibited on Darkover, since it used the advanced technologies of the Federation. Instead, it was a reasonable imitation of the noble ancestor of that instrument, crafted wholly on Darkover, of native woods and rare Darkovan metals, made from drawings Marguerida had obtained with great difficulty from the University archives. There had never been such a keyboard instrument on Darkover before, but now, after the struggle to create the first one, there were six in Thendara. Members of the Musicians Guild were writing music specifically for them. Yllana was not playing any of these home-grown compositions, but one of the Klieg Variations from the twenty-fourth century—formal, structured and a challenge for ten small fingers.

There was nothing whatever to disturb the serenity of the moment, as a speedy mental sweep of Comyn Castle assured her. The Alton Gift, which she had resented so bitterly when she first discovered she had it, had turned out to have its uses, one of which was the ability to scan the environment around her. Perhaps she was just being anxious for no reason. It had been a troubling year, with a summer that was the warmest in recent memory. The farmers had fretted over the possibility of drought, and the fire danger in the hills had been very great. There had been disturbances of another kind as well—some small riots in the markets of Thendara and reports of an uprising in Shainsa in the Dry Towns. But the rains had come in from the west at last, the balmy, near-sixty degree temperatures had vanished, and there had not been any outbreak of large fires.

She really must get down to work! This woolgathering was wasting valuable time, and her time was at a premium just now. Marguerida looked down at the stack of pages in front of her. They were staff sheets, covered with musical notation and accompanying lyrics. After nearly two decades of doubt and hesitation, she had finally succumbed to her great, secret ambition and written an opera. It had taken all of her nerve and a great deal of encouragement from Ida to get started. But once she began, it had been nearly impossible to stop. Mikhail Hastur, her beloved companion and husband of nearly sixteen years, had complained that her composing was a greater rival than any living man could be, and Marguerida knew he was only half joking.

Writing the music had been fairly easy, but finding the time—the peace and quiet to do so—had been difficult. She had a great many duties, as wife of the heir designate to Regis Hastur, and the mother of three children. Somewhat reluctantly, Marguerida had also taken over some of the task of running Comyn Castle from Lady Linnea Storn-Lanart, Regis' consort. In the years since she had been married to Mikhail Hastur, she had done so many things she had never imagined doing when she had been a young career academic. Foremost among these things, she had learned how to manage her unique and potentially dangerous *laran* talents, guided by the Keeper Istvana Ridenow. Her friend and confidant had come to Thendara from Neskaya to help her and Mikhail right after they were married, to train them and teach them. Istvana had remained in the city for eleven years, and they had been wonderful ones for Marguerida. But now she was back in her own Tower, pursuing her own calling, and Marguerida still had to work hard at not missing her.

Reflecting for a moment on years past, she decided she had not done so badly in facing her challenges. She had read ancient texts written in the rounded alphabet of Darkover with one hand while she cradled a baby at the breast with the other. She had learned to sit through Comyn Council meetings without losing her fearsome temper, even in the presence of her mother-in-law, Javanne Hastur, who remained an enduring thorn in her side. The shadow matrix which was blazed upon her left hand, the thing she had wrested from a Tower in the overworld, still remained something of an enigma, but she had found ways to control it so that she was no longer afraid of it. It remained beyond the considerable knowledge that had been amassed over the centuries by the *leroni* of Darkover, a thing which was both real and unreal at the same time. She could heal with it, and she could kill as well, and coming to grips with both extremes had been very difficult. The years had been hard, but she had accomplished things she had never dreamed of, and she had a deep sense of satisfaction in that.

During those years of study and motherhood, however, there had been no time for the music which had once defined her life and still remained her ruling passion. Instead, she had channeled her considerable energies into less personal efforts. With the help of Thendara House, the Renunciate center in the city, she had founded a small printing house, and several schools for the children of tradesmen and crafts people. She had helped the Musicians Guild get permission to erect a new perfor-mance hall much larger than anything which had existed before, and en-couraged the preservation of the fine musical tradition of Darkover in any way she could.

Marguerida's choices had been neither altruistic nor uncomplicated. When she had returned to the world of her birth over sixteen years be-fore, there had been a great vogue for everything concerning the Terran Federation, a condition which perturbed not only the more conservative rulers of several Domains, but bothered the craftsmen and tradesmen as well. They feared their way of life would be lost in a flood of Terran technology, and had gone so far as to petition Regis Hastur to restore the Comyn Council, which had been disbanded two decades earlier. Their demand had been unprecedented in the history of Darkover, and Regis had listened to their arguments, and restored the Council. This had kept Darkover on a path that satisfied most of its inhabitants.

But a complete return to the pre-Federation past was impossible, although there were a few members on the Council who sincerely be-lieved otherwise. Javanne, for instance, seemed consumed with the idea that if everyone would just do things as she wished, and make a real effort, then somehow the glories of an earlier time would reappear, and the Federation would cease to trouble their minds. Francisco Ridenow, the head of the Ridenow Domain, was almost as bad.

Marguerida understood both her mother-in-law's curious nostalgia for a time which she had never actually known—for the Terrans had arrived four decades before Javanne had been born—and her almost atavistic fear of change. She also knew it was much too late to turn back, and that Darkover needed increased knowledge, not unlettered ignorance, in order to prosper. The Federation was not going to go away just because Javanne Hastur wished it to, although there seemed no way to make the woman grasp this fact.

The space madness which had possessed the previous generation of youngsters had faded, however, and the populace had returned to their normal pursuits, with, Marguerida was sure, a silent sigh of relief. The number of young men and women who wanted to learn the intricacies of Federation technologies had diminished, too, and while there was always a pool of adolescents eager to obtain employment at Federation Headquarters, they were principally the offspring of Federation people who had married Darkovans.

The Federation itself was responsible for this. The political body she had been familiar with during her years at University was gone, replaced by a tangle of bureaucracies, each jealously guarding its own privileges, and unwilling to welcome newcomers into its ranks. This reorganization, which had taken place twelve years before, had brought them Lyle Belfontaine, the Station Chief at Headquarters. She had never actually met him, but her father had, and Lew Alton had given her a very poor impression of the man. Belfontaine had made it quite clear that he regarded the Darkovans as backward and useless. The organizational shift in the Federation had made him the most powerful Terran on the planet, superseding even the Planetary Administrator, who, while he still retained his position, had no voice in the actual running of things. Belfontaine had closed the old John Reade Orphanage, out of pique at a decision of Regis', and then closed down the Medical Center to any except Federation employees as well.

Much of this had passed by Marguerida unnoticed until recently. She had been much too busy rearing her three children, and studying with Istvana. She had found an unexpected kind of satisfaction in both activities, and had been happily willing to leave larger matters to her father, Lew, to Regis, and to Mikhail. It had been enough, with her other more public activities. But now, finding that she could compose music with the same hand that was her curse and her blessing, she had discovered a depth of pleasure that nothing else afforded her.

She had never wanted to participate in the administration of Comyn Castle, but Lady Linnea had persuaded her that she must. Eventually it would become her job, in some misty future time when Regis Hastur had gone to his rest, or his consort was too old to continue. The idea remained unreal in her mind, as if she could not bear the idea of their inevitable ends.

She had tackled her new duties as she had approached everything else in her life—by learning everything she could as quickly as possible. It had helped that she had spent ten years assisting Ivor Davidson, her long-dead mentor, on his journeys around the backwaters of the Federation in search of indigenous music history and tradition. More, Marguerida had the advantage of knowing Comyn Castle in a way that no one else did. She had ancient memories of the building imprinted in her mind, a leftover from her overshadowing by the long dead Keeper, Ashara Alton. These ancient memories had cursed her youth and adolescence, appearing in dreams and nightmares. Only her return to the planet of her birth had released her from the torment of inexplicable thoughts and images, although for a time it had given her more problems than she had ever imagined. She had nearly died from adult-onset threshold sickness—an experience Marguerida had mercifully almost forgotten.

Ashara had been present at the construction of Comyn Castle, and after she had died, her shade had remained present in the now ruined Old Tower that stood on one side of the castle. So there were forgotten byways and unremembered rooms and passages that were as familiar to Marguerida as her own hand. It was a disquieting knowledge, one that she had to take pains to conceal because it made the servants uneasy. Dealing with them had been a real challenge, since she was more accustomed to doing things herself than to ordering them done. And the actual administration of Comyn Castle was a much larger project than keeping travel papers and baggage in order. In many ways the building was a self-contained small town, with its own brewery, bakery, and even a small weaving loft. It was always stocked as if for a siege, and one of her duties had been to keep it ready for any eventuality.

Although she had been born on Darkover forty-two years before, Marguerida had lived half of her life off that world, and part of her still felt like an interloper. Her father said he often had the same feeling, and sharing her sense of alienation with him was a comfort to her. She had been estranged from him for all her years at University, but when they had met again, soon after her return to Darkover, Marguerida had found him changed. Now she could not think of life without him—his ironic sense of humor, his profound insights, and most of all, his steady affection for her, for Mikhail, and for his grandchildren. He was no longer the drunken, tortured man who raged in the night, and even the death of his wife, Diotima Ridenow, ten years ago had miraculously not returned him to that earlier state.

But despite the understanding presence of her father, Marguerida's sense of being a stranger had never entirely gone away. Part of this was the result of her difficult relationship with Javanne Hastur. Mikhail's mother had never really accepted her into the family, although his father, *Dom* Gabriel had finally broken down and welcomed her with genuine affection. Javanne always managed to convey to Marguerida a sense that there was something wrong with her, and with Domenic, her oldest child, whose conception had occurred under such unusual circumstances— during her journey back through time to the Ages of Chaos. She might even be correct about Nico, although Marguerida would have bitten her tongue rather than admit it. He was an odd lad, older than his years, self-contained and remote. But the difference ran deeper than that, and Marguerida knew it. There was something just a bit eerie about her oldest child, a quality of stillness that made it seem as if he were listening to some distant voice. Maybe he was, or perhaps, as *Dom* Danilo Syrtis-Ardais had once suggested, half seriously, he was the reincarnation of Varzil Ridenow. She rather hoped he was not, for her single encounter with that long dead *laranzu* had not left her with any desire to meet him in another form, and certainly not as her son.

She tried to accept and come to terms with her mother-in-law's dislike of her. After all, she was Regis' older sister and part of the family. She took some comfort in the fact that Javanne treated Gisela Aldaran, now the wife of Mikhail's older brother Rafael, with even less courtesy. It was about the only thing she and Giz had in common, for she had never managed to become friends with her sister-in-law, and having her in Comyn Castle all the time could, at times, be a real trial. Marguerida had done her best to reconcile with her sister-in-law, taking an interest in Gisela's researches into the geneologies of the Domain families, and also into the game of chess. She had even managed to procure a three-dimensional chess set as a gift for her one Midwinter, and the other woman had unbent for a brief time as a results.

But Gisela remained an aloof and disruptive presence in Comyn Castle, which already housed enough strong personalities to overwhelm anyone. She understood some of Giz's melancholy and sizzling rage. The woman had set her sights on Mikhail when she was only an adolescent, and had failed to achieve her ambition. That was hard enough. But she and Rafael lived in the Castle, and had to see both Mikhail and Marguerida almost every day. She was a kind of gentle hostage for the good behavior of the Aldaran Domain. Regis had never come to trust *Dom* Damon Aldaran entirely, and as difficult as having Gisela underfoot might be, it gave him a lever to hold the old man in check. Marguerida managed to forgive her difficult relative much of her ill-temper, recognizing in her both intelligence and ambition, and only wanted to strangle her once a tenday.

Her mother-in-law was another matter entirely, and even though she was not present at Comyn Castle very often, the thought of the woman always roused her to rage. Javanne doted on Roderick and Yllana, Marguerida and Mikhail's younger offspring, but she treated Domenic as if he were invisible, or worse, as if he smelled bad. And Nico was such a good lad, so serious and thoughtful, unlike Rory, who was born for mischief. Yllana was still too young to be fully formed, but was of reasonable intelligence, clever with her fingers, quick-tongued like her mother, and cautious like Mikhail.

Grimly, she pushed aside these distracting thoughts. It was time to begin a clean copy of the entire manuscript, and while she could have given the job to someone from the Musicians Guild, Marguerida wanted to do it herself. She had managed to sort out the usual morning's work quickly—the menu for the evening meal with dishes that would not unsettle Regis' now finicky stomach, an ingress of mice into one of the flour bins in the kitchens, and several other minor matters. It was a normal day, full of trivial problems.

For the present, the children were occupied, although there was always the chance that her difficult foster daughter, Alanna Alar, would interrupt her. Nico, her secret favorite, was doing his Guard duty, and Rory was scrubbing a wall he had adorned with chalks and paints a few days before. It was rather a nice mural, and she was sorry to tell him to destroy it, but she could not allow her troublesome middle child to get in the habit of defacing walls. It was bad enough that he gorged himself to illness on stolen tarts from the kitchens, showing every sign of taking up thievery as a fulltime occupation. Marguerida wondered if some of that tremendous energy might not be channeled into art, at which Rory seemed quite talented. But this was an idle thought, for in a few months he would go to Arilinn for his first training, and after that, the Cadet Guards would be his future. His life was laid out for him, as much as it could be with things so uncertain.

Marguerida's years on Darkover had not been untroubled, and the Terran Federation had been at the root of most of it. In the prior two decades the Federation had increased pressure on Darkover to give up its Protected status and join the Federation as a full member. This would have meant paying taxes into the coffers of the ever more rapacious Terrans, as well as making drastic alterations in the way in which Darkover was governed. When a planet became a part of the Federation, it became subject to the Federation, and essentially lost autonomy over its own resources and governance. For that reason, Lew had strongly advised against surrendering their Protected status, a choice which had allied him with Javanne Hastur. It had not particularly pleased Javanne to have Lew agree with her, since her youthful dislike of him had now hardened into something approaching fanatic hatred, but at least it had ended rancorous argument between them during Comyn Council meetings. Council meeting "debates" tended to be emotionally heated and often vindictive, leaving Marguerida with a profound desire for peace and quiet. But as Lew calmly told her, there was no peace on Darkover because if everyone agreed, it would be unnatural.

Instead of starting to work, Marguerida found her thoughts drifting toward the problems the Federation continued to create for Darkover. It was very annoying, really, not to be able to concentrate. Then she paused, frowned down at the music, and then gazed at the fire in the hearth. She had become extremely disciplined while she studied with Istvana Ridenow, and it was unusual for her mind to go off on tangents like this. Perhaps there was some reason for her fussing.

Marguerida kept abreast of the deteriorating relationship between Darkover and the Federation, even though she tried to remain in the background as much as possible. One of the things which Javanne disliked about her was that she was in a position to influence the views of her husband, her father, and others in Comyn Castle. Javanne assumed she *would* interfere, because that was just what Javanne would have done, given the same opportunity. To counteract these suspicions, Marguerida had done her best to pretend she was a proper Darkovan woman, interested in domestic matters, not those of state. She readily admitted she had not succeeded very well. She was too strong-minded to sit quietly during Council meetings, even though she promised herself each time that she would.

It was funny, really. She and Javanne were very similar in disposition, and while Marguerida had the advantage of a Federation education, her mother-in-law knew Darkover down into her aging bones. So, they disagreed on almost everything, often painfully. Javanne just could not understand that the Federation had to be dealt with; it could not be wished away or sent off.

Even when they were in agreement, as when the Station Chief had installed some media screens in taverns in the Trade City, and Regis had ordered them dismantled since they violated the treaty with the Federation, it was grudging and unpleasant. Something niggled in Marguerida's mind as she thought about this incident and she wondered if Belfontaine was about to attempt another intrusion into the Darkovan way of life. There was no information she had to suggest such a thing, but sometimes her unconscious mind seemed much more canny than her waking mind.

Of course, there were those odd disturbances this past summer. A small riot in the Horse Market, and all manner of rumors, which had come and gone like the clouds across the sky. It had been a summer fever, and the usually peaceable populace of the city had turned ugly and resentful for a brief time. But why should that trouble her just now, when she had a few uninterrupted hours to work? She felt a frisson of unease, not the first since she had sat down, she realized.

Something was troubling Marguerida, and it was not the Federation or her children, or Mikhail or anything she could put her finger on. She had just the hint of a headache, and her belly was queasy, almost as if she were pregnant again. Since she knew this was not the case, she could not account for the unease, unless she was coming down with some medical complaint. She dismissed the idea abruptly and turned again to the work on the desk.

She really must bear down and focus. Marguerida had a self-imposed deadline to meet. In three weeks it would be Regis' birthday, and it had become the custom to present an evening's entertainment of music for the occasion. She planned to premiere her opera then, since the subject was the legend of Hastur and Cassilda, the legendary forbears of his house, as a gift for him. It was fortunate that an increase in the number of musicians coming to the Castle was a perfectly normal part of the preparations for the event, and more fortunate yet that the singers and players of instruments regarded Marguerida as an *ex officio* member of their Guild. Thus far, the whole project had remained a secret from Regis, although she was sure he suspected something was going on. In a castle containing many varied telepaths, it was difficult, but not impossible, to plan a surprise.

Marguerida closed her eyes and leaned back in her chair. Once again she let the Alton Gift reach out, seeking the source of her unease. She had discovered this particular feature of her Gift years before, in a long-destroyed keep, in the distant past, where her life had changed forever. Nothing seemed to be wrong, so she decided she was just being foolish, shrugged her shoulders, opened her eyes, and picked up a pen.

Dipping it into the inkwell, she started to copy the first page. Darkovan musical notation was unlike the form she had learned at University, but after all this time, it was quite familiar to her, and easy to do. Yes, she had been right to do this herself—there was a place on the page where it was unclear what she had intended. Hardly surprising, since she had edited the original half a dozen times. She hummed the notes to herself, vocalized a stanza softly, and made the necessary corrections.

After half an hour, Marguerida had made clean copies of four pages, when a shaft of ruddy sunlight came through the narrow window, brightening the desk and making her blink. She got up to shut out the blinding light, but instead of pulling the curtains, she stood for a moment, looking out. Her ivory wool gown fell around her still slender body in comforting folds, and the apron she had donned to prevent ink stains was crisp over her waist. There was a brisk breeze snapping the pennons on the opposite roof, and the smell of autumn was everywhere. On any other occasion, she would have been out riding with her groom and two Guardsmen, chafing about having the escort, but enjoying the freshness of the air. Her beloved mare, Dorilys, was eighteen now, and feeble, so she rode one of her several foals, Dyania, a frisky, pewter-gray mare with a white star on her chest. It was hard to spend such a fine day indoors, and she turned back toward the desk with enormous reluctance.

Yllana's playing had ceased, and it was very quiet as she sat down once again. Once more she had a stab of unease, but tried to ignore it. Perhaps she was just anxious about the opera. Well, it was more of an oratorio, since there would be neither sets nor costumes. Marguerida very much wanted those, and a public performance of the work as well, in the newly built Music Hall on the other side of Thendara. But in her position it was probably not a good idea. Javanne Hastur and some of the other, more conservative members of the Domains, would likely think that it was unseemly for her to compose something to be publicly performed, as if she were a common musician and not the wife of Mikhail Hastur. There was nothing she could do about the animosity of Javanne except, she hoped, to outlive the woman. That might be a long time coming, since the Hasturs were famous for their longevity. It would be decades before Mikhail became ruler of their world, if he ever actually did. As things presently stood, he was Regis' right-hand man, and Lew Alton was his left, with Danilo Syrtis Ardais, as always, guarding his back.

Marguerida did not mind that, since once Mikhail was in control, her life would become even more circumscribed than it already was. Fortunately, she expected to be a very elderly woman by that time, and hoped she would not mind very much being a virtual prisoner in Comyn Castle. Now, however, she minded a great deal. Sometimes she wanted to scream. And occasionally, in the middle of the night, she went out into one of the back courtyards and howled at the moons, just to relieve herself, to be utterly alone and free of Guards and servants and the fractious personalities that filled the Castle.

She returned to the work, and found a very rough passage that needed attention. Maybe it would be a good idea to delay the thing for another occasion—next year even. Marguerida took a fresh sheet and sorted out the parts on it, found where the problem was, and fiddled with it until she was satisfied. How could she have been so clumsy? She wondered if Korniel, the fine composer of operatic works from Renney, in the previous century, had had these problems. Very likely. *The Deluge of Ys,* his best known work, was her standard of excellence, and she knew she was unlikely to ever achieve anything so grand and moving. Still, there were some bits in what she had done, drawing on the lengthy ballad tradition of Hastur and Cassilde, that were not half bad. She had expanded the lyrics slightly—not enough, she sincerely hoped, to offend the sensibilities of her audience too much—and introduced a few diverse elements she had collected from sources in the north. Erald, the son of the deceased former head of the Musicians Guild, Master Everard, had been very helpful. He was not in Thendara very often, since he lived with the Travelers, the wandering jongleurs of Darkover, but when he was, he always came to the Castle and talked with her. A strange man, but she thought of him as a friend.

Yes, this refrain she had introduced was quite good. Either that, or her eyes were filling with tears for some other reason. Marguerida put down the pen, lifted her left hand, mitted in silk, and now soiled with inkstains, and wiped away the moisture. It was really very silly to be moved by one's own creation. On the other hand, if it brought tears to her eyes, it would likely have the same effect on her audience. Thus heartened, she returned to the copying with fresh enthusiasm.

But between one stanza and the next something changed. One moment Marguerida was deeply focused on her copying, and the next she felt a chill in her body that made her hand shake violently. The pen sputtered, left several blots, and slipped from her fingers. There was a sharp stab of pain above her left eve, gone so quickly she almost thought she had imagined it. She blinked several times, and the room went from fuzzy to clear at last.

For a few seconds, she just sat there, too surprised to think at all. It had felt like a seizure of some sort, but she had not had one of those in years. It took Marguerida a minute to realize that what she had just experienced had not actually happened to her, but to someone else. Her first thought was of Mikhail, or the children. Her earlier unease, she decided, was almost certainly one of those unwelcome visitations of the Aldaran Gift of foresight. She did not have them often, and they always seemed to center around events that affected her directly.

Then, without any clear understanding of how she knew, Marguerida realized what was wrong. She stood up abruptly, banging against the edge of the desk and knocking the inkwell over. Dark liquid flowed across the blotter, the freshly copied pages, and the front of her gown, but she barely noticed.

Mikhail! The Alton Gift soared from her mind, breaking into the attention of every telepath in the great building.

What is it?

Something has happened to Regis!

2

A blast of cold air struck her face, and Katherine Aldaran gasped. After the heated port building, it was a shock. The fear that had gripped her since Herm had awakened her in the middle of the night and told her to pack for Darkover seemed to loosen its hold on her throat for an instant, and anger rushed into the breach. She would never forget the way he looked in the dimness of their bedroom that terrible night, the way his pupils had been constricted even in the inadequate light. The desperate expression on his usually calm, familiar face had terrified her so that she had not even questioned him but just done as she was asked.

She had endured her fear in the tiny cabin on the ship, and through the change at Vainwal. Katherine swallowed hard and opened her mouth to demand an explanation at last, but the frigid wind snatched the words away as it pulled her hair from where it had been coiled. She saw that the porter assigned to them was right behind her, and forced herself not to ask the questions that hovered in her mind. Instead, she swore vividly in her Renney patois, releasing the fear and anger in colorful phrases, not caring if her son learned some bad language. "You might have warned me we were coming into a storm!" The words sounded lame to her when compared with those she would have liked to voice.

Herm watched Katherine capture her long black hair, drawing the strands out like whips around her exhausted face. She had a keen temper, his Kate, and being dragged out of her bed in the middle of the night, then taken halfway across the galaxy with no reasonable explanation had strained her control to its limits. He had caught the questions which rose in her mind a few times—for all telepathic purposes she was practically shouting—and knew what it had cost her to hold them back. Only her own understanding that her diplomat husband was unlikely to speak frankly with the Federation listening had saved him from a grueling cross-questioning thus far. Instead he had been treated to cold silence, which was, in his opinion, even worse.

But Herm laughed in spite of himself, even knowing it would enrage her further, smelling the wonderful clean scent of autumn coming in from the west. He could not help himself. The cold stung his cheeks, bracing and familiar, but it had no hint of snow in it yet. He had forgotten how it felt, and until that moment had not realized how the ache of homesickness had been his daily companion. He had not been home for over two decades, and that was too long a time.

He put his arm around her slender waist, drawing her against him. He could feel the warmth of her flesh, and smell the faint chemical odor from the ship's fresher. She resisted his touch, and he let her go reluctantly.

"A storm? Nothing like, Katherine. This is merely a refreshing breeze." He sniffed knowingly, speaking with more ease than he felt. "But I would be surprised if it did not rain before nightfall."

Amaury, who had his mother's dark hair and pale skin, gave his step-father a skeptical glance, while Terése leaned against his leg, shivering. Herm bent down and scooped up the girl, even though she was rather big for that now. She was a pretty thing, with the red hair and green eyes so common in the Aldaran clan. Indeed, she very much resembled his sister Gisela when she was the same age. "Is it always this cold, Daddy?" She huddled against his shoulder trustingly. She had never seen snow, and rain never fell in the controlled climate in which they had lived their lives.

"No, little one. This is nothing compared to winter. But soon we will be in a warm carriage—assuming that Lew got the message I sent from Vainwal—and after that, in a nice warm house." He pointed across the peaked roofs of Thendara. "Do you see that big building up on the hill? That is where we are going, I believe." He had never seen it before, but he knew the vast structure must be Comyn Castle.

Even at a distance, it was enormous. The white of the stonework gleamed in the afternoon sun, and he could make out the movement of pennons and flags flapping from the towers and buttresses. On one side there was a dark ruin, as if part of the building had been struck by lightning and never repaired. For no reason he could name, the sight of it gave him a sudden chill of unease.

"That is not a house," Amaury protested.

"No, it isn't. It is a castle."

"Is that the castle you grew up in, Father?" Amaury had stopped calling him Dad a few months earlier, and adopted this more formal means of address. He was almost thirteen now, and was acting just as Herm had at the same age, finding ways to distance himself from his parents and starting to become a separate person.

"No. Aldaran Castle is far away, up in the Hellers—tall, tall mountains—and you cannot even see them from here. Come along. We will be inside soon, and we can have a nice hot bath and some food that did not come from a dispenser." He signaled to the porter, assigned to him by the Customs officer because he was, it appeared, still a Senator. The man, a civilian employee of the Federation, had a cart piled with the few belongings they had brought.

They had left so much behind! Herm had promised he would have things shipped later, but he knew that this was unlikely to happen. Everything they had not taken would be confiscated. He was still amazed that he had gotten Katherine away without so much as a quarrel, bringing only those things which were precious or irreplaceable. She had not even questioned him after being awakened so abruptly, as if she sensed the urgency of his mood. "I have been called back to Darkover, dearest," he had said. "I must leave immediately and I don't want to leave you and the children behind." It had been enough in the rush to leave, to get her moving and packing. He knew how frightened she must be, unlike the children who seemed to have decided this was a fine adventure. She really was incredible, his Kate.

The meanness of their habitation had prevented the accumulation of much, but their luggage was still considerable. There were Kate's oil paints and brushes, her sketchbooks and charcoals, Amaury's collection of Rennian warrior figures, and two of Terése's rather ragged dolls, as well as a volume of clothing entirely unsuited to Darkover's climate. The dreadful synthetics they wore in the ever-warm rooms of Terra were no protection against the sharp bite of wind around them. There were holos of Katherine's enormous family on Renney, and even his own collection of tiny ceramics, little bowls and vases no larger than his thumb. It was a foolish thing to bring, but he had found he could not leave the precious objects behind. Besides, a few of the pieces were rather valuable, and he could not see any purpose in letting them either molder in some warehouse, or be sold on the block for the profit of the Federation.

What there was not were any of the technological gewgaws of the Federation—no communicators, computers, recorders, or broadcasters. These were forbidden by Darkovan statutes, and the only contraband in the bags was a tiny box of lumens, little light-emitting dots that could be applied to any surface. Herm was fond of reading in bed, and the lumens allowed him to do so without disturbing his wife. He spent a moment wondering how the children would react when they finally realized how different Darkover was from what they were accustomed to. All their young lives they had been surrounded with access to enormous amounts of data at the touch of a finger, and instant reports of the planets in the far-flung Federation. He wasn't sure that he was going to be comfortable himself anymore, without mediafeeds. He shrugged the thought away.

Katherine had managed to collect her hair now, twisting it into a roll at the back of her head. He never failed to be amazed at the cleverness of her fingers. Fortunately, the collar of her Terran tunic came up high on her neck, so she would not seem immodest. After so many years of seeing women wearing low-cut dresses, with their napes exposed in a way which had shocked him when he first came to the Federation, he had almost forgotten that particular custom of Darkovan clothing. With a slight start Herm wondered if he would adjust to things he no longer thought were important—hiding the back of the neck for women or wearing a sword for men. Was he still enough of a Darkovan to survive?

They trudged across the tarnac, heading for the archway that separated the spaceport from the portion of Thendara called the Trade City. It was not a great distance, but they were all thoroughly chilled by the time they reached it. He nodded lazily at the black-clad Terran guards, and flashed his papers and documents, refusing to allow himself to show the slightest hesitation.

Herm had forced Katherine and the children to remain in the small cabin during most of the tedious journey. They only ventured out to get their meals in the first class dining area. Despite its grand title, it was only a narrow galley with plastic tables anchored to the floor, disposable plates and cutlery, and a very limited menu in the food dispensers. The food had been nearly tasteless, although nourishing, he supposed, and he allowed himself to look forward to some real Darkovan cuisine.

When they had gone to Renney almost nine years before, to present Terése to her great-grandmother, there had still been a semblance of amenities on the ships they had traveled on. But the austerity measures that were now commonplace within the Federation had made themselves present on the ship. It seemed to Hermes symptomatic of all that was amiss in the Federation, and he had been vastly relieved to climb down the curving passageway, through second and third class, and out into the port building half an hour before.

The other passengers in first class had been bureaucrats and business people, suspicious and unfriendly. There had been no buzz of civilized conversation in the dining area, as there had been on the earlier trip, but only the steady drone of a mediafeed reporting stale news, and the click of small computer touchboards from the other travelers. Herm had listened more from habit than from anything else, hoping to catch some clue as to what was occurring beyond the void in which they journeyed. There was nothing to suggest that anything monumental was occurring, and he had begun to wonder if he had made a stupid and expensive mistake. But on the third evening of their dull passage, he had caught a tidbit that set his nerves thrumming. There had been a sudden, seemingly inexplicable sell-off on the Intersystem Exchange, one of the large interplanetary stock markets.

Strange, he reflected. When he had been a boy, running wild in Aldaran Castle, he had never heard of a stock market, and when the term had first come up, had imagined pens of chervine and sheep. Even his father's tame Terranan had never mentioned this particular institution. And yet, he discovered, these commercial enterprises were an uncanny bellwether of events, almost as if credits could see into the future before their owners did. He could have made himself very rich by combining his own Gift with the sense he got by watching the fluctuations of the exchanges. Instead, he had refined his understanding over the years, until he could extrapolate a great deal of useful information from something so apparently irrelevant as a sudden shift in gallium futures, or the crop failure on a minor planet.

Watching the feed scroll across the crystalline face of the monitor, he had a sure sense of the disruption in commerce that Nagy's announcement would create. No one, including her Expansionist advisors, could predict the economic havoc they would wreak. He was sure someone in the know had leaked the word, in hopes of making a quick fortune, and his broker had begun something that would spread shock waves across the Federation. It might be months or even years before the extent of it was realized. That was good, as far as he was concerned, because if the Terrans were in economic crisis, they would not have time to bother with Darkover for a while.

His worst fears had not come to pass—he had not been arrested. But he had hardly slept during their passage, his ears on alert for a chime at the portal of the cabin, signaling disaster. Kate, frightened and furious with him, had been very silent, and the children had imitated her at first. Then boredom had set in, and they had started asking him questions about Darkover. That had helped to pass the dreary time, and even to ease his heightened senses a little. Upon their arrival at Vainwal, both Terése and Amaury had begged some credits to play at the many games of chance that stood everywhere in the port building. Vainwal was famous for its gambling and other leisurely pleasures, and he had handed each of the children enough money to keep them occupied while he sent word of his imminent arrival to Darkover. It had been a great relief to herd his small family onto another ship, and the last leg of their journey.

Herm tensed until his papers were examined. He was still on Federation territory, and subject to its laws, not Darkover's. He had not made too many enemies during his years of service, but he was acutely aware that until he was actually off Federation soil, he could still be arrested, declared an enemy of the state, and carted off to one of several penal worlds to languish, without trial, forgotten, until he died. It had happened to more than one of his colleagues, enough of them to know that the reach of the Expansionist arm was nothing to be taken lightly.

The wind gusted as he crossed the division between the Federation and Darkover, causing his all-weather cloak to flap wildly around him. He paused to yank the useless garment down, and set Terése on the cobbled stones, experiencing a lessening of the tension which had defined his life for months. No matter what happened now, he had brought his family to the safest place he could think of, and if he died that minute, they would be taken care of. His brother, Robert Aldaran, would see that they were fed and housed, and no one would threaten them with the possibility of imprisonment or death. It was a mistake to relax, he realized belatedly, for the full weight of his exhaustion settled on his broad shoulders immediately. It was all he could manage to remain standing upright.

Herm saw a large carriage which seemed to be awaiting them in the plaza beyond the archway, with four horses stamping their feet, their tails and manes fluttering in the wind. Their Terran luggage porter pulled his cart to a halt, unloaded the baggage efficiently, and scuttled back through the arch, as if being at the edge of the Trade City made him nervous. He did not even wait for a gratuity, which was just as well, since Herm had only a small number of credit chits still in his pocket. Then the door of the carriage swung open, and a man Herm had never seen before stepped out. He was about Herm's age, stocky and cheerful looking, with brown hair and blue eyes that twinkled.

"Senator? I am Rafael Lanart-Hastur, and Lew Alton asked me to meet you. He could not get away just now." The twinkle in the eyes faded a little, clearly troubled by something he did not wish to say. He gave the Terran guards, standing about ten feet away, a quick look, and Herm knew that even though he was speaking in Darkovan, he did not want the nearby guards to hear what he was saying.

"Well, we meet at last! Kate, this is my brother-in-law, my sister Gisela's husband." His voice sounded overly hearty and utterly false in his ears.

"I don't care if he is the King of Ys, so long as we can get in out of this cold!" She snapped the words in *casta,* which she had learned from him, then favored Rafael Hastur with her brilliant smile, the one Herm always thought could light up the world.

"Of course!" If Rafael was surprised by her command of the language, he showed no sign, but instead offered her his hand gracefully, not waiting for any further introductions. He helped Katherine into the coach, and the children scrambled in after her. The driver was already loading the baggage onto the roof of the vehicle, and Herm stepped in out of the wind. Despite being a large carriage, it was rather crowded with five people.

Herm and Rafael took one bench, with their backs to the driver, and Katherine and the children huddled on the other. Rafael picked up a large woolen blanket from the seat beside him, unfolded it, and handed it across carefully. Amaury took it and spread it across their laps, tucking it around his mother solicitously while the thump of the baggage being piled on the roof seemed to go on and on. When it ceased, it was followed by the sound of the driver mounting the box. The vehicle shifted as the horses began to turn around, and through the window Herm saw a large, derelict building on one side of the plaza, with the words John Reade Orphanage carved above the lintel of the door. Its windows were covered with boards, and it looked sad and empty.

Terése's eyes were large with wonder as she examined the carriage. She only knew of such vehicles from her ancient history texts, and clearly thought it was delightful. It was made of dark woods, mountain dur and rhowyn, and there was a small brazier set in a fire box in the floor, giving off a smoky smell and a little warmth. He watched her reach out and stroke the smooth wood, then smile her secret grin. At least one of them was enjoying herself.

Katherine took a long breath, pulled her all-weather cloak closer around her, thrust her hands under the blanket, and looked at her husband and brother-in-law. "Don't you think it is about time you told me what the hell is going on, Hermes?" She had returned to Terran, and her deep voice was calm. Still, he recognized the danger signs. His wife was never more fearsome than when she seemed reasonable. "Surely there are no listening devices in this carriage."

"Yes, I should. You have been very patient with me."

"I am not stupid," she snarled, her cheeks flushing in a very becoming manner. "You wake me up in the middle of the night with a look in your eyes like . . . the demon cats of Ardyn were at your heels." She sputtered to a halt and shuddered all over. "Then you tell me to pack, that we are leaving because you have been called back to Darkover. How? When?"

Hermes found the children watching him with wide and curious eyes, and sensed the mild amusement of Rafael beside him. *At least he did not marry a faint-hearted woman,* came the wry thought.

"Well, I could hardly tell you the truth in the ship, Katherine."

"Well, you can now!" She was fighting her fear, concealing it with anger as best she could.

"I had reason to believe that the Premier was about to disband the Senate and the Chamber, Katherine, and it did not seem to me to be a good idea to wait around until it happened." He used his most reasonable voice, but he could see that it did not satisfy her—she had been stewing for too long.

Rafael cleared his throat. "It has been— We received word just a few hours ago, after we knew you were arriving. All the members of the Senate and the lower house are being detained, I believe, including a few of those who represent Protected Planets. I don't have any information about what is going to happen to them. Lew only had a few minutes to brief me. It all sounds quite mad to me."

"What!" Katherine exploded, her gray eyes blazing in the dim light of the carriage. "Are you certain?" Her homeworld, Renney, was a Protected Planet, like Darkover, and a cousin of hers was a Deputy. Herm regretted that there was no way to have warned the woman, Cara, whom he liked.

"As sure as I can be, since I got the word from Lew, and he from Ethan MacDoevid, who is at HQ—which means I only have thirdhand knowledge. I wish Rafe Scott was still at HQ, for he could have been a great help just now." Rafael Hastur shrugged. *Rafe is a strong telepath, and could have been very useful.*

"I am surprised that I was not detained, then, even though Darkover is Protected." Herm voiced the question he knew was in Katherine's mind as well.

"We have a few sympathizers yet at HQ, and bribery is still possible," Rafael answered tersely. There was something guarded about him now, and his pleasant face looked grim and sad. *Regis picked a damned inconvenient time have a stroke! And I don't know how much longer we can keep it a secret.*

Herm heard his thought and winced. *Something* has *happened to Regis!* The remembered words rang in his mind. So, his clairvoyance had been correct. Whose voice had he heard, across the light-years between Darkover and Terra? Odd. He was gripped with profound sadness for a man he had never actually met. A stroke—so at least he was not dead. That was good. But from the turmoil in his brother-in-law's mind, it was also clear that he was not expected to recover. It did not seem possible. He could not imagine Darkover without its white-haired monarch. And clearly Rafael did not want to discuss it.

Rafael cleared his throat and continued speaking. "I am not privy to all the details—Uncle Lew has been quite close-mouthed." His face twisted in an odd grimace. *I will never be completely trusted because of Gisela. The only reason I was sent on this errand is because Herm is my brother-in-law, and my presence would rouse no comment. Damn all the Aldarans!* Then he flinched, as if aware that he was, for all intents and purposes, shouting his thoughts to those who could hear them, and gave Herm a helpless look. "All he told me was to meet you, and to distribute enough substantial bribes to make sure you were not detained."

Visibly shaken, Katherine huddled against the wall of the vehicle. "This is insane. Why didn't you find some way to tell me! And how did you know, when no one else did?" *I know that he couldn't have told me. Why am I being so unreasonable? Wasn't there some way he could have suggested . . . no. Did he even try?*

Herm shifted uneasily on the bench. All his hens and chickens were going to come home to roost, much sooner than he wished, it seemed. He should have told Kate the truth years before, but there had never been just the right moment for the revelation. Or so he had convinced himself. He would have to lie—again. And he was so tired that it seemed impossible. "I was warned by a clerk of the Premier's I have been culti-vating," he answered, surprised his voice did not quiver at all. There was a clerk whom he had gotten information from in the past, a pretty woman who liked to flirt with him. He had never been unfaithful to Katherine, but he had skirted the edges of it more than once for political reasons.

"And you could not tell me?"

"No. I could not put you and the children at risk—there are too many listening devices in too many places, dearest." She knew that per-sonal privacy had nearly vanished in recent years, and was aware that their apartments were not safe, but she was not in a mood to be mollified. It was not just the Security Forces either, although they were the most obvious spies. There were other groups, covert bunches of shadowy peo-ple, nameless and faceless, who nurtured their own suspicions of the Senator from Darkover and anyone else whom they did not own. He had found hints of them in the unguarded thoughts of clerks who were noth-ing of the sort, as well as in those of his fellow legislators. Herm wondered if the Expansionist Party knew that there were traitors in their midst, plotting for power over the decadent Federation. It did not matter any longer, did it? They could all plot themselves to perdition, for all he cared. By Aldones, he was tired!

As a Senator, Herm had taken a different tack than that of his predecessor, Lew Alton, and cunningly played at being a *bon vivant,* a pleasant fellow who could be bought occasionally. For Herm did not possess Lew's gift of forced rapport—could not bend minds to his bidding—which he knew that Lew had done more than once, with great subtlety and not a little remorse. But Lew had used what he had, and paid the price. Lew's powers had cost him a great deal, and he had been a heavy drinker during the years Herm had known him. He wondered if he still was.

Instead of force, Herm used deviousness. For the most part he had managed to keep Darkover from becoming a planet that demanded attention, that appeared as a threat in any way. It had not been easy, for the paranoia of the Expansionists now bordered on obsession. They saw enemies everywhere, and many of them sincerely believed that Protected Planets were getting away with something. They were never able to define exactly what that "something" was, but that did not keep them from thinking that they were being cheated somehow.

Herm had fought with his own peculiar talents, pretending that Darkover was just a backward planet, poor in the metals that might be useful for building ships or armaments, barely able to provide enough food to feed its inhabitants. He painted a portrait of an impoverished world, and Darkover was far away and still obscure enough that few had inquired too closely. During Lew's term as Senator, he had cleverly managed to get a great deal of information about Darkover either suppressed or classified in some fashion, so that access to it was limited. And thankfully, Darkover did not have any particular strategic value, although that might change soon. If the Federation fell apart, or split into factions, who knows what the future might hold?

The real problem was in the mind-set of the Expansionists themselves. They imagined enemies everywhere, and much of their energies for the past decade had been devoted to building ships of war, not commerce, and to preparing for combat. Their argument was that just because the Federation had never encountered another space-traveling power, this did not mean that they would not. Herm knew that they were wrong, that the enemies they feared were already at work within the Federation, that it was almost inevitable that some ambitious planetary governor was going to rebel and start the war they expected. He suspected it would be a very unpleasant surprise, and could only hope that it would happen on the other side of the galaxy. The last thing Darkover wanted was to become involved in an internecine conflict.

The carriage rattled across cobbled streets, and the wind shifted the vehicle back and forth. They went down the wider streets, and through the window he could see the open shutters of the shops, adorned with gaily painted signs. They were passing Tanners Way, and the pungent smell of boiling vats of leather filled the crowded interior. Terése made a face, but said nothing. Amaury gazed out the rather misted window, his blue eyes alight with interest and curiosity.

At last Katherine stirred. "I am sure you did the best thing, Hermes," she said in a voice full of exhaustion. Until that moment, he had not known how much her silence during the journey had cost her. *What about my family? I wish we had gone there, instead of to this godforsaken place—but why couldn't Herm have warned me somehow? No, I must not blame him. He has always kept his own counsel—I wish it were otherwise. It is not as if I didn't know that things were going badly, that the Federation was starting to come apart at its seams. I just refused to believe it was as bad as it was. I did not want to know, even though I kept noticing things in the news-casts that disturbed me. Even with the rebellion on Campta, and the riots on Enoch. And I only knew what the Federation wanted me to know! Still, I must make the best of it. At least he has taught me some of the language, and the children have never been able to sort out what words are from Renney and what are from this place. It's so cold! What will happen to Nana and the rest, if they try to house Federation troops at the Manse? She will probably put a curse on them, or add some of her potions to the food. Nana may be ancient, but I suspect she can take care of herself and my sisters. When are we going to arrive? So cold and so tired. Surely I will feel better when I am warm and really rested.*

Herm reached across the carriage and patted Katherine's hand through the wool of the blanket. She opened her eyes and looked at him for a long minute, then slipped her hand out and grasped his wrist, feeling the warmth of his skin against hers. "It will not be long now," he said quietly, as if he had heard her disjointed thoughts. And perhaps he had, for often in the past he had seemed to know what she was thinking without her speaking any words. No, it was impossible! He was just very intuitive. Whatever it was, it made him a fine lover. Nana had told her Herm had the Sight, on their single visit to her home planet, and while she dismissed that as the old woman's superstition, she could not deny that her husband was a very unusual man. When Terése was an infant, he would frequently get out of bed before the child began to cry, rushing to her cot and catching her up against his broad shoulders just as the pink mouth rounded for a wail. And he always seemed to know if she was wet or hungry or just wanted to be rocked.

Ever since the day they had met, when he found her doing a portrait in the offices of Senator Sendai, Katherine had realized that Hermes Aldaran was unlike any man she had ever known or was ever likely to know. His eyes seemed to see everything, down to details she herself had overlooked. She had found him charming and intelligent, but also mysterious in a way she still could not define. That had made him nearly irresistible.

And now, after more than ten years, she still felt that she did not know very much about her husband. She knew he had several siblings, his sister Gisela and his brother Robert, plus others who were *nedestro*, whatever that meant. But that was about all. At first, he hardly spoke of Darkover, and when he did, he talked of great snows, high mountains, and vast wilderness. His childhood was something of a mystery, although he was very interested in hers, and there always remained a certain remoteness in him. It was both frustrating and fascinating, and she had learned not to demand more of him than he was willing to give. Now, looking at his behavior with the ruthlessness of exhaustion, she felt cheated and more than a little lost. Katherine chided herself for being unhappy then and tried to let the nasty emotion go.

Herm had begun to teach her *casta* soon after they were married, and they had discovered that it was akin to the Renney dialect, related to old Breton. The inflections were subtle and different, but much of the vocabulary was similar enough that she had picked it up quickly. She, in turn, had instructed him in Rennian, and the two tongues had mingled into a harmonious stew that the children used in preference to the less colorful Terran one.

But Katherine had never really expected to come to Darkover, and she was still in shock over the sudden journey. A first class cabin on a Big Ship was not a large space, and the carriage was not an improvement. She felt claustrophobic, as if she could not get enough air in her lungs. Every time they hit an unevenness in the street, the motion jolted her aching bones, and although the brazier in the floor afforded some warmth, she felt chilled to the bone. It was all she could do to contain her anger, but she refused to argue with Herm in front of the children, and certainly not with this near stranger listening. But she longed to raise her voice, to proclaim her still pent-up sense of ill-usage, to express her fury and her fear. Hermes-Gabriel Aldaran was going to be fortunate if she let him kiss her for weeks to come.

Herm sighed as he watched his wife and children, realizing that perhaps he should not have been quite so secretive. It was a policy he knew was going to cause him regret, and soon. But for twenty-three years he had portrayed Darkover as a rather primitive place, with few resources worthy of exploitation, in order to keep the curious uninterested. He had no desire to see the Hellers deforested, nor to have Darkovan foodstuffs shipped to other planets to feed the ever enlarging populations. And certainly he did not want to have knowledge of the Towers of Darkover to become general, as it nearly had a generation previous. The Expansionist forces would occupy the planet in a flash, eager to co-opt Darkovan telepaths for their own dreams of dominance.

The carriage rolled to a stop, and the door was opened. A gust of cold wind billowed across them, and the children shivered. Katherine just drew herself further into her shining all-weather cloak and looked grim. There was a servant in the livery of the Castle waiting, and they climbed out one by one.

Two flights of broad steps led up from the cobbled court, and Herm herded his family swiftly up them. Behind him, servants were unloading the luggage. Rafael led them through a door and into a modest entryway. There were tapestries hung along the stone walls, and a checkerboard pattern of tiles under their feet. It smelled of woodsmoke and damp wool, and there were a number of heavy woolen capes hung on pegs beside the door. But after the chill outside, it was deliciously warm and cozy.

They followed Rafael up a long flight of stairs to the next floor, then down a corridor, and up another set of stairs. He sensed the bewilderment of the children at the flight of steps, since even the meanest hives, where the poor huddled in misery, all had lifts. Herm had never been in Comyn Castle before, but he had heard that the place was a regular warren of halls and stairs. The children shucked off their cloaks and observed their surroundings with interest, but Katherine just walked with her eyes straight ahead, her back rigid, and her face empty, like the survivor of some unnatural disaster.

"We did not have much warning of your arrival, Herm, so your quarters are probably a bit chaotic. The bed linens will be clean though, even if the hangings are a little moth-eaten."

"After days in the berths of a cabin, it will seem quite luxurious, Rafael. Where have you put us?" He wanted to make conversation, meaningless noises to ease the tension in himself.

"The second Storn apartments, which have not been used except during Midwinter, for ages. The ones that were done up for Lauretta Lanart-Storn years ago. Giz and I use the Aldaran Suite, and it really is not large enough for another family." He sounded faintly ashamed of this, and Herm just grinned at him.

"Who is that, Lauretta Lanart-Storn?" Amaury asked.

"She was the wife of my grandfather, although she is not a blood relation of mine," Herm replied.

"How can that be?"

"My father was not her son, Amaury."

"Sounds confusing."

Herm chuckled, happy to find anything to be amused at. "It is. Darkovan geneologies are rather difficult, and often bewildering, even to those of us who know them from the cradle."

"Why is that, Father?" Amaury appeared genuinely interested as they continued down the long hall, past burning lampions and rather faded tapestries.

Herm looked at his stepson, and for the first time, wondered if he had done the right thing, bringing the boy to Darkover. He was a rather sensitive child, with his mother's quick mind and deep intuition, and who knew what from his father. The tension between his parents had left him anxious and concerned, although he was hiding it rather well. He was trying to ease things, as Herm himself had done with his own father, long before. What kind of place could be found for him here? He was just too tired to think about it. "We are a small population, and the families of the Domains, like the Aldarans or Altons, and the lesser families, like the Lanarts and the Storns, have been intermarrying for centuries. Everyone is related to everyone else, if you go back far enough. For instance, Rafael here is a Lanart on his father's side, but I cannot guess just how he might be connected to Lauretta."

"Neither can I," Rafael put in, grinning easily, "but Gisela would know. She is very good at that sort of thing."

"You amaze me, for the last thing I would have suspected my sister of is an interest in geneology," Herm answered. "When I left Darkover, she was still a girl, and her only pursuits seemed to have been hunting, reading Terranan novels, and getting new clothes as often as she could cajole our father to allow her."

"That has not changed," Rafael admitted, "but she is too intelligent to limit herself. She has been working on a book on chess for several years, and what I have read of it is very good. And she has read just about every book in the Castle Archive, I think."

"My sister an author? Amazing!"

"She tells me it keeps her from getting bored, for she does not find minding the children at all to her taste."

"How many are there now—I have lost count."

"There are Caleb and Rakhal, her children by her first husband, and our daughter Casilde, and our sons Gabriel and Damon. Rakhal is at Arilinn and intends to remain, and Casilde will go there soon." *I hope she gives up this mad idea of becoming a Renunciate. A pity that Marguerida's friend Rafaella is so attractive, and makes the Renunciates seem so romantic. She will outgrow it, for it cannot be a pleasant life. Fatherhood is much more difficult than I ever imagined.* "And the boys are just being boys, and it is all I can do to keep them out of too much mischief."

"And Caleb?"

Rafael frowned. "He is at Nevarsin," he said somewhat abruptly. Herm understood his unwillingness to go on, for Caleb must be above twenty by now, and if he was at Nevarsin, then likely he intended to become a *cristoforo* monk. Although the sons of the Domains had been educated by the *cristoforos* for generations, it was rare these days for them to join the odd community in the far north, in the City of Snows as it was sometimes called.

"Here we are at last." Rafael stepped forward and opened a pair of doors, pushing them aside and gesturing them into a large sitting room. There was a fire burning in the grate, and the smell of recently applied beeswax rose from the heavy wooden chairs set around it, belying Rafael's suggestion as to the state of the accommodations. The carpet beneath their feet was thick and free of dust, and the curtains across the window looked relatively new.

It was a pretty room, furnished with a woman in mind. The walls were painted a pale golden color, and the tapestry that hung along the wall portrayed a group of ladies bent over an enormous embroidery frame. There were small footstools, upholstered in thick velvets, and several little tables as well as a longer one that would seat half a dozen people in comfort. A small arrangement of flowers sat in a vase in the center of it, and the faint smell of them mingled with the odor of the fire.

Katherine looked around, her artist's eye refreshed after the barrenness of the ship's cabin. She turned and relaxed in the warmth of the room, then favored Rafael with a bright if tired smile. "This is very nice. Thank you. You cannot know how . . . this room is nearly as large as our entire quarters on Terra. And wood, real wooden furniture. We have that on Renney, and I think I must have been missing it without knowing. I hope it was not too much trouble."

Rafael shrugged easily. "The servants did everything. Now, the main bedroom is through that door, and the bathing chamber and privy are down the hall, second door on the right. You can't miss it. There are robes and towels and all that, and I will have some food brought up as soon as you tell me whether you want breakfast or dinner. Lew says the food on the ships is abysmal, and that you would certainly want something tasty immediately."

"What is that other door?" Terése pointed to a closed portal on the far side of the sitting room.

"Those are the other bedrooms, and you can choose the one you like," Rafael answered. It was clear he had a great deal of experience with children, as well as a natural talent with them, despite his own doubts.

Terése's face lit up. "My own room? I won't have to share?"

"You are old enough to have your own room, Terése—such a pretty name." Rafael gave Herm a look which spoke volumes, and he felt mildly embarrassed, even though the sparse living arrangements permitted him on Terra had not given him much choice. But Rafael was right. His daughter was much too old to be sharing a bedroom with a brother.

Herm watched Katherine remove her cloak and look for a place to hang it. At that moment a servant appeared, a rosy-cheeked girl with her hair caught back in a wooden butterfly clasp, and she took it from Katherine. She bobbed a quick curtsy. "Welcome to Comyn Castle, *vai domna. Dom* Aldaran."

"Thank you."

"I am Rosalys, and I have been sent to look after you. *Domna* Marguerida told me to come. She said to say that she regrets she cannot come to greet you herself, nor *Domna* Linnea either, and hopes she will be forgiven."

"Of course," Herm answered. "We understand entirely." He gave Rafael a quick glance. *Is Regis really dying?*

Yes, he is. It was a massive stroke, and the healers are unable to do anything thus far. Even Mikhail and Marguerida, with their incredible abilities, have been unable to help him, and, believe me, they have tried. My poor brother is beside himself with frustration, and I do not blame him. He has all that power, yet he is still helpless.

This last thought made no immediate sense to his fatigued mind, so Herm shunted it aside. *I don't suppose there is any chance that the Medical Center at HQ could be useful?*

Them? They have not allowed Darkovans to use the facilities in over five years—ever since the new Station Chief tried to install some media screens in one of the taverns in the Trade City, and Regis ordered them dismantled immediately. Belfontaine retaliated by closing the hospital to any except Federation personnel. That includes a few Darkovans, of course, but . . . we could hardly trust them under the circumstances, could we?

No—stupid of me to even suggest it. They would likely jump at the chance to finish him off.

Herm became aware that his wife was watching him closely, and realized that she must be aware that the sudden silence between him and Rafael was peculiar. He had slipped into the easy habit of unspoken conversation without thinking—it was easier than talking just now! But his Kate was observant and intelligent, and she had had a decent amount of sleep during the journey, unlike himself. Herm knew she had used sleep to escape the terror in her mind, to still the voices of protest that rose in her throat. He cleared his voice to conceal his chagrin. "I think something in the way of lunch would be right—soup, bread, tea. They gave us a breakfast of sorts just before we landed."

"I will see to it, *vai dom,*" Rosalys answered quickly. She gave another curtsy, opened the door of the main bedroom for them, then left the suite.

Herm followed Katherine into the bedroom as the children went off to the other side of the suite. She rounded on him, her cheeks red and her eyes glittering. "What the hell is going on, Hermes! Don't give me that hurt look! You drag me off in the middle of the night, refuse to explain anything except that we must leave immediately for Darkover, and you and that man . . . What were you doing?"

"Doing?" He gave her a hurt look, and tried to appear innocent, his heart sinking down somewhere in the region of his navel. Damn the woman for being so observant!

Katherine audibly ground her teeth. "Just tell me the whole of it."

"Ah, err . . . Rafael was just . . . informing me of . . ." He did not feel very clever, just exhausted and rather stupid.

"How? Secret hand signals? What were you two up to!"

Her voice was uncannily like that of his old nurse in Aldaran Castle, a sound of authority which would not be satisfied until it got to the bottom of the matter. It made him feel small and young and powerless for the first time in decades. "No, not hand signals."

When he did not continue, she looked into his face, searching it with her penetrating eyes. He looked down at the floor, at the pattern of the carpet, and shuffled his toe around. He had to get the words out now, before he lost his nerve completely, but he feared the uproar that he knew would follow. If only it could have waited until he was more rested. "Well, if you must know, I was having a conversation with Rafael telepathically." So much, he thought bitterly, for being a cunning man.

Katherine was silent for a moment. "Tele . . . Of all the . . . you really mean it, don't you?"

"Yes, I do."

Katherine sank down on the edge of the bed and clutched a handful of the hangings between her trembling fingers. "So, that's it. I've always wondered how you could anticipate me so well . . . I could just kill you, Hermes! How could you not have told me you were reading my mind all these years? All my private . . ." He could sense that she did not really believe him, that her mind wanted to refuse what she had just heard. "Surely I would have sensed . . ." she whispered.

"No, no!" he protested quickly. "I can't invade your thoughts at will, although there are those on Darkover who can. But I can pick up on your surface thoughts from time to time. Think of all the paintings I have not interrupted," he begged, trying to deflect her ire.

"But why did you never tell me?" The pain and betrayal in her voice cut him right to the heart.

"If I say it was a matter of policy, you will murder me." He sighed and sat down beside her. "You know as well as I do that the Federation has ears everywhere, and this was a secret I did not wish to share with them."

"Why?" Her voice was cold and distant.

"I did not want to vanish into some laboratory, which would have been my fate if I had been discovered." He held back a sigh, and tried to think of what to say next. "First, not everyone on Darkover is a telepath, and indeed the Gifts occur in only a small part of the population. And of those, few have great powers, although there are enough of these to . . ."

"How many? And how is it that the Federation doesn't know about this?"

"I don't know an exact number—maybe two percent of the entire population." He rubbed the top of his bald head. "As for the other, it is a long tale, and not a happy one. Once, years ago, we agreed to participate in something called Project Telepath. Just in time we realized that the Federation could not be trusted not to abuse our talents, and Lew Alton managed to persuade certain influential scientists that the claims had been exaggerated, that there were many fewer telepaths on Darkover than had been thought, and that it was a rare and inconsistent ability, hardly worthy of pursuit. Then he got the funding for the project cut off. He was afraid, as was I when I took his place, that if it became known that we here on Darkover possessed a population of capable telepaths, we would find ourselves occupied, the way that Blaise II was."

"But I am your wife! I did not think we had secrets between us." *No, that isn't true! I knew there were secrets, and I was afraid to discover what they were! But I never imagined this. . . .*

"I am sorry, Katherine. I did try to tell you once, when we were on Renney, but I just couldn't find the right words to begin." He paused, aware of how feeble it sounded from him, the glib and clever Hermes Aldaran. "I wish I had kept a mistress and fathered a bunch of illegitimate brats instead of not telling you about this." He sighed again, deeply this time, and forced himself to tell the whole truth, fearing he would not have the courage another time. "I would have had to soon enough, because there is a high probability that Terése has inherited some of my *laran,* my paranormal capacities. I have no idea what the nature of it might be, but I just have a strong . . ." He wanted to deflect her anger now, to direct her attention away from his folly.

"For a mistress, I would indeed have killed you." Katherine interrupted, almost as if she could not bear to hear the words he was going to say about their daughter, and tried to lighten the mood with a soft, feeble chuckle. "You promise you have never invaded my thoughts willfully?"

"I swear it, word of an Aldaran! No more than I would read your personal journal, dearest. You must understand that in order for a community of telepaths to continue, we learn to respect the privacy of others from a very young age. We are a very ethical bunch, we Darkovans."

"You? Ethical?" Katherine went off into a peal of mirthless laughter. "You are the most devious man in the Federation, Hermes-Gabriel Aldaran, and you know it! Nana told me that there was something about you that you were hiding, but I did not believe her. No, I did not wish to believe her!" She gave him a look, a mixture of sorrow and mistrust that wrenched his heart. Then she squared her shoulders and lifted her chin, as if bracing herself to make the best she could of things. "I suppose I might forgive you in a decade or two—but then again I might not. Telepaths! This must be the best kept secret in the Federation."

"Yes, I suppose it is."

She was able to hold the stiff posture for perhaps half a minute, then weakly sagged against him. He could smell her weariness and the stink of the ship on her skin. The knot of hair she had made slipped down, and he could feel the silkiness of it brush his hand. "What else? There is something more, isn't there?"

"Yes, there is. Regis Hastur, who has guided Darkover for two generations, is dying. At least Rafael says he is, and I do not think he would exaggerate such a terrible thing. That is why his consort, Lady Linnea, is not able to welcome us, as she would have under any other circumstances, and why Lew Alton deputized Rafael to greet us."

"Did you know that he— Herm, what really made you yank us out of our beds and rush here?"

"A vision, my dearest, if hearing voices can be called that. I have what is called the Aldaran Gift, which is the occasional power of foreseeing, although in this case I foreheard rather than foresaw. I suddenly *knew* that the legislature would be dissolved, and realized what the implications of that were. So I did the best thing I could think of, which was to get us all as far away from Federation territory as quickly as I could."

"Then you did not know that Regis was sick?" *Nana knew he had the Sight—but this is too much . . . first telepaths and then clairvoyants. I wonder what else he is not telling me. No, I don't want to know! Not now, not today. I could not bear another revelation.*

"I had an inkling, you might say, and while I got both the sense of some terrible thing about Regis and Nagy's move at the same time, I did not have anything to tell me when. For all I knew, Regis' illness might be weeks or years in the future, or might have already happened. The Aldaran Gift is not precise, and not all foreseeings come to pass. For instance, I might see that someone would be in an accident—an aircar crash, maybe—but on the day of it, this person decided to stay home instead. I was on fairly firm ground about the dissolution of the legislature, because we had not been able to do any real business in nearly two months, and everyone was sort of holding their breath, waiting for the ax to fall. I suspect that some of my colleagues with no paranormal abilities whatever were anticipating something of what happened to occur. I just had the advantage, if you can call it that, of a little more warning than they did. It was more a leap of faith on my part than anything else—that I believed what I foresaw and acted on it. That is the most I can tell you."

"Who will take over when Regis is gone?"

Herm chuckled. "My brother-in-law, Mikhail, who is the younger brother of Rafael. I met him just before I left Darkover, when he was in his early twenties. A good man."

"The younger brother? Isn't that a little odd?"

"Yes, it is. You see, long ago, Regis named his youngest nephew as his heir, before he married Lady Linnea. Mikhail is the son of his sister, Javanne Hastur. Regis had other children, but they were murdered in their cradles, along with any number of other people, by the World Wreckers—a covert organization run by Terranan. Then he married Linnea, and they have three children: a son, Danilo, and two daughters."

"But, then, why is this Mikhail going to succeed him?" Katherine let herself be distracted almost unconsciously. She desperately wanted to think about something, anything, but telepaths. It was too much just now. And she had to keep talking, to keep herself from thinking.

"It is a very complicated affair, but essentially Danilo Hastur abdicated the direct succession in favor of becoming the heir to the Elhalyn Domain, through his marriage to Miralys Elhalyn. The Elhalyn have been the kings of Darkover since the beginning of recorded history, but the power of rule has always remained in the hands of the Hastur family. The two families are related, and Regis' mother was Alanna Elhalyn. . . . Your eyes are glazing over."

"Are they? I suppose they must be, for my head feels full of buzzing bees. Herm, I am so tired! I slept and slept because I knew you would not tell me what was going on, and it frightened me so much. Every time I was awake, I wanted to strangle you! Yet I feel so wrung out. And afraid, too. What is going to happen to us?"

"Well, the first thing that is going to happen is that we are going to get something to eat, some *real* food, and then we are going to sleep in a real bed."

"You know what I mean!"

"Yes, I do. I believe that we are here, on Darkover, for the foreseeable future, my dearest. I am sorry that I could not consult you first, but I had to make my decision quickly, or risk ending up in a Federation prison as an enemy of the state. And, as suspicious as the Terranan have become recently, you and the children would probably have been locked up with me."

Katherine nodded. "Yes, with my connections to the Separatists, you are almost certainly right. But what is going to happen to Renney?"

"I have no idea. I think that the Protected Planets are on their own, or will be soon enough. My best guess, and it is only a guess, is that the Federation will threaten to withdraw its presence, take away its beloved technologies in the assumption that it will force the Protected worlds to submit to its will, and give them what they want most, complete domination of all the planets. I can only guess if they will actually carry out such a threat, and, frankly, I am just too tired to worry about it."

"This has been coming for a long time, hasn't it?"

"Yes, it has. The Federation has been jumping at shadows for years, even before I took over Lew's position as Senator. They have been looking for a fight of some sort, in order to justify all the pillaging they have been engaged in for the past two generations. They have been preparing for a war, and there is no one to fight with except themselves. So they have chosen to believe that the colonies are the enemy, or the potential foe, and that they have to be brought into line by force."

"The occupation of the Enki system?" Her voice was low and weary.

"That is one example. Now, enough of this. Let's eat, go take a bath, and get the stink of the ships off our bodies. You will feel much better, I promise. Darkover may be a bit backward in some matters, but in terms of comfort and cleanliness, we are the most civilized world in the galaxy."

Gisela Aldaran-Lanart sat with her feet resting on an upholstered stool, her knees draped with a soft woolen throw. She stared at the glassy plates of the chess game Marguerida had given her three Midwinters before without really seeing it, so familiar was she with the object. It was a beautiful thing, the playing pieces carved by a master's hand, so the folds and draperies caught the light, making them seem almost alive. They were not, but trapped in stone, and she often felt as if she were one of them.

Often, when she was feeling lonely, she would hold the figures, stroking the draperies, feeling the bone and wood from which they had been carved. She had always liked statues, and when she was little, she had made small things from bits of firewood, until her nurse told her it was a dirty habit and forced her to stop. Gisela had always thought that the forms were already in the woods, just waiting to be released. As she longed to be let out of this pretty prison of a palace.

There were only a few people in Comyn Castle who understood this complex game of chess for her to play with—Lew Alton, Marguerida, Danilo Syrtis-Ardais, and her husband's nephew, Donal Alar, the paxman to Mikhail Hastur. She avoided her sister-in-law as much as possible, although it was safer to meet her over the eight transparent levels of the game than in the halls of the Castle. Lew Alton was a good opponent, but his playing was erratic, and Danilo was much too clever, so her own playing disappointed him. That left Donal, who had little time away from his duties, although he tried to engage her as often as he could. They were fairly matched, and she almost enjoyed their encounters, as much as she allowed herself to enjoy anything.

Everything was so dreary! She was tired of chess and ancient genealogies, tired of being nothing more than a pawn in the shifting games of power that were played in the Castle. She should have been a queen, of course, and might have been, if only Marguerida had never existed. This thought was threadbare, so often had she dragged it from her mind, and she let it go.

If only she could force herself out of the doldrums that had possessed her for years now, since the birth of her last child. Gisela had consulted healers, drunk filthy tasting draughts, and had deep massages—to no avail. She had no interest in the sort of public efforts that Marguerida indulged in, and thought them nothing more than a way for her rival to show what a gracious lady she was. The worst part was that, after fifteen years of living in Thendara, with almost daily contact with her rival, she could not even manage to hate her. Dislike, certainly—a mean and petty emotion that left her feeling nasty and soiled. If only Marguerida were bossy and demanding, like Javanne Hastur, instead of so damned decent. How galling!

Something like a chuckle rose in her throat, and her dark mood began to break apart. For a moment she tried to hold onto it, to dwell in its somber pleasures, but she was bored with it, and it fled away to wherever such things went. She needed something to do, something real, not the pallid intrigues she had attempted at her father's behest in her first decade in the city. They had brought her nothing except the distrust of Regis Hastur and, by association, the exclusion of her husband from any actual power. Rafael had never complained, never mentioned it, but she knew it rankled and that she had hurt him deeply.

And she had not wished to. Although she had been completely infatuated with Mikhail Hastur in her youth, she knew now that this was all it had been, a girlish affection combined with the even stronger desire to be powerful. After her mercifully short marriage to her first husband, who had had the kindness to break his neck while hunting before she found a means to murder him, she had sworn to herself that she would never again be her father's pawn. And the best way to achieve that had seemed to be to marry Mikhail and become the consort of the heir designate. What a fool she was!

Nothing satisfied her, and Gisela knew that this was her own character, not anything else. Years of bitter introspection had left a mark on her soul, even as she struggled to find something worthwhile in her existence. There were the children, but she had never managed to conjure up more than a pretended interest in them. And there was Rafael, the single constant in her life. Strange, really, how she had come to cherish the man, although his patience and silent endurance made her grind her teeth. If only he would shout at her sometimes. She wished he would make her behave, and knew that he never would. That was his character flaw, as envy was hers.

Gisela heard his tread before he entered the room, the particular rhythm of footfalls that she would have known anywhere. Then he was beside her, his clothing smelling of the fresh air beyond the Castle, of charcoal smoke, and the warm scent of horses as well. He had gone to fetch Herm from the port, and now he was back. He bent and kissed her forehead.

"So, is my brother well?" She forced herself to be interested, dragging herself as if through glue back into the present.

"He is, although he is very tired. His wife and children all look as if they have been through hell."

"It is hard to imagine Herm married, Rafael. What's she like?"

"Well, I only had an hour with her, and much of that time she was ringing a peal over his head for dragging her to Darkover." He chuckled softly. "She is very lovely—dark hair and pale skin and a fine smile. Smart, too, I believe, and tough as well. I liked her."

"Why?" The envy demon extended its talons, jealous of everything.

"Umm . . . I can't really say. She is tired and confused, but she—her name is Katherine, by the way—kept her head very well. I listened to the questions she was asking him, about why he had brought her and the children off as he did, and she didn't miss much, even though he was trying very hard to dissemble his way out of it."

"Well, at least that hasn't changed. Herm likes to . . . fiddle things. I suppose I should go meet her, shouldn't I?"

"If you can bestir yourself, yes." She caught the faint criticism in the words and flinched—sometimes she thought she would almost prefer it if he beat her. "Tomorrow is soon enough though."

"Yes, tomorrow." Lovely and smart—Gisela almost hated her already.

3

Mikhail Hastur stood up slowly and stretched. His spine popped audibly in the stillness of the sick room, and Lady Linnea, seated on the other side of the bed, looked up, her face drawn with exhaustion. He had been sitting absolutely still for hours, concentrating his mind on the unmoving form resting on the bed. His right hand, where the great matrix which had been passed to him by Varzil the Good was mounted in a huge ring, ached from the energy he had driven through it.

As had so often happened since he had been given the matrix, Mikhail had imagined he had heard Varzil's calm voice, reaching through time to counsel him. He was never certain whether it was just his own fantasy, or if somehow the long dead *laranzu* actually spoke to him from the overworld through the matrix which had once been his. After fifteen years, it no longer mattered. Yet it remained disquieting to hear the words in his mind. This time they gave him no comfort or reassurance, but only the certain knowledge that Regis Hastur was dying, and there was not a thing he could do to prevent it. He wanted to rail against the cruelty of the fates, to weep for the beloved mentor who would speak to him no more, but he was just too tired.

The chest of the man beneath the covers still rose and fell, but very shallowly now, and he sensed that the end would not be very long in coming. Mikhail would have given a great deal to see his uncle's eyes open, and the familiar twinkle gleam from beneath the eyelids. He wanted Regis to sit up and demand a haunch of chervine, and a butt of wine. Could Mikhail have accomplished that miracle, he was sure that Lady Linnea would have carried the meat in with her own small hands.

Mikhail had a moment of relief at this foolish vision, and then the grief rose in his throat once again. The smell of the room, thick with burning herbs and candlewax, suddenly threatened to make him gag. He swallowed convulsively and ran the fingers of his left hand through his curling hair. Then he glared at his right, at the ring, and clenched his hand into a fist. It was infuriating. He had spent most of the last fifteen years studying the arts of healing, trying to discover as much as he could about the matrix he had been given by Varzil the Good, and he had become very skilled. But what was it all worth if he was not skilled enough to save his uncle.

Had he tried everything? Mikhail racked his brains again, the futility of it mingling with his own weariness. Yes, he had, and so had Marguerida, who had her own talents in the healing arts. She had also brought in every capable healer in Thendara, and two from Arilinn. The body was still alive, but Regis was barely within it.

He did not want to accept that, and he raged silently, like a child, not a man of forty-three. He had known Regis all his life, and he suddenly found that he could not imagine Darkover without him. He had been preparing to succeed his uncle for decades, but he had not expected it to happen so unexpectedly, nor so soon. The old doubts nagged at him, fears he had thought were long gone. He was not ready to lead Darkover!

The rustle of fabric behind him made him turn. Marguerida came into the chamber, carrying a tray with several mugs on it, doing a servant's task in spite of all that she had learned through the years. There were dark circles beneath her golden eyes, and deep creases beside her normally smiling mouth. Her fine red hair lay slackly against her skull, the curls barely visible. Without a word, she handed him a mug, and he smelled the refreshing scent of mountain mint and the distinctive odor of Hali honey. Their eyes met for a moment, hers asking an unspoken question and his answering. *No change.*

Lady Linnea glanced up from her study of the body of her beloved companion of more than three decades. Her shoulders drooped and she rubbed her eyes, as if they ached. They were the color of harebells, blue and pale, still as young as they had been when he was a lad. But there was no hope in them, only a sorrow that wrenched at him desperately.

Marguerida went to her with the tray, and Linnea took a mug of tea in silence. Then she went to the man standing in the shadow of the bed hangings beside the carved headboard, Danilo Syrtis-Ardais, and offered him one. Mikhail watched the six-fingered hand of his uncle's paxman slip into the handle of a mug and saw exhaustion and despair in the familiar face.

Marguerida set the tray down on a small table and came to stand beside him. "Dani has just arrived," she whispered. "He'll be here in a moment."

"Good. I think Regis is hanging on for him. You look terrible, *caria.*"

"Probably—but have you glanced in the mirror lately? I finally got Father to lie down for a while. Oh, yes—Herm Aldaran has arrived in Thendara—with his wife and children. Rafael met them and took them to a suite."

"What? Why?" The world had stopped for him, four days before, and he had nearly forgotten that anything outside this room existed.

He received no answer to his incredulous question, for at that moment, Danilo Hastur, Regis's son, came into the room. He was wearing a brown tunic and heavy trousers, and he smelled of sweat and horse, a healthy scent against the stuffy air of the chamber. He was a sturdy man of thirty now, not the slender boy that Mikhail remembered so fondly. He and his wife and children lived in the Elhalyn Domain, which stretched from the west side of Lake Hali to the Sea of Dalereuth, and it was clear that he had ridden long and hard to get to Thendara.

Linnea dropped her mug from nerveless fingers at the sight of her son, spilling tea down the front of her rumpled gown, tears welling in her blue eyes. Dani embraced her gently, as if afraid she might break in his grasp, and placed a soft kiss on her cheek. They stood together for a moment, her head resting on his shoulder. Then he released her and approached the bed.

Dani Hastur stood beside the bed, looking at the still shape of his father beneath the linens. Then he sat down and took a hand in his own, stroking it softly. Regis did not stir. Only the subtle rise and fall of his sunken chest gave evidence that he still lived.

"Father." Dani's voice broke over the word. "It's me, Dani."

The silence in the room was disturbed only by the ragged sound of Dani's breathing, and the sobs of Lady Linnea now beside him. Mikhail watched the tableau and sensed a slight change in the man in the bed. For a moment his heart clenched with the hope that Regis was going to rouse, to wake and speak to his son. But instead he saw a faint shudder ripple along the form beneath the covers, and knew that his desperate hope was in vain. Regis-Rafael Felix Alar Hastur y Elhalyn was no more.

A strange sensation gripped him then, a brush of warmth on his face, and a tingling in his right hand. Mikhail looked down at the gleaming matrix on his finger, and watched in wonder as it flashed brightly, coruscating in the dim light of the bedchamber. He had never seen the stone do that before, and the intensity of it was painful.

Mikhail turned his eyes away, unable to look any longer. He glanced back toward the bed, his eyes aching. In the hangings behind the headboard something flickered, a play of light and shadow. For a moment he thought he saw two women, one fair, one dark, in the folds of the textile. They seemed to be transparent, and he might have thought it was some trick of the light. But the fair face was one he had seen before, long ago, in another place and time. He drew a sharp breath of startlement and the vision vanished. His heart pounded and blood rushed through his veins, making him dizzy. Evanda, Goddess of Spring, was the fair one, and the other must be Avarra, the Dark Goddess. Even as grief began to seize him, Mikhail felt another emotion, one of otherworldly calm, arise within him.

Beside him, Marguerida wept silently, the tears coursing down her pale cheeks. Mikhail put his arm around her shoulders and drew her against his chest gently, allowing himself to feel everything all at once, only for an instant. He could not really believe it was over. Somehow, in the deepest recesses of his heart, he had expected some miracle would occur, and all he could feel now was a vast sense of emptiness and failure that it had not. What a fool he was.

Danilo Syrtis-Ardais moved from his place in the shadow of the bed-curtains. The paxman set aside his mug and bent over the body in the bed. He put his hand around the wrist of his lifelong friend and held it in his grasp, his lean face alert and resigned at the same time. After a minute, he took Dani's hand off of his father's, and folded Regis' arms carefully across his chest. Danilo stared down into the still face of the man who had been his best friend and companion for more than four decades. He touched the brow softly, stroking the white hair, his face filled with infinite tenderness. Then he bent down and kissed the pale cheek of his lifelong friend, and turned away, his shoulders shaking with grief.

Dani Hastur gazed at his father for a long time, a look of yearning on his face. He continued to sit on the side of the bed, dumbstruck, and then finally he lifted the sheet tenderly and drew it over Regis Hastur's peaceful face. He stood shakily, then mastered himself. He took Lady Linnea into his arms again, and she seemed to collapse into his grasp, as if, at last, her legs would no longer support her. She leaned against him, her head pillowed on his shoulder, and wept uncontrollably.

The vivid details remained before Mikhail's eyes for several seconds, and then began to blur, as if rain were falling. He realized that the tears he had held back while he struggled for the life of his uncle would not be denied any longer. The overwhelming power of his feelings was too much, and, abruptly, he turned and walked out.

Mikhail sat in his uncle's shabby study, behind the large desk where Regis often worked, stared into the fireplace and wept. The carpet was rather threadbare, but Regis had refused to have it replaced, or to have anything done to the room. Servants were only permitted to come in to sweep and dust. It gave him an odd feeling to remember the rather pleasant arguments between his uncle and Lady Linnea about the state of the room—it had been such a cheerful and caring dispute.

He had come there hours before, unable to sleep or think or function, fleeing duty, fleeing life. There was no fire in the hearth, so the room was cold and the air was chill and stale. He had a bottle of firewine on the desk, and a glass beside it. The level of the wine was much diminished since he had arrived, but it had not lessened his paralyzing, aching grief at all. He was not even drunk. Such was the power of Varzil's matrix that he could not dull his senses, no matter how he tried.

Distantly, Mikhail could sense Comyn Castle bustling around him. Even the death of Regis Hastur could not halt the steady function of the huge complex completely. He knew that his young paxman and nephew, Donal Alar, was standing outside the door of the study, to guarantee his solitude, even though poor Donal was surely ready to drop in his tracks. Fostering the young man had been Marguerida's idea, and he was glad of it now. Prying Donal and his sister Alanna out of Ariel Lanart-Alar's anxious grasp had been difficult, but Mikhail believed it had probably saved their sanity. Ariel had never been the same after Alanna was born, and he was deeply saddened by that.

Somewhere he knew that Marguerida was doing her best to deal with all the arrangements that must be seen to. There would have to be a funeral, but not until all the lords of the Domains arrived, and that would be several days at least. His mother and father were still at Armida, even though he knew that Javanne should have been informed as soon as Regis fell ill. But Lady Linnea, usually the most sweet-tempered of women, had been adamant. "It is all I can bear to see him like this, Mikhail. I will not have that woman in Comyn Castle until I must." Under the circumstances, he had bowed to her wishes. And with a slight sense of guilt, he had agreed with Linnea. His mother was not an easy person at the best of times, and having her underfoot would have been intolerable.

His mind went to Marguerida, knowing she was as tired as he was himself, yet shouldering the burden of preparing for the funeral. There had not been such an event for decades, and although he knew that the *coridom* of Comyn Castle would do his best to help her, the man was ancient and likely so grief stricken he would be of little use. He would have preferred she was in bed, with a hot brick at her feet, but she was probably up and about, doing those things he himself should be managing. He tried to think what those duties might be, and found only sorrow and despair. *He was not ready!*

It was dark outside, and his belly was grumbling. How long had it been since he had eaten? Mikhail could not remember, and even though his body needed food, he had no appetite. His eyes were swollen with crying and lack of sleep, and his shoulder muscles were taut with tension. The candles were unlit, and he could not summon the energy to rise and set them aflame.

The light from the corridor made a bright band on the floor as the door of the study opened, and Lew Alton entered. He stared at his father-in-law dumbly, annoyed by being disturbed, and for a moment, furious that Donal had permitted even this special person to enter his sanctuary. Then he realized it was not his, but Regis' place, this battered desk and worn carpet. This room was still so filled with the presence of his uncle that he ached with it. It seemed to him it was all he had left of the man, and he did not wish to share it with anyone just yet. Donal followed Lew into the room, unwilling to let even this most trusted advisor alone with his master, and closed the door. Then he leaned against the jamb, folded his arms, and tried to become invisible.

Lew said nothing, but got a firestarter and knelt beside the cold hearth. There was a flash, then a flicker of flame in the kindling laid there. Mikhail watched the fire lick at the logs, curling around them, eating them up with light and color. He watched Lew take a small brand from the fire and start to light the candles. The comforting smell of hot wax and burning wood began to fill the room.

Lew poured himself a glass of wine and took a chair on the opposite side of the desk. His hair had turned completely gray, and his facial scars were almost invisible, buried in the wrinkles that seamed his face. He was a weathered man, his skin rough and dry, and tonight he looked his age. Mikhail saw the redness around his father-in-law's eyes, and knew that he had been weeping.

"Marguerida sent me," Lew said after swallowing half of the contents of his glass.

"Are you here to tell me I must put aside my grief and think of my duty to Darkover?" Mikhail snapped, startling himself with his own vehemence. He felt his face redden with embarrassment, and Donal roused from his place by the door and gave him an odd look.

"Certainly not! You can sit in the dark for the next week for all I care—although I hope you will not. But your absence is disturbing."

Mikhail hunched his shoulders. "I just couldn't bear to see him laid out—not yet. I am still in shock."

"There will be plenty of time for that later, Mikhail. It will take the better part of a week for everyone to arrive, for the bier to be constructed and put in place. And I do understand. When Dio finally died, even though I knew she was going to, even though Marguerida had restored her to me for five years, it took many days before I could believe it had actually happened. There were times when I cursed my own daughter for bringing her back, because I had to lose her twice. But I had time to prepare—although I did nothing of the sort! There is, I think, something in us that denies death. We convince ourselves that it will somehow be avoided or delayed, that everyone we love will outlive us, so we won't have to suffer the loss or perhaps admit that the ones we love are mortal. When my father died on Vainwal, I was completely stunned, and furious. And for you, as close as you were to Regis, this is probably more like the death of your father than anything else."

Mikhail heard the words, but they did not seem to penetrate his mind. All he could feel was a vast and endless numbness. But after a few moments of consideration he realized that Regis *had* been like a father to him, more than an uncle. For a time this had estranged him from *Dom* Gabriel, his actual father. And he realized that he knew now, as he had not before, that the Old Man would die, too, and he would be bereft again. And Lew, sitting across from him, sipping firewine. He had become so close to Marguerida's father during the past fifteen years that he was as dear to Mikhail as either Regis or *Dom* Gabriel.

At the same time, there was something else that troubled him. He prodded at it, trying to bring to consciousness the vagrant wisp that perturbed him. It was, he decided, guilt, though why he should feel that way he could not say immediately. Had he done enough? Was there anything he could have done to extend Regis Hastur's life?

Mikhail glanced down at his right hand, encased in a thin glove of finest leather once more, now he was no longer doing the healing work he had performed in the sick room. The great, glittering matrix that rode on his finger was hidden, but always he could sense its presence. It was so powerful that there had been times since he received it that he had wanted to cast it away, to be relieved of the burden of it. It had made him the most powerful person on Darkover, too powerful for the comfort of some of the lords of the Domains, like Francisco Ridenow, and certainly for the peace of mind of his mother, Javanne. More, it had kept him a near prisoner in Comyn Castle for fifteen years, surrounded by Guards and watchers, always aware that anything he might do would be measured and analyzed. He was respected, but he was also feared, even by the uncle he had loved so much.

And now—what? He would succeed Regis. Hadn't he prepared for this moment for his entire life? Why did it feel so wrong, so empty and frightening? He was no longer the boy who had dreamed of ruling Darkover, nor the man who had, for a time, given up those ambitions. He was someone else, and Mikhail wondered if he knew himself at all. He did not wish to think about it any longer. He was too weary for self-examination, and he suspected it was closer to self-indulgence in any case.

He forced himself to stop dwelling on his aching sense of loss, and searched for some topic of conversation. At last he said, "Marguerida told me that Herm Aldaran had arrived. What is going on?"

"Ah, that." Lew gave a grim smile and reached across the desk for the wine. The bottle was nearly empty, and he poured the last drops into his glass. "Herm and his family, actually. I received word that he was coming only hours before he arrived, and it did not seem important enough to tell you immediately. You had enough on your plate, Mikhail. But it seems that the entire legislature has been dissolved, by executive order of the Premier, until new elections can be held. My best guess is that this means that there will be no more Federation Congress— ever—or that if it exists, it will be filled with those who toe the Expansionist line completely. This coup was almost inevitable, given the Expansionist mind-set, and I fear that whatever survives of the Federation will be a military dictatorship or something even worse."

Mikhail's mind was too fatigued to completely grasp everything Lew was saying, so he focused on what he did understand. "Elections? Half the worlds in the Federation have no more use for democratic government than a donkey for dancing shoes." It felt like a blessing to channel his remaining energy into a mild sense of disbelief and concern over this new development, even though he was perfectly aware that it would have unimaginable ramifications for Darkover. Those fears would keep until his mind was less muddled.

"Precisely, Mikhail. Many of the Senators and the rest were appointed, just as I was, by kings and governors and oligarchs. And those hereditary or appointed positions have long been a thorn in the side of the Expansionists, one they appear to have plucked out for the moment. I think the Premier's action was ill-considered, and likely will have consequences that she will regret later. Sandra Nagy does not realize that she has set the fox loose in the henhouse, but she has. Probably she believes she has control of the Party, and when she discovers otherwise, it will be rather too late." Lew had been gloomily predicting all manner of dire things for the Federation for as long as Mikhail had known him, and appeared to take some grim satisfaction in what had now happened.

"Then she must be a fool! Does she think that worlds like Darkover will comply with this transparent plan?"

"Not being privy to the most recent thoughts of Sandra Nagy, I cannot say, Mik. I knew her years ago, when she was an appointee on the Trade Board. She is canny and extremely clever politically, but has little if any moral sense. I never liked her, but I had a certain respect for her cunning. I am saddened that my worst fears about the Federation seem about to be realized, but I find I am less disheartened than I expected."

"What does it mean for Darkover?" Mikhail did not particularly care what happened to the Federation, which remained an abstract conglomeration of places he had never seen or, in many cases, even heard of. No matter how much Marguerida or Lew told him about it, it remained more imaginary than real in his mind. More to the point, after he had received the great matrix stone, he had realized that he would never be able to travel off-world, as he had longed to when he was younger. So, although he remained interested and even curious, Mikhail had discovered that it pained him to talk about faraway planets he would never see. He was envious that Marguerida had traveled so extensively, and sometimes he even resented his wife's travels a little, enough that that feeling shamed him a good deal.

Lew shook his head. "I cannot guess. The Terranan might imagine we can be brought to our knees by the removal of their technologies, by closing the port and withdrawing."

"That's ridiculous—we've never had any use for their technology! It would probably be a blessing for us if they left."

Lew gave a gruff chuckle, a slight growling noise in his throat, like a bear trying to laugh and failing. "Bodies politic are rarely logical, Mikhail."

"Then how can they function?"

His father-in-law looked thoughtful for a moment. "They run on ideals and power struggles—often political movements are born of ideals, but deteriorate into power struggles, megalomania and the dissolution of the very ideals which gave birth to the political movement in question. Here, I believe, the ideal is that everyone in the Federation will be alike—without diversity—and that it is possible to achieve consensus by decree. The Expansionists believe that this can be achieved by everyone agreeing to do it their way, the Expansionist way. And since they have experienced strong opposition, they are seeking to force their 'ideals' down people's throats."

Mikhail frowned over this. His mind felt soggy, but he was glad of this distraction, this unwieldy problem to focus on, however poorly. "I am not sure I understand you. Do you mean to say that these people really believe that they can coerce entire planets to give up their customs, to be just like Terra? That is the most ridiculous thing I have heard in ages."

"I know—it sounds impossible. But I don't think you have any idea of how powerful the effect of propaganda can be on a populace, because Darkover has never experienced the effect of constant newsfeeds, which only tell what the government wishes its citizens to know. It has happened over and over in human history, like some recurring nightmare."

"Tell me." Over his father-in-law's shoulder, he watched Donal come to attention, and knew his paxman was listening intently. He felt a flutter of pleasure, the better for being completely unexpected. Donal had wisely chosen to make Danilo Syrtis-Ardais his model, and realized already that his task was much more than merely guarding the person of Mikhail Hastur. With time and experience, Donal would become a wise advisor. Oddly, this notion comforted Mikhail more than he would have thought possible.

Lew Alton made a kind of grunting noise, a familiar prelude to the conveying of information. Oddly, the ordinariness of the sound, and the anticipation of the words to follow soothed Mikhail's frayed nerves. At least this was the same. "First, someone in power announces things are going to hell in a handcart, and that the reason is the fault of some group or tribe or opposition party. Morals are decaying, or parents are not rearing their children properly. They propose that the answer lies in reformation, in everyone behaving according to some ideal that suits their notions of a good society. They demand conformity, and anyone who does not submit is regarded as a potential enemy, if not an outright traitor. It has happened in our own times, on places like Benda V, about thirty years ago, for instance."

"I've never heard of that planet." There were several hundred members in the Federation, and Mikhail had only read extensively about twenty or thirty. But although he was quite well-informed for someone who had never left Darkover, it always made Mikhail feel terribly ignorant when a planet was mentioned he knew nothing about. It was rather silly, since there were so many planets in the Federation, and even widely traveled people like Marguerida and Lew did not know about all of them.

"I'm not surprised, since it is a pretty out-of-the-way place. Here is what happened, as well I can recall. The Orthodox high priest announced he had had a vision from God, that the only way to save the planet from utter destruction was to wage a holy war against all members of the Church of Elan, which were the rivals of the Orthodoxy, and had become very powerful on Benda. They were accused of everything from poisoning the grain to murdering Orthodox babies and drinking their blood. And since the media was controlled by the Orthodox, this resulted in a planet-wide bloodbath. About sixty million people were slaughtered in a three-month period—men, women, children."

Mikhail was stunned. "But didn't the Federation intervene? I mean, I thought that was something they were supposed to do in . . . such situations?"

"Yes, I know. The taxes collected from the planets of the Federation are supposed to be used to maintain the Spaceforce, so that they can keep events like this from ever happening. However the real function of the Force is to keep Terran coffers full, to see that trade is not disrupted, that taxes are collected, and that resources continue to flow to Terra. They did not intervene because it was decided that it was a planetary matter, not a Federation one. So for the past three decades, as far as I know, Benda has been a theocracy where everyone spies on everyone else, and you can be executed for belching during services. These, I understand, take up at least four hours of every day. Needless to say, this has created great economic hardship, because if you are stuck in church, you can hardly be tending your fields or selling your goods, can you? And the loss of all those poor folks who belonged to the Church of Elan did not help either, since they were productive members of the community."

"Sixty million? That is three times more than the entire population of Darkover!" Mikhail stared at Lew, unable to quite believe what he had just heard. "And no one tried to fight back?"

"Mikhail, anyone who risked that was going to die." He sighed again, seeing the incomprehension in Mikhail's eyes. "I know—you cannot really grasp this sort of thing because it is beyond your experience. Darkover is a very special world, and one of the wisest things Regis ever did was to keep us out of the Federation except as a Protected Planet."

"When I was younger, I always thought he did it to keep people like my mother happy, or at least quiet!" Mikhail let himself chuckle softly at the ridiculous thought of Regis making so momentous a decision just to appease Javanne Hastur. She was never quiet, and now she would come to Comyn Castle and make his life miserable. He did not feel he had the strength to stand up to her intrigues and passions just now.

Lew nodded, as if he understood what Mikhail was thinking perfectly well. "He felt it was potentially too costly, that Darkovan culture would not survive if we embraced Terranan values completely. The plain truth is that we don't need the Federation. What do you think would happen if there was no longer a Federation presence here, Mik?"

"As far as I can see, if the Federation pulls out there would not be any more Big Ships, and the hospital at HQ would cease to exist. The Terranan would not pay us for the lease on the spaceport any longer. Not that they have been any too consistent with the payment in recent years." After a moment's reflection, he added, "And Marguerida would no longer be able to procure coffee at exorbitant cost for her occasional pleasure. It is a shame that we have never been able to cultivate the plant on Darkover." Mikhail had never taken to coffee, but he knew his wife loved the strange, bitter stuff. "None of that seems too earth shattering to me."

Lew chuckled. "That is a fairly good assessment of the impact, since the Federation controls the spaceways. There are quite a number of inter-system trading companies, but between the stars, one must have the technology of the Big Ships, and only the Terranan have that and guard it jealously. As for the other, the lease is about to end, and Belfontaine was trying to jigger Regis into concessions, as he should. It is part of his job."

Mikhail found himself amused at the memory of the excuses for the lateness of the payments that had been offered. "Regis told me that Belfontaine had suggested that when the lease is renewed, that Darkover should pay the Federation for maintaining a base, instead of them paying us. He got a big kick out of it." It hurt to remember that, but it touched his heart at the same time. It made him remember Regis' smile—his smile had always been one of his greatest assets.

"That's true enough, and I will never forget the look on Belfontaine's face when I had the pleasure of telling him the answer was a definite no. But, Mikhail, what economic effect would the Terranan leaving have on us?"

"Well, not much, I believe. The Trade City would certainly lose considerable business, and the pleasure houses would not be happy. Lady Marilla's pottery would not be exported any longer, but the Aillard and Ardais Domains would survive. We haven't really developed much trade, have we? I suppose that is why the Terranan want us to be a member world instead of a protected one, so they can market their products. We don't produce enough food to export, and we don't have enough metal to build ships or other things. Marguerida says that the sand up in the Dry Towns would be useful for silicon-based technologies, but somehow

I can't imagine a factory in Shainsa. Besides, if I understand the process correctly, it would need a lot of water, and there isn't any to spare in that region."

"No, there is not. And that is one major problem with adopting Terran ways—the impact on the ecology would be tremendous and devastating. You have never seen a manufacturing world, but I have. The air is thick with smoke and foul smells, and the people live in wretchedness. We don't have slums on Darkover—you don't even know what that means, do you? Believe me, Mik, the poorest family on Darkover lives better than many people on advanced worlds. We are a marginal world, for which we should be thankful, because if we had more obvious resources, we would be more attractive to interlopers. Our timber would be hewn, exported to places we never heard of, our crops taken to feed people on other planets, and when the land would no longer support our populace, because the rivers were full of silt, we would either be abandoned or forced to pay enormous prices for food from other planets."

"You mean this has happened?"

"Absolutely. I know of at least two planets which have been almost destroyed by the greed of the corporations that owned them, then left to struggle along with a ruined ecosystem, where the population can hardly feed itself. And since I left the Senate, there have likely been several more."

"I find that hard to believe. Why? I mean, it seems very short-sighted."

"Exactly. The Federation has kept going through expansion, by finding new planets to exploit. This has been the policy for the last hundred years, give or take a decade. But in the last fifty, only a handful of habitable worlds have been discovered—the rest were places where establishing a new colony would either be prohibitively expensive, or so unattractive that the only way to get people there was to ship them out and force them to live there, which is quite costly. But the basic idea is that restraint is unnecessary. This is the foundation of the Expansionist philosophy, which is that unlimited growth is not only possible, but is also desirable. They remain blind to the actuality, which is that there are fewer and fewer habitable planets to be had in this region of space. And because the worlds they are exploiting are farther and farther away from the center of the Federation, the governing of these places becomes more and more difficult, demanding more and more resources to maintain contact, longer and longer journeys between worlds, with greater and greater cost to haul the raw materials home to Terra. So they want the member worlds to surrender everything they have, and be taxed for it as well. The home world, and a few other planets have become parasites on the rest of the Federation."

"Taxed to send their food to Terra?" Mikhail knew he was tired, but he was not sure he had understood his father-in-law.

"Yes."

"But, Lew, that is insane. Why would anyone pay to have their wheat sent somewhere else?"

"By using the media to convince the population that they derive some benefit from being taxed and starved at the same time."

"But what possible benefit . . . ?"

"They are persuaded that by being taxed to support the Spaceforce, they are being protected from some imaginary enemy—aliens that are destined to appear in the skies and conquer them. They do not see that the real enemy has become the Federation itself. There are, at present, weapons that can reduce a planet to molten slag in hours, things created to defend against this phantom race, which are actually being used to keep the member worlds in line. The only thing that keeps the whole situation from dissolving into chaos is that the expense of such things is enormous—sending a fleet of ships to destroy a planet costs a great deal, not to mention that it is poor policy. It is very hard to keep the knowledge of something that monumental out of the newsfaxes, and it tends to make other worlds more anxious, rather than more obedient. The Federation has become rather like a big bully, kicking smaller children around just because it can. And, until now, the existence of the Senate and the Chamber of Deputies has acted as a restraint on such insane undertakings."

"Do you think that we will have Federation Marines invading Thendara, then?" Mikhail was only half serious.

"I hope not. And I do not really expect such an assault, although it could happen, if someone decided that Darkover had strategic importance. No, the greatest danger is that the Federation itself will crumble, and that there will be splinter groups, with their own ambitions for power and dominance. A planetary governor or some local king with a few captured dreadnoughts could be real trouble. Or worse, if some admiral in the Force decides to mutiny and go adventuring for his own profit." There was a grim look on his father-in-law's face now.

"Do the Terranan know that?"

"Some of them certainly do. There are people within the Federation who have likely given as much thought to this, over the years, as I have. The problem is, however, these people have no power and do not make policy. It's probably the nightmare of the General Staff, that some planet will manage to get hold of enough armaments to be a threat to Terran security. There have been a few rebellions in the last fifteen years, planets where the populace revolted, or the governor went off on his own hook. They have been put down with force, but with enough restraint to keep things from getting completely out of hand. Again, it was the function of the Senate to keep things from getting to that point, to restrain the Premier and the General Staff from making overt war on too many worlds. But I think you must talk to Herm since his information is more recent than mine."

"I suppose I must. I just don't feel as if I am ready. Everyone has been telling me for years how powerful I am because of this accursed ring," he said, making a fist of his gloved hand. "But I do not feel powerful. I don't have Regis' charm or cunning, nor his experience, although I have tried to learn all I could."

"You will do very well, Mikhail. Regis believed that, and I do as well."

"I am glad I will have you to advise me, Lew, and Herm as well. And I am even more glad I do not have the Aldaran Gift because I think that if I could foresee the future, I would be too frightened to do anything at all. I would give a great deal to have some of my youthful certainty back again, instead of all these doubts."

"If you did not have doubts, Mikhail, I would be very concerned."

"That is an odd thing to say, even for you." Lew was notorious in Comyn Castle for voicing outrageous opinions as if they were the merest commonplace.

"The man who is absolutely sure of himself is much more dangerous than the one who entertains uncertainty. Robert Kadarin was such a man, and so was old Dyan Ardais. They paid a great price for their pride and vanity, and nearly ruined this world in the process. You are a thoughtful man, and that is exactly what is needed at present."

"Thank you for your confidence. It means a great deal to me, especially now." He was too tired to think about the future any longer. It was too big and very frightening. He need to change the subject, talk about more mundane matters. "You said Herm brought his family? Have you met them yet? Have they been seen to properly?"

"I stopped in and greeted them before I came to you. Since I did not feel I could leave the Castle myself, I let Rafael do the welcoming, which I think he was glad to do, since it got him out of Gisela's clutches for a short time. The wife, Katherine, is a very lovely woman from Renney, with hair like night and a forceful chin. She has a son, Amaury, from her first marriage—she was a widow—and she and Herm have a daughter, Terése, as well. A pretty child, and so like Marguerida at the same age that it nearly made my heart turn over in my chest. They are all exhausted and I suspect that Katherine and the children are more than a little frightened at the prospect of being exiled on Darkover for the rest of their lives. Herm, however, seems very glad to be home—and I can certainly understand why!"

"Renney? Why does that planet sound familiar?"

"Because one of Marguerida's favorite composers, Korniel, was born there, long ago. It is another Protected Planet, and has a history of uprisings and rebellions, and a strong movement, called the Separatists, which caused trouble from time to time, while I was still in the Senate. It was settled by colonists from Avalon, New Caledonia, and some other places, several hundred years ago. That exhausts my entire knowledge of the place, except that I understand it is very beautiful."

"I must make them feel welcome." Regis would have wanted him to greet them, he was sure. Besides, he hadn't seen Herm in years, and wanted to reacquaint himself with the fellow. Mikhail was disgusted to realize that, for all the will in the world, he could not even attempt this small courtesy.

Lew shook his head. "The first thing you should do is bathe and get some sleep, and perhaps a decent meal. Marguerida has arranged for their needs, and she is planning a small supper for them tomorrow night. Until then, you do not have to do anything except rest. Comyn Castle will run just fine without your attentions for a day or two. The world has not ended with Regis' death."

"Maybe not, but why does it feel as if it has?"

There were tears in both men's eyes as they rose from either side of the desk. Lew blew out the candles and damped down the fire. They stood, shoulder to shoulder for a moment, united in their desire to guide their world through the difficult times that lay ahead, and then Donal opened the door and they left the room.

4

Lyle Belfontaine, Station Chief at Cottman IV's HQ, leaned back in his rigid and uncomfortable chair and stared west through his large window, toward the afternoon sun, which was almost hidden behind some watery clouds. It would rain soon, or perhaps a little snow would fall. From his office he could see all the plain, square buildings that made up the headquarters complex—the power generator, the barracks, the hospital, and the rest. It was a good view, in his opinion, because from here he could see nothing of the native "city" of Thendara itself. This suited him very well. He loathed the city, its inhabitants, and, in particular, Regis Hastur and all the other recalcitrant lords of the Domains. Nothing he had done in the years he had been exiled to this godforsaken place had made any more impact on them than a gnat, and he hated being ignored.

After several minutes spent in futile musing, Belfontaine turned around and leaned forward to pick up the skimpy sheet of messagefax that lay on his otherwise empty desk blotter. He read it again, in utter dismay and disbelief. He shifted miserably, for the chair had been constructed for a taller man than he, and was bolted to the floor. He had requisitioned a new one several times, but it never had come. The chair seemed symptomatic of everything he thought wrong with the Federation at present—it was too rigid, and the wrong size.

His features twisted with discontent, and the scar he had gotten in the disastrous mess on Lein III itched across his cheek and brow. Belfontaine could have had it removed, but he had chosen not to. He believed it made him look dangerous and commanded respect. And it was a reminder of his fall from the good graces of the Federation, his removal to this benighted planet with its miserable climate, and his complete failure to execute the plans that had danced in his mind before he arrived. He had been determined to do what no one else had managed—deliver Cottman IV to the Federation on a platter. But thus far he had not succeeded, or come even close. If only he was not forced to act through underlings, and work with stupid, obstinate people like Lew Alton. At least he had gotten rid of Captain Rafe Scott—forced him to retire. Let him run his mountaineering expeditions to the Hellers—he hoped he'd break his arrogant neck or freeze to death. In fact, if the entire population turned to icicles, he would be very pleased. The place was marginal at best, but if there were no native people, then the planet could be colonized, and he could be made Governor-General, at least.

Now everything he had hoped for was ruined! The entire Federation staff was being ordered off Cottman, in only thirty days. He shook his head, ran nervous fingers through graying hair, then crunched up the missive and tossed it toward the disposal chute. It missed, falling short and dropping to the floor. The crumpled message lay there, mocking him. His chance to redeem himself, to get back in favor, was slipping away, all because of Premier Nagy and her ruthless ambition! Maybe it was a mistake. This was not the time for the Federation to pull back!

He only needed another year—two at most—and the title of Governor-General would surely be his. Not, of course, that this was what he wanted. Being governor of a place like Cottman IV would not satisfy his ambitions, but it would have been a beginning. He was sure he could have parlayed it into a better position, one on a planet where he could wield real power and influence. Cottman was as worthless a piece of rock as he had ever seen.

God, how he hated the planet. Sometimes he dreamed of calling in a Strike Force, to slag the whole place down to radioactive magma, boiling away into the void. It seemed such a suitable fate for a damned cold place, where the filthy natives believed that Hell was a freezer. It was only a fantasy, and a wasteful one at that, but the idea kept him from going crazy. Or, failing that, Belfontaine longed for a Task Force, at least. He had done his best to create a situation to justify such an order, so he could at least get a couple of regiments of Marines to "preserve order." That had worked very well on other worlds, even on members of the Federation itself. But the damned Protected status tied his hands, and unless he could demonstrate that the spaceport was in danger, or Headquarters was besieged by hostiles, it was pointless to request help. All he got was form refusals from some clerk on Alpha, telling him that the present economic problems made it impossible to fulfill his demands. He doubted anyone in charge even saw the reports he was at such pains to generate.

He was surrounded with incompetents! He had agents—true, not many, and not the best that the Security Services had to offer—and he had sent them out to make just the sort of trouble that should have brought him the power he wanted. They had failed him, for the riots he had managed to get started had ceased almost as quickly as they were begun, and Regis Hastur had never applied to him for help. He had used his own Guards, and kept order in a way that won him Belfontaine's grudging respect, or would have if he had not hated the fellow quite so deeply. He had never met Hastur, and knew of him only through the eerie Danilo Syrtis-Ardais or that damned Lew Alton, who had been appointed to a position that seemed to be the equivalent of Secretary of State, except that Cottman IV didn't use titles like that. He loathed the tall, one-handed man, and tried to avoid meeting with him whenever possible. There was something uncanny, almost unnatural, about him, something that set his nerves on edge. Alton was a wall that Belfontaine had never managed to get past.

He toyed once again with the idea of sending in a false report. His personal clerk was stupid and obedient, chosen for these qualities, actually, and would not question his orders. She likely would not even read the message, but would only type in the code. Belfontaine shuddered a little. That was exactly what had gotten him sent to Cottman in the first place, with a reduction in rank from Lieutenant General to Colonel, and a black mark on his record. His punishment was this backward, frozen hell where the populace never saw newsfeeds, and could not be influenced except by word of mouth. And Cottman had proved quite resistant to the rumors his agents had tried to spread—almost as if they knew the falseness of them.

Belfontaine's single attempt to get around the technology restrictions directly had been a complete failure. He had installed mediafeeds in a few of the taverns in the Trade City—even though this was a direct violation of several agreements—and they had been dismantled within a day. It had been a costly mistake, and he was sure that Alton was at the bottom of it. If only he could have had direct access to Regis Hastur, he was sure he could have persuaded the man of the advantages of media screens, which would have easily led to electrification of the city of Thendara, and given the Federation a grip on the attention of the people. But despite many requests, Belfontaine had never been invited to Comyn Castle, and Regis Hastur could have been an imaginary person for all the contact he had had with the man. In a fit of spite, he had put the Medical Center off limits to any except Federation personnel, thinking that the natives would be loath to forgo the conveniences of the place. He'd shut down the John Reade Orphanage as well. That hadn't worked out either. They were so stupid that they didn't care about Terran medical technology and they took care of any abandoned children themselves! They didn't even use Life Extension treatments—except that old fool up in the Hellers, Damon Aldaran—and got old and died!

This, among many other things, offended him. He intended to live for at least a hundred and fifty years—longer if possible. Hell, he'd sell his soul for immortality, if he still believed in souls or gods or any of that other claptrap. But if he did not find some way to get Cottman in his hands before the deadline, some means to destabilize the government, such as it was, he was going to find himself on another backwater world, and never have the money needed to afford the treatments at all. He was close to sixty, after thirty years in various arms of Federation Service, and he would need treatment soon. But the price had risen enormously during the past decade, which he found peculiar. Coming from a corporate family, he had a grasp of basic economics, and knew that the LE treatments should have become cheaper with the passing of time, not more expensive. Someone was clearly making a huge profit on the process. Belfontaine Industries had nothing to do with pharmaceuticals, so he could only speculate in fury.

He had been told, in a burning interview with his father, that he lacked the sort of mind that was needed for the vast empire that was

Belfontaine Industries. Otherwise, he would not have been on Cottman IV, but would instead have been dragging the molten guts out of some planet, like his brother Gustav was, producing the raw materials for the Big Ships and the dreadnoughts the Federation was busily creating.

He would never forget the day his father had told him there was no place for him in BI, that the corporate psychprobes had determined he was unsuitable for any position in the company. At least he had not suffered the unspeakable insult of a plant managership. Vividly he remembered standing in front of the huge desk behind which his father was buttressed, waiting to be told he would be appointed to the Federation legislature from one of the many planets that the corporation owned. That was the usual path for those who did not go into the company.

But apparently he was not suited for that either. He could still feel the shock at his father's words, the roughening of his skin and the shrinking of his testicles. "We can't do a thing for you, Lyle. And we certainly won't support you—no wastrels in this family. I think your only option is Federation Service—not the military side, obviously—too many possibilities for conflicts of interest that might embarrass the company. Belfontaine Industries has to come first, of course. I know you'll understand. But there should be *something* you can find, some post or other. That's all—I have a holoconference in thirty seconds."

Numb, he had taken his dismissal without a word, and walked out of the office. Federation Service! That was for people who couldn't succeed anywhere else—who were *incompetent*. He had been raised to regard the Service with contempt, and now he was being ordered to apply for it. He longed to turn around and go back, to smash Augustine Belfontaine's smooth, life-extended features into a pulp. But his father was tall and strong, and Lyle was not. He had never seen the man again, and had tried to assuage his injured feelings with plots to make them all sorry for treating him so badly.

Oddly, the Service had actually suited him rather well, after he got over his initial humiliation. He discovered he had a certain skill for administration—so much for the value of the psychprobes. He had risen rapidly through the ranks, until he made his stupid mistake on Lein III. He never should have tried to unseat a planetary ruler, especially not with explosives that could be traced to his offices. And the false reports he had sent to Alpha had been revealed for the fabrications that they were.

He had been lucky to get Cottman IV. If he had been less well-connected, he might have ended up running a penal colony, or worse, inhabiting one.

He was smarter now, and with his background in Information Technologies and Propaganda, he knew what he could have done on Cottman with even one media screen and the right sort of entertainment. He could have had the occupants of Thendara in a fury in less than a month, he was certain, and probably ready to storm Comyn Castle with pitchforks and truncheons. He had switched over to the security arm that administered outposts like this, after the incident on Lein III, and found it much to his liking. True, he had never used a weapon, although occasionally he fantasized about what he might do with a blaster. He would have liked to flame his father, still running Belfontaine Industries in his nineties, and Lew Alton, and a few other people. But he despised soldiers almost as much as he loathed hereditary rulers like Regis Hastur. They were just disposable men and women, like the workers in the factories of Belfontaine Industries. And he was aware, in moments of rare self-examination, that there was some flaw in this attitude, and occasionally wondered if the corporate psychprobes had known this about him, and that was why he had been denied his rightful place in the company.

But it was not his fault! It was people like Lewis Alton, who wanted to preserve their own power, who were keeping the Federation from achieving its destiny, to rule all the planets with an iron hand. That was just how things were supposed to be. But no—they insisted that their own customs suited them just fine, and they could not see that they were only delaying the inevitable. How could one small, backward planet stand up to the Terrans, in the long run? And he, Lyle Belfontaine, wanted to be the man who destroyed Cottman's Protected status and brought them into the Federation, where their rightful masters would make them toe the line!

It troubled him deeply that they had managed to resist thus far, for it flew in the face of what little he really believed in. These were simple things—duty, loyalty and obedience—and beyond that, Belfontaine knew that the destiny of the Federation was to control completely the lives of several trillion people spread over hundreds of planets. Anything less was unacceptable and virtually unthinkable. The Federation was the best structure to keep things running smoothly and efficiently, which to him meant that the huge corporations, like Belfontaine Industries, could do as they wished, to survive and show a profit. He had learned that almost as soon as he could walk, and nothing had ever dislodged the idea from his mind.

He was aware that sometimes this caused pain and suffering. But, in the larger view, it did not matter to him if a few million backward, ignorant people starved to feed those trillions on more developed and enlightened planets. People were a disposable commodity, after all. Not, he felt, people like himself, who were born to make important decisions and shape the future. It was the farmers and merchants and soldiers—the faceless masses—who were unimportant. Even local bigwigs like Regis Hastur were disposable. If he could just get rid of that self-important little man, he could probably take out the rest of them pretty easily.

Lyle sighed. As delightful as the idea of placing an explosive device under Comyn Castle and blowing it into well-deserved smithereens was, he knew better than to attempt it. Even in its present state of disarray, the Federation was not so disordered that questions would not be asked, a Board of Inquiry seated, and probably disgrace to follow, if such an event took place. It would be impossible to blame the thing on the locals themselves—their technology was not up to the job. No one would believe that one of the natives had gotten into HQ, stolen a shaped charge and timer, and gained the knowledge to use it properly. There were a couple of them, like Captain Rafael Scott, who had had a free run of HQ for decades before he resigned, who might, but even he could not imagine anyone believing that Scott would do such a thing. He had taken that route once, and learned his lesson. There had to be another way. He just hadn't thought of it yet.

The chime on the door rang softly, and he looked up, annoyed by the interruption. "Enter," he snapped.

A tall, broad-shouldered man stood in the doorway, leathers gleaming. He came in with an easy grace that Belfontaine envied, and his six foot frame never failed to remind him of how short he himself was. It was Miles Granfell, his second in Information, and his principal agent in fomenting discord on Cottman. He was shrewd and capable, but rather too ambitious for comfort, and Lyle did not entirely trust him. Still, he managed to smile brightly for the sake of appearances.

"So, what is going on?" Granfell was never one for chitchat and pleasantries, a trait that Belfontaine appreciated. It was a waste of time to ask how one was. And, very likely, he already knew the contents of the crumpled official communication, but wanted to pretend to ignorance for his own reasons.

"Unless we can convince Hastur to come into the Federation as a full member, we have thirty days to pull out of here."

"Is it worth trying?"

"I don't think so, but I will summon Lewis Alton tomorrow or the next day and give it one last attempt. I wish I could get to Hastur directly, but that seems to be impossible. And since the Federation is tied up with other problems, we can't get much support right now."

"Tied up?"

"It seems that the dissolution of the legislature has not been received well, and some of the member worlds are showing signs of revolt. This whole thing was ill-planned, and I can't help wonder if Premier Nagy knows what she is doing. That's what comes of putting a woman in charge! They are far too emotional for the job of governing."

Granfell nodded. "If only we had been able to get a new lease on the port lands before this happened, our position here would be much better."

"Well, we didn't. And this iceball is hardly worth the effort. They have never really traded with the Federation, and Hastur's resistance to accepting our technologies has not helped a bit. If someone else were in control of their Council—someone more in tune with the Federation—we might have a chance. But not this way." That fool, Damon Aldaran, had made a lot of vague promises, but so far he had failed to deliver on them, and now he would never have the chance. Belfontaine had never really believed the old drunk anyhow.

"The problem is not that these stupid people are anti-Federation, Belfontaine, but that they insist on being pro-Cottman. They don't give a damn about other planets, except for a few individuals, and even those still seem to love this place. I've been here ten years, and I have never, understood the attraction. It is hellishly cold and its people are backward—most of them can't even read! Hardly worth the effort, in my opinion, except that it sets a bad precedent to allow any inhabited planet to be outside the control of the Federation."

Belfontaine chuckled. "Cottman is hardly going to start building Big Ships—they don't have the resources—and challenging us. But I hate to withdraw. It feels like a failure, and I hate that."

"You said something about some of the other worlds rebelling."

"It has not come to that—yet. And frankly, I can't get much out of the head office." Odd, how the language of his corporate upbringing lingered in his speech. "But I think that there is a very real chance that a few admirals are looking at this as an opportunity to set themselves up in power, to oppose the Federation now that things are in transition. And I have managed to find out that there are huge riots on some of the worlds with Liberal representation. It won't be long before that is put down, of course, but it is troubling. We might find ourselves lifting off with nowhere to go."

"Or worse—we might not be able to leave. Have you thought of that?"

"What do you mean, Miles?" He studied the larger man suspiciously, wondering if Granfell knew something that he did not. Was it possible that Granfell had his own sources of information within HQ, or worse, some contact outside that he did not know of? The idea made him uneasy, but it bore thinking about.

"If the Federation Security Forces are busy putting down riots and rebellions, they might not be able to send ships to lift us off. We could be abandoned here for several years." Granfell spoke simply, as if the notion were a familiar one to him.

Lyle stared at the other man, aghast. He had not even considered that scenario. And it was not impossible either. In the recent past, the Federation had shown itself willing to withdraw from a few marginal planets when it could not get its way by any other means. The idea of having to remain on Cottman was distasteful, and the other was even worse. He could find himself sacrificed—unthinkable as it was! There must be some way to turn it to his advantage.

If the Federation left them behind, what would he do? He knew the answer to that almost before the thought formed in his mind. He would take out Cottman's ruling families in short order, and declare himself Governor. Without the fear of a Board of Inquiry, he could do as he pleased. It was so tempting that he almost wished, for just a moment, to be abandoned. Not that Cottman was any prize, but he could endure that—if he had the power to run things as he wished.

Granfell was looking at him oddly, so Belfontaine schooled his narrow face to look concerned, knowing well that sometimes his avidity betrayed him. "I doubt it will come to that."

"Did you know that Hermes Aldaran returned and got through customs sometime yesterday?"

"Yes, I heard about it. What does that matter?"

"Don't you think it is a little odd, him returning just now? I mean, he left Terra before the announcement was made."

Belfontaine shrugged. "He was probably lucky, that's all. If he came through the port now, we could arrest him. But it's too late. And the port is closed until we leave, so that's that." The germ of an idea began to play in the back of his mind, but Granfell's words sent it flying.

"If we *can* leave. I would not put too much dependence on the Federation at the moment, myself. I was on Comus during the evac, Lyle, and it is not a pleasant memory. Just keep in mind that you and I are disposable, unless we can think of some way to turn this situation around."

Lyle gaped at him for a second. Granfell might think himself disposable, but he refused to! Then he recovered his composure. "Do you have something specific in mind, or are you just being wishful?"

"Nothing yet, but I have been listening in the streets, and so have my agents. Something is going on. Damn. Do you know, I think that Comyn Castle is probably the only seat of government in the galaxy where we don't have eyes and ears. We've tried everything, but the people are either too stupid to be bribed, or too loyal to the Comyn. I'll try to find out more. We have a month, after all, and a lot can happen in that time."

"A pity we can't just take out . . ."

"I know. But there are no more than three hundred Marines on the whole damn planet, and even with our superior armament, that is not enough."

"True. Perhaps I'll see if I can get some reinforcements." He knew it was a vain hope.

"You do that, and I'll try to contact Vancof. It's a shame that our efforts to cause a rebellion have been so spectacularly unsuccessful, isn't it?"

"It is hard to make people who think they are content unhappy, Miles. And, frankly, these people are just too ignorant to know how much better off they would be with good technology. I thought I would bring them to their knees when I put the Medical Center off limits, but it did not work. They just don't know enough to care."

"Incredible, isn't it? Half of them are illiterate, have never seen a vidram, and they look down on us as if we were . . . barbarians, I suppose."

"Arrogant bastards! I want to bring them down!" His control left him suddenly, and his fist crashed down on the desk, startling both Belfontaine and his companion. "They don't know what is good for them!"

"True enough," Granfell replied mildly, as if he were amused at his superior's outburst. "But I am not ready to try storming Comyn Castle with the men I have at my disposal—not until I have exhausted all the other possibilities. I am going to make another try to get someone into the place—not that I have much hope of succeeding. The pile appears to be entry-proof. Sometimes I think that old rumor about there being mindreaders on Cottman has more truth in it than we have believed."

He glared at Granfell for several seconds. Where had he gotten the idea that he had the right to storm the castle? Was his second pursuing his own ambitions, or trying to usurp his authority? No, he must just be speaking generally. Unless he was up to some scheme of his own. That was a disquieting thought, much worse than imaginary telepaths or magicians.

Belfontaine shook his head, suppressing a shudder. "That is impossible. Project Telepath was a complete bust, and a waste of money. Oh, yes, there are a few mutants around, but nothing to worry about. I just think that, for primitives, the Cottman have excellent security." He smiled grimly, knowing that it infuriated Granfell that he had never been able to penetrate the castle. Still, he could not shake off the way Miles had spoken, as if he were in command of the Marines, not Belfontaine. He would have to keep an eye on Granfell during the coming weeks—the man was too ambitious and too clever.

"We'll see. Dirck Vancof has been almost useless, but maybe he can get us the information we need. I'll talk to you later."

After Granfell left, Lyle sat at the desk, staring at the empty blotter, and feeling a churning in his guts. The idea that had come into his mind returned after a few minutes, and he turned it over. Hermes Aldaran could now be considered an enemy of the Federation. Could he use that as an excuse to force Hastur to do something rash, and then bring in a Task Force?

It was unfortunate that Lew Alton knew Federation law as well as he did, but it would not hurt to demand that Aldaran be turned over, would it? It might upset old Lord Aldaran, but he had already proved himself to be a useless ally. His son Robert, the older one, was no better. A dull fellow without an ounce of imagination. There was the sister, who lived in Comyn Castle, but she hadn't been nearly as useful as he had hoped at first. Besides, women were not to be trusted. There had to be a way to topple the Hasturs—he just needed to find it!

5

When Mikhail escorted Marguerida and his children into the smaller dining room the following evening, he was pleasantly surprised to discover that he felt almost human. There was an ache in him that was not physical, which he recognized as grief. He had experienced it long ago, when his nephew Domenic Alar had died, and later again over Emun Elhalyn and Emun's mother, Priscilla. He had felt it again ten years before when Diotima Ridenow, Lew's wife, had died. Neither rest nor food would banish it, only time. And Regis would have expected him to go on, to keep things going smoothly. He only wished it were easier.

At the same time, he was looking forward to seeing Hermes Aldaran again, after so many years, and to meeting his wife and children. Lew had been right to send him to bed the previous day, and to insist on keeping him secluded for a time, but he still felt a bit guilty that he had not gone to the old Storn suite and greeted them personally. He had seen no one except his wife and children, and that had been hard enough.

Domenic, his firstborn and heir, seemed deeply affected, and somehow angry. That was puzzling, but he did not have the energy to puzzle it out right now. He knew better than to ask Nico, who had been a very quiet child, and was now an extremely private young man. Rory, his second child, insisted on making really dreadful jokes, as if he could not bear the general gloom that had settled over Comyn Castle. He had managed to annoy everyone, provoking his sister Yllana, his foster-sister Alanna, and Ida Davidson, who was usually impervious to the behavior of adolescents. Even Marguerida, who ordinarily found Rory's antics amusing, was ready, she said, to send the thirteen-year-old to Nevarsin, where the *cristoforo* monks would teach him some manners. Rory just grinned, completely unafraid of this threat, as he was of almost anything. It was a shame he was not quite old enough for the Cadet Guards yet, because even Mikhail admitted his middle child was sorely lacking in discipline.

Alanna Alar was already present in the dining room, her auburn hair burnished like pure copper, her green eyes taking in everything. She had been a fretful baby, an anxious child, and now had bloomed into a vigilant and restless adolescent. He glanced at her, standing on the far side of the room and gave her a smile. To his pleasure, she returned it. Mikhail was fond of her, but he had to admit he found his niece rather eerie. He was relieved to see her in a good mood. Yllana had been completely disconsolate at Regis' death, but Alanna behaved with something closer to indifference, which was peculiar, since she had been close to her great-uncle. He suspected that she was numb with shock, and that when this condition finally wore off, she would make up for her present calm with a double helping of the hysteria for which she was well known in Comyn Castle. There seemed, to his mind, little question that she had inherited some of the instability that blighted so many of the Elhalyn line, and he could only be grateful that she seemed merely high-strung, instead of clearly mad, as some of her cousins had been. And time might cure that. Mikhail hoped so, for he was genuinely fond of the girl.

She really was a beautiful young woman, and aware of it as well. She had just completed the first part of her training at Arilinn, where her powerful and remarkable *laran* was being disciplined, he sincerely hoped, into something manageable. She was already both a teleport and a firestarter, a combination that was potentially deadly, and one which was so rare that it was difficult to limit. She had a hot temper, as well, which made her extremely dangerous. He worried more about his niece than he ever did about his own children, for her quicksilver disposition reminded him rather too much of some of the Elhalyn children, Vincent in particular. She had some of the same egotism, but none of the bullying tendencies of that now deceased man.

Mikhail watched Nico smile at Alanna, brightening as he always did around his difficult cousin and foster-sister. Eight months separated them in age, and she had lived in Comyn Castle since she was five. They were, together, more like twins than otherwise, and had an uncanny ability to either cheer one another up, or send each other into foul moods that no one else could understand. Tonight she seemed to be on her best behavior, despite the general air of sorrow that was everywhere. He thanked the gods for that favor, and turned toward the doorway of the dining room.

Herm and his family came into the room, and Mikhail put everything else out of his mind. Behind him, Donal came to attention, alert in every muscle, examining the newcomers with a very jaundiced eye, much too suspicious for such a young man. Mikhail held back a sigh, for like himself, Donal had never really had a childhood. He knew he had made the right decision for himself, taking his young relative for paxman, but he was not as sure that he had made the best choice for Donal.

Mikhail studied Hermes Aldaran, trying to fit the image of the man before him with his memories of a much younger person he had known briefly over twenty years before. He had much less hair on the top of his head, and a softness above his belt that spoke of little physical activity. There were interesting wrinkles around his eyes, and the mouth almost hidden in his curling beard was generous, made for laughter. But there was no merriment in his face now, just a sort of tension, as if he were uncertain of his welcome.

Beside him stood a very attractive woman, with black hair and, as Lew had mentioned, a square and stubborn jaw. Two children stood next to her. The boy, who looked about thirteen, had gray eyes that went immediately to Alanna with interest and admiration, and the girl, who might be nine or ten, seemed a little bashful in the presence of so many strangers. Lew was right—the girl looked like an Aldaran and could have easily been mistaken for a child of either Marguerida's or Gisela's.

They were dressed in Federation garb, which looked outré and exotic to Mikhail. The girl, Terése, wore a brief skirt of some shiny stuff, and her still gawky limbs were covered in stockings of a woven material with a vivid pattern in it. Her mother wore a close-fitting gown of dark red velvet, cut low over the shoulders, and clinging across her bosom. The lower portion of the dress dropped from knee length in the front to floor length at the back, showing off elegant calves and feet clad in shiny shoes. Her obviously long black hair was elaborately braided and coiled behind her head, decently concealing her nape, and long metal earrings dangled beside her graceful throat. Herm and the boy wore jackets that ended abruptly at the waist, over pleated shirts and narrow trousers that looked rather uncomfortable to Mikhail. All in all, it was a bizarre presentation, and he had to school himself not to stare at Katherine's legs.

Katherine glanced at Marguerida, then at Alanna and Yllana. Her face clouded with dismay for a moment, and when he saw Gisela and his brother Rafael come through the door behind her, he realized that his ever mischievous sister-in-law had been up to one of her tricks. She had probably told Katherine to wear these clothes. Still, as he watched, he saw the woman's face become composed, her spine stiffening a little in the lovely but unsuitable gown. She had been a Senator's wife for over a decade now, and could probably handle herself in situations he could not even imagine.

Oh, dear—she is upset, Mik.

Anyone can see that, caria.

Gisela offered to look after her, and I just assumed she would tell Katherine what sort of dress was appropriate. I was so tired that I could not think straight! I know it doesn't matter to you, but we women take these matters very seriously. Damn!!

My darling optimist! After all these years, you should know better than to trust Giz. Katherine has very nice legs, don't you think?

Should I be jealous?

Never, my dearest, never.

Herm cleared his throat. "Hello, Mikhail. It has been a long time, hasn't it? I would like to present my wife, Katherine Korniel Aldaran, and our children, Amaury and Terése."

"Welcome to Comyn Castle. I only wish your arrival had been a little less hectic, and I apologize for not coming to meet you earlier. I was sent to bed, frankly, although thankfully not without my supper." Mikhail exerted himself to be friendly, hoping to ease the awkwardness away.

"Korniel? Are you by chance related to the composer of that name?" Marguerida wondered.

"He was my great-uncle," Katherine answered.

Marguerida repressed her lively interest, her eyes almost sparkling, and stepped forward with both her mitted hands outstretched in greeting. "Where are my manners! How are you, after your long journey?" She paused for a moment, waited for Herm to speak, then when he did not, went on. "*Domna* Katherine, this is my husband, Mikhail Hastur, and my children, Domenic, Rory, and Yllana. Yllana, why don't you take Terése and get her a glass of berry juice? Or watered wine, if you do not mind, Katherine?"

"I think a little watered wine would not be a bad thing—not too much, Terése," Katherine answered in a deep alto voice that was heavy with tension.

Over her shoulder, Mikhail could read the faint disappointment in Gisela's expression. She was plumper now than when she had been a girl, her waist thickened with child-bearing as Marguerida's had failed to do, and her face had lost some of its earlier winsomeness. He gave her a stern look, and she had the grace to redden a little. Katherine caught his expression, and her eyes widened in surprise, apparently thinking he was glaring at her. Then she looked quickly over her shoulder, saw Gisela's blush, and turned back toward him with a splendid smile.

Yllana's pale blue eyes twinkled, and she gave the other girl a quick grin. Terése answered with a relieved smile, as if she were very glad to remove herself from the orbit of her parents, and to be in the company of someone her own age. The two girls slipped across the room as if they had known each other for days instead of moments, and Mikhail sensed that Yllana was pleased to be out of earshot of any adults.

Roderick made a decent bow in front of Katherine, his eyes sparkling with mischief. "Come on, Amaury—the grown-ups don't need us underfoot. Nico and I will be glad to answer your questions, and I'll wager you have a lot of them."

Amaury glanced at his parents, then started to follow Rory toward the fireplace. "I have one—who is that girl watching us from over there?" Mikhail heard him ask.

"Oh, that's just Alanna," Roderick replied. "She is our cousin and our foster-sister." Then he passed out of earshot, and Mikhail glanced over his shoulder at his foster-daughter. She should have been beside them, to be introduced. Oh, well, the children would make their own way. Then Mikhail turned back to Herm and Katherine. There was an awkward silence for a moment.

"Have you begun to recover from your journey?" Mikhail asked.

"We have caught up on our sleep, and enjoyed eating real food." Katherine spoke in *casta* easily, but her accent was unfamiliar. She rounded the vowel sounds more than was normal, and in her mouth, the language sounded unusually musical. "We offer our condolences, *Dom* Mikhail, on the death of your uncle."

"Thank you, *domna*. It has been a great shock and a terrible loss for all of us." He paused, feeling this formal response was a bit cold. "I cannot really believe it, yet. It all seems like a nightmare from which I cannot manage to awaken."

"Of course it is! If I understand what Gisela told me, there was no warning, no signs of illness or anything."

"Nothing whatever," he answered, moved by her immediate understanding.

"That makes it all the harder to bear."

A silence fell heavily among the four of them then, as if no one could think of what to say. Finally Marguerida stepped into the breach. "I am sorry that that I could not greet you upon your arrival, but things are in such a state. And I am sincerely happy that you are here, and hope that you find Darkover to your liking." She paused and the shadow of a smile graced her lips. "It might take some getting used to for you," she continued, as a servant appeared with a tray of wineglasses. She took one and offered it to Katherine, who gave her a speculative look, as if she suspected there might be some hidden meaning in the last words. Donal picked one up and handed it to Mikhail. Herm helped himself, looking more at ease now. "I can remember my own difficulties, when I came back sixteen years ago," she added, smiling and shaking her head at the vivid memories at the same time.

Gisela and Rafael moved forward, and from the petulant expression on her face, Mikhail suspected that his brother was giving her a telepathic lecture that she was not enjoying. He had a stab of guilt, that Rafael had ended up with this difficult woman, but he knew that his steady, older sibling genuinely cared for her. At the same time, he was sincerely glad he had not been shackled to Gisela, because he was certain he would have strangled her long since. He could only admire his brother's patience in silence, resisting any impulse to eavesdrop even a little.

"Herm tried to explain things to me," Katherine was saying to Marguerida, "and so did Gisela, but I still feel quite disoriented." She gave Herm a stern look, then favored Gisela with one that was openly hostile.

Mikhail could just imagine what sort of nonsense Giz had offered, and admired Katherine's firm control on her temper. "My husband has been keeping secrets from me for years, and I am only now discovering them." She moved restlessly and brushed her free hand across her brow, as if she was afraid of something.

"I have tried to reassure her that her thoughts are safe, but Katherine is a very stubborn woman," Herm commented dryly. "She will probably forgive me in a few decades."

Marguerida nodded and gave a soft laugh. "If you are fortunate, *Dom* Hermes. *Domna*, trust me. No one is going to invade your privacy." *She's very frightened, Mik, but I must say she is concealing it very well.*

"Would I know if they did?" Katherine asked with candor. Mikhail could sense her heart beating a little faster, and felt his liking for the woman increase further.

"No, you would not," Marguerida admitted calmly. "And your uppermost thoughts are audible to me, if I focus my attention on you. Still, you are worrying yourself for no good reason. Darkovans are most scrupulous in these matters."

"I suppose they must be, or else everyone would be quite mad." Katherine sighed and drank off half her glass with a nervous gesture. "I will be all right as soon as I can get back to work."

"Work?" Mikhail looked at her, watching the wine begin to ease her discomfort.

"Katherine is a very fine painter, and she left much of her clothing behind so she could bring along her paints and brushes." Herm smiled fondly at his wife. "I met her when she was doing a portrait." *Damn Gisela for setting us wrong—I should have known she was up to something. I don't care about my clothing, but I think my Kate will take my sister's eyes out the first chance she gets. I had almost forgotten how spiteful she could be, for no good reason.*

"An artist. How wonderful. Then we must give you a room in which to work," Marguerida insisted. "Let me think. Ah, yes. There is a pleasant chamber on the second floor, with decent north light. It is very quiet, so you will not be disturbed. Will you need an easel? I don't suppose you brought one, what with the restrictions on baggage."

"You are right—I didn't." Katherine looked at Marguerida with relief. "Herm did not tell me what was going on—he could not have risked it, really—just told me to pack, and we were at the spaceport before I knew what was happening. It is a very good thing I trust my husband, for if I had not, we would probably not be here now. But it was very . . . unsettling."

"I am sure it was," Marguerida said with sympathy. Better than anyone in the room, she knew what it meant to be uprooted, to be dragged out of bed in the middle of the night without explanation. Her memories of the Sharra Rebellion were vague, for she had only been a child at the time, but they remained disturbing, even after so many years.

She set aside these thoughts firmly and concentrated on making Katherine feel more comfortable. "We must have an easel built for you immediately. The Castle carpenters can probably manage that in a day, although they will complain that they have been rushed and that it is not a good job, that the wood is not of the proper sort, then stand around and mutter darkly. They will tell you that it would have been better if they had had oak, but that only pine was available, most likely."

Katherine laughed at last. "I know. Craftsmen are such perfectionists. I don't suppose I can get any canvases?"

"We have canvas, but it is not of a quality for painting, only for making awnings and tents. Can you manage with board? Wood we have in plenty, and our painters here use panels of it."

"Perhaps Master Gilhooly can provide some," Mikhail offered. "He is head of the Painters Guild, which I confess is a very small company. They can probably supply you with panels and anything else you need, including pigments."

"That would be wonderful, since my supplies are limited, and it does not seem that I am going to be able to get more when these are exhausted. I confess that I am very spoiled, since all I needed to do was sit down at the console of my computer and order what I needed, and it would be delivered in a few hours." *I cannot believe I am standing here discussing paints with these complete strangers, as if nothing were more important. Why is Mikhail wearing a glove indoors—maybe his hand is scarred or something? And Marguerida has mitts, but Gisela does not. It is not cold in here, but perhaps she has poor circulation. Will I ever understand these people? It is all too confusing. I wish I were somewhere else!*

"There are no computers here since that is a restricted technology, forbidden except to the people at HQ," said Mikhail. "And we have nothing resembling a depot of art supplies on Darkover. The Painters Guild grinds and mixes their own colors, and the Brushmakers supply the tools. I believe the Woodworkers Guild is charged with creating the panels. And that entirely exhausts my store of knowledge on the matter."

"Then you have never visited the Painters Guild yourself?" Katherine seemed surprised by his knowledge and then by his ignorance.

"No, I have not." Mikhail shrugged his shoulders. Like Regis before him, he had been a virtual prisoner in Comyn Castle for years, except for a few trips to Arilinn, and one to Armida, ten years before. Now he would be even more restricted, he knew, and the prospect did not delight him. "I would know nothing at all, except that I was a very curious boy, and I absorbed tidbits whenever I could. I know who is head of the Guild, because it is part of my duty to know, but I have never actually met Master Gilhooly. I met his predecessor long ago, when he came to arrange for a portrait of Lady Linnea, and I asked him a great many questions, the answers to which have long since faded from memory." Mikhail shook his head and laughed softly.

"I think we are about to sit down, Mikhail. Will you show *Domna* Katherine to her place." *And keep charming her,* cario. *It's working. She is starting to relax a little, which should improve her digestion.*

That will not be any burden. I like her. Do you?

Oh, yes. And it is taking all my discipline not to ask her more about Amedi Korniel right now. His official biography is rather dry and she probably never actually met him, but maybe she knows some family stories about him. But it gives us some common ground for further conversation.

It is good to hear you sounding excited, my dearest. These last few days have been so hard on you.

On both of us, Mikhail.

Mikhail offered Katherine his arm, and she took it cautiously, acutely aware of the young man just behind him, watching her suspiciously. Who was he, and why had no one introduced him? Katherine let herself be guided toward the table as her husband fell in beside Marguerida with conscious grace, as if this were no more than a state dinner of the sort they had attended hundreds of times before.

There was a quiet scraping of chairs, as everyone got settled. Mikhail saw Nico get Alanna seated, while Roderick helped Terése. Amaury, taking a cue from the boys, helped Yllana, and then sat between her and Alanna, casting an admiring glance at the Alar girl. Mikhail seated Katherine to his right, in the place of honor, while Marguerida did the same with Hermes.

Gisela started to take the place at Mikhail's left, but just then Lew Alton appeared with Ida Davidson, the widow of Marguerida's mentor, on his arm. He seated Ida next to Herm, then subtly shifted Gisela one place down, getting a very dirty look for his pains. Danilo Syrtis-Ardais trailed behind them, and took the empty place on Gisela's other side. She did not look as if being buttressed by the two men pleased her, but she shrugged and seemed to choose to make the best of it. Mikhail observed her green eyes as they flashed toward the other side of the table, where Rafael was taking his place on Marguerida's left, with the children ranged beside him.

The servants went around, filling glasses, and the soup course was brought. Except for the children, there was very little conversation around the table. Roderick was telling Herm's daughter about his horse, and she was round-eyed. Horses were almost extinct in much of the Federation, and it was clear the girl had only seen one in the Menagerie.

Lew gave Mikhail a quick look, his eyes troubled. *What is it, Lew?*

I just received a most interesting message from Belfontaine—addressed to Regis, of course. Thus far I have managed to keep word of his death from getting to HQ, but I won't be able to keep it from them for much longer.

Why bother, they'll find out eventually?

Because I do not wish us to be perceived as being vulnerable, Mikhail. The Federation has a history of using events like Regis' death to try to further their own interests. I am especially glad that Dani is here, and not at Elhalyn Castle. And Gareth Elhalyn showed up an hour ago, so he is safe, too.

I don't understand.

It is not beyond imagination that they might kidnap him and try to have him put into power. They have done such things on other worlds. I believe that the situation in the Federation is too chaotic at present for anyone to attempt such a coup, but the sooner Domna Miralys *and her daughter get here, the happier I will be. Gareth is with his father and Lady Linnea for the evening. I am probably jumping at shadows, and giving Belfontaine more credit for imagination than he deserves.*

So, what was in the message?

It was closer to a demand—he wants me to hand over Herm, as an enemy of the Federation. He made a few veiled threats about what would result if we did not, but since I know that the Federation is going to be leaving Darkover in the very near future, I don't think he can really act on them.

Pull out? Did Belfontaine say that?

Hardly. That I learned in a note from Ethan MacDoevid just ten minutes ago—our intelligence is still better than Belfontaine's! He seems to have charmed the information out of Belfontaine's personal clerk, immediately before he was ordered out of Headquarters for good. He said he will come around tomorrow, and tell me everything he has managed to pick up. I praise the day Marguerida decided to send him to Rafe Scott, for he has been invaluable since Rafe was forced to retire, even though he has no laran *and cannot eavesdrop that way. But it does mean we now have no one actually in HQ, and any information we get will have to be acquired unscrupulously.* There was a kind of merriment in this last remark, and Mikhail knew what his father-in-law meant.

Mikhail realized that Katherine was watching him intently, and that she must suspect something was being said that she could not hear. Her earlier discomfort had returned, and he cursed himself silently for letting his attention wander. She was an intelligent woman, and for all he knew, might be a Federation spy. No, he was being overcautious. She was just a woman in an unfamiliar setting, yanked out of her familiar world without warning and dropped down in the middle of a political crisis.

"Lew mentioned that you were from Renney, *Domna* Katherine. I confess I know nothing about it, except that your ancestor, the composer, came from there. He is a favorite of my wife's, and she is yearning to interrogate you about him, but that will keep. Please, tell me about your home world."

Katherine set down her spoon, her bowl empty, looking quite relieved to be asked about so ordinary a subject. "Well, there is not a great deal to tell. It is a small place, at the edge of the Pollux sector. We are farmers and dairymen and seafarers, much as our ancestors were when they were still on Terra. We speak a tongue very similar to your own—it astonished me when Herm demonstrated the likenesses. I lived there until I was sixteen, and then I won a scholarship to the Fine Arts Academy on Coronis. I studied painting with Donaldo dePaul, and then met my first husband, Amaury's father. He was killed in an accident when Amaury was a baby, and two years later, I met Herm. My life, until the past few days, has been extremely uneventful."

"I am sorry that you did not come to Darkover under better circumstances, *domna*."

"When I married Herm, I took a vow to be with him at all times, good and bad, but I confess I never expected that to mean I would be dragged out of my bed in the middle of the night and end up on the other side of the Federation, far away from everything I know, and with very little chance of ever seeing Renney again." There was no mistaking the sadness in her voice now, and the undertone of worry as well. "Except for the children, and my cousin Cara, who was in the Chamber of Deputies, my entire family is still there, for we are not a world that produces very many travelers. We have everything we need on Renney, or almost. When I left, my Nana just shook her head and said she hoped I would not rue the day. I can imagine what she would say now."

"I hope you will not miss it too much, and we must both pray that things do not get completely out of hand."

She shook her head, and the coil at her nape shifted, so Mikhail got a glimpse of the soft flesh at the back of her neck. "I overheard Lew Alton and Herm talking, and they did not sound very cheerful. I can barely believe that the Premier has disbanded the Legislature. It seems so . . . extreme. And, for all that I am the wife of politician, I have managed to keep myself in relative ignorance, because worrying about political strife interferes with my work." She looked faintly embarrased at this admission, and glanced at the now empty glass in front of her, as if she wanted something to focus on. A servant started to refill it almost immediately.

Domenic, who was seated beside Katherine, spoke for the first time. "It was a crazy thing to do, *domna*." A puzzled look came into his face, as if he was surprised by his own outburst. He glanced at his father, and when he found no look of disapproval, he relaxed.

Mikhail looked fondly at his oldest child, the most mysterious of his offspring. He did not know if it was because the child had been conceived in the distant past, or because he had spent several weeks of time suspended in his mother's womb while both she and Mikhail were in the misty waters of Lake Hali, but he was much more mature than his years suggested, and he was a remote boy. No . . . not remote, but just having a hard time making the transition from childhood to adulthood. Sometimes he was shy and other times he was outspoken, although he was never bold in the way his brother Roderick was.

Istvana Ridenow, who had first tested him, said he had a unique *laran*, one she was unable to define to her own satisfaction. True, he had the Alton Gift of forced rapport, as strongly as his mother, but there was something else as well. Mikhail wondered from time to time if Nico had the living matrix of the Hasturs, but Istvana said it was not that. Whatever it was, it was developing in its own way, slowly and almost painfully. He had a kind of shyness around everyone except his cousin Alana that made him quiet and reserved.

Katherine looked at Nico with interest. "I agree, but I would like to know your thoughts." *What am I saying? I can't know his thoughts, because I am not a telepath, but he can probably know mine, even though Marguerida said that . . . damn Herm for not warning me! And what about Terése? Is my little girl going to be a mindreader or some other sort of witch, like Great-grandmother Lila was supposed to have been? Nana's stories about her always gave me the creeps, and here I am on a planet where some of the people have the ability to look into my mind whenever they choose, and I can't tell who can and who cannot. Even though I have nothing to hide, it is still intolerable! Well, I would not be disappointed to give that Gisela a piece of my mind, except she probably has just enough scruples not to snoop when I very much wish she would! I really must try to be more consistent—one second feeling naked in this room, and the next expecting these odd folks to hear my thoughts. I wonder what that man next to Gisela is saying. Whatever it is, she doesn't look very happy about it—serves her right, the cat! She deliberately tried to embarrass us!*

Nico considered her question without speaking, as if trying to find the best approach. These days he often appeared very sullen, alternating without reason toward sudden bursts of pungent observation that surprised his elders. Remembering his own adolescence, Mikhail knew it was normal for his age. At least he thought about his words first, unlike Rory who said the first thing that came into his head, without any thought of the consequences. Mikhail loved them both, but he knew he favored Roderick, just a little, because Domenic was so very opaque and distant.

"I have been listening to Grandfather Lew. And thinking. It seems to me that the Terranan have leaped before they looked." Nico frowned and hesitated. Then he continued. "Granddad says that most of his mistakes came from acting before he considered what might happen, and that the Federation has done that now." He glanced across the table at Lew, to see if he had said anything untoward, but Lew just continued consuming his soup in pleasant silence.

"Aren't you a little young to be thinking about political ramifications?" Katherine sounded both amused and genuinely interested. It was clear she was at ease with the boy. Mikhail could tell that Domenic was starting to respond to her friendliness, to abandon his normal reserve and actually enjoy himself.

"I am fifteen, and I have been thinking of politics all my life, or so it seems to me." He gave Katherine one of his rare and charming smiles, then ran his fingers through his hair, unconsciously imitating Mikhail. His hair was a little long, touching the collar of his green tunic, because Nico loathed the barber. "You see, with our long winters, with the snow up to the window sills for months, we are all devoted to intrigue here. Just ask Aunt Giz sometime, and you will get an earful." He cast a look across the table at Gisela, and to Mikhail's surprise, there was something like real malice in his son's gaze.

"Aunt?" She looked slightly confused for a moment. "Of course. Do you know, I believe that makes me your in-law as well. I had not thought of that before. I have lots of sisters, and nieces and nephews by the bushel, but it hadn't really penetrated my brain that I would have instant relations on Darkover." She turned her head gracefully and looked Gisela up and down, managing to convey without a word that her new sister-in-law was a mere country girl, and something of a dowd into the bargain. Mikhail dabbed his napkin to his mouth to conceal the broad grin on his lips, while Gisela simmered with fury. Then Katherine turned back to Mikhail, her dark eyes flashing in a very attractive way, as if she had paid off a score and was quite pleased with herself. "Indeed, I believe Amaury and I are the only people at the table who are not some sort of relation to you by blood. Is that right?"

Mikhail nodded. She was as intelligent as Lew had suggested. "Almost correct. The elderly woman seated next to Hermes is not a native of Darkover, but the widow of Marguerida's musical mentor. But everyone else is a relative, yes. Young Donal here," he said, gesturing over his shoulder, "is both my nephew and my paxman, and Alanna is his sister. You could say that most gatherings of the Domain families are family gatherings, and not be too far off the mark." It seemed like a safe topic, and he decided to pursue it further, just to keep Katherine from dwelling on her fears. "And since the arrival of the Terranan over a century ago, we have intermarried with them as well. For instance, Lew's mother, Elaine, was a daughter of Mariel Aldaran and a Terran man, Wade Montray. Lew's first wife, Marjorie, was also an Aldaran, on her mother's side, and her father was Zeb Scott, a Terran. So, my Marguerida is a cousin of your husband through her grandmother."

Katherine frowned over this. "But not an Aldaran through her father's first wife, I take it."

She was quick! "No—Marguerida's mother was Marjorie's half sister, Thyra."

"Mother does not like to talk about her," Nico said very quietly, the remnants of his usual shyness vanishing in the warmth of Katherine's attention. "She was a very strange person, and wicked, too."

"Thank you for telling me—I can see that it would be easy to make a mistake and mention something that would offend her. Now I finally understand why she and Gisela look so similar—they are cousins as well as sisters-in-law. I thought that Renney kinships were convoluted, but I think that Darkover might just have us beaten, fair and square."

"Father was almost forced to marry Gisela, but he went away instead," Nico answered, his tongue loosened with wine and his dark eyes glittering with something like his brother's devilment. He knew that the subject still made Mikhail squirm. Then he glanced at Katherine's face and grinned. "Father and Mother ran away together in the middle of the night and got married by . . ."

"Domenic!"

"Oh, Father, she is sure to hear the tale from someone, and you would not want the servants telling her, would you?"

"I am sure *Domna* Katherine does not wish to be bored with events in the past."

Domenic laughed aloud, and everyone stared at him for a moment. "The past! That is a good one, Father."

For a moment, Mikhail had the wish to strangle his firstborn. Katherine was not yet easy in their company, and he was sure that hearing a tale about a trip into the Ages of Chaos, in Darkover's distant past, would only increase her discomfort. Accepting telepaths was surely enough for the present. At the same time, he realized, Nico was right. If she did not hear the story from him, she would find out from another source, likely embellished with details that were more fancy than truth. He could just imagine Gisela's version of their adventures.

Katherine looked from son to father and raised her eyebrows. She really was a handsome woman. "Now I am very intrigued. My Nana always said that I was as curious as a bag of cats. And, in truth, I would rather hear about anything except the follies of the Federation. I am throughly sick of that subject."

A servant removed her soup bowl and replaced it with a plate of fritters and broiled fish. Mikhail had already been served his portion, and picked up his fork with his gloved hand. He cut off a bite of fritter, lightly flavored with herbs, and speared a piece of fish.

When he had swallowed and sipped some wine, Mikhail spoke. "Domenic means that Marguerida and I were drawn into the past—about seven hundred years—and were married by an ancient *laranzu* called Varzil the Good, who was of the Ridenow Domain. It all seems quite fantastic to me, and I was there!" Then he cursed himself for the clumsiness of his choice of words, and knew how very weary he still was.

Katherine choked, and Domenic gave her a few firm pats between her bare shoulders. She gasped for air and her eyes bulged. Then she recovered her breath, emptied her refilled glass in a few gulps, and stared at Mikhail. "You are serious, aren't you?"

"Very. But I do not expect you to believe me, when my own mother very much doubts the truth of it. I can only say that I was there, and I know what happened. You do not have to believe me." He glanced at the heavy *di catenas* bracelet that encircled his wrist, made for another man whose name was a variant of Mikhail, then looked down the long table toward his wife, remembering that strange, magical time.

"You traveled in time?" She was both amazed and disbelieving, but her curiosity got the better of her.

"Yes."

"What was it like?"

Mikhail was rather taken aback by her question, for it was not the reaction he had anticipated. "It was very uncomfortable."

Katherine began to laugh, and tears formed in the corners of her eyes. After a few moments, they began to trickle down her cheeks, and she dabbed at them with the corner of her napkin. Finally she regained control of herself and turned to Domenic. "Is he always this terse?"

"Almost, unless he is lecturing Rory." Domenic gave his father a fond look, which took most of the sting out of the words. But not all. Mikhail could remember vividly the day Dani Hastur had told him that his father never seemed to have time to talk to him. Was this how Nico felt? Mikhail had promised himself he would be a great parent, that he would not neglect his children that way. Now he felt that he had failed.

It is all right, Father. You listen more than you talk, that is all. And you worry too much.

Thank you, Nico. You do know that you can always come to me, don't you?

Yes, but I don't have much to say.

Are you happy, son?

No, but there is nothing you can do about it. And I don't want to discuss it, either now or any other time.

Very well. Mikhail returned to eating glumly. Then he remembered himself at fifteen, and how prickly he had been. He forced himself to relax and let the matter go, for it was likely just the normal problem of being an adolescent, and would take care of itself in time. Was any teenager happy? Probably not.

Mikhail looked up from his plate and found Marguerida looking at him from the other end of the table. She gave him one of her wonderful smiles, a look that never failed to reassure him and comfort him, then turned her attention back to Herm Aldaran. The deep pain of his uncle's sudden death, and the actuality that he was now the real ruler of Darkover seemed to lessen a little with her look. With Marguerida beside him, he knew he could face anything, no matter how impossible it seemed at the moment. He turned his attention to the food on his plate, while his son and Katherine talked, and let himself think of nothing in particular.

At the other end of the table, Marguerida observed her son and husband, and sighed softly. She wondered what had provoked Katherine's outburst of merriment. The woman struck her as very serious, but she seemed less angry now, and Marguerida was glad of that.

"I don't know what Mikhail said, but it is good to hear Kate laugh like that again. I was beginning to think . . . well, no matter." Herm smiled at Marguerida as he spoke.

"She must be beside herself."

"Do you know, I have never understood that phrase. How can one be beside themselves? But, yes, she has been very troubled, for which I cannot blame her. When I first met her, she was a young widow, and very sad. From all I can gather, Amaury's father was a very good fellow, and his sudden death was a great blow. I have often wished I had known him, although if he had still been alive, I would never have had the opportunity to marry Katherine, and that would have been intolerable for me!" He chuckled to himself. "I might have had to challenge him to a duel, or something equally preposterous."

"You do not strike me as a marrying sort of man," Marguerida commented.

"You are right on that, though how you could have discerned it after such a brief acquaintance I do not know. I was quite happy in my bachelorhood, until I encountered Katherine, and then the only thing I could think of was to marry her as quickly as possible, before someone else snatched her away."

"Were there other suitors, then?"

"No, not at all. But I kept imagining hordes of them, lurking in the corners of the ballrooms and drawing rooms. She is so beautiful that I could not help it. And why she agreed to marry me remains a mystery. I know I am not a handsome man." He gestured at his shining pate. "Whatever good looks I had, Robert damaged in a fist fight when we were lads." He rubbed his nose, which had clearly been broken at least once.

"Robert in a fist fight? Now, that is a remarkable notion, for he has always seemed to me to be the best-tempered of men."

"He is, but I was a very provoking boy. Not unlike your Rory, I suspect. But, tell me, how did you arrive at the conclusion that I was not the marrying type? My curiosity demands satisfaction."

"Gisela suggested to me, long ago, that you were a confirmed bachelor. Indeed, I did not even know you had married, let alone were a father, until you arrived. Somehow you never mentioned it in your messages to my father, or in your infrequent letters to your sister. Why did you keep it such a secret? Didn't you want your father to know he had another granddaughter?"

Herm grunted. "My father and I parted on poor terms, *Domna* Marguerida, and one reason I took the position in the Chamber of Deputies was to escape him. And because it was the chance of a lifetime for me. I had wanted to travel to the stars since I was a boy, all full of the tales told by the spacemen who frequented our home. But, I never wanted to be a spacer at all—the idea of being cooped up in a ship for long periods of time made me cringe. Besides having no talent for the mathematics and other disciplines that are needed. And it seemed that this was the only way to leave Darkover, until Regis decided to appoint me. I jumped at the chance, and, frankly, my father was furious with me."

"But, why?"

"I suspect it was because he never liked Regis, but I cannot say for certain. All I know is that he went into one of his rages, a drunken fury that had the servants scrambling for cover, and called me a number of things I cannot repeat in polite company."

Marguerida grinned. "There is nothing you can say that would shock me, and Mikhail can tell you that occasionally my language would shame a drayman. But I appreciate your restraint, since I do not particularly want Rory learning any more choice phrases than he already knows. Do not be fooled by his pleasant demeanor—he was born to mischief." She glanced at her red-haired son fondly, and Roderick blushed deeply.

"All boys his age are like that, even Amaury."

Marguerida shook her head. "Not my Domenic. He has always been the best child, so much so that I worry about him. I know it sounds silly, but I have often wished he would get into trouble of some sort. He is just too good sometimes."

"Do not borrow trouble, *domna*. It is a very dangerous thing."

"I know. But sometimes I cannot help myself." She cast a fond look at Lew Alton. "I am, after all, my father's child."

To her delight, Hermes Aldaran roared with laughter, making everyone at the table stare at him. "Born to trouble. Yes, I know that one very well," he chortled.

6

Domenic stood at his post outside the Guard's Barracks and stared at the stonework of the buildings opposite, across the narrow street. A steady stream of foot traffic moved past him, the familiar faces of local merchants and householders, cheerful in the mild autumn weather. Distantly he registered the pleasant smell of woodsmoke, carried by a brisk but not unpleasant breeze. It was coming from the direction of the kitchens of Comyn Castle, so the odors of roasting fowl and baking bread mingled with the smoke. Usually this made his mouth water, but today he had no appetite.

He shifted and stamped his feet, which were slightly cold from standing in the shadows at attention for over an hour. He wriggled his toes in the tips of his boots, trying to restore some circulation. The problem which had troubled his sleep returned to his mind, and he bit his lower lip, trying to find some answer to it. He glared at the white bulk of the Castle to his right, swore unconsciously, making his companion look at him curiously.

"Something the matter, *vai dom?*"

"No, Kendrick. I didn't sleep well and am feeling rotten, is all."

"At your age, you should be sleeping like a log, no matter what, lad. Fire or flood."

"If you say so." Nico shrugged and turned away. He had pulled his hair back tightly and bound it with a small thong, since Cisco Ridenow, the head of the Guards, did not approve of long hair. The tautness of it was giving him a headache.

Nico wished he knew every aspect of what was bothering him, but he could not pull all the threads together, and that made it all the more maddening. Part of the problem, he knew, was Regis' sudden death, because that had changed everything for him. He was deeply saddened, but that was not all that was disturbing his mind. It was, primarily, the feeling that he would never have the opportunity to do anything that was not laid out for him by custom and heredity. Funny, that had never made a difference before. And he could not actually think of anything he wanted to do particularly, except not be Domenic Gabriel-Lewis Alton-Hastur. Rory was the lucky one, for he could do whatever he pleased.

He shuffled his feet again and stared at the cobbles under them, trying to sort out the muddle in his mind. He had drunk more wine than he was accustomed to the previous night, under the pleasant influence of Katherine Aldaran, who was the most interesting woman he had ever met, except for his mother. And brave, too, because he could tell she was simply terrified of being around telepaths, but she managed to keep herself in hand. Her quiet steadfastness the previous evening had left him feeling a bit cowardly by comparison. Was this what was disturbing him, and might there be some truth in it? Might he be a coward?

In moments, the thought grew from being a pebble in his mind into a boulder. He wondered if he were brave enough, good enough to be the heir of the Hastur Domain and all that entailed, now that Regis was gone. While Regis still lived, the prospect of ruling had remained distant and remote. And, he admitted to himself, he had very little ambition for the position in which fate had put him. He had assumed that Regis would live for another two decades, at the very least, by which time he would have been a father himself, and his own son could be made heir to the regency. How odd that he had never before acknowledged this fantasy— that he had never really believed that the task of governing Darkover would actually be his.

He knew what Regis would have told him—that if he didn't want the life he had, he should have arranged to have different parents. He had heard this more than once, but now it failed to make him smile. All he could say for certain was that he felt as if the walls were closing around him, as if he were an animal trapped in some snare, ready to bite his paw off in order to escape. He would be watched over, even more than he already was, and that seemed intolerable. Hadn't he been a near prisoner in Comyn Castle all of his life? It had not bothered him before—so why now did he have this strange desire to run away, just to walk down the street, into a city he barely knew, despite having lived in it all of his life, and just to keep going until he reached the Wall Around the World. He wondered briefly if his father would change this arrangement—he knew that the Hasturs had not always immured themselves as Regis had—but decided it was very unlikely.

There were dangers on Darkover—he was well aware of that. There were Terranan agents around, although they were few and apparently not terribly good at their jobs, if the mess they had made of causing troubles in the city were anything to judge by. There were beasts like catamounts and banshees—except that if he stayed in Comyn Castle he would never know what they looked like. And there were people on the Comyn Council who would do him harm, if they could. His own grandmother, Javanne, occasionally let herself wish him dead. But that was only an unhappy old woman's foolishness, and he was fairly certain she would never actually try to hurt him.

Domenic shuddered. She would be arriving shortly, for the public ceremony and then to accompany the funeral train of Regis Hastur on its journey to the *rhu fead*. He had never seen that place, and it had an eerie reputation, but it was where the bodies of Darkover's rulers were laid to rest. And doubtless she would once again bring up the remarkable circumstances of his conception, and suggest that his status was *nedestro* rather than legitimate. If only his parents had been married in the ordinary manner, instead of being wed by Varzil the Good in the distant past. Even though several *leroni*, including his aunt Liriel, had attested to the truth of the experiences that Mikhail and Marguerida had reported, there were still people who chose to disbelieve them. And although he did not like to admit it, even to himself, he sometimes wondered if his grandmother was right. Not that it mattered, now that his father had named him heir designate, but the doubt and suspicion about his conception hurt him more than he cared to confess.

His mother said that once Javanne got an idea in her head, nothing short of a bolt from Aldones could shake it loose, and that pretty much summed it up. And she was bound to make trouble in the Council. He had attended his first meeting of that body at Midsummer, right after he had his fifteenth birthday, and had been startled by the amount of shouting it included. Somehow he had always imagined it was stuffy and boring, but instead it had been a series of arguments about everything from the state of the Towers to the status of the Guilds in Thendara.

Afterward he had asked his father,"Is it always like that?"

Mikhail had grinned ruefully and shaken his head. "This was a fairly orderly meeting, Nico."

"Then I hope never to see a disorderly one. I thought Francisco Ridenow was going to try to punch Uncle Regis in the nose!"

Part of the argument had been about the lease on the spaceport, which was due to run out in two years. Regis and Grandfather Lew had been in favor of extending it, at a greater fee, and Francisco had been against that. Domenic understood why—the Federation had failed to pay the rent for two years of the past five. They did not particularly need the money, since Darkover had kept her economy as free of Federation dependency as possible, but it was the principle of the matter. For its own part, the Federation had proposed that they be given the spaceport in perpetuity, and without any rents, since they had "developed" it. No one had even entertained that notion for a second—it was almost the only point of complete agreement in the entire meeting.

And who knew what would happen, now that the Federation had dissolved its legislature. They might pull out, which would please people like his grandmother and Francisco Ridenow. Domenic didn't really care one way or the other, because the few Terranan he had known had not impressed him as either pleasant or particularly clever. He did not include Ida Davidson, who was like an aunt to him, and had even managed to teach him how to carry a decent tune. He thought glumly of the "advisor" who had been foisted off on Regis a few years before, a dry, clerkish man who had asked a great many questions and never given any answers at all. He still wasn't sure why his uncle and his grandfather had allowed the man into Comyn Castle. It seemed to be one of those grown-up things, some plot that he could not really grasp the purpose of. And where he would, when he had been younger, have asked any number of questions, Domenic now found himself tongue-tied a good deal of the time.

His thoughts drifted toward Lyle Belfontaine, away from the unpleasant specter of Javanne, and more, he admitted to himself, from young Gareth Elhalyn, Danilo's son. They had met at Arilinn the previous year, and he knew he did not like the boy, and that the feeling was mutual. There was something in the way he looked at Domenic, a sidewise glance, that made him want to squirm. More, Gareth gave himself airs, expecting to be deferred to, which had not sat well with his fellow students at the Tower. It was better to think about Belfontaine, because it did not seem proper to dislike his grandmother and cousin as much as he knew he did.

Lew had taken Domenic with him to HQ during one of the meetings he had, telling him to observe everything, and passed him off as a page. It had been rather fun, pretending to be just a nobody, catching the random thoughts of the Terrans in the halls and offices. It had not been very interesting, though, because most of what he picked up was incomprehensible to him. But the Station Chief had been fascinating, in a sort of repulsive way, trying to get Lew to agree to let him come to the Castle and meet Regis Hastur. He watched his grandfather dodge the issue and change the subject so skillfully that Belfontaine hardly realized he was being deflected. It had been, Nico felt, a good lesson in diplomacy, but seeing the Station Chief had left him with the feeling that the man was a dangerous fool, and that all Terranan were equally irresponsible and treacherous.

He had been more interested in the machines that were everywhere, beeping and humming to themselves, while grinding out sheets of flimsy paper that Lew told him would turn to ash in less than a day. Until he saw the relays at Arilinn, Domenic had never seen anything similar, and he was impressed in spite of himself. The only piece of advanced technology he knew was his mother's now ancient recording device, gathering dust, since she could no longer obtain the batteries that enabled it to run.

It seemed futile to think about Belfontaine, and he let his mind drift in another direction. There were so many things he did not understand, and questions he could barely formulate, let alone find someone to answer. Everyone was so busy, and expected him to look after himself, now that he had reached his majority. And, in truth, he was a little afraid of the things that were in his mind, the thoughts and memories that dwelt there.

There were times when he thought he could remember the moment he had been conceived, although he was sure this was impossible, and he wondered silently if he might be a little mad. But he could not shake a sense that he knew things he *could* not, and no one, even such wise people as Istvana Ridenow, were able to answer the questions that had begun to trouble him about five years before. He missed the old *leronis*, who had tested him before he had gone to Arilinn, and she had returned to Neskaya. He wished, sometimes, that he could go there and study with her, but he knew that he would never be allowed that far away from Thendara.

Grandfather Lew referred to the way Regis had spent the last years of his life as a "siege mentality" and frequently rued it within Nico's hearing. He knew it was the result of events that had occurred long before he was born, when the World Wreckers had tried to ruin Darkover. As he had aged, Regis had become more and more anxious, as if the past were gnawing away at the present, destroying his peace of mind.

Lew admitted the necessity of keeping the ruling family safe, and away from the Terrans, but he still seemed to think there should be some less restrictive way of handling the problem of security. Domenic could not imagine being able to come and go as he pleased, nor even suggesting that he might be allowed to. He was still only a boy, or a man only legally, not a full adult. He was never going to have any adventures, or see more of Darkover than he already had. It was a very depressing thought, and he decided he had better get hold of himself, or his mother would become alarmed and make him drink something foul-tasting.

There was no cure, he was certain, for the way he was feeling, except, as his mother often said, time. He was sad over Regis' death, and that was normal. It was rather reassuring to think that what he was experiencing was perfectly ordinary, because recently his emotions had seemed to swing wildly, back and forth between elation and depression, without any reason. But Alanna's moods did that, too, so maybe it really was just his age, and not anything more serious.

Of course, his cousin and foster-sister worried him a great deal. They were very close, having been reared together for ten years, and he probably knew her better than anyone else. Thinking of Alanna's fits of temper did nothing to reassure him of his own mental stability, and he could not help thinking of the stories he had heard over the years, about the Elhalyn branch of the family, which was well-known to be rather odd. Maybe great-grandmother Alanna Elhalyn had passed some strange gene through her daughter Javanne, that showed up in him and his foster sister.

Thinking about Javanne Hastur was not a good idea, because she always made him feel perfectly dreadful. She had, as far as he could remember, never touched him, let alone hugged him the way she did Rory and Yllana. Mother said that was Javanne's problem, not his, but he admitted to himself that it hurt. Anticipation of his grandmother's imminent arrival at Comyn Castle, and the already prickly presence of Gareth Elhalyn, was making him feel worse by the second. If only they did not seem to hate him!

But his father's mother seemed to hate a lot of things, sometimes even including Father. Well, at least he was in good company! He would endure her visit as he had all the previous ones, by avoiding her as much as possible. Let her make a great fuss over Rory. He was not jealous of his little brother . . . was he?

All of this anxiety was likely due only to the great upheaval in his life, and that he was fifteen, and feeling unsure of himself. Uncle Rafael had told him a few months earlier, in a pleasant way, that he was a perfectly normal adolescent young man, which was a comfort. He would surely grow out of it, as he had started to grow out of his clothes every few months, although he was still short for his age. But his uncle did not know the shape that Domenic's *laran* seemed to be taking—no one did except a few *leroni* at Arilinn—and they were puzzled by it. And no one knew how it had grown since he returned to Thendara! Grown and changed into something so strange that half the time he was sure he was going to go mad. He could not really *hear the planet*, could he? No, that must be impossible, or the result of an overactive imagination. Human beings could not listen to the movements of the earth, could not hear the roll of the distant Sea of Dalereuth against the shore. Maybe, if he got the chance, he would ask Lew about it. Probably not. His grandfather was pretty busy, and there was no way to discuss this without revealing his fears about his own sanity.

The rattle of wheels brought him out of his reverie sharply, and Nico looked down the narrow street that ran past this entrance to the Barracks. He knew all the delivery schedules by heart, and none were expected. He stiffened into alertness and peered into the shadows, as did his watchmate.

"What's this?" Kendrick was a career Guardsman, a sturdy man in his early thirties, and one of Nico's favorite people. Nothing ever seemed to bother him, and standing guard with him was usually pleasant, restful almost. He followed the direction of the older man's eyes.

Now Domenic could see what troubled the older man. It was a mule-drawn wagon with a painted panel behind the gaudily garbed driver on the seat. Travelers! What the devil were they doing in the city now? They were only permitted into Thendara during Midsummer and Midwinter. In the warm part of the year, they went about, entertaining in small hamlets and the lesser cities. Except for Midwinter itself, he did not know where they wintered. His mother, who was curious about many things, had been trying unsuccessfully to gather some real information about them for a long time, and had not succeeded. Most of the little she did know she had learned from Erald, the son of the prior head of the Musicians Guild. He must remember to tell her that he had seen them.

Still, they should not be driving along on this particular street, even when they were welcome in the city. The only traffic permitted along this route were those who had business at the Castle, draymen bringing in supplies or Guildsmen. This was interesting because it was out of the ordinary, and Domenic felt his black mood start to dissipate in the face of his curiosity. He had seen Travelers twice, during his time at Arilinn, where they performed some rather scandalous songs and a play which he remembered was funny but seemed to delight in making fun of his Uncle Regis, among other things. What he had really liked was the rope dancer, a pretty girl in a skimpy costume, and the juggler who said poetry while he tossed more and more balls into the air. No one told the Travelers what to do, except themselves, he believed. What was it like to be that free of duty?

They did not seem to belong anywhere, unlike everyone else he knew. They did not have any permanent homes, and the organization of their troupes was a mystery. They belonged to no Guilds, answered to no authority, not even the lords of the Domains, and did as they pleased, so long as they did not violate the few laws which applied to them. There was something wonderfully attractive about that. For a moment, Nico wondered what it would be like to have the liberty to go where one chose whenever one wished. Then he decided it was probably cold and wet and hard.

He peered into the shadows made by the walls of the Castle, trying to make out more details. The wagon had come far enough up the street that he could see the figures painted on the sides of it now. There were puppets, the strings picked out in flaking gilt, and a garland of flowers ran around the topmost edge. The side of the wagon was lowered, and he saw a girl leaning out, grinning. She was red-haired and freckled, and seemed to be about his own age. She gave him a wave of greeting as Kendrick stepped away from the barrack entrance.

"Just what do you think you are doing, there, my good man?" he demanded of the driver. He gestured to Nico to remain in the shadows, and even though he wanted a better look, he remained where he was. He did not sense any danger from the skinny man, but he knew that he should obey the older Guard.

The man just shrugged and gave Kendrick a surly look. He was a small man, with a narrow face and a beaky nose. "We broke a wheel and had to stop in Wheelwrights Row to fix it. It didn't seem worth going out of the city and around to meet the rest of our troupe."

"You are not permitted in Thendara at this season! And this street is out of bounds to the likes of you in any case." Kendrick sounded outraged, but Domenic suspected he was enjoying the break in the rather boring task of standing guard at this post.

"We ain't bothering nobody," protested the driver. "You ass-kissing servants of the Comyn are all alike, telling us what to do for no reason than that you don't do no real work!"

The words were rude, and the attitude of the driver was that of a man looking for a fight. But there was more. Nico caught just a hint of fear from the man, and some muddled overthoughts that were strange. It took him a moment to realize that the man was not thinking in *casta* or *cahuenga*, but a mixture of both, with a good amount of Terran as well. Peculiar, but he was probably from up in Aldaran country, where Nico knew there were quite a few Terranan. Maybe he had a Terran father. Or maybe he had come this way for a reason. What if he were a spy or something? Nico laughed at himself quietly. That was a ridiculous idea— just because the man's uppermost thoughts were confused was no reason to suspect him of any mischief. He was jumping at shadows.

"That is enough! You get on, or I'll have you . . . "

"Don't get your trews in a twist," sneered the driver. "We are only going to the Old North Road, where we will meet up with the rest of our folk."

"Stop being provoking," the girl called from behind. "I told you we should have taken the other street!"

"And I told you it was too far. Keep your tongue between your teeth, girl, or I'll take a switch to your behind."

"You and what army, Dirck? I can outrun you any day, even in ten petticoats." She laughed at the driver and grinned at Nico, her gray-green eyes alight with amusement. He smiled back. Domenic wondered who she was, and how she had become a Traveler. More, he wondered about the flaming hair, so often a sign of *laran* in the Darkovean populace. He had never heard of any Travelers coming to the Towers to be tested or trained.

The hair itself was fascinating. It was very curly, like his mother's, but wiry where Marguerida's was as fine as a babe's. It stood out around her face like an aura of flames, even though the back of it was held in the confines of a wooden butterfly clasp. She was, he decided, a very pretty girl, but in an odd sort of way. She looked rough, not smooth like his cousin Alanna or his sister. And her features were not in any way remarkable—a slight turned-up nose, luminous eyes, and a generous mouth. There seemed to be nothing serious about her, and he decided that this was why he thought her pretty. She looked as if she found life very interesting and never worried about much, unlike Alanna.

Domenic sighed. Every time he thought about Alanna, his belly clenched and his heart ached. He had feelings about his foster-sister that he suspected were foolish as well as inappropriate. He did not care that she was regarded by almost everyone as a difficult child, and that sometimes his parents were ready to despair of their charge. She was bold where he thought himself timid, willing to say things he wished he had the courage to speak. More, he knew, he was almost her only real friend in the world, because her sudden shifts of mood had alienated even his mother to some degree. Would he grow out of his feelings for her? He had better, for he could not marry her. They were too closely connected by blood.

"Can you really defend this place?" the girl in the wagon asked him saucily, peering toward him still in shadow. "You look a little small for a Guard."

"Here, now—don't you go being rude to your betters, girl," Kendrick growled as he stepped toward the wagon.

She shook her head, setting the curly mass of hair in motion, illuminated by the strip of sunlight that was making its way down the center of the street. It flashed brightly, like a nimbus of fire around her face. "Some overbred sprout of the Comyn isn't *my* better, Guardsman."

Kendrick made a soft growling sort of noise in his throat, but it was clear he knew he was not going to win any arguments with the Traveling girl. She was not going to give him the least respect. "Go along with you, now!"

As the driver slapped the reins against the hindquarters of his mules, and they started to move forward again, Nico caught a feeling of frustration coming from him. He looked uneasily over his shoulder at the girl still leaning out, and muttered something to himself. *Dratted wench!* That thought came through quite clearly, and Nico smiled to himself. In spite of knowing that he shouldn't, he felt himself admiring her rudeness. He wished he had the courage to be rude to anyone, instead of always doing what was expected of him. And for a moment he enjoyed the notion of this girl encountering Lady Javanne Hastur and tried to imagine what she might say.

"If you come to the old Tanners' Field by the North Gate, we will be putting on a show tonight," the girl shouted at him as the wagon pulled away, sending his delicious fantasy right out of his head. "You aren't on duty all the time, are you?"

Nico shook his head, suddenly mute and feeling rather like a dolt. He was getting the oddest set of impressions, and there was a thrumming in his head, an annoying sensation, and something more. He had an impulse to use the Alton Gift, to penetrate the girl's mind, if only for a moment—just to discover her name. Or did he wish to know more? The girl was so unlike anyone he knew that he found himself drawn toward her for a moment.

The girl waved at him boldly, and the desire to do anything foolish faded away. He took a deep breath, relieved. His secret wish to do something unexpected did not extend to consorting with a Traveling lass. While that might have been acceptable in another, he knew that as his father's heir, it would never be. What a scandal!

I wonder who he is?

"Who are you yelling at, Illona?" The girl turned and looked into the dim interior of the wagon at the older woman lying on a narrow bed.

"Oh, just one of the Guards, Aunt Loret."

"You keep away from them, lassie. And don't go being forward, unless you want to be mistook for a whore."

"Yes, Auntie."

He caught the edges of her curiosity and found himself amused. Then, as if annoyed at being ignored, his bleak mood returned. What in Zandru's coldest hell was the matter with him! He had felt completely miserable for weeks, even before Regis had died—restless and, worse, profoundly angry. He resented everything and everyone most of the time, keeping his emotions under an iron grip that left him exhausted and furious. Why couldn't he be easygoing, like Rory? He was too serious and dull. Well, not dull, exactly. He just never got into trouble, and much to his disgust, Nico discovered that he wanted to.

If only there was someone he could talk to without fear of feeling naked and vulnerable. His father had asked him on several occasions if he wanted to talk. Busy as he was, he always tried to make himself available for discussions, but Nico knew that this was impossible for him. How could Mikhail understand the silent rebellion that simmered in his belly and wracked his mind? He knew that his father would listen, because he always had, but he was certain that Mikhail would be distressed if he ever knew how unhappy Domenic was. Surely Mikhail had never felt like this! It did not matter how unhappy he was, he was still the heir, and he had *obligations*. Disgusting word! He had to put aside his own hazy yearnings and buckle down. He couldn't burden his father with his own childish problems—especially now!

The sense of those duties was a heavy weight to bear. And he would never be free of them, so long as he drew breath. That made it even worse. He was trapped and alone, a prisoner of his heritage. . . . and his peculiar *laran*, which no one seemed to be able to understand, and which made quite a number of people uncomfortable, made it all much worse. Even Lew Alton, whom Nico adored, could not help him. Besides, how could someone as old as his grandfather even begin to understand what troubled him? He could not really explain his feelings to himself, so how could he explain them to someone else?

By the time the shift was over, Nico was deep in the doldrums. He yanked the thong out of his hair, left his post and returned to the Castle, climbing the long stairs from the entry to the upper floors. He knew he should be hungry, but he wasn't. All he wanted to do was find a closet and get into it, shut out the world and the oppressive sense of his own obligations. He simply had no business feeling so unhappy, but he could not shake it away.

As Nico approached the family apartments, he heard a shrill shriek, followed by the sound of something smashing. Alanna, in one of her tempers. And no one could calm her down except him. For once he did not wish to play peacemaker, even for his beloved Alanna. He just wanted to be left alone, in the vain hope that he could find some solution to the inner fury which plagued him day and night.

Then a bubble of amusement seized him. He and Alanna were really a perfect match—she was rarely in a good humor and he always pretended that he was. Nico envied her the freedom of her tantrums. Her mother, Ariel, had spoiled her badly when she was small, then surrendered her reluctantly into the charge of her brother when the girl became completely unmanageable. Even the instructors at Arilinn had been unable to discipline her beyond certain basics.

When he entered the apartment, Alanna was standing in the center of the sitting room, scowling. There was a smashed teapot at her feet, and a stain of spilled liquid on the carpet. Her hands were clenched into fists, and her shoulders hunched beneath the fine linen of her blouse. She fairly bristled with energy, seemingly radiating from every cell of her slender form. It was an all too familiar and increasingly frequent sight these days.

"Are you single-handedly trying to support Lady Marilla's pottery works, Alanna? That is the fourth teapot you have broken this month." He looked at the shards at her feet. "I rather liked that one, too." Maybe he could jolly her out of her mood, and help his own at the same time.

"The sixth, actually." Her beautiful voice was thick with tension. "It is better to smash pottery than people, isn't it?"

"If you absolutely must destroy things, than I suppose that innocent cups and pots are best, *breda*. But for the sake of the carpets, you might at least wait until the vessel is empty. What's the matter now?" He spoke jovially, trying to tease her into a better mood, but his own patience was worn and frayed, and he wished himself in some other place—any other place!

"I can't breathe! Everyone is walking on tippytoe, trying to be solemn. It makes my head hurt." She spoke with great drama, but there was no question that she was genuinely suffering. Alanna had inherited much of her mother's anxious disposition which, combined with her volatile temper, was an unholy mixture. He thought it a great pity that she could not become an actress, then wondered where that remarkable idea had come from. Daughters of Domain families, or even lesser ones, such as the Alars, were not free to join the Players Guild, or any other.

Alanna had voiced this complaint before, and no one, not even his mother, who was a powerful healer, had been able to discover the source of the girl's discomfort. It was very real, however. There was no doubt of that. "Perhaps we should order a gross of crockery for you to throw, *chiya*."

"I feel like I am going to burst, Nico! Bang! Into a million bits!"

"I can see that." He was not unfamiliar with that sensation, for he often felt it himself, though not as strongly as his foster-sister. Perhaps it would be good for him to break a few cups himself, just to relieve the inner turmoil. No, that would not help. What Domenic wanted was to break the rules, and that he dared not do.

"Was it something specific, Alanna, or just the general atmosphere of hushed solemnity that provoked you?"

The girl unclenched her hands at last and shrugged. "I was playing the clavier, and my fingers seemed all thumbs, and that made me furious. But it is more. I feel . . . like I am coming apart. As if there are two of me, or perhaps more. And each wants something different." She lowered her head after this admission, and began to cry quietly.

Nico put an arm around her shoulder and leaned her proud head down a bit. She felt warm in his light embrace, but she smelled of rage, a distinct odor which was unmistakable and rather unpleasant. Alanna was stiff, her muscles taut, as if she held herself in by will alone. Even as she wept, there was no lessening of the tension.

His mother came into the sitting room, looking very tired. She paused and looked at the two of them, and a slight shadow seemed to cross her fine features. It was gone almost as soon as it appeared, but Nico suspected that Marguerida knew something of his feelings for his foster-sister and that they worried her.

No need to fuss, Mother.

I can't help it. You are my firstborn. There was more, something deep in her mind which perturbed her, but he could not guess what it might be.

I mean that you need not worry about me letting my feelings for Alanna get out of hand.

No, you are much too disciplined for that—even though the temptation must be frightful. Sometimes, Nico, I almost wish you were just a little bit less restrained.

What do you mean? Do you want me to be more like Rory?

Certainly not! One hellion is all I can manage. I only want you to be yourself. And I cannot quite escape the feeling that you are holding yourself in check—you are too abnormally good!

Should I start seducing the maids, or go drinking with some of the Guardsmen?

I would prefer it if you did not. It would cause talk, and we don't need that. But I wish you would kick over the traces, just once. You never surprise me, Nico, and I wish you did.

What a disappointment I must be, so stuffy and sober.

Never a disappointment, son! I suppose I have too much of my father in me, and am a covert rebel. Don't you ever want to do something outrageous?

Often. But I know my duties. Domenic felt Alanna stir against him, and was relieved for the distraction. He did not want his mother to discover how much he resented his duties. She had enough to think about, what with the death of Regis Hastur, and Alanna being impossible more often than not. She never complained, but he knew she chafed under her obligations, that no matter how much she loved him, his siblings, and his father, she wanted to devote more of her energy to her musical compositions and less to being a wife and mother.

She had never neglected him or his brother and sister, not to mention fostering Donal and Alanna. She had listened patiently when he boasted of his small accomplishments—the training of his beloved hawks or learning to take his horse over a hurdle. Marguerida had sat up with him when he had a bout of fever, refusing to let a servant press wet cloths to his hot brow, but insisting on caring for him herself. He was loved—well-loved—and he knew it.

At the same time Domenic knew that she had often been torn between her own ambitions and her duties. She did not like to sit in Council meetings, listening to disputes and smoothing ruffled feathers. She hated having to take a carriage everywhere, that she could no longer walk through the streets of Thendara even with an escort, as she had before he was born. Sometimes, he knew, she went down to one of the Castle courtyards in the middle of the night and paced across the cobblestones, just to release herself from the tension of a kindly confinement.

It had been thirty-five years since the World Wreckers had been on

Darkover, murdering children in their cradles. Nothing that had happened since then was so threatening to the families of the Domains, but an attitude of alertness, of wary watchfulness, had taken possession of Regis as he had aged. They were embattled, although no foe had yet presented itself. Still, if some of the things he had overheard from his parents and Grandfather Lew were accurate, they might find themselves being very glad of their paranoia. The only problem, as far as Nico was concerned, was that it meant he could not go where he pleased, as his father had been able to do when he was younger. Right now, that chafed him more and more, and he almost shared Alanna's feeling of being unable to breathe.

The desire to get away rose in his throat, and he swallowed it. There was no good thinking about it. He was stuck in Comyn Castle for the foreseeable future, and he must resign himself to that. And he must not complain of his captivity either, or envy Rory his relative freedom. Bile soured his mouth.

Alanna straightened up, pulling away, and he could feel her distress. She glanced at the mess on the floor, her mobile face becoming stiff and expressionless. "I am going to go take a bath."

"That should relax you," Marguerida replied placidly.

Alanna's face turned into a mask of barely suppressed fury. "Nothing will relax me, nothing except. . . . I can't even think of anything. I hate it here!" With that she turned and left the room.

"As dearly as I love that child, Nico, there are times when I despair. I tell myself that it is just adolescent hormones running amuck, but truthfully, I don't believe that for a second. I don't foresee Alanna settling down into marriage—the very idea is too fantastic—and she does not belong in a Tower, even with all her gifts. There is no place for a girl like Alanna on Darkover." Marguerida frowned and her shoulders sagged. "Nor anywhere else I can think of."

A girl like Alanna. It was a strange thing for his mother to say, and not for the first time he wondered if there were something about his foster-sister that Marguerida knew and he did not. Domenic wanted very much to comfort his mother, but he could not think of anything to say that would help. He was glad she did not think that marriage and children were a solution to his cousin's ills, unlike many of the other women in the Castle. And living in a Tower would drive his nervous cousin stark raving mad. It almost had when she had been at Arilinn. She did not seem to belong anywhere, really. "Maybe she will grow out of . . . whatever it is. And me, too."

"You will, I believe. But Alanna is another matter. My sense is that as she gets older, her talents will become even more difficult to manage." She gave a little sigh. "Long ago, when I was first on Darkover, I had an experience of the Aldaran Gift. Your aunt Ariel was pregnant with Alanna, and it was the day your cousin Domenic was injured in that terrible carriage accident. It was one of the worst days of my life, and I have always tried to persuade myself that the vision I had was more the result of my own frayed emotions than anything real. But I remember thinking at the time that she should be called 'Deirdre,' not Alanna."

"Why?" So, she did know something she had never told him. Domenic realized that his mother was worn down from the demands of the past several days, that she had lowered her guard a little, and it gave him a peculiar feeling as he waited for an answer. After a second he decided that he was being spoken to as an adult, not a child, and he was not really sure he was ready for that.

"Because it means 'the troubler.' It was a fancy of mine, and I never told anyone. I *knew* that Alanna was going to be difficult, even before she was born. And I have never felt comfortable with that. Do you know what set her off?"

"She said she felt smothered, but she also told me that she felt as if there were . . . two people inside her, fighting with each other. If I did not know better, I would suspect she had been overshadowed, Mother."

Marguerida shuddered. "If I never hear that term again, it will be too soon, son. But you are right—she has not been. I would know, I think . . . I hope."

"I am sorry that Alanna and I are being so much trouble. You look very tired, Mother. Headachey?"

"Just a bit. And you are not any trouble, Nico. Never that. But the desire to take to my bed with a sopping kerchief full of lavender on my brow is very attractive. The preparations for Regis' funeral are perfectly exhausting, and Lady Linnea is so sad it nearly breaks my heart. If it were not for Danilo Syrtis-Ardais, I think I would collapse completely." She gave a soft laugh.

"Share the joke, please." He did not want to put an end to this particular conversation just yet.

"I was just thinking how the first time I ever set eyes on Danilo, I nearly fainted from terror. I had been on Darkover less than a week, and I had no knowledge of catalyst telepathy or anything like it. I just felt he was a danger to me, an inexplicable foe. The Alton Gift was starting to manifest, and I was doing everything in my power to deny it—telling myself I was imagining things, or going crazy, or both. I wanted nothing to do with him, and now I don't think I could manage without him. It struck me funny—that's all."

"Is there anything I can do to help, Mother?"

"Not really. The casket has been ordered, and the hangings. We would have used those from Danvan's funeral, but the moths had been at them, and they were tatters. Just another detail to occupy my mind. It keeps me from thinking about other things, like Alanna, or the fact that your father and mine are closeted with Hermes Aldaran, trying to hammer out some policy without even a clue as to what the Federation might decide to do. And your grandparents have just arrived from Armida, so I wish to be several places at once."

"There isn't a *laran* for that," he said kindly, ignoring the chill that the mention of his grandmother aroused in him. She could not do him any real mischief, could she?

Marguerida chuckled. "Just as well. Can you imagine the chaos if we were bi-locational?"

"Oh, I don't know. You could be taking a nap while attending a Council meeting."

"I don't need any special talent to do that. I've had any number of snoozes during some of the more boring parts, and been rudely aroused when the shouting started. Tell me, son, what do you think of Katherine Aldaran?"

"I like her very much. I think she is finding Darkover difficult, and making the best she can of it."

"I have not been able to spend more than a moment with her, and had to deputize Gisela, which was probably a mistake. But they are sisters-in-law, so it was logical. After that nonsense of the clothes at dinner last night, they are likely not even speaking to one another—which is just one more thing that I don't have time to deal with!" *Damn Giz for being such a troublemaker! I wish she would grow up and start behaving like a woman instead of a spoiled brat!*

"You worry too much, Mother. Go take a nap and have a cup of tea.

Domna Katherine can take care of herself. And Aunt Gisela never likes other women, especially if they are beautiful. She cannot help it."

"You are very wise for your years, Nico. Yes, a nap is in order—if only no further upsets occur."

Marguerida left the room as a servant came in and started to clean up the mess on the floor. Domenic sat down, then jumped back to his feet a minute later, and began to pace. The entire weight of Comyn Castle seemed to press against his skull, and he tried to shake the feeling away.

What was the matter with him? Nico tried to discover the source of his oppression, and at last it came to him. He did not want to attend the last rites of Regis Hastur. He could not bear the thought, even for a moment. It was more than just his sorrow at losing a man who had always been there for him. The grief was real, but beneath it there was a well of barely contained fury and fear, as if the walls were closing in on him.

His mind went to the red-haired girl in the Traveler's cart. How fortunate she was to be free, without obligations or duties. How wonderful it would be to go where he wanted, when he wanted.

An idea began to form, a wicked and wonderful notion. Nico shook his head at himself, and tried to make it go away. Could he really sneak out and go to see that night's performance? He really should not, but the more he tried to persuade himself out of it, the more attractive the idea became. Of course he could go with his usual contingent of Guards—that would be almost acceptable. But he wanted to go alone, unaccompanied. He wanted to have at least one adventure before he was shut up forever.

Then he chuckled. It was something Rory would do, never Domenic. Well, he would show that he was not as stuffy as everyone thought, not the "good" son. His mother might just get her wish, that he would do something which surprised her. Now all he had to do was find a way to exit the Castle without being noticed. The sense of oppression almost vanished as he drew a deep breath, and began to plan his escape.

7

The carriage rattled over the cobblestones, and Katherine Aldaran studied her sister-in-law, sitting languidly on the opposite bench, her lower body draped in a furred blanket. What a complicated woman she was turning out to be. First she had played a mean trick, and then apparently to make amends had appeared right after breakfast that morning with an armful of garments and the offer to take Kate to met Master Gilhooly, the head of the Painters Guild. She had not apologized, nor even alluded to the previous evening, but instead had seemed to only be interested in being helpful.

She had shown Katherine how to deal with the multiple petticoats every Darkovan woman was expected to wear. Each one was dyed a slightly darker hue, and when Katherine put them on, with a fine chemise beneath them, the effect was not only quite pretty but warm as well. A skirt, embroidered with leaves, and tunic to match completed the ensemble. The colors were more suited to a redhead than to Katherine's coloring but they did well enough, and when Gisela sat her down and dressed her hair, pulling it back and fastening it with a very lovely butterfly clasp, she was both pleased with the reflection in the glass and forgiving of her new sister-in-law as well. The nagging suspicion that Gisela might be up to something faded back, but Katherine thought she would be a fool to drop her guard completely around this obviously complex woman whose agendas were unknown to her.

The trip to the Painters Guild had been pleasant, and Gisela had pointed out things of interest, and told her some of Darkover's history as well. She had been animated, clever with her words, and not at all like the coyly manipulative woman who had visited her the day before, and given her the impression that wearing Federation evening clothes to the welcoming banquet was the correct thing to do. But now Gisela seemed weary and out of sorts, as if returning to Comyn Castle was something unpleasant.

Katherine tried to think of something to say, wanting to restore the previous mood, which was more comfortable for her. She noticed, in a distant way, that Gisela, like Herm, was an oddly restful person for her. Kate had always appreciated it that her husband managed to hide his feelings so well, and it appeared that Gisela had the same quality. That absence of emotional need had made their marriage tranquil. She resented that Herm had kept so many secrets from her, but that was a different matter altogether, one she would deal with in her own way.

"Thank you again for taking me. Even though Herm has taught me rather a lot of *casta*, I could never have managed without you. My vocabulary was not up to it."

Gisela smiled vaguely and nodded. Then she plucked at the hem of her tunic and shifted on the bench. "He would not have thought, if he even knew the terms himself, which I rather doubt, of how many words are specific to painters. And, truthfully, I would not have known myself, except that for the past decade I have been so bored that I have read anything I could get my hands on, whether I was initially interested in the subject or not. One of the books I found in the Castle archives was a treatise, about three hundred years old. 'Concerning the Limner's Craft.' The parchment is yellowed and starting to crumble, so I had to be careful. And I don't suppose anyone but me and the archivist even know it exists. I have picked up a great deal of information that I never expected to use. It was rather amusing to find an application for some of it at last." She did not sound amused, in fact she was clearly discontented. But somehow Katherine was not made uncomfortable by these feelings. Maybe it was a family characteristic, this containment. She wondered for a moment if their brother, Robert Aldaran, and his father would be the same.

Katherine tried to imagine a life as confined as she knew Gisela's must be, and felt more than a little sorry for the woman. "Well, I am happy that you were bored, then, because it was a great treat for me. Are you bored often?"

Gisela looked at her, green eyes glinting in the light that came through the windows of the vehicle, as if she were seeking some hidden meaning in the words. "Most of the time, yes, I am."

Katherine could sense a sudden tension in her sister-in-law and realized she had to tread warily. "I am sorry, but I don't understand. I would imagine that living in Comyn Castle would be . . . pleasant."

A bitter laugh answered her. "You might find it that, but I have never done so." Gisela drew her fine brows together and pursed her lips. "I am there because Regis Hastur wanted some way to guarantee my father's good behavior, not because I am wanted or needed. I have no purpose but as a pawn, and I suppose I have never had one—it makes me very cross."

"That would make me cross, too, Gisela. But I still don't quite understand."

"What?" Gisela sat up on her bench, her face twisted with hope and wariness at the same time.

Kate wondered what had happened to this obviously intelligent woman to make her so untrusting. "Well, why you think you have no purpose except as a pawn, I suppose."

"I am not like you, Katherine, or like Marguerida. I don't have anything that matters to me the way I know now that art matters to you, or music does to Marguerida. Watching you talk to Master Gilhooly—the way your face lit up—made my . . . stomach hurt." She reddened, looked mildly ashamed, and gave a little sigh. "I was not raised for such things. I was never encouraged to find an avocation—something which would fill my life with passion and meaning. My father spoiled me very badly, and I always believed I could have anything I wanted. It was only later that I understood that I could only have what *he* wanted, *if* I was fortunate. I am just a woman, and on Darkover that doesn't count for much."

"How were you unfortunate, then?"

Gisela stared her for a second. "You are really interested, aren't you?"

"Of course I am. Why would I pretend otherwise?"

"You wouldn't, I guess. You are a very odd woman, Kate, and I cannot think of anyone like you. I just don't know what to make of you."

"There is nothing to make of me, Giz. But, you see, I was born on Renney, where women hold the reins of power, and I am having a great deal of trouble understanding Darkover. The things you told me when we were going to the Painters Guild were more than a little disturbing, and if Herm expects me to turn into some sort of subservient wife, doing whatever he wishes without asking questions, then I want to know about it beforehand, so I can box his ears. He seems different already."

"Women have the power . . . what a peculiar notion. Hmm. I rather fancy that. It sounds very attractive." She paused for a moment, her face reflective. "I'll wager Herm is probably not telling you things you think you should know, am I right?"

"The number of things that Herm has not told me during the course of our marriage so far is already enormous, and I am quite angry with him." She bit off the words before she said more, surprised by her own candor. She did not know Gisela very well, and had already learned that the woman was capable of being spiteful, and that she was a chancy ally at best. But she needed to talk to someone, and her new sister-in-law was the only one she had found so far. "We have had a happy marriage until now, and I feel . . . betrayed."

"Poor Katherine." There seemed to be a genuine compassion in the words. "Herm is a good man, but he has always been very secretive, even when he was a boy. I think it was his way of dealing with our father, who is a difficult man at the best of times." She laughed mirthlessly. "And in Aldaran Castle, it is never the best of times! Our family was mistrusted—cast out—by the other Domains, long before I was born. That drove my father into fits of fury. Then Regis Hastur decided that the Aldarans should not be punished for things that had happened in the past, and his first gesture toward reconciliation was to appoint Hermes to the Chamber of Deputies. It was a small thing, and it did not satisfy my father, whose desire was to be a power to be reckoned with on Darkover, instead of sitting up in the Hellers like a hawk in jesses. I think he expected Herm's appointment to lead to something immediately, but it didn't. And I don't think Father has ever understood my brother's character."

"And what is that?" Katherine was fascinated now. True, Gisela had not known Herm for over two decades, and was several years younger than her brother. But the earlier part of their journey had raised her opinion of the other woman considerably. More, she had always been curious about her husband's history, and frustrated that he refused to discuss it.

"It is not easy to put into words. I would say that he is very solitary. Indeed, I was stunned to find out he had a wife and children—it was so unlike the Hermes I remembered. We have an animal in the Hellers, the scavenger-wolf, which runs in packs and howls in the night. But sometimes, for no reason anyone knows, one of these beasts leaves his pack and goes off on its own. When I was little, I always thought Herm was like one of those."

"A lone wolf—yes, that makes sense. And your father did not understand that?"

"Well, it made him uncomfortable, because he could not command Herm to do his bidding. But I don't think that was the problem, for my father is not an introspective man, and he does not give much attention to anyone other than himself. No, it was another matter entirely." She took a breath. "Again, it is difficult to express exactly. I think that my brother loves Darkover more than he can ever love a living person, Kate. Please do not suspect me of malice, although you would be completely justified if you did. I do not mean to hurt your feelings in saying this—and you did ask me."

"No, I don't. It fits in with what I know of my husband. Not happy knowledge, but at least I no longer feel I have misjudged him completely. Thank you." She sighed, letting some of the tension leave her body. "Now, tell me your sad tale, please."

"It is not sad, exactly, although I often feel as if it were, when I am in one of my black moods. It isn't even very interesting. I fell in love with Mikhail Hastur when he came to visit Aldaran Castle. I was sixteen and he was the first person outside my family, other than some Terranan who visited my father, I had ever gotten to know. My father approved, in his way. He encouraged me in my folly, and I was young enough to think that something would come of it. Mikhail was Regis' heir, and marrying him would make me the greatest lady on Darkover! Regis wanted to bring the Aldarans back into Darkovan society, and it seemed to me a perfect solution. I had no idea what kind of opposition such a notion would arouse, because my father had filled my head with some extremely silly things, and I was too young to understand the politics of the situation. Politics!" Gisela spat the word out.

"I quite agree. So what happened then?" Katherine sensed that her sister-in-law was revisiting something old and painful, that she had longed to speak of it and had had no one she could open up to. It was not the first time she had heard things she had no business knowing—the models for her portraits often became positively garrulous while posing. And though she was uncertain whether she wanted Gisela's confidences, Kate could see no harm in learning more about her husband's family.

"Absolutely nothing! Mikhail went away, and Herm became a Deputy and left. Time passed, and Mik did not return, not did he send me any messages and my father grew impatient. In one of his furies he decided to marry me off to an old drunk who had already buried two wives, to get me off his hands, since I had not furthered his dreams as he thought I should have. Those were the worst four years of my life." She shuddered all over and reflected for a moment. "That part was rather sad, I suppose."

Kate felt the pain in the words and wondered if this new relative knew how very courageous she was, to have endured such a trial. She shifted a little on the hard bench of the carriage, trying not to let her usual discomfort with people in general influence her too much. "I take it the old drunk died. Or did you divorce him?"

"We don't have marriage dissolutions on Darkover, or at least not very often. No, he broke his neck out hunting before I had time to find a way to poison him, and good riddance! So, there I was, a young widow with two sons, and Regis reformed the Comyn Council, and invited my father to come to Thendara. I came with him, all ready to recapture Mikhail's interest, and there was Marguerida, in what I imagined was to be my position!" She shrugged her shoulders, as if trying to relieve herself of some old burden.

"That sounds completely miserable for you. What happened then?" In spite of her now increasing unease, Katherine was fascinated and did not want her sister-in-law to stop talking.

"There was a ball, for Midwinter," Gisela began, her voice distant now. "My father had backed Regis into an agreement to announce that Mikhail and I would be married, to heal the breach between the Domains, you see. I have never been so anxious in my life as I was that night, because I had a sense of dread, a certainty that it was not going to

happen the way I wished. We Aldarans have the Gift of foresight. Gift—
it's often more of a curse! And then Marguerida and I ended up in an
alcove, glaring at each other, and she told me that I had put my heart on
the wrong Hastur. Before I could reply, everyone in the ballroom who
had any *laran* heard this terrible, booming voice—it was incredible! The
next thing I knew Mik and Marguerida were dashing out of the room,
and Mikhail's sister Ariel went into labor with Alanna, and people were
fainting and screaming and having fits. Mikhail and Marguerida left the
Castle and rode away to Hali Tower, where somehow they . . . managed
to get away into the past."

"Yes. Mikhail said something about it at dinner last night, and at first
I thought he was pulling my leg. Then I realized he was serious, which
was even more difficult to take than being the butt of a joke. They really
did?"

"Well, they went somewhere—somewhen? I still have a hard time
imagining it, and I always wished it were me, not her, of course! When
they returned, several weeks had passed for them, but only a night had
for us, and they were married and she was pregnant with Domenic! I tell
you, this was a lot to believe, and there are a few people, like my mother-
in-law, who still don't, even though the best *leroni* on Darkover have
attested to the actuality of these events. Javanne didn't want Mik to marry
Marguerida any more than I did, but for different reasons, and she still
insists that it was not a valid marriage. That is mostly spite, because she
had not given her consent."

Gisela paused and shifted on the bench. "So there we all were, stuck
with the situation. Rafael was very kind to me then, though I had never
done anything to warrant it. And I knew then that Marguerida was right,
that I had misinterpreted my foreseeing, and that Rafael was the man in
my visions. I had *known* all along, but I had refused to see it."

"How had you known?"

"The Aldaran Gift, as I mentioned before. I saw myself married to a
Hastur and I persuaded myself that it had to be Mikhail, because I
wanted it to be. I was well aware he had two brothers. I just pretended
to myself that Gabe and Rafael did not exist—what a goose of a girl I
was!" The self-loathing in her voice made Kate want to cringe.

During the ride to the Painters Guild, Katherine had almost managed
to forget that the people around her had peculiar "gifts," that the woman
sitting across from her was a telepath, and perhaps more. She had let

herself be persuaded by Marguerida's assurances that her thoughts were safe. Now all her doubts and fears returned, at the mention of the Aldaran Gift, and she swallowed hard, and forced herself to sound calm and casual. "Yes, the Aldaran Gift. Herm told me a little about it, but I am not sure I believed him."

Gisela gave a genuine laugh this time. "Oh, it is very real, but interpreting it is pretty chancy. And I never told anyone—I can't imagine why I am speaking so openly to you." She looked into Katherine's eyes then, a piercing gaze full of fear and a deep longing as well. "The only person who knows the most of it is probably Marguerida, and she is much too tactful to ever throw it in my face. Sometimes I wish she were not quite so . . . disciplined. Or that I could be more like her and less like myself."

Kate returned the look, trying to put into it her unspoken intention to be a good friend, for the more she listened to Gisela, the more she found her to be both brave and lonely. "It is easier, sometimes, to tell things to strangers than to people you know well."

"You see, that is exactly the problem. There are no strangers in my life—only folk I know so well that I can anticipate what they will say before they speak the words. Sometimes I think that if Rafael clears his throat before he asks me how I am today one more time, I will . . . go mad."

"Please don't do that."

Gisela laughed quietly and her shoulders drooped a little. "No, I guess I won't, I would surely have done so years ago if I were going to. All in all, life has not been terrible, just not terribly satisfactory. My husband cares for me a great deal. Even with all the naughty things I did."

"What sort of things?"

"Well, I listened to my father, which was my first mistake, and I did a few things that were . . . impolitic. They did not do serious damage to anyone except that Rafael was embarrassed and no longer completely trusted, because of me. He is a proud man, and I shamed him in the eyes of his own brother. There are days when I would give anything to undo that. But I can't, and I have to endure the consequences of my own stupidity."

"What exactly did you do that was so terrible?" Katherine asked.

"I suggested that perhaps Mikhail should not be Regis' heir, because of his travels into the past and his marrying Marguerida, but that Rafael should instead. To anyone that would listen." The pain in her voice was unmistakable. "And the most terrible part is that he has never chided me for what I did, never made me ask for forgiveness for being a foolish, immature, conniving wretch. All he has done for fifteen years is try to make me happy, to help me be content with my lot in life, as he is with his."

"Umm . . . that rather goes beyond impolitic, Gisela."

She spat a bitter sounding laugh from between white lips. "I know—it was near to treason, except that I wasn't taken very seriously. I never do anything by halves. And when I understood that it was hurting Rafael, I stopped and tried to be good. I studied chess, pretending that the pieces were the inhabitants of Comyn Castle, until I grew weary of that, and then I started to write a text on chess, which filled the empty hours, and read my way through the archives. I am probably the most well-read woman on the planet." She gave a feeble smile. "Marguerida even consults me on old books, sometimes, which should make me happy, but nothing really does."

"But haven't you ever found anything you loved to do?" The words came out before Kate could restrain them. She could hardly bear the anguish in the voice of the other woman, and the sense of her pain.

"No."

"Even when you were a little girl?"

To Kate's surprise, Gisela blushed along her high cheekbones and looked down at her hands. She mumbled something, but the folds of her cloak muffled the words.

"I'm sorry, but I didn't quite catch that," Kate said.

Gisela lifted her head and looked directly at Katherine for a minute without speaking. "There was something." She flexed her hands, with the extra finger that Herm had told Katherine was common in the Domain families, and which looked so peculiar. "I liked to carve—such a common thing. My nurse made me stop, because it was dirty and she said I might cut myself with the knife. I was so ashamed. I hadn't thought about that in years, until a few days ago." She stopped talking and looked out the window of the carriage. "It was the day you came, and I was looking at this fantastic chess set that Marguerida gave me for Midwinter, and thinking how lucky it was that the figures had escaped from the stone and bone they were made from. I felt as if I were somehow trapped in stone . . ."

Kate was nearly squirming with discomfort now. She was angry, that a perfectly intelligent woman was caught in such a dreadful trap. Stone, indeed. She drew a harsh breath and said, "I think it is terrible that your nurse shamed you, Gisela, and I also think it is high time you stopped letting what other people expect of you rule your life. I think you are terribly brave, too. I don't know if I could have been married to a drunk, and then held hostage!" The ugly word hung between them, almost visible, for a moment. "And as for wanting to be more like Marguerida and less like yourself—nonsense! If anything, you should want to be *more* like yourself!"

Gisela managed a shaky laugh. "I think if I were any more like myself, someone would strangle me, Kate."

"I don't mean being your lowest self, but being your very best." Kate could feel her impatience rise. Nana had always said it would be her downfall, and she had tried very hard to master it. Now she felt as if she had learned nothing over the years.

"My best self? You are either the most generous woman ever born, or you just don't understand!"

"Perhaps I don't or maybe it's you who don't understand. I was raised so differently than you were!"

"Tell me about that, please."

Katherine knit her brows for a moment, forcing herself to become calm again. She could not change the past for Gisela, but perhaps she could find a way to help her sister-in-law into a better future. "On Renney we believe that each person has a purpose, or more than one, and that we are obligated to discover what that is. We have a lot of complicated rituals that we use to find out what we are supposed to be. The idea of someone else deciding what we are going to do with our lives, of being trapped in place, is very hard for me to imagine."

"So, how did you find out you were supposed to become a painter?" There was a friendly glint in the dazzling green eyes of the other woman, and Kate had no doubt she was genuinely interested. Gisela smiled encouragingly, and some of the tension between them faded.

"I fasted for three days and then sat in a cold grove of trees for the night and waited. It was very unpleasant, but it was expected, so I did it anyway." She chuckled, more comfortable now. "My toes felt like ice and my belly was growling and nothing happened for hours and hours. I was just starting to feel as if I were going to fail when . . . something happened. Between one second and the next I wasn't cold any longer, and my head was filled with images, of people and places that I had never seen." She paused for a breath. "I was terrified and happy all at the same time, and my heart leaped in my chest. I just sat there feeling this incredible thing, and then it started to dawn, the light coming through the trees, making long shadows and coloring the trunks gold. And then I looked at my hands and discovered that I had a stick in one, and that the ground in front of me was covered with scratchings that I did not remember making, little figures of people and buildings. And I knew in my bones what I was supposed to be, and I went home and told my Nana, after eating a huge bowl of stew and giving myself a belly ache."

"Your Nana?"

"The mother of my mother."

"It sounds very interesting, except the part about the fasting." She patted her waist and sighed. "And no one asked you if you were sure, or wondered if you had just made the whole thing up or anything?"

"The Rennians believe that visions are a gift from the Goddess in her many forms, and to question one would be . . . unthinkable."

"I see. How old were you when this happened?"

"Twelve."

Gisela sighed. "Well, we don't have that sort of vision here on Darkover, and I am much too old to start, I think. It does sound wonderful, though."

"You are never too old to start something, Gisela. Stop talking as if your life were already over. You are younger than I am! I do not know your customs here. What harm would there be in you doing something that genuinely pleased you, instead of sitting around . . . feeling sorry for yourself."

Gisela winced. "There is that. How did you get to be so wise?"

"I'm not, but when you spend your days painting people, trying to capture them on canvas, you discover a great deal. The way they fold their hands or purse their mouths tells you something about them, often something they would rather not know."

"Oh." Self-consciously, Gisela tucked her hands under the edges of her cloak, then shrugged. "I guess it is too late to escape your eye, isn't it? What have you divined about my character that you think I would prefer not to know?"

"Are you sure you want me to answer that?"

The other woman thought for a moment. "Yes, I think I do. All my life I have been . . . other people's Gisela. I was my father's pet, when he noticed me at all, and then his pawn. I was a wife, then a widow, and a wife again—but none of that seems to be about me. I can't explain it better than that."

"You did fine. What I see is a very intelligent woman who does not really like pleasing others."

"You mean that I am selfish? I already knew that."

"No, because if you were really selfish, you would please yourself and not worry about the consequences. Instead you keep trying to be what other people expect of you, and it ends up making you angry. So, you punish yourself by doing mean things that make you dislike yourself."

"Ouch!" Gisela started, then looked reflective.

"Are you sorry you asked?"

"No, but you are much too close to the bone for my comfort. Do you talk like this to Hermes?"

"Not often enough!"

Gisela shook her head in wonder. "It must gall him dreadfully."

"Yes, it does. Now, tell me why you are afraid to do something you want to do?"

"When I was little and I carved, I lost all track of time and got so . . . far away. I didn't pay attention to anything except finding the thing in the wood. And that is unwomanly, or so my nurse told me time after time."

"Lost? Obsessed? Totally unaware of anyone else on the planet?"

"Oh!" Tears swelled in Gisela's eyes. "You do know what I mean!"

"Of course I do, and I am sure Marguerida would as well, although I can see that you never could have told her what you just told me. Now, I do not know Rafael very well yet, but somehow I can't see him objecting, as long as you don't come to bed with splinters in your nightdress."

"You make it sound so easy," Gisela almost moaned.

"Do you really want to spend the rest of your life being bored and . . . getting into mischief?"

"No!"

"Then, for Birga's sake, do what you wish."

"Birga?"

"The goddess of craftsmen on Renney."

"Do what I wish . . . I don't know if I dare."

" 'She who dares nothing is truly lost.' I mean, it is not like you are proposing to establish a . . . joyhouse in Comyn Castle or something, is it?"

"A . . . joyhouse?" Gisela laughed and laughed, until tears fell from her eyes. She hugged her sides and rocked from side to side. "Oh, my! What an idea! I am almost tempted to suggest it, just to see the looks on the faces of . . . no, that is more mischief, isn't it."

"My Nana always told me that shocking people just to get attention was very naughty, and she is a wise woman." Then her own demon of wickedness stirred a little. "On the other hand, if you did suggest it, then the idea of you whittling or sculpting would seem perfectly wonderful by comparison!"

"Quite right." She fell silent for a moment, thinking. "Katherine, what if I am no good at it?"

"Irrelevant. What matters is the doing."

"But I want to be good!" Her face twisted, as if she had heard her own words and grasped the depth of desire within them.

"Of course you do—but you dare not let your fear of failure corrupt your intention. Renney is a world of forests and seas, and we use wood for everything we can. We have a great tradition of wood carving, therefore, and lots of proverbs as well. One is 'Be true to the wood, and the wood will be true to you.' "

" 'Be true to the wood!' How beautiful! Oh, Katherine, I am so glad you came to Darkover!"

"Do you know, I am starting to be glad I came here, too—although I confess I find some of your customs . . . distasteful. Well, you might feel the same if you went to Renney. Married off to a drunk! I have a feeling that my father-in-law and I will never see eye to eye."

Gisela smiled fondly at her. "You will be part of a large group, then, for hardly anyone sees eye-to-eye with him!" The light through the carriage window caught her features for a moment, the green eyes gleaming and the mouth relaxed almost completely for the first time Katherine had seen.

"Will you sit for me, for a portrait?" The impulse was irresistible because the subject was beautiful, and she itched to start to work.

"Really? I would like that very much. Thank you, Katherine—for everything!" Gisela's hands stroked the fur on her lap and her eyes unfocused slightly. Her taut shoulders drooped softly now, as she mused. Then she roused, leaned across the carriage, and took Kate's hand in hers, tears brimming in viridescent eyes. "You have given me hope, at last."

8

Herm Aldaran sat down on the edge of the bed, bent over, and pulled off his boots. He wriggled his toes sensuously, then leaned back across the covers, his arms extended above his head. He gazed up at the hangings, and at the plastered ceiling, enjoying the utter silence of the suite. Katherine was gone, and he did not know where the children were, but he was too drained to worry. He had been with Lew Alton, Mikhail, and Danilo Syrtis-Ardais for hours, and his tongue ached from talking. He was parched, and wanted a pitcher of good beer, but lacked the energy to sit up and ring for a servant. Instead he closed his eyes and tried to relax.

Overall, he was pleased. Mikhail Hastur had matured from the callow young man he remembered over two decades earlier, and seemed to have a good head on his shoulders. He had been preparing for the task that lay ahead of him for years. If anyone could guide Darkover through the difficulties that lay ahead, it was he. He had listened to Herm intently, and his questions had been both informed and intelligent.

Unfortunately, no one could accurately guess what the Federation might do next, although everyone at the meeting was attempting to anticipate it. He hoped they would just ignore Darkover, but doubted that the Expansionists would be that cooperative. And Lew Alton had said some disturbing things about the current station chief, Lyle Belfontaine, at HQ, including his demand that Herm be turned over for arrest as an enemy of the Federation. He tried to be amused by the whole idea, but his guts had churned with fear when he heard about it. He had lived with this kind of terror for years now, and had believed that once he reached the safe haven of Darkover, he would no longer be subject to its claws. The more fool he—the Federation was not going to let him go!

This was a time when he wished he could provoke the Aldaran Gift into activity, but unlike other forms of *laran*, it was almost impossible, without the use of certain dangerous substances, to cause it to manifest. He might see more than he desired, or find out things he did not wish to know at all.

So much for coming home to peace and quiet. Why had he ever gone into politics, and when was he going to be allowed out? He chuckled to himself, knowing that he would never be able to give up meddling and intriguing. It was in his blood, like some strange disease, and from all reports, might even be genetic. His little sister Gisela was of the same ilk, and he wondered exactly what she was up to at the moment. He had seen her twice now, and each time he had come away with the distinct feeling that she was looking for trouble. There was a kind of guardedness about her he mistrusted, as he had when she was a girl. He knew that expression, that catlike narrowing of green eyes that boded no good. And it would be some time before he forgave her for her mean trick on Katherine the previous evening. He did not want her to embarrass the Aldarans, or give her long-suffering husband any more grief than he suspected she already did. Really, Gisela needed a good spanking—except it was years too late for that remedy. If only their father had not alternately spoiled her and neglected her!

A soft rustle of fabric made him open his eyes. Katherine walked into the bedroom and gave him a smile. Her cheeks were rosy, and she smelled of fresh air. "What have you been up to?" He sat up and studied her. She was wearing an outfit of typical Darkovan garments, a green tunic and shirt over russet petticoats. The colors did not really become her, but she looked healthier and more alive than she had for days.

"Gisela and I went to meet the head of the Painters Guild, Master Gilhooly."

"Giz and . . . I'm surprised. After the stunt she pulled by not telling you how to dress for dinner last night, I assumed you would not speak to her for about a month."

Katherine smiled and her shoulders lifted in a slight shrug. "Gisela appeared right after breakfast with these clothes—but no apology. She ordered a carriage and went with me. It was rather enjoyable, actually, and we talked over a good many things. I don't know what caused her change of heart, but I rather suspect it was something that man next to her at dinner said to her."

"Danilo?"

"I don't know—he arrived late, and somehow I was never introduced to him."

"That was Danilo Syrtis-Ardais, paxman to the late Regis Hastur, among other things. Having just spent several hours in his company, I can well imagine him putting Giz in her place."

"Paxman—I've heard that term several times, but no one has bothered to tell me what it means, Herm—like so many other things." Her good mood seemed to recede a little, and she looked as if she might be nursing a grievance. Well, he could hardly blame her if she were.

"Umm—it is a bit hard to define. The paxman is a personal guard, and in the case of Danilo or young Donal Alar, also an advisor, constant companion, brother-in-arms. When Mikhail was a young man, he was paxman to young Dyan Ardais, even though he was also Regis' heir. I suppose it is one of the ways in which we keep ourselves connected to one another. And, Katherine, I am sorry about how badly my sister has behaved."

"She's just a little jealous, Herm." *And restless, like you are most of the time, my dearest.*

"Of what?" He sat up.

"Of me. You are her brother, and her favorite one, if I read things correctly."

"I hadn't thought of that. Hmm . . . yes, she never favored Robert, who is the best of men, but a bit . . . ponderous, and our other brothers—the *nedestro* sons—never gave her much attention, I suppose. But I still don't understand why she should be jealous of you."

"It is a female thing," Katherine answered easily. She had ended her trip with Gisela in a good mood, and she wanted to keep it.

"Ah, one of the mysteries."

"Yes."

Herm looked at her, trying to read her expression, realized she was not going to say more, and decided not to press her. "And how was your visit with Master Gilhooly?"

"Delightful. He showed me around the workshops and we talked technique. It strained my vocabulary to the utmost, and without Gisela's help I would have had a much more difficult time. She told me she had read some old book about painting and had picked up the words from it. She can be very charming when she wants to."

"Gisela read a book on painting? Amazing."

Katherine gave him a look he recognized. She was beginning to become annoyed with him, and he had better mind his words. "She tells me she has read just about everything in the archives during the past fifteen years, out of boredom, as near as I can gather. Poor thing."

This was completely unexpected, and Herm did not know what to make of it. Something had clearly happened between the two women during their outing, and it worried him more than a little, although he could not decide why. Still, she had come to no harm, and apparently found his sister interesting. "This is the first time I have seen your eyes really sparkle in days, Kate. Just promise me you will not come to the table smelling of turps, or with a smudge of charcoal on your lovely nose."

Katherine grinned broadly. "I will try not to disgrace you, my lord. But, remember, I was not raised to be a great lady, or even a medium one. I feel a bit stifled by all this formality, which made my visit to Master Gilhooly all the more pleasurable. After he recovered from the initial shock of *Domna* Aldaran—I haven't adjusted to the title yet, being bowed to and treated like I was important—entering his establishment, and in the company of Gisela as well, and realized that I was a serious artist, he unbuttoned completely. He stopped bowing and scraping and fell to discussing important things that are his passion."

"It is a bit unusual for a woman of the Domains to pursue anything other than childrearing, unless she chooses to become a *leronis*. Or a Renunciate," he added, still puzzled by the change in his wife. "I have never heard of a Darkovan woman who pursues art seriously. Our more artistic women satisfy themselves with vast amounts of unnecessary needlework. Lady Marilla Aillard has a pottery works in the Ardais Domain, but I do not think she throws bowls or glazes them personally. She might. You can ask her when she arrives."

"She is coming for the funeral, I assume."

"That is part of it. She holds the Aillard seat on the Comyn Council, which will meet in order to confirm Mikhail Hastur's succession to Regis. Her son, Dyan Ardais, will come as well."

"*Domna* Marilla Aillard and *Dom* Dyan Ardais? Different last names? It is a good thing I have had so much practice keeping such things straight. Gisela told me your father and brother are expected, too— though from what she said I am not really looking forward to meeting your parent—or is it parents? No one has mentioned his wife yet."

"There isn't one, as far as I know, although he probably has a *barragana* or two up in Aldaran Castle. Gisela's mother died a long time ago."

"I see." She frowned at the word for concubine, then shrugged. "The children seem to be adjusting well. Rory and Amaury are thick as thieves already, and I think Terése and Yllana will amuse one another."

"They will probably get into mischief." He had taken a liking to Roderick Alton-Hastur after dinner the previous evening, and thought that it would be good for his stepson to have someone his own age to play with. But he was fairly certain that Rory was a little too frisky for his own good, and could only hope that he would not lead Amaury into anything too dangerous.

"Will that be good or bad?"

"Neither. We Darkovans indulge our children a good deal, because we have always had a high infant mortality rate. A certain amount of wickedness is expected of the boys, though not of the girls, I confess."

"I had noticed that the attitude toward women here was a wee bit backward," she answered very dryly.

"What do you mean, precisely."

"Gisela gave me a thumbnail sketch of the proscribed roles of Darkovan wives and daughters during the ride. It is so different from Renney, which is my only real experience with a Protected Planet."

"I hadn't considered the matter, but since Renney is, for all practical purposes, a matriarchy, I can see that you would find it strange. We guard our women closely, and confine them in odd ways. There are a good many historical reasons for that, which we seem not to have overcome. I hope you do not find it too oppressive, darling Kate."

She sat down on the bed beside him and leaned her head against his shoulder. "Only if I am forced to spend all my time in this . . . outrageous building! It seems very odd not to be able to come and go as I please, to have all these servants and guards everywhere. I confess to feeling a bit stifled. And watched." Her voice dropped sharply and she shifted uncomfortably.

"What?"

"You grew up with this, but frankly the idea of being with a bunch of telepaths still gives me the cold grues. You would think, after living for years with invisible eyes observing my every move that I would not be bothered, but I am. The Federation was not interested in my thoughts, just in my actions. I keep thinking that someone is spying on me, trying to discover my secrets. I know I am being paranoid, Herm." *I was almost easy around Gisela, as I always have been with you, but now. . . .*

"That is not what is really bothering you, Katherine."

"No, it isn't." She stiffened slightly, as if bracing herself. "For the first time in my life, I feel . . . crippled. Unequal. I wish you had told me, before we came, about *laran* and all the Gifts and . . . everything. And about the Towers." She jerked her head away from his shoulder abruptly as if she no longer wanted to be touched by him. Gisela had told her something about these peculiar places, and she wasn't really comfortable with the idea yet.

"It was not something I was free to explain, even when we went to Renney. I was always worried that I could have been overheard by a spying device of the Federation. And it is not as if I didn't want to tell you the truth, Kate, but only that I could never find the words. Besides, you will have lots of time to learn about the Towers, and soon."

"Why?"

He sensed a trace of anger and hostility now. "Terése will have to be tested for *laran*, and we will go to Arilinn Tower, which is east of here, for that. I've never been there myself, so I am looking forward to it." As soon as the words were out of his mouth, he knew he had misjudged the situation.

"Damn you, Hermes! Were you going to tell me, or just wake me up one morning and announce we were going to this place? This is my daughter we are talking about. What's the matter with you?"

"Why are you so angry?"

"Because you are behaving in a high-handed way that makes me . . . want to bite you! Why does Terése need to go to this Arilinn?" *This is intolerable. Just when I get my feet under me, I get knocked down again!*

"I told you, Kate! She almost certainly has *laran*, and it is important that she be tested to determine the nature of her gifts."

Katherine sat in stunned silence for a moment. "You mean my little girl . . . ?" *He tried to tell me the other day, but I would not listen!*

"*Our* little girl, Katherine. She is my daughter, too, and has inherited as much from me as from you."

"I can't stand this!"

"Be reasonable, Kate. Believe me, the last thing you want is a wild telepath in the family. An untrained telepath is a danger to herself and everyone around her. If she has *laran*, she must learn how to use it properly."

"A wild . . . it sounds so odd." And abruptly she began to weep. *My little girl, my baby! This is a terrible world, and I am so afraid. What will they do to her—how do they test! I have to stop it! Terése has never been away from me, and she will be frightened. And what will she be like, if she learns how to read minds? If only I could talk to Nana right now. I don't even know this man, and I will never understand this world.*

In despair, she covered her face with her hands and made a wailing sound that Herm had never heard from her before, so terrible that it wrenched his heart. He wanted to comfort Katherine, but he knew that no mere words would help. Perhaps he should not have brought her to Darkover. He had not thought through the problem of being head-blind, how frightening it must be for her, no matter how many reassurances she received. And Amaury, too. How was the boy going to feel if his sister turned out to be a telepath? Herm had not explained things to his stepson yet, and he did not look forward to doing so. With a sinking heart he realized that the budding friendship between Amaury and young Rory might lead to some upsetting revelations. And he was so tired!

Internally, Herm shrank away from all the possible outcomes that rose in his mind. He had always loathed the messiness of other people's emotions, and was deeply grateful he did not have the Ridenow Gift of empathy. He knew that he had left Aldaran Castle and Darkover as much to escape the swirls of drama that seemed to fall like the snows, no matter what the season. Now, with a wrenching start, he understood that what had drawn him to his Kate was her reserve and self-containment. She made no great demands on his feelings, and had rarely displayed her own fiery temper. It had been a relief to find a person who was so absorbed in their own work, as she was in her painting, that she did not bother him with petty arguments.

Somehow, in the back of his mind, Herm had expected Katherine to . . . what? To stop being herself, intelligent and independent, and become obedient and passive? To let him rule the roost? Why? She never had before, not really. She wasn't going to turn into a nice Darkovan wife, and he was a fool for imagining that she would. It was going to be unpleasant, and he knew it, and knew, too, that he was not going to be able to get out of it. He wished himself far away, in some distant place where there were no problems to disentangle.

Then Herm spent a futile moment berating himself for being selfish and a stupid bastard. Why had he never told Katherine before? Was it really because he was afraid of listening Terranan ears, or something more? He had a rare moment of introspection, and decided he had been afraid of Katherine's reaction, that he had suspected that she would feel just exactly as she did right now, angry and frightened. He had never been willing to risk losing her, and had hoped that the situation would never arise.

What an idiot he had been. How would he have tried to lie his way out of Terése's threshold sickness when it began? If he had remained away from Darkover, his precious daughter might have died!

Hermes realized he had hurt his wife deeply, with his own avoidance and denial. He would have had to bring his daughter back to Darkover in a couple of years, for her own safety, but he had refused to think about it until a crisis forced him to. And he had blundered badly.

He was shaken again, as the enormity of his folly finally blossomed in his mind. It gave the lie to the great confidence Herm had always had in himself, in his inate cunning and cleverness. These seemed worthless now, the wrong tools for the task. "As well carve a roast with a spoon," as they said in the Hellers. This was not dissembling before the interested eyes of some political foe, but a different sort of problem, a human one, full of conflicting feelings. And, he admitted to himself with great reluctance, he was not really very good with strong feelings. It put him too much in mind of the endless tensions of Aldaran Castle in his childhood, where loud voices and passions were the order of the day. He had left Darkover as much to escape those as to serve the planet of his birth.

Katherine mopped her eyes on her sleeve and sniffed noisily. Herm reached into his pouch and took out a square of linen and offered it to her. This ordinary object—an "obsolete" cloth handkerchief brought with it a sense of powerful distinction, for there were no paper tissues available on Darkover, unless there was a supply at HQ. Nothing on Darkover was easily disposable, not nose wipes or people. And that was a profound difference. To the Terran mind, almost everything was replaceable except power. By contrast, Darkovans were pack rats, saving everything and using it until it just wore out.

Herm had become accustomed to the ease of life in the Federation, but never completely comfortable with it. He thought it very extravagant to discard a perfectly good object just because there was a newer one available. He preferred the soft feel of real linen bedsheets to the paper-cloth ones he had slept on for twenty-three years, and the faint smell of age in the stones and plaster of the walls, saturated with centuries of woodsmoke and seasons, to the sterile one of a typical Federation apartment. He liked being home, but this was not Katherine's home, and it must seem very strange to her. Houses on Renney were made of wood, not stone, and castles were virtually unknown there. There was nothing he could do about that, short of letting her leave Darkover, to return to Renney with her son. And that thought was unbearable, and probably impossible now, if what he had learned in the meeting was accurate.

Katherine blew her nose several times. "Forgive me, dearest. Just when I think I have myself under control, I go all to pieces again. I can't bear the idea of Terése going away—she's still a child. And, quite truthfully, I hope she will have no talents at all, and will just continue to be a normal little girl." She hesitated, and Herm saw both fear and great sorrow in her beautiful eyes. "Of course, a normal little girl here can read minds or do . . . the goddess only knows what!"

Herm patted her awkwardly on the shoulder. "Kate—I am the one who needs forgiving. I should have told you years ago, before we married, I suppose. Yes, that would have been the wisest thing. Or not married you at all. My only excuse is that I fell passionately in love with you the second I saw you, and I was not thinking very clearly. Later . . . well, I was too scared I'd lose you."

She gave a little snort. "You are claiming the triumph of hormones and emotion over reason, then?"

"Something like that."

"I suppose I should feel complimented—since you are the most calculating person I have ever known—that you did one thing just because you wanted to. Nana told me you were keeping some secret from me, but did I listen?" She gave a gusty sigh. "At least I will never see her again, and be spared hearing her say 'I told you so.' That's very chilly comfort, Hermes."

"I am sure it is. Your Nana is a very smart woman, and she almost saw through me."

"What do you mean?" Katherine sounded a little less despondent now, although still not her usual lively self.

"A few times she almost penetrated my secret, and I know she thought I had second sight, which is an old tradition among your people. It is my guess that the Rennians, who are not unlike the population of Darkover in several ways, including linguistics, have some genetic predisposition toward what we call *laran*."

"Why?"

"Some of the stories I heard when we visited, about those old witches and sorcerers, sounded remarkably like *leroni*. It is just a guess, but not a bad one, I suspect."

"But, Herm, those are folktales. Surely you did not take them seriously! My great-great-grandmother was not really able to charm animals or turn herself into a white cat when the second moon was full—that is all nonsense." Her dark eyes were rather wide as she spoke, as if she saw the world of her birth in a new light, and found the prospect not very comfortable.

"True, about the cat. But we have a few people here on Darkover who can make contact with animals in such a way as to influence their actions. And I think that telepathy is probably more common in humankind than is generally believed."

"Then why hasn't the Federation . . . ?"

"Why haven't they discovered it and exploited it, as they do everything else? Because it is intangible, I suppose, because you cannot hold it in your hand and grasp it. And they almost did, once. There was a thing called Project Telepath, back when Regis was first in power, in which we agreed to participate. But Lew Alton, who was our Senator then, decided it was too dangerous to Darkover, and managed to get it shelved. The Terranan are convinced that the products of their material technologies are superior to anything else, and they have stopped looking for other ways to do things. Lew just persuaded a few key people that real telepaths were rare, much too few to be worth the expense, and that those who were gifted in this way were usually emotionally unstable, and ultimately valueless. And it is true, that if you are unfortunate enough to be born on a world where paranormal powers are not cultivated, and you are a telepath, you end up pretty crazy."

"But that's terrible! I mean, if there are other people in the galaxy who have such powers . . . ? How could he?"

"With the greatest difficulty, and a lot of sleepless nights, I assure you. He had a whole planet to think about, Kate—his world."

"I see, I guess. But it seems pretty selfish to me." Katherine decided to reserve judgment on the interesting and complex man she had met the previous night.

"The alternative, to his mind and mine, was to risk an invasion. Can you imagine how tempting it would be to certain people to be able to read the minds of their opponents at will? Oh, the Federation knows that telepathy happens, but they have no idea what a Darkovan with trained *laran* can do consistently. If the Federation had really guessed the extent of Darkovan talents, they would have come in with force and taken away anyone they felt could be useful to them."

"What did Nana say—government is a beast without a conscience?"

"Did she say that?"

"Yes, but she was talking about the plan to clear-cut one of the old groves, back when I was still a girl. Some Federation corporation wanted the wood, to make into furniture." She chuckled briefly. "Good thing they did not get their wish."

"Why?"

"It was a grove of nightwood."

"You mean those gigantic trees we visited. That is fine lumber, and I can see how it might attract some greedy developer. Is there something wrong with nightwood?"

"Oh, no. It is a wonderful wood, very hard and durable. But there is a belief on Renney that a chair made of it will drive you mad if you sit on it. Just a superstition, of course." *Well, perhaps, but one I would not risk going against—what a silly woman I am.*

"What was it used for, then?" Herm was relieved that the subject had moved away from *laran* and other things that made Kate uncomfortable, and would have discussed wood or bones or just about anything at that moment, just to keep her happy.

"Spears, back when we still did that sort of thing. A nightwood spear was supposedly able to pierce the heart of a foe all the way through. And shields, too—to protect against the spears. But never chairs, and especially never cradles!"

"You must be sure to tell Marguerida about that. Mikhail says she is a great collector of tales."

Katherine sighed, settled her shoulders firmly, and braced herself. "Herm, does Terése have to be tested? Is it absolutely necessary?"

He kept himself from cringing. Herm should have known that he could not distract Katherine for long. "Yes, it is. But it is not difficult or painful—they do not strap anyone into a machine. And it is more dangerous not to know what her talents might be than otherwise."

"Will they let me be with her?"

"That is a bit unusual, but I think I could arrange it. In fact, it might not be a bad idea to have both you and Amaury checked out, dearest." *You might not be as head-blind as you think.*

"Don't be ridiculous, Hermes! I am no kind of telepath, and I don't want to be one! The idea frightens me!"

"Are you entirely sure?"

"What is that supposed to mean?" She glared at him, furious and more than a little scared at the same time.

"Well, it has occurred to me occasionally that some of the portraits you have done have elements in them that . . . are remarkable. Remember how Dame Hester could not get over those flowers you put in the background of her picture."

"I must have seen those in a book and knew they came from her world."

"But how could you have known she was particularly fond of them?"

"Blind luck," Katherine insisted, not sounding very convincing. "They just felt right. . . ."

"It might be intuition, my Kate, and it might be something more. Don't you want to find out?"

"No, I don't. I could not bear it if I found out I had been snooping on my sitters, all these years." He was just trying to make her feel less like a cripple, suggesting that she had more than mere intuition. How dare he! The urge to throttle him came and went, and she glared at him accusingly. Kate felt almost ill for a second. What a disgusting notion. And she certainly was not going to be tested by anyone!

Herm recognized the set of Kate's jaw, and knew he would be wasting his time if he tried to suggest more than he had already. Let her think about it for a while. "Very well. I will not force you, but I hope you will change your mind."

"Damn you! I hate it when you do that."

"Do what," he answered, trying to look innocent and, he knew, not succeeding at all.

"Be all reasonable and calm, when in fact you are manipulating me, playing me like your favorite fiddle." She was wary now, but her fear was slipping away slowly.

"I never do that when we are both dressed," he said huskily.

"Oh, no, you don't! No fiddling for you. I won't be pleasured out of . . ."

He began to laugh, and after a second she joined him tentatively. But when he reached for the laces on her tunic, she pushed his hand away roughly. "You are not nearly as irresistible as you imagine! And if you don't behave, I will make you sleep on the couch in the sitting room."

"But, darling, it is so short. Think of my bad back."

"There is nothing in the least wrong with your back!"

"There would be, if I tried to sleep on that dumpy bit of furniture!"

"Hermes-Gabriel Aldaran—you are hopeless!" She grabbed both his ears and tugged—not very gently. "What am I going to do with you?"

"I don't know, since you are in no mood for fiddling. Are you trying to reform me, woman?" He tried to look stern, but it was impossible. She was too lovely, and she still took his breath away, whenever he looked into her eyes.

"No. Yes."

"That is honest, at least. Let us agree that I am beyond reclaimation, that I have the morals of a fell-cat. But remember that I love you, and that I would not have brought you here if I had had any other recourse. You are my life, Katherine."

"Very prettily said, and perhaps even true." She traced her fingers across his mouth, touching him sweetly. "Just promise me that you will always tell me things, that you will never keep me in the dark again. I don't think I could forgive another secret, not now."

"I will tell you my secrets, Kate, but not those of others."

"I'll settle for that. Now, I am starving! Let's order some lunch, and you can tell me about your meeting with Mikhail and Lew Alton. Was there anyone else there?"

"Danilo Hastur and Danilo Syrtis-Ardais were present, as well as Mikhail's paxman Donal. It went well." Herm knew he should tell her that there was a price on his head, as it were, but he could not bring the words to his mouth.

"And?"

"I can't get anything past you, can I?" He had just given his word, and now he knew he was going to break it immediately. Herm could not tell her that Belfontaine wanted him turned over, since there was no chance that Mikhail Hastur would ever agree to such a thing. She did not need to know! It would give her more to worry about, and she deserved better than that, after all she had endured. Later, when the crisis was past, then he would tell her . . . .

Katherine was giving him a penetrating look. "Not any longer, Herm. I will not be kept in the dark again, even if matters of policy are not precisely my business. I have myself and the children to think about—and I do not give a fig about the larger picture, not really. I think all of this is just some great game that you males enjoy playing, trying to achieve dominence over your fellows."

"You might be right, though you ladies are not above the game. I've never understood why you girls won't just stand quietly on your pedestals and be admired." He decided that he had better distract her, and quickly!

Katherine narrowed her eyes even further. "Because we don't want complete strangers looking up our petticoats. Stop trying to annoy me and distract me from my purpose. It won't work! 'You girls' indeed!"

"I had not thought of that." He grunted softly, trying to decide how much to tell her. "The situation is complex. There are a great many people on Darkover who have never been enchanted with the Federation, and who will likely try to take this opportunity to persuade us to withdraw from it completely. This is a very conservative culture, which is one reason that there has been no proliferation of Terran technology. And one of the most powerful advocates of isolationism is Mikhail's father, *Dom* Gabriel Lanart-Alton. You will meet him in the near future. And his wife, Javanne Hastur, who is the older sister of Regis, and, by all accounts, a formidable foe. From what I have heard, she might not be entirely stable. And she has never entirely resigned herself to Mikhail being Regis' successor, for reasons I will not go into. It would be better if you asked Marguerida about that, when you have the opportunity. But Javanne is all for restoring the Elhalyn kingship to power, although it never possessed any real power in the past. Even though Mikhail is her son, she would rather see Danilo Hastur running Darkover, because she imagines he is weak enough to be manipulated by her. From what I learned today, I believe she is mistaken. But the truth is that Dani was never trained to run a planetary government, and never wished to be a ruler."

"I don't understand. Are Dani and Mikhail rivals?"

"They do not see themselves as such, but there are others who would love to churn things up. You see, the Elhalyn kingship has always been a largely ceremonial position, and the Hasturs have always had the real power. There are good historic reasons for this, since the Elhalyn line produces some very unstable people. Dani married Miralys Elhalyn with the intention of breeding some health into the line—which sounds very cold, I suppose. He was in love with her, so it was not terrible and calculated. But he resigned from the heirship of the Hastur Domain in favor of Mikhail, when he could have fought for it, and perhaps even gotten it, because he did not want the task of running the planet. He is a man who understands his own limitations, and I admire him for that."

"So the matter was settled a long time ago?"

"It was, but not to everyone's complete satisfaction—particularly not to Javanne Hastur's. Time has not mellowed her, by all accounts, And she has a few allies on the Comyn Council, so there is likely to be a great deal of shouting and table pounding before the dust settles."

"But that is not what troubles you."

"No, it is not. Darkovans are very pragmatic, and they will do the sensible thing eventually. The real problem remains the Federation. We have never had an intelligence agency here—the entire idea is foreign to us. Instead we have depended on a few well-placed people in the Terran Headquarters, plus Lew Alton, who has been keeping his finger on the pulse of the Federation ever since Captain Rafe Scott resigned. Now those people are going to be 'released from active duty,' which is a pleasant euphemism for being tossed out on their butts, and we won't have anyone who can keep an eye on Lyle Belfontaine and his minions. Without a few people in HQ, we won't know what the Federation is up to, and will be dependent on only the information they permit us to hear. Lew, who is very good at reading between the lines, thinks we will be handed some sort of ultimatum soon. We have managed to keep word of Regis' death from getting out, thus far, but that cannot last, and once word does get out it is likely that the Federation will try some sort of maneuver. So it is in our best interests to settle the matter quickly, and nothing on Darkover ever happens fast. Mikhail cannot make any unilateral decisions."

"Why not, if he is Regis' successor?" Katherine was concentrating very hard on his words, trying to bring her intelligence to bear on the subject, and for a moment, all her fears were pushed into the background.

"He may be the most powerful man on the planet, but he must answer to the Comyn Council, which is divided. We have never had a tyrant on Darkover, and Mik hardly wishes to be the first."

"This doesn't make complete sense to me, Herm. I would think that a planet of telepaths would have no trouble penetrating any intelligence agency in a flash."

"It is not that easy, even setting aside the ethical considerations."

"Why?"

"Because you can't just close your eyes and start plundering people's minds—unless you have the Alton Gift of forced rapport. Proximity is required, as well as some familiarity with the mind you would like to explore. What you get when you don't know the subject is just a lot of noise—their argument with their lover, or how much they liked the most recent encounter, how much they loathe their work, or just that they have a terrible headache from too much drink the night before. Spying on other people is something that Darkoveans with *laran* learn is unforgivable very early."

"So you have an advantage, but you don't use it! That's a little hard to believe. The temptation must be huge."

"No, not really. For the most part, you don't want to know what is in the minds of others, because much of it is too trivial or distasteful. If someone is mentally shouting, you can't help hearing it, but most of that is emotions and not information. I mean, no one at HQ is going to sit at their desk, reading the most recent orders, broadcasting their thoughts at a roar. Instead they are going to be focused on the impact of those orders on their immediate circumstances—where they will be posted next or whether they can take their Darkovan spouse and children with them."

"I see. It is kind of a relief to know, Herm. It makes me less anxious."

"Good. I realize it will take you some time to believe that no one is going to invade your mind in the hall or at dinner. Very few of us can do that at will. Marguerida has the Alton Gift, and so does her father and her son Domenic, but none of them would ever violate you."

She nodded, as if reassured. "I like Nico, but he certainly is a serious young fellow. And Marguerida seems very nice, the little I have seen of her."

"She is very busy just now arranging for the funeral rites, but she lived in the Federation for twenty years before she returned to Darkover, so she will probably find interests in common with you. She was at University, a Fellow in Musicology, when she came here, and I understand that she has continued to transmit ethnographic papers for years now. And she can hardly wait to grill you about Amedi Korniel just as soon as she has a free moment."

"I think Mikhail said something about that, last night at dinner. That, at least, is something I feel I can handle. I know a number of really scandalous tales about him—he was a great musician, but he was not really a very nice person." Realizing, then, that there were still things of which she was unaware, she brought the discussion back to the original topic. "Is there more, Herm? I have the feeling there is something else bothering you."

"Yes, dearest. How did you guess?"

"You always twist your fingers into knots when you are uneasy."

Herm looked down at his hands and discovered that they were indeed interlaced. How had he never noticed that before? "As I said, we don't have a real intelligence force of our own, but we know the Federation does. I don't mean those at HQ. Lew suspects that someone is running a covert operation, but he has no idea who or how. We are not even certain it is a Federation agency."

"What else could it be?"

Herm chuckled. "If I had not spent the last two decades in the Federation I could not even attempt to answer that. The Liberal Party as well as the Expansionists, the New Republicans, the Monarchists, and just about every other political power have spies of various sorts, trying to ferret out the secrets of the others, in order to expose them. How do you think that banking scandal on Coronis Nine got into the media? It was not some eager newshound that sniffed it out, but an agent of New Revelationists who leaked the thing. They love to discredit the Expansionists—it is practically their only form of sport." They both chuckled, since the New Revelationists were famed for their fundamentalism and their disapproval of play of any sort. "Not that the rest of us did not enjoy it, of course. So, whatever is afoot on Darkover could be anything from Federation to a group I never heard of. Unlikely, in truth, because none of the various groups is likely to be interested in Darkover. Yet it is the not knowing that is disturbing."

"But why would anyone want to do that? I mean, Darkover is not a very important planet, Herm. Wouldn't spies be more interested in Aldebaran Five or Wolf? Places with a lot of industry or important resources?"

"Darkover is a very mysterious place, Kate. Our very policy of information limitation, which Lew put into place and I have continued, was bound to provoke some curiosity somewhere. We just did not see the problem at first. You know—you do something to solve a situation, and then, ten or twenty years down the line, it starts to have consequences you never anticipated. We don't know anything for certain, but Lew said there have been some disturbances recently that made him suspicious. He hoped I could confirm these, but I had to tell him I don't know of any specific group that is casting its eye on Darkover. So, we don't actually know we were being spied on."

"But you think you might be."

"Yes, that was our tentative conclusion, for all the good it did us," he agreed reluctantly. "Let's eat. All of this will keep." He felt a profound sense of guilt, mingled with relief and weariness. He had kept his Kate from finding out he might be arrested, but he did not feel happy about his deception. And he knew that when he did finally tell her, there would be hell to pay.

For a brief moment, Herm wished he had never come back to Darkover at all. He felt a kind of dreadful restlessness seize him, a desire to be anywhere in the galaxy except where he was. Kate was upset. He hated that, and he knew it was not going to go away just because it made him squirm. It was as he had said—he had solved one problem, the security of his small family—without imagining clearly the consequences that would follow. And it had not taken years, but only days, to discover that his solution had created fresh trouble.

True, he felt himself born to discord, to deal with it as a cunning fellow should. But it was not supposed to affect those he held dearest in the cosmos—his wife and children. How could he have been so short-sighted not to see this coming. And how was he going to resolve it? His belly grumbled then, and Herm gave up in exhaustion. He had had no choice but to do what he had done. He was not going to fix things soon, or on an empty stomach—so he might as well eat. That, at least, was something he could do without hurting anyone.

9

Domenic spent the rest of the afternoon plotting his escape from Comyn Castle, with a kind of glee he had never felt before. His grief and his fears faded into faint shadows, even though finding a way out of the vast building was more complicated than he had imagined. There were servants everywhere, and most of the exits were closely guarded. He would have to do a lot of sneaking, something he had very little practice in. The more he thought about that part the more attractive the entire scheme became. It was odd, really, and he felt possessed by some imp of wickedness in those occasional moments when he allowed himself to reflect.

If only there were not a banquet planned for the evening, it would have been simpler. But the arrival of his grandparents as well as several other members of the Comyn Council demanded such a meal, and Domenic knew he was expected to be present. He could think of nothing he wished for less than to spend several hours with Javanne glaring at him, or worse, pretending he was not even in the room. And Gareth Elhalyn was likely to be there as well. What was it about his cousin that made him so uneasy? On the other hand, it would certainly be an interesting meal, since Herm Aldaran and his family would be present, and perhaps that would distract Javanne from paying too much attention to him.

For several minutes he came close to abandoning his foolish idea. Nico found himself alternating between excitement and despair, fearful of the consequences and yet enthralled at the same time. Then he scolded himself for faint-heartedness. Rory would not hesitate over such minor considerations as duty and good manners. Maybe he should ask Rory to help him. His brother knew all the back ways and little used corridors of the building, and often employed them for his own mischief. But he rejected the idea. Certainly Rory would show him how to escape, but he would insist on coming along. It would not be an adventure if he went with his younger brother, would it? More, his brother was almost always in some sort of trouble, and it would not sit well with his parents if he got his sibling into more. Nico chuckled a little over this, knowing he was making excuses to himself. The plain truth was he wanted to get away with no one being the wiser, including, or perhaps especially, his brother.

But, how was he going to get out of attending the meal? He wracked his brains and could think of nothing immediately. Just when he was almost ready to give it up completely, Ida Davidson came to his rescue. The ancient woman had been a part of his family for as long as he could remember, and Nico felt she should have been his granny, instead of Javanne. He could barely remember Diotima Ridenow, Lew's late wife, who had died when he was about five. So Ida had filled in the space where he felt a grandmother should be, listening to his small complaints without making him feel like a dolt, giving him music lessons, and when he turned out to be fumble-fingered at the clavier, the guitar, or any other instrument more complex than a drum, she had schooled him in song. Both his parents were very musical, but he and Rory seemed not to be. Ida's kindness and patience had helped him over his feelings of inadequacy and now he could sing well enough not to disgrace himself. After his voice changed, he had turned into a reasonable tenor, and actually enjoyed the little quartet consisting of himself, Rory, and his uncle Rafael's two younger children, Gabriel and Damon.

"Nico," the old lady said, peering at him a bit short-sightedly, "are you quite well? You look a bit peaked."

"Do I?" He considered her remark briefly, and brightened internally. "I am feeling a bit off. Achey, you know?" He did not ache at all, and knew his appearance was the result of his internal struggle. Ida had no *laran*, and was never suspicious of him. Why hadn't he thought of this sooner? Roderick often played sick when he did not want to do something, but Nico had never employed that ruse. Part of him hated fibbing to Ida, but another was practically bouncing with joy. Maybe Alanna was not the only one who felt she was more than one person.

"With all the furor we have had, I am not surprised. Now, off to bed with you. The last thing you need to do is sit through a long dinner, and if you are getting sick, you will just share your germs with everyone. I'll have one of the servants bring you a tray."

His heart sank. The servants! That would ruin everything. "My appetite seems to be gone, Ida." The lie rolled off his tongue as if he had been doing it for years. "If I get hungry, I'll ring for something."

"Not hungry?" She shook her head. "You must be coming down with something, if you aren't hungry. Scoot. I will tell your mother."

Nico scooted, going off to his bedroom. He listened to the sounds in the suite, the movement of servants and his parents and siblings. Then he got into his nightshirt and crawled into bed, sure his mother would come to check on him before she went to dinner. He could hardly contain his excitement, and tried to relax.

Marguerida came in, wearing a long blue gown embroidered with silver flowers, the Hastur colors. As she came toward the bed, he could smell her particular perfume, lavender mingled with musk. She bent over him and swept his forehead with a mitted hand. "Poor Nico. You do not feel hot, but you look rather pale. What is it?"

"I haven't been sleeping very well, and I think I am just tired, Mother." He could get away with telling Ida a lie, but with Marguerida it was more difficult, and he had never even tried before. And it was close to a real truth, for in sleep he could hear the fire in the heart of the world, and the rumbling deep inside the earth, or thought he could. Worse, in dreams he found himself trying to halt the sea in its endless motion, and do other things that were too incredible to be considered. So, he avoided sleep as much as he was able, using the trance states he had learned at Arilinn as a substitute.

"Not sleeping well? You should have told me. Shall I get you a sleeping draught?"

"I don't think I need that, and besides they leave me feeling stupid in the morning." If Marguerida ordered a draught, and stood over him while he drank it, his plan would be ruined.

"Very well. I hate the things myself, although these past few days I have drunk more of them than I wished. Just when I am ready to drop off, I think of something else that I should have attended to and start up in the bed. Which wakes your father, and he really needs his rest."

"I'll be fine. I think I'll just read for a while. I have this really boring book I started about six months ago somewhere around here, and it should have me asleep in five minutes. Save your fussing for our guests, Mother. I am sure you have better things to do than worry about me." He gave her a droll look, and she answered with a wan smile. They both knew he meant Javanne Hastur, who was never easy to deal with, and with Regis' death, was likely to be even more difficult than usual.

"What book is that?" Nico knew that when his mother had come to Darkover, books had been uncommon except in the homes of the Domains, and most of those had been imports. She had made it one of her projects to promote literacy, and with her friend, Rafaella n'ha Liriel, the Renunciate who had been her guide and friend during her first months on Darkover, had started a small publishing enterprise. The Renunciates had begun printing handbills and other single pages years before, but had never expanded beyond leaflets into actual books. Until Marguerida had founded the Alton Press, most books had been handcopied, slowly and painstakingly, and were kept in the archives of the Castle or the various Towers.

Now there was a young Binders Guild, separate from the Tanners Guild which had always done that task before, and editions of five hundred volumes were not uncommon. With the help of Thendara House, the Renunciate headquarters, two small schools had been established, one near the Horse Market and one in Threadneedle Street, and the sons and daughters of tradesmen were encouraged to attend. It was a small step, she had told him, but at least a beginning. Marguerida had written a volume of folktales for publication and use in the small schools, stories she had collected in her travels around Darkover and from other worlds as well, and it was now in its fifth printing.

"Oh, that tome that Hiram d'Asturien wrote about the evolution of *laran*."

She laughed, and the sound of it was wonderful. His mother had not laughed very often in recent days, and he had not known how much he missed it until now. "What he has to say is useful, but I agree that his style leaves something to be desired. Positively soporific, actually. But I am a little surprised to find that you were looking at it. Any particular reason?"

"I was just curious." Another fib, though not a very big one. He was curious, but the actuality was that he had hoped to discover some clues to his own uniqueness, to find out if anyone before him had been able to hear the planet. He could not discuss it with anyone, even his mother, whom he trusted completely.

"Good. Never lose that quality, Nico." Then she kissed his brow lightly and left, apparently satisfied.

He waited impatiently until the suite was quiet and he could hear no nearby thoughts at all. Then Nico scrambled out of bed, took off his nightshirt and put on his oldest tunic and some patched trousers, plus his riding boots. He took a shabby cloak that he was particularly fond of and refused to stop wearing and looked around the bedroom. He stuffed several pillows down under the covers, in the shape of a body, and pulled the blanket over the head. He studied his handiwork and thought it would do until he returned. Then he snuffed the candles, sending the room into near darkness. The light from the little fireplace hardly reached the bed, and cast several nice shadows that concealed his deceit. Nico was quite pleased with himself.

He slipped out of the suite by the servants' stair, and started down the back corridor in the direction of the huge kitchens. Even at a distance, he could hear the clamor of pot and pans, the shouting of the head cook at her minions, all in preparation for the meal to be served. Then he heard someone coming toward him and he darted into the first doorway he found, his heart hammering with excitement. It was very dark within, and from the smell of it, he was in the stillroom. After a second he heard footfalls pass the door, and knew who it was. Just one of the lads who turned the spits in the kitchens, all his thoughts concerned with fetching something for Cook.

As soon as silence returned to the corridor, Nico slipped out and tiptoed along. When he crept past the great door to the kitchen, he heard Cook swearing a bit at someone's clumsiness with the dessert tarts. His mouth watered. He should have eaten before he set out. Maybe he could get something at a foodstall. He had done that a few times before, not nearly as often as he wished, for he found the taste of street food much more interesting than what was served in the Castle. Had he brought any coins? Yes, there were a few in his beltpouch.

Despite the chill of early evening, the door to the alley that ran from the kitchen past the bakery was propped open a bit. He darted into the shadowed way, feeling more excited by the second. Was this why Rory did the naughty things he did? What a fool he had been to let his little brother have all the fun!

The heat from the walls of the bakery was pleasant, and he almost regretted it when he passed beyond. He pulled up the hood on his cloak and moved quietly behind the barracks where the Guards lived, praying he would not meet anyone. From the noise, he knew the off-duty Guardsmen were eating their evening meal. It was a friendly, jocular sound, and he thought how much he enjoyed it when he ate with them. They did not defer to him at the table, but treated him as just another young man, and please pass the platter.

At last he came out into a narrow street, and turned right. It was deserted, but the houses on either side were alight, and he could hear occasional voices. A few minutes of walking, and Comyn Castle was behind him, and his fear of discovery began to evaporate. The street wound around and came back to a larger thoroughfare, and went on into a little square. There were torches on the faces of the buildings, and he saw a foodstall on the far side.

A pair of burly draymen were standing in front of it, waiting for the old man who ran it to serve them up pockets of flat bread stuffed with chunks of roasted fowl. It smelled wonderful. Nico was glad he had not eaten first, because it seemed more of an adventure to get his supper on the street.

In the flickering light from the torches, he realized he looked quite ordinary in his old and disreputable garments. No one would ever suspect who he was. When the draymen had been served, he stepped forward, sniffing hungrily. He listened to the conversation of the men, talking with their mouths full. They were complaining in cheerful tones which belied their words about how poorly they had been tipped for some moving job they had done. He guessed that they were enjoying their mutters of discontent about the stinginess of their employers, and that this was a normal subject of conversation.

Nico asked for a serving, and the old man slipped several pieces of meat off a slender wooden skewer and plopped them onto a crusty slab of bread, rolling the bread around the filling to make it easier to eat. He dug out his smallest coin and handed it over. Then he sank his teeth into the rolled-up bread, tasting the spices that the fowl had been marinated in. It was delicious. Why didn't they serve such good things at the Castle?

He left the square still eating, and walked quickly down the street, heading for the North Gate. The evening wind cooled his face and ruffled his unbound hair, but he barely noticed. He was having a wonderful time, just being alone and listening to the night sounds of Thendara. He finished his food, found his face was a little greasy, and grinned. Then he wiped his sleeve over his cheeks. No napkins or linens for him tonight! And, even better, no Javanne ruining his appetite!

After half an hour of unhurried walking, he saw some people ahead of him on the street. They were heading toward the Gate, and he slowed so as not to catch up with them. When they passed beneath some torches he realized that they were dressed in Terranan leathers, and wondered what they were doing outside the Trade City. It was not forbidden for off-duty Terrans to venture into Thendara proper, but even Nico knew it was a bit uncommon. Well, maybe they were bored and had heard that the Travelers were performing.

But it was a bit puzzling. He had overheard a few things in the last couple of days, from his father or Grandfather Lew, and had gotten the impression that there was some sort of order from the Federation that restricted their people from leaving Headquarters. Oh, well, perhaps he had misunderstood, or the Terrans had changed their minds. The only thing he was really sure of was that Darkovan personnel had been ordered to leave both the space port and the Headquarters complex. He had seen Ethan MacDoevid, his mother's protegé from Threadneedle Street, coming into the hall just as he was going out for his Guard duty, and was sure that he had come to tell Grandfather Lew something interesting.

He knew the story of how Ethan and his mother had met very well, for she was very fond of recounting it. Ethan and his cousin Geremy had met Marguerida coming out of the port the day she returned to Darkover, and the lads had guided her to master Everard's house in Music Street, becoming friends along the way. She had a way of telling the tale that made her first impressions very vivid. The boy—he had been a bit younger than Nico was now—had confided to her his longing to go on the Big Ships, and later she had been instrumental in getting him the chance to learn the things he needed to become a spacefarer. He had acquired the skills, but the opportunity had never come to him, since the Federation had changed its policies about allowing personnel from Protected Planets to man their ships, so he had never gone into space.

When Rafe Scott had been forced to retire from HQ, Ethan had taken over many of the duties of Liaison that Scott had performed. Nico knew, from a few conversations with him, that this had not entirely pleased Ethan, but he did his work with a good will. The appointment had annoyed several people on the Council, since Ethan was the son of a tradesman, not the Domains, and Marguerida's protegé as well. However, it had turned out to be a good choice, and he could only wonder what Ethan was going to do now, if the Federation left, and there was no need for a Liaison officer, and even if they didn't, they weren't going to let any native Darkovans stick around HQ. He could hardly go back to his father's tailoring business after so many years.

Domenic noticed that there was something hasty and nervous about the men ahead of him, and it sent all speculations about Ethan's future right out of his mind. He found their behavior very interesting, and puzzling as well. One second they were moving along like two fellows out for a good time, and the next they were peering into the shadows, as if they expected to be attacked. If they had wanted to be anonymous, they should not have come in their distinctive leathers. Typical Terranan arrogance. What were they up to? If they wanted female companionship, they would have stayed in the Trade City. He gave a slight shrug under his shabby cloak, and decided it was not important, and that it just added a bit of spice to his thus far unadventurous evening.

Nico was beginning to feel slightly foolish about the whole thing. Just because his mother said he was too well-behaved was no reason to be sneaking out in the night, leaving some bolsters in his place on the bed, was it? He was tempted to turn around and go back before his absence was discovered. But that was hen-hearted, and besides he was not doing anything very terrible.

This whole thing is a waste of time—we could be back in the barracks now, warm and comfy, instead of out in this wretched cold. Vancof will not have anything to tell us—he never has before. God, I hate this planet. I won't get reassigned to anything better, since I haven't managed to make any kind of name for myself here. Belfontaine is crazy if he thinks he can turn this around before we have to leave. I will be glad to get off Cottman. The sooner the better. Damn fool backwater place.

Domenic heard this jumble of thoughts, the usual disorganized muddle, and almost stumbled. Cottman? He must be picking up one of the men ahead of him—only Terranan called Darkover that. And who was Vancof? Were the men expecting to meet someone outside the Gate? Why would they do that? It did not make any sense at all.

The name was strange, and clearly not a Darkovan one. Why would these men go to meet a Terran outside the gates? Suddenly the whole episode took on a darker tone. The men were not in search of entertainment, but were going for some other purpose. He moved faster, hoping to overhear them speak, or catch another snatch of thoughts. It was not as if he were spying, since he could not help listening to the uppermost thoughts of other people. Still, it made him feel slightly uncomfortable.

The men passed through the arch of the North Gate, and Nico followed them. Beyond the Gate there were half dozen firepits blazing away, as well as torches set in stands. After the relative darkness of the streets, it seemed more light than it really was. Nico could see several of the painted wagons of the Travelers on one side of the huge field. On the other there were foodstands and booths that sold trinkets. Just beyond the stands there were groups of mules tethered to ropes and a couple of wagons piled with goods. Briefly he wondered why the muleteers were camping out there. Then he decided that it likely saved them the cost of stabling for the night. There seemed so many things he did not know, and he felt rather annoyed. Some education he had had!

One of the Travelers' wagons had its side lowered, and there was a juggler standing on the platform, fearlessly tossing small lighted torches in the air. He had four of the things in motion, and was declaiming at the same time. Nico moved toward this display, fascinated. The redheaded girl was nowhere in sight, and the side of the puppet wagon was pulled up and shut. Maybe they had already performed, and he had missed it.

He joined the crowd of watchers, listening to the jibes of the juggler and the catcalls of the audience as well. The smell of cheap beer and unwashed clothing was all around him. It was a rough bunch of people, men and women both, and even a few children, wide-eyed with wonder. But it was not an unruly crowd—they were just having a good time on a not unpleasant evening. In a few weeks, it would be too cold for this sort of thing, so everyone was making the most of the mild weather and a chance to have some harmless fun.

The two men in Terran leathers stood in the crowd for several minutes, their backs toward him. They were both big men, broad shouldered and well-muscled. One had dark brown hair and the other was a blond, but other than that there was very little difference between them. They stared at the performance dully, as if they were waiting for something or someone.

Just when Domenic was starting to think they had come to see one of the girl acrobats or dancers in the scanty garments that had scandalized some of the people at Arilinn, one of the men made a gesture with his head, signaling his partner. They slipped off quietly, and vanished between two of the parked wagons. They did not look like men seeking the company of a woman, and, as far as he had ever heard, Travelers did not offer that sort of custom. Of course, with his abysmal ignorance of things beyond the walls of Comyn Castle, almost anything seemed possible. But there were easier pickings in the taverns in the Trade City, if all they wanted was a bed-warmer.

For just a moment, he hesitated. Then he could not resist. He wanted to find out what they were up to. Nico slipped through the crowd unnoticed, and went toward the space between the two wagons. Then he leaned against one and bent over, tugging at one of the laces on his boots, as if it had become undone and needed to be retied. His cloak fell around him, concealing his movements. No one seemed to be paying him the least attention, and he was relieved.

Nico's blood was pounding in his ears, and for a minute he could hear nothing but the noises of his body. Why was he spying on these men? Because they did not belong where they were and, he admitted to himself a little grudgingly, because he was extremely curious as to what had brought them there. He could just catch the sound of whispering, hushed and cautious, speaking in Terran. He had learned that language from his mother and grandfather, but he had a little trouble following the words at first. He leaned toward the narrow passage between the wagons and strained to hear. Finally he was able to distinguish three males, as they stopped whispering and began to speak in low tones.

"You haven't sent a message in six days." The voice was harsh, and sounded a little angry.

"If I had a shortbeam, it would be easier," one voice whined. Nico wondered what that meant.

"Too risky, and you know it. Besides, the damn things only work half the time."

"I've been busy. And there hasn't been anything much."

"Busy?" The harsh voice sounded disbelieving.

"Driving the wagon and managing the mules is a full time job! I broke a wheel to get into Thendara, and managed to drive across the city, but I did not find out much. The old bastard, Regis Hastur, is dead, but you already know that." Now, as the whining voice spoke further, Domenic recognized it. It was the driver of the puppet wagon he had seen that morning! What had the girl called him—Dirck?

Domenic nearly gasped and almost missed the reply. "No, we did not know that! Damn you, Vancof. You are incompetent. You did not think it was important, when we have been waiting for an opportunity like this for years. A pity it had to happen just when we are getting ready to pull out."

"Pull out? Are you sure?" He did not seem very much like the unpleasant fellow who had been so rude to Kendrick now, but sounded uneasy, as if he were frightened of the men with him.

"Of course I'm sure! That's the word from Command, and we will leave at the end of the month." *If the Federation doesn't desert us!* The speaker sounded annoyed and amused at the same time. "But if Hastur is gone, then maybe those plans will change. What's going to happen?"

There was a hacking noise and someone spat. "He is going to be buried in a few days, and then his heir will be his nephew, Mikhail Hastur."

"I see." Domenic was almost certain this was the man whose thoughts he had overheard earlier, though he could not have said how he knew. "We don't know much about him." There was a thoughtful pause. "They take their kings to that thing up north, don't they? The roo something."

"Yes, they do." The driver sounded alert now, and wary as well.

"This has possibilities, Vancof—real possibilities. You might finally start earning the enormous salary we pay you."

"If you say so," came a sullen reply. *I haven't been paid in three months, and what I do get, when I get it, is hardly enormous. He's up to something. Damn him.*

The other man went on, thinking aloud. "Our problem has always been that we have never been able to really get into Comyn Castle. We have tried seven times to put an agent into place, and failed. The servants don't bribe, and they rarely talk." He sounded extremely disgruntled by this, even speaking in a near whisper. "And all the positions are inherited, so we can't do anything. But once this fellow is out of the Castle, it should be fairly easy to take him out."

"Take him . . . ? How?"

"Oh, an ambush along the road, I think. You should be able to manage that. Find a good spot, Vancof, and the Chief will think you are a wonderful fellow." Even in a hushed voice, there was no mistaking the contempt in the words.

There was a snorting sound, a derisive and humorless laugh. "You expect me to get through a few hundred Guardsmen and find one man I've never even seen?"

"I'll get you some help."

"Granfell, have you lost your mind? Do you really believe that you can just . . . you think that killing is the answer to everything." *This is bad, very bad. I don't want to be involved. But Granfell will stick a knife in me without thinking twice about it.*

"When's this funeral thing?"

"There will be some kind of ceremony in Thendara in a couple of days, and then they'll carry the body north. It hasn't happened in a long time, but if what I have heard is right, all the heads of the Domains are supposed to accompany the body to the *rhu fead*."

"Really—that is even better! We have time to make some preparations. Good. With a little cleverness, we can destroy not just this Michael person, but most of the rest of these . . . "

"Planning to land a troop of fighters up the road, are you?" The driver was sneering in spite of his own fright. "Think that no one will notice? You don't understand Cottman, Granfell, and you never have. And I don't think the Chief will like your plan either. He got into trouble before, and if he wants to advance, he can't afford to do it again."

This is my chance to make a name for myself, and I am not going to let this bastard get in my way. We can destablize Cottman, or take out most of their ruling class, and then the Federation can step in and take over. Then I'll be able to have my pick of any posting. I'll jump three grades of rank, at least.

Granfell is out of his mind! I can see it in his face. He was always a little crazy. He is going to get me killed with his ambitions! He just wants to impress the Chief. But I have my own skin to think about. Trying to assassinate Mikhail Hastur is just plain stupid. He won't believe me, though, so I better pretend to go along for mow.

Nico was so startled by what he had just overheard that it took him a moment to realize he was catching the thoughts of both of the men in leathers. His heart was pounding with fear and excitement now, and he felt frozen in place.

"You better talk to the Chief, Granfell. And don't come back here in those clothes. You stand out like a virgin at the orgy." It was the driver again, holding back his fears. Nico could sense a desire for wine in the man's surface thoughts—a great deal of wine.

"You whining . . . you don't think I'd go around wearing the rags these barbarians do, do you?"

"Fine. It's your neck."

With these words, Domenic decided that he had heard enough, and moved away quietly. He slipped back into the crowd, trying to appear inconspicuous. After a few moments, he knew he had succeeded, since no one was paying him the least attention. The juggler was done now, and had been replaced by a skinny man who was telling a long story. The audience did not seem very interested, but they were not ready to start booing just yet. He barely noticed, his mind racing.

What should he do now? Part of Nico wanted to race back to Comyn Castle and tell someone what he had overheard. But how was he going to explain being there? And why would anyone take him seriously? They'd probably just think he was making the whole thing up to keep from getting punished for his adventure.

Who would believe him? Well, his mother would, after she recovered from being very angry. He shivered lightly in anticipation. Danilo Syrtis-Ardais would also realize that he was not joking. He had never lied before, unlike his little brother. But what could they do? His father? True, Mikhail had told him not a day before that he was always ready to listen to his eldest son, but somehow Nico did not feel that he could just walk into Mikhail's study and announce that there was a plot to kill him. The words stuck in his throat. He was afraid of upsetting his father just now. Things were not right at Comyn Castle, and he did not want to add to the tension. Once all the heads of the Domains arrived, there would be a Council meeting to confirm his father's succession, and after that everyone would be less jumpy. One did not need to be a Ridenow to know that anticipation of that meeting, which promised to be loud and probably acrimonious, was weighing heavily on his parents' minds.

Still, he had to do something, and quickly. He turned and started to leave, then stopped. He was thinking like a scared child. First, he needed to get a grip on himself, before he did anything! *Calm down, Domenic, and slow down, too—nothing is going to happen tonight.*

After a minute, during which his mind raced in several directions at once, he began to sort out his feelings from everything else. No one but him knew what Vancof looked like. And the others, too. He glanced around, looking for the two men in leathers, but they seemed to have vanished. No, there they were, walking back to the Gate—and he had never gotten so much as a glimpse of their faces! Some spy he was. Would he know them again, from the backs of their heads and the way they held their shoulders? He was torn for a moment—should he track them back into the city, go back to the Castle, or remain where he was? At last he decided he might know the men again, and that it was probably best to stay where he was for a while longer. His hoped-for adventure was turning into something unexpected, and there was no need to rush, was there?

How had a Terranan ended up driving a Traveler's wain? He wanted to know more now. Maybe he should have stayed near the wagons and listened a little longer, or used the Alton Gift to force information from the minds of the strangers . . . the idea repelled him. Mother was right—he was too good.

Domenic realized how frightened he was, and how alone he felt. He wanted to run away, and at the same time, he wanted to stay. He had to keep an eye on things, didn't he? It was his duty. But he could not just go off . . . well, why not? He was trying to protect his father, wasn't he? And all the others. And then he realized that he did not want to hand the problem over to the adults, that he wanted to be there—to have an adventure. If he went back now, he would be punished and perhaps not taken seriously.

If he had not been so curious about the redheaded girl, none of this would have happened, and the plot would not have been discovered. If it was a plot, if this Chief—they almost certainly meant Belfontaine— went ahead with Granfell's plan. And if he went back and told everyone, and was believed, he would be trapped. His parents would surround him with so many guards he would not be able to breathe. He would be relegated to being just a boy again.

Domenic could not bear the thought of that happening. This was his adventure, and he was determined to see it through to the end. He was sick and tired of being a prisoner in Comyn Castle, and returning guaranteed that he would remain so. On the other hand, running off in the night would make his parents both afraid and angry. He did not want to consider that fact, but he had to. It meant he had to tell someone who would understand and believe him, and who would not instantly drag him back.

There was only one person he could think of who would know what to do. Lew Alton. His grandfather always understood. He would keep Marguerida and Mikhail from worrying, and tell Nico how to proceed. It took some of the keenness out of the adventure, but he had to act responsibly, didn't he? There was a small sense of relief at this thought, the decision to trust Lew.

Nico walked across the field toward the foodstalls. Then he hunkered down beside one of the open fires, pulled his hood over his head, and concentrated. He hoped he looked like some weary boy, warming himself, because he wanted to remain invisible for the present. He closed his eyes and focused.

Grandfather!

Nico? What is it?

I . . . I'm not in bed sick. I just pretended to be sick so I could sneak out and . . .

Visiting the fleshpots of Thendara, are you? There was a sense of amusement in that thought.

No, Grandfather. The idea shocked Nico slightly, that he would sneak out to visit a joyhouse, but he knew from things the Guardsmen said that other boys his age did such things. *I am out at the field by the North Gate—I wanted to see the Travelers perform. But I heard something—there were two men in Terran dress just ahead of me in the street, and they came and talked to someone there, a man called Vancof. I saw him earlier today, driving a Traveler's wagon. I think he is a spy or . . . an assassin.*

A spy? If Rory was telling this fabulation, I would not believe him, but you, Nico! Go on.

The Terranans watched a juggler, then snuck off behind a wagon. So, I went and listened. I mean, it seemed strange to me that two men in those uniforms that look like leathers would come out here to see the Travelers. One is named Granfell, but I don't know the other one's name. And Vancof said that Regis had died—which I guess Granfell did not know—and Granfell said that it seemed like a good idea to try and kill Father on the way to the rhu fead. *And others, too. Vancof tried to persuade him this was a bad idea, but Granfell seems very ambitious and . . . this Vancof thinks he is a little mad, too.*

Slow down, Nico. Are you telling me that there is an agent of Terran Intelligence masquerading as a Traveler?

I guess I am.

There was a silence from Lew Alton, as if he needed time to digest the information. *That explains several things which have been troubling me for some months. Why haven't you come back to the Castle?*

Well, I did not think anyone would take me seriously.

And?

And I know what Vancof looks like, and no one else does. Well, maybe Kendrick. He was standing guard with me when the wagon came through this morning. I want to stay here and keep an eye on things. Grandfather, they want to kill everyone, so they can grab Darkover! Vancof asked Granfell if he was going to land troops on the road or something. Could they do that?

In the past, they would not have dared. But now—I refuse to speculate.

Again there was a ruminative silence, and Domenic waited tensely. What would he do if Lew ordered him to return?

Well, Nico, it sounds as if you have gotten yourself into a very peculiar situation. And, even with the risk, I agree with you that you ought to remain where you are for the present. A night away from home won't kill you.

I hope not! I am scared, Grandfather, but not too much. I mean, the driver saw me, but I was just a young man in a Guard's uniform, and he was so busy being obnoxious that he probably won't remember me. And I won't go near. I can keep an eye on things from a distance. Or pretend I am interested in the girl I saw this morning—she is very pretty. I would not mind being interested in her! This admission surprised him and pleased him at the same time.

You are having an interesting time, aren't you?

Yes, Grandfather, I am.

Very well. Someone will join you out there before morning—you can't just go alone.

Who? You?

No, not me. Let me handle this, Domenic. And keep safe. I don't want to have to explain to your mother that I let her firstborn get himself . . .

I promise not to get killed!

Good.

Please don't let them make me come back!

No, not for the present. You are not in any danger that I can think of. And it is good for you to get some experience outside the Castle. I have never entirely approved of how embattled we have let ourselves become in recent years, as I have often told you and anyone else who would listen. The presence of a Terran spy among the Travelers just proves how right I was. What a perfect cover—why didn't I think of it sooner? And how many others have been wandering around Darkover for thirty years? Leave it to me, grandson. I am very proud of you, Nico.

Proud?

You have never shown a lot of initiative, which I believe is a valuable quality in a ruler. This shows you can handle yourself in a difficult situation.

I don't think Mother will agree with you. She will be furious.

Very likely, and ring a peal over my head. Be careful, and I will contact you later tonight.

10

Lew snapped back into focus at the table in the larger dining room, glanced at his hand, and realized that he had paused with his soup spoon suspended in midair while he communicated with Domenic. The noise of people eating and talking around the long table seemed like a raucous clamor after the intensity of mind-to-mind contact, an assault on his ears and senses. The room was warm, but he was chilled by the sudden wave of fear he felt for his grandson. He forced himself to shake it away, trying to think clearly and calmly. What an unexpected and undesirable development.

He sorted through the information Domenic had just given him, discovering that he was not really surprised by any of it. They had managed to keep news of Regis' death from reaching Federation HQ for almost three days now, but it was inevitable that they would learn of it, and now they had. And the temptation to try to take advantage of the emotional turmoil and transition of leadership in Comyn Council would be difficult for Belfontaine to resist. Unless he decided not to go along with Granfell's idea. He knew there was an unspoken rivalry between the two men, even if they were not aware of it themselves. A smile played across his mouth—sometimes there were real benefits to telepathy, although he rarely thought of them.

As he lowered his spoon, he considered the two men. They were both suspicious and ambitious, but Granfell was headstrong and had an explosive temper. Belfontaine, by contrast, was controlled, using his intelligence and cunning to best advantage. But he was frustrated, and that element would almost certainly sway him in favor of Granfell's plan. Being posted to Darkover was a dead end in the Federation bureaucracy, and if the Federation was going to pull out, Belfontaine had to act fast or admit defeat to his superiors. Had he learned anything from his misadventure on Lein III? Lew doubted it. Men like Lyle Belfontaine rarely learned much from their mistakes. And now he would be desperate. Desperate men were always dangerous.

Lew looked up and down the long table, and found Gareth Hastur-Elhalyn staring at him; his bright blue eyes seemed to bore right into him. The boy, Dani Hastur's son, looked away hastily, but not before Lew caught an expression of avidity on his face. It reminded Lew of old Dyan Ardais, and he felt a sudden sense of unease. Gareth seemed like a good lad, but Lew did not know him very well. He must have the wind up more than he thought, if he was being suspicious of a child of fourteen. And why was Gisela watching him? The last thing he needed was more of her mischief.

But she was smiling, and Lew could not remember the last time he had found Giz smiling at anything. There was nothing in her look that was alarming, and then he realized she was not actually looking at him, but at his dinner companion, Katherine Aldaran. Wonder of wonders, there was an expression of fondness on Gisela's face as she looked at her sister-in-law.

Kate was just finishing her soup, and she raised her eyes from her bowl, caught Gisela's look, and returned the smile. The tension in her shoulders slackened as her eyes met the other woman's. He realized that his abrupt silence had perturbed Katherine, that she must have understood that he was using his *laran,* and had probably assumed it had something to do with her. Still, she was containing her fears wonderfully, and he was impressed again. What had he been saying to her? He could not remember. . . .

Really, he was getting too old to maintain a normal conversation while he communicated telepathically. He felt a strange satisfaction in this realization—he was so very fortunate to be as old as he was! He had managed to outlive many of his foes, and had acquired a bit of real wisdom along the way. The biting grief was that he had lost so many precious friends at the same time.

Lew dipped his spoon and took another mouthful of soup. It was tepid and unappetizing now, and he pushed the bowl away. He considered Belfontaine and Granfell again, weighing what he knew of the two men from his visits to HQ. Their surface thoughts were similar, full of ambition and a longing for power. Lew had never really understood minds like theirs, no matter how many people he encountered who thought this way. He wondered if Lyle Belfontaine had the least idea of how eager his subordinate was to get ahead. Could he use this to Darkover's advantage?

Javanne Hastur was fixing him with a basilisk glare from the other side of the table, her rather protuberant eyes bulging with suspicion. Katherine shifted uncomfortably in her chair, thinking the look was aimed at her, and he heard the creak of the wood beneath her slender body. He returned Javanne's gaze with a bland smile, knowing this would annoy her enormously. It was a shame they had so many old scores to settle. Javanne was really an intelligent woman whose pettiness and wrong-thinking was born of her frustration and feelings of powerlessness.

Lew turned his eyes toward Katherine, and thought how very nice she looked in the white wool gown with black embroidery that he had given his daughter years before. The colors suited her perfectly, and the dress outlined the rise of her breasts in a modest way that was all the more provoking for being so subtle. He liked her, and thought that Herm was lucky to have found such a wife. Then Mikhail, at the head of the table, quirked an eyebrow at him, and the enormity of his easy promise to Nico swept through him. He should have told the lad to come back! How was he going to tell Mik, let alone Marguerida?

"Forgive me, *Domna* Katherine. I have no idea what we were talking about—something came into my mind and I completely lost my train of thought."

"What are you up to now?" Javanne asked suspiciously.

Lew did not answer immediately, but instead studied the woman he had known for over six decades. Time had been kind to her, and although her red hair was now almost as white as Regis' had been, her skin was still smooth and soft, and she did not look her age. He wondered if her combative disposition kept her youthful—certainly her personality had not mellowed with years, and he could almost forgive his eldest grandson for running off in order to avoid her. She had always been a headstrong and difficult person—a bully—even as a girl, but he had never thought her wicked or evil. Like himself, she was just quite pig-headed in favor of her own treasured opinions.

"Mother, do stop plaguing Lew, as if he been created purely to annoy you."

For a moment it appeared that Javanne was going to lose her temper at her youngest and least loved son. Instead, she held herself in check, as if the presence of Katherine Aldaran made her hesitate. Lew let himself marvel at his daughter's cunning in the seating arrangements. She had put Gabriel Lanart-Alton at her right, at the other end of the table, and Javanne at Mikhail's, separating the couple by the length of the board. Then she had put Lew across from Javanne, to draw her wrath away from Mikhail, and paired him with Katherine, to guarantee at least a semblance of courtesy. Under Dio's tutelage, during the last years of her life, Marguerida had turned from a rather awkward young academic into a capable and even masterful political hostess, able to be gracious under the most trying of circumstances. He looked down the board toward his daughter, and, aware of his regard, she gazed at him, a bit puzzled. He let his deep love for his only child hold him for a moment, then turned back to wait for Javanne's response.

"I do not imagine that Lew was brought to life just to irritate me, although it often feels as if he were." This admission had a ring of sincerity. "But he spent too many years away from Darkover for me to trust him completely. I believe he is too much a friend of the Federation for anyone's good." This had been her complaint for years, and it did not bother him in the least. More, Javanne was genuinely distraught over her brother's sudden death, and by the fact that she had not been summoned until he was gone. That Lady Linnea had been adamant on that matter she did not know, and he hoped she never would. Undoubtedly she thought it was Lew's fault, and that was for the best. What she really wanted was a good argument, the better to vent her churning emotions.

"Tell me, Javanne, if you had a choice, would you prefer a foe you could see, or one that was invisible?"

She blinked her large eyes once, then frowned at Lew. "One I could see, obviously. What sort of question is that?" The color rose in her cheeks, as if she suspected he was trying to trick her somehow.

"Very wise. And while the Federation maintains a presence on Darkover, we can keep an eye on them. But I fear you are about to realize your oft spoken wish to have them gone. At present, it is their intention to withdraw in a month, by their reckoning."

Her eyes narrowed. "And when were you going to share this wonderful news?" She did not sound very pleased, but instead seemed even more wary.

"At the Council meeting, Mother, when everyone was present, and could hear it at one time, with all the details that we know thus far," Mikhail explained patiently.

"Very proper," she admitted grudgingly. "I suppose you are disappointed by this development," she shot at Lew, still seeking something to dispute.

"Not in the least. The Station Chief has been a headache since he arrived, and the Planetary Administrator is nothing but a figurehead and can do nothing to control him. The political changes that have occurred in the Federation have not been to our benefit at all. And I will not miss Lyle Belfontaine for one moment. But I confess I am more than a little alarmed by the planned pullout." He could sense Katherine listening intently to what he was saying. A servant whisked away his empty bowl, and replaced it with rabbithorn forcemeat in a tender crust, a serving of carrots surrounding it. It looked very tempting, and he hoped that Javanne would not ruin his appetite with her persistent needling.

"Alarmed?" There was a note of caution in Javanne's voice, for however much they disagreed on almost everything concerning Darkover, she had a decent respect for his political acumen.

"Yes, Javanne, alarmed. Once they abandon the spaceport, we will not be able to watch what they are doing."

"But, why should that matter?"

"You are not a stupid woman, cousin. Think! Without a presence on the planet, and their own people to consider, there is nothing to restrain the Federation from attempting to conquer Darkover by force."

Her eyes bulged dangerously. "I had not . . . you are trying to frighten me, Lew Alton!"

"No, I am not!" He paused, filled with the longing to avoid a real confrontation, no matter how much Javanne wished for one. There would be enough shouting and disagreement when the Comyn Council met to satisfy everyone. He decided to take a different tack, to see if he could distract the woman. "Although if I were, it might pay you back for that ghost story you told me when I was twelve. I had nightmares for weeks afterward. Javanne is a superb storyteller," he informed Katherine, wishing to draw her into the conversation, "and can chill your blood with a minimum of words."

I can believe that. She reminds me of my Aunt Tansy, always so sure she knew best how to run other people's lives. "We have a lot of such stories on Renney, but I never have acquired a taste for them. When I was five or six, we visited one of the ghost groves on the coast, and I was frightened out of my wits," Katherine replied. She gave him one of her remarkable smiles, as if she understood what he was doing, and Lew found himself thinking again that Herm was a damn lucky man.

"Fancy you remembering that," Javanne said, preening slightly, and looking rather fine, with a blush on her pale cheeks and a glitter of pleasure in her eyes.

"It was a formidible influence on my life," he answered dryly.

"Do you really believe the Federation would try to . . . invade Darkover, Lew?" She was sufficiently mollified by her own memory of the ghost story to be civil instead of spiteful.

"I don't know, but I confess to being worried."

Javanne stared at him, her face a mirror of conflicted emotions. "You are serious, aren't you?"

"Very."

Javanne lowered her head and took a bite of her rabbithorn. She chewed and swallowed, sipped some wine, and then looked at Lew again, her face thoughtful and less angry now. "I believe I have misjudged matters somewhat, in my efforts to keep the Terranan from . . . forgive me, cousin. I see I have not respected your efforts as I should have."

"There is nothing to forgive," he answered, startled by her uncharacteristic apology. He ignored the slight stab of conscience at the lie on his lips. There was a great deal to forgive, starting with Javanne's rejection of Domenic. But he thought it wiser to take advantage of her good humor of the moment than to settle any old scores. She would likely be conspiring with Francisco Ridenow before the dishes were cleared, for she simply could not resist the urge to meddle. "We see things very differently, but we both want what is best for Darkover."

Javanne nodded, then looked down the board, at Danilo Hastur, sitting next to his mother, toward the center of the gathering and well away from the most volatile of the guests. "Yes, we do," she finally answered, casting a sudden and unloving look on Mikhail before she turned her attention to her supper.

I need to see you after dinner, Mik—it is important.

Oh, no! More alarms and excursions? By Aldones, I wish that Regis had never made me his heir! Very well—in my study. At least it will get me away from Mother.

Two hours later, Lew Alton and Mikhail Hastur were sitting in the cozy and shabby study where so many important matters had been decided over the years. Danilo Syrtis-Ardais, Donal Alar, and Herm Aldaran were also in attendance. Lew looked at Mikhail and chewed his lower lip reflectively. His son-in-law looked exhausted, and he was not feeling too chipper himself. The dinner had seemed interminable despite the excellence of the food, and the pleasant company of Katherine Aldaran. He had been restless, aware that his grandson was alone in uncertain circumstances. It was unlikely that any harm would come to him with so many people around him. Still, he wondered if he should have just ordered the boy to return, instead of taking it upon himself to tell him to remain by the gate.

Javanne had recovered from her good mood, returning to her earlier one of confrontation, and it had taken all of his energy to keep from arguing with her. It had ruined his pleasure in the food, until he had thought to ask Katherine about the ghost groves she had mentioned. This had led the conversation onto less treacherous paths, and after a while, Javanne had given up the effort to berate him or Mikhail for things entirely beyond their control.

After dessert, Javanne had descended on Dani Hastur, all smiles and charm, and Lew had watched, caught between amusement and annoyance at the transparency of her actions. She had never resigned herself to Dani's choice of the Elhalyn Domain over the Hastur one, and it was now clear that she was going to try to get the man into her clutches. Dani had shrunk away from her attentions politely, and Gareth had said something that made her laugh and ruffle his fine, golden hair with a tender hand. Lew, observing the action as Javanne returned to harrassing her nephew, Dani, had found the boy looking back at him again, with an unreadable expression on his handsome features. Dani looked haggard, and ready to lose his usually calm temper, and finally *Dom* Gabriel had intervened and almost dragged his tiresome wife out of the dining room and back to their suite.

That inconsequential moment came back to Lew now. There was something going on, something he was missing, and he knew he could not bring his attention to the problem at hand until he solved the puzzle of Gareth Hastur-Elhalyn to his own satisfaction. The boy had never shown any interest in Javanne on his two previous visits to Comyn Castle. So why was he hanging close to her now—he had been by her side before they started eating, too!

Looking around at the comfortable furnishings of Regis' study, Lew remembered another gathering in that room, fifteen years before. He could recall the tension in the chamber, and the sound of Dani Hastur's voice, anxious and fearful, as he told his father he did not wish to be the heir of Hastur. And, with this, Lew suddenly knew the answer to the puzzle. His belly knotted. How could they have been so stupid not to have anticipated that perhaps Dani's son would feel cheated of an inheritance he would otherwise have had. The Elhalyn kingship was nothing compared to the real power which Regis had wielded, and it never would be.

If he was correct, and Lew now felt certain he was, then Gareth would regard Javanne as a natural ally. The boy had not been proclaimed as Elhalyn heir yet—he was almost a year away from that—and so he could nurture hopes for a reversal of the agreement that Regis and Mikhail had entered into! And Javanne would seize the opportunity in both her skillful hands. He held back a groan.

What a dreadful time Nico had picked to do something uncharacteristically mischievous and probably very foolish. Fortunate, in that he had discovered a plot—which still might come to nothing—but unfortunate in that his absence was certain to cause problems. He weighed the matter in his mind again, considering various possible scenarios. After several seconds, Lew decided he did not like the expression on Gareth's face one bit. Perhaps Domenic was safer away from Comyn Castle than in it. For a moment he was aghast by the deadly direction his thoughts had taken. Gareth was only a boy! He must be more tired than he thought, to entertain such ideas. On the other hand, accidents could occur, and it was better to be safe than sorry. If he was wrong, then he was wrong, but if his suspicious mind had turned up something worth worrying about, then he must proceed cautiously.

Ruthlessly, Lew played out the possibilities. If something happened to Domenic—Aldones forbid—Mikhail still had another son. But Roderick, fine lad that he was, did not have a head for governance, and he could not imagine anyone, even Javanne, suggesting that he should be named heir. Without Nico, the logical person to follow Mikhail would be Gareth Elhalyn, which would find favor with Javanne Hastur and several others on the Council. Keeping Nico out of reach suddenly seemed a very good idea! He was probably imagining plots where none existed, and he would keep his peace on the matter for the moment, but he would keep an eye on Gareth, just in case.

Having settled the matter in his own mind, Lew went over what Domenic had told him again, trying to make sure he had not forgotten anything important. The more he thought about it, the surer he became that Belfontaine would take action. Perhaps not precisely what Granfell suggested, but he could think of several things that Belfontaine might attempt, including trying to occupy Comyn Castle. Lew could not be certain what Belfontaine would do, but he was sure the little man would not be able to pass up an opportunity to further his own ambitions. It would be just too tempting. So they must proceed as if the plot that Dominic had overheard was real until they learned otherwise. Lew felt a flush of excitement—something that lessened the ever-present grief over Regis' death for a moment. Suddenly he was glad that his grandson had gotten into mischief. Even if nothing happened, it was excellent experience for the lad.

Lew had told Nico he would handle the matter, but now that the time had come he was not sure how to begin. He had taken so much on himself, and in the past this had not always been a wise choice.

He glanced around the room. Donal Alar stood behind Mikhail, his young face solemn. Danilo Syrtis-Ardais looked dreadful, his normally pale skin was gray and drawn, and only Herm Aldaran did not look ready to fall over. The grief over the death of Regis Hastur had taken a toll on all of them, but Regis' lifelong companion, Danilo, was probably the hardest hit.

"Why did you want to talk to me, Lew?" Mikhail sounded tired, his voice tense and a little hoarse. "I have had enough speaking to last me until Midwinter, and the end is not in sight."

"Yes, I know. It is almost as bad as when you came back from the past, isn't it."

"Worse. I was twenty-eight then, not forty-three, and I recovered more quickly."

"Well, son, I have some news."

"What is it? I saw that something made you stop in the middle of the soup. Couldn't it have waited for tomorrow?"

"Domenic has run away from home." He wanted to soften the blow, but there really was not any way to do it.

Mikhail gaped at Lew, and Danilo gave a little gasp. Donal did not react except to raise his eyebrows, and Herm looked puzzled.

"What the hell do you mean, Lew," Mikhail snapped, the color rising in his cheeks. "Nico is upstairs in bed with a cold or something."

"I'm afraid not. He only pretended to be sick, so he could sneak out of the castle and go to watch the Travelers perform outside the North Gate."

Mikhail was clearly outraged, at the ragged edge of control, and Lew now regretted his impulsiveness. "Domenic is off in the middle of the night with . . ."

"Hush, son! Just because Nico has never done anything on a lark before is no reason to assume he never would. He is safe enough. And he had the good sense to tell me what was going on, rather than you or his mother. He knew you would get angry." Lew stifled his own worries about his eldest grandson, alone in a field outside the city. It was unlikely that anyone would recognize him, since Domenic was only outside Comyn Castle during his Guard duties, but there was still a chance. But he was just one in a crowd, and if he knew Nico, the boy was probably being very careful not to draw attention to himself. It would have to do for the moment.

Mikhail quelled his outrage with a visible effort. Then the start of a smile began to play across his face. He shook his head and ran his ungloved fingers through his thick, curling, and still golden hair. "Snuck off, did he? He picked a dreadful time to get into mischief, but I never expected . . . Rory yes, but not Domenic. If he got in touch with you, why didn't you tell the little scamp to get himself back here?"

"Well, there's more to the story, and the rest is not quite so innocent, I'm afraid."

"You don't mean he's been kidnapped or something?" Danilo interjected.

"No, he is quite free, sitting by a fire pit and keeping warm, the last I knew. No, the bad news is that Nico stumbled into a conspiracy."

"What!" The partial calm that had quieted Mikhail vanished. "Conspiracy? All the more reason to make him . . ."

"Mikhail, he is a man, albeit a young one. And if he had not been there, we might never have suspected that the Terrans were considering an assault on the funeral procession and an attempt on your life!" The words came out in a rush, more abruptly than Lew had intended, and they had the effect of halting any further questions. Instead, everyone just stared at Lew as if he had lost his mind. "That is why Nico did not run back here—he decided it was best if he remained in place and kept an eye on things. He knows the face of one of the conspirators, and he can describe the others. And I promised him that someone would join him at the North Gate. The only question is who."

"Kill me. . . ." Mikhail was stunned. "But, why?"

"How better to gain control of Darkover?"

"But I thought the Federation was going to leave."

"That is our current information, yes. But it appears that Federation Intelligence may have been using the Travelers as spies, and I have to wonder how long that has been going on. It would explain a few incidents which have troubled me during recent years."

At this, Danilo nodded in agreement, his exhausted face actually brightening, as if the news distracted him momentarily from his grief. "That does answer some questions, doesn't it? The Travelers! What fools we were not to have thought of them before."

"Well, why should we suspect a troup of entertainers of being anything but what they appeared? In truth, most of them likely are just that—players and jongleurs."

"What happened, exactly?" Mikhail cut in angrily. "Start at the beginning, before I completely lose my mind!"

"Yes, of course." Lew ordered his thoughts carefully. "It seems that this morning, while he was on duty, Nico saw a Travelers' wagon pass by the castle—yes, yes, I know they had no business in Thendara at this season. There was a girl, and . . ."

"Oh, a girl," Donal exclaimed, grinning. "About time."

"Perhaps." Lew gave the young paxman a swift glance, pleased that the interruption dissipated some of the tension in the room. "Anyhow, she seems to have told him there was a performance at the North Gate this evening, and, on a lark, Nico decided to go see it—to avoid Javanne as much as anything, I believe. He saw two men in Terranan garb, and that aroused his interest. When they left off watching the Travelers, he got curious and snuck over and tried to discover what they were up to— rather brave of him. The spy, who is a driver of one of the wagons, and the two men had a conversation in which the driver told them that Regis was no more." Lew paused, trying to organize his words carefully.

"That news was enough for Miles Granfell . . ." he began.

"Granfell—I am not surprised!" Danilo looked grim as he spoke. "My contacts with him have not been as many as yours, Lew, but I have always thought him driven and ambitious."

"Yes, all of that, and opportunistic as well, it seems. He knows that we take our dead leaders to the *rhu fead,* and he seems to have realized that it would be a fine opportunity to attempt a massacre of the Domains families, since most of us will accompany the funeral train." Lew paused, waiting to see if anyone reacted, but everyone seemed too stunned to speak. "It seems to have been an impulsive idea, and he does not yet have the approval of Lyle Belfontaine. But knowing our Station Chief as I do, I find it hard to imagine him passing up what may be his last chance to try to get Darkover into the Federation instead of leaving in defeat in a month's time. At the moment, it is only a plan, not yet an actual plot, but Domenic felt that Granfell was sincere in his intentions."

"Nico knows nothing of spies and intrigues! He must come back at once!"

"Just a moment, Mikhail," Danilo began quietly. "By the time you were Nico's age, you had fought on the fire lines in the Kilghards, joined at least one catamount hunt that I can remember, and done any number of other dangerous things. I believe that it is good for Domenic to continue in this venture, for I, like Lew, have never really approved of Regis' insistence on keeping all of us shut up in the Castle, getting on one another's nerves, and looking over our shoulders for assassins. Certainly he must not be left alone, but I can see no useful purpose in dragging him back here and acting as if he were incapable of looking after himself for a night. The only question is who is the best person to go after him. I don't believe that letting the news of his absence become common knowledge would be helpful, but I think he . . ."

Donal, looking quite self-conscious, interrupted. "*Dom* Danilo is right. Nico needs the experience, and he really is very clever."

Mikhail turned and looked over his shoulder at his paxman, his expression troubled. Then he looked back, stared at Lew, and his face changed. "Perhaps, but I do not like it." *There is something more, isn't there, Lew? Something you are holding back.*

Yes, there is. It is only a suspicion, but I really think Nico is safer out of Comyn Castle than in it, for the next few days.

What! You don't imagine that my mother . . .

No, it is something else, Mikhail. But sparing your son from Javanne's fury will be a kindness to them both, don't you agree?

Damn you, old man! Very well. Keep me in the dark for a bit longer. I trust you.

Believe me, Mikhail, I will tell you if I am right or wrong as soon as I am able.

At least I don't have to start looking at my mother as if she might be planning . . .

Murder is not Javanne's style, son, but there will be others present who might not be so choosy.

Dom *Damon?*

He is one, and Dom *Francisco Ridenow is another.*

There is that—I hope you are being overly vigilant.

I hope so, too—but keep Donal at your back!

"I'll go," Herm shifted in his chair and spoke very quietly, an unreadable expression on his face.

"You?" Danilo gave him a questioning look.

"Yes. My face is not well-known, and it would not be the first time I engaged in a bit of skullduggery, Danilo. And besides, if I am not in Comyn Castle, then you can't turn me over to Belfontaine for arrest." He gave a cockeyed grin, looking gleeful and a little uncomfortable at the same time. "Not that you would, I know, but you can now tell the fellow that I am not here, and to go to hell. You do want to do that, don't you, Mikhail?"

"More than you can imagine."

"But, Herm," Danilo began, "you have been away from Darkover for so long. Don't you think that I, or someone . . ."

"Forgive me, but you are much too well known, Danilo. Someone would almost certainly recognize you, or Lew, or just about anyone else you could trust with this. But me—I have kept my ugly face out of the mediafaxes, so the number of people who might know me is very small even in the Federation, and on Darkover, I am a nobody. Good Lord— Gisela barely recognized me! And besides, there is no one on Darkover more in touch with Federation schemes."

"Well, there is a certain wisdom in that, I guess," Danilo admitted grudgingly. "Yes, if you go out and find out what is going on . . ." He trailed off, his vivid eyes more lively than they had been a few minutes before.

"Zandru blast the Terranan and their filthy, vile plans!" Mikhail's face was white with anger. "What would have become of us if Nico hadn't been there to uncover this plot?" He lowered his head into his hands and shook all over. Then he straightened up slowly. His face was pale, the anger was gone; only despair and resignation remained. "My impulse is to find these men and arrest them—which is precisely what I must not do. Damn Regis for dying anyhow!"

"My sentiments exactly, Mikhail," Lew said dryly. The worst was over, he knew, although he did not look forward to telling his daughter what was going on. "Herm is a good man for the job. Between his knowledge of the Federation, his native cunning, and Nico's intelligence, we should be able to avoid any disasters. And perhaps it will all come to nothing, it is still possible that Belfontaine will not want to risk a Board of Inquiry, or that there will not be time to arrange an ambush along the road. But I don't intend to assume that, and neither should you."

"Very well. You go out there, Herm, and get Nico to tell you everything, and then . . ."

Danilo cleared his throat softly, and everyone looked at him. "It strikes me that it is perhaps best if Domenic remains with Hermes—a man with a boy is less likely to draw attention than a man alone. Plus let's not forget that Nico has the Alton Gift. That is very useful under these circumstances."

"But the danger—"

"Is minimal, Mikhail," Danilo said very calmly, as if he had already evaluated the possibilities and found them to his liking. "He has already shown that he is clever enough to get out of Comyn Castle unnoticed, and smart enough to inform Lew when he encountered a situation he could not manage on his own. He will be safe enough with Hermes, and between the two of them, they can discover whether this plot is anything to worry about. I am sure that Herm will not allow Nico to get into harm's way."

"I don't like it! But you are probably right." Mikhail grimaced. "Which leaves me the delightful task of telling Marguerida. Go, now, before I change my mind!" He groaned dramatically, then let something like a ghostly chuckle rise in his throat. He shook his head. "The ironic part is that, under any other circumstances, I would be tickled pink by Nico's mischief."

"We all would, son," Lew answered.

Herm did not move for a moment, his head lowered as if he was thinking deeply. Then he rose from his chair and nodded. "I'll take care of the lad as if he were my own."

11

When Herm reached his suite, he found Katherine on a couch in the sitting room, with a tablet of paper on her lap, sketching. She had removed the white gown she had worn at dinner, and replaced it with a shapeless and much-worn garment in a brown that did not become her. Her long hair was braided into a queue down her back, and there were smears of charcoal on her cheeks, like the marks of some tribeswoman preparing for a rite. She looked up at the sound of his footfalls and smiled in greeting. "Where did you get off to? You just vanished after dinner, leaving me to the mercies of Lady Javanne, who pretended she wished to know all about me. Fortunately, Gisela came to my rescue by distracting her. It must be very hard having that woman for a mother-in-law, and I pity both Marguerida and Giz." She sounded amused by the whole incident, and more relaxed than she had been in days.

"Lew needed to discuss something with me," he replied, falling back into the long habit of never revealing anything to anyone, even his beloved wife. Then he braced himself, realizing that his sudden decision in the study had been reached without much consideration for her needs.

What had he been thinking? "And now I have to go away for a few days, dearest."

"Away? Why? Where?" She gave him a sharp look.

"Something has come up, and I have to deal with it."

Katherine set her tablet aside and rose, frowning now. "I do not like the sound of this."

"I'm sorry, Kate."

"You aren't going to tell me what is going on, are you?"

"No, I am not."

"Why?"

"Because the less you know, the less chance there is that you will be tricked or induced to say something to the wrong person."

"And who might that be?" she replied dangerously, the anger welling up slowly.

"I cannot say." He did not want to remind her that there were telepaths all around them, and that she might disclose something without ever intending to. She was far too uncomfortable with that situation as it was. Nor did he choose to reveal that he found his sister's sudden interest in Kate very suspicious. It seemed out of character, somehow, for Gisela. The little he had seen of her since his arrival had puzzled him. She was almost frantically gay one moment, then silent and removed the next. Certainly she was nothing like the young woman he remembered, and he wanted to warn his wife against trusting her overmuch. At the same time he knew it was important for Katherine to fit into this new life, and for her to make friends, so he held his tongue. He would have to depend on the good sense that Kate had always demonstrated in the past in dealing with people. Unfortunately, this was not easy for him, since he trusted very few people beyond his wife and children, and this did not include his father or his sister.

Herm did not want to believe his sister was capable of real treachery, but she had been reared with all of *Dom* Damon's thwarted fury at his lack of real power. And marrying Rafael, which he knew had not been her first choice, must have been a blow to her pride and ambition. Gisela had never in the past settled for second best, and he suspected she was quite unhappy. He sighed softly.

His thoughts turned away from Gisela, to his father, who would be arriving at Comyn Castle in the next few days. With a little start he acknowledged to himself that one reason he had jumped at the chance to go and find Domenic was that it put off for a while this dreaded encounter. Even though he had not seen *Dom* Damon in almost a quarter of a century, he had never lost his own sense of alienation from the old man. If the little that Lew and Danilo had let slip was any indication, time had not mellowed the head of the Aldaran Domain at all. *Dom* Damon had always insisted that the Hasturs were the only thing that stood in the way of his own plans, although what these might be remained something of a mystery.

There was more to it than the desire to put off encountering his father, however. While they had been on the ship, all his attention had been directed toward reaching Darkover and keeping his wife and children safe. Now this was accomplished, but he felt that nothing had turned out quite right. Comyn Castle reminded him too much of his adolescence in the Hellers. The Aldaran Keep, full of conflicting and outspoken personalities, snowed in for most of the year, had been miserable for him. Rationally, he knew it was different, but even after only two days, it felt the same.

And then there was the other problem, the one he had refused to consider for ten years—that Kate was not a telepath. He remembered their conversation earlier in the day, and wished that she had not told him her fears. There was nothing he could do to cure the problem, and he hated things over which he had no power.

He walked into the bedroom and started sorting through the closet, looking for something plain to wear. The servants had unearthed a good many garments from the cluttered attics of the castle, and he now had a decent selection of both formal tunics, like the embroidered and rather uncomfortable one he was currently wearing, and the more ordinary clothing that was the daily garb of Darkovans. Katherine followed him, and stood looking at him as he pulled out a rather shabby tunic, unadorned and a bit worn along the cuffs and hem.

He could feel her eyes on his shoulder blades, trying to penetrate him, furious and frustrated. She cleared her throat a little. "Hermes, I think it would be better for me if I took the children and left for Renney while I still can. At least it is warm there, and no one keeps secrets from me."

He spun around, startled and deeply frightened. He stared at her, suddenly feeling helpless. He had never imagined it would come to this! Then he shook his head, refusing to take her seriously. "No, don't—don't threaten me, Kate. I don't have time right now!" He could feel the anger pulsing in his blood, and beneath it the sheer terror that she might make good her threat.

"You *never* have time, damn you! Ever since we got to Darkover, you have been closeted with other people, plotting something I have no knowledge of. I have never seen this side of you so clearly before, and I do not like it. You may be having a wonderful time, but I am not! And you cannot keep me from leaving, if I choose to." Her face, always pale, was chalk-white now, with her held-back fury.

Herm stood with the tunic in his big hands, twisting the old fabric between them. "Yes, I can. And I will, if you force me." He had to control this situation, somehow.

Katherine walked across the room and slapped him across the face before he realized what she planned to do. It stung, and he could feel his skin redden. "Damn you to hell! You are treating me like a stranger."

He raised his hand to his burning cheek and rubbed it gently. She was right, and he hated that. "If I am, I am sorry, Kate. But I have to do what I think is right. And at this moment *that* is to keep my secrets to myself. Ask Marguerida in the morning, and she will tell you what is going on."

"That's wonderful," she sneered. "Just wonderful. My husband dashes off in the middle of the night and I am supposed to ask a woman I barely know where he has gone. If this is how wives are treated on Darkover, I do not wonder at how unpleasant your sister and Javanne Hastur are. And if you imagine I am going to put up with this sort of nonsense because you want to . . ."

"What?"

"I don't know." She looked away for a moment. "Ever since we arrived, you have been different. Restless—you are often that—but something else too. Distant." The word seemed to hang in the air between them. "Are you missing all the intrigues of the Senate?" There was a tone of supplication in her voice, as if she were begging him to explain himself to her.

He had his shirt over his head, pulling off the fancy garment to replace it with a plainer one, and he paused, face hidden in the folds of fabric, unwilling to meet her eyes. Herm stood unmoving for several seconds while he considered her words. He could not explain himself to her—nor to himself either. And he did not dare let her know that. It would leave him too vulnerable, and he had sworn never to let that happen to him. He finished removing the garment, and remained with his bare chest exposed, looking into her black eyes.

Herm let his wide shoulders sag a little. "Yes, I suppose I am." He thought for a moment. "The reality of Darkover is not quite what I remembered, Kate."

"You mean that it is a cozy little bunch of agoraphobes, inbred and full of itself?" The glitter in her eyes was dangerous and attractive all at once. A blush rose along her throat and ascended into the white cheeks. There was something about Kate in a temper that never failed to arouse him, and he regretted he did not have time to follow through with his impulse to clasp her about her slender waist and press his mouth against the soft skin of her neck.

"I would not go that far," he admitted. Then he chuckled softly. "Actually, you are nearer the mark about us than you know, in several ways." He wanted to molify her now, not argue with her. "While I was in the Federation, I was doing something useful, but here . . . here I am less so."

"I don't understand."

"In the Senate, I was working against the Federation, outfoxing my fellow Senators whenever possible. It was . . . fun. Now, it is different." He could feel his own conflicted emotions, and he did not like it. It was something he had tried to avoid most of his adult life.

She looked at him as if he had suddenly sprouted a second head. "Fun? What a strange man you are. I think you are just looking for an excuse to get away from me and the children. And wishing you had never met me!" The pain in her voice was unmistakable and completely mystifying.

"Kate, why would I want to do that?" He felt his heart lurch. He had hoped she would not bring up her feelings of inadequacy again.

"It was fine to have a non-Darkovan wife while we were still in the Federation, but now I must seem a cripple to you, because I am not a telepath. Why didn't you just divorce me, or leave me behind? Why did you drag me halfway across the galaxy to somewhere where I am . . ."

She held back her tears, pushing away her sorrow and clinging to her fury as hard as she could. Herm put his arms around her and drew her against his chest. She was stiff and unbending now, determined to remain angry. And he did not have the time or energy to tease her out of her present mood. "I married you because I truly love you, Kate, and whether you were a telepath or not was irrelevant to me. Why can't you believe that?"

"Because you never told me the truth," she hissed. "Why should I believe you now, when you have been lying to me for years?"

"Does it really matter that much to you?"

"That I am blind in a room full of sighted people? Of course it matters, Herm. That my daughter might turn out to be able to read minds? Why can't you understand?"

Herm did understand the torment which was wracking his wife, but he could not bear to confront it. He told himself she was magnifying the problem, making a fuss about it, instead of just accepting everything, the way he wanted her to. Why did she have to complicate matters? "Why can't you just trust me, and let me do what I must?" He wanted nothing more than to escape the turmoil within him. If she would just be reasonable! But he knew, even as he thought this, that expecting Kate to be reasonable when her feelings were so troubled was asking too much.

"Trust you? Oh, Herm! I don't believe I will ever be able to trust you again."

He flinched—it was even worse than he thought. "Why?"

"Because every time I think that I can, you do something else that you won't explain."

With a sinking feeling, Herm realized she was right—again. He had kept his own counsel too much already, and he had damaged the thing he held most dear—all to preserve the control he needed to have. "I'm sorry, but there is no help for it, Kate. Just let me do this thing, and don't ask any more questions. I'll be back in a day or so."

Do I have the strength to leave him, to take the children and just go? What if he is right about Terése? I have the credits to book passage, I think, but can I get off Darkover? We came on Herm's diplomatic passport, didn't we? I should have paid more attention! I should have insisted on knowing everything years ago. And now it is too late! Now I am trapped here, perhaps forever, and I don't know if I can bear that.

"I can't stop you," she said bitterly. Then she turned away and left the room, her shoulders hunched.

Herm did not move after she was gone, just stood beside the bed, feeling as if he had swallowed a ton of broken glass. Why had he volunteered? He knew the answer, and he did not like it. He knew he wanted to get away from Katherine for a while, to think things through. No, that wasn't true—the last thing he wanted to do was think! He just wanted the entire problem of a head-blind wife to magically solve itself!

Should he go back to the study and tell Mikhail that he could not go? Was his marriage more important than making sure Domenic was safe? And could their marriage survive this crisis? He could not guess, but he suddenly knew that he must leave the Castle, leave his wife and children for a while. The future was out of his control, and the present seemed very bleak. He just had to get away from everything right now.

Herm grunted. He was not going to get away from anything, and he knew it. He would take the problem with him, and perhaps he would find some solution on the way. And, with a sigh of relief, he realized that Kate could not leave Darkover at present. She would be there when he returned, and she would find it in her to forgive him. He could not bear to think otherwise.

He finished fastening the clean shirt, then tugged the tunic over it and replaced his belt and pouch around his middle. There was a cloak hanging in the closet, a brown wool garment that should keep him warm enough. He assembled a few other things he thought he needed—a knife, a firestone, a second shirt, and quite against half a dozen Federation regulations, the lumens he had smuggled in. He spent a futile moment wishing he had a blaster, even though such a device went against the Compact, and everything Darkovans held dear. He wondered if the spies had advanced weapons, and hoped they did not. Then he shrugged away the thought. He would just have to depend on his native cunning. At the present, that seemed like a poor thing to use against real firepower.

He went down the corridor and found his way, after several wrong turns, to the stables. Herm used the time to devise an identity for himself, and another for young Domenic. They would be uncle and nephew, if anyone asked, on their way to the Hellers for a wedding. That would explain the subtle differences in his accent, the occasional *cahuenga* words that still slipped from his tongue.

The horses peered out of their stalls, curious at this late evening arrival, and a groom who was repairing some tack by the light of a lamp jumped to his feet. "Greetings, *vai dom!* How may I serve you?"

"I need two horses. They should be steady and unremarkable."

"Sir?" The groom looked confused.

"I don't want a mount that would draw attention to me."

"Ah, I understand now." The man looked relieved and curious as well. "Let me think. I have a mare, about ten years old, whom I keep for the old ladies. She's small and not very good looking, but she is a hardy beast. And there's a gelding, too—he doesn't have a very good gait, but he can go forever. This way."

Herm followed the groom to the far end of the stable, and opened a stall. Several horses poked their muzzles out and pricked their ears. One was a small dun, with a straggly mane, and the groom brought it out. It was, Herm decided, the ugliest horse he had ever seen. No amount of currying would make it lovely. Then the groom took out a leggy steed, piebald in gray and white, which regarded him a bit suspiciously until he let it take his scent. Then it snorted roughly.

Between the two of them, they had the animals saddled with some rather worn equipment in short order. "I'll want a couple of bedrolls as well."

"Very good, *dom.* We have many of those." Without being told more, the man brought out two neatly tied bundles with nothing about them to suggest either wealth or station. Clearly the groom understood that Herm was on some sort of clandestine errand, and he could tell that the man was rather enjoying the whole event.

As soon as they were attached behind the saddles, Herm mounted the gelding, took the reins of the ugly mare in one hand, and asked, "What are their names?"

"The mare is called Fortune, and your gelding is Aldar, because he comes from up in the Hellers." *What a tale this is going to be.*

Herm caught the thought and frowned. "Not a word of this to anyone, you understand. You never saw me."

"Oh. Saw who?" There was disappointment in the groom's voice, and the hint of uneasiness in his mind. Herm knew he was weighing the value of a juicy bit of gossip against a direct order, and then wondering how he was going to explain to the stable master about the disappearance of two animals which were his responsibility.

"Speak with Danilo Syrtis-Ardais if you have any questions, and he will tell you everything you need to know."

"Very well, *Dom.*" *Catch me bothering* Dom *Syrtis-Ardais! I think not!*

Herm rode out of the stableyard, and hoped that the groom was trustworthy and loyal. The worry of it brought back Katherine's stinging accusations, and he felt quietly miserable as he rode through the now silent streets of Thendara, heading for the North Gate. The groom had not exaggerated the poorness of the gelding's gait. It was dreadful. It almost spoiled the pleasure Herm had in being on horseback again, until he adjusted his body to conform to it a little. The mare trotted along behind him, the sound of hooves on the cobblestones echoing between the buildings.

It took him less than an hour to reach his goal, but even in that short a time his thighs were protesting this unexpected exercise, and he was ready to regret his impulse. It was not cold, he knew, for the time of year, but after two decades in the heated confines of Federation buildings, he felt like he might freeze to death. The breath of the horses barely misted the air, and he told himself he would readjust soon.

He looked around. There were two fields, one on either side of the road. He saw the brightly painted wagons of the Travelers in one, and some food vendors and muleteers in the other. Several fire pits were blazing, and he saw a number of figures standing around them. There was a sense of quiet about the scene. Someone was telling a story to a fascinated audience beside one fire, and a deep voice carried through the stillness.

Finally he spotted a small figure sitting beside one fire, cloaked and hooded. There were a couple of old men sitting across from him, on stones that had been there for ages, arguing about some small matter, but they paid no attention to him. Herm dismounted and led the horses over.

"Well, nephew," he began quietly, "I see you got here before me. I was delayed in the city."

The head beneath the hood moved at the sound of his voice, stilled, and then lifted. "I was starting to think you had forgotten me, Uncle."

"I would never do that. I hope you were not bored, waiting."

"Oh, no. I just watched the performances, and got something to eat."
Herm! You are not who I expected!

I know. Now, we are going to be pretending to be quite ordinary people, on our way to a wedding in the hills.

We? Does that mean you aren't going to send me back?

Not immediately, Nico. I promised your father I would keep you safe—he was not very pleased with you. Now, I want you to be called Tomas, and I will be Ian MacAnndra. It occurred to him then that there was something he had missed earlier, during the discussion in the study. Herm wondered why Danilo and Lew wanted Domenic away from Comyn Castle. Then he decided they probably had good reasons and stopped worrying about it.

I understand. That's a good choice—there are hundreds of MacAnndras in the hills. I've been keeping an eye on the wagons while I waited, and nothing has happened so far. What are we going to do?

We are going to remain here until morning—there's a bedroll for you—and then we are going to decide our next move. Tell me everything you have learned thus far, Nico.

Tomas! Not Nico. You might forget and say the wrong name—Uncle Ian!

Damn, but the boy was quick! Herm sat down next to the young man and stretched his hands toward the fire. Then he listened intently to the voice in his mind. The tale unwound clearly, beginning with how the Travelers' wagon had passed Comyn Castle that morning and ending with what the boy had heard later. Domenic seemed to have a good memory and an eye for detail. As he went over his story, Herm could sense that Nico was starting to relax, and even enjoying himself a bit. He asked a few questions, and discovered that Nico had never seen the men's faces, but thought he could identify them anyhow.

At last they stood up together and got the bedrolls from the horses, spread them out beside the fire, and prepared to sleep. Herm discovered he was very tired, and that his legs ached from riding, but he was excited as well. The pleasant smells of woodsmoke and horse dung, cold air and a light breeze, refreshed him. He ignored the rocks under his bedding and thought about Katherine and the children. His spirits started to plummet, but before he could pitch himself into despair, he heard the boy again. *I think something is happening over near the Travelers.*

What?

There is some sort of argument between the one called Vancof and another driver. They both seem a bit drunk, and their thoughts are not very clear. But it seems as if Vancof is picking a fight on purpose. There is an undertone in his mind—he's afraid. No, he's drunk and torn up inside. He wants to get away from here, but he thinks he has to stay at the same time. It is all muddled up with remorse and firewine.

A moment later loud voices erupted in the other field. There were shouts from within the wagons to be quiet, and the noise of wooden doors being opened and closed. Everyone who was awake looked over with interest. A few of the muleteers began to wander across the road, abandoning the storyteller at the fire pit in favor of more lively entertainment.

Herm sat up and looked, and Domenic as well. Two shadowed figures were struggling in front of one wagon, fists flying and mostly missing the mark. Then several other people got out of the wagons and joined in the fray, trying to separate the combatants.

The fight was over quickly, though the loud voices continued. One man swore at everyone, and shuffled away. He vanished into a wain, and reemerged a few minutes later with a rather clumsy bundle. He started to trudge away from the encampment, and a woman screamed at him. He turned and shouted back at her.

That's the man, uncle—that's Vancof. I don't know who the harridan screaming at him is. It's not the girl I saw earlier, but someone else. I never heard a woman, even Mother, say such things!

You have led a very sheltered life, Tomas. Never be surprised at what a woman can think of to say when she is angry. Can you sense anything more from him?

Not much. He really is pretty drunk. He just wants to get as far away as he can. But I can't tell if he wants to get away from the Travelers or from the men he talked to before. He just seems disgusted with everything.

We can't follow him without drawing attention to ourselves.

He is too drunk to get very far, I think, Uncle Ian. Sometimes Uncle Rafael gets like this, after he has had a row with Aunt Gisela. He drinks himself into a stupor, and falls asleep. Vancof seems to be in a similar state.

Good. Then let's get some sleep. Tomorrow promises to be an interesting day.

12

Lyle Belfontaine stared at the stack of sheets on his desk. They were the messages he had sent during the past two days, and all of them had been returned without any reply. This was something that had never happened before, and it left him with a knot in his belly and a raging headache. It was as if the Federation had vanished from the galaxy, leaving him stranded on Cottman IV. He had not felt so helpless since his father had dismissed him over thirty years before. And he had not felt so frustrated since just before the disastrous events on Lein III, when he had tried to overthrow a planetary government against all the rules of the Federation. It gave him an anxious feeling, a roughening of the skin at the back of his neck, an almost prescient sense that he might revisit those events, and this time make them work out to his advantage. Strange—this planet must really be getting under his skin, if he was starting to think like the superstitious natives who believed in such nonsense.

Miles Granfell walked into the office without announcement, his face sober, but his eyes gleaming with surpressed emotion. His boots were soiled, as if he had been walking on dirt, and his usually tidy hair was wind-tossed. Without a word, he took the chair on the other side of the desk and stretched his long legs forward.

"What is it?" Lyle growled the words, glaring at the stack of returned messages, aggrieved and almost eager to take it out on his underling. "Where have you been?"

"Oh, 'walking to and fro upon the earth.' "

Belfontaine recognized this as some sort of quotation. The last thing he wanted to do was play literature with Granfell, but he decided he had to be patient. "What is that supposed to mean?"

Granfell grinned and crossed his ankles. "I have some good news. Regis Hastur is dead."

Belfontaine found himself angry at the man's words rather than pleased. Surely he should have known about this before his subordinate! With an effort, he mastered his emotions and asked only, "Are you sure?"

"Vancof is, which will have to do for now."

"I see. Well, that is news indeed," he conceded with as much grace as he could muster. When he did not say anything further, the other man shifted in the chair, as if trying to gauge Lyle's mood.

After a minute of silence, Granfell asked, "What's all that clutter? I've never seen so much paper on your desk in all the years you have been here."

Lyle eyed the other man with thinly masked dislike. Granfell's tone bordered on insolence. Then he dismissed his feelings—it was just Miles' way, after all. "It is every message I have sent out in the past thirty-six hours. Regional Headquarters seems to have . . . vanished."

Granfell came to attention abruptly. "Is there some problem with the relay station?"

"I don't know. Our transmitter appears to be functioning perfectly, but whatever I send out just bounces." He did not need to add that the transmitter for Cottman IV was ancient by Federation standards, that all the equipment at Headquarters had been there for ten or even twenty years without replacement. Fortunately, most of it still worked, but recently they had had to scavenge parts from some mechanisms to keep others going—all because of the austerity measures that had spread across the Federation.

"This is serious, Lyle."

"I am well aware of that," he answered as icily as he could. "It makes your concerns that we might be abandoned here take on a whole new dimension."

"Precisely. And I think we should . . ." Miles' voice faltered, and he looked around the office slowly. "It makes planning anything very diffi-cult," he said at last.

Belfontaine looked at him dumbly for a moment, until he realized that Granfell had something he wanted to say that he did not want to have heard or recorded. Even the chance that they were going to be stuck on Cottman instead of removed did not relieve him of the fear of being suspected of working against the Federation. There were automatic de-vices in the walls of the room which heard everything, and he had no control over them, even though he was part of the Security Forces. If Lyle had been able to, he would have turned off the listeners long since. And just because the Federation was out of touch at present did not mean it would remain so. They had to proceed with caution.

"My head feels like I have been on a three-day drunk. Let's take a walk, and consider our options," he replied after a moment.

"The hangover without the pleasure of the booze, you mean?" The words were spoken casually as Granfell unfolded his long body from the chair, smiling without humor.

"Precisely."

Belfontaine picked his all-weather cloak off the hook beside the door. They walked out of the office together, down the corridor, and took the lift to the ground floor without speaking again. Then they exited the building, coming into a chilly night, the sky overcast as usual, and the wind brisk. They moved across the tarmac in silence, until they were well away from everything, and had some assurance of not being overheard.

"So Regis Hastur is dead. And I never even got to meet him."

"Yes. And if the Federation has left us behind, we have our own lives to think about. Vancof told me that Regis' heir is Mikhail Hastur, and we know even less about him than we did about Regis. What I do know is that they are going to take the body up to some place near Lake Hali, some religious site."

"Who is?"

"All of them, the entire Comyn Council, is my understanding, with their wives and children, and who knows how many else."

"You mean that the Castle is going to be . . ."

"I'm not sure if it will be empty, but I suspect that it would be comparatively easy pickings. But that is just a building. The real power here is in the Domains." After stating this obvious fact, Miles paused for several seconds, as if experiencing dificulty in continuing.

Belfontaine waited as patiently as he could, sensing the tension in his subordinate. "And?"

"What I think you should do is . . . arrange for this funeral train to be attacked along the road somewhere." The words came in a rush, as if Granfell wanted to release them as fast as possible. When Belfontaine did not react, he went on. "I told Vancof to scout out a likely ambush site—which he did not like very much. But if a substantial part of the ruling class were removed, there would be no obstacle to Federation rule—assuming that there still is a Federation in a few weeks. I confess that this sudden silence makes me very uneasy. What do you think is going on out there?"

Belfontaine moved more quickly to keep the chill out of his bones. He thought about this sudden proposal, wary and suspicious. He did not like his underlings to have ideas of their own, and he was aware that such a plan was very dangerous. If it went awry, it was his head that was in the noose, not Granfell's.

There was something about this sudden proposal that rang alarm bells in Belfontaine's mind. What if Regis Hastur was still alive, and the entire thing was some plan to discredit him as Station Chief. It would not be the first time some ambitious subordinate had tried to further himself at the expense of his commander. He had never entirely trusted Granfell, had he? The whole thing seemed too good to be true, and Lyle had learned very early in life to mistrust anything he had not learned firsthand, for himself.

Still, he should be able to determine if, indeed, Hastur was dead. If he was, he knew why he had not been informed—Lew Alton was behind it, of course. It would be just like the man to keep him in the dark. He felt surrounded by enemies and incompetents, suspecting everyone, even the Planetary Administrator, Emmet Grayson, whom he had managed to neutralize effectively for the most part. The reorganization of the Federation bureaucracy had made it easy for Belfontaine to exclude Grayson from any real authority, but he still had a few loyal followers among the personnel at HQ. It seemed an unlikely prospect, but one which would bear considering when he was alone.

"I can only speculate about what is happening in Federation space,

Miles. My best guess is that in order to keep things going they have simply closed down intersystem communication for the time being. That would keep any ambitious admirals or planetary governors from conspiring or causing trouble."

"You think they have isolated all the member worlds, then?"

"Those that might be disloyal, certainly."

"But why take us out of the loop?"

"A sound question, for which I have no answer. For all I know, some group has seized control of the relay station itself. The dissolution of the legislature may have triggered some crisis we cannot imagine—it was an ill-considered move, in my opinion. I have no doubt that Nagy's Expansionist advisors assumed that they could control the situation, but I have never had a great deal of respect for most of them."

"Politicians," Granfell sneered.

"Exactly." He weighed his next words carefully, wishing to seem neither too eager nor too reluctant. Granfell's reaction to them would tell him a great deal. "Do you seriously think this funeral train can be attacked successfully?"

"I think it worth a try, yes."

"I don't want a try, Miles. I can't risk violating Federation policy. It would have to appear as if it were a local action, not a Federation move."

"Yes, that's true. I thought that we might take advantage of our Aldaran friends in this." The wind gusted and the words were muffled.

"What precisely do you have in mind?" Aldaran friends? He meant *Dom* Damon, who was no friend to anyone but himself. All of Belfontaine's suspicions hardened—why bring *Dom* Damon into it? What was Granfell up to?

"If we fly some of the troops down from the Hellers, land them along the road, and attack the train . . ."

Lyle was shocked for a second as Granfell paused. This did not sound like a spur of the moment plan, but something that had been thought out far more completely. On the other hand, from the evidence of his boots, Miles had walked from wherever he had met Vancof, and perhaps he had used the time to think it through. He had never underestimated the intelligence of his subordinate before, and he was not going to begin now. "We have about a hundred useful men up there," he answered reasonably, as if he were thinking about it, when instead his mind was racing with fresh suspicions. "The funeral procession will be heavily guarded,

won't it? The natives here may be backward, but they know how to fight."
He waited to hear Granfell's reply, to measure it. The strange prickling
he had had earlier on the back of his neck returned.

"Dress the men up in local clothing and pass them off as brigands.
God knows there are enough of those up in the hills. And I am sure that
a couple platoons of trained soldiers could take out these paltry guards
without using blasters. We might mine the road or . . ."

"And if the Federation appears, and there is a Board of Inquiry, what
then?"

"If you aren't ready to take the risk . . ."

"I did not say that, Miles. But we have to be extremely cautious. I
just want to be certain that, whatever happens, nothing can be traced to
us. The idea of using men from the Hellers complex is a good one, since
we can blame *Dom* Damon if anything goes wrong. We all know that he
thinks that he could run Cottman if he ever got the chance. He would
make an excellent scapegoat, particularly if he were dead. But I don't
want to move precipitously. It might be possible that this Mikhail Hastur
would be more agreeable than his predecessor, and we could save ourselves a lot of potential trouble by trying to deal with him first."

"I thought you would jump at the chance to get Cottman into the
hands of the Federation." Miles sounded disappointed, and a little angry,
too.

Mine the road? Use blasters? Had Miles lost his mind? "There are
too many random factors for my peace of mind." When he saw the expression on the face of the other man, the look of eagerness fading away,
Belfontaine felt a certain smugness. Granfell had to learn who was in
charge here. "Still, it is an excellent opportunity, and I agree we should
not ignore it. Go ahead. Get Vancof to work on finding a good site for
an ambush, and we will try to gather more information. I want definitive
proof that Regis Hastur is dead. Vancof's word is not enough. And if I
hear from Regional Headquarters tomorrow, we might have to scrap the
whole idea."

Granfell grunted, then nodded. "I'll send Nailors out first thing in
the morning."

"Why not go yourself?" The introduction of Miles' next in command
disturbed him, for the more people who knew of the conspiracy, the
greater was the danger of failure.

"Vancof hates my guts, and would do almost anything to annoy me.

He was very reluctant when I suggested the idea a few hours ago—the man is a coward and a drunk. It is a pity we don't have a better agent in place, but he is the only one that is on the route the procession will take. And we don't have time to get another band of Travelers into position to spy for us."

"Can Nailors be trusted?"

Granfell did not answer immediately, and Belfontaine felt a sudden thrust of unease pierce his belly. "I believe he can be," the other man finally said.

The reply did not reassure Belfontaine, but instead caused the faint bud of unease in his mind to bloom into a full-fledged anxiety. Granfell was holding something back. He must be! What was it? He had a yearning to grab the taller man by the throat and throttle the truth out of him. For all he knew, the entire story was a fabrication, some plot to discredit him. Lyle chewed over this, hating the wind blowing against his back, the smell of woodsmoke drifting across from the city choking his throat. He looked at the decaying surface beneath his feet, the weeds that had pushed through the ancient concrete, breaking it, and held back a sudden sense of helplessness and fury.

The dilemma before him seemed hydralike. If Granfell was telling the truth, and Regis Hastur was dead, why had he not heard of it from other sources? True, Lew Alton had stonewalled him on certain matters in the past, but it seemed out of character for him not to have informed Headquarters. The man was just a bureaucrat, full of his own position and power, wasn't he? Was there some sort of struggle going on in Comyn Castle? Perhaps this unknown Mikhail Hastur did not trust Lew Alton— which would suit Belfontaine well enough. Alton was Regis' advisor, but was he also a confidant of this unknown man? He needed better information, and he could think of no way to get any immediately. If only that daughter of Damon Aldaran's had been as useful as her father had suggested she might be.

On the other hand, if Granfell were playing him false, then this whole thing might be a plot to discredit him and take his place. Belfontaine played that idea out quickly. With his personal history, it would not be difficult for Granfell to convince their superiors that he had been the instigator of an unauthorized attack on the planetary rulers of Cottman IV. That was assuming that the Federation had not abandoned them to the cold winds of Cottman forever.

Why was he suggesting using troops from the Aldaran Domain? Was Granfell in league with that old fool up in the Hellers? Miles had gone to the Hellers a few months before, ostensibly to evaluate the situation there. But what if the actual reason had been to see *Dom* Damon and involve him in Granfell's personal ambitions. If Belfontaine were removed, Miles was the logical person to step into his place as Station Chief.

What if the Federation's planned retreat had forced Granfell's hand? With a sick feeling, Belfontaine realized that his hatred of Cottman had led him to isolate himself, to depend on Miles Granfell, whom he knew to be a discontented and ambitious man. But until now he had always believed he could trust the man not to overstep himself.

"Let us take one thing at a time, shall we?"

Miles was not satisfied, if the angry jerk of his shoulders was anything to judge by. "Why wait? I thought you would jump at the chance."

"There are several ways to approach this situation, Miles, and not all of them involve the wholesale slaughter of a hundred or more people."

"Very well. But I will send Nailors off in the morning to tell Vancof to scout out a possible site for an ambush." He paused, as if something disturbed him, something he did not want to say. "Uh, there is a little problem. Vancof says he wants written orders from you before he goes ahead. And a shortbeam transmitter, too. Funny, isn't it, how much of our current technology fails to work on Cottman, but things we abandoned hundreds of years ago still do."

"A transmitter? I don't much care for that idea. The locals are backward and self-absorbed, but not so much so that they would fail to notice illegal technology . . ." Written orders? Was that really Vancof's idea, or was Miles trying to create trouble for him? One thing the disaster on Lein III had taught him was to never leave any evidence behind, and here was Granfell suggesting that he do exactly that. The whole thing smelled. No, it stank!

"I don't think there is much real danger that it will be discovered and recognized as prohibited technology, do you?" Granfell brushed aside Lyle's mild objection with an abrupt gesture, his face animated in the yellow glow from a nearby light. "And perhaps we might see about creating a bit of havoc in Thendara itself—something to keep those stupid City Guards busy."

Belfontaine gave the taller man a hard look. On the surface he seemed just as he always had, a ruthless, restless man with grand ambitions. But underneath—Lyle sensed a tension that he could not quite read. Granfell was too eager for Belfontaine's comfort, and the more he thought about it, the more certain he became that Granfell could not have come up with such a plan on the spur of the moment. He didn't believe Granfell was that clever. And suggesting sending a piece of offworld technology to a man who was a poor spy, although an efficient assassin when he was not drinking too heavily, made no sense and roused a finger of unease in his already unsettled belly.

Yes, it was clear now. Granfell could not be trusted, and he was probably in league with either the Planetary Administrator, Grayson, or with Lord Aldaran. Hmm . . . for all he knew, Miles was in league with Lew Alton, and this was why the news of Hastur's death had not reached him. Stranger things had happened. He drew a breath, forcing himself to keep his imagination in check.

"Do what you can," he answered with as much outward indifference as he could manage, while inwardly seething. "And have Nailors see me before he leaves—I'll think about the shortbeam."

Granfell turned and walked away without a word, leaving Belfontaine alone in the cold. After a minute, he turned and walked toward his own quarters, deep in thought. Surely he had neutralized Grayson sufficiently. Besides, the man was not much of a schemer. So it must be Aldaran. Unless Alton was part of the plot, too. No, this seemed unlikely in the extreme. It had to be *Dom* Damon, didn't it, with his desire to become the real power on Cottman.

Abruptly, Belfontaine turned and went back into the HQ Building. He had to find out if Granfell had been in secret communication with *Dom* Damon—the idea had never occurred to him until now. What an idiot he was! He had such contempt for the old man that he had not seen the danger at all. And there were those sons of his, too. Why had Hermes Aldaran returned so suddenly? Or perhaps it was the older one, Robert, who was conspiring with Granfell. Just because he appeared the soul of probity did not mean he had no desire to succeed to his father's place.

They must all be in this together! There was no other reasonable explanation for Herm Aldaran to have come back so conveniently. Somehow the old man or Robert must have sent for him—his return had nothing to do with the dissolution of the legislature! That had been a mere coincidence. He must find a way to get Hermes away from Comyn Castle. He knew ways to get information out of a man!

Frustration welled up in his throat, leaving his mouth sour and dry. Lew Alton had not even bothered to reply to his demand for the return of Herm Aldaran. He felt ignored—no, worse—dismissed as unimportant. Well, he would just have to do something—perhaps send a message to this Mikhail Hastur instead. Or go to Comyn Castle himself and demand a meeting. He shuddered all over. He would not risk his dignity by going—no, he would make someone come to him! And if it was Lew Alton, the man would never leave HQ alive.

For a moment, he dwelt on this satisfying idea, enjoying the images that danced in his mind. Then Lyle scolded himself. Alton was too smart to risk it, and he knew it. And he was being hasty, jumping to conclusions without enough real evidence, wasn't he? No! On the contrary, he knew in his gut that he was right—that his constant fear and paranoia had some foundation.

As his chilled feet hit the floor of the corridor leading toward the Communications Office, Belfontaine felt the enormity of the plot swell in his mind. The heat of the building was almost stifling after the cold outside, and he felt a bead of sweat trickle down his narrow brow. He pulled off his cloak with an angry yank, then wiped his forehead with his sleeve. The water-resistant fabric of his uniform refused to absorb the moisture, and he was forced to use his hand, which he loathed doing.

The Communications Office was empty except for one sleepy-eyed clerk who stared at him with a gaping jaw before leaping up hastily and saluting gracelessly. Belfontaine ignored him until he found a tissue and wiped his hands. "Has there been any word from Regional?"

"No, sir. It has been quiet all during my shift." The clerk looked uneasy, as if he wanted to ask questions but dared not.

"No news is good news, perhaps. Why don't you take a break—have some synthecaf or something. Bring me some, too."

The clerk didn't react at first, just looked mildly surprised. He was not supposed to leave his post unless he was relieved. Then comprehension stole over his face. "Yes, sir. That would be very pleasant."

Belfontaine watched him leave, and realized that it had been a mistake to come there. Too late. He knew the clerk would talk unless he could find a way to stop him, and he did not want his visit to be the gossip of HQ by dawn. He would worry about that later.

He sat down in the still warm chair vacated a minute before and tapped a few commands into the keyboard. The thing was old, the keys soiled with use, and some of them were sluggish to respond. Another economy—the keyboard should have been replaced long since.

It had been several years since Belfontaine had actually used a communications array, but he had not forgotten how. This pleased him. It took only a few strokes to call up the records he had in mind, then transfer them to the display in his office. There was no way to remove the traces of his use, however, if anyone wished to discover what he had been up to. He could only hope that the clerk's evident boredom and sleepiness would prevent him searching for what had occurred.

When the faint tattoo of approaching footsteps came to his ears, he cleared the board, rose, and returned to the spot where he had been standing before. He whistled tunelessly, a nervous habit he had never quite managed to break. When the clerk came in with two disposable containers a moment later, Belfontaine took one calmly.

"It must be rather boring sitting here all night," he commented.

"Yes, sir, but I am used to it now."

"Still, I have been a little lax about rotating the shifts, I think. How long have you had the night shift?"

"Eight months or so, sir. Ever since I was posted to Cottman."

Ah, good—he was a recent transfer. And from his nervousness, probably easily intimidated. "That is much too long! I'll see about having you transferred to days for a while."

"But, sir . . . aren't we . . . I mean?"

Lyle gave him a coy look, trying to appear amused. "I think you deserve to be put on days for the foreseable future," he announced. "If that would suit you."

The disconcerted clerk looked down into his cup. "It does rather interfere with my social life, always being awake at night and asleep most of the day," he admitted. "And I don't have the seniority to get a better shift, so I didn't even ask."

"Got a lady friend in the Trade City, do you?"

"I wouldn't call her a lady, sir."

Belfontaine laughed as lewdly as he could manage, and the clerk smiled timidly. "Well, tomorrow I'll change your shift. I am glad I came in tonight. I have had so much on my mind that I haven't been giving as much attention to my men as I should." The words were as sour in his mouth as the revolting liquid in his cup. He hated synthecaf.

"Was there something you wanted, or were you just . . . restless, sir?"

"I could not sleep, so I went for a walk, and then I just found myself here. Habit, I suppose. I began my career at a message array, and a room like this seems very homey to me. Why do you ask?"

"Oh, no particular reason, sir, except I've never seen you around at night. But I think we are all a little restless, with things being so unsettled."

Belfontaine nodded, as if he accepted this explanation. "Unsettled. That's a good word for it." Then a worm of suspicion uncoiled in his mind. "I suppose I am not the only one wandering around in the corridors."

"No, sir. Clerk Gretrian said that Captain Granfell stopped in during her shift, and then he came back again a while ago. Just looked in and gave me a hello."

"Did he now?"

"Yes, sir. And two nights ago, or maybe three—they all start to run together after a while—I saw Adminstrator Grayson's assistant, too. Hmm. It seems to me that she's been here other times as well, even before the order to get the indigines off the complex came through."

"My goodness! I had no idea." Belfontaine wanted very much to ask if Grayson's assistant, a half-Cottman woman who had been raised in the John Reade Orphanage, had tried to access anything. No, he decided, it would be foolish to display any real interest. Perhaps Granfell and Grayson were indeed up to something. The suspicion he had discarded only a short time before returned with a vengeance. "Well, good night. And thanks for the synthecaf. After the outdoors, it was very welcome. Beastly climate, isn't it."

"You can say that again, sir."

"Good night, then." Belfontaine walked out of the CommCenter before he realized that he had no idea what the name of the clerk was, and that he did not really care. But he would find out, and put the man in for a transfer to days. Perhaps that favor would keep him from talking, or defuse his interest in why the Station Chief had stopped in so suddenly.

A wave of weariness washed through him, followed by a mild nausea. He dropped the now tepid synthecaf cup into the closest disposal chute and made a face. There were too many variables, suddenly, after years of things being stable, and he did not like it. No, that was too mild a reaction. He hated this situation. He hated not knowing who his foes were, and he hated not being able to predict what would happen in the near future.

Belfontaine's small hands curled into fists, and he wished there were something nearby that he could hit. But the walls of the corridor were unforgiving, and he was not of a mind to injure himself out of sheer frustration. He needed to have a plan of his own. The problem was he had no clear idea where to begin.

His office was silent, and the stack of papers on the desk did not improve his mood. Why was the Regional Relay Station returning his messages unanswered? If the Federation was really going to pull out of Cottman, he should be receiving lots and lots of directives, shouldn't he? Unless they were somehow being rerouted to Grayson.

That, at least, was something he could check out. He pushed the papers aside, intent on finding some answers. He keyed into the comm in his desk and began a search. No, Grayson was not sending out separate requests, nor receiving replies, other than one two days before, when everything had stopped cold. And that one, when he accessed it, was perfectly correct, exactly what a Planetary Administrator should be asking from Regional HQ . . . unless it was in some code.

Belfontaine toyed with the idea for a moment, then rejected the possibility. Emmet Grayson was from a family that had been in Federation Service for generations, and he took his duties seriously. He was, as far as Lyle had ever known, a rather dull man who was honest to a fault. Worse, he actually believed that Cottman was fine, just as it was, and had done as much as he had been able to prevent Belfontaine from changing things. Really, the notion of him conspiring with Granfell or anyone else was laughable.

He keyed up the records he had caused to be transferred to his unit, looking now for any communication between Granfell and the Federation outpost in the Aldaran Domain. There were a few things, but they were the normal sort of communication. There was nothing alarming or even interesting in them.

This did not mean that Granfell had not met with *Dom* Damon while he was up in the Hellers, though. Miles was clever enough not to leave traces of any subversive activity.

Was it possible that nothing was going on? Could it be that Miles' plan really was a spur of the moment thing, conjured up opportunistically when he learned that Regis Hastur was dead. Was he being overly tortuous, or just plain paranoid?

Perhaps the best thing would be to let Granfell go ahead, bring a few troops down from the Hellers to attack the train, and see what happened. If it succeeded, fine. If it did not, then he could claim he knew nothing about it, that Granfell had acted on his own, without authorization, should it come to a Board of Inquiry.

Of course Granfell would try to implicate him, and with Belfontaine's past record, he might even be believed. It would be better if Granfell did not survive, wouldn't it? He was much too eager for Belfontaine's comfort. And there was Nailors to consider as well. He was Granfell's man, and would back him up.

A slow grin began to pull at the corners of his mouth. He could see a way out now. Vancof wanted orders, did he? Well, he would get them, and they would solve the entire problem. If you have an assassin, you might as well use him. And Nailors would never have any idea that he carried his own death warrant, and Granfell's as well.

Pleased with his own cunning, Belfontaine turned his mind to the other problem, that of Mikhail Hastur. He had never seen the man—could have passed him in the hall without recognition. He might be manipulable, and he might not. And wasn't there a son of Regis' somewhere?

Annoyance replaced his good mood abruptly. He had not gathered enough information during his years on Cottman, and now he had to work without it. True, Granfell might manage to eliminate most of the ruling class of Cottman, or at least those who were adults. But would that get him what he wanted?

He could not depend on that, could he? And if the members of the Comyn were away from Thendara, bearing the body of Regis Hastur north, then the castle should be easy pickings. And there were at least a hundred and fifty men in the HQ Barracks, eating their heads off and whoring with the local women. They were a match for any number of sword-carrying guards, even without high energy weapons.

What justification could he claim for attacking Comyn Castle? For several seconds he was thwarted, and then he realized that the solution was Hermes Aldaran. He was a wanted man, and, as far as Belfontaine knew, he was holed up in the castle. Therefore, he would be justified in storming the blasted place—if the Federation ever questioned his actions, they would never know that Hermes most likely would be riding north with the rest. Yes, that was the answer.

As soon as the funeral train was out of the city, he would order an assault on Comyn Castle. The unfilled warrant for Hermes Aldaran was all he really needed, wasn't it? And there would be no real opposition, just a few servants and a handful of Castle Guards. And once they occupied that great white pile on the hill, he would be in the perfect position to make any demands he wished. With any luck at all, it might be a bloodless coup.

Belfontaine leaned back in the too-large chair, feeling it hit his spine in all the wrong places, and sighed. Then he leaned forward and pressed a thumb lock on the lowest drawer of the desk. It slid open silently, and he took out a bottle of rare Fontainian brandy and a small glass. Slowly he poured himself a tipple. He raised the glass, toasting the air, and tried to convince himself that at last his ambitions were going to be realized.

13

Herm felt a weight on his arm, and for a moment thought it was his Kate. Then he opened his eyes, saw a clouded dawn sky above his head, and found that the boy had rolled over in his sleep and pillowed his head against Herm's shoulder. There was something very trusting in this, and he was moved by an unexpected rush of tenderness. He barely knew Domenic, and now here they were, alone together, involved in a covert operation.

The events of the previous night flooded into his mind, filled with fear and regret, but also a profound sense of relief. He was glad to be away from Katherine for a time. Then, just as he began to enjoy the relief, guilt crept into his consciousness, destroying the mild pleasure of having escaped the situation for a while. He saw his choice as somewhat cowardly now, and was ashamed. Katherine was right. Everything had changed between them since they had come to Darkover. He had just been too stubborn and too self-involved to admit it before. It was a bitter pill to swallow so early in the day.

The tension which had thrummed along his nerves for weeks, was still there, but subtly altered. He had escaped one set of problems only to be saddled with another. Herm had not anticipated how difficult it was going to be, not just for Katherine and the children, but for himself. He loved Darkover deeply, but his homecoming had not been what he expected. He felt sad and angry at the same time, the very emotions he had tried his best to avoid most of his adult life.

And now he was uncertain of his decision, wracked with doubts that rarely troubled him. He had taken the easy way out of the conflict with his wife. Why? Ultimately it would only make things worse. Reluctantly Herm acknowledged to himself that he had put his world before his personal life—again! There was no other rational explanation for why he had kept Kate in the dark about the talents that gave the Comyn much of their authority. He was the cunning man, wasn't he? Surely, if he had really wished to, he could have found a way to tell her the truth, even with Federation spy eyes and ears all around him. He hated himself for leaving Katherine the way he had. He felt drained now, bewildered, and full of self-loathing. It was too many conflicting emotions to contain. He would have killed for a cup of synthecaf, if he could have gotten one.

Nico stirred, interrupting Herm's dark thoughts. He opened his eyes, and then rubbed them with a rather grubby hand. He had gray eyes, flecked with gold, the iris rimmed in black. His black hair went back from his brow in a peak, very like Lew Alton's, giving the boy something of the appearance of a hawk, with his prominent nose and small mouth. Not a handsome lad, but there was a lot of character in his face, and his eyes shone with intelligence.

"Uh, sorry." Nico shifted his head off Herm's shoulder. "Tell me, is having an adventure always this uncomfortable? There must be a million rocks under me."

It was cold, even under the blankets, and the rocks Herm had noticed when he slipped into sleep seemed to have indeed multiplied during the night. He sat up and looked around, the covers falling off his chest. "I don't know, since I have not had a great number of adventures. And thus far, this one is pretty tame, Tomas. But I agree about the rocks. Perhaps we were lying on a migration path of stones." It was a feeble jest, yet Herm was quite pleased that he had managed it.

To his surprise, this bit of levity provoked a look of alarm on the boy's face. It was gone in an instant, but for a moment he thought that Domenic had taken him seriously. It was a troubling notion for no reason he could immediately understand. He opened his mouth to ask about it, then silenced himself. Herm remembered himself at fifteen, how secretive and spiky he had been, and decided that Nico should be let alone for the present.

"What are we going to do now?"

"Now we are going to get some breakfast from one of the foodstalls. I don't believe our friend got very far, as drunk as he was, and if my guess is correct, he is suffering from a bad hangover and wishing he were dead. Later, I think we might make a few cautious inquiries among the Travelers—you spoke of a pretty girl. Maybe she can tell us something about him."

"What if she recognizes me?"

"A good question, and one I had not thought of. You might have a real talent for subterfuge, boy."

"Thank you, Uncle. But if I do, no one has ever noticed it before. Rory is the one. . . . He is going to be furious when he finds out what I've done. And jealous." There was a certain quiet satisfaction in the words.

"No doubt. You are the 'good' one, aren't you, like my own older brother? And I was like Rory when I was your age, always into some trouble or other."

"Yesterday . . . it seems longer ago . . . Mother was saying that I must be abnormal because I never gave her a minute's worry. If she had foreseen what I was going to do, she would have bitten her tongue."

"Well, she didn't, and saved herself a pot of bother. Now, roll up the bedding and put it back on the horse, and we will fill our bellies. The Travelers seem to be late risers."

Among the footstalls there was a booth that offered a pail of heated water for the refreshment of wayfarers, and they afforded themselves of its services. As Herm splashed the warm liquid over his face, he started to feel better, and Nico removed most of the grime that he had somehow acquired during the night. Then they got bowls of porridge, thick stuff, rich with dried fruits, and slabs of warmed over flatbread. They ate in silence, until the food was consumed. It was a peaceful moment in what promised to be a tense day.

Herm—you were right. That man, Vancof, only went up the road a little. Here he comes, and he seems to be in a very bad mood.

How do you know?

He is practically shouting his thoughts. I think he is afraid of something. He was frightened last night as well—of the other man, Granfell, but mostly of getting killed. He is cursing the day he ever came to Darkover, or joined Intelligence.

Good. Angry men make stupid mistakes.

They went to the horses and got them fed and watered. After a few minutes, the skinny driver came down the road, muttering to himself, and went to the wagon with the puppets painted on its sides. A female voice from within began to abuse him roundly.

"Is that the girl you mentioned?"

"I don't know, Uncle. It doesn't sound like her voice. And she didn't look like she could swear like that. She seemed rather nice."

The driver backed away from the wain, and a plump woman emerged. Her voice was lower now, so they could not overhear the words, but it was obvious that she was berating the man. After a minute another figure came out of the wagon, the slender redhead Nico had seen the previous day. She was knuckling sleep from her eyes, and looked very cross.

"Auntie, leave off!" Her voice carried across the field, as she tugged at the older woman's sleeve. Then, suddenly, she dropped her hand and looked around, scanning the booths and stalls, as if she was looking for something. The expression on her face seemed puzzled and a little frightened.

At her movement, Nico ducked behind his horse and looked alarmed. Herm watched and saw the girl shake her head, and turn back to the now sullen combatants. The driver was red-faced with fury, and the older woman seemed about to shake him by his slight shoulders.

She sensed me!

Were you probing her, Nico?

No, just sort of . . . hovering around. It is something Mother taught me. But she noticed it. She must have some laran, *otherwise she wouldn't have. And if she sees me, she is going to wonder why I was standing guard yesterday. What's she doing here, and why isn't she in a Tower?*

That's a very good question, Nico. Another is who is she? She does not have the appearance of a commoner, does she?

I don't know. I mean, she looks ordinary, like other people, to me, except for her red hair. And even though I know that red hair often goes along with laran, *it is not always so. My Aunt Rafaella has pretty red hair, and not a lick of* laran—*although her sister was in a Tower for a time. And my hair is dark, yet my gifts are strong. That girl certainly is pretty, and she has a really sharp tongue.* He gave the mental equivalent of a sigh. *I don't have much experience with anyone except the people in the castle and at Arilinn. I feel totally ignorant about a lot of things.*

No, I suppose not. Very likely she is some nedestra *child of the Comyn, but I agree that her presence among the Travelers is a little peculiar. When I left Darkover, there were only two or three groups of them, and they were more an amusing source of light entertainment than anything else. Still, I suppose that some randy sprig of the Domains might have fathered her and given her that fiery head of hair and a bit of* laran, *and never known he had done it.*

You mean her mother was likely a Traveler?

It is a reasonable idea—in light of our total lack of real information!

By now both sides of the road were abustle with activity. The muleteers were loading their animals, and a wagon was pulling through the gates, loaded with barrels of beer or wine. Then several women with cropped hair and weathered faces rode out.

"Oh, hell!"

"What's the matter, Tomas?"

"It's Aunt Rafi!"

"Who?" Herm looked back at the troup of Renunciates whose appearance had so clearly alarmed the boy.

"That woman in the lead, that's Rafaella n'ha Liriel, my aunt of sorts. She is freemated to Great-Uncle Rafe Scott. I'll just bet Mother has sent her to drag me back and lock me in the Castle!" There was no mistaking the bitterness in his voice.

"They might be on another errand, lad." He agreed that the appearance of the woman was suspicious, but he was less ready than Nico to leap to any conclusions. During the dinner where he had sat beside Marguerida Alton, he had taken her measure, and thought her a sensible if somewhat forceful person. He had liked her a great deal, and he hoped that she and Kate would talk when Marguerida had the time. He suspected that once they knew one another, they would get along well. Herm did not want his sister to be the only confidant his wife had.

He wondered again if he should have told Katherine what he was doing, but after a few moment's reflection he decided he had made the safest decision. Although only those with the Alton Gift, like Nico or Lew, could force information out of the minds of the unsuspecting, he was acutely aware that any telepath could overhear the topmost thoughts of another. And, for no reason he could put a finger to, he did not want his sister Gisela knowing what he was about.

Herm watched the Renunciate woman stand up in her stirrups and scan the fields. She had very curly hair, red but starting to gray, and a cheerful expression. Then she urged her horse forward and rode over to them. She dismounted and walked up to Herm, her callused hand extended in a friendly way. He allowed himself a silent curse at this confirmation of Nico's suggestion. He did not really want a pack of women, however capable, tagging along. But he clasped the offered hand and made his mouth smile.

"We are your escort," the woman said quietly. "Sorry we are a bit late." Her blue eyes were twinkling as she spoke, and she ignored Nico completely after giving him a swift examination.

"Yes, I see."

"It was decided you might be less noticeable if you were in the company of some Renunciates," she went on, speaking so quietly that he knew no one would overhear them. Then she gave Nico a friendly smile. "It was a compromise, you see. To keep Marguerida happy." She chuckled softly, as if some memory amused her. "There is no one else I would allow to drag me out of a warm bed in the middle of the night to form up an expedition on a moment's notice."

"Then you aren't going to take me back," he whispered.

"No, those are not my instructions." Rafaella did not explain any further, but there was something a little guarded in her expression.

"I see. I am Ian MacAnndra, and this is my nephew Tomas," Herm told her, to forestall the use of any names that might prick the interest of bystanders. And it was a good idea. An escort of Renunciates would be a good cover for their activities, as well as added protection for the boy. His respect for Marguerida Alton-Hastur went up a notch. She must have been frantic when she learned what her usually sensible son had done, and yet she had found a solution that was both simple and useful. Herm's earlier resentment at the sight of the Renunciates vanished. He had been sent out to assure the safety of Domenic, not to have a bit of excitement for himself. What a selfish bastard he could be sometimes.

"I am Rafaella n'ha Liriel. I will introduce you to my sisters later. Perhaps you will fill me in."

Before Herm could reply, Nico stiffened beside him. *Look!*
What?

That man coming through the gates is one of the men who talked to Vancof last night. He was wearing leathers then, and sneered at dressing like a "barbarian," or maybe it was the other one who said that, but I guess he has changed his mind.

Very good, Nico. Is it Granfell or the other one?

I don't know—I never really saw their faces. But I recognize the walk. Look. He is nodding to Vancof. What do you think it means?

I believe it means that they have decided to try to attack the funeral train, son.

But, how?

We will just have to find out, won't we?

Nico gave a brief nod. Then he smiled at Rafaella. "Father must have done some fast talking."

"From the little I know, Tomas, he did more than that, and your grandfather, too." She gave the boy a friendly smile, as if she understood both his relief and his anxiety, and only restrained herself from ruffling his unbound hair with an effort.

The rest of the Renunciates had dismounted and were standing beside their horses a short distance away. They were talking quietly among themselves. They had several mules with them, loaded with baggage, tents and bedding, and a supply of feed for the animals. Herm was pleased and slightly amazed—they must have been up most of the night getting things together. They were a hard-looking bunch, their faces weathered. From the well-worn look of their scabbards, they were probably experienced fighters as well.

Vancof was meandering across the road toward the foodstands, walking gingerly, as if his head hurt. The man Nico had pointed out was already standing in front of one. He watched them drift together, very casually to any eye but his own. Then he saw Nico's face go grim.

Vancof is very worried, and the other man is telling him that he has to find a good place for an ambush. He says not to worry, that once a site is chosen, they will take care of the rest.

How is he supposed to communicate the information?

The man is giving him something—a device of some sort. It is very small.

Probably a signaling beacon—quite illegal on Darkover.

Yes, and I think that this worries Vancof a great deal. I think he is afraid that one of the Travelers will see it and start to ask questions. What do you think they are going to do now?

I don't know, Nico. Bring in some soldiers and dress them up like brigands—that's what I would do, if I were going to attack. But if they plan to use Federation weapons, such a subterfuge would be useless. Of course, once they had successfully killed everyone, there would be no one left to complain, would there? He did not like the drift of his thoughts, and there was no way to effectively conceal them from Domenic.

How can they even think of such things—it is so cowardly!

To you and me, yes. The Federation sees things very differently.

Herm recognized the futility of trying to explain the ways of the Terranan to Domenic. He had lived with them for over two decades, and he still did not completely understand them himself. All he was certain of was that Federation Intelligence was always eager to distabilize the rule of planets, just for the power of it, as near as he could tell. The Federation did not want Darkover for any reason other than that it was something that was not under their control. He had opposed a great many bills in the Senate, intended to curtail the rights of Protected Planets, as well as those which further oppressed the lives of those living on member worlds. The reasoning was always the same—people did not know what was good for them, and they needed to have wiser heads decide what was best. Anything different was looked upon with suspicion, any deviation in thinking was considered a threat.

He sniffed the smoky air, felt the light breeze touch his face, and felt more alive than he had for years despite his worries. He was glad to be home, to be there to thwart the plans of these men. It would make up for years of frustration in the unending battle to keep Darkover free of outside intervention. But he still felt conflicted, torn between his desire to do something purposeful, and his fear that Katherine would never forgive him. Had he jumped at the opportunity to get away because on Darkover she was, as she insisted, no longer his equal? Did part of him really believe she was a cripple, and was that the real reason he had never told her the truth? He wished he could control his mind enough to stop thinking about that, but every time he relaxed just a little, it came back to haunt him.

His pleasure at the brisk morning breeze and the smells of the encampment vanished. Herm let himself chew on this undigested morsel, tasting the bitterness of it, almost savoring it. Yes, he wanted very much to discover the full extent of the plot against Mikhail Hastur. He loved Darkover and knew himself to be utterly loyal to the world of his birth.

But, was his love of Darkover worth destroying his marriage? He had known before he told her that Kate was going to be angry, and he had assumed that his ability to manipulate her would keep things from getting out of hand. But that had not worked out as he expected, had it? Now he might have to pay a greater price than he ever imagined for his desire to serve his world.

Herm remembered his younger and more idealistic self, the man who had gone to the Federation to work for Darkover. He had always hated the way the Aldarans were isolated from the rest of the Domains, how they were treated with mistrust and suspicion, and he had been determined to change that attitude. Less than a year in government had disabused him of most of his idealism, and the self-serving cynicism of many of the others in the lower house had given him a low opinion of humanity. But now his earlier idealistic vision flooded back, warming him, heartening him, and the fear that he might fail in his ambition began to gnaw at his assurance. This was his chance to redeem the Aldaran Domain, to prove to the Comyn that not all the members of his family were treacherous.

It was very dangerous, and Domenic might get injured or even killed. Ruthlessly, he evaluated the situation, sparing nothing. He knew in his heart he would die for Darkover, for Mikhail Hastur and the Comyn. If the assassination plot succeeded, Kate and the children would be in more danger, wouldn't they? And what about Domenic? Should he send the boy back into the city? He was torn. He needed the availability of the Alton Gift, certainly. But did that need justify putting the lad in such peril?

Herm had not felt so unsure of himself in decades. His mouth tasted like vinegar, and his belly churned around the heavy porridge he had eaten. He must be mad, thinking of challenging the Federation with one young man and a band of Renunciates as his allies. But he was not alone, and it was not entirely his decision to make. The very fact that the Renunciates had arrived, and that Domenic had not been told to return to Comyn Castle after his night away suggested that there was something going on to which Herm was not privy. What had Danilo Syrtis-Ardais said—that it might be a good idea for Nico to be away for a few days. He had barely listened to the remark, but now it had a sinister sound. Nico might be safer here than in his bed—an idea that rocked Herm down to his scruffy boots.

His mind raced. What was going on? Did the boy have some enemy in Comyn Castle that he did not know about? He remembered what he had learned, of Javanne Hastur's opposition to both her son and her grandson, and that although Mikhail was Regis Hastur's designated heir, there were some who felt he should not be. Satisfied that he had found a logical reason for things, he eased back a bit. All he had to do was keep Nico safe and put an end to the plans of the Federation.

With this thought, Herm's wry sense of humor began to reassert itself. Next he'd be imagining he could fly without benefit of Terran technology! "We need to find out where the Travelers are going to go next," he said.

"That's easy. I have picked up the name Carcosa from the thoughts of several of the Travelers, and they seem to be intending to perform there this evening." Nico smiled, pleased with himself for knowing this.

"That's less than a half day's ride on horseback, but it will take longer for the wagons to get there," Rafaella added. "And they appear to be preparing to leave." She nodded slightly, setting her wild curls in motion beneath her knitted cap.

Herm glanced across the road and saw that the mules were being put into the traces of the wagons. There was a good deal of shouting and a pleasant bustle of activity. "Then I suppose we should start out ahead of them."

"Good." Rafaella turned away and moved toward her sisters, apparently satisfied with this plan. At the same time, the stranger who had come to meet Vancof turned away, and started to walk back in the direction of the gate, his task apparently completed.

Domenic took a good look at his face as he passed, and then mounted the mare Herm had brought for him with a little snort of derision. He glanced at the piebald gelding and shook his head. "Did you have to choose the worst nags in the stable?"

"I did not want to draw attention to us, which bringing a splendid steed would certainly have done," he answered a bit defensely as he mounted.

Nico gave a snort. "You will be regretting your choice before we are halfway there. That gelding has the poorest gait of any horse I ever knew."

"I think I have already discovered his shortcomings, Tomas," Herm admitted. They left the field and started up the road at a leisurely pace.

There were heavily laden wagons ahead of them, and one party of muleteers followed behind, so the going was slow. Herm was glad of this, since they looked quite ordinary in such company. When he looked over his shoulder a few minutes later, he could just make out the first of the brightly painted Travelers' wains pulling onto the road.

Nico rode beside him, silent and sharp-eyed. After a time, Rafaella dropped back, to ride on his other side. "I am not very familiar with this part of Darkover, *mestra.*"

"I know. That's one reason Marguerida sent me." She grinned broadly, and the freckles on her fair skin stood out in the faint sunshine now breaking through the overcast. She had a pert, upturned nose, a generous mouth and laugh-lines beside her eyes. "What do you want to know?"

Herm hesitated. How much had Rafaella been told already? Then he realized he must trust her without any assurances, that if Marguerida had sent her, she must be loyal and dependable. "Our opponents are looking for a good place for an ambush."

Rafaella did not seem surprised by this statement. "I can think of a dozen between here and the ruins of Hali Tower. Not right here, so close to the city, of course." She fell silent for a moment, thinking. "There is a goodly stand of forest about eleven miles beyond Carcosa that would appeal to me, if I were of a mind for such things. It is dense enough to conceal a hundred men with no trouble at all. And beyond that, there are some portions of the road on the way to Syrtis, where the low hills and the trees give a lot of cover."

"I take it that these areas are not havens of bandits already?"

"Oh, no. The country this close to Thendara has been quite safe for years. The bandits keep themselves to the hills, mostly. The worst we have had is the occasional footpad hoping to discover a solitary merchant or some lady of the Domains with a modest escort. It is pretty poor pickings."

He looked from one side of the road to the other, taking in the fallow fields, the occasional house or barn, and the presence of animals. He could see a little rise dotted with white blobs that were undoubtedly sheep. The smell of the empty fields, horse dung on the road, and the warm scent of his own mount mingled pleasantly, and he began to relax just a little.

"Uncle," Nico began, getting Herm's attention. It still felt odd to be addressed by that title, even though, since Gisela was married to Rafael Hastur, it was a genuine kinship.

"What is it?"

"That man, Vancof, is thinking about the terrain, just like you are, but not as clearly. I just thought you'd want to know. I can't be certain, but I think he rather likes that bit of forest that Aunt Rafi just mentioned. He is not absolutely sure, because his mind is going in several directions at once—but I got 'just outside Carcosa' a couple of times."

"That's a useful piece of information. Have you ever considered becoming a full-time spy?"

Domenic looked horrified, and then realized that he was being teased. "No, but I can see how it might be attractive to some people. I feel very uncomfortable, doing what I am doing. It doesn't seem right. I mean, I have been able to overhear the thoughts of others for a long time—can't really remember not being able to—but I learned not to listen. For one thing, most thoughts are pretty boring. Or embarrassing." He blushed all the way to the roots of his dark hair. "And most of the people I have been around were trained, too, so they kept their thoughts to themselves. Even the servants in Comyn Castle are pretty quiet. But, this—it is a god-awful racket! One of the muleteers up there has the runs, and I can't seem to block it out."

"But surely you learned how to do that at Arilinn, Tomas."

"I did, but . . . maybe I am just too excited to concentrate."

Herm frowned. Nico was only a boy, and he had been thinking of him as an adult. He puzzled over what he had heard. He was depending on Domenic's gift to keep him informed of the plans of Vancof and the other Terrans. But what if he became overwhelmed by the input? He could go into shock, and then they would really be in a mess.

"You say you can't remember not being able to hear thoughts. You mean that before your threshold time, you were already . . . ."

The boy laughed. "I forgot that you don't really know much about me." *You did not hear the story, but your wife did—part of it, anyhow. When Mother was pregnant with me, when she and Father were in the distant past, they hid out in Lake Hali for a long time, and the* leroni *at Arilinn think that it changed my* laran *somehow. No one knows quite what to make of it, really. Oh, I have the Alton Gift, certainly. But there seems to be a lot of other stuff in my brain that no one can explain. I've been tested over and over, and no one has ever been able to define the real limits of my* laran, *I am something of a freak, although no one dares to say it.*

Herm considered this. He could remember his own adolescence, his own sense of his difference from others, and suspected it was something that all teenagers experienced. But he caught the undertone of anxiety in Nico's thought, his fear of himself. He hid it well, but not completely.

Don't be afraid, Nico.

If you could hear what I do, you would think you were going mad, Uncle Hermes!

And what is that?

Sometimes I can hear the planet groaning.

I see. Have you told anyone this? That, at least, explained the look of anguish at the mention of migrating rocks.

No. And I don't know why I am telling you, except I just know you won't tell me I am imagining things, or that I will grow out of it!

Herm was more touched by this expression of trust than he dared to examine. He hardly knew the boy, and yet Domenic was willing to confide in him. After a moment's reflection, he understood. He had reacted that way to Lew Alton, years before, telling him things he had never been willing to voice to any member of his own family.

Perhaps you will be able to grow into it instead, Nico.

You don't think there is anything too strange about hearing the world?

It does not seem to be harmful. As a matter of fact, it sounds fascinating.

I hadn't thought of that. Thank you.

The boy looked much more cheerful, and Herm was pleased with his diplomacy. At the same time, he was troubled. How could one hear the planet? His ever-present curiosity wondered what it sounded like. Did it groan and moan, or roar like a great fire? Both, probably, if Domenic did not merely imagine the whole thing. Then he put the worry away for another time, and returned to mulling over what he had done to Katherine. Gloom descended over his mind, and for several miles he forgot everything except his wife and children, and how much he loved them.

But after a time the pleasures of the road reclaimed his attention. In spite of the miserable gait of his mount, and his concern for both his family and the young man riding quietly beside him, Herm started to cheer up again. There was, he knew from long experience, a part of him which remained irrepressible, no matter what, and riding in the ruddy light of the morning sun, he allowed it to come to the fore.

14

Domenic was enjoying himself enormously. The sounds and smells of the Old North Road were new to him, and in the pleasure of the moment he nearly forgot about his actual reason for the journey. When he realized this, he immediately felt guilty, pulled in two directions at once. It was hard, he decided, to feel properly serious or gloomy while riding along in the company of Herm Aldaran and Rafaella n'ha Liriel.

He knew that if Regis had not chosen to be so cautious in his last years, this experience would hardly be anything new or remarkable. When his father had been a young man, he had gone everywhere, even up to the Aldaran Domain high in the Hellers. Nico was mildly resentful that he had been denied such opportunities, and was determined to get as much out of this trip as he possibly could. He might never have another chance, unless his father decided to change things. True, he was not alone, but he was not surrounded by servants or guards either, and Uncle Herm did not treat him like a child. That made a great deal of difference. He had always been fond of Rafi, but he had never encountered her outside the confines of Comyn Castle. Here she seemed like another person altogether. He could not quite explain just how, but she was certainly more relaxed on the road. As for the rest of her band, they were strangers, and he was looking forward to getting to know them.

More than that, he was fascinated by the people around him. His encounters with the common folk of Thendara had been few, and a proper distance had always been kept by his many guardians. Most of what he knew he had learned during his Cadet duties, and that consisted of nodding to the various merchants and suppliers who brought things to the Castle rather than actually meeting them. Their concerns and ambitions remained largely a mystery to him, and he knew that he would be a better ruler—if he ever became one—if he had an idea of what they wanted and needed. No one here would bow or scrape before him, and he decided that being ordinary had a great deal to recommend it.

He listened to both the voices and the random thoughts of the bustling people ahead of him on the road. They worried about the weather, or if the dun mule would go lame, and if the load were properly balanced. No one seemed to have a single thought about the things that were always being fussed over at Comyn Castle. It was as if both the Federation and the Domains did not even exist. The tenor of these thoughts was restful, and he decided it must be rather wonderful not to worry about plots and schemes, or what sort of terrible things might happen in the future.

Toward midmorning they encountered a train of grain merchants on their way to Thendara. Nico listened to the exchange of greetings between the muleteers ahead of them on the road and the drivers of the wagons, friendly and informal. They appeared to know one another well enough to toss jokes and insults back and forth before they passed, and to ask about each others' families. If he had had a finer horse, he thought, he would have been completely happy.

By the time they reached Carcosa just past midday, he was very glad to get off the sluggish mare. The muleteers had arrived ahead of them, and the courtyard of the small inn was crowded with braying beasts. Mules were more vocal beasts than horses—they seemed to complain about everything! He looked all around, and noticed a painted sign above the door of the inn, a bright and cheerful thing with a picture of a handsome rooster on it, its proud head thrown back.

The inn itself was a large stone building with a slate roof. The main section rose to three stories, with narrow windows overlooking the yard. He could see half a dozen chimneys above the line of the roof, with smoke rising from them. Two arms extended out at angles from the structure, one for the stables, and another housing a fowl run full of cackling birds, and cages of rabbithorns as well. The stink was incredible, but he was sure that he would become accustomed to it, as the people who worked there surely must be.

Nico studied everything, as his instructors had trained him to, taking in the strong wooden door of the inn which could be closed and bolted from inside, the thick walls, and the small size of the windows, set too high off the ground for anyone to climb through. Even though it seemed to be a friendly place, he could see that it had been built with defense in mind.

When he had been about eight, he had been taken to Armida, and he must have passed through this town. But they had gone in a closed carriage, and he had seen nothing except the inside of it. He did not like to remember that trip, for while he had loved the home of his Alton ancestors, his grandmother had made him extremely uncomfortable. Now he hung back, a little shy in the presence of so many strangers, and watched a middle-aged man bustle out of the building and approach them. He was tall, nearly bald, and what was left of his hair was gray. When he drew closer, Nico could see he had twinkling blue eyes and a small nose above a friendly mouth.

Rafaella greeted him cheerfully. "Hello, Evan. This is Ian MacAnndra and his nephew Tomas—Evan MacHaworth, the best innkeeper in all Darkover." Then she grinned broadly.

"Pah—you say that to all the innkeepers, *mestra*. Welcome to the Crowing Cock," Evan said pleasantly, and reached out to shake Herm's hand without any hint of a bow. Then he ushered them inside.

The entry room had whitewashed stone walls, a flagged stone floor, and dark beams overhead. It smelled of roasting fowl, woodsmoke, and beer, plus the sweaty essence of the mule drivers who had arrived earlier. He could hear voices from a room to one side. They were a noisy lot, but he rather liked the racket they made, and was disappointed when Evan showed them into the room on the far side.

A roaring fire lit a chamber with long tables in it. The walls here were paneled with dark wood, polished so much they gleamed in the reflected light of the fire. He glanced at the stone floor, then up at the beams overhead, and found that they were carved and painted with bright designs. On the mantle he spotted a collection of roosters, made of wood and stone and pottery. They struck him as amusing, and he smiled.

Evan noticed his fascination with the figures. "Do you like our cocks?"

"I have never seen anything like them," Nico answered, wondering uneasily if he had made some sort of mistake by displaying his interest.

"An idea of my wife's. She started with one—that large fellow with the red glaze—that she found in Thendara, and then she began asking our frequent guests to look for others. So, often, some merchant or wagoneer will arrive and present her with a new one. We have cocks from the Dry Towns, and two from up in Ardais country. And this wee one here is a gift from Rafaella." He pointed to a very small rooster made of some green stone.

"They are wonderful," Nico answered.

"She'll be tickled that you like them. I'll be sure to tell her when she gets back—her sister is ailing, and she has gone off to take care of her."

Herm had already sat down at one of the tables, and a serving boy put a large mug of beer in front of him without being asked. Across from him, Rafaella was sitting down, so Nico decided he should join them. The warmth of the fireplace was pleasant after the chilly morning's ride, and he realized he was very hungry.

A girl brought in wooden trenchers and napkins of coarse linen, and another followed her with a platter of roasted birds. He watched Herm dig out his belt knife, spear a whole fowl onto his platter, and begin to tear it apart with his strong hands. He picked up a leg and started to eat, and Nico imitated him.

It was wonderfully messy. Grease slimed his fingers and ran down his chin. And the taste was different than what he was accustomed to. The cook had put some herbs on the skin of the bird that he was unfamiliar with, something very spicy. Nico slurped at the smaller mug of beer the boy put down in front of him, and grinned. Accustomed as he was to more formal dining, he found the whole experience delightful. When a bowl of boiled grain with several wooden spoons in it appeared, he helped himself to a serving, using the spoon he served with to eat, copying Rafaella's manners carefully. A basket of hot rolls was served, and he speared one with his knife.

Rafaella was watching him from beneath her lashes, hiding a smile, which was difficult with her generous mouth. "Good, isn't it?"

"Delicious!"

"Evan MacHaworth's birds are known the length of the old North Road. And his fowl pies are famous. I have even heard that cooks from Thendara have come up and tried to steal the recipe."

"That doesn't surprise me," Herm muttered, speaking with his mouth half full.

The rest of the Renunciates had seated themselves at the other end of the table and were eating and talking quietly. Nico heard their voices, and those of the now somewhat rowdy muleteers across the hall, and felt replete and content. Not to mention greasier than he had ever been in his life. He wiped his hands and mouth on the rough napkin, then cleaned his knife and put it away.

Beside him, he could sense Herm's weariness. *Are you well, Uncle?*

Oh, yes, but I have gotten quite soft over the years. I am not used to sleeping on the ground, or riding for several hours. My legs ache, and I have a stitch in my back. But the beer seems to be helping.

Satisfied, Nico relaxed. *Are we going to go on, or wait for the Travelers?*

A good question, Nico. I had not thought about it yet—I confess I do not have a real plan, but am improvising as we go along. Clever of your mother to have sent these Renunciates—they are a good cover. I think we will remain, since you believe the Travelers will perform here tonight. They should catch up with us in an hour or so.

You could tell Aunt Rafi that you are tired, or that you think your horse is going a bit lame. Then our remaining here would not arouse any interest. And you could take a bath—I am sure the inn has one.

You are a genius! Just what my poor back needs is a long soak.

Your hands and face, too—you are gleaming with fat!

Disrespectful imp! You are a grubby sight yourself!

No one had ever called Domenic either an imp or grubby before, and he decided he liked it. Herm was not like the other adults he knew, not so grown up and serious. Even Grandfather Lew, whom he adored, and who had a good sense of humor, was always thinking about terribly important matters. And no one except Lew had ever really teased him. He could not decide if it was because he was too serious himself, or whether it was his status that prevented such comfortable exchanges. He envied

Amaury, having Herm as a father. As much as he loved Mikhail and respected him, there was always a kind of distance between them, as if his father were afraid to get too close to his eldest child. He was his mother's son more than his father's, and Rory, he knew, was Mikhail's delight. It had never disturbed him much. Rory was a much more amusing person than he was, especially with all his mischief, and Nico had always accepted this. But now he was the wicked one, and equal to Roderick in mischief. Domenic had a moment's deep satisfaction in this thought, even though he was sure his irrepressible little brother would think of something outrageous to do in the near future. Let him—Rory hadn't uncovered a plot against their father's life!

"I believe I have thrown my back out, *Mestra* Rafaella," Herm announced, bringing Domenic back to the present. "Do you think there is a good healer in the town?"

She looked startled for a moment, then seemed to grasp the intent beneath the casual words. "No need. We have our own." Rafaella gestured down the board, pointing to one of the woman. "Danila takes care of all our aches and pains. But we will stay here for the night, I think. I don't fancy having you fall ill along the road. I'll go arrange with Evan for rooms."

She rose and went out of the room, humming to herself. A few minutes later she returned with the innkeeper, all smiles. MacHaworth took them upstairs, showed them to a pleasant bedchamber. It had a large bed, a worn bureau, and a stand with pitcher and washing bowl on it. There were heavy curtains over the narrow window, and a small hearth on one side. The room smelled of balsam and a recent cleaning. He told them where the bathing room was and left.

One of the Renunciates knocked on the door almost immediately. She had both their bedrolls in her capable hands, and Nico took them from her with a quick thank you. "When you wish, call me, and I'll come up and see about straightening your back, *Mestru* MacAnndra," she said. She was a big woman, with large hands, and looked quite capable of yanking a spine to rights in a trice.

They sorted out their few belongings, put things away in the drawers of the chest, and headed for the bathing room in companionable silence. Nico was pleased to discover a cabinet with thick towels, and a closet with several heavy robes hanging in it. He undressed and wriggled his toes against the planked floor of the room. Then he got into the steaming communal tub and ducked down under the water.

Herm joined him, groaning with pleasure. "I have missed this."

"Missed what? Don't the Terranan have bathrooms?"

Yes, of course they do, but nothing like this. I think we had best not speak aloud, because while I doubt there are any Federation spies lurking in the woodwork, there are servants who might gossip, Nico. And terms like Federation and Terranan would make their ears prick up. After twenty-some years of living in a tiny, cramped apartment, and cleaning myself in a sonic shower, this is a real luxury!

But why? Domenic had no idea what a sonic shower might be, but he did not want to reveal his ignorance. A tiny apartment? This did not jibe with his impression of the Federation, gleaned from comments made by his mother and grandfather.

You cannot imagine how crowded it is on most Federation worlds, despite all attempts at population control. It is one reason they are so eager to exploit other planets. There are over eighteen billion people on Terra alone, and the strain on their resources is enormous. Water is taxed and rationed, as is everything else. A room like this would be considered an extravagance, even in the wealthiest home, and for a mere government functionary like myself, it is inconceivable. Oh, there are a few Senators who are rich enough to afford a proper bathroom, but few of them would dare to risk it.

I still don't understand, Uncle.

My, that has a wonderful sound to it, that Uncle business. It is rather difficult to explain how things are, but I will try. You see, many in the Federation insist that austerity is necessary in order for things to function. This is part of the Expansionist philosophy—that the Federation does not have enough resources to care for its citizens, and so must get more by exploiting other planets. As a result, water is rationed and taxed, food is limited and heavily taxed, although no one goes hungry. There are programs to feed the poor, and part of the taxes are used to support that. The meal I just ate would cost a whole day's wages on Terra, and would have had to feed four people, not one. If they could get anything like that delicious chicken at all.

But, what do they eat, then?

The poor exist on artificial slop that would sicken a dog, Nico. It is grown in enormous vats and smells like beer gone bad, and . . . well, I don't know what it tastes like, because I never could make myself try it. It is nourishing enough, I suppose—it keeps them alive and reasonably healthy.

Was it always like that?

No, it wasn't. When I went to the Chamber of Deputies, before the Expansionists got back into power and the austerity policies were introduced, things were different. Water was already being rationed, but goods were less costly then, and you could afford to eat in a restaurant from time to time. It just got worse and worse. There are millions of people on Terra who cannot find jobs, and cannot earn money, and have to live on public support programs. There are waiting lists for colonists, but they have not found very many new habitable planets recently. And most of the older worlds in the Federation are in the same shape or worse. There have been food riots, and water riots—things you simply can't imagine. Last year the entire grid went down on one of the continents, and no one had any power or light for three days.

What's the grid?

The grid is a network of power stations and connections that covers the entire planet. Due to the deliberate stinginess of the Expansionists, there is said to be no money for enlarging the grid, even though everyone agrees it should be done. Thus, in recent years, the demand for energy sometimes outruns the capacity of the grid to supply it. One substation will go off-line, then another, and soon everything grinds to a halt. That means that the lifts which carry people to their homes cease to function, and since many of the buildings are more than fifty stories off the ground, there is no way to get in or out until the power comes back on. And that is just one example.

Nico scrubbed his arms with a rough cloth and considered this information. He had never longed to visit other worlds, unlike his brother who was a bit space mad. And since he had begun to think he heard Darkover in his mind, he had had no desire to leave at all. There was a part of him that felt if he ever left the soil of Darkover entirely, he would die or go insane, as if he were bound to the world itself. Although the noises that echoed in his mind made him uneasy and often fearful, there was at the same time a sense of rightness in them. True, he could not imagine why he, of all people, seemed to have this particular ability, but the longer it continued, the more accustomed to it he became. He had not entirely accepted the idea, but as Herm had told him that morning, there did not appear to be any harm in it. And Herm was the first person he had told of his strange condition—he had not even confided it to Alanna, who had shared so many of his secrets when they were younger.

But he had always imagined the planets of the Federation as being places where everyone flew about in aircars, and lived in light-filled palaces with lots of devices which provided every conceivable comfort. Somehow he had never thought that anyone was poor or lacked enjoyment, which he realized now was pretty stupid. What did those people do with their time, if they did not have jobs?

It sounds terrible! Why do they live like that? I mean, if everyone has to measure their water and are taxed for it—I don't understand that at all, Uncle—why don't they just do it differently?

A good question—one that has troubled better minds than mine. The only answer I have is that the Terrans are in love with their technology, and they truly believe that all problems can be solved with it—that and the resources of the member planets. They never consider if the idea that everything can be made right with technological advances might be an illusion. So they take the grain from one world to feed the masses of Terra, and the metals from another to build their ships, so they can continue to explore the galaxy, looking for more planets to colonize. No one has addressed the plain fact that they haven't settled a new colony in eleven years, because there hasn't been anything but worlds so marginal that no one in their right mind would agree to go there.

What's a marginal world? Domenic felt overwhelmed with the information he was learning, as well as the strange words that Herm used so casually, but he was fascinated and determined not to miss this opportunity.

Oh, one that is even colder than Darkover, or where the air is not quite breathable, or has little arable land. Thetis, where your mother grew up, is one example, and she would not recognize it if she went there now. Has she ever talked about it?

Oh, yes. I know all about the islands and the delfins. It sounds very beautiful.

It was a paradise, when Lew and Diotima lived there, Nico. Not much land, just about ten medium-sized islands and one very big one, and lots and lots of ocean.

And now? Ocean was a difficult concept for him, despite having gotten glimpses of such a thing from a few of his mother's memories, and the occasional moments when he was sure he could see the Sea of Dalerueth rolling against the shore. He had taken a ride, while he was at Arilinn, along the banks of the Valeron, and knew that if he been allowed to ride west along it, it would have ended at the sea. There had been a moment when he had wished he could do just that, ride toward the set-ting sun until he reached the river's terminus. Foolish, of course.

It made him rather angry that he had spent so much of his life cooped up in Comyn Castle, and was so very ignorant, but after a moment he shook the feeling off. It was not worth bothering about. He was free now, and since he might never again have the opportunity to sleep in an inn, or ride along the North Road with a band of Renunciates in search of Terranan spies, he might as well enjoy it while he could. He turned his attention back to his uncle.

They discovered a rare element they needed for weapons development about ten years ago, and started mining it from the oceanbed. Now there are no more delfins, Nico, because the sea has been poisoned, and they think in five years, most of the rest of the life in those waters will be dead, too. Worse, the cancer rate on Thetis has increased greatly, and people are dying for no more reason than that Interworld Mining was too greedy to take measures to avoid destroying the ecology. Once the plankton stop using up the carbon dioxide, the air will become unbreathable on Thetis, and in a short time the place will become uninhabitable.

Nico was puzzled over several of the terms his uncle used, but he fastened on just one. *What's plankton? Mother never mentioned that.*

Nico sensed Herm's gentle amusement at this question, but did not feel stupid. He felt safe with his newest uncle, and found his mild teasing to be very pleasant. He only wished he could be as comfortable with everyone as he was with Hermes Aldaran.

They are very small organisms, so small you can only see them with an optical device. Some of them are plantlike, and others are really tiny animals, but on a world without great forests of trees, like Darkover, these provide breathable air. We've had three bills in the Senate in the last three years to provide money to clean up Interworld's mess on Thetis, and two of them have been defeated as being too costly. And the last one was in committee when the legislature was dissolved, so it is dead now as well. Basically, the Federa-tion has decided that it is not worth throwing good money away on a losing proposition, particularly when Thetis is considered an unimportant world.

It isn't unimportant to the people who live there!

No, of course it isn't. The problem is that there are a great many people who think that money is more important than anything, and that human beings are a disposable resource.

It sounds like they think that planets are disposable, too, Uncle.

"My fingers are starting to turn into prunes," Herm said aloud. "Are you clean enough now?"

"Yes, I am. I just wish I had some cleaner clothes."

"Then why don't we go out and see if there is a stall in the market and get you some new ones." *We can do a bit of snooping at the same time.*

"Good. I like that idea." Nico scrambled out of the tub, dripping, and stood on the planked floor, watching the droplets slip off his skin. Then he wrapped himself in a large towel and dried off. He redressed, trying not to feel too disgusted by the state of his garments. If he had known when he left that he was going to be away overnight, he would have brought a fresh shirt, at least.

"How's your back feeling, Uncle Ian?"

"Much better, thank you. I believe I will forgo Danila's ministrations for the present. She looks strong enough to snap me in half."

Nico chuckled, for indeed the large Renunciate was rather intimidating. She did not look like any healer Domenic had ever met before. Herm got his clothes back on, and they went downstairs again. It was much quieter now that the muleteers had left to continue their journey.

They stepped out into the courtyard of the inn into watery sunlight. There were thin clouds overhead, and heavier ones mounded toward the western horizon. It would rain before the next morning, but he was not weatherwise enough to guess how soon. Nico just hoped it would not prevent the Travelers from performing. He hadn't gotten to see much the previous evening, and he was looking forward to more.

Herm asked a groom about the local marketplace, and got directions. They walked away from the Crowing Cock in companionable silence, both of them relaxed from their baths and full bellies. After getting slightly lost in one of the winding streets of the town, they finally found their way to an open square, bustling with commerce. There was a glass blower near the entrance, and Nico stopped for a few minutes to watch the work. The heat from the open air oven was tremendous, and it felt good against the growing chill of the day.

They found a clothing stall, and purchased undergarments, a cheap shirt, two woolen tunics, a pair of trews for Domenic, and some things for Herm as well. It was rather exciting to him, since he had never been allowed to explore the marketplaces in Thendara, and he was disappointed when Herm said it was time to go back to the inn.

But when they arrived at the inn, the yard was blocked by the colorful wains of the Travelers, and he forgot his disappointment in having to leave the market. He saw the man called Vancof get down from the seat of the puppet wagon, and stepped quickly into Herm's shadow, to avoid being seen. Then the red-haired girl climbed down from the back of the wagon and stretched luxuriously. He hoped she would not notice him, or ask any questions if she did, for the few glimpses he had gotten of her mind told him she was quick and a bit headstrong.

The driver looked pale and pinched, and he shuffled away from the wagon, heading toward the inn. He probably wanted some beer, Nico thought, although after all the drinking he had done the previous night, the boy felt he oughtn't. The plump woman who had been arguing with him during the morning came out of the wagon and shouted at him. "You lazy good-for-nothing! Damn you for a sot!" She made a fist and shook it at him.

Vancof ignored her and vanished into the doorway of the inn. The woman looked unhappy. "Now, how am I going to manage those animals without him?" She looked around rather helplessly, since all the rest of the Travelers were busy with their own wagons and teams.

Herm took this in with a swift glance, and walked over to the angry woman. "I'm not unhandy with a mule, *mestra*. Perhaps I could be of assistance."

To Nico's surprise, she laughed, making her face transform from miserable and angry to quite pleasant. She must have been very pretty when she was younger, he decided. "You don't know what you are thinking of," she told Herm. "Those mules are the meanest animals on Darkover, not counting a hungry catamount. Only my driver can manage them, and he gets bitten six times out of seven." *He's been nothing but trouble since he joined us, that Dirck, and I wish we had someone else. Even if he did come from Istvan's troup—they were probably glad to be rid of him.*

"Well, let me give it a try. If I get bitten, then it is my own fault for not listening to you."

"No one listens to me," the woman moaned, shaking her head and setting her grizzled braids in motion. "Not my flighty niece, or anyone. I am only a woman, and almost alone in the world, except for the girl, who is more trouble than she is worth, even though she is a very good puppeteer. If only she were as good a girl as she is a string-twiddler."

"She's very young," Herm said sympathetically. Nico watched the man, and would have sworn that charm was oozing out of his freshly-bathed pores. "She will grow out of it."

"Not soon enough for me. Well, I am Loret, and I will take you up on your offer, even if I think you are crazy to make it." She was clearly persuaded by Herm's pleasantries, and Nico wondered if she was flirting with his uncle.

"Ian MacAnndra at your service, *Mestra* Loret." He walked away toward the animals, who were indeed an evil-looking pair of underfed mules. They snorted and brayed, and one snapped its large teeth when Herm's hand reached for the traces. The man deftly avoided the attack, and said something in a low voice. The mules pricked their ears, stamped their hooves, and shifted from side to side uneasily. Their eyes rolled mistrustfully, but they offered no further resistence, and in a few minutes Herm had successfully removed them from the long bars of wood on each side, and led them away toward the stables.

"Well, I never!" Loret looked amazed. Then she turned on the girl, who had been standing quietly, watching all of this. "Are you planning to grow roots and flowers there, Illona? Get inside and work on the costumes. It will be dark soon, and you won't be able to see well enough to sew."

"Oh, Auntie! I've been cooped up for hours!"

"No sauce, girly! You do as you are told, or there will be no supper for you."

Illona did not appear in the least frightened by this threat, and from the well-upholstered appearance of her aunt, it was probably an empty one. She just stuck out her tongue, as she had the first time Nico had seen her, and shrugged. "The dolls are fine," she muttered sulkily.

"Nonsense! The ruffle on Cassilda's costume needs mending."

"I hate sewing!"

"We all have to earn our keep. Now do as you are told."

Illona looked as if she might refuse for just a moment. Then she gave a large, dramatic sigh and started to go back to the wagon. She glanced at Nico as she went past, and her eyes widened. "Don't I know you?"

Domenic shook his head. "Not unless you saw me last night." She had only seen him in the shadows of a doorway, and his hair had been pulled back, not hanging loose beside his face as it was now, but he had the feeling that very little escaped her sharp eyes. "I watched some of the performance while I was waiting for my uncle."

"Oh. That must be it. You look very familiar."

"Maybe I just have a common face."

She giggled softly. "Hardly that." *I know I didn't see him last night, but where? Oh, well, I am probably imagining things again. Still, there is something about him.* "I'm Illona Rider."

"Tomas MacAnndra."

"I have to go sit in the wagon and sew," she complained.

"And you hate sewing. Are you good at it?"

"Yes, very skilled. That's why I have to do it. Aunty doesn't understand that just because you are good at something doesn't mean you enjoy it."

"Yes, that's true." He was struck by her remark, because it had never occurred to him before that having the ability to do something might be a burden instead of a gift. Then he remembered a few things his father had said about the powers that Varzil's matrix had presented him with, and decided she was probably more right than she guessed. Domenic wanted to continue talking to her, but felt hopelessly tongue-tied, at a loss for anything to say. "I never heard of any Riders before."

"There are a lot of Riders in the Travelers, Tomas—hundreds. And it is not really my name, because I don't know what that is. I mean, I am an orphan, and I was adopted by Aunt Loret when I was a very little girl." She paused, thinking about herself, wondering as she had many times who her parents were. "And she isn't bad, actually, just bossy."

Herm was returning from the stables, striding confidently across the courtyard, looking amused. Nico watched his uncle, and shifted from foot to foot, eager to continue the conversation but unsure what to say next. "It must be very exciting to travel around and perform."

"Not really, Tomas. It is very boring after a while. The performances are fun, but even they get stale. And Mathias keeps writing these new pieces, and I have to memorize them—odd sort of things, they are."

"Are there scripts, then? I sort of had the idea that you made things up as you went along, getting the audience involved." There, that was better, and he did not sound quite so idiotic.

"That's how it used to be." She looked troubled for a moment. "But since Mathias joined the troupe, he has been doing—"

"Illona!" It was an angry yell.

"Yes, Auntie! I'd better go, before she gives herself a fit. Come out and watch the show tonight."

"Oh, yes, if my uncle says I can."

"He will—he seems very nice." She gave Nico a ravishing smile and scrambled up the folding stairs at the back of the wagon, her curiosity about him fading as she thought about thread and needles and lengths of fabric.

Herm rejoined Domenic and said, "What was that all about?"

"Oh, we were just talking, Uncle." *She almost recognized me, but I managed to make her think she didn't. And I am sure she has no business with these Travelers.*

What do you mean?

Well, she told me she was an orphan, and that the woman adopted her when she was very young. But I can sense her laran. *It is completely untrained, but pretty strong even without any discipline. It makes me wonder how many other telepaths are roaming around, getting into trouble because they do not know how to manage their gifts.*

I bow to your greater knowledge.

Father encountered a woman, years ago, who was a wild telepath, and she nearly killed him. He won't talk about it much, but I have heard him remembering it a few times, and it was very scary. I asked Aunt Liriel about it, and she said that this woman was a kind of sorceress, that she could make your mind go all fuzzy and helpless, but that she could only do it with a small number of people. But it made Father aware that there were probably more telepaths on Darkover than anyone thought before. And he and Great-Uncle Regis made an effort to find them, but it was not very successful.

Why not?

Grandfather Lew says it is because the men of the Domains have been altogether too generous with their favors over the years, and they have fathered children they never knew about. And after a few generations, laran *has spread out in the general population more and more. And if, say, a mother died in childbearing, and hadn't told anyone that the father was the* nedestro *of some Domain, then no one would know until the child was grown and had thresh-old sickness. And then, if the sickness did not kill him or her, which is possible, since there is no way to predict the severity of it, then they would grow up and make more children, and pass it on. It is all very simple in theory, but as the generations pass, it becomes more and more complicated.*

Why was the effort to locate these people not successful?

I'm not sure, but I think that perhaps there are not enough leroni *to manage the job. What Grandfather Lew says is that in the past, there were so few people with gifts that no one ever made a good plan for it becoming part of the greater population. And Mother thinks that we Darkovens still tend to think that only those of the Domains have gifts worth bothering about, so that ordinary people like, for instance, the innkeeper, never really think about it. So, if they have a small gift, they either ignore it, or turn to being streetcorner seers.*

But wouldn't such a person go to a Tower?

They would, if they had any sense, or if they had a substantial Gift. And in the past, of course they would. But what if someone has just a little bit of laran, *enough to start a fire, perhaps, or to be good with animals? Lew thinks that there are a lot of lesser powers, that are just so minor that we have never paid attention to them, because we were so focused on the Gifts of the Domains. He said something about recessive genes, which I don't understand. And if two common folk, with minor powers, got married, then their children might be more powerful. He says that generations of inbreeding have made us complacent.*

I see that I will have to have a long talk with Lew when we get this thing settled.

Uncle, is there a back way out of the inn?

I don't know, but there probably is a way through the kitchens. Why?

Let's go see if Vancof is really drinking beer in the common room! I think he is up to something else.

Why do you think that?

It is just a feeling I have.

As they started for the entrance to the inn, there was the sound of hoofbeats on the cobbles of the yard. Nico glanced over his shoulder, and saw a wide-shouldered man awkwardly astride a sweating animal. He had a scowl on his broad face, and he dismounted gracelessly, swearing a little. A groom raced out and took the horse, gave the man a glare, and began to lead it away.

"Uncle, that man we saw talking to the driver this morning just rode in."

Herm grinned without the slightest humor. "Yes, so he did. The pot is really starting to boil. Come on—don't stare! Let's get inside before we attract attention." *What's on his mind, I wonder?*

Nothing much, Uncle, except that he doesn't ride well and is afraid of horses, that his bladder is ready to explode, and he wonders where the hell Vancof is.

All that?

Yes. And he is worried and puzzled, too—he doesn't understand why he was ordered to ride after Vancof. Something changed since this morning.

Well, he is going into the building, so we will just wander in and keep an eye on him, won't we?

15

Marguerida stood outside the closed door of the room which had been given to Katherine Aldaran for a studio, and took a deep breath. She had gone to the suite to find the other woman, and the maid told her that *Domna* Aldaran had left right after breakfast, saying that she needed to start working. Lucky Katherine. Marguerida would have loved to be in her own office, although working on her opera was impossible now. A chill swept over her—would she ever be able to complete it, now that Regis was dead? She hadn't written the work for him, but for herself, but she had been so looking forward to seeing him hear it for the first time. The pages were still on her desk, inkstained and ruined. It hurt to think about it.

The strain of the past few days weighed on her body, giving her aches that Marguerida knew were a combination of exhaustion and sorrow. Right now she did not want to see Katherine, or anyone else for that matter. She wanted a nice quiet cave and utter stillness. Marguerida grinned at herself. She was worried about Domenic, and Kate was probably worried about Herm, so she had a duty to try to ease Katherine's fears. The problem was that she was sick and tired of duties, not to mention fractious personalities.

When Mikhail told her what her son had done, she had been furious with both of them. How dare her husband make a decision concerning Nico without consulting her! And sending Herm to join him? What good was that? It was only when she had thought of sending Rafaella n'ha Liriel and some of her sister Renunciates to follow them that her fears had lessened. And then Mik had told her that Lew suspected that Gareth Elhalyn might be up to some mischief where Nico was concerned, and her hard-won calm had gone up in smoke. She could not believe it for a second, and then she grasped the implications, and remembered how young Gareth was behaving with Javanne. As if I don't have enough to worry about, she thought, but I have to look at a fourteen-year-old boy as a potential enemy of my child.

Marguerida's only comfort thus far was that the Aldaran Gift had not manifested, as it often did concerning those dearest to her. It was a feeble and undependable lack of information, however, and she wished she was free to pursue her eldest child along the North Road, and shake him until his teeth rattled. Right at that moment, she would have welcomed a vision, so long as it was rosy. Unlikely. The Aldaran Gift never seemed to show itself with good futures, only ambiguous and frightening ones.

She lifted her hand to knock, then lowered it. Marguerida was not ready to see Kate just yet. She wanted to be more serene before she encountered the other woman. If only she had not bumped into Javanne Hastur, on her way to the studio, and had an exchange of discourtesies that had left her trembling with rage and biting back cruel words. Her mother-in-law had demanded to know where Nico was. It would have been amusing, under any other circumstances, since she usually avoided the boy as much as possible. Mikhail had been adamant that his mother must not know about Domenic's adventure, and Marguerida agreed.

Lady Javanne always managed to make her angry, but now she just felt slightly nauseated. She knew her mother-in-law was working against Mikhail, conniving with Francisco Ridenow to overset the agreement that had been reached years before. Javanne would do almost anything short of murder to unseat her youngest son from his position. And Francisco might even go that far, if he thought he could get away with it.

So much had fallen on her shoulders. It seemed unfair, and Marguerida banished that thought sternly. She was overseeing the arrangements for the public funeral, which would take place after the Council meeting. With all the servants in Comyn Castle, this should have been rather easy, but Regis' death had been a shock, and the servants were less useful than they might have been. Everyone from the *coridom* to the head cook seemed to need her direction, until she thought that just one more question would drive her mad. But dealing with mourning servants was simple compared to her other duties.

She had to keep Javanne from driving poor Lady Linnea mad with her attentions. Marguerida had to reassure Katherine that Herm was safe, without revealing anything about the actual nature of his mission. There were so many secrets she had to keep—Kate did not know that there was a Federation arrest warrant for her husband, and Mikhail wanted to keep it that way. The fewer people that knew about that, apparently, the better. And it was all for the good of Darkover! Men! Just at that moment she would have cheerfully consigned every male on the planet to Zandru's hells, even her beloved child, just to get a little peace and quiet, as long as she could have sent Javanne along with them.

Marguerida decided she couldn't put her present task off any longer. She knocked, and heard a voice answering. Marguerida opened the door and stepped into the room. It was a spacious chamber, with several windows facing to the north, and the wan sunlight of autumn spilling onto the stone floor. An easel, sent over the previous day from the Painters Guild, was set up near the windows, with a whitened board on it, ready to be painted. There was a cracked vase with brushes sticking out of it sitting on a small table, tubes of paint laid out on a wooden palette on another, and the unfamiliar scent of turpentine mingled with the more pleasant one of woodsmoke from the small fireplace burning in one wall.

Katherine Aldaran looked at her, then started to stand up from the chair where she had been sketching on a tablet. She was wearing a shabby brown tunic, a divided skirt of dark green, and an apron. Her long fingers were smeared with charcoal, and there was a dark, sooty mark on her high forehead, where she had brushed her black hair back.

"Oh, hello. Have you come to discover what I am doing and make me stop?" Katherine's question was both playful and a bit hostile. There were dark circles under her eyes, evidence of a poor night's sleep, and she looked as if she were afraid to hear what might be said.

Marguerida forced herself to laugh at this, and found that she felt better for it. "No, I have not! I would not have intruded at all, since I know how annoying it is when one of the children comes in while I am trying to compose. But I thought you might be worried about Herm, and came to tell you that, as of an hour ago, he was well."

"The devil take Hermes-Gabriel Aldaran! He is probably having the time of his life, and not thinking of me at all." The voice was sullen, and the words lacked conviction.

"Katherine, I doubt that very much. Well, I suppose he probably is glad to be out and about, since he struck me as the kind of man who likes to do unusual things, but I am sure he is thinking of you." Marguerida was not really certain of this, but it was a tactful thing to say.

"Only because I threatened to leave him last night, and I would, only I know that I cannot. He would not tell me anything, except that he was going away for a few days, and I could have strangled him, I was so furious." There was no tone of complaint in her voice now, just a righteous indignation which Marguerida thought was perfectly appropriate. This was not a woman given to self-pity.

"I know all this is hard for you. It was hard for me when I first came to Darkover as an adult."

"But you are a telepath, have this *laran*-stuff. I don't, and I never will."

"That is true, but it does not make me a different person than I was when I returned to Darkover. In fact, it nearly killed me."

"Now, that sounds like the start of a story." Her voice eased, as if she was glad to think about something other than herself, and she looked at Marguerida with guarded but not unfriendly eyes. "I forgot that you have not lived all your life here, but were at University."

The room was largely unfurnished but there was a stool standing in one corner, and Marguerida pulled it out and sat down a few feet away from Katherine. The other woman picked up the tablet again, settling it over her lap, and Marguerida made a mental note to get a proper work-table moved in as soon as possible. One more thing to remember—she was sure her brain was going to melt if she asked it to do much more.

Katherine had tucked the stick of charcoal into her hair, so it stuck out of the bun at the back of her head, and now she plucked it out, turned to a fresh page, and studied Marguerida. She started to sketch again, not looking at the paper at all, but moving her hand across it while appearing to give Marguerida her complete attention. She wondered how Katherine did it, and got the mental impression that the woman's eyes gave directions to her hand without any other part of her mind being engaged.

Marguerida forced herself to ignore her fascination with the movement of the fine hand across the paper, and marshaled her thoughts. "Yes, it is. I was born on Darkover, but I left when I was a little girl, and my father and stepmother deliberately concealed my history from me—for reasons that seemed logical to them at the time, but which caused me a great deal of trouble later." She sighed and then smiled at some of the memories. "The Old Man says he regrets it now, but that at the time it was all he could think of to do. Some things had happened when I was a child that were very bad, and one of them was that I had been overshadowed by a long dead ancestor of mine, which did some things to my mind I still have the occasional nightmare about."

"Overshadowed by a dead . . . and I thought the stories we had on Renney were fantastic! What is that—overshadowing?"

"Umm. It is hard to describe. This ancestor, Ashara Alton, lived and died over seven hundred years ago. She was an incredibly powerful *leronis,* and she managed not to die entirely when her body failed her. Instead, she left the imprint of her personality in a matrix array in the Old Tower of Comyn Castle. You can still see what remains of it—blackened and broken." Marguerida shuddered a little, remembering the sight of the ruined structure when she rode into Thendara just before Midsummer sixteen years before. She had gone into the overworld, torn a great jewel from a building that existed only on that plane, and in the process, she had destroyed the link that kept Ashara Alton tied to present-day Darkover. In some manner that no one could explain, she had absorbed the energy of that jewel onto her left hand, and brought across the boundaries between the worlds a matrix that was part of both. She glanced down at her mitted hand, then looked up again.

"Over the centuries, she . . . well, manifested is a reasonable word for it. She would latch onto the energy patterns of someone, and use them to fulfill her will. And she had a very, very strong will," she finished dryly, reflecting that she had at last reached the point in her life when she could speak of these events without starting to tremble. Marguerida did not feel the need to add that Ashara had a personal grudge against her, that she had foreseen the existence of one Marguerida Alton and had been determined to destroy her. Kate could only take so much information, and besides, she didn't need to know.

Katherine paused in her sketching and frowned. "Does that happen very often? I mean, do a lot of your people go around and muck in the minds of . . . ?"

"No, it is rare, and considered extremely unethical. What Ashara managed to do to me, when I was still a child and too young to resist her, was reconfigure certain of my brain patterns, so that I did not go into the usual threshhold sickness at puberty. I almost did not go into puberty at all! I came back to Darkover a twenty-eight-year-old virgin, because her interference affected my sexuality." Marguerida gave a grin. "I have been trying to catch up for years now."

"That must make Mikhail a very happy man." There was no bite in the words, and Katherine sounded amused.

"A very tired one occasionally," Marguerida agreed. "But when I got here, I had no idea of any of this, and I thought I was losing my mind more than anything else. Then I did become sick, and let me tell you, adult-onset threshhold illness is not a pleasant experience. I nearly died, and I would have except that I was helped by several people, including Mikhail, and miraculously, I survived."

"I can see that. And your son Domenic said you and Mikhail went into the distant past, too—which I would have found utterly incredible two weeks ago. I keep having the dark suspicion that all of you are playing some trick on me, for reasons I cannot figure out."

Now why would we do such a cruel thing?

Katherine jumped and the charcoal slipped from her fingers and skittered away across the floor.

"What! How did you . . . what did you just do?"

"Damn! Forgive me, Katherine! I am very tired, and my control seems to be . . ."

"What did you do!" Oddly, there was no fear in the question, just a single-minded rage.

"I possess the Alton Gift, which is the ability to force rapport with another mind, even the mind of a nontelepath. But I did not intend to . . ." Marguerida was ashamed of herself, and very cross as well. She should never have come to see Katherine so soon after encountering Javanne. She was upset, more than she wanted to acknowledge, and that made her careless.

Katherine bent down and recovered the charcoal. "Don't do it again!" Her cheeks were pale, and she was breathing shallowly.

"No, I won't—unless necessity forces me to." One of the things she had learned over the years was never to make a promise that she could not be sure she could keep. "Still, I am curious. Why would you imagine that we would make up stories just to distress you?"

"Herm never told me much about Darkover, and certainly not about this whole *laran* business, Marguerida," Katherine began, drawing her brows together and looking troubled. "He says he could not have, and this is almost true, because in the Federation now, there are eyes and ears everywhere. They spy on everyone, and everyone is assumed to be up to no good! He dragged me out of bed in the middle of the night, told me to pack, and the next thing I knew, we were on a Big Ship." She drew a shaking breath.

"That was difficult, but Herm has always been rather secretive, and I just assumed that was his character. Now I discover he really has a secret—one that makes me . . . useless!"

"Useless?"

"Well—what do you call it . . . head-blind? Goddess, what a filthy term!"

"I think you should speak to Ida Davidson."

"Who?"

Marguerida shifted on the stool. It was hard and uncomfortable, and she added to her list of things to remember to have some nice chairs brought in soon. "The small elderly woman you have seen with me the past two evenings."

"Isn't she your nanny or something? There are so many people, and I haven't really been introduced to most of them—which I do understand, actually. I could have gone a whole lifetime without meeting Javanne Hastur," she finished rather bitterly.

"Quite," Marguerida answered dryly. "No, Ida is not a nanny or a servant. She is the widow of my mentor, Ivor, who died shortly after he and I came to Darkover. She is a musician, a fine one, and when she came to Darkover to reclaim her husband's body, she remained here, because things in the Federation were already becoming difficult. She has no *laran,* and she has felt many of the same emotions I know you must be going through. But she has lived here for fifteen years, and I think she can reassure you much more than anything I can say." *And it will take some of the pressure off me. I should have thought of it sooner—if I were not so damn tired!*

"Doesn't she mind being . . . how can she not feel like cripple?"

"Ask her."

"You are probably right—I am being overly anxious." Katherine swallowed hard. "I don't like things being out of my control," she admitted gruffly.

"Who does?"

"There is that, isn't there? I keep trying to keep my thoughts very . . . small."

Marguerida shook her head. "I am sorry to tell you this, Katherine, but you are not doing a very good job of it. And that is because you are afraid—fear is like mental yelling."

"So I should just relax and pretend that everything is wonderful!"

"I did not say that, and I wouldn't. What I want you to do is get enough information to ease your fears of being . . . examined."

She shivered all over for a second. "That is exactly it! And Herm wants me to be tested—he thinks I might have some latent paranormal talents or something—when Terése . . . I can't stand this! I don't want my little girl to hear my thoughts!"

"But, Katherine, she never would if she were trained properly. And if you really object to being checked out, then no one will force you. Do you know, I think you are actually more afraid of discovering you might have some sort of ability than of being . . . otherwise." Marguerida was loath to use the term head-blind just then.

"Maybe," Katherine answered reluctantly. "Herm pointed out how often my portraits have elements in them that I have always thought were from my imagination, but which have turned out to be . . . significant to my subjects. I had never considered that, and, truthfully, I was disgusted by the idea. My Nana did not raise me to be a snoop!"

"I am sure she didn't." Marguerida paused, carefully considering her next words. "But does it occur to you that you might be overreacting somewhat because you are afraid you have been inadvertently . . . snooping on your sitters. I mean, if you thought all your life that you were an honest person, and then one day you found yourself in a shop putting a trinket into your purse, you would be horrified, wouldn't you?"

"Absolutely. You know, Marguerida, you are not doing a very good job of reassuring me right now."

"Well, perhaps you don't need reassurance as much as you need forthrightness. Tell me, do you know what empathy is?"

"Of course—it is the ability to share the emotions of others."

"That is one definition, and valid as far as it goes. But here, on Dark-over, it is one of the Gifts, that of the Ridenow Domain, and it is much more than the intellectual capacity to agree with the feelings of another."

"I don't follow you."

"There is a great distinction between 'I know how you feel' and 'I feel how you feel,' wouldn't you agree?"

Katherine's eyes widened. "Yes, but . . . I see now. So that's it!"

"What?"

The other woman rubbed her cheek, leaving streaks of charcoal along the skin. "When I met Herm, the first thing I noticed about him was that he did not make me feel tired, the way many people do. He was so *restful*," she went on, shaking her head. "And after we married, it did not change. He made no demands on my emotions, but was just this good man. After a while I realized that he kept a tight rein on his feelings, that he was remote and secretive, but it did not matter because I loved him. He was my safe haven."

"And it never occurred to you that you might have chosen him be-cause he *was* remote and distant? That you had some natural empathy, which is normal, but that you had an extra helping of it, shall we say, and that a husband who kept his feelings to himself was a real blessing?"

"No, not when you put it that way. Do you mean I don't really love him?"

"Of course not! The way the two of you look at each other has such love in it that no one could imagine you do not adore one another. But we all pick partners, or try to, who suit us. Mikhail and I . . . well, the first time we met we had this ridiculous argument, but I think both of us sensed that we were meant for each other. And we still fight, too."

"Really? Do you know, Herm and I rarely had any disagreements until we came to Darkover. Oh, there were a few times, and I lost my temper, but for the most part, it has been very nice."

Marguerida laughed again. "Then you are very blessed."

"Am I? I never thought about it like that. You have given me a great deal to consider, and I am not sure I am grateful, Marguerida."

"I didn't expect you to be, Katherine. But you still have not told me why you imagined that anyone would tell you tales that would frighten or amaze you." Marguerida wanted to move away from the subject of the

Aldaran marriage as quickly as possible. She felt uncomfortable, that she was meddling where she had no business.

"It is probably cultural. On Renney we have a body of folklore that is hardly believable, and I schooled myself to be a skeptic even before I left there. One of your ancestors managed to survive in . . . what did you call it . . . a matrix array, but one of mine supposedly could shape-change into a large cat! I always thought that that story was something to keep us children from being wicked, and I hated it."

Marguerida smiled. "As far as I know, we don't have any shape-changers on Darkover."

"That's good! I don't think I could have stood that. I feel a little better now, but it probably won't last. I keep rocketing back and forth, between fear and rage and back again. And even though everyone has assured me that I am safe, that my mind will not be . . . explored by strangers, I don't believe it entirely. I hate it. And, more, I hate it that Herm has been lying to me for years and years." She snapped the slender stick of charcoal between her fingers and threw the pieces onto the floor.

Marguerida waited to see if Katherine would do more, considering her own next move with a kind of calculation that shamed her just a little. "If I said that your fear and rage were entirely reasonable, would that help?"

"A little." The admission seemed reluctant, as if she were unwilling to let go of the emotions.

"I was furious when I discovered I had the Alton Gift, Katherine. And there were times when I would have traded it for a warm bed and a good meal, or almost anything, except that it cannot be transferred or given away. Inherited, yes. Domenic has it, and Yllana, too."

"And Roderick?" Katherine was very curious, in spite of her fears.

"Rory does not have the Alton Gift, but seems to have gotten a variant of the Aldaran one."

"Oh, *that!* Herm told me it was the ability to see into the future, but I still find it hard to believe. If he had been able to really peer into tomorrow, he would have known we were going to come to Darkover, and at least have told me about it years ago. Wouldn't he?"

Marguerida shook her head. "It doesn't function like that. Yes, the Aldaran Gift is that of foresight, but it is rarely nice and clear. At least my own experience of it has never been very precise—I get a burst of information, all sort of jumbled, and then I have to try and figure out what it means. That often has turned out to be something other than I thought at the time. And what Rory has is kind of a backward version."

"Backward? You mean he can see the past?"

"Sort of. It is more than just psychometry, although that is part of it."

"Psychometry—now that one I have heard of. That's where someone can touch an object and tell how old it is, or something. It always sounded pretty far-fetched to me. But Rory's isn't exactly like that?"

"No, it isn't. He can pick up something and not only tell you how old it is, but a great deal about the history of the person who used the thing. There was a time when I thought it would be a wonderful skill for an archaeologist, and even considered sending Roderick off Darkover to study. But now I am glad I changed my mind, because I realize that such a talent could cause more trouble than it is worth, in places other than here."

Katherine looked thoughtful for a moment. "I think it would likely get him killed, if he were not careful. And from the little Amaury has told me, your son Rory is not a careful boy."

"No, that's true enough." Marguerida smiled and ran the fingers of her ungloved hand through her hair. "I have always been grateful that Domenic had a cautious disposition, and was not so hasty as Roderick." *I never should have told Nico he could never surprise me!* "He would make the sort of ruler that causes ministers to go early to their graves."

"But Domenic will succeed Mikhail? I mean, there is no question about that?"

"Yes, he will, always assuming he lives long enough." *Bite your tongue! Nothing is going to happen to Nico, and you are borrowing trouble again!* "Fortunately, my mother-in-law is almost alone in her insistance that Nico is not a legitimate heir to my husband."

"But why? I have to say, Marguerida, that the little I have learned about Darkovan politics already is enough to drive me slightly mad, if I were not already well down that path on my own."

"Nonsense! You are perfectly sane. You have been plunked down in a situation for which you were totally unprepared, and which probably violates some of your ideas about the nature of reality. I know that mine were seriously unsettled during my first months on Darkover. My father kept so much from me, my history and my potential as a telepath, so I can make an educated guess as to how you feel." She sighed and then smiled a little. "I have almost forgiven him now. He was well-intentioned, but totally wrong. Not that I would have believed him, mind you, if he had sat me down and said, 'Marja, you may discover that you can read minds, and you must not be afraid,' or something equally logical. The problem is that human beings are not really logical."

Katherine seemed rather puzzled by this for a moment. "We aren't?"

Marguerida smiled and shook her head. "While I was at University, and afterward, I behaved in what seemed to me to be a logical manner. But I now realize that what I did was do things irrationally, and then after I would arrange the events in my mind so they seemed to follow some sort of reasonable path. That is not logic—it is wishful thinking, and involves rewriting one's own history as one goes along. Life is not logical—it just goes along happening, and the best anyone can do is try to deal with the present as well as they can."

"Very wise, and very difficult," Katherine replied thoughtfully.

"Yes, it is. And especially for someone as intelligent and strong-minded as I believe you are. Herm spoke of you as Kate during dinner, and I think I can make an educated guess. . . ."

"As opposed to picking my brains, you mean?" Katherine's face underwent a transformation, going from serious to reflective to amused in only a second. "We met over a portrait I was doing, but the first thing we did together was attend a performance of *The Taming Of The Shrew*. A very poor production, but after that I was his Kate. But I never realized until a few days ago how like Petruchio Herm actually is! Not a fortune hunter, of course, since I haven't one. I mean, I have watched him connive for ten years now, and I always thought it was charming, the way he could manipulate his fellow Senators. Now I discover he was gulling me, too, deceiving me just like he did those men and women, and it isn't the least bit charming! I want to kick him in the shins!"

"Katherine, people deceive one another all the time, for much less important reasons than the safety of a planet. If a week goes by that Mikhail does not keep something from me that I believe I should be informed of, it is a miracle." *Right now, he is closeted with my father and Danilo Syrtis-Ardais and Dani Hastur and who knows what other people, plotting and scheming, and when he tells me what he wishes to, I will have to pretend to be delighted.*

"But, you could . . ."

"Yes, I could listen in—but I wasn't raised to be a snoop either! And

I have to tread carefully, Katherine, because there are many who mistrust me, who think I have too much influence as it is, over my husband and my father." She looked down at her hands again. "I was granted a peculiar power, and Mikhail was given another—so between the two of us we can do remarkable deeds. There are quite a number of people who refuse to believe that we would never use what we have to force our wills on others—my mother-in-law among them. I think this is mostly because if she had the capacity, she would use it, and she cannot imagine that we would not." She sighed softly.

"But you haven't? It must be very hard to resist the temptation, Marguerida."

"No, not really. Oh, if I could turn Javanne into a toad, that might be pretty irresistible. Fortunately, *laran* doesn't function like that. It still follows all the rules of the universe."

"What do you mean by that?"

"You know—all that matter into energy stuff. With my particular *laran,* I can convert, with a great deal of effort, some matter into energy, or the other way around, and so can Mikhail. Hmm . . . I could, for instance, cause your tablet to burst into flame—well, in theory at least. I have never tried such a thing. But I can't turn my mother-in-law into something else."

"However much you might like to."

"Exactly. But everything in Darkover society comes down to keeping the various parties in a balance of powers. Otherwise we would tear the fabric of our culture to shreds. In the past, we have almost done just that, and the gifts that Mikhail and I possess are all too similar to things that come from our history for anyone's complete comfort. So I still have to act like a proper Darkovan female, and defer to the menfolk! All right— pretend to defer!" Marguerida felt her face redden with fury. She had to get a grip on herself before she said more. "I have learned to trust Mikhail to manage his part of the job, and to spend my energies doing mine. It is the hardest thing I have ever done in my life."

"Trust?"

"Do you trust Herm?"

"I did, until a week ago."

"No, Katherine, that is not what I mean. Do you think that your husband is a capable man, who can make decisions well?"

"Yes, he is that. Actually, he is so sharp it's a wonder he doesn't cut himself, as we say on Renney. And he hasn't done things in the past to make me worry. No mistresses or fiddling with the account books. But he isn't the same man I married any longer."

"Yes, he is. Herm is exactly the man you married, only now you are aware of a portion of him that you didn't imagine existed before. He is still a bit of a rascal, a charming fellow who cannot help being manipulative. No mistresses? He must love you very much."

"As far as I know, he has been a paragon of faithfulness. Oh, I've seen him flirt occasionally, but it was usually with Senators from other planets, whom he wanted to vote a certain way." She paused for a moment. "My Nana said he was like a cattle trader, always looking for a good purchase, feeling up the legs and checking the teeth."

"But did she think he was an honest trader?"

"Umm, not entirely. She said he had a secret, and that it was probably a wife and six children here. I think I would have been relieved if that had turned out to be the case. Another wife I could deal with. The six children would have been a bit of trouble, I suppose." She chuckled softly over the idea. "I could have been a wicked stepmother, after I poisoned the other wife, and drove the children into exile or something."

"Well, to be really truthful, Herm might indeed have some *nedestro* offspring up in the Hellers, although I think that Robert Aldaran or Gisela would probably have mentioned it to me if they knew of any. He was in his twenties when he left here, and likely he was not celibate. But it seems to me that you already knew he was concealing something from you, at some deep and almost instinctive level."

"*Nedestro.* I know the word, but I never really thought about the ramifications of it. Hmm . . . I guess I did know something was going on. Oh, Marguerida, I know I am being difficult. And maybe after a few years I will adjust to Darkover. But right now, I just want to scream with frustration."

"Go ahead. The walls of Comyn Castle have heard things over the centuries that would curl your hair. And do not hesitate to come to me when you are troubled, please. I want to help you."

"Thank you. I'll try. But it isn't easy for me, because I am not a confiding sort of woman. Actually, except for my Nana, I haven't ever found the company of my sex very interesting, and I don't make friends easily. I love my husband and my children, but truthfully, I am more comfortable with my pigments and brushes than with most other people.

Hmm . . . if what you suggested a few minutes ago is real, and I am extra empathetic, it would explain a great deal."

Katherine looked at Marguerida for a moment after she stopped speaking, and realized that in time she might indeed become friends with her. It was a somewhat surprising realization, and it was followed by another—that her troubled sister-in-law had become another. Funny—two nights before Gisela would have been the last person she could imagine liking, but after their talk in the carriage, everything had changed. And now Herm was away on some mysterious errand, leaving her alone among strangers. That most of them were relatives of some kind made the whole thing even more difficult. She had better just stop fretting and start learning how to cope with Darkover! Kate had her children to think of, didn't she?

"I feel the same way about music. And I will take your words as a hint to go away and let you get on with what you are doing. I won't press you any further." She wanted to ask questions about Amedi Korniel, but decided that it would keep for the present. "Well, I do have a favor to ask you—two, really."

"What is it?"

"My son Roderick shows a certain talent for drawing—at least when he gets bored and can't think of any mischief to get into, he takes colored chalks and puts them on any wall he likes. They are rather pretty, even though I cannot allow them to remain. Could you bring yourself to tutor him a bit?"

"I would be happy to. And the other favor?"

"Do you think you might ask Gisela to sit for a portrait? I know you did not get off to a good start, but she is so unhappy, and I believe it would please her."

Katherine gave Marguerida a bemused look, with something secretive but not unpleasant in it. "She would make an excellent subject," was all the answer she gave, but her dark eyes glinted with interest.

"Fine. And now I will leave you to work. I will see you later in the day."

Marguerida was rather puzzled as she left Katherine's studio. But she was satisfied that she had eased some of Kate's fears, and let the matter go from her mind. She had not gone ten feet down the corridor before all her own concerns rushed back. Katherine had distracted her for a brief while, and she realized that she had gotten as much relief from the visit as she had given. She had to wait, to be patient. It was very hard to be a middle-aged woman with duties, when she really wanted to rush off and do something—anything! And then the grief returned, as if it had been waiting to capture her emotions once more. "Damn you for dying, Regis. Your timing was off for once," she muttered, and felt her eyes go blurry with fresh tears.

Katherine did not return to her sketching after Marguerida left, but sat and stared out the window, thinking about what had been said in a disordered sort of way. Her mind was tired and she knew that she could not make sense of anything right away, which irritated her greatly. Talk to Ida Davidson, Marguerida had said. It sounded simple and sensible, but Kate was not sure she could just walk up to a total stranger and voice her concerns. No, she would wait for a while and see what happened. But it was good to know that she was not the only inhabitant of Comyn Castle who was frustrated and angry.

For a time she considered the matter of empathy. That was a normal human trait, wasn't it? And yet on Darkover it seemed to be something more—one of these Gifts that people kept mentioning. She could endure being empathic, she supposed. Marguerida's explanation sounded plausible at least.

When another knock came at the door, she could not decide whether she was glad or annoyed at a further distraction. "Come in."

It was Gisela, looking a little shy and wary of her welcome. She was wearing a russet tunic and darker skirt, not dissimilar from the clothing she had brought Katherine the previous day. "Hello. Am I interrupting you terribly?"

"Not at all. I was just woolgathering." Had Marguerida told Gisela to come so quickly? Katherine was not ready to start a portrait yet—she would require something for the model to sit on, and there was only the stool—but she could make a few sketches.

"Good." Gisela looked her up and down. "Kate, why are you wearing a riding skirt?"

"Is that what this is?" Kate tugged at the folds of her lower garment. "I was looking for something comfortable, that wouldn't show the dirt. Is it improper?"

"No, not exactly, but it looks rather eccentric with an apron!" She gave a little giggle, then sobered. "I hardly slept last night."

"I am sorry about that."

"Don't be! I was thinking about what you said in the carriage and I was just too excited to close my eyes until nearly dawn. Are you well, Kate? You look like you did not get much more sleep than I did."

"Yes, I am fine." Katherine repressed a yearning to talk to Gisela about Herm. She liked her new sister-in-law, but she was not yet sure how trustworthy she was. "It is just taking me a while to get adjusted to Darkover, I think."

"You seem worried."

"Do I?"

"Still fussing about people poking into your mind?"

"Yes, a little, I suppose." With a slight start, Katherine realized she had managed to go for nearly half an hour without thinking about that problem at all. How unkind of Giz to remind her of it.

"Well, don't." She hesitated again, shuffling her feet back and forth under her long skirts. "Can I show you something?"

Katherine looked at her, and now she noticed that she could sense something of the mood of the other woman. It was very odd, and she felt very uncomfortable for a moment. But all that she could feel was excitement in Gisela, with none of the other darker emotions Kate now realized she had noticed on the previous day. How much, she wondered, of this sort of thing had she refused to acknowledge over the years? Maybe Marguerida was right. "Certainly, as long as it is not something horrid."

Gisela looked stricken and shook her head. "Kate, I swear to you that I will never do anything mean again! I want you to be my friend! I need you to be my friend!" Tears glistened in the vivid green eyes and she trembled.

Katherine set aside her sketchpad and stood up slowly, moved and just a little frightened by this outburst. Then she crossed the space separating them and put her arm around Gisela's shoulders. She could smell the faint scent of lavender in the cloth and some perfume as well. "There, there. Don't cry, dear. Marguerida just asked me to do your portrait," she added, frantically trying to think of some way to stem the wave of despair that was wracking her sister-in-law and grasping at the first thing that came to mind.

"Really? And did you tell her you already asked me to sit for you?"

"No, I didn't. She thought it would please you, and I didn't wish to . . ."

Gisela straightened against her. "That was very kind of her, wasn't it? After everything?"

"I think that Marguerida is probably a very kind person, Gisela, and genuinely wants everyone around her to be happy."

Gisela wiped her eyes with her handkerchief. "She hasn't had much luck with me, has she?" There was a rueful tone to her voice. "Do you know how much time I have wasted hating her?"

"No, and I really don't want to."

"Good—because it makes me very ashamed. And I don't like that at all." She sighed, shrugged her shoulders under Kate's light embrace, then made a comical face. "You see before you a reformed Aldaran."

Impulsively, Kate took Gisela's chin in her hand, looked intently into her face, and said, "Yes, I can see the virtue almost seeping from your pores."

To her delight, Gisela giggled. "There is not another person, even Rafael, I would let tease me like that, dearest sister. Somehow, from you, it does not hurt."

"I am glad of that. Now, you were going to show me something." Katherine released Gisela, finding that she was not entirely at ease with the intimacy of contact. *Is this why I paint portraits then, to be close but not too close?*

Gisela plunged her hand into her beltpouch and took out a small object. "It was in my jewelry box, and I remembered it when I was getting dressed this morning." She opened her hand. A little figure, about six inches in length, lay across her palm. The wood was dark with age, and the carving was crude, but it was powerful nonetheless. "It is the last thing I made before my nurse . . . made me stop."

Kate took the small figure and turned it over. She noticed how Gisela had used the grain of the wood to good advantage, only removing enough to suggest folds of cloth below, and a face above that was simple but moving. On the back of the carving, there was still some bark left, rough and dark. She could see the marks left by some crude instrument, not a carver's chisel but something less deft. One of the belt knives that everyone seemed to wear, Kate suspected, and not a very good tool for the job demanded of it.

"I don't think you need to worry much about being good, Giz. Any sculptor I know would have been pleased to make this."

"Thank you."

"Will you tell me something now?"

"Anything."

"Why did you come to me yesterday?"

"Oh, that."

"Yes, that."

"I . . . don't know, not really. I was ready to hate you, and after I saw you the first time, it got worse. And then, at dinner, when Danilo Syrtis-Ardais took me to task, because he took one look at you in your Terranan finery and knew exactly what had happened, I suddenly realized that I was behaving like a fool—that I didn't need to have you for an enemy." She shivered slightly. "It didn't cross my mind, when Rafael came back from the spaceport with all of you, that you could even want to be my friend, because I never imagined anyone would want that. I always wanted a sister, you know. But I had ruined things for myself with Marguerida, and here I was, starting off to mess everything up with you. So—I took a risk. I was scared to death, but I knew if I didn't at least try, I would regret it for the rest of my life."

"I am glad you did, Gisela. I have several sisters, but they are halfway across the galaxy, and I expect I will never see them again now. You were very brave."

"You said that yesterday, and I didn't believe you, but if you say it a few more times, maybe I will start to."

Katherine smiled and leaned over and planted a gentle kiss on Gisela's warm cheek. Then she stepped away. "Now . . . how do we get you some proper carving tools?"

16

The air in the little study was stale and filled with the smell of tense bodies. Lew Alton watched Mikhail, standing in front of the fireplace, fiddling with some small carved figures that stood along the mantle. The younger man looked more rested than he had the night before, despite the looming anxiety about Domenic. He smiled at his father-in-law, as if he understood Lew's concerns and was trying to reassure him. Donal stood a few paces away, alert and watchful. Then, aware of Lew's regard, he winked. It must be wonderful to be twenty-three, Lew thought, although his memories of himself at that age were so painful that he dreaded their recollection.

Mikhail turned and took his place behind Regis' scarred desk. He looked from face to face, studying each intently for a moment, as if measuring his advisors and weighing their strengths and weaknesses in his mind. Satisfied that his son-in-law was in as good a frame of mind as could be hoped for, Lew relaxed a little. Now they must decide how to proceed, and he had to find a way to keep himself in the background, to allow Mikhail to take the lead. Otherwise, he felt, Mikhail would not be confident in his own decisions, and he would need to be for the sake of all their futures.

Rafe Scott, formerly of Terran Intelligence, was sitting lazily in one chair, and Dani Hastur occupied another. Time had been kind to Scott, and while his hair had grayed and his tanned face was a bit wrinkled, he seemed much the same man that Lew had known decades before in a time so removed, so different, that it might as well have been another universe. When Lyle Belfontaine had forced him to retire from the Service, Rafe had started a venture with Rafaella, taking occasional parties of Terranan on mountaineering expeditions into the Hellers. It had made him rich by Darkovan standards. He had an additional pension from the Federation, which was even occasionally paid to him, much to his amusement. The loss of Scott at HQ had made things more difficult, for he possessed strong telepathy. Until a few days before, they had used Ethan MacDoevid, who while he did not have any *laran,* was quick and kept his wits about him. The man from Threadneedle Street had been a good channel of information, and they all regretted that his observations were no longer available to them.

Beside him, Dani Hastur, now thirty, was still the rather quiet person he had been in his adolescence, but he had more assurance than before. The death of his father was a blow, one that Lew knew he would only recover from with time. But Dani hated Thendara, and it was obvious from the set of his shoulders that he would rather be almost anywhere else than in what had been his father's study for so many years.

The sixth person in the room was Danilo Syrtis-Ardais. Regis' death had taken its greatest toll on him, and he had aged visibly in the past few days. But the look in his eyes remained vigilant, and it was clear that he was not going to allow his very real grief to impede the workings of his fine mind.

Mikhail sat, clenching and unclenching the hand that bore the great matrix of Varzil the Good, his lean jaw rigid. He seemed to be looking for something that Lew could not discern. Finally, he cleared his throat and began to speak. "As soon as *Dom* Damon favors us with his presence," he began, the irony in his words evident to all, "we will have to hold a Council meeting. The question is, what are we going to tell them?"

"That is succinct and to the point," Danilo replied crisply. "If we tell them that there is a plot to assassinate you, there is going to be hell to pay. Francisco Ridenow and Lady Javanne will demand proof, or action of some sort, and we all know it. And Nico's absence must be explained soon. So far we have managed to keep it secret, but eventually one of the servants will let the cat out of the bag, and then we will be up to our hips in wild speculation." He gave a narrow smile. "I confess I have even toyed with the idea of telling your meddlesome mother that he has been kidnapped by the Federation, just to see the expression on her face. If only she would keep out of things!"

Dani Hastur nodded. "Yes, exactly. Gareth was asking me this morning where Nico was, and I hardly knew how to answer him, since I realized we did not want this information to become common knowledge just yet." He gave a shrug of his shoulders. "Life would be a great deal easier if everyone minded their own business, wouldn't it?"

"Truer words were never spoken," Mikhail answered. "Let's get on with this—the longer we remain here the more wild speculation we will create. I have no doubt that Francisco, Lady Marilla, and my dear mother are already imagining all manner of things. The floor is open to suggestions, information, and even jokes, so long as they are relevant."

Rafe Scott shifted on his chair. "I have a little information that might be useful. I spent an hour in a tavern in the Trade City last evening, sipping beer and keeping my ears and mind open. I frequent the place enough to be taken for a regular, although the quality of the beer is not nearly as good as that of the gossip. Something is most assuredly up at HQ. There has been a veritable flood of messages going out for three days. What is most interesting is that, as far as I can gather, there has been no answer to them. The result is that the Terrans are becoming agitated, and are ready to jump at any shadow."

"Do you have any idea what was in those messages?"

"Most of them were in code, and the people I eavesdropped on were too lowly placed to have access. It would be very useful if you or I could take a stroll through HQ, Lew, but that is out of the question, I suppose."

"Perhaps. We've had several messages from Belfontaine, each one more shrill than the one before, and it seems clear from the most recent one that they now know that Regis is dead. He wants Herm Aldaran handed over to them, and an immediate interview with Mikhail, to discuss the future of the Federation on Darkover. It would be funny under other circumstances. It is a good thing I do not take offense easily, because the last message was extremely rude."

Rafe Scott chuckled softly. "That's Belfontaine all over. It sounds as if he thinks we are not aware that the Federation is planning to pull out—does he mention that?"

"No, he didn't. Any more than we have told him of Regis' passing. It is clear that his second, Miles Granfell, told him last night. It is a shame that we could not have kept Regis' death secret just a little longer," Lew answered.

"Why couldn't you go to HQ and see him," Dani asked.

"Oh, I could get in and speak to Belfontaine. The question is, could I then get out? Frankly, I am just a little too old to be a hostage. The same is true for Rafe." If necessary he would die for Darkover, but he was not willing to waste his life in a futile exercise.

"Once you were on what is still Federation territory, they feel they could pretty much do as they wished." Dani sounded uneasy at this idea.

"My information is that the port is shut down—is that right, Rafe?" Mikhail looked at the older man intently as he asked the question.

"Your information is correct. The port is closed, and there has not been an incoming ship for two days. Herm was lucky—his was the last Big Ship to come." Scott shook his head. "I don't like to think what this is doing to Federation trade, if this situation is occurring on planets closer to the hub."

"That is the Federation's problem, not ours," snapped Mikhail impatiently.

"No, Mik, not entirely. Even though we are largely independent of the Federation, we can't foresee how a large economic disruption within it might affect us. But that is for the future. What I observed is that low-ranking guards are still coming to the Trade City for recreation, and there is a certain quality of recklessness about them. They are aware that they will be leaving shortly, and act as if that gives them leave to do anything they wish. Already the City Guard have had to put down several brawls, and a few of the joy girls had bruises that were unusual. I popped in and called on *Mestra* MacIvan of the Red Sun House, and she said she was almost ready to close her doors, because things were getting ugly."

"But why? I don't understand that," Dani wondered.

Rafe shifted in his chair. "My guess is that they think they can get away with anything, perhaps even murder, and not have to worry about any consequences."

"Yes," said Danilo. "The Commandant of the City Guards sent word this morning, wondering what to do with the Terranan he has already arrested, because his lock-up is getting rather full. And Belfontaine demanded, in another of his messages, that they be released immediately. His errand boys must be getting footsore, running back and forth between the castle and HQ." He gave a wry grin. "I answered that they had destroyed property, and would not be let go until it was paid for, which should give him something to chew on for an hour or two. Still, I don't quite know what to do about the problem. We can't build another jail overnight, and if we let these men go back onto Federation territory, they will likely just return and cause more trouble."

"What about the orphanage?" Donal asked this, then looked self-conscious.

"The John Reade Orphanage? What about it, Donal?" Mikhail asked.

"It has been standing empty since the Federation shut it down two years ago, and it is built like a fortress. It has lots of rooms, and from what *Domna* Marguerida has told me about it, it was little better than a prison to start with." His cheeks were rosy, but he was standing his ground, and Lew gave him an approving nod.

A slow grin crept across Mikhail's tired face, and years dropped away, leaving him looking very youthful instead of middle-aged. "A very elegant solution, which will no doubt amuse Marguerida greatly. Danilo, tell Belfontaine that his men are going to remain in our custody until payment is made, or until the Federation leaves. That should put him off-balance for a few minutes, since he does not yet know that we know they are pulling out. It will give him something to think about other than trying to kill me. Is there more, Rafe?"

"A bit. Most of the people I watched are low level, without any access to really sensitive information. They are worried, I would say, and what they seem to be worried about is that the Federation will not send ships to remove them at the appointed time, but will instead abandon them here. It has happened on other worlds, and even though it was not common knowledge when I left, it seems to be that now. The overall impression I got was that no one knows what is going on or what is going to happen. This has left them anxious, and reckless as well."

"Interesting," Lew said, leaning forward, so he could look at Scott around Dani. "It sounds as if those at the top are keeping those at the bottom in the dark, doesn't it?"

"Exactly. The rank and file are clearly uneasy, and I did not see any officers."

"Is that good or bad?" Mikhail asked.

"Bad, I suspect. If Emmet Grayson still had any authority, we could approach him. But since the reorganization of the Federation bureaucracy, most of the real power has been in Belfontaine's hands, and we know him to be our enemy."

"How many trained fighters can Belfontaine muster in Thendara?" Mikhail leaned forward across the desk as he spoke, his eyes intent.

"Now, that is a very good question, and one I cannot answer accurately. When I retired, there were about two hundred, but I don't know if this number has been added to or reduced. Then there are those up in Aldaran territory. I tried to get a count the last time I took a party into the Hellers, and I wold guess that there are between seventy-five and a hundred men there, many of them no better than raw recruits. But there are some veterans of the Pali Uprising, marines and soldiers both, and they know their business. There might be a few more, since I suspect that some of the technicians are actually combat trained."

"What is your opinion of Belfontaine, Rafe? You have had more contact with him than anyone except Lew and myself." Danilo spoke the question before anyone else could.

"He is shrewd and ambitious, and he has long wanted to advance his position. He got into some sort of trouble when he was Adjutant on Lein III, and was sent to Darkover in disgrace. He has been chafing to find some action for years now, and he will see Regis' death as an opportunity to end Darkover's Protected status, by claiming that the Federation needs to step in and keep order, or some other fabrication. It would not be the first time a Terran official acted in his own best interest. The Federation usually doesn't interfere with this sort of adventurism, since bringing all the planets into the fold is their aim anyhow."

"Is this Belfontaine an Expansionist?" Dani asked the question, wrinkling his brow with concentration. He had never had much interest in the problems of governance, and his years in the Elhalyn Domain had put him out of touch with current information.

"I don't think he has any politics, or even political alliance, just a driving ambition to become a general before he is sixty," Scott answered dryly. "He comes from an industrial family, one that owns entire planets, and essentially even the people who live on them, which gives him a particular way of seeing things that is incomprehensible to me. In the usual circumstances, he would have gone into the business, but from something he let slip once, it seems they did not think him suitable, and he ended up in the service of the Federation instead. I have the impression that in his family, working for the Federation is regarded as a step down, something that is only for people who are not sharp enough to survive the corporate environment. I think that gives him something to prove. What I am certain of is that he hates Darkover, has a very low opinion of our people, and sincerely believes that we would be much better off under the dominion of the Federation, rather than continuing on as we have for centuries."

"Then it is safe to assume that if someone came to him and suggested that it would be possible to assassinate me on the way to the *rhu fead,* he would jump at the chance." Mikhail said the words slowly, as if they were sour in his mouth.

"Possibly."

"Only that?"

"He is not a stupid man, Mikhail. He has to step with a little care, because the last thing the Federation would want is some ambitious fellow setting himself up as a warlord. He might succeed in killing you, and then find himself facing a firing squad for treason."

"In other words, he needs to make it appear that he is acting in the best interests of the Federation, not his own?"

"Yes, Dani, exactly. He has enough trained men to attack the funeral train—but I can't guess if he would do it. I suspect that some of these unanswered messages he has been sending are an attempt to get some sort of authorization for intervening in Darkover's affairs, and that he has also asked for reinforcements. It must be very frustrating for him to have no reply. Lew, do you agree?"

"I do. I assume that since disbanding the Legislature, the Federation has been in too much of a turmoil to worry about some little backwater like Darkover—for which we should be very grateful."

Mikhail gave a grunt. "I don't like this, but I can't think of anything to do to change it. Lew, have you had any further word from Nico and Herm?"

"I know they joined up with Rafaella this morning, and headed toward Carcosa. If there have been developments beyond that, I have not been informed of them."

"That was a good idea of Marguerida's," Scott offered. "Rafi was thrilled to get out on the road."

"Does anyone have any ideas to propose?" Mikhail asked.

Young Donal cleared his throat and everyone looked at him with surprise. The paxman turned slightly pink with embarrassment at being the center of attention. "I don't want to talk out of turn, but ever since Nico left, I have been thinking, and I've spent some time looking at maps of the route to the *rhu fead*."

"There is no need to be hesitant, Donal," Danilo said kindly. "You will have to learn to advise Mikhail as I have done for Regis for all these years. It is one of the more interesting duties of the paxman, you know." He grinned wryly, but his eyes were filled with memory and sorrow. "You are even permitted to offer unpleasant thoughts to Mikhail, without fear of censure."

"That's right, Donal," Mikhail said. "I remember a night, right here in this room, over sixteen years ago, when Danilo told my uncle that he must abandon any hope of me marrying Gisela Aldaran. He did not like it, but he took it well enough." Mikhail and Danilo both chuckled at the memory. "Go on."

Instead of speaking, Donal reached into his beltpouch and took out a folded piece of very thin paper. He opened it out and laid it on the desk in front of Mikhail, smoothing it carefully. "I traced this out last evening, using one of the old maps that the Terranan did years ago, and another that Rafaella gave to *Domna* Marguerida."

"Why did you use two?" Dani wondered.

"The map from the Terranan is what is called a contour map, which means it shows the shape of the land, but does not have a lot of information about towns and farms. It is pretty old, but since the land remains the same, it should still be accurate."

"It must be something done from one of their geosynchronous satellites, when they could get the infernal things to function," Scott suggested. "It used to drive their people almost mad, for just when they got one up and running, they would have peculiar failures, and go off-line again. It gave me a poor notion of their technology at first. But someone explained to me that our sun gives off a strange radiation that blouxes up the readings or something. Personally, I think Aldones doesn't want strangers taking pictures of Darkover."

Everyone chuckled at this, except Donal, who remained serious.

"I don't know about that. The Federation thing shows how the ground rises and falls, and I made the best copy I could. Then I took Rafaella's map, which is just a sketch of things along the Old North Road, and added that information to the first one. By using both, we can look at the landmarks and such, but also can see more about the terrain." He pointed at one section. "For instance, here Rafaella marked a big farm, a small village, and suggested the shape of the road. But on the Terranan map, you can see how the farm is spread over several hills, that the land rises and falls, and that the road winds in a slightly different manner than she drew. I just thought it would be useful to us to look for places where an ambush might be possible. And there are a couple that I found."

Scott stood up and looked at the map from his side of the desk. "The places marked in red, Donal?"

"Yes, sir."

"You are right. Those are logical places for an ambush."

"I thought that perhaps we could . . . put some of the Guardsmen in ordinary clothing, a few of them, and send them ahead to scout out things," Donal said. "I mean, why should we go into this with only Nico and Herm and Rafaella's Renunciates? Let's outguess the Terrans, and spike their plans." His young face was fierce now.

"That is a clever idea, Donal," Danilo said, his voice warm with approval. "And do you have any suggestions as to who these men might be?"

"I made a list." Donal pulled another piece of paper out of his pouch, rather wrinkled, and with a great many crossouts, and offered it to Mikhail. "I would have consulted Commandant Ridenow, but I thought I had better not, since it would raise questions and get back to Francisco. And after I could not think of a way to get any of the Guards from the barracks assigned, it struck me that there are a lot of loyal older men, no longer on active duty, who are living in Thendara right now. I picked men who have had experience fighting bandits, who are seasoned and smart as well, and whose absence would not cause comment."

Danilo stood up, circled the desk, and leaned over Mikhail's shoulder. "These are good choices, for the most part. The only problem I can foresee is how to do this in secrecy."

"Are you afraid of Terranan spies, Uncle Danilo?" Dani Hastur asked, "Or are you worried about some members of the Council getting wind of what's happening?"

"Both, Dani. These men have families, and if they say anything, it will be gossip in an hour. You were wise not to talk to the Commandant, Donal."

"I knew that Cisco would tell his father something was up, and then Grandmother Javanne would hear of it, and then the fat would have been in the fire." He spoke simply but with great feeling.

"Your discretion does you credit, Donal."

The young paxman grinned broadly. "I learned that from watching Lew all these years."

"Did you now?" Lew was pleased and amused.

"When I was ten, you told me that information was the real power in the world, not kings and Domains. I have tried to remember the lesson. And when I was chosen to be paxman to Mikhail, I watched how Danilo was with Regis, how he listened more than he talked, but always seemed to know everything."

"You have all the makings of a fine advisor," Rafe Scott praised.

Danilo Syrtis-Ardais stood up. "I think that I can accomplish what needs to be done without arousing too much talk. I can think of a few additions to make to Donal's list, but for the most part, it will do very well indeed. And, just to muddy the waters a bit, I think I will suggest to Cisco that he go over the reserve list."

"Why that?"

"It will give him something to do, for one thing, and we may find we need to have those men mobilized, if the Terranan continue to misbehave in the Trade City."

"Danilo," said Lew in admiration, "I am very glad you are on our side, and not theirs."

"Make it so," Mikhail said quietly. "Now all we need to do is decide what, if anything, we are going to tell the Council, and when."

"That is the sticky point, isn't it?" Lew answered. "The funeral is planned for three days from now, so I suggest you delay any meeting until the day before that. You know that Javanne is going to try to overset you, and that she has at least two allies on the Council—Francisco and Lady Marilla Aillard. She has not budged an inch over the years."

"You are right, Lew." Mikhail looked sad at this. He had managed to reconcile with his father, *Dom* Gabriel, but his mother remained ada-mant in her refusal to accept the agreement that had been worked out fifteen years before, where Danilo Hastur became the Elhalyn Regent, and Mikhail was Regis' heir designate. It was her ruling obsession, a kind of blind fury that drove her to bouts of near madness. Had she been anyone other than the sister of Regis Hastur, and the wife of *Dom* Gabriel, she would have been confined long since.

"I spoke to her this morning," Dani said. "I found her in the dining room with Mother, insisting that . . . It was a very distressing encounter. And Mother was ready to collapse. It made me wish I were a more forceful person."

"What happened?"

"As soon as she saw me, Aunt Javanne became very . . . friendly. It made my skin crawl. She told me that she was sure that wiser heads would prevail, and I would be made to take Mikhail's place. I could tell she meant herself when she said wiser heads, and I tried to explain to her that I did not want to govern Darkover, that I wouldn't have the job for all the gold in Carthanon. She didn't listen, but at least it gave Mother a chance to escape back to her rooms." He frowned. "She said I must not think of myself so much, but should consider my heritage and that of my children. Do you know, I think she imagines that if she cannot twist me to her will, she will go after Gareth! Forgive me. I have said too much." He looked stricken and miserable.

"My poor mother thinks that she is the wisest woman on Darkover, and also imagines that she will live forever. The temptation to give her a powerful sleeping draught is almost irresistable."

"That might not be a bad idea," Lew said, completely seriously, and found himself the object of five pairs of startled eyes. Then everyone realized he was teasing them, and a chuckle came from Mikhail, followed by an eruption of laughter in the room. It eased the tension, and everyone began to relax slightly.

"It would be a wonderful thing if my mother were unable to be present at the Council meeting, wouldn't it?" Mikhail looked almost happy for the first time in several days.

"Yes, wonderful. And quite scandalous," Danilo murmured, his pale eyes alight with merriment. "Unthinkable," he added.

"If I find Aunt Javanne troubling my mother again, it will not be in the least unthinkable, Danilo. I'll put enough sleepweed in her soup to keep her dead to the world for a tenday!"

"We will have to hope it will not come to that, Dani," Mikhail answered. "Besides, I think you would have to get in line for the honor."

He looked from one face to the other, and what he saw seemed to satisfy him. "I think we have accomplished as much as we can at present, until we get further information."

There was a scraping of chairs at this dismissal, and everyone except Lew and Mikhail stood up to leave. When they were gone, Mikhail looked at the older man. "Was there something else?"

"Yes, there is. I believe that you should include your brother Rafael in any further discussions."

"But . . ."

"He has never been disloyal to you, Mikhail, and you know it. Yes, you have suspicions of his wife, for her scheming when they were first married. But you need him, and I think that he has been punished more than enough for her actions. She hasn't really caused any problems for several years now, and I don't expect her create any now." Lew sighed and shook his head. "We distrust her because she is an Aldaran, but how long must she be forced to . . . Mik, it has to stop somewhere! We can't continue to nourish wounds from the past, not when we have so many problems in the present!"

"What Regis did, keeping her and Rafael here as hostages, wasn't really right, was it?"

"I don't know any longer, son. There was a kind of logic in it, at the time, but that time is past. It certainly was not kind! I have no wish to dishonor the memory of a man I loved and valued as a friend, but some of the decisions Regis made in the last fifteen years were extreme, and both of us know it!"

Mikhail nodded. "I have always been torn between my loyalty to Regis and my affection for Rafael. He had never done me ill."

"Mikhail, if you are going to rule Darkover, you have to begin making your own decisions, not keeping to the policies that your uncle put into place. I don't want to influence you against your own judgment, no matter what your mother believes, but I do wish to advise you as well as I am able. And truthfully, if I had to choose between Gisela and Javanne right now, I would take your sister-in-law in a moment! Something has changed for her—I have no idea what—but she suddenly seems almost happy instead of restless and dissatisfied."

Mikhail shrugged. "All that might mean is that she intends to return to her earlier insistence that Rafael would be a suitable person to take my place."

"That is certainly a possibility, of course, but if it is, what better way to interfere with her plans than by bringing Rafael close to you? No matter how much he cares for his wife, your brother would never act against you, particularly if you mend your fences with him."

"How fortunate I am to have you for an advisor, even when you tell me to do difficult things that I would rather avoid. I am so ashamed of how Rafael has been treated, not just by Regis, but by me as well."

"I understand. But, Mikhail, you are a wise and decent man, and a stronger one than I think you realize just now. And one thing that separates the strong from the weak is the ability to admit fault, ask forgiveness, and get on with life."

"Have you ever . . . ?"

"Yes, of course I have. Don't you think that the way I denied Marguerida any real knowledge of her childhood does not make me cringe with shame? She was generous enough to forgive me, and then to trust me again. I think that is a miracle."

"Yes, I suppose it is, but my wife has a very big heart—or otherwise we would never have ended up fostering Alanna, would we?"

"Go to your brother and make peace, Mikhail. I don't think you will ever regret it."

"Will he forgive me, do you think?"

Lew smiled. "Of course, Mikhail. If he does not welcome you with open arms, I will be very surprised."

"Do you know, I have wanted to approach him many times over the years, and more in the past few days. But I was afraid to risk it. Thank you for . . . for everything."

"There is nothing to thank me for, son. I have nothing but your best interests in mind . . . and heart."

"No matter what my mother believes?"

"No matter what anyone thinks or believes or imagines, Mikhail."

Mikhail took a deep breath and knocked on the door of the suite where his brother and sister-in-law lived. Then he opened it and entered. Gisela was sitting at a small table, looking at a little carving, her brows knit together, and Rafael was reading a book. They both looked at him, and the woman shrank back a little, her green eyes bright with wariness.

"Good afternoon," Mikhail said quietly.

"This is an unexpected pleasure," Rafael answered, smiling slightly. "You have been so busy the past few days."

Mikhail felt the strain between them. It made his heart ache, and he wondered if he had a way to mend the inadvertent injury that Regis' choices and Gisela's mischiefs had brought about. "Yes, I have been, and I would rather have not."

"Have you come about Hermes?"

"Why do you ask that, Giz?"

"I don't know, really. I was visiting Katherine a little while ago, and she seemed . . . worried about something. I just assumed it was about Herm, because she is so devoted to him." There was nothing in her look or voice except genuine interest. Lew was right—there was something different about Gisela. He had not seen her so relaxed since she had been a girl, when they had first met. No, not even then, because she was always tense, waiting for one of *Dom* Damon's frequent outbursts of temper.

"Well, you are right. Did she tell you that Belfontaine wants him given over to the Federation?"

Gisela looked alarmed. "No, she did not, and I don't think she knows that either! My dear brother! He hasn't changed a bit in twenty years. I'll bet he didn't tell her. Where is he?"

Mikhail considered before he spoke. "He felt it would be better for everyone if he were not in Comyn Castle at present, so I sent him ahead to oversee preparations at the *rhu fead*." It was the best he could think of at the moment.

Gisela fixed him with a penetrating look, more like her usual self. "I'll wager he wanted to be away when our father appears—a pity I could not go with him!"

"That may have been part of the reason he took the task, yes," Mikhail agreed.

"You did not come to discuss Herm, did you, Mik?" Rafael said.

"No, I didn't. I came to beg your pardon."

"My . . ."

"Rafael, the past is past. I cannot have you sitting around the Castle twiddling your thumbs, looking disgruntled."

"Do you want me to leave, then?"

"Certainly not! I am going to need you now, to advise me, to listen to me when I have a problem. I have missed your good sense terribly—and more, your company, *bredu*."

At Mikhail's statement, Rafael seemed to hold his breath. "I have waited a long time to hear that word from you, Mik."

"I should never have let Regis . . ."

"You could not have changed his mind about my trustworthiness, Mik, and we both know it."

"That does not change the fact that I regret it very much."

"As you said, the past is past, *bredu*." Rafael walked across and embraced his brother firmly. Over his shoulder, Mikhail could see that his sister-in-law was smiling and that tears were falling from her green eyes. There was no calculation in her expression, just relief and joy.

As Mikhail hugged his older brother, he felt a knot of tension in his belly uncoil. Yes, he needed Rafael, but more, he loved the man, and was glad that he could now have him and his counsel close by. And he knew he was forgiven for the years of estrangement, for Rafael had a great heart with nothing petty in it. And that, he decided, was a gift that outweighed anything else.

17

Domenic was fretting with restlessness. After they had entered the inn, Herm found one of the Renunciates and told her to find Vancof and keep an eye on him. Then he had ordered Nico to change into his new clothes and stay out of sight. This had not pleased the boy, but he was so accustomed to doing what he was told that it took a while for his feelings of resentment to manifest. Herm himself had settled into the common room of the Crowing Cock with a mug of beer, relaxing before the wide hearth, and somehow managing to appear unremarkable. Nico had been able to observe him before he went up the stairs, and had wondered how the man did it. He just seemed to melt into the woodwork.

Nico felt let down, the way he often did after a celebration in Comyn Castle. The excitement of the previous evening and the ride along the Old North Road had sustained him, but now he once more felt like a child, sent off to his room and told to be quiet. There was even, he decided, hard logic in Herm's instructions. Vancof had seen him the previous day, and might recognize him if they met in the halls of the inn, but he had never seen the Aldaran man.

Still, there was the evening's performance to look forward to—unless

Herm decided to keep him away from that as well. Nico tried to marshal a few good arguments as to why he should be allowed to attend, and decided that the Alton Gift was probably the best. He scanned the inn again, as he had done several times since he came upstairs, and noticed the Terranan who had ridden in earlier sitting in the taproom, looking uneasy and fidgety. He was probably waiting for Vancof.

Time passed, and he wished he had something to read. He closed his eyes and slipped into a light doze. After a while, he sat up, refreshed but also somewhat unnerved by his nap—had he slept too long? Domenic peered out the narrow window, facing west, and saw that the sun was sinking behind heavy clouds. Soon it would set, and twilight would creep over the town. He could not stand it a second longer! He ran a comb roughly through his hair, and then opened the door of the room.

He was just coming down the stairs from his room when he heard a familiar voice in the entry. Domenic stepped into the shadowed door of the dining room and peeked around the jamb. Yes, it was one of the older, retired Guardsmen, Fredrich MacDunald, dressed in worn and ordinary clothing. Nico had never seen him without his uniform before, and he was rather surprised by how different he appeared.

Nico hesitated. Should he expose himself and speak to his friend, or stay out of sight, as Herm had instructed him? When Aran MacIvan followed Fredrich into the inn a moment later, he decided that he had better tell Herm of this new development before he did anything else. This spying stuff was more complicated than he had imagined.

Uncle Herm!

Yes, Nico.

I think some reinforcements have arrived. A couple of retired Guardsmen from Thendara have just come into the inn, dressed like common folk, and I cannot imagine any reason for them to be here—unless they have come to drag me back to Comyn Castle. Should I speak to them or not?

Have they seen you?

Not yet. I am sort of lurking in the shadows.

Then let them alone, for the present. We don't want to call too much attention to ourselves, or to them. Has Vancof come back yet?

I haven't seen him, but I was upstairs, like you told me. He could tell that even in telepathic communication his sense of ill-usage came through.

Poor Nico. I am not letting you have any fun at all, am I? Why don't you venture into the kitchens.

Why would I want to do that?

Because growing lads are always hungry, and your being in there will not cause any comment. Then, if Vancof comes in through the back door of the inn, you will certainly see him.

What if the cook chases me out? And what if Vancof notices me?

Be creative. You've already shown you can be.

It was better than sitting on his hands in the room, and he was a bit hungry. At least Uncle Herm had not sent him back there! Domenic followed the smell of fresh bread into the back portion of the Crowing Cock, and found himself in a large, very clean kitchen. Two girls sat on one side of a long table, cutting vegetables and chatting quietly. On the far side of the hot room, a boy was pulling loaves from a great beehive oven, using a long wooden paddle to keep from burning his hands. The cook, a very skinny man, was standing before the stove, stirring a pot, and the wonderful smell of chervine stew with dumplings wafted out from it. His mouth watered.

One of the girls looked up from her work and gave him a friendly smile. She appeared to be a year or so younger than himself, and by her features, must be related to the innkeeper. At least she had the same small, turned-up nose as Evan MacHaworth. She gestured him toward the table with the knife in her hand. "Can't wait for supper, huh?"

"I am a little bit hungry," he admitted, as he sat down on the bench across from her. "Can I do something to help?" The cook turned around at the sound of his voice, gave him a look, then returned to his stirring.

She giggled, as if she had never heard anything so funny in her life. Then she got up, grabbed a loaf of bread that was already sitting at the end of the table, cut it into two pieces, and put both in a basket. She took the basket in one hand, and another with something green in it in the other, and came back.

"You ever strung snap-beans before?"

"No, but if you show me how, I can probably do it."

"You must be really bored if you want to string beans. Here, this is how." She demonstrated with a few quick gestures. "I hate to do it, but the way our cook fixes them makes it worth the work. He fries them with bacon and it is delicious!" She turned and grinned at the back of the skinny cook, and Nico had the impression it was some sort of joke between them.

"That sounds good." He pulled a chunk of bread off, bit into it, and started to string the beans. It wasn't very challenging, but it was much better than sitting in his room, waiting for something to happen. He could see how the nameless girl would grow weary of it.

The other girl glanced up from the growing pile of carrots in front of her, gave him a nod and then looked at the first girl with a calculating eye. He sensed her watchfulness, her slight unease, and sensed without the least probing that she was keeping an eye on him with her younger sister. "We will get a big crowd in here tonight, what with the Travelers being here, and all the folks in the town coming around to see the show," she informed him.

"I saw some men come in just before I came back," he offered, "and I think they might be wanting dinner, too."

"Really?" She did not seem surprised or very interested in new guests. "I'm Hannah, and this is my sister Dorcas," the older girl announced. "This time of year we are always busy, and never busier than when the Travelers stop by. There won't be an empty room in the place, what with you and your uncle, and those women." She gave a big sigh. "Father has gone off to the market, so I'd better go find out if the men you saw will be wanting a place to sleep."

He watched Hannah get up and go out. Then Dorcas said, "She doesn't think much of Renunciates, but I think they are interesting. And a while ago, one of them marched right through the kitchen and out the back. I wonder what she was about?"

So much for not drawing attention, he thought glumly. "Who knows," he replied. "They go where they like, don't they?"

Dorcas giggled again, a titter that was going to get on his nerves if he heard it very much longer. "You woulda thought the kitchen was a lane this afternoon, because one of the Travelers came through, too. I've seen him before, but I woulda known he was one of them by his clothes anywhere. Came through town just before Midsummer and got roaring drunk. Dad had to send him out before he was sick on the hearth. A real nasty piece," she went on, giggling at the same time, for no reason he could discern. She probably did it in her sleep.

Then he sensed that she was just nervous, and knew that she wanted to impress him and make him like her. She was so different from his sister, or his cousins, that he did not really know what to make of her. But he felt a little ashamed of comparing her to Alanna, or even that Illona Rider, who was probably still sewing in the confines of the wagon. "It must be interesting living in an inn."

Dorcas shrugged. "I don't know. I've never lived anywheres else, or gone beyond the town even. Ma says it was good enough for her, and has to be good enough for me, but I would like to go to Thendara and see the sights."

Domenic bit off another mouthful of bread and did not answer until he had chewed and swallowed it. Even without butter or honey, it was very good, and the smell of the stew was tempting. "What sights do you mean?"

"There's Comyn Castle, and the spaceport, and Terranan, to be sure. I heard the Big Ships make a fearful noise when they land, and I would like to see if it is so. And they say there's a new hall built by the Musicians Guild, as big as a barn, but with seats in it insteada stalls and hay."

"I heard that, too, but I have never seen it."

"Have you ever seen a Terranan?"

Before he could answer, Domenic saw Vancof slip into the open door at the back of the kitchen, looking very furtive. He bent his head over the beans so his unbound hair concealed his features, and felt a burst of success as the man passed by him without a glance. He could hear the topmost thoughts in the man's mind, but they were disorganized, full of anger and fear, and not particularly informative. Vancof was so lost in thought, he realized, that he could have been naked and dancing on the table, and the man might not have noticed him.

A moment later he sensed another presence nearby, saw Samantha, one of the Renunciates, come to the door of the kitchen, peer inside at Vancof's shoulders, and then fade away into the growing twilight. If he had not been expecting her, he would have missed her completely, and he wondered if he could learn to do that. He thought she was going to circle around the Crowing Cock and come in from the front door.

Domenic spent a minute trying to make some sense of the troubled thoughts of the driver, to glean any useful information from them at all. There was something about orders that was bothering him. Then he used the Alton Gift to speak to his uncle again.

Herm, the driver is back, and so is Samantha.

I know. Vancof just came into the taproom and ordered a brew. Now he has noticed the man you recognized, and he does not look very pleased. I think he resents our friend here—there—he's sitting down at the table across from him and trying to look casual. Hmm . . . maybe resentment is the wrong feeling—Vancof looks very uncomfortable.

Good! From the little I know about him, he deserves to be! What about the Guardsmen I noticed?

I assume they are here, too, but since I do not know them, I can't say for certain. The room is getting very crowded, since half the village seems to have stopped in for a drink. This entire thing is becoming more amusing by the second. What are you doing?

I'm sitting across from a very giggly girl, cleaning up snap-beans and listening to her life story.

Well, finish your task, and then come out in front. It will be dark soon, and I want to keep an eye on our friends here, and see what they do. I'll need your help.

Domenic had almost emptied the basket by now, and there was a large pile of cleaned and broken beans on the table in front of him. He was needed—how gratifying! It occurred to him briefly that he had never felt particularly needed before, and then he wondered what they were going to do about supper. He chided himself for letting his belly get in the way of his good sense. Eating was not *that* important, was it?

"I'd better go see if my uncle is looking for me," he told Dorcas.

"Take the rest of that piece of bread with you. It should hold you until we start serving."

"Thanks. It was fun."

"You wouldn't say that if you have to clean beans six days out of ten during the season. I am always glad when they are done, all put up in crocks for winter." Dorcas seemed a little disappointed at his departure. "Will I see you at the show?"

"Probably," he replied vaguely. The last thing he needed was some girl hanging around. Now, if it were Alanna, it would be different. She might be high-strung, but she was not silly, and she never giggled!

He went through the rather dark corridor from the kitchen to the front of the inn, and was so intent on his movements that he nearly ran into the broad chest of Duncan Lindir, standing in the shadows. The old Guardsman gave him a startled look, a quick nod, and a slight grin.

"What's going on? Has my father sent the entire barracks up here?" he hissed to the man.

Duncan shook his head. "There's ten of us, that *Dom* Danilo ordered to come here. We started out right after midday, and rode much too hard for these old bones," he grumbled. "I don't know what is going on. All *Dom* Danilo said was that *Dom* Aldaran would tell us what to do—never thought I'd find myself answering to an Aldaran. And what are *you* doing here?"

"It's too complicated to explain now. Just keep your eyes and ears open."

"For what?"

Domenic hesitated for a moment. If Uncle Danilo had not informed the man of a plot to try to assassinate Mikhail Hastur, then he should not say anything, should he? Still, he could sense both curiosity and some bewilderment from Duncan, and it needed to be satisfied. "There are some Terranan here, and we believe they are going to cause trouble. Keep an eye on a big man with very new boots and short brown hair. He's in the taproom just now. I think, sitting with a ratty-faced man. There may be more—I don't know yet."

"*Dom* Domenic . . ."

"Don't call me that! I'm Tomas MacAnndra, and Hermes is Ian Mac-Anndra—and you never saw me before in your life! I am going into the taproom now, and I'll sit down with Herm, so then you will know who he is."

"Then I guess I don't know your name," Duncan replied, forgetting his aching bones and grumbling. His eyes startled to twinkle with great good humor. "Good thought—since I never set eyes on the man. What have you gotten yourself into, lad?"

Nico did not reply, but just left the corridor and walked toward the front of the inn. The noise from the taproom was tremendous, many male voices discussing the weather, the corn crop, the news of the death of Regis Hastur, and other matters. There were a few female voices as well, and he recognized Rafaella's before he came to the doorway.

Herm saw him and waved him over. Then he gestured to the serving boy and signaled for a short mug for Domenic. By the time Nico reached the table, the boy had brought the beer, and he settled down on the bench beside Herm and picked it up.

I bumped into Duncan Lindir in the hall, and he told me that Danilo Ardais has sent ten men up here, without any instructions except to obey your orders. He was not exactly pleased at having to answer to an Aldaran, so do not be surprised if you are greeted with some coolness, Uncle. I don't know why he did not tell them more, or why they were sent.

I don't know either, but I am not sorry that they have come. Hmm. If they were not told about the plot against your father, it was likely so that they would not inadvertently reveal it to anyone else. "What have you been up to, nephew?"

Duncan was not expecting to find me here, and was surprised, so I think you are probably right. "I went to the kitchens and got something to eat," Nico answered, holding up the remnants of the bread. "And I helped with the preparations, too."

"Your mother would be proud of you, lending a hand." *Is there any reason for Danilo to play things close to his chest?*

Umm. Well, Cisco Ridenow, the Commandant of the Barracks, is not exactly one of Father's friends. He would have preferred it if Uncle Rafael had taken the job, when it came vacant three years ago, but Regis decided against it, because of Gisela and all. Uncle Rafael isn't entirely trusted, which I think must hurt him dreadfully. I wasn't really paying attention, since I was at Arilinn then, and by the time I came back, Cisco was already in charge.

What sort of man is he, Nico?

I think I would call him smooth. He is an empath, like many of the Ridenow, but he is good on military matters. I learned a lot from him, about how to look at a building and find its weak points, for instance. I have always found him to be fair, but there is just something about him that is very remote.

What do you mean by smooth?

Well, there is something about him that I don't really like, and I can barely explain it. Nothing bad, but he is as slick as a glass ball—nothing seems to cling to him. I guess the most I can say is that I wouldn't completely trust him to back me up in a fight. Or maybe I just don't like him because his father was always fighting with Regis, and will probably make everything more difficult in Council. My judgment may be prejudiced, Uncle.

At least you have the wisdom to realize that you might dislike Cisco for no other reason than that his father was an adversary of Regis. There are a lot of people three times your age who would not be able to make such a distinction. What is the general feeling about Cisco in the barracks?

I don't know—it would have been impolite to ask, wouldn't it? I haven't overheard any real grumbling, though. As I said, he seems to be fair, but very . . . remote.

I see. I wish you were a little nosier, Nico. It would have been useful if you knew more. Still, the fact that Danilo Ardais is sending men up here with only a minimum of instruction is very suggestive.

Of what?

Something clandestine. Wouldn't Cisco be aware of these men being ordered to Carcosa?

No, he wouldn't. Those I spotted are retired from active duty, and only would be called for if there was a real need for trained men.

I see. Is Cisco trusted by Danilo Ardais?

I suppose so—but Danilo is so deep and cunning that I would never guess if he weren't. He's never done anything that I know about that would make anyone actively mistrust him. I think it is only that Francisco Ridenow, his father, is practically in Grandmother Javanne's pocket, and has opposed Regis for years now. I think giving Cisco the Commandant's position was intended to mollify Dom Ridenow—but it didn't work. He is just as bone-headed as he always was. And it's only natural that Danilo would assume that anything Cisco found out would come to his father's ears very quickly.

And do you believe that?

I'm not sure, Uncle. It seems to me that Cisco keeps his own counsel most of the time—that he doesn't trust anyone too far. And he might not trust his father very much either.

Why?

When Francisco was younger, the Ridenow Domain had several men who could have claimed it—two older brothers, and an uncle. They all came to grief, and a lot of people think that Francisco had a hand in their untimely deaths. Who knows if it's true or not.

I had almost forgotten how complex Darkovan alliances could become. They make the backroom dealing of the Federation look like a picnic in the park.

Domenic had never seen a park or been on a picnic, so he shrugged his shoulders and sipped his beer. *I described the man with Vancof, and told Duncan to keep an eye on them if they leave the taproom. Was that the right thing to do?*

Yes. Now, let's go eat something, since I think this might be a very long night for us.

When Herm and Nico came out of the inn an hour later, it was already dark, and the smallest moon, Mormallor, had risen. The smell of the night air was fresh, but heavy with the threat of rain, and it did not entirely conceal the pungent scent of the nearby stables and hen runs. This, added to the powerful scent of the growing number of people crowded into the courtyard was rather overwhelming at first. Then his nose stopped protesting, and he forgot about it.

Nico looked around with interest. He saw that torches had been set in stanchions around the broad courtyard of the Crowing Cock, and the wagons of the Travelers looked much better in that light than in the glare of day. The shabby paintings on the sides of the wains seemed prettier, and the worn costumes of the performers looked finer. He watched a fire eater stuff what seemed to be burning brands into his throat, and wondered how the trick was accomplished. Overhead, a slack rope had been drawn from the stables to one outjutting portion of the roof of the inn, and a slender female was just setting her comely foot on it, testing it for her acrobatics.

Half the town had turned out for the entertainment, and there was a great deal of noise. A juggler began to toss lighted torches into the air, and the crowd cheered, then jeered when he dropped one. The man, who had a comical face, just grinned and continued to perform. Everyone seemed to be talking at once, continuing discussions begun in the taproom, and a general air of anticipation ran through the crowd. Most of the people wore cloaks and capes, although the evening was not particularly cold yet, so the hoods were pushed back. The earlier wind had died away, and it was calm and almost pleasantly cool.

Domenic spotted the rest of the men whom Danilo had sent, mingling in the crowd. In spite of their ordinary clothing, they still seemed to him to be obviously Guardsmen, from the straightness of their backs and the alert way they watched the crowd. Still, he suspected that no one else would catch on immediately. And even though he almost resented their presence, part of him was very glad they were there. He also noticed the man who had ridden in during the afternoon, standing in a corner where the stables were connected to the wall of the inn and keeping an eye on everything. The entire scene began to take on a fantastic aspect to his eyes, as if the townspeople and the Travelers were a backdrop for a play which had not yet begun.

He closed his eyes for a moment, and swept the crowd with his mind, as his mother had taught him to do a few months earlier. It was a dizzying experience, with such a large number, but he was getting better at it. He sensed Rafaella, standing about ten feet away from him, keeping an eye on him as if he were her own child, and the other Renuciates scattered through the throng. From the Guardsmen he received the impression of puzzlement and a little worry, and realized that they were feeling more than a little resentment at their lack of directions. It was a shame that none of them had *laran,* and that the only way he could communicate with them was by using the Alton Gift.

Nico shifted his attention back to the Terranan, who was doing a reasonable job of fading into the crowd. He, too, was puzzled and annoyed, and waiting for something as well. Why did he keep looking up at the sky? And why was he looking to the north, toward the mountains, instead of toward Thendara and the spaceport.

He leaned his head back and scanned the dark sky, seeing a few bright stars poking through the light overcast that was moving slowly in from the west. In his present heightened state of awareness, he felt the earth beneath his feet and the movement of the clouds above him. There was a strong if brief temptation to let himself fall into a light trance, to listen to the planet itself, but he resisted it. Instead, he sniffed the air and guessed how long it would be before the rain arrived. Not long, he decided. The clouds were moving faster than when he had wakened from his nap, driven by a wind high up in the atmosphere. Then he returned his attention to the nameless spy hovering at the edge of the throng, turning so as to be able to observe him without being obvious.

Uncle Herm.

What is it?

The Terran man keeps looking north, at the sky, as if he is expecting to see something fly overhead. That's the wrong direction for Thendara and the spaceport. There is nothing that way except . . .

The Domains of the Aldaran and Ardais, as well as the estates of the Storn. And none of them have any Federation technology except my father. You need not try to spare my feelings, Nico. I'm just pleased that you are so observant, and are using your head.

Regis was always a little anxious about the number of Terranan in Aldaran territory, but since we managed to get your Domain back onto the Council, he thought it was taken care of. Your brother Robert is a good man.

My father, however, is another thing altogether. I know. It is one reason I jumped at the chance to leave Darkover when it was offered to me, to get away from him. There is no love lost between us, and I would not put anything past him.

But, Herm, surely he would not help the Federation kill my father!

I would not have thought so, but don't forget I have not seen him in nearly a quarter of a century. He might see it as a chance to further his own ambitions. I can't speculate, but I confess I have a very bad feeling about it. Do you have any idea how many Terranan are in the Aldaran Domain?

Several hundred, for certain.

And how many of those are soldiers and Marines?

That I could not say. I have always had the impression that most of them were technical folk.

We have been assuming that any attack would originate at the spaceport in Thendara, and we have overlooked the possibility that combat-ready men might be flown down from the Hellers. As soon as the performance is finished, you should get in touch with Lew and inform him of this possibility. This whole matter might be much more complex than we thought at first.

That is not a happy thought.

No, it isn't.

Domenic saw the side of the puppet van lower down on strong ropes, and the crowd began to press toward it, cutting off his view. He slipped through the people, using his still relatively short stature to advantage, and managed to elbow his way into the front of the throng. An enchanting vision was painted on a sheet of canvas, a vista of turreted castles and in the center, a very tall but recognizable Tower surrounded by a field of blue *kireseth* flowers. After a moment, a red-clad figure on strings began to cross the small stage. It was supposed to be a Keeper, obviously, but while the face was concealed beneath a veil, the skirts of the robe were indecently brief, revealing a pair of comely limbs sewn from some soft textile. He was not sure whether to be amused or scandalized.

The Keeper began to speak, and he recognized the voice of the red-haired girl, Illona Rider. What she declared made Domenic's ears turn red, and his cheeks burn with embarrassment. A young woman had no business saying things like that, especially one who seemed as nice as Illona! And they would never have dared perform such a play at Arilinn or any other Tower. He began to understand now why Regis had restricted the Travelers from frequent visits to Thendara.

Herm was standing just behind him now, with a hand on Domenic's shoulder. He could sense the Aldaran man's startlement and displeasure, and felt a little less upset. It was not that he was being a prig. What the puppet was voicing was disgraceful. Worse, the people in the crowd were laughing noisily and offering a few ripe comments of their own. He sensed a general feeling that the townspeople did not hold the Towers in great esteem, which was strange and puzzling to him.

Another puppet joined the Keeper on the stage, and they indulged in a verbal display of punning that had the crowd roaring with approval. He listened, wondering how Illona managed to create two such distinct voices, and then began to really pay attention to the wordplay. It was more than naughty, and came close to obscene. He saw a village woman nearby grab a young girl and haul her back into the throng, her face outraged. Around him others began to rustle with discomfort, and he saw that a few people were leaving the courtyard, casting glances over their shoulders as they hastened into the narrow street beyond the inn. They had clearly lost their taste for the entertainment.

Is this a typical thing, Nico?

I don't know. I saw the Travelers twice at Arilinn, but they never did anything like this. It is bad, isn't it? Hmm. Illona told me that a man called Mathias joined the troupe who has been writing some pieces for the players that she appeared to find . . . unseemly.

It is much worse than unseemly—it is subversive. It is one thing to make a little fun of an institution, but this goes far beyond that. If this is what the Travelers have been doing in the towns and villages, I am only surprised that they have been allowed to continue at all. All this stuff about keeping the common folk in their places, and taking their grain . . . is bound to whip up resentment. This is not my idea of amusement, and it isn't playing well with the crowd either. Who is that supposed to be?

A third puppet had entered, a male figure in fine but tawdry garments, wearing a two-pointed fool's hat with a wobbly crown around the it at the brow. The puppet was poorly made, and he had the impression that it had been constructed in haste, for it was not of the quality of the other two. It had a dissipated face, and legs that managed to mince in a very unmanly way. Domenic felt a rush of anger as he watched, for although the face of the figure was crudely carved and sewn, there was no mistaking the white hair beneath the hat. It could only have been intended to be Regis Hastur, and he was stunned and outraged at the same time.

Nico lowered his eyes and stared at the bare head of an urchin just in front of him, wondering what the little boy was thinking of what he saw. He probably didn't understand half of it, because the child seemed puzzled and restless. He did not want to watch the movement of the puppets any longer, and wished he were a hundred miles away.

Around him, Domenic could feel the crowd shift back and forth. The cheerful mood that had been present a few minutes before was gone, and there were mutters. In a few seconds, these turned to cries of outrage. Apparently, making fun at the expense of an imaginary Keeper was all right, but insulting the ruler of Darkover was not.

When he looked up, he knew that the puppeteers did not realize what was happening outside their wagon. The crowd was becoming very angry. It was all happening so quickly that the manipulators did not suspect a thing. In a sudden movement, half a dozen burly men, a little the worse for drink perhaps, rushed clumsily forward. One grabbed the offensive doll and yanked it hard. The strings snapped.

This action set off the rest of the audience. In a second there were twenty furious men around the wagon, and one pulled open the door at the end of it and climbed inside. Others tore at the painted screen, or the remaining figures, and the uproar spread through the crowd. The townspeople turned on the Travelers in a fury, seizing the innocent juggler and anyone else dressed in motley, and half a dozen fist fights broke out across the courtyard.

The man hauled a screaming, red-faced Illona out of the wagon, and slapped her hard across the face. Another man tried to pull the girl away from him, and the shouting between them degenerated into yet another fight. Two village constables tried to keep order, but there were too many fights going on for them to contain the fury of the mob, which was now howling for blood, without much concern as to whose was spilled.

Domenic took advantage of his size and darted between several infuriated men. Then he grabbed Illona's hand and yanked her toward him. She tried to snatch it back until she realized he was a rescuer, and not an enemy. "Come on," he shouted. "You are going to get hurt."

Illona glanced back, her eyes wide with terror, and then they dashed away, through the gates of the courtyard and into the dim light beyond it. She gave a short, sharp cry of pain, and he paused. It was then that he realized that she wore no shoes, and had stubbed her toe on a rock. All she was wearing was her undershift and drawers. He could just make out the rise and fall of small breasts beneath the thin fabric, as she gasped short, fearful breaths.

For a moment, he was too stunned to move. She just stood beside him, panting and frightened. Then Domenic whipped his cloak off his shoulders and wrapped it around her. A moment later Rafaella emerged from the darkness, and he realized that it had only been seconds since he dragged Illona away. He had never been so glad to see the Renunciate in his life.

The fracas began to spill out of the courtyard, and Rafaella seized both of them by the shoulders and herded them around toward the back of the building. The racket decreased as they went farther away, and the Renunciate drew them into a nest of shadows and halted. "I think it is better if we stay out of sight until things calm down a bit," she said, her voice shaking a little. "How could you have done such a thing, girl?"

"I didn't do anything," Illona snapped back, her fear fading into anger as she pushed a tangle of hair off her sweating face. She eyed the Renunciate fiercely, daring her to disagree.

"I don't call putting a puppet of Regis Hastur up for ridicule nothing. He has not been dead a tenday! And why aren't you dressed?" Domenic asked, letting his fury leak into the words.

Illona shrugged, shivered and drew the cloak more closely around her. "It gets very hot in the wagon, and close, too. I'd be a puddle if I wore all my clothes. As for the puppet—the Hasturs are a bunch of parasites."

To his surprise, Rafaella grabbed Illona by her shoulders and shook her hard, until he heard the girl's teeth rattle together. "How dare you speak that way! You are a stupid girl. I will have you know that Regis Hastur was a friend of mine, and one of the finest men who ever walked. Who put you up to that play? Tell me, or I will slap you silly."

Domenic had never seen his Aunt Rafi angry before, and he was rather awed. It reminded him a bit of his mother's infrequent rages, but there was a quality of restraint in her that Marguerida did not possess. He could sense the deep loyalty in Rafaella, a simple, steady emotion that calmed him enormously.

Illona, on the other hand, seemed to have lost both her earlier fear and her common sense. She pulled away from Rafaella's grip and glared.

"Everyone knows that the Domains are oppressing the people of Dark-over, and that we need to get rid of them in order to have a better life."

At first, Nico did not react. The words the girl used were strange, and he sensed that they had not come from her own mind, but from someone else's. She was parroting something she had heard, without any certainty or real understanding. But beneath the words, there was a core of a more personal emotion, made of fear and resentment, a puzzling mixture, fo-cused on the subject of the Towers. He wondered why she was afraid of the Towers; it was almost as if they threatened her.

The more he thought about it, the more confusing the text of the play became. Why would anyone suggest that the Towers were dens of vice—what purpose could it serve? Then he recalled the sense of mistrust he had noticed in the crowd when the puppet play began, the feeling from the townspeople that had puzzled him at the time. What had Herm said? That the play was subversive. Was someone trying to foment a revo-lution on Darkover? Who, and why? Had the Travelers been performing similar things whenever they were not in Thendara?

Rafaella's anger flared, and she lifted her hand to strike the girl, dis-tracting him from his thoughts. Domenic caught her wrist in his hand and shook his head. "Who told you that lie, Illona?" he asked. "And who is 'everyone?' " He managed to speak calmly, but his heart was pounding.

Illona looked at him, her eyes almost blank. "Well, our driver and a lot of the others, I guess. Mathias, who wrote the script for our play, says that . . . if it weren't for Regis Hastur, we would be able to fly about in aircars, and live in fine houses and . . ." Her voice was a monotone now, and Nico could tell she was pulling back into herself, that the violence she had just experienced was finally reaching her mind and sending it into a kind of shock.

"And of course Mathias is a knowledgeable man, and has been to Comyn Castle and seen this so-called oppression for himself," he com-mented. Despite his compassion for this girl, he was still very angry, and it helped to let his words release it.

"Well, no," she admitted meekly. Then she seemed to gather her energies, to shake off some of her fear and shock. "But the fact that we aren't allowed in Thendara except at Midsummer and Midwinter proves that the Hasturs are afraid of us, so it must be true."

"Your logic is impeccable, but your premises are false."

She narrowed her eyes and peered at him in the faint light from the back of the inn. Recognition dawned in her face. "I saw you in Thendara, didn't I? You were standing guard, hiding in the shadows near the Castle. You are one of them! You just look so different with your hair loose, and not in uniform. You are a spy for the Hasturs!"

I have to get away and tell Aunt Loret and the others!

"And who are *you* a spy for, Illona?"

"Me?" she squeaked, astounded.

Rafaella, impatient, demanded, "Who told you all these ridiculous things? And, more to the point, when did you hear them?"

An expression of confusion came into Illona's face. "People . . . like Mathias, I guess. When?"

"Have you been listening to this seditious nonsense all your life, or is it a recent thing?" Domenic could sense Rafi's puzzlement at his question, but he ignored it. He was determined to get to the bottom of the matter, and the girl was his best chance for that. He did not want to use forced rapport, but discovered, to his dismay, that he was willing to if he must. All the lessons in ethics he had taken at Arilinn rang in his mind, and for the first time, he realized how dangerous a thing the Alton Gift could be in the hands of someone who could set aside any consideration except their own needs. He hoped that Illona would tell him the truth without force.

Who is this boy, and why is he asking me this? There is something wrong here, but I can't figure out what it is. He's right—I never heard a word against the Hasturs before this spring, when we were in the Hellers, up in Aldaran country. Everything changed after that, didn't it? What are they going to do to me?

Illona seemed suddenly subdued. "This spring was when I first heard it." *Why am I telling him anything at all? He seemed so nice, and I liked him right away. But that is no reason to talk to him, is it? Aunt Loret didn't like that play, and now I see why. I wish I was somewhere else. I'm scared.*

"And this Mathias fellow, who wrote the play, how long has he been with you?"

"He joined our band this spring."

The noise from the courtyard was decreasing a little, although some shouting could still be heard. There was also the sound of wood being smashed, and Nico suspected that the Travelers' wagons were being demolished by the angry townspeople. A moment later he saw a burst of fire rise above the wall around the inn. Someone had put a torch to one of the wagons. "Illona, you have gotten yourself into a real mess."

"I have guessed that much," she said, some of her earlier sauciness returning. She gritted her teeth, forcing herself to stand up straight, and glared at Rafaella and Domenic. Even in the rather dim light, he could see she was very pale, and the freckles on her strong nose were very apparent. He marveled at her strength, at her refusal to surrender to her terrors completely. He was not sure how he would have behaved in the same situation.

"You have been in some bad company," Rafaella said quietly. She had regained her self-control, and in the shadows she seemed stern and powerful, but less threatening than a minute before.

Illona looked up at Rafaella, defiant. "I've never known anything but the Travelers, so I can't judge. My Aunt Loret thinks that Mathias and some of the others are a little crazy, but I didn't pay her any mind."

Herm Aldaran suddenly appeared out of the darkness, his expression invisible in the shadows. "Ah, there you are. I saw you snatch the girl from harm's way, and a good thing, too! The constables and our *friends* have managed to get things under control, but most of the wains are firewood now." He cleared his throat and shifted from foot to foot uncomfortably. "Some people have been killed . . . including your aunt, Illona. I'm sorry."

She did not react at once. She peered from face to face and then tears swelled in her eyes and began to trickle down her grubby cheek. Illona made no sound, just wept silently, shrinking into Domenic's cloak, getting smaller and smaller, as if she might puddle down to the ground. Rafaella put a supporting arm around her and drew the girl into her embrace.

Who else was killed, Herm?

I'm not certain, except for the woman and the juggler, who was in the wrong place at the wrong time. The crowd went mad, and I was very glad for the presence of those Guardsmen, even if I fear that their intervention has destroyed their anonymity. There is still a lot of confusion, though, and per-haps they will not be too obvious. I don't know where Vancof or the other Terran have got to. I looked around, but they seem to have vanished.

Domenic hesitated then, conscious of an inner conflict. Hermes Al-daran was the son of Damon Aldaran, the head of that Domain. True, Herm had assured him earlier that he was loyal, but all the old stories about Aldaran betrayal rose in his mind. Regis had managed to force the Council to allow *Dom* Damon and Robert Aldaran seats on it, but there was still a great deal of bad feeling about the entire family. He liked and trusted Hermes, and he thought well of Robert, didn't he? It was old *Dom* Damon he did not like. But where would Herm's real loyalties lie if it came to serious conflict?

Domenic struggled briefly with the problem. Then he made his choice, deciding he did not have time to consult with Lew or his father. The Terran stranger had kept looking to the north, and this band of Travelers had come from Aldaran territory in the spring—there might be no connection, but he could not assume that. *The girl says that when they came down from the mountains this spring, there was a change. I think that someone in the Hellers is up to mischief.*

Domenic was rather pleased at the diplomatic way he phrased this, but he had not anticipated the quickness of his uncle's mind. *If you mean my father, I would not put anything past him. He has always resented the Hasturs, and thought that the Aldaran could do a better job of running Dark-over. But, truthfully, this mess is not his style, Nico. My father is not a very subtle man, and spreading sedition would, I believe, never occur to him.*

I have to agree, from the little I know about Dom *Damon. But maybe he is backing them somehow.*

Unless he has changed a great deal in the past twenty-three years, I doubt it.

Why?

My father is stingy to a fault, Nico. He would not spend a sekal on something unless he could be sure to see a return. No, my guess is that there is something going on in the Aldaran Domain that the old bastard knows nothing about—that the Federation complex up there is behind this.

I hope you are right, Herm.

I hope I am, too, because I would not like to see my own father, much as I dislike him, involved in a plot to destroy the Domains.

It was getting colder now, especially without his cloak, and Nico shivered, as much from the chill as from the words he had just heard. The distrust of the Aldaran went back for generations, and it had been very important to Regis Hastur to overcome it. If it were discovered that they were involved in planning the overthrow of the Hasturs, all that effort would have been for nothing. And using the Travelers to spread discontent was very clever. They went everywhere, and spread gossip as they did.

But Herm was right about one thing—it was not the sort of behavior that *Dom* Damon had shown in the past. He tended to bluster and bully his way around. Domenic felt very young and a little helpless for a moment, as if too much had been put on his shoulders. And, as if he sensed this, Herm put a firm hand on his shoulder. "Let's get in out of the cold, shall we?" *And let Lew know about the latest developments.*

18

Domenic looked at Herm for a moment, in the flickering light from the courtyard. Then he said, "We should make sure everything is under control first." His words surprised him, and the firm voice that came from his throat seemed to be that of another—some older, stronger person than himself.

"Yes, I suppose another few minutes will not matter," Herm agreed. "Rafaella, take Illona with you, please. She needs a hot bath—look how she is shivering."

"I don't want to go with her," Illona wailed, sounding suddenly very young and afraid. "I want my aunt!"

"I know you do," Rafaella began gently. "But you will have to make do with me. It is going to start raining soon, and if you stay out here, you will get an inflammation of the lung and have to drink all manner of nasty-tasting things to heal you."

"I wish I was dead, too," the girl moaned.

"No, you don't!" Herm was stern. "And Loret would not want you dead either—she wanted you to be safe, child."

"I . . . can't believe she is dead. Now I am all alone . . . what is going to happen to me?"

"Nothing is going to happen to you, Illona," Rafi told the girl almost tenderly. "Now come along." The girl hesitated, then finally allowed the older woman to draw her away.

It was growing colder, and Nico was sorry he no longer had his cloak. He wanted to follow the girl and the Renunciate into the warmth of the inn. Instead, his sense of duty gripped him—the very thing he had run away to avoid—and he marched back into the courtyard purposefully. There was a great deal of heat from the fire, and the yard was unnaturally warm. Destruction was everywhere. He needed to introduce Herm to the old Guardsmen who were helping put out the fires and carry the dead and wounded away.

Yet, the scene within the yard was less chaotic than he might have imagined. Most of the fires were beginning to gutter out from lack of fuel. There was a terrible smell, of burned wood, paint, and probably flesh as well. There had been people in the wagons when they went up, and not all of them had escaped. His stomach gave a slight lurch.

Domenic spotted Duncan Lindir first and went over to him. The man was very pale in the light that remained. "How many dead have you found?"

"Six Travelers, *vai dom,* and one man from the village. There may be more in the rubble—it is still too hot to handle—but I hope not. Then there are the injured—quite a lot, but I am not sure of the number yet. Mostly broken arms and knocked heads. The Renunciate healer is seeing to them with the help of the village healer."

"Very good, Duncan. This is Hermes Aldaran."

Duncan sketched a brief bow, as if reluctant to show respect to an Aldaran. "I was told to ask you for orders, but I did not have the chance earlier, *dom.*" His tone was barely civil, as if he was forcing himself to say the words without meaning them.

"Just as well, since I had none to give you," Herm answered, pretending he had not noticed the man's mild rudeness. "I would like to know the rest of your company."

"Well, they are rather . . ."

"I did not mean this instant, man! I can see they are very busy. Just point them out and tell me their names . . . if you would be so kind."

The irony of his answer was not lost on Lindir, and Duncan's mouth twisted in something approaching a smile. He nodded then, and Domenic could sense the old Guardsman's barely supressed hostility toward Herm begin to diminish. He watched the two men, speaking in quieter voices now, and wondered how his uncle did it. It was the same thing as had happened with Loret that afternoon. But Herm did not seem to be trying to be charming now, just businesslike and impersonal. If there was a *laran* for persuasion, then Herm had it, he decided. Nico moved away, restless and uneasy. Where had Vancof and the other man gotten to? Had they been hurt or perhaps killed in the riot?

He walked toward the corner where he had last seen the Terran man standing, an inky cluster of shadows where the stables met the wall of the inn. There was a low bench there, where the grooms and stable lads waited for wayfarers or rested from their duties, almost invisible except as a deeper shadow against the wall of the inn. He stood there for a moment to let his eyes adjust to the near darkness, and then he saw a boot.

Nico squatted down and peered beneath the bench. The boot had once been shining leather, but now was scuffed and a little muddy. It led to a leg, and as his eyes were able to see more, he realized he was looking at the body of the nameless man. There was no movement, no rise and fall in the chest. He swallowed very hard several times, then reached out and put his hands around the boot.

He stood up and used his weight to try to pull the body out from beneath the bench. The man was heavy, but at last the corpse slithered out across the uneven stones of the courtyard. There was the sound of footfalls behind Domenic, and a moment later Abel MacEwan was beside him, shouldering him firmly out of the way and taking the burden of dead flesh into his larger and more capable hands.

The torso of the dead man was slumped forward, but now it fell back, and Domenic could see the hilt of a knife thrust into the chest. A stain spread around the wound, dark against the brown cloth of the tunic. Someone brought a torch, and he looked down into the face of the stranger.

The eyes were still open, and the mouth gaped a little. He seemed, in death, to be surprised. Nico could not drag his eyes away from the sight, until someone finally took the shoulders of the corpse and Abel the feet and, between them, began to carry it away.

No, not surprised—betrayed. Swaying a little from the shock of it,

Domenic knew that no one from the village had killed the man. It must have been Vancof—though why was a mystery. Then he remembered that morning, seeing the dead man give the driver something. He closed his eyes, trying to recall every detail. There had been something folded, a paper, and another object, something square.

As the fires went out, the chill of the evening began to make Domenic shiver. Despite his discomfort, he did not move, frozen in place with sorrow and horror. Instead, he forced himself to try to remember anything he had overheard from Vancof. Most of it was a useless muddle, but a few phrases seemed to be important. The word "orders" kept cropping up, something the driver did not like, which made him afraid. What had he been ordered to do—kill his ally? That was insane! Still, there seemed no other explanation, and he forced his mind to accept it.

Almost shaking with chill and emotion now, Domenic trudged into the inn. The warmth of the entrance seemed almost feverish for a few steps. He brushed his sleeve across his face roughly. Then, too weary to continue, he sank onto a bench near the door.

Nico felt his control slip away in a flood of unfamiliar emotions. He wanted to weep, but no tears came. He felt as if he had turned to stone, and he ached for release. People were dead, innocent folk like Illona's Aunt Loret, whom he had known only for a few minutes. The Terran man, whose name he had never discovered, was dead also. He had not seen the others, but he had seen the unknown Terran, and knew, deep down, that he had not deserved to perish.

The deep grief for the death of Regis Hastur, which he had held at bay for days, rose in his throat at last. He remembered incidents, pleasant moments when his great-uncle was at ease, telling tales of the Sharra Rebellion, to Grandfather Lew's obvious discomfort, but somehow making them seem less painful than they must have been. Nico recalled Regis' charm and swift wit, the way he ate his meals, and many other small things. It did not seem enough, somehow, for such a great man.

His chest ached, and there was a pounding pulse in his forehead. A tear rolled down his cheek and he swept it away with a trembling finger. All he had done was run away for a bit of fun, and now there were dead people and injured folk, and too much pain to endure. This was not an adventure—it was a nightmare from which he could not escape!

If only Lew or his mother could be with him, to tell him how to feel, to help him. Logically, Domenic knew that the riot would have happened whether he had been present or not, but he still felt responsible. After dwelling on this unsettling event and feeling worse by the moment his good sense tried to assert itself, and succeeded a little. He was being morbid over things he could not control! He had to get a grip on himself and inform his grandfather of the events in Carcosa. Now, if only his cold and tired body would cooperate!

Domenic forced himself to stand and half stumbled up the stairs to his room. Once there, he slammed the door shut and sank down on the edge of the bed. His breathing was ragged and he tried to control it. At last the rapid beating of his heart started to slow, and the dreadful thoughts that were racing through his mind began to subside. He closed his eyes hard, pinching the lids down almost angrily, trying in vain to squeeze the images of destruction out of his mind's eye.

From below, he could hear voices, townspeople and Guardsmen both. The sickening smell of the burned wood and flesh lingered in the air. Then he realized that the stench was in his clothes, his hair, his skin, and he almost vomited. He pulled his tunic over his head and threw it across the room into the far corner. The movement energized him enough to shed all his garments, and to pour cold water from the ewer into the basin and wash himself. Then he put on a clean shirt from their purchases in the town market, and the trousers he had worn the previous day. The comforting smell of horse from the garment seemed to dispell the miasma of death in his discarded clothing as well as the scents that wafted through the window.

After several minutes he heard a soft rain begin to patter outside the window, a sweet sound after so much horror. He just sat and listened to it, his mind almost empty. All he wanted to do was fall into the bed and pull the covers over his head. But he still had something to do—if only he could remember what. Oh, yes, he had to contact his grandfather. Where was he going to find the strength?

His mind drifted, refusing to focus, and he found his thoughts return-ing to the girl, Illona. He was glad she was safe with Rafaella. If the Carcosans had discovered her and recognized her for a Traveler, she might have been hurt or killed. Domenic could not have endured that, although he wasn't sure why he cared so much about someone he barely knew. Then it occurred to him that he liked her, even if she was just a silly uneducated girl. No . . . not silly—just very foolish and ignorant. If only she had not looked so fetching in her undershift! Why couldn't she be ugly or at least plain? Then it would be easier to despise her, as he was sure he should. Instead, he had the same urge to protect her he always felt about Alanna. It was all very puzzling.

No, it was more than that. After a few moments of ruthless self-examination, Domenic realized that his thoughts about Illona verged on the lustful. This surprised him, and then it disgusted him. How could he be thinking such things at a time like this! What kind of unnatural man was he?

Furious with himself, Domenic dragged his mind away from the memories of Illona's young breasts and slender body beneath her shift. Herm had told him to inform Lew of the latest developments and he had not yet done so. He was there because he had the Alton Gift and could communicate with his grandfather with much less effort than anyone without that talent. For just a moment he resented his Gift, then shut away the thought abruptly. Why couldn't he have just one feeling at a time, instead of this morass! And why couldn't he get the image of the dead Terran out of his mind?

At last his mind began to quiet, and while he knew it had taken only a few minutes, it felt like he had undergone hours of fruitless struggle. There was a sour taste in his mouth, and his belly was in a complete knot. Domenic had wanted to be treated like an adult, not a child, and here he was, feeling angry at having adult responsibilities. At last he admitted to himself that he was more than a little frightened by the sudden violence he had seen, and realized that he must have been crazy to have dashed over to rescue Illona. He let the sense of fear spend itself, and wondered if he were a coward, or if it was normal to be scared after the fact. There was no one at hand to ask about it, and finally he let it go. Fear was a luxury to be indulged some other time.

He got up and rinsed his mouth in the basin, then splashed cold water over his face. After he had dried it on a towel, he went back to the broad bed and forced his mind into the stillness he needed. It was hard, but the Alton Gift could span great distance, and after only a brief time, he touched the familiar mind of his grandfather.

Lew!

Hello, Nico. you seem . . . upset. Did our reinforcement arrive safely? The mental voice sounded overly hearty, and Domenic felt his heart clench sharply. Had something terrible happened in Thendara? Was he overreacting to Lew's concerns about him, jumping at shadows instead of acting like an adult? He made himself slow down, and tried to order his thoughts.

I am. I just saw my first riot, and I hope I never see another. The Travelers tried to put on a play that infuriated the crowd—it was disgusting and indecent. They were making fun of Regis—it was not funny at all. It was so ugly. Uncle Herm said it was subversive and that the intent was to turn people against the Comyn! What began as a pleasant evening's entertainment turned the townsfolk into a mob in a flash. They tore apart the wagons and burned them. People got killed.

Are you all right? The tone of the question was alarmed, even if the words were commonplace.

Yes, I'm fine, but don't tell Mother about it, please. She'd be on her horse and traveling the North Road in a minute. But there is more, and it is worse, I think. It seems that this troup of Travelers were up in the Hellers, in the Aldaran Domain, last winter, and when they came back, they had not only this Vancof I told you about, but some other people who were spreading a tale of . . . well, I don't quite know how to put it. It's like they were trying to make people mad at the Hasturs, and at the Domains and the Towers in general. I don't know if it was just this bunch, or other groups of Travelers as well.

There was a small fracas in the Horse Market involving the Travelers at Midsummer. Regis was even thinking of banning them from the city completely, because there have been incidents recently as well. So, unless it was the group you have there, it might be . . .

Grandfather, I think someone is using the Travelers to upset people. It is either the Terranan or . . . or Dom Aldaran.

I was afraid of that. Poor Dom Damon—so ambitious and so thwarted. It is funny, you know, that all of Javanne's fears that Mikhail might hand Darkover over to the Terrans are much more likely to be fulfilled if Damon Aldaran ever gets his hands on some power.

But that could never happen, could it?

The Hasturs have been ruling Darkover for a long time, Nico, but nothing lasts forever. And yes, if something happened to your father, you and Rory, and a few other well-chosen people, then Damon Aldaran might be able to declare himself in command.

How?

Through Gisela, in her marriage to your uncle Rafael, of course. That would have the illusion of legitimacy. But we don't need to speculate. You and your brother are very much alive and well, and so is your father. He has just arrived, by the way.

Who? Father?

No. Dom *Damon and Robert Aldaran. They flew down, which was a mistake on their part. The landing field has been closed for two days, the Terrans nearly clapped them in chains. Robert was able to talk his way out of that, but Damon is in a rare temper.*

It's a pity he is a lord of the Domains, or otherwise you could put him in the cellar until after this mess is over.

A temptation, to be sure. There never seems to be a moldy dungeon available when you need one. There has been quite a bit of trouble from the Terrans here since you left, and we are going to turn the old Orphanage into a jail.

Grandfather! Be serious!

I am not joking. I wonder if Dom *Damon knows about this plot . . . no, I think not. But, if the funeral train is attacked, he will be in as much danger as the rest of us. The problem in a battle is that you cannot plan who will survive and who will not, and if the Terranan think to set up* Dom *Damon. . . .*

Grandfather!

Sorry, Nico. I am feeling extremely harassed just now. Rafe Scott has found out that the Federation has cut off communication with Darkover, for reasons which remain unclear, and perhaps the plot to attack the funeral will turn out to be nothing at all. I don't know if Belfontaine would risk taking action without approval, and I can't pop over to HQ, as I might have in the past, to see how the wind is blowing. I sincerely hope that it will all turn out to be a tempest in a chamber pot, because I don't particularly want to go up against energy weapons with my rather rusty sword.

Herm and I were thinking about that a little while ago. So much has happened, Grandfather, and my mind seems so muddled.

Take your time, Nico.

It started because the Terranan spy from Thendara . . .

The what?

Remember I told you I saw two men last night—one was Granfell and one wasn't? Well, the one that wasn't rode in here late this afternoon, before the old Guardsmen arrived.

Go on.

He came out to watch the Travelers, and I noticed he kept looking up at

*the sky, but he wasn't looking south, toward Thendara, but north instead. I
mentioned this to Uncle Herm, and he asked me how many troops there were
up in the Aldaran Domain. He suggested that perhaps the attack could come
from them, rather than from HQ.*

*Yes, that makes a kind of sense, now you say it. Herm has the most
devious mind I have ever encountered, and I have always been grateful he was
on my side, and not my enemy.*

Do you trust him?

*I do, Nico. He has proven over and over, in his time in the Senate and the
Chamber of Deputies, that he had nothing but the best interests of Darkover in
mind. He has had at least a dozen opportunities to sell us out, and he never
did. There is more, isn't there? What are you holding back?*

Domenic paused, trying to control the upwelling of sorrow within
him. *The Terranan man is dead. I never knew his name, and now I never
will, because someone—Vancof probably—stuck a knife in him during the
riot. I . . . found the body.*

*Poor Nico! The first time you look at death is always hard, and it never
gets easier.* Nico caught fragments, images of several bodies, and knew
that his grandfather was remembering the Sharra Rebellion. *No wonder
you are upset.*

He looked so surprised, Grandfather! And that isn't the worst part.

Tell me everything.

*It's so awful, and I feel . . . ashamed. I found him, and I was sorry and
sad. But afterwards . . . I started having these thoughts about Illona—that's
the Traveler girl I saw yesterday in Thendara—and they were . . . when the
crowd attacked the puppeteer's wagon, she got pulled out, and she was only
wearing her underclothes! She was almost naked! One second I was feeling
terrible, and the next, I was . . . excited.*

For a moment, there was no answering thought, and Nico wondered
if his grandfather were disgusted with him. *Nico, I do not know why it is,
but close contact with death often makes men very randy. Men going into
battle often resort to the couch before, and again after. I think that love or sex
or whatever we call it is about life, and when you are near to death, then you
wish to . . . renew life. In a young man your age, sexual feelings run very high.*

I don't like how I was thinking!

*I did not suppose you did, Domenic. And all I am telling you is that it is
a perfectly natural reaction, not something to be ashamed of, or worry over,
unless you pursue your instincts and force yourself upon a woman.*

I wouldn't!

I did not think so. Now, let the matter go, and stop being so hard on yourself. You will wear yourself out, and you need to save your energy for other things.

Yes, you are right. Grandfather, I am very confused. I don't understand why the man was killed like that. I think Vancof did it, because no one here in Carcosa knew the stranger, and the others who died in the riot were hit with sticks . . . I mean . . .

I understand, Nico. If you are right, and your spy did the killing, than I think it was probably that he took advantage of the uproar. You suggested last night that this Vancof was afraid, and very reluctant to go along with Granfell's plan. Perhaps his idea was to get rid of this fellow, and then try to vanish. Or maybe he was just evening up some old scores. Nico, one thing you will have to learn is that people sometimes kill one another for no good reason at all. It is a sad reflection on the species, but we don't seem to outgrow it, even here on Darkover, where murders are few.

I'll try, but it is very hard to understand. And I just hate it. Grandfather . . . Herm just came in. Wait a minute.

Herm Aldaran, his balding pate gleaming with rain, was holding a small object in his hands, a collection of metal and brightly colored wires. "Just look what I found in the remains of one of the wagons."

"What is it?"

"A communication device, for sending messages. It is called a short-beam and quite illegal on Darkover. I wonder where the receiver is? A pity it is ruined, since I might have been able to use it to create some trouble at the other end."

"Was it in the puppet wagon?"

"No, in another. It was under a stack of pages that had the most incredible filth on them."

"Then it was probably the one called Mathias, who wrote the plays. But why would he have it . . . ?"

"This was nothing like a play—these were broadsheets."

"Do you think Mathias and Vancof were working together?"

"I've no idea, but Duncan grabbed the man before he could hare off into the night, and we can ask him." His usually pleasant face had an expression on it that Domenic found most disquieting. "Now, where did I put my thumbscrews?"

"Your what?"

"I have shocked you. Forgive me. I don't really intend to torture the man, but he doesn't need to know that, does he? I am just working myself up to scare the filth out of his bowels, Nico. It's that, or else ask you to go into his mind and find out what we want to know."

Domenic considered this evidence of a ruthlessness he had never suspected, and decided he would rather scare Mathias than plunder the man's mind. "But what if he lies," he managed to say at last.

"You would be able to tell if he did. So, come along. This is going to be very unpleasant."

"Just a minute. Let me finish talking to Lew."

"Of course."

Domenic closed his eyes again, although he did not need to, and completed his interrupted conversation with his grandfather, feeling more and more uneasy as he did. He did not want to interrogate anyone, because he was afraid of what he would learn. The sense of adventure which had sustained him the night before vanished, and he was left with the reality, which was not nearly as comfortable. Odd—the people in the books he had read never seemed to have such conflicts.

There was a third floor in the inn, and Herm led him up to it. The raucous sounds of the still agitated townsfolk receded a little as they ascended. Nico discovered that he was sweating slightly, and the stink of it told him how anxious he was.

There were several small rooms along the corridor, and they went to one at the end of it, a tiny chamber that was occupied by three Guardsmen, as well as a man he had never seen before. The stranger, who must be Mathias, had pale hair and the look of the Dry Towns about him. His light blue eyes were constricted almost to pinpoints, and he looked frightened out of his wits. Six people in the small room was too many, and the heat of their bodies was almost overwhelming. It was like stepping into an oven, but instead of the nice smell of bread, there was only the stench of fear and anger.

With no spoken word of command, two of the men stepped out into the hall, leaving Duncan, Herm, and Domenic alone with the hapless man. They were standing, and he was seated on a rush chair, his hands bound with a rope. The atmosphere in the room seemed a little less stifling now, and Mathias looked from one face to another, seeking some sign of release and finding nothing to lessen his terror. Nico thought he did not look at all like a spy or a revolutionary, but was just an ordinary man. And clearly he was not a very brave one.

Hermes smiled, but there was no friendliness in it. He looked like a wolf, and a hungry one at that. Mathias shifted on his chair, squirming. "I trust you are comfortable," Herm said very quietly, his voice menacing in spite of the pleasant words.

"Why have you dragged me up here?" Mathias half snarled, half whined. "I have done nothing wrong."

Herm laughed. He had a deep, rumbling chuckle that Domenic was fond of, though now it seemed to take on a sinister quality. "That's rich! Nothing wrong. You've been writing scandalous plays, and we found broadsheets that will have you on the gibbet."

"I don't know what you are talking about." *How am I going to get out of this?*

"You are a filthy spy for the Terranan," Herm announced.

Mathias seemed to brighten a little. "I am no such thing. I am a Son of Darkover, and I don't have any truck with any Terranan."

"We are all sons of Darkover here, aren't we?" When he received no response, he asked, "What do you mean by that?" *Nico, have you ever heard of these Sons?*

Curse it—why did I say that? "We are people dedicated to the betterment of Darkover."

No. From what I can gather from his mind, they are some sort of fraternal organization, dating back to the time of Danvan Hastur. Maybe Danilo Syrtis-Ardais knows more about them. Their aims seem to be . . . the establishment of some government with themselves as rulers. But I am not sure of that, because unless I actually probe him, I can only get a vague sense of things.

Ah—revolutionaries! Thanks, Nico.

"And what betterment do you intend?"

"Why, to stop slaving for the lords of the Domains and be free. There is nothing wrong with that, is there?" Mathias sounded less frightened now, as if Herm's behavior was lulling him into a false sense of calm.

"How many lords have you encountered, and how did they make you slave for them?" Herm sounded almost amused now.

"Everyone knows that the Domains exist on the hard work and sweat of the common people, who are too stupid to realize that they are being kept in servitude."

"That is a pretty poor opinion to have of the people you would like to save, don't you think?" Herm sounded quite disinterested now, almost as if he were inviting the man into an intellectual discussion. Then without warning, he shifted, learning forward toward the bound Mathias, and raising his voice menacingly. "Now, tell me about the broadsheets! Where were they printed, and who wrote them?"

This change in tone made Mathias cringe back in the rush chair, and it creaked almost musically under the movement. Domenic realized that he had been prepared to declare several more outrageous sentiments, and had not expected to be asked about the damning papers. "What broadsheets?" *I knew those damn things were going to get me into hot water! I wish Dirck had never persuaded me to write them. I wish Dirck had been strangled by his birthing cord. I would not be in this mess if it were not for him!*

"The ones we found in your wagon," Herm answered calmly.

"I don't know what you are talking about. I am just a Traveling man, a poor scribner. You have no right to haul me around and tie me up like this. Who the hell are you, anyhow?" It was bluster, and needed no telepathy to be deciphered.

Duncan rolled onto the balls of his feet. In spite of his gray hair and slight paunch, the impression he gave was of a man who had just run out of patience, and was prepared to use his fists if necessary. "Don't you take that tone. You are in enough trouble as it is. Answer the question. Where were those sheets printed?"

Mathias flinched and shivered, looking from Herm to Duncan and back again, seeking any hint of mercy. He cast a glance at Nico, frowned slightly, and swallowed hard. "I don't know anything." *They'll never find the press in a million years. They will never think to look in Aldaran Castle.*

Domenic conveyed this fresh information to Herm, and saw his uncle's shoulders sag a little. Then he straightened and glowered. "Tell me about the driver of the puppet wagon."

Now Mathias looked confused, as if he had expected more questions about the papers, and worried as well. "What about him?"

"Who is he, and where did he come from?"

"He's just a man. He came from another band of Travelers, and he joined up with us this spring." *Curse him. I always thought there was something wrong with the bastard. He said he was one of the Sons, but I should never have believed him. But he knew all the passwords! This is all his fault.*

"What troupe of Travelers is he from?"

"I don't remember." *Dirck said he used to drive for Dyan Player, but he died two years ago. What do these people want from me?*

"Did he put you up to writing that puppet play tonight?"

"Yes. No."

"Which is it?"

"Dirck said we needed something stronger, that it would get the people riled up more if we told how the Towers were full of wicked people, who lived off the backs of the poor, and . . ."

"That's enough. I don't want to hear any of your silly cant." Herm shook his head dismissively. "So, this Dirck suggested you write a play that involved a Keeper and Regis Hastur, and you actually wrote it. Is that right?"

"I suppose."

"Why did you choose Regis Hastur?"

"He's dead and can't squawk—and a good thing, too! Everyone knows he's been keeping behind the walls of Comyn Castle so as no one would kill him, all these years."

"What a truly disgusting creature you are," Herm said quietly. "Now the only question is what do we do with you?"

"I'm not afraid to die for what I believe in," Mathias sniveled, looking perfectly terrified. "I'll be a hero." *The Sons will save me—if I can just get word to them.*

"No one will even miss you, you sack of dirt." Duncan growled these words, then turned away in disgust. After a moment, he turned back. "You are a disgrace to an old and respectable fellowship."

Herm and Domenic looked at Duncan in surprise, but the man said nothing more. Instead, the old Guardsman made a gesture, suggesting that he wanted to talk out of hearing of the miserable captive. Herm nodded slightly, stepped to the door, and ordered one of the men outside to come in. Then he and Duncan left the room, and Domenic followed them.

"I take it you know something about these Sons of Darkover, Lindir."

"Not really, *dom,* and it took me a few minutes to remember that I had heard of them before. But I think that Istvan has a brother who is a member—shall I fetch him?"

"Yes, that would be very useful." Duncan walked away and went down the stairs. The second Guard remained beside the door, trying to fade into the paneling on the wall behind him, but was clearly very curious.

"Well, nephew, what do you think?"

"I think that we might learn more from Mathias, but I don't think it would be very useful. I don't believe he knows very much, not really." Nico paused and thought for a moment. "What we do not know is how many other of the Travelers are involved in this. It might be that there is only Vancof, with this group, but it could be that there are Federation spies in others. So, I think that all the Travelers need to be found, wherever they are, and detained."

"A good idea. How do we go about that?"

"I'll tell Lew what we have learned, and he can get the Tower relays humming, and before morning, they can be located. I will leave it to someone else to decide what to do with them—I am so tired, Uncle!"

"Of course you are. You have been pulling extra duty being the message center for our little effort."

"Little!"

"All right—that was too modest a word. Would 'enormous' please you more?"

"Nothing would please me except another bath, a second supper, and bed for about three days."

Duncan returned with another man, introduced him as Istvan Mac-Ross, and looked very pleased with himself. He gave Nico a droll look, and Domenic smiled back at him. It felt very good to have trusted retainers around him just then.

"Tell me what you know about the Sons of Darkover, Istvan."

Istvan grinned. He had a scar across his forehead and cheek, and the smile make him look very frightening. "Not much, *vai dom*. My younger brother was a member, years back, and since it is a secret fellowship, did not tell me a great deal. They call themselves the Ancient and Loyal Sons of Darkover, and they came into being during the final years of Danvan Hastur's rule. A fine-sounding name for a rabble of discontents who have never done much that I can tell except gather together to piss and moan about how they could run things much better if they could only think of how to do it."

"What do they want?"

"There I am not sure, except something different. They do not regard the Domains with any love—that was what made my brother leave them after a couple of years—but I never heard of them doing anything against the Comyn. I think what they really like is being secret—having pass-words and all manner of nonsense."

"Do you think there is a branch of the organization here in Carcosa?"

"Might be. See, the way they do it is like this. They never get together in groups larger than six, and only one of those six knows how to reach another. They call the divisions rhowyns, after the six-petaled flower of that tree. Pretty silly, really, for if something happens to the man who knows, they are out of luck."

"I see. A pretty ordinary secret society setup—and no way to find them unless you know the passwords or something."

"Just so, my lord."

"Thank you."

Herm, it sounds to me as if Vancof just took advantage of these Sons, and they are not really a serious threat.

I agree. Which is a great relief, because I think that the Federation is all the trouble we can manage at present. I suspect that Federation Intelligence tried to infiltrate these Sons, then decided that the Travelers were a better bet. Who knows—I can think of a hundred possibilities.

I can also—and I am rather relieved that it is all nonsense, Uncle.

It is not all nonsense, Nico. There is a real plot, a dangerous one, even if the plotters are not very capable. We must count ourselves fortunate that we stumbled into it—that you were a very naughty lad with a good head on your shoulders—before it turned into a massacre. Even if the Sons and the Travelers are neutralized, there remains the Federation. Why did I imagine that return-ing to Darkover would be a pleasant and peaceful experience?

Yes, I know. What should we do about Vancof?

Since he seems to have vanished, there is nothing I can think of, unless you have some means to track his whereabouts, nephew. "Tell me, Istvan, do you believe these Sons are any real threat to the Comyn?"

"I could not say, *dom,* but from what I learned from my brother, they are more talk than action."

"Do you imagine they might use the excuse of Regis Hastur's death to foment some sort of uprising?"

Istvan looked horrified. "I don't, but I might be wrong."

Why is that important, Herm?

It is just an idea, and probably not a very useful one. If the Federation has been trying to use either the Sons or the Travelers to destablize Darkover, then they might create some sort of situation which would justify them using force here. They would not have to assassinate anyone, just say that they were keeping the peace here on Darkover. They might have been planning such a thing, but with the dissolution of the legislature and the planned pullout in a few weeks' time, they would have to rush things. Under such circumstances, they would just declare a state of emergency and use force outright. Did you get any sense of such a possibility from our captive?

He thought about the passwords a little, and I had the impression there were hand signals, too. Vancof knew enough of them to convince Mathias he was one of the fellowship. But how Mathias would contact another rhowyn I don't know. I mean, standing in the middle of the marketplace and putting your little finger in your ear until someone came up and scratched his nose doesn't seem like a very good system to me. I think his hope of contacting them is the wish of a desperate man. And even if he did, how would they rescue him, if they are as foolish as Istvan makes them seem?

Never underestimate your foes, Nico. If I were running a secret society, I would make sure that no one felt threatened by it until the time was ripe. I would make it appear feeble and foolish, so that no one would pay it the least mind.

Grandfather was right—he said he was glad you are on our side, and not that of our enemies. I will tell Lew what we just learned, and he can get things in motion. Nico paused, anxious and hesitant. *Do you think your father is involved, or is he . . . ?*

I don't know, but secret societies are not really my father's style—he is too impatient for that. Besides, if they really do want to overthrow the Comyn, he would hardly want them for allies, since his ambition is to lead the Comyn and run Darkover to suit himself, not a bunch of half-baked revolutionaries.

Istvan thought they were mostly tradesmen . . . I caught that impression when he was talking.

Humph! Catch my old man consorting with merchants and weavers! I think not. He's too proud for that.

A wave of fatigue struck Domenic, and his knees trembled. He sucked in a deep gust of air, and started down the hall. As he reached the head of the stairs, he overheard the thoughts of the man tied up in the room. *Who is that boy, and why is he here? I saw him talking to that bitch Illona earlier. Where did she get to? He is probably a spy for the Hasturs. I hope I will see them in Zandru's coldest hell before the week is out! I must find a way to reach the Sons and warn them. But how? Maybe when they feed me—if they don't starve me to death—I can signal. Surely someone in the inn must belong to the Sons.*

Herm—Mathias thinks that someone in the inn might be a contact—keep him away from everyone but our own people.

Oh, I intend to— but good thinking, Nico. Yet that presents a fresh problem, doesn't it?

Anger flooded through Nico. It took all of his will not to use the Alton Gift in a way he had never done before, to plunder Mathias' mind of everything it knew. He felt Herm's mental flinch as his emotions reached the other man, and was ashamed at the loss of control. *Yes, it does. It means we have to suspect everyone—I hate that, Herm.*

Not necessarily—you are very tired and are forgetting our companions, the Renunciates.

Would Rafaella know about the Sons? Domenic felt incredibly stupid for not thinking of the Renunciates sooner. *Well, she and her sisters know how to find things out, so I'll ask her.*

No, Nico. You deal with Lew and then try to get some rest. I will talk to Rafaella after I have a few more words with Mathias.

Domenic stood at the head of the stairs for a minute, feeling too dizzy to start down. Overhead, he could hear the rain falling on the roof tiles, a pleasant sound that seemed to clear his mind. He was sweating again, and knew he was close to the edge of his own endurance. He wiped his face on the sleeve of his shirt wearily. There was still a great deal to do before he could rest.

As he came down the stairs, he heard the sound of boots coming from the lower floor of the inn, up the stairs. For no conscious reason, he halted in his own descent and waited to see who it was. He knew the Renunciates had taken two rooms at one end of the corridor, the one next to his, but there were other guests at the Crowing Cock that night.

Briefly he chided himself for being so jumpy. Then he saw the shoulders and head of a man appear, and then the rest of the body, illuminated by the lampions along the hall. He had never seen the face before, but as soon as the stranger turned and walked down the corridor, he knew it must be Granfell. The shape of his skull from the rear, and the way he strode were unmistakable. He was wearing Darkovan clothing now, like the dead man had, but they looked wrong. Granfell tugged at the edge of his tunic, as if he found it uncomfortable. His light-colored hair was wet, and it was clear that he had just arrived. He knocked at a door at the far end of the corridor, and Nico wondered how he knew which room to pick. When there was no answer, he quickly opened the door and entered.

Uncle Herm, I just saw the man called Granfell go into the room on the back of the inn, at the other end of our corridor. He's wet, so I think he just rode in. He must be looking for the other man, the one that was knifed.

Wonderful. I told MacHaworth that if anyone came looking for the stranger, he was to tell him what room to go to. I am glad he can follow orders.

So, that's how he knew. I was wondering about it. Are we going to grab him and use your thumb screws? Domenic was startled by the sudden change in himself, although he knew perfectly well that Herm was not going to torture anyone. His fear and grief seemed to have vanished, and in their place he found a peculiar desire to hurt someone or something. It was gone almost before he could understand it, but it revealed to him a part of his character he had never suspected he possessed.

Don't be bloodthirsty—it does not become a future ruler of Darkover. No, I think not. We will let him think that their plot is undiscovered for a while yet. And see if Vancof turns up again. Go and get the Towers alerted, and then try to get some sleep. You will need all your strength tomorrow.

Yes, I will. Nico felt shamed for a moment. Herm should not have to tell him not to be bloodthirsty. Then he realized that his uncle had been teasing him gently, that it had not been meant to be the rebuke he took it for. He just was not used to being spoken to as Herm spoke to him, and he took it too seriously.

Someone—was it Danilo Ardais?—had said in his hearing "Violence begets more violence," so perhaps his momentary lapse was something normal. But between that and his earlier thoughts about Illona's scantily clad body, he felt as if he did not know himself any longer. Domenic hoped he was not becoming some sort of monster, as unnatural as Javanne had frequently intimated he might be.

After he had reached Lew, telling him everything that had happened since their earlier contact, he collapsed back onto the bed. His belly growled. Domenic was ravenous, despite a large supper only a few hours before. It seemed like he hadn't eaten in at least a day! Then he knew that he had not been using his *laran* correctly, in the manner which his mother had been teaching him, which required less energy than the method still taught at Arilinn and the other Towers. He wasn't grounding himself right.

The air in the room seemed stifling, and he knew he had to get away from everything for a time. In spite of the temptation of the pillow, he dragged himself off the bed. His mind was filled with images of the dead stranger, and he wanted to banish these. He hadn't even known the man, but his murder seemed to have affected his thoughts to a degree he could not seem to control.

He went down the stairs and out of the inn. The courtyard was empty of people now, except for a groom sweeping a pile of ash off the stones. He looked up at the sound of Nico's footsteps and shook his head at the young man. "A sorry business, this."

"Yes, it is." One of the Guardsmen appeared from the shadows and gave Domenic a nod. Then he moved to accompany the boy, and halted at a gesture. "I'm just going to get a breath of air."

The smell of burning was dissipating with the rain, and the sodden heaps of debris were barely visible in the gloom. Domenic walked across the scene of destruction, out through the walls around the inn, and away until he found a little stand of trees a hundred paces from the inn. He could sense that the Guardsman was dogging him at a distance, keeping an eye on him without intruding.

Domenic stood, ignoring the rain and his lack of a cloak, as well as the cold that was seeping into him, and closed his eyes. He breathed slowly and deeply and thought of nothing except the earth beneath his feet. After several minutes, a sense of restoration began to flow up his limbs and into his body. He could hear, faintly, the distant murmur of the heart of the world, burning and burning, and for once he did not doubt it.

Lost in the sounds and sense of the world beneath his boots, Domenic emptied his thoughts of everything that had happened that night. It was difficult at first, even with the calming rhythm of the planet running along his veins, but after a while he felt balanced once again—neither monster nor spy, but just himself, Domenic Gabriel-Lewis Alton-Hastur.

Despite the lightness of the rain, he was drenched by the time he turned back toward the inn, as serene as he could hope to be. The Guardsman was standing with the hood of his cloak pulled up, watching him. He smiled and nodded to him, and wondered what the man thought about his going out in the rain. Nothing, very likely.

In spite of the refreshment of his energies, Domenic was still hungry for another meal. He walked into the taproom, and found it occupied by three or four of the retired Guards from Thendara and one of the village constables, all drinking quietly together. The older girl, Hannah, was there too, and she grinned at him, shook her head at his wet clothing, and handed him a small towel. He asked for some food, and in a few minutes she brought him a bowl of stew with some bread and cheese, and a half mug of brown ale.

Just as Domenic was finishing his food, he saw Vancof passing into the inn, coming from the back and making his way to the stairs. He quickly bent his head over his bowl, but the Terran agent did not spare a look toward the taproom. He appeared preoccupied from the brief glimpse Nico had of him through the strands of his dark hair.

He scooped up a mouthful of stew with his spoon and listened to the mental static around him for a moment. Then he separated Vancof's particular mind from those around him to try to discover new information. Unfortunately, all Vancof was thinking about was his aching feet, the fact that his belly was sour with tension, and his general displeasure with everything. If he had killed the other man, he was not thinking about it at all. And to learn more, Domenic would have had to force rapport with the man, the idea of which revolted him so much that the remnants of his appetite left him abruptly.

Domenic listened to the footfalls as they continued up the stair, then heard them move overhead, toward the end of the corridor where he had seen Granfell go. After a second there was a slight noise of a door opening and closing, then nothing more. He looked down at his bowl, saw there were only a few mouthfuls of stew left in it, and forced himself to finish eating. Then he headed for his own room.

Herm was sitting on the only chair in the room, looking weary and disgruntled. "Where were you? And why are you wet?" he growled.

"I went out to clear my head, and then I was hungry and went to get something to eat. Vancof just came back. He went down the hall. I wonder what he will do when he finds Granfell there," Nico announced, feeling suddenly very certain of himself.

Herm gave him a hard stare, reassessing him in some fashion. Then his face twisted in something like a smile, although it was more like a hound baring its teeth. "With any luck, he will kill him, and then we will have one less enemy to worry about. Did you get to Lew about alerting the Towers."

"Who's being bloodthirsty now?"

Herm just shrugged. "You reached Lew?"

"Yes, Uncle, and it gave me an appetite."

Herm gave a barking laugh, which only increased his resemblance to a snarling cur. "You should not have gone out alone. If anything happened to you . . . I forget that you are a growing boy, not a man, and need your vittles." Then he gave a little sigh, ran his stubby fingers through his thinning hair, and grunted softly.

"I was not alone precisely, because one of the Guardsmen followed me on my walk and kept an eye on me from a discreet distance."

"That's better. This situation is becoming more and more dangerous, and I don't think I can take on worrying about your safety at the moment. I don't know which way to turn, and I realize I have gotten altogether too dependent on technology during my years in the Federation. I keep wanting to have a communicator, not to mention a blaster or two."

"You wouldn't use a blaster, would you?" Nico was rather startled, both at the admission of frustration, and at the ruthlessness that seemed to have emerged without any warning. The cheerful companion of the road seemed to have vanished, and he was at a loss. All the tales about the Aldarans that the servants told danced in his head for a moment, and then he came to his senses. Herm was a man, no matter what his family name might be, and he was probably no more ruthless than any other—than Grandfather Lew, for instance, or even Mikhail. It was only that Domenic had never seen them in dangerous circumstances.

"Probably not. But you can bet your life that Granfell is hiding one somewhere on his person, and will have no hesitation in using it. I suspect that the only reason that Vancof was able to knife the other fellow was that he never suspected he was in any danger."

"Is that why you didn't want to grab him when I told you he was down the hall?"

"That's one reason, Nico. The Guardsmen are brave fellows, but I did not want to have them trying to use swords on people armed with blasters. And I want to see what they are up to."

"But if we stop them here, then they won't be able to attack the funeral train."

"That is true in theory, but we have no idea what has been planned by now. There are too many players on the board—Belfontaine and perhaps others in Thendara, as well as whomever is involved up in the Aldaran Domain. Capturing Vancof and Granfell would not stop things if there are troops up in the Hellers preparing to descend on this little town."

"They couldn't get here unnoticed, could they? I mean, someone would see the flyers." Domenic knew about the vehicle which *Dom* Damon owned and used to come to Thendara, although he had never actually seen it.

Herm shook his head. "They would not come in little flyers, but in machines that are much larger, capable of transporting fifty men, armed with weapons that could lay waste to this town in about three seconds. I don't know exactly what they have here, but for decades now there have been transports that are virtually invisible to the naked eye. I have no idea if any of those are on Darkover. But, if there are such here, you can wager that those are what they will use to carry the ambush party."

"Invisible? You mean like those cloaks that legend says we once had, only bigger?"

"Pretty much."

Domenic chewed this idea over for a moment. "So, basically, what you are saying is that swords are no match for Federation machines, and we might as well try to throw rocks! What are we going to do?" He had a terrifying vision of great bolts of lightning blasting his father and mother to cinders as they rode toward the *rhu fead* with Regis' body. It seemed very real, and the helplessness he had experienced earlier returned with a vengeance.

Herm flinched, as if aware that he had frightened Nico. "Try to outsmart them. And hope that they do not dare to use high technology weapons, but will dress themselves as brigands and meet us on equal terms. The one thing that is to our advantage is that they do not know we know they are up to something. The Federation does not have much respect for Darkover, and they do not know much about our secrets. Lew led them to believe that the Towers were religious establishments rather than anything else, and fortunately for us, the people of Darkover have not told them any different."

"I hate them! Why are they doing this? We've never done any harm to the Federation, have we?"

Herm sighed gustily. "None that I am aware of, Nico. As for the whys, that is more difficult to answer. One is because they can, and the other is that the leaders of the Federation have, over the past two decades, begun to mistake power for authority."

"I don't understand."

"It is the difference between force and cooperation, Nico. The Domains have managed to continue on Darkover because they have been wise enough to keep a balance between themselves, through cooperative efforts, so that no one Domain became too strong and could overwhelm the others. Regis' decision to get the Aldarans back into the Comyn is part and parcel of that idea—that we all inhabit the same planet and have to get along, in spite of our differences. My father, damn him, has never believed in such ideas, and what he would like is for Darkover to be ruled by a strong man—he always thought Regis was a lightweight—who would just make people do what he thought was best for them. And he imagines himself to be that man, probably. Or plans to set Robert up as king."

"I don't think your brother would agree to that."

"That is reassuring, since I haven't had any contact with Robert for over twenty years, other than the occasional letter."

"This makes me so mad, Uncle Herm. I want to blast those men to bits—turn their brains to jelly."

"Could you do that?" Herm looked alarmed.

"Yes, I could, and so could Mother and Grandfather Lew. The backwash would be terrible, and besides it would be wrong, but it is possible. I don't think anyone has done such a thing, but I know my mother burned a man to death with her touch, years ago, before I was born. And used the command voice to turn some bandits into statues in the snow."

Herm stared at the boy, as if he was unsure whether to believe him. "Hmm. That raises some possibilities I had not considered—I've been away too long."

"And then there is Father's matrix."

"Mikhail's matrix? What about it?"

"I'm not totally sure, but everyone, even Uncle Regis, is afraid of it, and what it can do. It came from Varzil the Good and . . . well, maybe I should say no more."

Herm waited for a moment. "Varzil? That doesn't make any sense—if you mean his matrix. All the legends in the Hellers say it was lost centuries ago."

"It was—before it came back into our time."

"And here I thought I was past the point of ever being amazed again. No, don't tell me. If Lew had wanted me to know, I am sure he would have told me everything. Are you catching any useful tidbits from down the hall?"

"No. In fact, for the first time in years, I am hardly able to hear anything. I believe I am too tired to do any effective snooping, Uncle, for the moment."

"As well you should be! I have been using your Gifts without much thought of how so much effort might affect you. Now, let's get some sleep. Nothing else is going to happen tonight—I hope."

Nico knuckled his itching eyes. Then he bent down and pulled off his boots. "I wish I were not so ethical and so very tired, Uncle Herm. If I weren't, I'd just let my mind drift down the hall, and . . ."

"Leave being immoral to me, son. I've had more practice. You just going on doing what is right, and I will do the dirty work. We will come out of this mess, somehow."

19

Domenic's eyes snapped open abruptly, and he went from deep sleep to complete wakefulness without his usual intervening muzziness. He sat up, puzzled, and peered around the darkened bedroom. Herm was snoring on the other side of the bed, a pleasant, rhythmic noise which had not disturbed his rest. The wind had risen, driving the rain against the windows, and rattling the shutters. He heard rain gunneling from the downspouts along the eaves, then splashing into the courtyard below. He knuckled his eyes and scratched his head, noticing how tired he still felt, and started to settle back again.

What had roused him? It was not a noise, but more of a feeling, a shift somewhere nearby. Ah, his mental balance had returned, and he could once again pick up the random thoughts of those nearby. Nico was almost regretful for a moment—it had been restful to be too weary to hear thoughts without effort. But he felt more like himself, and that pleased him.

Vancof and Granfell were at the other end of the corridor—were they up to some new mischief? He let his mind reach out, sweeping through the inn like a feather, briefly touching the dreams of the inhabitants.

Several people besides himself were awake—Vancof, it seemed, but not Granfell, and at least two of the Guardsmen. But there was another mind, a troubled one, and after a second he knew it was Illona. She was creeping out of the room she shared with the Renunciates, and she was not looking for the privy!

Her surface thoughts were jumbled, fear-filled and anxious. She intended to put some distance between herself and her rescuers, although he could not catch any hint of an actual plan. Ungrateful wench. For a moment, Nico was tempted to let her run away, and go back to sleep. Where could she go? The Travelers were in the village lockup and she did not know anyone else.

Then it occurred to him that he could not be sure of that. The Travelers had been through Carcosa earlier in the year, and in previous ones as well. She might have made friends he did not know about, or she might be acquainted with some of the Sons of Darkover. Unlikely, he decided, after brief consideration. From the tone of Mathias' thoughts about that organization, he didn't think any young girls were involved. But she might encounter Vancof, who would not hesitate to attack her.

She could come to some harm. Domenic found he was a little surprised at himself, that he cared as much as he did after only knowing her so briefly. Somewhat reluctantly, he examined his feelings about Illona. He had liked her from the first second he clapped eyes on her, and that had not changed. There was just something about the girl—her courage or maybe just her difference from the young women he knew already. She was rough and ill-mannered, but she was also quick-witted and brave.

He swung his legs off the bed, pulled on his tunic and boots, and decided to follow her. Carefully opening the door of the room, Nico peeped out into the dim corridor and saw her reach the top of the stairs. She was waiting, listening for sounds from below. He could see she had on a tunic that was too big for her, over her shabby undergown, and her feet were bare in the faint light that came up the stairs. Silly girl. She was not going to get far that way. She must be really desperate to try to escape without shoes.

And where did she think she was going? He waited until she started down the stairs and slipped out of the room, closing the door softly behind him. His boots made a little noise on the wood of the floor, and he realized that the girl was smarter than he had thought. It was hard to sneak around in boots or shoes.

Domenic managed to get halfway down the stairs before he heard a scuffle below. There was a feminine squeak followed by a muffled cry of pain. He scrambled down the rest of the steps and found the girl in the hands of Gregor MacEwan, one of the Guardsmen. He was swearing a blue streak, under his breath, as Illona had her teeth firmly on his forearm, as well as aiming a knee at his groin.

"You little catamount," snarled the man, shaking Illona hard as he tried to avoid her flailing legs. She reached out her fingers and tried to scratch his face or gouge his eyes, but his greater height prevented it. As it was, she tore the top of his tunic out of its lacings, the ripping noise of fabric seeming very loud in the silence of the inn.

Somehow Illona managed to wrench herself free of Gregor's grip for a second, and she would have been able to run if Domenic had not grasped her around the middle and held her tight. It was like holding a sack of furious ferrets, as she kicked backward, struggled to pull away, and clawed at the arms around her waist. She shoved an elbow back into his ribs as hard as she could, and Nico was shocked by how much it hurt. Then he fell backward with a thump, and Illona landed on top of him. All the air was knocked out of his chest for a second. She was heavier than she looked!

Before she could turn around and attack him, Gregor grabbed her by the front of her tunic and hauled her off, holding her at arm's length, so she flapped her feet helplessly above the floor. She continued to claw and scratch, but held at arm's length, the girl found nothing except Gregor's well-protected forearms. Nico sat up slowly, rubbed his ribs where she had struck him, and then started to get up.

I have to get away from these people. I have to get back to the Travelers.

The terror and pain of this mental shout shook Domenic. He had not been prepared for the strength of it, nor the violence either. How could he or anyone convince her that she would come to no harm, when it was clear she believed herself to be in mortal danger. Well, if a strange man grabbed him in the dark, he would probably think the same thing. He wanted to calm her, to reassure her.

Illona jerked suddenly in Gregor's grasp, and turned her head sharply around. She glared at Domenic, her eyes huge in the faint light of the lampions. "Don't touch me," she shrilled and stopped struggling.

For a moment, he was puzzled. Then he understood that she had sensed the touch of his mind and was outraged. How clumsy of him! He had sensed her nascent *laran* earlier, but had completely forgotten about it in the heat of the struggle. His previous idea that she might be the *nedestra* daughter of some man of the Domains, with her red hair and pale skin, returned. His father had often said there were many more telepaths on Darkover than anyone suspected, but no one, as far as he knew, had ever thought to look among the Travelers.

It was a problem that had troubled both Mikhail and Regis Hastur in recent years. They had known there were many undiscovered talents in the general population, but no one had ever come up with a method to unearth them. The number of *leroni* in the Towers was too small to test a population of twenty million—an estimate at best, for no real census of Darkover had ever been completed. More, most people seemed uninterested in the matter, or resented it. A farmer did not want to lose a son who was a useful laborer, and a tradesman wished his children to follow in his footsteps, not depart for a Tower. He had encountered a few sons and daughters of both these classes during his time at Arilinn. They had been uncomfortable in the company of so many scions of the Domains, eager to get their training done with and return to the lives they had been born to. Oh, one or two had been ambitious, or wished to remain, but the majority of them had not.

"Calm down, Illona," Nico said. "No one is going to hurt you."

"I would not go that far, *vai dom*," Gregor growled.

"Put her down now," Domenic instructed, brushing off the front of his tunic a little, and scowling at Gregor for using the honorific. Then he shrugged to himself—the girl was smart and likely she already knew he was not the person he had pretended to be. "Just where did you think you were going to run to, Illona?" The Guardsman released his grip and lowered her feet to the floor, watching the slight girl carefully.

"Back to my people," she mumbled.

"All of your people are in the local lockup, and unlikely to be released for some time to come," he answered, pitching his voice carefully. It was a thing he had trained himself to do, in order to keep his foster sister Alanna from her all too frequent bouts of fury, a calming use of the command voice.

"Why? We did nothing wrong."

Domenic could sense that she was less angry now, but still intractable. What a stubborn girl! She reminded him somewhat of Alanna, except that there was nothing about her of the boiling confusion he always sensed from his cousin. Instead there was a certain single-mindedness to her, as if when she got hold of an idea, nothing could make her let go. "Come on. Let's go sit in the taproom and talk for a while. The fire is still going in there, and we can be comfortable."

"I don't want to talk to anyone," she snarled. Despite her angry words, she turned and walked into the taproom, shivering a little. It was chilly in the hall, and in bare feet, she probably felt it more than he did. Domenic followed her, and they sat down in front of the grate, where the embers of the previous night's fire still glowed. Gregor plopped a small log onto the irons, then withdrew at Nico's gesture.

Domenic thought for a minute while the fire started to grow, trying to decide how to approach this wary girl. She was defensive and hostile, but these were very clear emotions in her, not muddled the way they would have been in Alanna. Finally he said, "Illona, do you know anything about yourself?"

"What a strange question. Of course I know about myself. I am fifteen, a foundling, and . . . what exactly do you mean?" She was immediately alert, curious and puzzled at the same time. He could sense her trying to discern his intent, and at the same time planning to elude it. It was an interesting juxtaposition of thought and emotion, and he found himself admiring the clarity she was holding onto.

"Do you know where the Travelers found you?"

"What does that matter?"

"I am curious. Humor me, won't you?"

"Why are you talking in that . . . peculiar way, as if you were very serious. You can't possibly be interested in me." Now there was an air of confusion in her words and, beneath it, a fresh prickle of alarm.

Domenic was surprised. No one, except his mother, had ever caught him using the command voice, and yet he was sure that Illona could sense that he was. He shrugged, wishing he knew better how to test for *laran,* or that there was someone nearby who could, and relaxed his throat. "I am interested in you. You are a very remarkable person."

"Huh? Me, remarkable? That's rich." She gave a little frown. "Are you trying to seduce me, *vai dom?*" She spoke the last words with enormous contempt, as if she were cursing.

Nico coughed with startlement. "That idea had not crossed my mind," he admitted. No, he hadn't thought about anything so tame as seduction—it had been much less subtle than that. He felt himself redden slightly and hoped she would not notice it in the light from the hearth. She was pretty, in a waifish kind of way, but his present intentions were not in the least dishonorable. "Why would you think that?"

"Aunty Loret told me to watch out, that's all. And everyone knows that the lords of the Domains can do as they please with girls, and no one can stop them." She appeared to be nursing a grievance. *And that nasty man who grabbed me called you* vai dom, *so even if you are young, I know you are one of them!*

"I've never seduced anyone, Illona, and I'm not sure I'd know how to begin." The subject was making him feel uncomfortable, putting him subtly in the wrong somehow, so he went back to his original question. "Where did the Travelers find you? Did your aunt ever say?"

Illona did not answer right away. *He is such a strange boy, so old seeming, though I don't think he can be more than sixteen. There is something about him. . . . Why does he want to know where I come from . . . ? I suppose it can't hurt to tell him.* "Yes, she did. They came on a village that was burned out by brigands, and found me screaming my lungs out in the ruins of a house. That was up in the Kilghards, toward the Ardais Domain. My mother, whoever she was, was either dead or taken off by the bandits. And that is all I know about it."

"I see. Have you ever . . . been tested . . . ?"

"I wouldn't go into a Tower for all the gold in Carthon," she snapped before he could finish his question.

What has made you so fearful and hostile to the Towers?

Illona jumped a little and shivered all over. "What are you doing to me," she whispered.

"Nothing. You heard my thought just then." He tried to sound calm, and was tempted to use the Voice again, but remembered how sensitive she was to it and refrained. Frightening her further would not help him. Toward the Ardais Domain? That was very suggestive—was it possible that she was a child of young Dyan Ardais'? According to Mikhail, *Dom* Dyan had been something of a rascal in his youth. And the other Dyan, the old one, dead for years now since the final battle between Sharra and Aldones had had the Alton Gift himself.

Domenic turned the idea over in his mind, and decided it would certainly explain several things about Illona that he had observed but been too tired and busy to really consider. He restrained a shudder at the idea of an untrained mind with the Alton Gift being on the loose.

"Oh, no!" Her voice was a wail of despair, breaking into his thoughts. She swallowed hard several times, and he could see she was fighting back tears. So much for not scaring her. *I have* laran, *and I've known it for years. But it can't be very much, so maybe I won't have to be shut up in one of those places and forced to work for the Keepers. I have to get away before he drags me off and . . . he seems so nice, too. But that is just a sham, because he is one of* them, *and all he wants is to order me around and tell me what to do.*

Nico was glad she was too agitated to notice his eavesdropping now, and tried to think of something comforting to say. "It is not the end of the world, Illona," Nico said softly. He had heard his mother's tales of her first experiences with *laran,* and how she had been afraid and angry at the same time. The emotions boiling off of Illona must be close to what Marguerida Alton had gone through, and he felt a deep empathy for her.

"I won't go to a Tower! I won't! You can't make me. I don't care who you are!"

"Why are you so afraid of the Towers?" It was genuinely puzzling to him. He had never encountered anyone who expressed such a tremendous fear and antipathy for the Towers before. Those students at Arilinn who were there less than willingly had not been afraid, only uncomfortable and out of place. Still, he did not have a lot of experience from which to work. Perhaps it was a more widespread feeling than he could imagine.

He had grown up with Istvana Ridenow, the Keeper from Neskaya, always present, and had never had a time when he was not aware of *laran* and its potential around him. He knew her almost as well as he knew his own mother. He had nothing but respect for her, and for the other *leroni* he had met during his time at Arilinn. He was particularly fond of his cousin Valenta Elhalyn, who was now Underkeeper there, even though she was only twenty-eight. She had a keen sense of mischief and was rarely serious about the matter of matrix science, even when she was teaching it. He could think of half a dozen others without straining, all sober, hard-working men and women who had given their lives to serve Darkover.

"I don't want to slave away in a Tower."

"Slave? You make it sound as if you would be forced to . . ."

"The Towers are even worse than the Domains! They are parasites, and they do nothing except keep people locked up."

"That is a very strange thing to say, Illona. I trained at Arilinn, and I am not locked up, am I?" Parasites? The term startled him, and more, it disquieted him more than a little. He wondered if this was only the idea of the thin, frightened girl sitting opposite him, or if this opinion was common.

Domenic felt out of his depth and wished that there were someone he could consult at that moment. Herm could not help him. He had been away from Darkover too long. Should he ask one of the Guardsmen? They might have heard such remarks. Rafaella? No, if she had heard such talk, she would have told his mother.

"But you are some sort of lord, and can do as you please."

The words put his questions right out of his mind, and Domenic found himself laughing. It felt good, except that it made the spot on his ribs where Illona's elbow had struck him hurt. As far as he could see, his entire life had been planned for him, before he was even born, and he had not been allowed to stray from it until he snuck off in the night for this ill-fated adventure. He had been closeted in Comyn Castle for years, except for his time at Arilinn, and one visit to the Alton Domain years earlier. He knew that building very well, but the city around it was largely a mystery to him. He almost envied her wider experience. He also knew that there was no way he could convey this reality to her, even as he knew he had to try.

For a moment he wondered why he felt compelled to persuade her of anything. Why couldn't he leave it to others, people more skilled than himself. Illona was only a girl, uneducated and rough, and not really any concern of his. Yet he didn't believe that, even for a second. And if she really did have the Alton Gift, then he had a duty to help her.

Did he like her because she was unlike anyone else he knew, or was there some other reason? It made no sense, and all he had to go on was a feeling in his belly that it was important to keep her from harm. It was similar to the way he felt about Alanna, but without the feeling of despair he so often had about his difficult foster-sister.

"That is not true, Illona. I've never done as I pleased. I have had duties and obligations since the day I was born, and I have honored them as well as I could. But I think you have been listening to the wrong people. Have you ever actually talked to anyone who worked in a Tower?"

"No. I always stayed in the wain when we went there, because I was afraid." *If I had been noticed, then someone would have grabbed me and dragged me away from Aunty. I knew that since I was eleven. I've always been afraid that I would get caught.*

"Caught?"

She glared at him in the flickering light from the fireplace, aware that he had overheard her thoughts once again. "Yes. I knew that I had a tiny bit of *laran,* even if I didn't want it. And everyone knows that they want to keep anyone with *laran* locked up, or breeding for them."

"Illona, I think if you say 'everyone knows' one more time, I am going to be very angry. *You* don't know anything at all!"

She glared at him fiercely, the light playing across the freckles on her sharp nose in a pleasing way. "I am just an ignorant girl, huh? And you are some *vai dom* who knows it all. You are not much older than I am, or maybe younger, even. Who are you!"

He hesitated for a moment, caught between the need for secrecy and his enormous desire to gain her trust. Then he threw caution to the winds and used his Gift. *Domenic Gabriel-Lewis Alton-Hastur.*

The expression on her face would have been comical if it had not been so frightened. "How did you do that," she whispered, shrinking back on her seat. "I didn't do that—you did—on purpose!"

"It is something I learned at Arilinn." The slight lie came easily to his tongue. "It is something you might learn as well, if you were not so mule-headed."

"I am not going to listen to you! You are a nasty boy, and I hate you." *This is even worse than I thought—he's a Hastur. He could turn my mind to dust in a second, if he wanted. What does he want from me?*

"A nasty boy would not have rescued you from that mob, Illona." Domenic refused to let himself be drawn in by her fear or anger, but it was difficult. He felt a sudden, powerful need to defend himself, to say something that would dissuade her from her odd beliefs about the Towers and his own family.

Several emotions flickered across her mobile features too quickly for him to name them. She pleated the front of her tunic between nimble fingers, weighing something in her mind. "That's true, I guess. But it doesn't change anything. You are still my enemy, and you want to force me into servitude."

"What does that mean?"

"If you have your way, you will either lock me up, or marry me off to someone so I can have babies with *laran*."

He shook his head. "No, that is not true. I wish you could meet my mother. She and I have had any number of interesting discussions about that subject, and she does not approve of breeding for *laran* any more than you do."

"So, why did she submit and have children, then?"

"I believe that she was in love with my father—and, truthfully, submit is not a word I would ever use to describe her! She kicked and screamed about going to Arilinn, or so I have been told. And I am glad she had children, or else we would not be having this fascinating conversation, because I would not exist."

"That would suit me just fine." She chewed on her lower lip and thought for a few seconds. "Look, why don't you just pretend to look the other way, and I will leave, and you can forget about me?"

"And then what would happen?"

"I'll go find another troupe of Travelers. I am a good puppeteer, even if I don't like it very much."

"I can't. It wouldn't be right."

"Why not?"

"Because letting a wild telepath just wander off into the night would be wrong, that's all. And that is what you are, right now. Your talent isn't going to go away, Illona. You need to know how to use it properly, or else you are going to be a danger to yourself and everyone around you."

"No! I want to go back to the Travelers!" She paused and peered at him intently. "You know something about them, don't you? Damn, damn, damn! I can *almost* hear your thoughts, which is the most revolting thing in the world. It is like you are nearly whispering in my head. I don't want this!" She whimpered slightly and clenched her teeth to hold back the sound.

Nico swallowed hard and thought about this piece of information. His own mind, he knew, was well-shielded and he was not forcing rapport with her. Without training and a matrix stone, she should not be able to hear him, unless his earlier suspicion was correct. And if he informed her of the nature of her Gift, she was going to collapse. She was too near the

ragged edge of her own endurance as it was. After giving her some time
to think, he asked "Wouldn't you rather be able to control your Gift than
be at its mercy all the time?"

"Gift!" She spat the word out, as if it was foul on her lips. "I'm not
at the mercy of anything! I just keep my concentration on something, and
then I don't hear anything hardly at all."

"That sounds very tiring, Illona." Domenic felt a tremendous sympathy for her now, and a regret that she was so conflicted.

Illona's shoulders slumped forward a little. "Yes, I guess it is," she
admitted grudgingly. Then a little of her normal defiant attitude returned.
"But it is better than sneaking around listening to things that are none of
my business, or making people do things they don't want to do, like the
leroni."

"Is that what you believe?"

"Everyone knows . . . oops, I did it again, didn't I?" She shrank back,
afraid of his earlier threat. When he made no move to strike her, she
relaxed slightly, wriggling her bare toes over the lower rung of her chair.
Fear and curiosity warred in her sharp features, and he caught wisps of
memory, of beatings and hunger, cold and constant fear of those around
her. Only Loret seemed to have treated her with any real kindness.

Nico felt sick and ashamed of himself. He had no idea until that
instant of how really hard her life had been. No one had ever struck him
for no better reason than that they were angry or drunk. He had been
frightened, but only of the strange things within himself, never of his
parents. Even his grandmother had never done him any more injury than
to hate him.

Domenic wondered what words would reassure her. Perhaps silence
was the best answer, that and not making any move that would threaten
the girl. She was very quick, and perhaps she would work it out for herself.

After several minutes of quiet, Nico saw her relax slightly, and sensed
that her curiosity might be the victor for the moment. "But how else does
a Keeper work? I mean, no one would really want to live in a Tower
unless they were forced to, would they?"

"Have you ever gone to Nevarsin?"

"What a strange thing to ask. Yes, I have. We went there once, about
three years back. Why?"

"Did you see the *cristoforos*?"

"Certainly."

"Was anyone making them stay there?"

"That's different. They don't have anything anyone wants. They are just a bunch of crazy old men who believe in some weird god."

"The biggest difference between a Tower and a monastery is that a Tower is not concerned with religion, Illona. But both are communities of people who have things in common."

"You will never convince me of that. The Towers take the best people and make them into slaves, and then expect the rest of Darkover to support them. They don't *do* anything!"

"You don't know that since you have never been in a Tower."

"Then tell me what good they are, except to keep the Domains in power?"

This novel idea had never occurred to him, but he could see now how someone living on the edges of Darkovan society might believe it. "They are schools for people like yourself, Illona, who would go mad if they did not receive training."

"I've done fine so far."

"Then you have been very fortunate."

"I don't want to spend the rest of my life locked up!"

"Lots and lots of people take training in the Towers and then leave."

"I don't believe you." She was absolutely determined to hold to her own fears.

"Fine. Ask Rafaella. She has a sister who spent some time at Neskaya, then left and married and is very happily living her own life, up in the Kilghards."

"She would say anything you told her to."

This was too much for him, in his tiredness, and he found himself laughing while the girl glared at him, outraged and furious. When he finally managed to get himself under control, he said, "I am sorry. I was not laughing at you, though you probably don't believe me. It is just that the very thought of me telling my Aunt Rafi what to do struck me as very funny."

"Your aunt? You have an aunt who is a Renunciate?" Illona seemed to be having a great deal of trouble taking in this relationship.

"She is my mother's best friend, and she is freemated to a great-uncle of mine, Rafe Scott."

"The same Rafe Scott who runs expeditions?"

"You know of him, then?"

"Sort of. I . . . have heard of him."

"How?"

"Dirck thought about him sometimes, and I kept catching the name when we were still up in the Hellers." She seemed troubled now, as if something about Vancof's thoughts unsettled her.

Nico waited for her to continue, but Illona became quiet and thoughtful instead. He forced himself not to even brush her mind, letting her sort things out for herself. At last he said, "Tell me about Dirck's thoughts, why don't you?"

"He drinks, you know."

"I had that impression."

"Well, when he does, it is like he is throwing his thoughts all over the room. Nasty things. I tried not to hear anything, because it made me want to throw up. And it was all muddled, with a lot of things I didn't understand. But I do know he was afraid of Rafe Scott for some reason, and often thought about trying to kill him, when he was really in his cups. He thought about killing people a lot, and I think he has done it, too." Illona shivered. "He is a very bad man, but after our regular driver left, we didn't have a lot of choice."

"Your driver left?"

"I guess. He just didn't show up one morning, and the next day Dirck showed up and said he was from Dyan Player's troupe, and Aunty—you think that Dirck . . ."

"It does seem very convenient, doesn't it?"

Illona pulled her knees up against her chest and wrapped her arms around her legs, as if trying to make herself as small as possible. She seemed very small and afraid, but her fear was no longer of Nico. He looked beyond her, toward the wall, staring at the paneling and refused to let his mind catch even the slightest thought that ran in her brain. "Yes, I suppose it was," she said softly. "I never liked him, and neither did Aunty—and just look where it got her! But I told myself that I was being silly, because, you know, he looked at me so . . . strangely. Like he wanted to do something bad to me, only he dared not because of Loret." She paused, swallowed hard, reliving those moments, he was sure. "And I never took the things I heard him think seriously."

"Why not?"

"It was too scary." She trembled all over for a moment, then forced herself to stop. "What would you do if you were riding around the countryside with a man who seemed to be a . . . murderer? And who thought about—"

Domenic received a clear and unwelcome impression of rape, and it was all he could do not to march up the stairs, enter the room where he knew Vancof was at that moment, and kill the man. He controlled his own feelings with an effort. Aware that he did not want to frighten her again, that he was beginning to gain her trust, he only said, "You couldn't very well tell a village constable, I suppose."

Illona gave a feeble laugh. "We Travelers stay as far away from them as we can, because they are always looking for a way to make trouble for us. It is bad enough that we have to bribe them half the time, to let us perform. Not the ones near the Towers, though. But the ones in the smaller towns are greedy bullies as often as not. Except to smile and say good day, I have never spoken to a constable in my life!"

Nico chewed on this for a minute. It gave him a perspective on life outside the walls of Comyn Castle that was strange and uncomfortable. Had it always been like this, or had the withdrawal of Regis Hastur during the final years of his life allowed these actions to occur? He had never experienced any situation where he could not have asked for help, and he knew that this was not true for the girl, and for others like her as well. He could not even start to imagine what her life had been like, and the little he had learned so far only made him feel sick and sad. Domenic had never really thought about common life on Darkover, had merely assumed it was pleasant—certainly better than his life of endless duty. Now he realized how really ignorant he was.

If only his mother were there! She would reassure him—or would she? Marguerida Alton-Hastur was, in private, blunt and forthright. If she perceived a problem, she tried to remedy it, not tidy it away under the nearest carpet. Then, suddenly, he understood more of why Lew Alton had been so unhappy about Regis Hastur's last years—the way he had withdrawn and become wary and anxious. His grandfather probably knew that things on Darkover were not perfect, nor even very good for some people. And he knew now that Regis' refusal to actively rule the Domains, his insistence on hiding within Comyn Castle, had led to resentment in the common people. In another few years, or a decade, it might have even gone far enough to turn into the revolution that Vancof was attempting to foment.

Domenic was too tired to sort it out completely, and too confused. He felt as if a great weight were bearing down on him, grinding him to dust, and snatched himself back from that downward spiral with a sharp mental jerk. The girl was watching him now, her face a study in curiosity.

"You are a very strange boy, Domenic."

"How so?"

"Well, you are about my age, but you feel years older, like some ancient trapped in a boy's body. I think you know a lot of things, but I also think you don't know anything about the real world."

"You might be right about that." He grinned stiffly. "I will gladly bow to your greater experience."

"You will?" Her eyes got round as she considered this seriously. "But, why? I am just a nobody—an orphan girl."

He rubbed his chest reflectively. "With very sharp elbows. For no reason I can say, I like you, Illona. True, you have a bunch of foolish ideas in your head about the Towers, but I just like you. And I want to help you."

You do! I know it, and it scares me nearly to death. Her eyes widened as she sensed her own touch against his mind. *Did I do that?*

Yes.

I'm doomed.

Domenic could not help the bubble of laughter that rose in his throat at her horrified expression, even though he tried to stifle it. *No, not doomed Illona, just overly dramatic. I suppose that comes from doing all those plays with the puppets.*

She balled a fist, started to punch at him, then paused. *Aunty said something like that, too. I can't believe she is really dead. What is going to happen to me? Wait! It's that damn Dirck, and he is up to no good!*

What? Ah, yes. I almost missed him. Illona had distracted him, but now he could sense the driver leaving the room overhead, and he was not alone, from the sound of more than one pair of faint footfalls. "Gregor," he hissed.

"Yes, *vai dom.*"

"Get out of sight and let the men who are coming down the stairs do whatever they wish."

"But. . . ."

"That's an order."

An order, but it is going to be my skin that gets racked up for not following Dom *Aldaran's. Still, he's a good lad, and probably knows what he is doing.*

Domenic took Illona's arm and drew her away from the fire, and to his surprise she did not resist. He could feel her fear of the driver, and he realized that without the protection of Loret, the man represented a real danger to her. He pulled her behind the long curtains that hung over the windows at the front of the inn, and hoped that Vancof and Granfell were not going to come into the taproom at all. It was cold next to the glass, and the girl pressed against him, pushing her knuckles into her generous mouth to keep from making the slightest sound.

Illona huddled against him, shivering from more than cold. He could smell the warm woolen tunic and the scent of balsam and lavender on her skin. Rafi must have made her take a hot bath before bed. His senses were so heightened now that it seemed he could feel her blood surging through her veins, and if he had not been quite so alarmed, he would have thoroughly enjoyed her nearness.

"I stashed a couple of horses behind the inn earlier," a voice murmured. Domenic twitched the curtains slightly, so he could peek through a gap in the fabric. He could see the bottom of the stairs, and part of the hall that led to both the front door and the kitchens at the back. There was a small circle of light, then two, moving eerily across the polished floorboards. After a second he could see the shine of a pair of Terranan leather boots in the strange light.

"It's raining, Vancof! I still don't see why we can't stay in until morning," another answered.

"We don't have far to go—just a few miles. There is an abandoned croft where we can hide. I don't think we dare remain here. After the riot they might start looking for me."

"That's your problem, Vancof."

"No, it is *our* problem. Now, be quiet. We don't want to wake up the innkeeper and have to explain to him why we are sneaking out in the middle of . . ."

"A knife will . . ."

"Shut up! Do you want to draw attention to us?"

A gusty sigh followed. "Where the hell is Nailors?"

"He must have run off during the riot. This way. And try to be quiet!"

The noise of their footfalls faded away, and the strange lights with them. Both Illona and Nico let out aching breaths as they emerged from the curtains. The girl noticed she had her hand clutched around his upper arm and snatched it away as if it burned. *I am glad he is gone away! But I am still here.*

Illona, I promise you nothing is going to happen to you.

Stop that! I don't want to talk to you! I wish I was dead!

No, you don't. You only think that because you are afraid!

She shuddered all over, the color draining from her cheeks. Nico felt a whirlpool of blackness begin to rise in her mind and caught her slender body firmly, holding it against him, supporting her head against his shoulder and speaking softly into her ear. Grief and fear and rage poured into him, an overwhelming rush of emotions that had been held in check for hours. It touched the same feelings in his own mind, releasing them abruptly.

They clung to one another for comfort, drowning in a sea of emotions, so close that it seemed to Domenic that there was no separation between them except their flesh. It was a shocking experience, one greater even than the intimacy of working in a Tower circle, and when it began to abate as suddenly as it had begun, he had a pang of loss as well as another of great relief.

"It will be all right, Illona, I promise," he whispered feebly.

She snuffled, and he realized she was crying softly. Illona pulled away, a little reluctantly he thought, and gave him a bleary gaze. "Well, if you *promise,* that will make it fine, won't it!" Even in tears, she was tart as a green apple.

I am your friend, whether you like it or not, Illona Rider. And you are going to be a fantastic telepath.

Whether I like it or not! I wish I had never waved at you and told you about going to the North Gate!

But, then, who would have saved you from those men?

There is that. My friend? Aunty always said you can't have too many friends or too few enemies. Are you really my friend?

Word of a Hastur!

She gave a fluttering sigh, too tired to go on arguing. "That will have to do for now, I suppose."

20

Domenic stood in the dining room of the Crowing Cock and looked out the small window onto the courtyard. The rain which had begun so quietly the night before had turned into a real downpour when he had finally risen at midmorning. He could see pools of water which had collected on the stones, and piles of sodden debris which had not yet been cleared away. He sighed resignedly. It was a fairly common early autumn storm that would last for a day or two, turn the roads into mud, and keep everyone indoors until it spent itself.

A slow smile played over his mouth. Vancof and Granfell had left the inn when the rain had only begun. Now they were huddled somewhere, in some crofter's cot, he assumed, cold and cheerless. Perhaps they would fall to arguing and kill each other. He wondered if they would come back to the inn, and decided that possibility was unlikely. Vancof was known in Carcosa as a Traveler, and after the riot the night before, he was smart enough to realize that if someone recognized him, he would likely end up in the lockup. Where else might they go? There was another village, about fifteen miles farther up the Old North Road, according to Aunt Rafi. He must remember to pass this information to Herm.

At last he turned back to the long table and sat down. He picked up a sheet of thick paper, the best that MacHaworth could provide, and read through what he had written. It was a letter to his mother, containing surprisingly little of his exploits since leaving Comyn Castle, and nothing at all about finding the body of the dead man the night before. Instead, Domenic had written about subjects which he could never bring himself to speak of, either verbally or telepathically. He had written about his strong feelings for his cousin, Alanna, but more about how much he disliked living in Comyn Castle, and one short paragraph concerning the disturbing auditory experiences he had been having. It was the first letter he had written to Marguerida in his entire life, and he had discovered he was able to say things more clearly on paper than he could in any other way.

He read his words over and realized that he had left a great many things unsaid, despite his determination to do otherwise. Domenic had not mentioned the riot, because he knew it would worry his mother, and he felt she had enough on her hands already. He had not addressed his feeling of distance from his father for similar reasons. Mikhail had a lot of problems just now, and Nico did not want to add to them. In short, he decided, it was not as complete as he intended, and it was therefore dishonest by omission.

He wondered if he should just crumple the whole thing up and toss it into the fireplace. He was aware of his own self-consciousness, anxious at both saying too little and too much, but relieved that he had been able to write anything at all. No, he would send it. When Duncan Lindir rode back to Thendara later in the day, he would give it to the old Guardsman. His mother would be pleased to receive it, and that was enough.

Domenic was just finishing his reading when Illona came into the room. Her wiry red hair had been brushed and combed into a semblance of order, then pulled back ruthlessly from her forehead and braided down her back. She was wearing a green tunic and skirt that fit her well enough, belted around her slender waist, and there were soft slippers on her feet. He wondered where she had gotten the garments, for the town market was closed for the day, because of the riot, and then realized that they were rather fancy for everyday. She must have borrowed them from one of MacHaworth's daughters. He saw dark circles beneath her green eyes, as if she had slept poorly. He suspected he did not look much more rested himself.

"What are you doing?"

"I have written a letter to my mother—which will amaze her, since I have never done such a thing before. But, then, except for my years at Arilinn, I have never been away from her, and there was no need to write."

"What does it say?" She seemed anxious and curious, and did not appear to realize that she was being nosy.

"Nothing about you, if that is what is worrying you."

Illona looked surprised and almost disappointed. "I . . . I suppose I thought . . ."

"I would have told her about you, but I assumed it might make you frightened." In another mood, he knew, he would have described all the events leading up to this moment, and made rather a good tale of it. But after the previous night, Domenic's immediate impulse was to protect Illona, and he had followed it.

"That is . . . kind of you. It would have. I've been thinking about last night a lot, about what you said and all. And I think that I don't need to go to a Tower at all, not really, and that you were just being . . . what would a girl like me do in such a place? I think I'll join the Renunciates instead. It can't be any harder than being a Traveler." She eyed him closely, watching for his reaction with the wariness of a half-wild cat.

Domenic gave her a hard look. "What makes you think they would want a wild telepath in their company?"

"Are you always this unpleasant? Or just in the mornings?"

"No, I am not. In fact, I am ordinarily a very nice fellow, polite to my elders and courteous to fault. I even manage to be pleasant to my grandmother who hates me and wishes me ill. But when someone is deliberately being buffle-headed, Illona, I speak my mind."

"Is that what you think?"

"Your *laran* is not going to go away, no matter how hard you will it to. Anymore than your hair is going to turn soft and manageable."

Illona gave a slight grin. "Samantha tried to put it into order, and she did a good job, I think. How did you know that my hair was a trial to me? I hate it!"

"Well, I don't. I think it is very attractive—and you are changing the subject."

"I'm not the one who mentioned my impossible hair."

"True." Domenic looked down at the letter again, wondering if he could rewrite it in some other way, if he could be more honest without causing hurt. "My friend, you and I are more alike than you imagine."

"What? I am not the least like you!"

"Yes, you are. We are both stuck with Gifts we have to learn to live with. If you read what I have written, you would see that."

"Well, I can't read, so that's that."

"Not at all?"

"No."

"But how do you learn the scripts that Mathias writes if you cannot read?"

"Oh, that. I have an excellent memory. He would read the plays to me several times, and then I knew what to say. And sometimes I improved the words, which always annoyed him. He is not nearly as clever as he thinks."

Domenic remembered his encounter with the man the night before and had to agree. "I see. Well, then, I will teach you to read." He folded the letter in half and pushed it aside. Then he took a second sheet of paper and the pen in his hand. "Come and sit next to me."

Illona stared at him for a second, then walked around the table and slipped onto the bench beside him. "Why do I need to learn to read?"

"Because when you go to a Tower, you will need that skill. And we are not going to argue about that subject—you are going, if I have to drag you there myself and show you that it is not a terrible place." He was surprised at himself, because he knew he was not usually so forceful.

A mulish expression filled her face, then faded. "I think . . . I could go if you went with me. Mind you, I don't wish to, and I believe you are being very stubborn because you are used to getting your own way."

Domenic gave a snort of laughter. "I know you won't believe me, Illona, but I have rarely gotten my own way in my whole life. Now, this is your name, Illona Rider." He pointed to what he had just written. "Here are the letters, and you already know how they sound."

"Is that what it looks like?" She peered at the glyphs on the page. "Write yours."

Domenic did as she asked, putting the whole long name on the page. He watched her as she studied the letters closely. He reflected that he was very much his mother's son, just at that moment, trying to teach someone to read. She put her finger on the glyphs from her own name and then found the same ones in his, moving the digit back and forth between the two, and subvocalizing the sounds. After a minute she asked, "Why are the starting letters tall and the rest short?"

"In a name, you make the beginning of each word a capital, and the rest in another form. Do you know, I have never thought about this before—I've always just done it."

"What do you do when it is not a name, then?"

"Here—I will write a sentence."

"What does it say?"

"All mules bray."

"I see . . . the big letter at the beginning is the same one as in part of your name, and the next two are like the small ones at the first part of Illona. So, when you write something that is not a name, you make the first letter big, and all the rest small." She nodded, and he could sense she was enjoying herself.

"That is right, except if you are putting the name of a person or place in a sentence—here—I will write 'Illona and Nico are in Carcosa.' You see?"

"Is this word Carcosa?" She pointed.

"Yes, it is. But how did you figure it out?" Domenic knew she was very intelligent, but she seemed to be learning much faster than he had anticipated. Was she picking up clues from his mind—no, there was no sense of her overhearing him. Then he realized he was enjoying teaching her, and that he did not want her to learn so quickly, only because he did not want to end the time with her.

"I . . . uh . . . just matched the end of your first name with the letter you made bigger, because you told me that places started with capitals. That's all. Did I do it wrong?"

"No, Illona. You are a very good student."

"Write down ordinary words for me—bread and rain and . . . I want to know what they all look like!"

Domenic did not move for a moment. Then he pulled the folded letter to Marguerida toward him, opened it, and wrote above "Dear Mother," "Please send me a copy of your book of folktales as soon as you are able." Then he turned back to the other sheet of paper and began to pen the words Illona had requested.

"What did you just put in your letter?"

"I asked my mother to send me a book she wrote. You will like it because it is full of stories, and by the time you get done with it, you will be able to read very well."

"You asked . . ." she gave a little gasp of astonishment. "Your mother is Marguerida Alton-Hastur, isn't she?"

"Yes."

Illona shook her head. "And you just asked her to send a book, as if she was . . . a nobody. You are a very strange person, Domenic."

"Call me Nico—all my friends do."

"And I am your friend?"

"I told you that last night, didn't I?"

"Yes, but I didn't really believe you then. Now, write 'bread' for me."

It was late afternoon and the rain had been pouring down for hours. Katherine Aldaran put down her brush and rubbed the back of her neck. She had lost track of time. She gave a quick look at the panel on the easel, taking in the shapes she had placed there, and decided it was not a bad beginning.

"Are you tired?" Gisela asked, from where she sat on a thronelike chair across the room. "I know I am. I never imagined that sitting in one position could be so wearing!"

"Forgive me—I got caught up in the work! I am not usually so thoughtless of my sitters."

"I didn't mind, really. It was very interesting watching you. And I will tell you a useful thing, if you like."

Kate put the brush into a jar of turpentine and swirled it around. "What's that?"

"When you are thinking about painting, your mind gets extremely quiet."

"Quiet?"

"Well, maybe more like you are walled away. Shielded."

"I see. So if I walk down the corridor thinking about yellow ocher, no one can hear my random thoughts? That is useful! Thank you."

"I am glad you didn't mind, Kate. Can I look at what you did, or must I wait until it is done?"

"You won't see much at this stage, but you can look if you like." Actually, Katherine did not usually let her sitters see the preliminary painting, because it was just forms and was difficult for those who were not artists to understand. At present, she had blocked in the shape of

Gisela's head and shoulders, the carved posts of the chair, and a little of the draping of the violet tunic she had chosen to wear. What color there was in the face did not resemble any human being yet, since green was not a hue that people ordinarily thought of when they looked at themselves.

Before Gisela could rise and come toward the easel, there was a knock on the door, and a second later Roderick stuck his red head into the room, his eyes sparkling. Then he saw Gisela and he hesitated slightly. "Oh, sorry—Mother said you might be working."

"It is fine, Rory—we are finished for today, aren't we, Kate?"

"Yes, we are. Did you come about learning to draw, Roderick?"

The boy grinned and glanced around the studio, taking in the panel on the easel swiftly. "No, I didn't. Mother asked me to bring you this. She just got a letter from Nico, and this one is for you—from Herm." Rory held out a thick packet and shifted restlessly from foot to foot. He watched Kate with an air of anticipation. When she did not immediately react, he looked very disappointed. "Aren't you going to take it?"

"Thank you," Kate answered rather stiffly, and took the object from his hand.

"Aren't you going to read it?"

"Roderick Rafael Alton-Hastur—you are being a pest!" Gisela scolded him, but there was no real anger in her voice. "It is private, you little scamp!"

"But, I just wanted to know how many Terranan he has killed so far!"

Gisela looked scandalized. "Shoo! Get along with you, you imp of Zandru! Both of us are going to swallow our curiosity and leave Katherine to enjoy her letter in peace."

"Ah, Aunty Giz, that's not fair! First Nico goes off and gets into trouble, and I am stuck here in the castle, and then . . ."

"Enough!" Gisela was on her feet, shaking out the folds of her tunic and petticoats.

"Please, Giz, don't go." Kate held the letter between her fingers, suddenly cold all over. She did not want to be alone right now. "Why don't you make us some of that nice tea we had earlier, while I . . ."

"Of course! Just what we need on a rainy afternoon." She walked over to the fireplace, shook a kettle sitting on the hearthstones, and poured some water into it from a jug nearby. Then she hung it on a hook, and turned around. "Are you still here, Roderick?"

"You are so mean," he muttered, and then retreated and closed the door behind him. Once he was gone, Gisela began to laugh, and in spite of her own tension, Katherine joined in.

She sat down in the chair Gisela had been posing in and the merriment faded away. Kate looked at the packet in her hands, dreading what might be within its pages. She had said so many terrible things, in her fear, the night Herm had left Comyn Castle. What would she do if he decided she was right—that being married to a *laran*less wife was indeed impossible for him? And, knowing how much her husband disliked emotional conflict, it would be just like him to tell her in a letter, to avoid the inevitable confrontation it would mean.

"Kate, read your letter and stop your fretting." Giz spoke in a gentle voice, and then turned away to clean out the pottery teapot.

Katherine sighed and broke the paper wafer which sealed the packet. Three sheets unfolded on her lap, and Herm's large scrawl danced before her eyes. He had written to her a few times when they were courting, but she had not seen his handwriting since then, and the sight of it now made her heart leap in her chest. She remembered how the sight of one of his notes had made her blood race ten years before, how girlish and excited she had felt whenever she received one.

> Dearest Kate—
>
> I am a fool. I hope that you can find it in your heart to forgive me for being a coward and running away at the first chance I had. Please understand that it was not your fault, that nothing you did, including point out my many stupidities, was the cause. It was me, my fears and habits, that was the problem, and never you, my *caria*.
>
> There are so many things I want to tell you, that I should have told you earlier, and I don't know if I have the courage to do it now. The paper under my hand seems like a vast field of snow that I cannot get across.
>
> Just at this moment, I am sitting in my room at an inn called the Crowing Cock. It is in a little town called Carcosa, about a half day's slow ride from Thendara—so I am not very far away, although it feels to me as if it were a great distance.

Last night there was a riot in the courtyard of the inn, and people were killed. The rain came and freshened things up a little, but I can still smell the stench of it. Perhaps that is my imagination, or maybe it is that my clothes are filthy with ash and sweat and a lot of other unpleasant things.

I am delaying getting down to business. First, I have to tell you that the Station Chief at Federation Headquarters there in Thendara has an arrest warrant out on me. I did not tell you about it when I learned of it, and you somehow knew I was holding something back, even though I managed to distract you by telling you that Terése would need to be tested for *laran*. You were already so tired and worried that I could not bring myself to add to it—well, that is my excuse anyhow. I am hardly a threat to Federation security, and this man knows that perfectly well, but he wanted to use my presence in Comyn Castle to cause trouble for Mikhail Hastur.

Katherine stopped reading and looked up. "Did you know that Herm had an arrest warrant out for him?"

"Yes, *breda,* I did, but Mikhail asked us—Rafael and me—not to tell you, because he felt you didn't need to know about it so you wouldn't worry."

"I do wish everyone would stop keeping things from me and not meddle in my life!"

Gisela chuckled and then took the kettle off the fire to pour hot water into the teapot. "I'm not sure if that is possible on Darkover—everyone seems to meddle just for sport."

"Sport!" Kate spat out the word and felt much better for it. "I suppose it is something to do when you are snowed in for weeks at a time," she added, less angrily but with great feeling.

"It is better than killing each other, Kate."

"I'm not completely sure of that." She picked up the letter and went on reading.

But it was more than keeping Mikhail out of a mess he had no hand in. I came home, expecting to feel at ease, and instead I found myself feeling trapped. No, it was not you, but everything! After years dealing with the intrigues of the Senate, you would have thought that those of my own people would be simple for me. I only wish that were true. I felt more alienated in Comyn Castle than I did when we were still in the Federation — exacerbated, I must add, by your own entirely normal reaction to discovering that you were married to a telepath. In short, you were only making things harder, Kate — and I just couldn't deal with it.

That is not a very loving thing to write, but it is a true one. I hope you can forgive me eventually. I behaved selfishly. I jumped at the opportunity to get away from everything for a few days, and I do not regret the choice, even though I caused you grief. I am not perfect, and I have been more imperfect these past few days than I ever have before in my life.

"He says he isn't perfect," Kate told Gisela as the woman approached her with a mug of steaming tea, the pleasant minty smell wafting toward her.

"He is only now discovering that?"

"I don't know, but he is admitting it now." She took a sip and found the tea too hot to drink yet.

"I suppose that is progress of some sort," Gisela answered with her usual tartness.

It seemed to me that too much was happening, and I was overwhelmed. I could not bring myself to deal with the problem of your lack of *laran,* or how it might affect our lives or the lives of our children. More, I could not cope with how I suddenly felt about life here on Darkover. And then Nico discovered a plot against Mikhail Hastur, and I offered my services.

I ran away, Kate, ran away from you and the children, who are my life, and I confess that I was enormously relieved, even though I felt like dung. It was the wrong thing to do, but also the right one. Can you understand that?

Probably not. I feel that I am making a complete fool of myself, but I had to write and tell you as much as I was able. I want to come back to you, but just at the moment that is not possible. I have to remain here with Domenic until this matter is settled. But I hope that you can find it in your heart to somehow overlook my many flaws, my secretiveness and my cowardice, and to start anew very soon.

I remain, your adoring husband,
Hermes-Gabriel Aldaran

Katherine looked up and found there were tears in her eyes. She folded the letter over and picked up her tea. Then she wiped her wet cheeks with the sleeve of her blouse. The soft spider silk brushed across her skin like a lover's kiss.

"Well?"

"He is very contrite."

"Herm was always good at that, when he was a boy. He was always sorry for the mischief he got into. And he always meant it, too! Are you going to take him back?"

"What choice do I have?"

"Kate, you can do just as you please—something I never had a chance to do. The Aldaran Domain is not the richest on Darkover—Aldones knows it is certainly the coldest!—but you will never want for anything, should you decide that he has to sleep in the hawks' mews for the rest of his life. My brother Robert will see that you are well provided for. So you don't have to take Hermes back just because he says he is sorry. The question is—do you want him, imperfections and all?"

Katherine did not answer immediately, but drank some of her tea. Then she answered, slowly, "Yes, I do—as maddening as he is."

"Well, then, that settles it."

"Not exactly. Things can never be the same between us, Gisela, and I don't know if he understands that. He is so good at manipulating me—everyone, for that matter—and being clever, that he doesn't seem to realize the hurt it causes. So, I am going to have to insist that . . ."

"What?"

"That he not treat me like some adoring little woman who can be pushed aside when it pleases him!"

"That may be very difficult, Kate."

"I know." She bent her head forward and her shoulders drooped.

"Here, now, don't go falling into the dumps on me. Why, if things don't work out, there are always the Renunciates!"

"The Renunciates!" Gisela had told Kate about those women, and she had been fascinated. But the thought of herself living in a community of females was so bizarre that it was funny, and she began to chuckle. "What, and cut off my hair?"

Gisela rolled her eyes drolly. "There you are—saved by sheer vanity!"

Mikhail came into the sitting room of the suite and found Marguerida in a high-backed chair, with a sheet of thick paper in her lap. He realized that it was the first time, except for meals, that he had seen her seated in days. He studied her, noticing the slightest redness at the tip of her nose and the puffiness around her eyes—she must have been crying. And she looked so tired. He wanted to kill anyone who made his wife weep. She would not like that thought, since she preferred to take care of herself, but he could not entirely stem the feeling of outrage. After perhaps half a minute he realized that he was just using it as an excuse to vent his own emotions. Why shouldn't she cry if she wished to?

"What's the matter, *caria?*"

Marguerida looked up, as if she had not noticed he had entered the room, and stared slightly. "Nothing, really. Or perhaps everything. Nico has sent me a letter."

"Really? Might I read it, or is it too private?"

"You may not like it."

"I don't like a great many things, dearest, but that does not prevent me from discovering them." He tried to keep the sharpness out of his voice, and almost succeeded.

"I had no idea he was so dreadfully unhappy," she said as she handed him the letter.

"All boys his age are unhappy, I think. I was, and Dani was. Fifteen is a terrible year. At least he does not have spots any longer—I still did, and my voice kept breaking, which embarrassed me no end." He looked down at the piece of paper in his hand, realized he was looking at the back of it, and turned it over. "I wonder why he asked for your book?" he asked, noticing the writing above the salutation.

"I have no idea—maybe he is bored. I hope he is bored and not in danger."

"Umm." Mikhail was already deep in the first page and barely heard her remark. He frowned over the words, admiring the care he knew had been put into them. There was nothing he found very surprising, for he had suspected for some time that Nico was perturbed about himself. He had assumed that Alanna Alar was the cause, and had been happy at the way in which Domenic had walked the taut rope between his affection for his foster-sister and propriety. He turned the page over again, and looked at the back of the sheet.

Yes, Nico was upset about his feelings for his cousin, but that did not appear to be the real problem. The words danced before his eyes, and Mikhail sat down on the couch with a thump and reread them. When he was done, he shook his head. "It is a shame we could not have fostered him to someone."

"I don't really think that that would have helped, Mikhail. Are you feeling as if you were a poor parent? I know I am."

"Yes, I am. If only he wasn't such a prickly boy, so hard to . . . and you are right. Who would we have dared to foster him to? My brother Gabriel might have done, except that that would have placed him near to Javanne, and besides, Regis would never have agreed, would he?"

Marguerida sighed. "Your brother is an estimable man, when he isn't being a complete jackass, but I don't think he would have made any better a parent than we have done. We might just as well accept the fact that we did the best we could, and it wasn't enough!"

"Marguerida, this is not the end of the world! I know you are exhausted, and that you have been wearing yourself out, handling all the arrangements and worrying about Nico at the same time. But he did manage to tell you that he feels like some sort of unnatural child, didn't he?"

"Is that supposed to make me feel better?" Her golden eyes sparkled with anger, and color came into her pale cheeks.

"Yes, it is. I don't know—maybe all boys that age feel to some degree unnatural." Mikhail rubbed his forehead and tried to will away his headache. He could heal anyone but himself, it seemed. "I could always tell Regis anything, when I was young, before this," he said, shaking his gloved hand. "Poor Dani couldn't. So Regis was a better parent to me than he was to his own son. And I have never been able to speak to my own father as I did with Regis, or the way I can with Lew. I think the fact that Nico can write you such a letter says that you have been a very good mother. I think he struggled over it, trying to find the right words. He is very brave, you know." He did not add how miserable he felt, after reading the letter, that he had done to Domenic exactly what he had sworn he would never do—kept the boy at arm's length and made it difficult for both of them.

"But what are we going to do?"

"I don't know. And right now, Nico's unhappiness is the least of our worries. We can think about it after we have . . . gotten past the rest of it."

"This is our son, Mik!"

"Yes, he is. And he has gotten all the best of us and the worst as well—he has Lew's dour temperament, your intelligence, and my own damned imagination! But, Marguerida, he will not die from being unhappy, and from this letter, I think he is likely more capable of knowing himself than I was at that age."

"He really has never been young, has he?"

"No. He has an ancient soul, and we both know it."

"Do you think that . . . ?"

"That he is Varzil returned? I don't know, but it would hardly be surprising if that had occurred. The timing makes it likely. And that would not be such a terrible thing, would it?"

"What do you mean?"

"Varzil was a great man, in his time, and, for a future ruler of Darkover, I cannot think of a better prospect. But, first, my dear, we have to get there." Mikhail was more troubled than he admitted. He stared at his gloved hand. He did not want to think about the future, about the possibility that his firstborn would want to wrest the ring from him. True, he would have willingly cast it aside a thousand times, but that was another matter. Then he relaxed, so suddenly it took him by surprise. His limbs went slack and the throbbing in his temple vanished. He knew his son better than that. Domenic was the last person in the world who would try to seize the power of that ring.

Mikhail turned the letter over in his hand, and reread a paragraph on the first side. It was brief, and mentioned only that Nico had been experiencing some sort of unusual hearing—something he had thought were hallucinations at first. The script was tight, the glyphs crowded together more than in the rest of the missive, and Mikhail suspected that his son had refused to expand on the subject. Domenic had hinted at rather than disclosed what was really eating at him, he decided, reading between the lines and letting his imagination go where it would, just for the pleasure of thinking about something different than the problems which had plagued him for days.

What had Nico heard, and why did it disturb him so? Mikhail wished he had been able to get the boy to talk to him earlier. Perhaps Lew knew something about it—Nico often confided in his grandfather. Well, it was clearly not some immediate matter. His son was safe for the present, and that was all that was important.

"Marguerida, it will all be behind us in a few days."

"That is true—and thank goodness for that. I don't know how much more strain I can manage without taking to my bed and refusing to move."

"I like the sound of that—we could both just retire to the bedchamber and make love until we were too tired to move."

"How can you think about sex at a time like this?" she asked, sounding both pleased and annoyed.

"How can I think of anything else when I look at you?"

"You still find me comely?"

"*Caria,* you are the most desirable women in the world, and perhaps in the entire galaxy, to me."

She rose and came to him, slipping her arms around his chest and resting her head on his shoulder. Then she lifted her lips and kissed him softly, then with greater passion, until he could think of nothing else."

21

Mikhail entered the Crystal Chamber with Marguerida, her hand on his arm, gripping his muscles between her strong fingers. He had been dreading this moment ever since Regis had fallen ill. No, longer than that! In a way, he had been moving toward this fate all his adult life. He had not expected it to come so soon, nor to find himself so unprepared.

It was one thing to plan for the future, and quite another to experience it. He had not been prepared for Regis to die for decades yet, and even though time had passed since the actual event, it was not until Mikhail entered the chamber that he felt the enormity of what awaited him. There had been a certain dreamlike quality to it all until he faced the empty chair which his uncle had occupied on so many occasions.

He glanced at his wife, noted the extreme pallor of her complexion and the tension in her neck muscles. This gathering of the Comyn was going to be difficult. They both knew that, and the strain of it showed in her face. Mikhail took in her flashing golden eyes, so full of intelligence, the curls of her still fiery hair, and the way the corners of her mouth were firmly tucked in. She looked just as formidable as he knew she was, and he felt his heart lift just a little, to have her beside him, fierce and determined. He knew how weary she actually was, and yet none of it showed. Now all he had to do was match her, strength for strength.

Out of the corner of his eye Mikhail glimpsed Donal Alar a few strides behind him, and, next to him, his brother Rafael. It was the first time Rafael had come to the Crystal Chamber in many years, since Regis had barred him because of Gisela's mischief. It was ironic, really, since Rafael's marriage to the Aldaran woman had been Regis' idea in the first place. True, it had been a political match—an attempt to keep *Dom* Damon happy and quiet. That had failed, of course, since the old lord of the Aldaran Domain would never be quiet, short of the grave. And it had caused a great deal of misery for Rafael and Gisela as well. He recalled the expression on her face, when he had come to speak to his brother. He knew now that she genuinely cared for Rafael. It gave him a deep sense of satisfaction to have his brother at his back, a feeling of support he knew he would need to get through the next few hours.

Mikhail decided to count his blessings—his wife, his father-in-law, his brother, his paxman, and the rest of his trusted advisors. He tried very hard not to think about the inevitable confrontation with his mother that would undoubtedly make the chamber ring with discord. At least, finally, all the tension that had made Comyn Castle so uncomfortable for the past several days would be released, but he wasn't sure if that was a blessing or a curse. Something like a laugh started up from his belly, but did not quite reach his throat. In spite of their brazen words, none of the men who had conferred in the study had actually had the nerve to drug Javanne Hastur into silence, not even Lew Alton. Beside, they were all too ethical and it wouldn't have solved anything in the long run.

He turned his attention back to his wife. It was almost a shame that they had both become so restrained over the years. Mikhail remembered their first quarrels now, with a kind of nostalgic pleasure. That first meeting, when he had accused her of intending to toss his parents out of Armida, came back to him. They had not fought like that in years, and he rather missed it. Instead, they held themselves in check, grinding their teeth, hissing and whispering, almost as if they were afraid to permit their furies into the light of day.

That thought made him actually chuckle, and Marguerida gave him a sharp look. The huge matrixes in the ceiling of the chamber prevented any form of telepathic communication, so she was unable to catch his thought. "Are you going to share the joke, Mik?" Her usually beautiful voice was thick with tension.

"Of course, *caria*. I was just thinking that if we were less controlled, and more like my mother, we could have a perfectly wonderful time shouting and screaming at everyone."

To his delight, he saw a small smile relieve the rigid expression on her face. "I would not demean myself in that way, but I confess that the temptation is very strong. I would just adore to have a nice bout of hysterics, or rant and rave. Alanna has all the fun!" He heard the tension begin to leave her voice, and knew that he had improved her mood considerably.

"She does, doesn't she. It is not fair."

"I almost wish I was back at Arilinn, in my wee cottage, with nothing more important to do than play my harp and eat my head off. Or that I could get on Dyania and ride and ride. If I had realized how hard it was going to be to act my age, I think I would have given up at twenty."

"Considering how much you loathed Arilinn. . . ."

"I said in my cottage, not in the Tower!"

"True, you did. We will be going to the *rhu fead* in two days, if we survive the council meeting without bloodshed, and you can have your wish to get on a horse, at least."

"You don't think . . ."

"I think my mother will do her best to oppose me, and I think that *Dom* Damon will be somewhere between difficult and impossible—but, no, I don't actually expect anyone to draw steel. Is it just me, or does it feel as if a thunderstorm is about to break?" He was glad, at that moment, that the dampers prevented her from knowing his mind. It had occurred to him that Francisco Ridenow might do exactly that, and although he knew that both Donal Alar and his brother Rafael would leap to defend him, Mikhail did not want to see anyone hurt.

"Since I have caught myself looking out the windows several times, and been very disappointed that all I saw was a light cloud cover, I think it is not just you. At least the rain has finally stopped—I believe it was making everyone even more fractious than they already were. Right now, Mik, I really wish we could travel a few hours into the future, and skip the actual council meeting completely."

"What a splendid notion! A pity we cannot manage it. Except that if I could, Mother would use it as further evidence of my unfitness to govern Darkover."

"I hoped that the news that the Federation was planning to depart would make her happy, and cause her to forget all about how much she mistrusts you," Marguerida answered, sighing deeply.

"Nothing will please her except to see someone other than myself in Regis' place, I am afraid. She has nearly driven poor Dani insane with her suggestions that he change his mind over the whole thing, give up the Elhalyn crown and assume the Hastur Domain, even though the Cortes Court settled the matter years ago. Once my dear mother gets an idea into her head, nothing short of a bolt from the blue will dislodge it. Dani is ready to throttle her, and poor Lady Linnea looks as if she wants to hide in the attic every time she has to see her." *And she is definitely cultivating young Gareth, which is not good for him or anyone else.*

Donal cleared his throat softly, to signal that someone else was coming into the room. Mikhail glanced over his shoulder at his young pax-man, and saw *Dom* Damon Aldaran and his son Robert coming through the door. Behind him were Lady Javanne and *Dom* Gabriel Lanart-Alton. His mother's cheeks were ruddy with suppressed fury, and her blue eyes sparkled with determination. She was dressed in her favorite shade of green, with a gold lace frill beneath her chin.

Javanne glared at *Dom* Damon, almost willing him to step aside and allow her to enter before him, but the old Aldaran man was completely unwilling to yield. He always treated Javanne as if she were a peasant, not a Hastur. For that matter, *Dom* Damon was just as rude to other women, including Marguerida, and Mikhail was happy to blame much of Gisela's mischief on her father. What a mercy Giz had been so well-behaved the past few days—spending time with Katherine Aldaran and staying out of trouble.

Robert Aldaran gave him a look of resignation as he allowed Javanne to precede him into the Crystal Chamber. He looked haggard in his plain brown tunic, and embarrassed as well. Why did they both have to have such impossible parents?

The exchange of glances heartened Mikhail. Robert was very sensible, and had, during recent years, become one of Mikhail's and Regis' strongest allies on the Council, often siding against *Dom* Damon. It was, he knew, a very peculiar thing, remarkable in light of the antipathy and mistrust toward the Aldaran Domain that had been a constant on Darkover for generations. The shifting alliances between the various Domains always made Mikhail shake his head in wonder; he could never reliably predict how they would go.

He found himself thinking again of Francisco Ridenow, and another gathering in the Crystal Chamber, when Regis had decided to reinstate the Comyn Council almost seventeen years before. Then Francisco had been Mikhail's friend, but now he was a foe—and it was all Varzil's fault! When Mikhail and Marguerida had come back from the past with the great matrix of the fabled *laranzu,* everything had changed. Francisco had felt that the great matrix should be riding on the hand of a Ridenow. It was irrelevant to him that it could not be given away, nor, he suspected, wrested by force without killing both the wearer and anyone who tried to take it. Mikhail's own matrix was integrated with the greater one, keyed to his particular energy, for as long as he lived. None of that made the least difference to Francisco—he felt it was an heirloom of the Ridenow Domain, and he, Francisco, should have it.

In light of Francisco Ridenow's rather checkered past, with the suspicion that he had had a hand in the deaths of his rivals, his uncle, and two brothers, for control of the Domain, Mikhail could only feel relief that there had been no attempt to do away with him thus far. But, now, with Regis' death, perhaps that would change, too. Francisco refused to believe that only Mikhail could wield the matrix, since it was set in a ring instead of worn about the throat like others. What if Francisco decided he could now get his elegant hands on the treasure he desired?

Mikhail shook his head, to clear away these ugly thoughts. He was starting to understand the concerns that had blighted his uncle's last years on Darkover, the fears that had wracked him, even while surrounded by trusted friends. Regis had survived the Sharra Rebellion and the attempts of the World Wreckers to destroy the planet and gain control of it. The experiences had profoundly affected his world view in his later years. Mikhail had no desire to imitate his late uncle by becoming paranoid, or even overly cautious, but Francisco was enough to give him pause. Mikhail refused to surrender to his imagination, as tempting as it was. It was hard, though, and he would have preferred to have the head of the Ridenow Domain with him, rather than against him.

What Varzil had not foreseen when he sent the ring into Darkover's present was how greatly the passing of the matrix would affect the delicate balance between the Domains. Mikhail did not blame the man—he had needed to get the ring away from the grasp of Ashara Alton. And he had succeeded in that. Mikhail just wished the ring could have gone to someone else, someone stronger than he felt himself to be—or been taken out of play entirely. It was a burden, one he had undertaken willingly but without really understanding the problems it would create.

He had gained a great power, for healing and, he knew, for destruction as well, but it had cost him the unquestioned trust of his uncle, and the friendship of several people he valued. Lady Marilla Aillard, who had been like a mother to him while he was Dyan Ardais' paxman, had chosen to side with Javanne and *Dom* Francisco, insisting that Mikhail was just too powerful to be trusted. The estrangement grieved him greatly, and he wondered if he could ever put it to rights. Worse, it had put his lifelong friend, her son, Dyan Ardais, in a most uncomfortable position, and the strain of that had made it hard for both of them. But he knew he could count on Dyan to remain loyal to him, and he silently numbered his allies, to reassure himself a little.

For years now the walls of the Crystal Chamber had echoed with argument—most of it concerning Mikhail and his place as Regis' designated heir. His uncle had been less and less able to control the Council, and the deteriorating situation had added to his growing sense of unease. Even though Mikhail had never done anything to threaten Regis' rule, the fact that he possessed the power to do so had disturbed his uncle's peace of mind. No one seemed to be able to grasp the actuality of his power except himself, Marguerida, and Istvana Ridenow. And neither words of assurance nor promises could convince his foes on the Council that he was no threat to any of them.

Mikhail indulged himself briefly in the sense of being misunderstood. People, Lew Alton had frequently informed him, always judged others by what they themselves would do. His mother and Francisco craved power, and so they believed he must as well.

So many harsh words had been said in the Crystal Chamber, and between the two generations there now stood an abyss of bad feeling that he feared would turn into vicious and potentially bloody infighting once the presence of the Federation was removed. Would they fall into civil war, as had happened in the past? The thought that he might be responsible for such an event, that his mother and *Dom* Francisco might take up arms against him, was very nearly intolerable. And although he had never tested the powers of his matrix to their fullest, he had the sinking certainty that he could use it to destroy his enemies, if he were forced.

He had never challenged Regis' authority by discovering all that his matrix was capable of. Instead he had trod a cautious and narrow path, careful never to cause his increasingly anxious uncle to feel threatened, while at the same time trying to retain his own self-respect. Now he was starting to understand the toll this interior conflict had taken on him, and he wondered if he were really up to the task of ruling Darkover. He had almost forgotten how to be forceful, and desperately wished he could reclaim his younger and less doubtful self. And he must, if Darkover were going to survive!

The years had not been wasted. Studying with Istvana Ridenow he had learned the vast healing capacities of his matrix. This had given Mikhail a deep satisfaction until he had been unable to save Regis. He knew of the remarkable tasks Varzil Ridenow had accomplished with the aid of the matrix, and suspected that he could do similar things. He still wondered how the man had transformed Lake Hali from a poisonous sink into its present peculiar condition. The knowledge of how to effect that change in energies, if it actually was possible, had not made itself known to Mikhail. But he knew that it meant that destruction was possible, even in a healing, and the idea did not make him rest easy. The sense that he might have to test the limits of his own powers in the near future was not a happy prospect.

Mikhail helped Marguerida into her chair, then took his place beside her. Donal put a goblet of cider beside his left hand, his young face calm and reassuring. He wished he could share his nephew's apparent serenity. Now, all he had to do was live up to his young paxman's excellent opinion of him. Oddly, this thought bolstered him and eased his endless doubts. He remembered how Donal had said that he had studied Danilo Syrtis-Ardais and made him a model for himself. That was very wise, for Danilo always seemed to be calm. Even when others lifted their voices, he never shouted or banged the table in rage. Perhaps he could do that as well.

Mikhail glanced at his mother's face, then at *Dom* Damon's, and realized it would be more difficult to keep his temper than he would have wished. They were both ready for a fight. His father, *Dom* Gabriel, was looking old and tired, and Mikhail suspected that Javanne had been driving the old man mad with her schemes and plots. At least he knew he could count on his father, no matter what his mother said in her rage.

Lew and Danilo Syrtis-Ardais entered the chamber together, followed quickly by Dani Hastur with his wife, Miralys Elhalyn-Hastur, on his arm. The pretty girl who had briefly been his ward sixteen years before had turned into a stunningly beautiful woman, confident and serene where she had once been shy and fearful. She was pregnant for a third time, and her skin glowed with the health and vigor of her condition. Marriage to Dani clearly agreed with her, as being Underkeeper at Arilinn agreed with her younger sister Valenta. It gladdened him to know that at least some of the people in the room were happy, and he rather wished Valenta were present as well. She was a fearless woman, tart-tongued, and utterly unintimidated by Javanne. But she was needed at the Tower, to oversee the relays for the present, and, he prayed, to prevent any of the Traveler troupes from causing more trouble.

Mikhail's brother Rafael helped his mother into a chair, and then took the one between them. Javanne gave her middle son a dark look, as if questioning his presence in the Crystal Chamber after so many years of absence. It felt very good to have Rafael between them, although he knew it would not protect him from Javanne's ire. Then he noticed that *Dom* Damon was staring at Rafael, and that he seemed none too pleased to find him there.

Mikhail was wondering why *Dom* Damon was looking daggers at his son-in-law when Marguerida placed her matrixed left hand over his engloved right one, and gave it a quick squeeze. The quiet gesture reassured him more than it had any business to. More people entered the room. *Dom* Francisco took the seat beside Javanne Hastur, and Lady Marilla sat on his other side. Dyan Ardais hesitated, and then sat down in one of the chairs which ordinarily would have been occupied by *leroni* from the Towers, putting a space between himself and his mother on one side, and the Alton seat on the other, already occupied by *Dom* Gabriel.

Danilo Syrtis-Ardais, who ordinarily sat where Rafael was now positioned, took the situation in with a swift glance, and placed himself on Marguerida's other side, with Dani and Miralys beside him. *Dom* Damon and Robert Aldaran took places between Dyan Ardais and *Dom* Gabriel, with several chairs left untenanted on either side of them, isolating them a little. The table could seat thirty without crowding, but the Keepers from the various Towers who would have been present if it were Midsummer were not there. Lady Linnea had excused herself, pleading her grief.

Mikhail knew it was something more—a desire to avoid Javanne Hastur which he shared with her.

"Are we going to sit here like stones," growled *Dom* Damon, "or get this foolishness over and done with."

"Father," Robert warned gruffly.

The elder Aldaran glared at his son. "What? We all know what we are going to say—it has been said here so often that I could likely recite to you the very words that will be spoken!" He glared around the table, daring anyone to challenge him, and looked very disappointed when no one did.

"*Dom* Damon is right," Francisco Ridenow began. "We have said everything, time and time again." He looked as if the words were sour in his mouth, for to agree with an Aldaran on any matter, even the weather, did not please him. "But I suppose we will have to go through the whole thing for form's sake."

Mikhail knew he must take charge of the meeting before it disintegrated into the all too familiar baiting and name calling that had become expected procedure at Council meetings. The lassitude in his limbs, and a certain fuzziness in his mind, almost overwhelmed him for a moment. Maybe Javanne was right—that in spite of his *laran*-founded power, he was not really capable of governing Darkover. But, if not him, then who? Dani was out of the question, no matter what his mother imagined, and Nico was too young. He had prepared for this responsibility all his life, and it was not fair that now he had the task, he felt unequal to it.

Then Lew Alton sat down next to *Dom* Gabriel. He gave Mikhail a look that seemed to mirror his own doubts and fears. Lew nodded at him, and suddenly the weariness that was crippling him vanished. His mind cleared completely, and if he had not known that it was almost impossible to use *laran* in the chamber, he would have thought that his father-in-law had somehow managed to use forced rapport to good effect on his flagging spirits.

"There is actually a great deal of new business to consider, and I hope we will be able to avoid our usual petty bickering," Mikhail began calmly, trying to imitate Danilo as he had planned a few minutes earlier. He saw his mother's cheeks redden at this remark, and knew he had scored a small hit. It was rather shameful how much pleasure he got from this little victory, so he put it out of his mind completely.

"First, I think everyone is already aware that the Terranan are planning to withdraw from Darkover in the very near future. While I realize that this will please some of us here, I believe that is a short-sighted way to look at it. When the Federation leaves, it will not evaporate, and it will not likely forget that Darkover exists. I realize that some of you imagine that will be the outcome, but you are wrong!"

"What do you mean, Mikhail," Lady Marilla asked in her soft voice.

"I mean that they will still have the capacity to return, hostilely if they should choose. If there are no treaties or agreements to honor, then they might feel free to do almost anything." He did not catalog the many possibilities—it was better to let their imaginations supply them.

"But why would they want to do that?" she said in a puzzled tone.

"Because they can, *domna*," Lew growled. "The Federation we are now facing is not the same one which came to Darkover during the time of Lorill Hastur, and we should not delude ourselves that it is."

"Yes, yes—you have been saying something of that sort for years, Lew," snapped Lady Javanne, "you old storm crow. I, for one, have never put much credence in it, and I do not believe you now."

"That is your privilege, Javanne, and I hope that you will never see Armida occupied by Federation forces."

"I do not frighten easily," she answered, yet she appeared uncertain to Mikhail's eye.

"Just a moment," Francisco Ridenow said before anyone else could speak. "We have not yet chosen a new head of the Comyn Council, and I think we should, before we begin any actual business. I nominate Danilo Hastur and . . ."

"Do you think you are in a democracy?" Lew interrupted sharply. "As Regis' chosen heir, Mikhail is head of the Council, and we need not waste any time discussing the matter."

Francisco gave Javanne a sidelong glance, and then went on as if Lew had not spoken. "I do not agree. Just because you have always assumed you would take Regis' place, Mikhail, does not mean that you will. The succession has *not* been decided. Therefore I propose we should select Danilo Hastur to be the new head of Comyn Council, because he is the most legitimate person to lead us."

Dani, who was ordinarily the quietest of men, turned an unlovely shade of red, and banged his fist on the table. "How dare you suggest such a thing—you maggot!" Then he rounded on his aunt Javanne, finally ready to let all the grievances of the past few days find an outlet. "This is your doing, and I will not be party to it! You are a selfish, interfering old woman, and it is just a shame that you did not die in my father's place! If you think you can manipulate me, think again. I want nothing to do with you, or with your filthy plans to run Darkover to suit yourself."

There was a shocked silence around the table at this outburst, although Miralys appeared quite pleased with her husband, and Lew Alton was having difficulty not laughing out loud at Javanne's discomfort. That redoubtable woman recovered quickly, however, the two spots of red on her cheeks fading as she got control of herself.

"You are just overwrought over your father's death, and do not know what you are saying," she answered, quite calmly under the circumstances.

"Is there nothing that will prick the bubble of your vanity, Aunt? You disgust me. My father was barely laid out before you started in with your vile suggestions that I renege on my sworn . . ."

"You were only a boy when you made the decision to resign as Regis' heir, and you did not know what you were doing. And now you must allow wiser and older heads to guide you," Javanne insisted.

"Go to Zandru's coldest hell," snarled Dani, his face losing all color. "You are the last person I would wish to guide me."

Dom Gabriel looked ready to burst, and Mikhail decided that he had to intervene. He managed to catch his father's eye, and watched him subside with an enormous effort.

"The matter was settled sixteen years ago, Mother, and you cannot change it. I regret that the idea of my following in Regis' footsteps causes you such grief, but that is how it must be. I have no intention of resigning, and Dani has none of taking my place." Mikhail was surprised by the steadiness of his own voice, and rather pleased with himself.

"You are not fit to . . ." Javanne sputtered.

"That is quite enough," Marguerida announced. "We will accomplish nothing by bickering with one another."

"You cannot silence me, Marguerida."

"Oh, but I *can,* and I *will* if you continue to be a nuisance!"

"A nuisance!" Javanne gasped. "How *dare* you!"

"You mean less to me than a gnat," Marguerida replied tartly, paying off years of old scores in only a few words.

This was too much of a strain for Lew Alton, and he tried to conceal his laughter by pretending to have a fit of coughing. But above the hand he lifted to cover his mouth, Mikhail could see his father-in-law's eyes sparkle with amusement, and only wished he could permit himself to openly enjoy the moment. Even *Dom* Gabriel looked less like a thundercloud, and he cast Marguerida a veiled look of approval.

Mikhail drew a long breath and said, "We are not here to debate who will rule Darkover in the future. If anyone imagines that they have the right to do that, they are quite wrong." He could feel himself choosing words as Danilo would have, as if the mantle of his uncle's paxman was somehow protecting him. "The problem that confronts us is that the Federation is departing. Yes, I know that some of you do not perceive this as a problem—but you lack all the facts." Mikhail caught the look on Danilo's face out of the corner of his eye as he continued, and was silently amused.

"What facts have you withheld from us, then?" Lady Marilla asked, her voice wary.

"I resent the implication, Lady Marilla, but I am going to ignore it. You all know that the Federation is planning to pull out in a few weeks' time, but you do not understand the reason. The legislature, which Lew and Herm served in, has been disbanded—and that changes everything!"

"What does that have to do with Darkover?" *Dom* Damon seemed genuinely puzzled.

"As the Comyn Council acts as an advisory body to the ruler of Darkover, so the legislature held the leader of the Federation in check," Lew said, as if speaking to a child, and a dull one at that. "Without that restraint, the Premier can do just about anything—and from what we have been able to learn, she is running the Federation by decree at present. That is tyranny, pure and plain!"

"I repeat—what does that have to do with Darkover," *Dom* Damon growled, glaring fiercely at Lew.

"I protest!" Dom Francisco banged his fist on the table, his pale cheeks flushed with anger. "We have not settled the matter of who is head of the Comyn Council, and until we do, everything else is . . ."

At that moment there was the sound of footsteps, and Gareth Elhalyn entered. He looked around as those with their backs to the door turned to look toward him, and smiled. "What are you doing here?" his father asked.

"He is here at my invitation," Javanne answered before Gareth could speak. Her eyes were glittering with pleasure, and there was a smug expression on her face. Mikhail thought that if she had been a cat, there would have been feathers poking out of her taut mouth.

"Of all the . . ." Danilo began.

"He has no business here, since he has not even been named Dani's heir as yet," snapped *Dom* Gabriel, favoring his wife with a furious look. "What are you doing, woman?"

"Sit down, Gareth," Javanne went on, as if no one had spoken. She waved at the vacant chairs. The lad looked somewhat uneasy now, his handsome face doubtful, but he sat down beside his mother, in between her and Lew Alton. "I have arrived at an obvious conclusion, which I cannot understand why no one else has seen." She looked around the table with a slight sneer, as if everyone except herself was stupid.

"And what might that be, cousin," Lew Alton asked with a kind of silky insolence that never failed to annoy Javanne.

"Since Mikhail is clearly too powerful to be allowed to rule Darkover, and since his oldest son is *nedestro,* and Dani refuses to do his duty, then we must agree that the rightful ruler will be Gareth Elhalyn—and all we need to do is appoint someone to be regent for him until he reaches adulthood." She paused, and looked less confident. "I think that *Dom* Francisco . . ."

"This is outrageous!" Gabriel Lanart-Alton's booming voice echoed off the great trap matrixes in the ceiling. "Gareth's life would not be worth a sekal with Francisco as regent!"

This pronouncement was followed by a stunned silence, since *Dom* Gabriel had voiced the unspeakable. Aware that he was now the center of attention, the old man continued. "I apologize for my wife's unseemly behavior—I was unaware of her plan until now, or I would have put a stop to her nonsense! Believe me, son, none of this is my doing." He looked tired and ashamed.

"I never imagined that it was," Mikhail answered calmly, reminding himself not to allow his temper to flare. "I think it would be best, and least embarrassing, if Gareth left now, since he has no right to be present."

"You stole my place, and I want it back," Gareth announced, glaring at Mikhail.

"You are much too young to understand, Gareth," Dani began quietly. "Mikhail is correct—you should not be present."

"No wonder he got you to give up the Hastur legacy! You are spineless, Father, and everyone knows it!" Gareth sneered at Dani as he spoke, leaning forward a little to see around his mother.

Miralys grabbed his golden locks in a firm grip and pulled his head back against the chair. There was an audible thump. "How dare you speak to your father like that." She slapped his face with her free hand. "Now get on your feet and get out of here, before I have the Guards drag you away! I have never been so ashamed in my life!"

Fighting back tears, the boy stood up. "I will have my rightful place, and no one is going to stop me. *I will be king!*" He turned on his heel and almost ran toward the door, cursing under his breath. "Damn you, Javanne Hastur—you promised me!"

Miralys and Mikhail exchanged a brief glance, and the woman bit her lower lip to keep from exclaiming. They had both heard those words before, from Vincent Elhalyn, her brother. And Mikhail knew, from her expression, that she feared that her firstborn might prove to be just as unstable as Vincent had been. Sometimes the Elhalyn defect took a long time to manifest itself, and he hoped that Gareth's behavior was only an indication of the boy's ambitions, fed by Javanne's treachery, and not something more dangerous.

"I hope you are pleased with yourself, Mother," Mikhail told the woman. He could see that she was trembling with rage and frustration, but also that she was unable to grasp why her plan had failed so dramatically.

Mikhail looked slowly around the table, measuring the expressions on the stunned faces of the Comyn Council. Even *Dom* Francisco seemed unnerved, running one hand through his pale hair and drumming on the tabletop with the other. From his look of unease, Mikhail guessed that he had not known of Javanne's plan to name him as regent for Gareth. Francisco was canny enough to know that such an appointment would never be accepted by the rest of the Domains, and would not have suggested it himself. After several seconds, *Dom* Francisco turned to stare at Javanne, and there was nothing kindly in his gaze.

Mikhail swallowed a sudden desire to laugh, to fall into cheerful hysterics, gather up his wife and children, and fly to one of the moons. Liriel, perhaps. He had always thought that his mother was her own worst enemy, and now she had managed to move Francisco Ridenow into that position! The irony was almost too much to be contained.

But he managed to control himself long enough to continue his examination of the rest of the Council. There was shock and outrage evident, but also an air of speculation that puzzled him for a second. Then he decided that both *Dom* Damon and Francisco Ridenow were trying to think how to turn this development to their own advantage. He knew these men to be his adversaries, even though they were not in any way allies. Mikhail felt he could handle them because he had come to know them over the years. A look at Robert Aldaran's face told him these thoughts were going through his mind as well, and that he would try to keep his father in check.

"When did you learn that the Federation had dissolved the legislature, Mikhail?" Lady Marilla asked, clearly attempting to get matters back in hand.

"I have known for several days," Mikhail said, "ever since Herm Aldaran arrived. Shortly after that, all Darkovan personnel were ordered to leave Headquarters. This is one of the things I intended to discuss at this meeting, before we became distracted by other matters." The sound of his voice surprised him, for it might have been Regis speaking in his particular way, chiding his adversaries like a stern but not unjust father. And from the way Javanne stiffened, she had caught the similarity as well, and was not at all pleased by it.

"Where is Hermes?" Dom Damon asked in a querulous voice. "I have asked several people, including that Terranan woman he married, but no one will tell me anything. Even Gisela does not seem to know where her brother has disappeared to." He gave Rafael a penetrating glance.

"Yes, Mikhail," Javanne cut in silkily. "Where is he?"

Mikhail looked at Lew, who gave a shrug. "He is doing a job for me at present," he answered, glad that the construction of the Crystal Chamber prevented anyone from reading his mind. "He volunteered for the task, and it seemed the best thing at the time."

"He volunteered? For what? When? Why?" Javanne was determined to get to the bottom of things. "He was at dinner three nights ago, and then he vanished."

"I don't understand any of this," *Dom* Damon grumbled.

Mikhail weighed things in his mind, and decided that he had better give them a bone to chew on, something to distract them. "Herm has the Aldaran Gift, and had a flash of warning—he left the Federation before Premier Nagy actually announced the dissolution of the legislature. He brought his wife and children with him, for he suspected that he would not be returning there in the near future. When the Station Chief realized Herm was on Darkover, he issued an arrest warrant, declaring him an enemy of the state—a unique distinction in Darkovan history, but one that I am sure Herm would have preferred not to have received." There were murmurs around the table, and a few mild chuckles. "Lyle Belfontaine had the audacity to send me a message demanding that I turn Hermes over to him for arrest and deportation. Or, to be precise, he sent Regis the message, not knowing at that time that Regis had died. I ignored it, since I have no intention of turning over any citizen of our world to anyone. But Hermes felt that it might be better if he were not here, so as not to cause trouble."

Lew gave Mikhail a heartwarming look of approval at this mixture of truth and half-truth. Everyone else was too busy digesting these revelations to comment for a merciful few moments, and Mikhail allowed himself to be quietly pleased.

"I don't believe this," bellowed *Dom* Damon, clearly surprised and outraged. "Belfontaine would never arrest my son!"

Mikhail drew a sheet of shiny paper from his pouch and handed it around the table. "This is the arrest order."

Dom Damon stared at it nearsightedly. "That treacherous bastard!"

"I did not realize you were so well acquainted with Belfontaine," Danilo Syrtis-Ardais remarked quietly, giving *Dom* Damon a piercing look.

"I would not say we were acquainted," Lord Aldaran blustered. "But unlike the rest of you, we have tried to maintain reasonable ties with the Terranan, particularly since there are so many of them living in the Aldaran Domain at present."

"Just how many of them are there?" Mikhail asked. Regis had never been able to get *Dom* Damon to name a figure, and it had annoyed him a great deal.

"Oh, I don't know. I never think about such things." The guarded expression on his face deepened.

Robert Aldaran gave his father a glance of surprise. "There are, at this time, approximately five hundred Federation citizens in the Aldaran Domain, most of them technicians of various sorts. That number includes about fifty spouses. There is a modest contingent of ethnologists and anthropologists, doing nothing very much, as near as I can gather, except annoying people by asking peculiar questions about all sorts of things that are none of their business. And there are about seventy-five Federation troopers, although I have suspected for quite some time that many of the technicians were actually fighting men pretending otherwise."

Dom Damon cast a look of unconcealed loathing at his older son. Then he rattled the paper in his hand. "I just don't understand this! Why in the world would Belfontaine issue an arrest warrant, particularly for a son of mine?"

"What better way to provoke an incident, and justify some action that would otherwise not be permitted," Lew replied almost smugly, as if he felt he had caught the Aldaran somehow. "Belfontaine has a history of overstepping himself, for being ambitious, and I am sure that being forced to leave Darkover this way, at this time, was not his choice."

"What in Zandru's coldest hell do you mean by that," growled *Dom* Damon, looking more confused and anxious by the moment.

"Well, if we did not turn over Herm, then he might think he could justify storming Comyn Castle itself. The law is rather ambiguous about the rights of individual citizens of Protected Planets, which means that Belfontaine might have decided to read it to his advantage." Lew looked grim for a moment. "We can only conjecture, I'm afraid, but I do know that Belfontaine has been sending frantic messages to his superiors, and that they have not, so far as I know, responded. I think he is trying to get permission to use force against us."

"Then you must be insane! Why would he want to do something so foolish?" The color of *Dom* Damon's face was alarming now, so red that Mikhail feared he would have an apoplectic fit. But he did not look like a man who was planning deliberate treachery. Whatever plan he had, it had nothing to do with the ambush that might await them on the road. He let himself enjoy a moment of relief.

"We must hope you are correct, with your greater knowledge of the Terranan, *Dom* Damon," Francisco said slowly, frowning over the words. "But if he is desperate, then who knows what he might decide. Are we just going to sit around and wait for him to make a move?"

"Hardly that," Danilo answered. "Both the City Guard and the Castle Guard are on full alert, as I am sure you already know, *Dom* Francisco. In the recent past the Federation has attempted to cause trouble in various ways on Darkover, but thus far they have had very little success. The Thendaran rumor mill is almost silent concerning the Federation, but very curious about . . . well, no matter." He fell silent and looked as if he had said too much already, but when no one questioned him, he went on. "If there is any assault, it will come from another direction."

"And just what is being done to prevent this," Javanne asked sharply, speaking directly to Danilo.

Mikhail looked at Lew, for they had spent hours together with Danilo, trying to decide just how to present the plot to the Council. Lew gave one of his speaking shrugs and answered, "First, we have started rounding up the Travelers' troupes, quietly and firmly, because there is some evidence that the Federation has been using them as spies and agents."

"The Travelers? I can hardly believe what I am hearing! Do you actually expect us to believe that a bunch of entertainers pose some sort of threat to the Comyn?" She looked triumphant, as if she felt she had scored a point.

Dom Damon looked alarmed at this revelation, since everyone knew that several of the Traveler bands wintered in the Aldaran Domain. Still, there was nothing guilty in his expression. The ruddy color in his cheeks faded, and now he was pale. "Spies? Agents? Have you lost your mind?"

"No, I have not. We have already uncovered one spy within the Travelers, and who knows how many others there are. Do you remember the riot in the Horse Market during Midsummer? Well, it was provoked by the Travelers—we know that now, although we did not then. But the danger has been nipped in the bud," Mikhail told them. Any troupe near a Tower had been dealt with, since he had received Nico's communication two nights before, but that still left those in more remote locations free to make as much mischief as they wished. But if his son were correct, then it was likely that the Travelers themselves were largely innocent dupes, and that no troupe had more than one or two Terranan spies with them, if that.

"Travelers! This is utterly ridiculous! You are making this up!" snapped Javanne. "I don't know what you think you are doing, telling us these stories, and . . ."

"*Silence!*" roared *Dom* Gabriel. "If you say another word against Mikhail, woman, I will drag you out of here by your hair."

Javanne's mouth gaped, pushing the little ruff under her chin askew. Then she clamped it closed, glared at her husband, and subsided, shocked. She gathered herself again, slowly and with difficulty, looking old and haggard, yet determined at the same time. "Son or not, I will not allow you to take my brother's place!"

Mikhail took a deep breath and looked around the table. "Let us be clear on one matter. I am Regis Hastur's heir, and I will do what he wished me to do. The matter is not open to further discussion. I will not waste my time debating my own fitness with those of you who imagine yourselves to have wiser heads, or the well-being of Darkover more to heart. This is hardly the time to start fighting among ourselves."

Lady Marilla cleared her throat. "I must disagree, *Dom* Mikhail, and very strongly. You are too much influenced by Lew Alton and your wife, and everyone here knows that. I am afraid that the matter must be debated, and that, in the end, you will have to step aside." Her voice was soft, as always, and it sounded as if she had prepared the words carefully.

This was too much for Dyan Ardais, who rarely said very much at Council meetings. "In whose favor, Mother? Have you completely lost your wits?"

Lady Marilla looked slightly surprised, for it was not often that her son opposed her openly in Council meetings. "Well, a regency, of course . . . until Roderick is . . . or perhaps Gareth . . ."

"Ah, so that is what you have decided, have you?" Dyan sneered. "Forgive my mother, Mikhail. That is the most foolish idea I have heard in months, and I can guess where she got it. I must point out that Mikhail named Domenic his heir when he reached his majority at Midsummer, so there is no question of . . ."

"Domenic must never be permitted to succeed, and neither must Mikhail." Javanne spoke firmly, and it was clear that she was sincere. No matter how many *leroni* assured her that the events that had taken place during Mikhail and Marguerida's strange adventure in the past had actually occurred, she refused to believe that her grandson was the legitimate issue of a real marriage. She had fixed her mind on the idea that Nico was *nedestro,* and nothing could budge her from it.

Mikhail felt his heart sink, and he felt slightly ill. He wanted her approval and support, and he wondered how she could hate him so much. Well, perhaps she did not hate him, but only hated that she could not influence him, could not force him to follow her own plans. But she did hate his oldest child, and his wife, and that was almost more than he could bear.

"None of you really understand, and think me a foolish old woman,"

Javanne exclaimed, anguish in her voice. "Regis cannot have been in his right mind when he named Mikhail his heir—it is impossible! Mikhail must have used his powers to . . ." Her voice trailed away and she began to sob.

Everyone at the table was looking at him, averting their eyes from the spectacle of Javanne Hastur's grief. Mikhail felt his cheeks flame with a combination of embarrassment and rage that made his hands tremble. No one had ever openly accused him of using his matrix to his own advantage before, although he knew that the thought had crossed their minds. The ancient *di catenas* bracelet encircling his wrist rattled against the tabletop as he tried to master himself, to refrain from saying anything he would regret later. It made his heart ache, that his own mother would think such things of him, could regard him as so dishonorable.

Marguerida put her left hand over his right one again, and, despite the dampers, he felt her healing power sweep over him. He felt his blood cease to roar in his veins, and his breathing returned to normal. He looked around the table, at his mother, Francisco Ridenow and Lady Marilla arrayed against him. Then he studied *Dom* Damon. It was almost enough to make him throw up his hands and storm out of the chamber in a rage.

"Is there anyone else who imagines I influenced Regis Hastur in his decision?" he asked, surprised to find his voice steady and even.

"It was very convenient for you, wasn't it?" Francisco commented, "when young Dani resigned and took the Elhalyn Domain, right after you showed up with that fantastic tale and what you claim is the matrix stone of *my* ancestor." Francisco glanced around the table, the center of all eyes. "And Dani was quite young, and so very malleable." His voice was soft with suggestion, and Mikhail wanted to hit him.

Dani Hastur glared at Francisco and nearly spat with rage. "How dare you! Is there no ill thought you will not entertain? Next you will be suggesting that Mikhail had something to do with my father's death," he snarled. His hand left the table and went to the hilt of his dagger, but Miralys touched his arm and he released his grip.

Francisco smiled narrowly. "So that thought crossed your mind, too, did it?" He tried to suggest a feeling of comradeship across the table with Regis' son. "It must have been so hard to wait for Regis to die, since the Hasturs are usually such a *long-lived* family."

Danilo Syrtis-Ardais shifted in his chair, leaned forward slightly so that he could see Francisco clearly, and spoke. "That is the most disgraceful thing I have ever heard. I was with Regis when he had his stroke, and there was nothing about it that was the least unnatural. To suggest such shows more than I wish to know about the nature of your thoughts, Francisco. I had no idea you were so filthy-minded."

If the words had any impact, *Dom* Francisco did not show it. Instead, he went on, speaking in a low voice, as if trying to persuade his listeners of the validity of his suspicions. "We do not really know what Mikhail can do with his matrix, do we, *Dom* Danilo? And even you can be fooled."

Dyan Ardais pounded his fist on the table again. "You keep that damned tongue of yours behind your teeth, Francisco, or I will personally pull it from your mouth! Mikhail has never done anything to anyone except to heal them."

"So why did Regis die? If Mikhail is so powerful, why was he unable to restore Regis? Your loyalty to Mikhail does you credit, *Dom* Dyan, but I think it blinds you as well."

"And I suppose you think that I would not have known if something was wrong, Francisco," Danilo Syrtis-Ardais almost snarled. "I assume you think I am blind as well? Considering how you managed to achieve the rulership of your own Domain, I suppose such thoughts are natural."

There was a stricken silence and everyone stared at Francisco Ridenow, even his usual ally, Lady Marilla. There was no one present who had not nourished suspicions about the deaths of those who stood in the way of Francisco, but no one had ever openly suggested that he had arranged them. The man flinched slightly, and his face paled as he realized he had gone too far.

Dom Damon's eyes narrowed, as if he were trying to find some advantage in this conflict. Then his face cleared quickly. "While I am sure that Mikhail did nothing to his uncle, we cannot pretend that we are entirely free of suspicion. And we should remember that Mikhail is not the only Hastur—that he has two brothers, both older than himself, who could easily . . ."

"Enough!" Rafael spoke for the first time. "I have no ambition to rule Darkover, and my brother Gabe has so little interest in politics that he did not even bother to attend the Council meeting. If you say another word, *Dom* Damon, against my brother, I will happily ram your teeth down your throat. I have been wanting to do that for years."

"What—and deny me that pleasure?" Robert snapped from the other side of the table, baring his teeth at Rafael, like a wolf challenging a rival. "The succession was decided, long ago, and not in some moment of weak-mindedness the way Regis's loving sister would have it. This is hardly the time to think about changing it."

Mikhail felt cold, as if a wind from the Hellers had just blown through his body. He had known for a long time that he was resented and feared, but the continuous barrage of violent feelings against him were eroding his strength. Despair flickered and burst into flame in his mind. How could he hope to lead the Domains, when he could not even control a Council meeting?

Suddenly there was a remarkable sound, and the great trap matrices in the ceiling of the Crystal Chamber rang like chimes. Everyone looked up, and then there was an explosion of noise and blinding light. The shining stones burst into shards and cascaded not downward, but outward, toward the walls of the room, shattering into bits as they struck. Reflexively, everyone at the table flinched, and Lady Marilla half ducked under the protective rim of the table before she stopped herself.

Mikhail heard a shout from one of the Guards near the doorway, and he sensed Donal rushing toward him. The young paxman flung himself against Mikhail's shoulder, throwing his body over Mikhail's, trying to protect him. He could feel the warm breath of his nephew against his cheek.

A wind seemed to rise from nowhere, tugging at garments and hair, plucking away the butterfly clasps of the women and the knives of the men as if they were no more than twigs. Mikhail felt a sharp tug at his wrist, and watched, round-eyed, as his glove was pulled from his hand and rose in the swirling air. A minor tornado funneled to the ceiling, then angled off, bearing away the debris it had collected. Finally, the strange whirlwind flung itself against the farthest wall, the collected implements clattering to the floor with a loud noise.

The silence that followed was broken only by gasps and a few screams. Everyone seemed too stunned to do more than stare at the destruction. Then Mikhail's ring quivered on his finger, and beams of light burst from it.

"What manner of mischief is this," shouted *Dom* Francisco, pointing at Mikhail's hand.

Before anyone else could speak, a shining cloud rose from the matrix and floated to the center of the table. It hovered there, about a foot above the carved wood, and then began to shift, to turn in place, spinning hypnotically. Mikhail found his mouth gaping in astonishment. The rest of the onlookers were just as stunned as he was, but he was sure they were going to turn and accuse him of using some trick on them as soon as they recovered their senses. The cold feeling in his muscles was gone now, but his mind felt numb.

"YOU PACK OF FOOLS! I AM NOT EVEN DECENTLY LAID TO REST YET, AND ALREADY YOU ARE TRYING TO TEAR THE FABRIC OF DARKOVER TO PIECES WITH YOUR AMBITIONS. SHAME ON YOU!"

"Father?" Although the volume was much greater than Regis Hastur had ever used in life, there was no mistaking the voice.

"SON, I AM SORRY I DID NOT REALLY SAY FAREWELL. THE SPIRIT WAS WILLING, BUT THE FLESH WAS MUCH TOO WEARY."

"How did you get into Mikhail's matrix?" Mikhail was glad that Dani was asking this question, because, for the moment, the power of speech seemed to have vanished from his mouth.

"VARZIL RIDENOW SENT ME FORTH FROM THE OVER-WORLD, TO MAKE ALL OF YOU STOP BEHAVING LIKE A PACK OF BRAYING ASSES. THE MATRIX WAS MERELY A CONVE-NIENCE. I BELIEVE HE WAS SO FURIOUS THAT A SPROUT OF HIS LINE WOULD BEHAVE AS FRANCISCO IS NOW, THAT HE ACTED, BUT I AM NOT SURE. CLOSE YOUR MOUTH, MIK. YOU LOOK LIKE A HOOKED TROUT."

The ball of light began to move, rushing first toward Lew Alton. The swirling light settled on Lew's brow, and a remarkable expression came over the old, scarred face as tears slithered down into the seams and wrinkles. Then it moved on to *Dom* Gabriel, leaving Mikhail's father looking stunned but not distressed. There was near silence as the cloud of light continued its circuit, touching the two Aldaran men, then Dyan Ardais and his mother.

Francisco Ridenow shrank back in his tall chair, trembling in spite of his efforts not to. When the cloud settled over his face, an expression of horror contorted his features, and he gave a bark of utter terror. He lifted a hand and tried to brush the light away, then snatched it back as if it had burned him. It seemed to cling to the Ridenow man for what seemed a long time, and when it finally drifted away, Francisco slumped forward onto the surface of the table.

Javanne Hastur sat stiffly, waiting and showing no fear. There was something in her countenance that spoke of a determination not to pay the least attention to what was going to occur, and when the light settled over her, she did not move. Then her hands, resting on the table, clenched into fists, and the cold expression in her face began to fade. Instead she looked very angry, as if she were arguing with her dead brother, and was getting the worst of it.

"How could you, Regis? How could you?" she murmured at last, as the shining energy departed.

Donal released his grip on Mikhail and stepped back as Mikhail waited his turn, too tired to feel afraid. What he experienced he could never afterward completely describe, but he felt a great, supportive affection that embraced him while simultaneously examining him ruthlessly. It was as if none of the previous years had ever happened. There was nothing of the anxiety and mistrust that had saddened both Regis and Mikhail, no rebukes or fault finding. The pain of the past was gone, as if it had never existed.

Mikhail barely noticed the reactions of the rest of the Council members as the cloud finished its journey, except that Danilo Syrtis-Ardais was smiling, and that Dani Hastur and Miralys were both weeping. At last he roused himself enough to turn and look at Marguerida. Her eyes were shining with unshed tears, but her face was as serene as he had ever seen it.

The cloud returned to the center of the table, and Mikhail watched as the light began to change once more. It folded into itself, until there was nothing except a spark, hovering above the polished wood. Then it sped back toward the ring, and the cold which had touched him earlier returned, and vanished a second later. He felt a moment's sorrow that Lady Linnea was not there to experience this last farewell, and then the thought was gone.

He found Dani looking at him, and Mikhail realized that with the dampers destroyed, the younger man must have overheard his regret for Lady Linnea. Indeed, now he could catch the uppermost thoughts of everyone; the mental silence that he was accustomed to in the chamber was no more. Then, as if the others realized this as well, he felt their personal shields go up, with a sense of relief.

Everyone began to speak at once, as if by unspoken agreement; they would not use their *laran* for the present. Mikhail made no effort to stop them. He was too busy trying to sort out everything which had been lodged in his mind. There was much more than Regis' love for him, and his belief in Mikhail. There had been an enormous burst of thoughts and emotions and knowledge as well, and he felt rather addled by the effect of it all. He reached out and took the cider Donal had poured for him earlier, draining the cup in three chilly gulps.

He knew now why Regis had died so young, that when he had wielded the Sword of Aldones during the Sharra Rebellion, he had paid a price that shortened his life, that same force that had turned a young man's hair white had stolen decades of his time on this earth. Mikhail wanted to weep with relief that he really had done all he could, but he held himself back. Instead, he focused on the import of the rest of what Regis had told him, and most especially that he must inform the Comyn Council about the plot against his life immediately, and without hesitation.

Mikhail looked across at Lew, and knew from his serious expression that Regis had told him some of these same things. So, he gazed around the table, and slowly the babbling ceased; all eyes were upon him. He took a long, slow breath. Regis was right. To put it off any longer would make him appear weak. He must take command now, no matter how he felt. If only he could find the right words to say, to get them to forget their own petty concerns and work together.

Then he looked up at the shattered remnants of the trap matrices overhead, and laughed deeply. It was going to be very difficult to keep anything a secret now, and he did not know if he was glad or sorry for it. His sudden burst of merriment was disturbing to several of the people seated at the table, but he refused to choke it back.

Finally, he regained control of himself. "We have spent much too long already debating decisions which were made years ago. *No more!* There is a plot against my life, but also against the lives of the rest of you. This is something which we have to deal with, and now!"

"A plot? First you try to frighten us with the threat of Comyn Castle being attacked, and then you say this! What a pack of nonsense!"

"Didn't you listen to anything your brother said to you, Mother?"

Francisco Ridenow had recovered himself, and was sitting up in his chair again, still pale but clearly nursing a grievance. "A plot against you—how convenient," he sneered. "And just how did you come across this purported plot, when you have not been outside Comyn Castle in months?"

"That is quite enough, Francisco," snapped Lew. "Don't be obstructive."

"I will be whatever I damn well please. Regis has been jumping at shadows for years, and I have always wondered how much of that can be laid at your feet, Lew. I think you fed his fears, in order to keep him in your own control. As for that little demonstration—I don't know how you did it, Mikhail, but I very much doubt that we heard the voice of Regis Hastur speaking from the overworld or anywhere else!" The expression on his face suggested that he did not believe a word he was saying, but that some inner demon forced him to speak as he did.

"Of course—it was all a trick, a cruel trick," screamed Javanne, her face twisting horribly. "How could you do that to me, Mikhail!"

"Yes—what just occurred proves completely that Mikhail must not be allowed to rule Darkover. He has too much power to be trusted. There is no plot, just lies and tricks!" Francisco roared the words with feeling, pounding his fist on the table to punctuate them.

"Silence!" Mikhail thundered, surprised at the volume of his own voice. "Believe me, if I had been in control of that manifestation, at least one person in this chamber would be dead now! I have endured your slights and suspicions without complaint for years, but I will not allow either you, Mother, nor you, *Dom* Francisco, to continue to spew your filth at me. You can choose to disbelieve that Regis Hastur shattered the trap matrices in the Crystal Chamber until all of Zandru's hells melt, for all I care. But that would be extremely foolish, and neither of you are complete fools."

"It was Regis," Danilo said very calmly. "He reminded me of things that no one in this room could know except . . . my dearest friend."

"That is true," Lady Marilla added. "My wits are slightly disordered yet, but I know that what touched my mind was Regis Hastur, and no other."

"So, even you were fooled," muttered *Dom* Francisco, glaring at his ally.

"What a paltry man you are," Marilla replied, with great dignity. "If Mikhail says there is a plot against him, and against the Comyn, why should we not believe him? What benefit would he derive from making up such a tale?"

"You stupid—"

"It is a very good thing that Regis disarmed me, Francisco," Dyan Ardais snarled, "or else your life would be forfeit already."

Dani Hastur cleared his throat. "I know it was my father, and I would like to know more about this plot. I realize that everyone is very shocked and frightened—and don't pretend you aren't, *Dom* Francisco! But if we start threatening to kill one another, then we might as well hand Darkover over to the Federation and be done with it!"

"At last—a voice of reason," Robert Aldaran announced. "Have you all lost your minds? As Lady Marilla asked, what possible purpose would be served by pretending that some plot existed when there was none?"

"I can tell you the answer to that."

"I am sure you can come up with some plausible explanation, *Dom* Francisco, because your mind is full of your own plots and schemes."

"That from Aldaran scum!"

"Why do you dishonor yourself this way, *Dom* Francisco?" Marguerida asked, her voice quiet but menacing at the same time. "You know in your heart that Mikhail has nothing but the security of Darkover in mind, and yet you continue with this irrational behavior."

"I know nothing of the sort, witch!"

"I have never done you a moment's harm, and still you hate me—why is that, *Dom* Francisco?"

"It would have been better if you had died years ago," he answered, snarling. Sweat now beaded his forehead, and his hands shook with rage and some less obvious emotion.

Javanne, who had sunk into a kind of stupor, roused herself with difficulty. "I don't believe in any plot, but I want to hear of it anyhow." The words came from her lips unwillingly. It seemed she was at war with herself. The pained expression on her face deepened, and she swallowed hard. *I have wronged my own child, and at last I know it.*

Mikhail caught her unguarded thought and felt more compassion for his mother than he had in years. He knew what it must have cost her to even allow herself to think those words, and then, with a kind of sorrow, knew she would not choose to remember them. Still, he could treasure them for as long as he lived, and would.

Mikhail looked across at Lew. He nodded toward the older man, gesturing him to begin the tale. "A few nights past, Domenic left Comyn Castle for a bit of mischief," Lew said solemnly.

"I should have known the little bastard was at the bottom of this," Javanne spat, her moment of self-awareness gone, and all her previous furies returning. "I've heard enough now!"

"One more word against my son and heir, Mother, and I will do something you will regret for the rest of your life."

She glared at him, then looked at the ring on his finger and shuddered, clinging stubbornly to her anger and her fears of him. "You are not my son any longer!"

"Thank you—I am greatly relieved that I need no longer give you any more respect than I would one of the servants. Please continue, Lew."

Javanne had intended to provoke him, and he could see the disappointment in her face. Then her eyes seemed to glaze over, as if the inner torment were too great for her to bear, and she leaned against the back of her chair and sighed.

"As I was saying, Domenic sneaked off to watch the Travelers perform. He observed some men in Federation leathers walking to the North Gate, and being a curious lad, he followed them. They met one of the Travelers, the driver of a wagon, who was, it turned out, a spy for the Federation. At that time, we had not let the word of Regis's sudden death reach as far as Headquarters, but this fellow, Dirck Vancof, told the men that he was gone. One of them, Miles Granfell, who is the second in command to Lyle Belfontaine, the Station Chief, suggested that since the Comyn accompany the body of their dead rulers to the *rhu fead,* that an attack on the funeral train might be a lovely idea. He has always struck me as the kind of opportunistic man who *would* think of such a thing, so I am not surprised that he did.

"Nico thought about what he had overheard, and, sensibly, told me—you recall that when we were at dinner the night you arrived, Javanne, I was interrupted? Yes, I see that you do remember. That was Domenic. And after the meal we closeted ourselves to decide what to do. Herm Aldaran offered to join Nico on the road, to see if there was anything other than wishful thinking in Miles Granfell's idea. We have now gathered enough information to believe that some sort of assault will likely be made against the funeral train, unless we can come up with some plan to prevent it."

"Forgive me if I do not believe you, Lew. It is just too fantastic."

Dom Francisco's face was white with fury and frustration, and his voice was thready. A look of desperation filled his eyes, and he looked like a man who was watching his favorite horse break its leg.

"I hope it does not demand a blaster shot in the guts to change your mind, then. If you even have time to consider the matter," Marguerida replied as if she were speaking of the weather.

The look of desperation increased. "Blasters are not allowed on Darkover."

"That is not strictly true," Robert Aldaran put in before anyone else could speak. "They are not permitted to the populace of Darkover because of the Compact, and we ourselves would never use them. But there are a goodly number of weapons of various sorts in the Terran complex in our Domain, and a greater amount at the spaceport. Regis has known this for years. Those, plus the presence of combat-trained troops in both places has been a source of concern for a long time. If you hadn't spent so much energy disputing him, you would have been aware of the problem."

"An Aldaran speaking of the Compact! When have any of you ever respected it?" No one responded to *Dom* Francisco's question, but Lady Marilla looked at him with enormous distaste.

Javanne tried to rouse herself from her near stupor. "Yes, that is true—but I have never understood why we did not change. . . ." She seemed too exhausted to continue, suddenly, and lowered her head so her jaw almost touched her collar.

"Because we do not have command of the Federation bases on Darkover, obviously." Mikhail shifted in his chair. "And we can hardly expect to overcome such weapons with swords and horses."

"Why should we believe you?" Francisco asked, trying once more to gain control of the meeting.

"You give me too much credit for deviousness, *Dom* Francisco, and not enough for common sense! There is nothing in the world that would cause me to endanger the lives of any of you."

"Mikhail is right," Lady Marilla said suddenly, "and you are wrong, Francisco. Everything he has said Regis also said when he brushed through me a few minutes ago—did he not tell you the same?"

"Yes, but I cannot . . . cannot bear . . ." He shuddered again and tried to get a grip on his emotions. "It must have been some sort of trick."

"Oh, do stop being a fool, Francisco," Lady Marilla snapped, her usually placid face twisted with anger. "I have known Mikhail Hastur for decades, and he is right when he says he is not devious. We have been waiting—you, Javanne and I—for him to do something with his matrix to confirm our basest suspicions, and he has never done so. The temptation must have been incredible." She cast Mikhail a fond look.

"Not really, Lady Marilla. In fact, the greatest temptation I have endured these past fifteen years has been the occasional one to give my mother laryngitis during her visits, since the sound of her voice has long since stopped giving me any pleasure." At this, everyone, except *Dom* Francisco and Lady Javanne, began to chuckle. The tension broke for the moment, and an air of relief traveled about the chamber.

"And just what do you intend to do about this supposed plot, Mikhail? Would you have us ride into the jaws of death for your sake?" Francisco's words sounded forced and thin.

"You are perfectly welcome to remain in Comyn Castle, or return to the Ridenow Domain, *Dom* Francisco," Marguerida said with false sweetness, "and I am sure that no one will think any the less of you for trying to save your own skin. And then, if we all get killed by the Terranan, you will have the pleasure of trying to survive while they hunt you down like a dog. Which, if they take over Darkover, they will certainly do."

Francisco Ridenow had the grace to blanch right down to the roots of his pale blond hair, and he glared fiercely at Marguerida. She had managed to imply that he was a coward without actually saying it, and there was nothing he could do about it.

Mikhail looked around the table again. There was a different atmosphere in the chamber than there had been just a few minutes before. The wariness that he was accustomed to feeling from Lady Marilla had departed, and there were other changes as well. Some of the fear and suspicion they felt toward him remained in several minds, but it was no longer as strong. Regis had reassured them, and they had believed him. More, the restraint he had demonstrated for years had finally made an impact. He had said he had only been tempted to silence his difficult mother, even though he had the ability to do much more, and they had believed him.

But there was more to it than a simple change of attitude. With the exception of his mother and *Dom* Francisco, he realized, these people *wanted* him to lead them. Regis' death had unsettled them, and they were intelligent enough to know that there must be continuity, and that he was the person to provide it. Regis' last gift to Darkover had been to tell the members of the Comyn Council to follow Mikhail Hastur, his heir. The alternative, everyone knew, was civil war of a kind that had not occurred on Darkover in centuries.

Mikhail experienced a moment of great relief, and also the sense that most of the people in the room were waiting for him to tell them how to proceed. Until this moment he had not realized how greatly everyone's mistrust had weighed on him during the past fifteen years. At last the Comyn would allow him to lead them, and he could only hope that he was worthy of their sudden trust. "I am completely open to suggestions as to how to proceed—even including canceling the funeral train altogether for now."

Dom Gabriel shook his grizzled head slowly. "Not that, son. You can't hide in here like your uncle did. No, we must meet this foe, but make it on our own terms, as much as possible. Indeed, if we can expose this plot for what it is, and embarrass the Federation with it, we will be in a much better position all around, won't we?" He turned to Lew Alton as he asked his question.

"True, and wise, *Dom* Gabriel, but very difficult to manage. The first thing, I believe, is that we must not take the youngsters along at all—that is too dangerous."

At this, everyone began to speak at once, offering their ideas, except for Francisco and Javanne. Mikhail listened and observed, and found that he was staring at *Dom* Damon. Something rustled in his mind, like a bit of paper in the wind, some tidbit that Regis had imparted earlier.

Dom Damon was innocent of plotting with the Federation—all he had intended was to try to place Rafael in Mikhail's position! He looked at his brother, the forgotten son, sitting stiffly beside him. It would not have worked, but *Dom* Damon was not clever enough to understand that. Still, it was a relief to know that while he could not trust the old devil too far, he was not part of the plot to attack the funeral train.

"We should call for *Dom* Cisco Ridenow," Danilo said, breaking into Mikhail's thoughts. Everyone looked at him. "His expertise will be very useful, I believe."

There were nods of agreement at this, and a look crossed *Dom* Francisco's face, as if he had been handed a reprieve. Mikhail caught the look as well as the whisper of thought behind it. Beside him, Marguerida was alert, and his brother Rafael, on his other side, turned his head toward the head of the Ridenow Domain with icy interest. *Dom* Francisco flinched—he had forgotten the absence of the dampers.

Don't worry, Mik—I'll see to it that he doesn't try to kill you himself. As he heard Rafael's angry thought, a kind of clarity began to fill his mind, a sudden, blessed calm, which he could only hope would endure long enough to hammer out a plan. With Marguerida on one side, Rafael on the other, and Donal at his back, he could bring all of his attention toward the immediate threat. Then, with a sickening certainty, he knew that he had been moving toward this moment all his life—not as he had anticipated in his youth, nor planned in early adulthood. Nothing was happening according to his own imaginings—and yet, this was his destiny.

22

Her dream was filled with an eerie wailing. Katherine reached toward the other side of the bed in her sleep. When her hand touched the empty pillow, she started to wake, and found there were tears on her face. Herm wasn't there, and she thought for a moment her heart would break. Then she remembered that she would be joining him soon, in some little town called Carcosa, and the ache began to subside.

But the sound from her dream had not stopped, and she sat up and pulled her knees up against her chest, hugging them and shivering all over. It was not wailing at all, but something else, something she had never expected to hear again in her life—seapipes, or whatever they called that instrument on Darkover. It was coming from some distance, but the melody carried, and then another pipe took up the tune, mournful and heartbreaking. No wonder she was weeping.

Kate rubbed her face dry on her nightgown and swallowed several times. More and more pipes were joining in now, until, after several minutes, it sounded as if there were thirty or more, playing in every quarter of the city of Thendara. Although she had never heard the melody before, she knew it for a dirge, and it made her ache for Renney. In her mind, she could hear the sea crashing near the old manse where she had grown up, and the sound of seapipes playing at her mother's death rites. She could almost smell salt in the air, so powerful was the evocation of memory and feeling.

A knock on the door of the suite interrupted her before she could completely surrender to the upwelling of emotions. Instantly she felt anxious. Had she slept into the middle of the day or had some terrible thing happened during the night? No, she was sure it was still morning, from the way the light came through the narrow window of her bedroom. Her heart raced as she pushed the covers aside, swung her long legs out, thrust her feet into slippers. The knock came again, sounding urgent, so she did not bother with a robe in the chilly room, but only grabbed a shawl from beside the bed and hurried to answer the door.

Gisela stood there, her arms filled with billows of dark fabric, her face chalky-white and stricken, her hair wild and half escaped from its clasp. There was a mark on one of her cheeks, the start of a bruise, and her eyes were puffy from crying. Without a word, Kate pulled her into the room and put her arms around her sister-in-law, so the pile of textiles was trapped between their chests.

"What is it?"

"I just brought you the clothes for the funeral," Gisela answered, her voice strained.

"No," Kate said, lifting her hand to touch the mark with tender fingers. "What is this? Rafael didn't . . ." She and the children had had dinner in Gisela's suite the night before, and her sister-in-law had not been hurt then. It had been a pleasant meal, much less formal than the lengthy suppers of the previous evenings. Meeting Gisela and Rafael's children, Casilde, the oldest, and the two boys, Damon and Gabriel, had been pleasant, and Terése and Amaury had become quite noisy in the presence of their new cousins.

Gisela looked horrified at this suggestion. "Oh, no! Never. Not even when I deserved it!"

"Who, then? And don't try to tell me you ran into the door or something—someone hit you!"

"Yes." Gisela did not speak further for a few seconds. "My father."

"Your father? But why?" Just then Rosalys, the maidservant, appeared from the other end of the suite, where she had a room near the children. "Will you get us some tea, Rosalys, and something to eat?" Kate took the bundle of clothing from Gisela, and held it out. "Please see that these are hung up, too."

"Certainly, *domna.*" The servant gave the two women a curious look, took the garments, then bustled off to attend to the matter.

Kate drew Gisela toward the chairs that were placed around the hearth in the sitting room. The fire had died down overnight, so Katherine added a small log and poked the embers into life. Then she turned around and began to chafe her sister-in-law's icy hands. She felt a callus which had begun to form across the right palm, where Gisela held her carving knife, and saw a tiny cut on one slender finger as well. A single tear swelled in one of Gisela's eyes and rolled down her cheek. "Will you tell me what happened?" She brushed away the tear with her fingers, then drew off her shawl and draped it around the shoulders of the other woman.

Huddled in the chair, Gisela just shuddered. Then she looked up and said in a small voice "I did not know where to go." And then, in a stronger tone, she added, "And I don't want any damned tea!"

"Oh." Kate glanced around the room, hearing the wailing pipes from outside the castle, and the soft sigh of the morning wind. Then she saw that there was a tray with a carafe of firewine and several glasses sitting on the table. She walked over, poured a glass, and brought it back to her sister-in-law. Gisela gulped it down in a few swallows, gasped, and began to cough.

Katherine pounded her between the shoulders until the fit passed, and the color began to return to Giz's cheeks. "Another glass?" A nod answered her. This time Gisela only sipped from it, then leaned back into the comforting chair and gave a long sigh.

"I haven't seen him like this in years," she began. "Whatever happened at the Council meeting yesterday put him in a fury, and somehow it was all my fault."

Katherine felt confused. "But you weren't even there—we were in my studio! They were all at that meeting, weren't they, your father and everyone, and they never came back for dinner."

Gisela gave a bitter laugh. "I hadn't told him that Mikhail and Rafael were reconciled, mostly because it wasn't any of his business. So he went to the Crystal Chamber all ready to propose that since Mikhail was not acceptable to all of the Council, then my husband should be instead. As near as I can tell, he never even got to suggest it before some sort of hell broke loose. I don't know exactly what happened, but the trap matrices in the chamber were smashed to bits, and there was a lot of shouting and table pounding. I am so glad I was with you!"

"I am, too." Kate had no idea what a trap matrix was, but it sounded frightening. There were so many things she did not know, and more she could not understand. "Rafael didn't tell you . . ."

"I haven't seen him, Kate. All I know is that everyone on the Council was in the Crystal Chamber until very late, and that after that, Rafael went off on some errand for Mikhail. He sent me a note." The wine seemed to have invigorated her a little, and some color was returning to her unnaturally pale skin.

"When did you see your father, then?"

"About two hours ago—he came slamming into the suite, dragged me up out of bed, and started screaming at me. That woke the children, and Gabriel tried to make him let me go, and got tossed on the floor. It was horrible, with the children screaming and my father shaking me by the shoulders and . . ." She stopped, drew a shuddering breath, and tried to calm herself. "I had taken a draught before bed, and I was so tired. He never *told* me that I was supposed to keep Rafael and Mikhail at odds, Kate! I don't know if I would have if I could. But, thinking it all over, I suppose that the reason he had me trying to get Regis to change his heir designate, all those years back, was just to make trouble between them. I feel like such a fool!" Gisela broke into fresh tears.

"Why? The only fool in this seems to be *Dom* Damon. He used you, Giz, and you fell into his plans without realizing clearly what it might mean. But, if there is any blame, I think *Dom* Damon deserves the larger portion." Kate could almost feel the waves of near-hysteria that were flowing from Gisela, and she was very glad that Marguerida had suggested the idea of empathy to her, or otherwise she might have felt she was going mad herself. And she wanted nothing but to make it cease—immediately. It was nearly a physical sensation—like being pricked by invisible knifepoints.

She had taken an almost immediate dislike to her father-in-law when she had met him at last the night after Herm left, and had come to the conclusion that one reason her husband had left was to avoid encountering the man. Now she was ready to hate him without reservation for upsetting Gisela and hurting her.

The sobs subsided slowly. Gisela mopped her wet face with a rather soiled hankerchief, then gulped down the rest of her glass of wine. "There is that, but it doesn't make me feel very much less dreadful and guilty. When I saw Mik and Rafael embrace three days ago, I was so happy for both of them. And when Rafael went to the Council meeting, after years of being excluded because of me, I was glad. Then my damn father had to try to ruin everything, and when he failed, he . . . punched me in the face." She lifted her empty hand and gingerly touched the bruise. "He called me terrible things, and I just wanted to kill him, Kate!"

"I'm so sorry, *breda*." The sense of being assaulted was fading now, and Kate was less uncomfortable.

"I should have. Mikhail would probably have given me a prize if I had."

"Maybe." She was glad Gisela had not murdered her father, even if he deserved it. She sat down in the chair across from the other woman, pushed her unbound hair off her shoulders, and shook her head in wonder. "Are things always this . . . dramatic?"

"Oh, no," Gisela said solemnly. "Sometimes nothing happens for years and years."

"Then I suppose they were saving it up for my arrival," Kate answered dryly. She hated raised voices and arguments but realized that the entire castle was full of people in the midst of a serious dispute. For a moment, Katherine wished she were back in the small apartment she and Herm had occupied, on an overcrowded world where everyone was very careful to be polite, lest the peace officers cite them with a civil violation and fine them. Or back on Renney, with the smell of the sea. The feeling passed, leaving her a little forlorn.

That was too much, and Giz gave a sputtering chuckle. Rosalys returned with a tray a minute later. There was a pot of tea and baked cakes on a plate. The scent of mint rose and floated through the air of the sitting room, mingling pleasantly with the smell of balsam from the fireplace. In the few days since her arrival, she had started to become accustomed to the odors of old stone and burning wood, and even to enjoy them. After years in a centrally heated building, the simple pleasure of the hearth, different from that of her homeworld but reminiscent as well, was a source of comfort.

Katherine rose and was beginning to fill mugs with tea when there was another knock on the door. She looked up, startled and with the beginning of a sense of ill-usage. People should not be calling so early, and while she was still in her nightdress! The maidservant darted over and opened it and Marguerida came in. A moment later Amaury wandered out from the other part of the suite, knuckling his eyes sleepily.

"What's that sound?" the boy asked his mother, then noticed that there were others present. He pulled his robe closer around his slender body and blushed a little. "It gives me shivers."

"Pipes, Amaury. We call them seapipes on Renney, but I don't know the name here."

"It sounds like someone hurting a cat," the boy announced, and then reddened as the three women laughed at his remark. "Well, it does," he added defensively.

"We call them bagpipes, Amaury, and you are not the first to have made that comparison," Marguerida told him wearily. She looked tired and faded, dressed in a robe of the same dark hue as the garments that Gisela had brought with her earlier. It was the color of twilight, a very dark blue with a purplish undertone, and the first clothing that Katherine had seen that was not adorned with embroidery. She glanced from Gisela to Kate, and back again, and if she was surprised to find them together, she seemed too exhausted to remark on it.

Remembering that Gisela had said that the meeting had gone on into the middle of the night, Kate guessed that Marguerida had not had much sleep. That, at least, was something she could deal with. "Here, sit down this instant, Marguerida. You look ready to drop in your tracks. Rosalys has just brought tea, and I insist you drink some. Have you eaten anything?" Katherine half shoved the other woman into the chair beside Gisela, and realized she had acted as she did as much for her own comfort as for Marguerida's. Where, on their previous encounters, she had sensed little or nothing, she now could feel distress of some sort. She went toward the table and the serving tray, and discovered that Amaury had seated himself and was already munching on a cake.

"I . . . don't remember," Marguerida said softly. She put her elbows on the arms of the chair and her capable hands hung listlessly from the wrists. "I've been up most of the night," she added, as if this explained everything. "And I need to tell you something that is likely going to upset you. . . ." She turned her head and studied Gisela briefly, and her weary eyes widened as she took in the bruise on Giz's cheek.

Marguerida half-rose, leaning on the arm of the chair, and extended her hand towards the other woman's face. *"Who did this to you?"* Her voice, faint a moment before, was furious. She was shaking with rage. She brushed the bruise with the fingers of her right hand and flinched.

Katherine moved swiftly, sensing that Marguerida's iron control had at last reached its limits. She was glad, at that moment, that all she possessed was empathy, because she was sure that if she could have read Marguerida's mind at that instant, she would have hated what she would hear. Instead, she forced the woman to sit down again. Then, pinning her down by putting her hands on the arms of the chair, she leaned forward, so their faces were only a handspan apart, and said, "Do not move for at least the next five minutes."

"You are very masterful, Kate," Marguerida murmured, submitting, and leaning her head against the back of the chair. She let her eyes close, breathing slowly and deeply, her hands resting in her lap. Then, after a couple of minutes, she asked, "Who hit you, Giz?"

"My father."

"Will you mind very much if I kill him?"

Gisela looked shocked, then amused, and Amaury suddenly got up and left the room abruptly, clearly uncomfortable. "No, but I would prefer to do it myself, actually."

"Yes, I should not be greedy, and try to have all the treats for myself. Do you think you could spare me a leg or an arm—just to properly vent my outrage? No, I suppose not. There was mention of tea, I believe." Her control had returned, and her voice was nearly emotionless. She might have been discussing the weather, not homicide, and Katherine was glad that her son had left the room before he heard the last remark. She didn't think either of the women were serious, but she was not absolutely sure.

Gisela smiled a little and nodded. "Perhaps we could tie him, hand and foot, to several horses, then drive them apart."

"That would be extremely satisfactory," Marguerida replied. "I do enjoy designing painful demises for certain people. Only those who deserve such treatment, of course, because I am not usually murderous this early in the day."

"No, only when bandits attack you in the middle of the night," Giz returned, and both women laughed pleasantly.

Kate listened to the conversation with some consternation, and wondered what they were speaking about. It sounded as if they were talking about an actual event—had Marguerida killed a bandit? As much as she wanted to demand an explanation, she held herself back. Instead, she laced the mugs of tea with a heavy-scented honey from a small pot that sat on the tray. Silence, except for the moan of the pipes, filled the suite. She noticed then that the steady beat of drums had been added, so deep that Kate had barely registered them at first. The tune had changed, too, to yet another slow, sad song.

The women drank their tea and ate still warm cakes, and except for Marguerida's mourning clothes, it might have been just an ordinary day. The maid had vanished into the children's part of the suite, and they were alone with their thoughts.

Finally, Marguerida roused herself. "Kate, after the funeral, we are going to send all the youngsters away to Arilinn, including your own. They will be safer there than here, if our guesses are right."

She didn't want to know what sort of guesses Marguerida was talking about, but she must find out what was going on. This sudden announcement seemed to come out of the blue, and she felt at a loss about how to react to it. Was she supposed to go with the children to this Arilinn place? Kate stood, torn between her need to remain with her children, and her desire to see Herm! Well, she could hardly let Amaury and Terése go off to this unknown place without her, could she? "Why won't they be safe here?" she finally managed to ask, then added, "They have never been away from me, in their lives."

"I did not realize that," Marguerida responded slowly. "I assure you, they will be completely safe at Arilinn." She shifted in the chair, and sipped a little tea. "We are concerned that while we are on the way to the *rhu fead,* the Federation may try to occupy the castle. We have prepared for this possibility, and I think that if Lyle Belfontaine decides to attempt it, he will be extremely surprised at his reception. But we do not want to risk the children." She seemed too tired to continue.

"I see." Kate wondered for a moment, finding the idea too overwhelming to absorb easily. "I believe you, but . . ."

Gisela interrupted. "But you want to see Hermes, so you can box his ears into the next tenday. I don't think my brother is nearly good enough for you, Kate! But you can't be in two places at one time." She thought for a moment. "I'll go with them, since my own youngsters must go to Arilinn as well. I'll manage somehow—even if I include Roderick, Alanna, and Yllana."

Marguerida gave Gisela a searching look. "That is very kind of you."

Then, as if unable to restrain herself, she added, "And quite uncharacteristic."

Gisela shrugged. "I am, as you probably noticed last evening, Kate, not a completely wonderful mother. Don't look so shocked. I know it's true. But, I can look after yours, mine, and Marguerida's until we reach the Tower—I'm just lazy, not uncaring."

"What has gotten into you, Giz?" Marguerida asked bluntly.

A sweet smile crossed the other woman's face, and there was a twinkle in her puffy eyes. "Kate has made me see the error of my ways— haven't you, *breda?*" Then she touched the bruise lightly. "I don't want people to see me like this, and ask nosy questions, or think Rafael has finally done what everyone hoped he would do years ago. So if both of you will entrust me with your offspring, I shall be a good aunty, and see they wash their faces before bedtime."

"Have you bewitched her?" Marguerida asked seriously, turning toward Kate.

"I don't think so," Katherine replied, still caught up in her own conflicted feelings. Was it safe to let Gisela take her children? After all, she barely knew the woman. And Herm did not completely trust her. Then she knew that the offer was genuine, that her sister-in-law understood how much she wanted to join Herm and was only being generous. "Yes, if you take the children, Giz, I will let them go. They like you, and they like your youngsters. Thank you—it is a kind thing to do." Then she frowned.

"What is it, Kate?"

"Herm told me, before he ran off like a thief in the night, that we were going to have to take Terése to this Arilinn for some sort of test." She bit her lip. "I don't want anything like that to happen when I am not around—I will not have my daughter frightened!"

"I can promise you, Katherine, that nothing will happen to Terése, and that she will not be tested in your absence." Marguerida thought for a moment. "She is a little young, and has not shown any sign of threshold sickness yet, so there is no need for it."

"I am going to hold you to that, Marguerida." Kate could hardly contain her sudden anxiety for her child. But she knew Marguerida to be a woman of her word, and she felt herself begin to calm.

"Now that everything is all settled, let's order up a proper breakfast. I'll help you dress for the rite, Kate. Doing your hair will probably improve my mood a bit. I wonder if anyone would mind if I wore a heavy veil, or perhaps a sack over my head?"

Marguerida sputtered over a gulp of tea. When she had regained her breath, she said, "Do Kate's hair?" She looked from one woman to the other, as if something had occurred between them which had escaped her notice, and she could not quite discern what it was. "I have never seen you so . . . helpful, cousin. It becomes you."

"I'd tell you I was reformed, but you wouldn't believe me, would you?"

"After what I witnessed yesterday, Giz, I would believe almost anything."

"Marguerida, what *did* happen in the Council meeting?" Kate asked.

"Aside from the damper matrices being shattered to pieces, and Regis Hastur manifesting out of the beyond and scolding everyone?" Marguerida sighed. "And Javanne disowning Mik, and Francisco Ridenow suggesting that Regis' death was suspicious? Other than that, it was a useful meeting. Don't look at me as if I have lost my mind—just give me a glass of wine. Tea is all very well, but not what I need just now. My bones ache with weariness."

"Regis . . . appeared?" Gisela looked startled.

"Didn't Rafael tell you?"

"No, because I haven't seen him since yesterday!"

"Oh, yes, I had forgotten. Mikhail sent him to Rafe Scott, and the two of them are trying to discover if the Sons of Darkover are a real threat to the Comyn."

"The who?" The name clearly meant nothing to Gisela, and she studied Marguerida keenly, her green eyes flashing in the light from the fire. "Kate, give her some wine right this minute! Now, Marguerida, begin at the beginning and tell us everything. Just pretend it is one of those tales you are always writing."

Kate poured another goblet of wine and handed it to Marguerida. Then she sat down, curved her hands around her still warm tea, and listened to the story. She felt suspended in time, as if she had nothing more important to do than sit and hear the tale. And when Marguerida stopped speaking perhaps twenty minutes later, she was not sure she believed half of what she had just heard.

The three women sat companionably in silence for several minutes, and then Gisela stirred in her chair. "Well, now at least I understand what put Father in such a rage. And why Lady Javanne looked so haggard when I passed her in the corridor."

Kate was struck by the oddness of the situation, to be sitting in her bedclothes with two women she had not known a week before, drinking tea and speaking of plots and ghosts, as if they were the most ordinary things instead of impossible ones. Or were they? She thought that Marguerida and Gisela were intelligent women and certainly not crazy ones. Maybe these events were not remarkable on Darkover. Some of the tales she had heard about the ghost groves on Renney would probably strike them as very odd indeed. Katherine decided she would accept the story, for the present.

"Kate, I am going to go tell the maid to pack some things for your children, and get them dressed for the funeral. They will likely be so bored with it that they will regard a carriage ride to Arilinn as an adventure." Gisela paused and smiled at Katherine. "Don't worry, *breda*. Just go and find Hermes and mend your fences with him, and leave the rest to me."

Katherine nodded in agreement. She knew she could stay in Comyn Castle, or go with the children herself, but neither of those choices would keep her from worrying about her husband. She had not really understood, until now, how absolutely vital he was to her, and if he were killed in what seemed to her to be an insane venture against the Federation, she would rather perish with him than live another forty or fifty years without him. She did not want to think about this possibility, but she had to. And, if the worst occurred, she was certain that Gisela would see that her children were cared for.

The enormous courtyard on the north side of Comyn Castle had not seen a gathering of the populace since Mikhail had been proclaimed the heir designate. Domenic's elevation to that status had been a much smaller event, almost private, due to Regis's fears, and had taken place within the castle itself, not in this public space.

Mikhail stood on the wide steps which rose from one end of the plaza, with his back to the high walls of castle, and looked out toward the crowd which had been gathering quietly up the length of the plaza for over an hour now. The lords and ladies of the Domains and the families of the gentry who had managed to come to Thendara were ranged on either side of him, and he could sense his nephew just behind his left shoulder, watchful even in his near-exhaustion. He felt safe under Donal's eyes, and grateful for such a devoted paxman.

Regis Hastur's body lay on a bier at the foot of the stairs, covered with a swath of fabric in the blue and silver of his house. There was no sign of deterioration on the corpse, for it had been placed in a stasis chamber immediately after death, and he looked as if he were sleeping. The white hair was slack around the quiet face, and the expression on it was calm and serene. There were guards on either side of him, and more stood along the path from the far end of the courtyard, keeping the crowd in order.

The people of Thendara, merchants and tradesmen, guild masters and their journeymen, women and children, moved along toward it. When they reached the body, they paused to express their grief and respect. For many of them, it was their first view of Regis Hastur in many years, and for the younger citizens, the only time they had seen him in their lives. He had been a stranger to those he governed during the end of his life, but that did not appear to have lessened the deep affection in which he was held, if the sad faces and tears were any indication.

Except for the wind fluttering in the awnings which had been hung from the wall, to afford some shelter in case of rain, there was little sound but the dirge from the pipes, the beat of the drums, the shuffle of feet, and the occasional cough. After they had looked at the body of their dead ruler, the people removed themselves to the other end of the plaza, crowding together and waiting patiently. Mikhail realized that these were his people now, his to govern and guide, and he felt very humble to receive their trust. He could only hope he would deserve it.

Mikhail was exhausted, and his feet ached, but he stood in his place, refusing to indulge himself by releasing his own sorrow. He felt he must not let go. Not yet, and not publically. He watched a woman bend over the body, and place a single white flower on it, adding to the collection of such offerings. He did not know who she was, although her clothing suggested she was from the mercantile class, but her sorrow was genuine, and it moved him, so he had to strain to continue keeping his face immobile.

Beside him, Javanne Hastur stood with clenched hands, clearly containing herself with enormous difficulty. No matter what their disagreements, he knew his mother had loved her younger brother deeply, and that his passing was a great blow to her. Then, without warning, he heard her begin to sob, and without thinking, Mikhail reached out and put an arm around her. To his surprise, she did not stiffen and pull away, but instead leaned most of her weight against him, turning her face into his shoulder. He shifted his feet to keep from falling backward and held her tightly, as he had not done since he was a very young man.

Javanne's hand clung to the laces of his dark tunic, and he felt her shudder with anguish. In his own weariness, her emotions flooded into him, and Mikhail felt his eyes moisten. Tears began to cascade down his cheeks, slipping down and falling into her hair. "It is my fault," she whispered.

"No, Mother. It is no one's fault."

"If I had not opposed him. . . ."

"Hush! It was his time—that's all." His voice was thick with tears and grief, and he barely believed his own words. There was no need to lay blame, but he understood his mother's guilt, for he shared it in his own way. Even though he now knew that wielding the Sword of Aldones had meant that Regis would be shortening his full measure of years, he could not help wondering if fearing his nephew had not also contributed to his uncle's untimely demise. He put his other arm around Javanne and held her close. "We will both miss him, Mother."

After several minutes, Javanne began to gain control of her emotions. She drew herself apart gently, brushing her cheeks with her fingers. She stood away from him and stared down at the continuing procession. Then she reached out and put her hand into his ungloved one, lacing her fingers into his and holding tight.

Mikhail returned her grasp carefully, not wishing to hurt her aging hand with his grip, and felt a moment of pure joy in the midst of his sorrow. After all that had been said the day before, he treasured the small gesture of her touch on his hand, of her turning to him in her grief.

Dani Hastur was standing nearby with his wife, his mother, and his son Gareth. Miralys and Dani were both in tears, but their child just stared blankly into the distance, as if completely unaware of what was happening. Mikhail could not help thinking about the previous day, and the way Gareth had behaved. Had he really stolen Dani's rightful place? Mikhail did not think he had, but he could see how a youngster would believe that. With a sickening certainty, he knew they had not heard the last of it either. And, covertly studying Gareth's emotionless expression, he was very happy that Domenic was not there.

The line of mourners still stretched to the end of the courtyard, and it would be some time before the final ceremony took place. It felt like it had been hours already.

He tore his eyes away, since the steady movement of people was starting to make him feel sleepy. To try to rouse his exhausted mind a little, he studied the members of the Comyn again. Their faces were somber, as befitted the occasion. No one would have guessed from their expressions how divided they had been a day before. They appeared to him to be like actors in some play, not the people he had known for years. Lady Marilla Aillard was standing beside her son, Dyan Ardais, her usually placid face troubled. For a moment he wondered what was bothering her. Then she shifted her stance and grimaced, and he realized that she was just as tired as he was, and that her bones were aching. Standing on cold stones in a chilly midday was a trial for her, as it must be for everyone.

Time slowed for him now, and the sound of the pipes was like the wailing of a hundred storms, sad and desolate. Mikhail lost himself in the dirge, forgot for a span everything except his sense of loss. He did not even think of the perils that might await them on the morrow, although he was aware that it remained in the back of his mind.

He came back to himself with a start, still holding Javanne's hand in his, and realized that the pipes had at last ceased. There was a stillness in the courtyard, a sense of waiting. The space around the body of Regis Hastur was vacant except for the Guards who stood at each corner of the bier, and the parade of mourners was a sea of faces at the other end of the plaza.

A chorus from the Musicians Guild began to sing, twenty men and woman giving voice to a hymn that had not been heard in decades.

"Oh, stars that in the elder days,
In Majesty unstained did blaze
And suns that in the deeps of night
Yet burn with uncorrupted light . . ."

It was a painfully sad melody, the ancient words rising in the air and drifting across the courtyard, wrenching him back into his grief again. Two harpers accompanied the singers, and it seemed to him that the gentle notes from the strings were even sadder than the pipes had been.

"Shine forth in splendor, show the way
Surpassing sight of mortal eyes,
For Hastur's Son departs this day
To seek his Father in the skies . . ."

A shiver of movement went through the crowd. Mikhail turned and saw that the great central doors of Comyn Castle were swinging open. The two sections swung ponderously on their hinges—they were only used for official occasions, and until this morning, when Regis' body was borne into the courtyard, Mikhail's proclamation as heir had been the last time they were opened. The singers continued—

"But darkness gathers here below,
Evanda's flowers are hid by snow,
The wounded sun sinks in the sky,
In fear the scattered moons do fly—"

Mikhail shivered, hearing in the song an echo of his own fears. The verse seemed uncannily appropriate to their situation. He wondered gloomily if the song was an exaggeration of Darkovan fears, intended to express conventional mourning, or whether the Hasturs had always left their heirs in such confusion.

But now white-robed figures were emerging from the dark rectangle of the doorway. They must be the Servants of Aldones, who had come down from the Shrine at Hali. They had arrived during the meeting of the Council, and he had not even had time to greet them, but at least they were there. He felt a pang of guilt at having left Marguerida to bear so much of the burden of arranging the funeral. He supposed he should be grateful to Gisela, who had found the ancient book describing the ritual in the castle archives. He knew he would have hated asking his mother if she could recall what had been done when Danvan Hastur had died.

"The banshee wails across the snows,
Kyorebni *gather scenting war,*
Oh, who will stand against our foes
When Hastur's son rides forth no more?"

The people lifted their voices once more in loss and longing, and Mikhail felt his gut clench with fear. They could not know how great a danger threatened them, but he did. Why had Regis laid this burden upon him? He was not worthy—he could never take the place his uncle had filled so well and for so long. He realized he was trembling, and in astonishment felt his mother squeeze his hand reassuringly, as she had done decades ago, when he was still a child and had come to Comyn Castle for the first time.

The five white-robed figures circled the bier, and as they did so, the Guards at its corners bowed and stepped away. The first, and youngest, of the Servants, carried a silver basin of water, which he sprinkled as he moved. The next, a tall man who strode as if he had once been a warrior, carried fire in a lantern. The third man swung a censer whose chains clashed and rattled as it circled, sending smoke swirling into the air. The one who followed him scattered sand from the shores of Hali. As they moved, the chorus began the next verse, picking up their tempo, so that the tune seemed less a dirge than a battle cry.

> *"Camilla weeps in darkest night*
> *But still Cassilda sings in light;*
> *Hastur's radiance shines above*
> *Blessing all below with love—"*

The fifth of the white-clad Servants of Aldones, an old man who seemed too frail for the weight of his robes, took his place at the head of the bier, arms lifted so that the wide sleeves rippled in the wind. The smell of the burning herbs began to drift across the courtyard, pungent and sharp. Mikhail's eyes stung, and he felt his mother's grip tighten as she swayed slightly. He caught a movement out of the corner of his eye, and *Dom* Gabriel stepped forward and put his hand against the small of Javanne's back, supporting her almost tenderly, his face colorless in the daylight.

> *"Though winter freeze the world in pain,*
> *The starflower shall bloom on the hill,*
> *Our foes shall shake their swords in vain,*
> *For Hastur's Children lead us still!"*

Mikhail jerked as twenty voices rose in triumphant conclusion. He had not expected those words, and they rang through his mind. The enormity of the moment was like a bright pain in his heart. *Someday,* he thought, *they will sing these words for me. . . .*

The last notes died away to stillness. The ancient man looked around, commanding all attention.

"Here lies the Son of Hastur, Son of Aldones, Son of Light, at rest from his labors at last." The thready voice carried across the courtyard.

The words bore echoes of Darkover's most distant past. Mikhail heard his mother take a sharp breath. He himself had never heard them before, for they were spoken only at the passing of those of the Hastur line, but his mother and a few others remembered them from the funeral of Danvan.

"In life he bore the name Regis-Rafael Felix Alar Hastur y Elhalyn, and these are his deeds—"

As the reedy voice continued, Mikhail tried to listen, but the man seemed to be describing a stranger, not the uncle he had known and loved. The eulogy proclaimed the power of Regis' wrath, but where was his charm? There were references in plenty to the craft with which he had outwitted the Terranan for so many years, but what about his wit? And though the speaker chronicled Regis' achievements, he said nothing of the love for Darkover that was behind them. Many of the people were weeping, but how much greater would their grief be if they had really known the man whose body now lay on that bier.

The style of the speech both magnified and distanced the man it praised, making Regis Hastur seem at once larger than life and less than human. But presently Mikhail realized that those measured phrases were beginning to ease his sense of loss. No doubt that was their purpose. How Regis would have laughed if he could have heard!

Or perhaps he did—Mikhail felt Varzil's ring throb on his finger, and clenched the fist within its glove. They were sending Regis to his rest, but would he go? He did not know whether the idea of another visitation would console him or make him more afraid.

He straightened his back, sensing that the eulogy was drawing to a close. His whole body ached with exhaustion, and his feet felt like two blocks of ice in his boots.

The Servant lifted his arms again. "We shall not see his like again, this child of Aldones—and so we bid him farewell!" The words were ancient, the sorrow in them like a fresh wound.

He lowered his arms, and as if he had released their voices, from thousands of throats came a great wailing, a ululation that rang against the stone walls of Comyn Castle in cascading echoes that battered at Mikhail's weary senses until his own throat opened in an anguished cry. For a measureless time thereafter he remembered nothing, heard nothing, and felt nothing except the wracking grief of their enormous loss.

23

Marguerida was chafing at the slow pace of the funeral train. It demanded all of her will and the discipline of a lifetime to swallow her impatience. They had been on the road since daybreak, and all she wanted was to reach the village where Domenic was staying and to see her beloved son safe. But there was no way to hurry the entourage. Twenty-five wagons and as many carriages were behind her, with about three hundred riders beside them. She was only grateful that she was mounted on Dyania, with the pleasant sensation of horsey muscles against her thighs, instead of enclosed in one of the vehicles as were *Dom* Gabriel and a few others. That would have been too much for her.

They had left Thendara at dawn, and ridden out of the city on the Old North Road, past fields covered with drifting autumn mist. It had been eerily quiet, and the soft folds of earth that were almost visible through the concealing veils of moisture had been empty of anything except flocks of sheep and cattle. This had gotten on everyone's already excited nerves, and when the sun rose and began to burn away the mist, she had sensed a little relaxation around her.

Now she rode beside Mikhail, surrounded by twenty Guardsmen, and Marguerida tried to force herself to think of something besides her son. Could it actually be only eight days since Regis had died? She turned in the saddle and looked back, to the coffin draped with the silver-and-blue Hastur colors, resting on an enclosed flat-bedded carriage, drawn along by six creamy horses. She knew that the funeral had provided closure for Mikhail, but she remained trapped with her own conflicted feelings, no matter how hard she tried to escape them.

There was something a bit puzzling about her emotions, for when Diotima, her stepmother, had died, Marguerida had been able to accept it almost immediately. True, she had been expecting Dio's death for several years, while Regis' death had come without warning, but surely after so many days she should be able to come to grips with herself. However, even after the astonishing intrusion of Regis during the Comyn Council meeting, she had not yet managed to absorb the sudden death of the man. And the lengthy and exhausting funeral the previous day had only left her tired, not free to mourn the man who had been so kind to her. She could only hope that once he was interred with his ancestors, she would at last be able to adjust her heart to the loss.

The Council meeting had given her husband fresh confidence, and he no longer seemed as doubtful and hesitant as he had in the days immediately following Regis' death. She did not understand all that had taken place within him, but she could see that he was ready to lead Darkover at last. Now, if they could just survive the expected attack—if it was not all a tempest in a chamber pot—and if she could keep herself in the background for the rest of her life!

She chewed on the problem, ruthlessly examining herself. She contrasted herself with Lady Linnea, who had never gone beyond the role of consort, and decided she could not imitate her very well. She was simply a different sort of person—too independent—and she was equal to Mikhail in the peculiar powers of her shadow matrix. Well, she could only be herself, and everyone would have to accept it. The thought refreshed her as the wind tugged at the hood of her cloak.

Marguerida wondered what Lew was doing right then. Pacing, probably. That was how he behaved when he was impatient. Would there be an attack on Comyn Castle? She hoped there would not be, yet, she was curious if the plan she had helped to conceive would be effective. She smiled slowly. Working closely with Cisco Ridenow for the first time had been a remarkable experience. He had grasped the nature of the problem immediately, swinging into action as if he had been preparing for such an eventuality for years. And, she thought, perhaps he had. She had not expected him to be so imaginative, nor sure of himself.

With the dampers in the Crystal Chamber destroyed, there had been no way to prevent a certain degree of leakage from the minds at the table, although everyone had been aware of this situation and done their best to shield their surface thoughts. So it had been something of a revelation to learn that Cisco was not nearly so much his father's creature as she and everyone else had always assumed. There was an undercurrent of mistrust between the two men which had surprised her. Watching the interplay between the two Ridenows, she finally decided that Cisco did not answer to anyone except himself, that he was stern and sober, confident in his own judgment, and wary of his sire as well.

It was Cisco who had suggested smuggling the children away from Comyn Castle in the carriages which had brought the *leroni* from Arilinn for the funeral, while the Tower people remained behind to aid in defending the castle. He had been able to give an exact count of the men available for both the defense of the castle and of the funeral train as well, and she suspected that he had independently considered the possibility of such attacks. Indeed, he had already organized the City Guards for this purpose, calling up the many retired Guardsmen who still lived in Thendara and putting them on alert.

He would bear watching, she decided, if they came out of this crisis in one piece. Still, she could not help mistrusting him just a little, because of his father, and after wrestling with her conscience for a moment, Marguerida decided she was probably wise rather than petty. It was always a good idea to keep a weather eye on cunning men, however loyal they might think themselves.

Getting the children away had been a great relief. Roderick had protested mightily, insisting he was old enough to go to the *rhu fead*. He was furious that Domenic was going to have an adventure from which he was excluded, but she was glad that she did not have him to worry about. And Gareth Elhalyn had been displeased as well. No, that was too puny a term to describe the boy's behavior. Gareth had been furious and had thrown something very like a tantrum. She almost pitied Gisela, and was still somewhat bemused by her offer to oversee both Katherine Aldaran's and Marguerida's children, along with her own. Marguerida did not envy her a carriage journey with eight youngsters, at least two of them in adolescent sulks.

It suddenly occurred to Marguerida that if they failed and perished in this mad adventure, then Gisela might see her youthful ambitions realized. As the aunt of Roderick and Yllana, and the wife of Rafael Lanart-Hastur, she would be one of the logical choices to care for the children, even though she was an Aldaran by birth. It would give her the power she had craved all her life. And, for no reason that Marguerida could bring to mind, she was not perturbed by this possibility. Giz would have to contend with Miralys Elhalyn, who had remained behind because of her pregnancy, as well as Javanne, who loathed Gisela even more than she did Marguerida. She let herself envision the encounter, for the sheer pleasure of it, to distract herself from other, even less wholesome thoughts. She succeeded for a short while, but then her doubts rushed back, and she started worrying again.

If they had been successful, then Lyle Belfontaine had no idea that the carriages were filled with armed men, not women and children as they ordinarily would have been. Six to a coach, and twenty coaches, gave them another hundred and twenty fighters who were not visible to any interested eyes, in addition to the two hundred and fifty Guardsmen and the company of Renunciates who rode at the rear of the procession. Not a great number to face the kind of armament that the Federation could bring to bear, although they did not anticipate there being more than a hundred of the enemy. And, too, the Federation had no idea of either Mikhail's powers, or her own. It seemed a slender thing on which to hang their future, but there had been no alternative, after hours of discussion that had lasted until every voice in the chamber was hoarse with weariness.

Suddenly Marguerida was struck by the irony of it all. For years people had feared Mikhail's matrix, so much so that they had almost forgotten the capacity of her shadow matrix. Lady Javanne, *Dom* Francisco and Lady Marilla had refused to believe he would not use his powers to further his own ambitions, and Regis had worried in his own way. Now they had turned about and decided Mikhail was to be their savior. It would have been amusing if it were not so terrible.

A cold wind from the west blew across her cheeks, and she breathed deeply, smelling the crisp air. It brought back memories of another journey up the Old North Road, sixteen years before, when she had gone to

Neskaya with Rafaella and her sister Renunciates. Odd that her mind did not go to that other occasion, when she and Mik had dashed off in the middle of the night, to tumble into history.

Marguerida knew she was thinking of the trip to Neskaya because of the bandits they had encountered up in the mountains. She had killed two men during the fray, and used the Command Voice to stop the battle, much to her dismay and surprise. And now, if they were attacked as Herm and Nico thought they would be, she would probably slay more. The Aldaran Gift had visited her briefly that morning, offering her the sight of blasted corpses on a seared hillside. It had been frightening and useless, since she could not see the faces, and had no idea of their identity or what had been the cause of their deaths. And it had come and gone so quickly, a flicker more than a real vision.

Everything depended on Mikhail, on his matrix, and on hers as well. What had seemed quite plausible in the security of the Crystal Chamber seemed less so now. Was it really a plan, or just a foolish hope, that they could overcome an armed force in the way they believed? She tingled with anticipation and chill, acknowledging her own fears with as much calmness as she could muster. This was no time to have second thoughts. She glanced at the grim faces of the Guardsmen around them and made a silent prayer to the thousand gods from a hundred planets whose names she knew.

Still, it was very good to be on the road, riding toward whatever destiny awaited them. A sense of ease began to seep into her, unexpected and welcomed. She turned and smiled at Mikhail.

"That's better, *caria*. Your frets were giving my nerves a workout."

"Oh, dear—was I that loud?"

"Only to me, I think. Actually you have yourself well in hand, my love. I don't know if I could have done this thing without you at my side. I wonder what is happening back in Thendara?"

"With any luck, absolutely nothing. That would disappoint my father, who really wants Belfontaine to do something foolish, so he can hang him out to dry in a cold wind. And Val, too."

Mikhail chuckled softly. "Yes, she was practically rubbing her hands together with glee when we left. How is Katherine holding up?"

"Pretty well, but she is as anxious to see Herm as I am to see Nico. Perhaps I should drop back for the present and ride beside her."

"Yes. We know that the attack, if it comes, will be beyond Carcosa, so there is no danger right now. She is a very brave woman, Marguerida."

"I know. I'm not sure I could handle being headblind as well as she has. Her painting helps, I think. And her friendship with Gisela, too—do you know, I never would have imagined that happening. She seems to have turned Giz into another person, and I don't really know what to make of it. Still, I am very glad of it. Very glad."

Marguerida pulled her reins and turned back two horse lengths, causing the Guards on either side to shift their positions. She rode back, past the catafalque, and pulled alongside of Katherine's rather pokey mount. Herm's wife claimed to be able to ride, but no one would call her a good horsewoman. She held her reins too tightly, and her knees were clasped tautly against the sides of the animal. She would have been in one of the carriages but for her insistence that the close confines of the vehicle would make her ill.

"Kate, the horse will not run away with you. You will be exhausted if you keep hanging on for dear life like that. Let go of the pommel, relax your knees, and take a deep breath."

"I am sure that is excellent advice, and I will try to obey it. I haven't been on a horse since I was five, and that was a moor pony, and much lower to the ground! We don't have real horses on Renney, just barrel-bellied ponies with shaggy coats and docile dispositions. They are used to pull wagons, and for children to ride as treats."

"Did you enjoy it?" Marguerida was determined to put Katherine at ease. It gave her something to focus on besides her own worries and those of the woman beside her. Those were a constant murmur of thoughts of Herm, and about the safety of her children. She felt sorry for Kate, torn by two competing loyalties. If Gisela had not offered to take the children, she would have had a harder time of it. And now, in hindsight and less weary than the day before, Marguerida felt that her sister-in-law's decision had been genuine, founded on her real affection for Kate Aldaran, and that there was no mischief in it. More, if Gisela was as determined as she seemed to behave better, she would have to learn to trust her more. With all the history that lay between her and Giz, it was a startling idea, one she was not sure she could accept easily.

"I'm not sure. I seem to remember being rather concerned about all those teeth—to a little girl even a pony seems pretty dangerous. And we rode bareback, without reins. I just grabbed the mane—I remember it was wiry in my fingers—and hung on for dear life." She laughed a little. "I did not tell you that, and pretended to skills I lack," Katherine admitted.

"That is all right. It was not a lie that was intended to injure anyone, and I do understand that being cooped up in a carriage would have been difficult for you."

"How far is it now?"

"To the *rhu fead* or Carcosa?"

"Carcosa."

Marguerida glanced knowledgeably along the movement of the train. "We will reach the town about midday, if none of the carriages loses a wheel, and if we have no other delays, we *might* get to Lake Hali by nightfall." Thus far she had not told Katherine about the possibility of an attack on the funeral train, nor that she would have to get into a carriage when they left Carcosa. It had been hard enough to suggest that the castle might be attacked, in order to get her to let the children be taken to safety.

"Nightfall?" Katherine shivered in the wind, as if the prospect of riding through the entire day was finally making itself known. "Where will we spend the night? Is there a city there? No one has said."

"Nothing like that—the only real city, in terms you understand, on Darkover is Thendara. There are a few largish places, like Neskaya, which are almost cityish, but for the most part there are only villages, towns and hamlets. I sent people ahead three days ago, to prepare things. By now I expect there is an encampment with its own kitchens, tents for sleeping, and latrines."

"You sleep outside in tents, in this cold?"

Marguerida managed to swallow a laugh. "This is not cold, Kate, not by Darkovan standards."

"Then what do you consider too cold for comfort?"

"Um, when the temperature is way below freezing, and there is snow up to your eyeballs, I suppose. I've gotten so used to it now that I hardly ever think about it. When I first returned to Darkover, I thought I would die from cold, but I adjusted, and so will you."

"I'm not so sure of that, Marguerida. You were much younger than I am now, weren't you?"

"Yes, I was, but I'm sure you'll become used to the climate with time."

Katherine scanned the landscape, her eyes going towards the horizon as if she were trying to see something very distant. "Herm used to rhapsodize about winter, and sometimes when he talked about snow, he got positively poetic. I never understood that, and thought he was exaggerating, the way you do when you are far away from home. I mean, when we took Amaury and Terése home to Renney nine years back, I was stunned by how small the Manse seemed, because in my memory, it was a much bigger house than it is in reality. True, compared to the average Federation dwelling, it was huge—seven bedrooms and two parlors. But the ceilings seemed lower, and the rooms less spacious than I remembered. Now I think that perhaps Herm did not even give me a true idea of how different Darkover is—that the Hellers are taller than he said, and colder, too." She shuddered slightly, looking north.

"You will get used to it. I did. Now I cannot imagine living in one room, or perhaps two, as I did when I was at University. My parents had a home on Thetis, with wide verandas facing the ocean, which I thought was very grand, but which would have fitted into a tiny fraction of Comyn Castle without a ripple. It all seems like a dream to me now, although a very nice one—warm and smelling of flowers and saltwater." She let herself sigh for the world she knew she would never see again. "We will rough it for a night, with decent cots and lots of blankets, so I promise you will not freeze to death, or even take a chill. And, with any luck, we will have your Hermes back, and you can bundle up with him."

"He will be very lucky if I don't make him sleep on the ground with one thin blanket, for all the aggravation he has given me." Her deep voice was twisted with conflicting emotions, too many for Marguerida to sort out without probing invasively.

"I would never dare to advise you on how to conduct your marital relations, Kate, but you must not be too hard on him. He is still a Darkovan male, and they are reared to be high-handed, to treat their women-folk like fragile bric-a-brac, and to do as they please, for the most part. He can't help not consulting you, any more than you can avoid resenting it."

"Bric-a-brac! Yes, that's how Herm made me feel once we arrived here—I just couldn't quite get my mind around it! And I don't understand it at all."

"It's our history, Kate. Darkover has a small population, and infant mortality has been high for centuries. Therefore women were protected fiercely—in some places more than others. Up in the Dry Towns they are shackled like criminals. Some of that has changed since the Federation came, but not as much as I would like. Even today, there is not a great deal of freedom here for females, unless they choose the Renunciate's path, which is not an easy one."

"You mean those women at the rear of the train? Gisela told me a little about them. We even joked that if things didn't work out with Herm, I could join them. They look tough as nails."

"Yes, those are Renunciates."

"There is so much I do not understand, which infuriates me and makes me feel even more . . . no matter. Tell me about this *rhu fead*. If it is such an important place, why is there no city or large town nearby? And, for that matter, why bury your kings there, instead of Thendara, if it is, as you say, the chief city? It doesn't make any sense to me, and I am driving myself to distraction trying to make heads or tails out of this planet my husband has plunked me down on."

Marguerida laughed aloud and nodded. "That seems perfectly reasonable to me, dear Kate. The short answer is tradition. Everything important on Darkover is done according to hoary traditions that no one remembers the reasons for any longer. One of these is that our dead rulers will be interred in the *rhu fead*, which is a very peculiar place to begin with. It stands near the shore of Lake Hali." She paused and took a slow breath. "I once spent several weeks submerged in the waters—except they are not really waters—of Lake Hali, and I know no more about it than I did before. So it is no good asking me about it. I wish I could tell you more. Just understand that Hali is a sacred place, and that Darkover is a planet which tends to be traditional rather than innovative." She grinned. "They don't examine their ideas much, and I think if you asked a hundred people at random why things were done in a certain way, ninety of them would just answer that if it was good enough for their grandfather, it is good enough for them."

"Oh, a religious site. Well, there is no explaining those sorts of things, is there? Even when you grow up with the beliefs, you never really understand them. I think that religion is just a box into which real mysteries are dropped, like old clothing."

Marguerida gave Kate a look of pleasure. She had nearly forgotten how delightful it was to have a discussion about ideas, for there were very few people on Darkover who had the education and intellectual curiosity she craved. And, until now, it had not occurred to her that Katherine might be a woman with unusual ideas of her own. "Now, that is a very interesting attitude. I never thought if it that way before, but you make good sense. I had the impression from a few things you said that Renney had a pretty complex religious life—your sacred groves and all. Don't you accept those things any longer?"

"Maybe my years living in the Federation have left me a bit cynical." Katherine gave a thoughtful sigh. "We have goddesses on Renney, and the people there believe in them. A day does not go by that my Nana doesn't offer her prayers and do her small rituals. When I was a child, they seemed to me to be wonderful, but when we went back there, so Nana could meet Terése, I was . . . almost embarrassed, I suppose. It seemed so backward and superstitious, and just a little silly. I would never suggest such a thing to her, of course. My Nana may be old, but she is still capable of reducing me to jelly without overly exerting herself." Katherine chuckled. "After living in the Federation for years, observing and being exposed to dozens of religions—the followers of which all insist that *theirs* is the only true religion—well, it all started to seem ridiculous to me. It is very hard to go on believing in the power of goddesses when you have never seen one, and are surrounded by people who believe so many diverse and contradictory things."

Marguerida did not answer, thinking about her own experiences. Her memory swept back to the moment when she married Mikhail, in the presence of Varzil the Good and another, the goddess Evanda. She had never doubted the actuality of that, but she found herself reluctant to share the experience with her new friend. It was a very personal remembrance, and even now, years after the fact, it was so awesome that she could not bring herself to speak of it to anyone except Mikhail.

At last she said, "The Darkovan mythology is fairly simple—two gods, two goddesses and no theology to speak of. They are more like forces of nature, invoked ceremonially on occasion, and otherwise not given much attention. There are other deities, lesser ones, as well. But I think that the general attitude of the people is that if the gods do not actively interfere in their lives, then they should just leave well enough alone." She paused for a second. "Up in Nevarsin there is a cult called the *cristoforos*. Their beliefs are monotheistic and not shared by most of the people of Darkover, but they have been a center of learning for centuries. In the past, many of the sons of the Comyn were sent there to be educated—including Regis Hastur. That custom has faded in recent years, although Gisela's oldest son, by her first marriage, went there and appears to have decided to join them. I can say, however, that there has never been a religious war on Darkover, although we have had several of the more ordinary sort."

"What about those men at the funeral yesterday—weren't they priests?"

"A good question, the answer to which is 'not quite.' The Servants of Aldones serve what on most worlds would be a priestly function, being the celebrants on certain important occasions, such as the Midsummer Festival. Where they differ from other religious bodies I have encountered is that they never tell the people what to believe or how to worship. There are no temples or churches on Darkover as you might know such places."

"So what do they do when they are not officiating at funerals?"

"They keep vigil over certain artifacts in a little chapel in the *rhu fead*, an eternal flame and some other things I don't know about. Yesterday was the first time I ever saw them in my life, even though I was the one who sent the message to them to come to Thendara."

"But they do not have religious authority?"

"No, they don't. For some reason I have never learned, the Darkovans have not developed a public religious structure. For them it is a private and almost a family matter."

"Marguerida, have you ever noticed that you speak of the Darkovans as if they were another people, not your own?"

"Do I? Yes, I suppose I do. For all that I have lived here for nearly seventeen years, I still feel a bit removed, something of an alien. Or perhaps it is the habit of scholarship, that I tend to try to assess everything as objectively as I can. Except for music. All I have there is passion, and Mik gets slightly jealous sometimes."

Katherine laughed. "Herm is the same about my painting, although he pretends otherwise. Once, when I was working in our apartment, the whole of which would almost fit into the studio space you gave me, and was staring at the canvas, trying to decide if a bit of vermilion would make the shadows better, he came in. I barely registered his presence, so after a few minutes, he cleared his throat and nearly scared me to death. 'You never look at me like that,' he said, and I wanted to clout him over the head, but I didn't. He is right, you know. As much as I adore him, from the top of his shiny pate to his extremely well-formed feet, there is a part of me that belongs only to my work. He never has to worry about infidelity, but he does have a rival."

"Yes. I know about that." Marguerida let herself sigh into the wind. "I was writing an opera for Regis' birthday when he died. I wanted to do something as grand as your ancestor's *The Deluge of Ys*, using the legend of Hastur and Cassilda, which is a very famous song cycle here. Now I don't know if I will ever be able to bring myself to complete it." It cost her a great deal to admit this, but somehow speaking the words eased an ache in her chest she had not noticed until it left her. She remembered the freshly copied pages of score, and how the ink had flowed over them when Regis had his stroke.

"You must, Marguerida. If you don't finish it, it will eat away at your guts and make you miserable."

"How do you know that?"

"Because I am an artist, and because I remember Amedi Korniel."

"I've been wanting to ask you about him, but it never seemed the right time," she answered, almost relieved that the topic had shifted away from gods and goddesses, or her feeling alienated on the world of her birth.

"Ask away—this is as good a time as any."

"What was he like, and why did he stop composing in his sixties?"

"My great-uncle was a very cantankerous man, who had an opinion about everything. He was in his mid-eighties when I was born, and he died just before I left Renney. Nana adored him, he was her older brother, but even she found him maddening sometimes. He was a complete egotist, and thought the world should revolve around him. And he did not stop composing—just refused to let any of his work after *Ys* be performed. There are boxes of his compositions sitting in the Manse."

"But why?" Marguerida's heart leaped at the thought of these unpublished compositions by one of her favorite musicians, then sank as she realized that she would never have the opportunity to see them. Years before, she had resigned herself to never leaving Darkover again, and the desire to travel to other worlds had left her, but now she found herself aching to go to Renney and rescue the works of Amedi Korniel. She shook the feeling away sharply, but it lingered like the aftertaste of some bitter fruit.

"He was never satisfied with anything he did after the success of that opera, Marguerida. And it ate at him, like some terrible disease. He was paralyzed by the fear that his next work would not be as good. So learn from his mistake. Don't let your music get corrupted by Regis' death, or anything else!"

Marguerida was moved by the fervor in Katherine's voice, and it gave her a sense of kinship as well. "I never realized until this second how much I have wanted another artist of some kind to talk to about : . . my work, Katherine. And you are right, of course, it would eat at me." And then she realized it was more than just having similar drives. At last there was someone who understood her *need* for the music, for as much as Mikhail loved her, he had never been able to know that part of her mind. Even her friends in the Musicians Guild could not share the urgency of her work, regarding her only as a well-born amateur.

"I wish we could travel faster," Kate said.

"If it were not for the wagons and carriages, we could. Mikhail and I covered the distance from the gates of Thendara to the ruins of Hali Tower in about four hours of hard riding, long ago, in the middle of the night, too, with a snowstorm coming in!"

"That sounds very exciting."

"If being cold and terrified and under a compulsion is exciting, then yes, it was. Don't fuss. We will get to Carcosa soon enough, and you can ring a peal over Herm's head as much as you please."

"And will you do the same with Domenic?"

"Probably not. I will just be so glad to have him back in my maternal clutches that I will forgive him. Except for this one instance, he has always been a very good boy."

"That doesn't surprise me, from my brief acquaintance at dinner that first time. He and Roderick are so different, aren't they?"

"Yes, they are. There is something I have wanted to ask you, and not dared to, Kate."

"Ask away."

"What have you done to my sister-in-law? I was only half jesting when I wondered if you had bewitched her."

"Well, in the first place, I haven't *done* anything, except perhaps see her as a person instead of an Aldaran." She hesitated, as if concerned she had been offensive. "When you are a portrait painter, you learn a great deal about people, because they will talk about themselves, even when I am trying to get their mouths down on canvas. So, I have been rather good at listening. And when Gisela took me to see Master Gilhooly, we talked during the journey, and I discovered that she was not a bad woman at all. She only needed to be heard without being prejudged because of her family." Kate hesitated briefly. "I think you are right about my having a great deal of empathy, by the way. I've noticed that I seem to have a sixth sense about people that was always there, only I did not pay much attention to it, except to be aware of which people made me squirm and fidget. Gisela doesn't, in the same way that Herm never did."

"And being listened to reformed her?" Marguerida was amused and somewhat disbelieving.

Kate laughed. "No, I don't think so. I gave her things to think about other than feeling unhappy about herself. And I believe that Mikhail coming to see Rafael and bringing him to that Council meeting was important as well. Giz really cares for Rafael, and she has felt perfectly miserable because she was the cause of his . . . estrangement from his brother." She gestured ahead, to where Rafael Lanart was riding a horse length behind Mikhail. "That's why *Dom* Damon hit her, you know."

"What?"

"From what Gisela told me, her father put her up to mischief, years ago, because he wanted Mikhail and Rafael to be at odds although she did not know she was to deliberately estrange the two! And when he discovered that they no longer were, he took it out on her."

"I am a fool! I should have guessed that something like that had happened! Of course, it all makes sense now!"

Kate shook her head. "I'm glad it does to you, because I am still rather in the dark. I don't understand your ways yet, if I ever will. But I do grasp the fairly obvious—that my father-in-law had some intention of unseating Mikhail and putting Rafael in his place."

"And Gisela walked right into his trap—poor woman."

"My *breda* is not any sort of poor woman, Marguerida. She is just a very intelligent person who has had nowhere to put her energies except to cause trouble. And, I gather, Lady Javanne is in a similar position."

"Yes, I believe that is true. You call her *breda*, and I think you mean it, in all its several possible interpretations. That is so remarkable to me, for you have only known her for a few days. And she is not an easy person to know, Kate. I still think you bewitched her."

"No one is easy to know, Marguerida. But Gisela is not as difficult as you imagine—all she needs or wants is to be treated fairly. And I have not ensorcelled anyone. If I were going to do such a thing, Gisela would not have been my choice."

"I have seen the way Herm looks at you, Kate."

The other woman chuckled softly. "And I have seen the way Mikhail looks at you. That isn't sorcery—it's sex!"

Marguerida shook her head. "It has to be more than that!"

"Of course it is, but . . . well, I just think that you and Mikhail are a good match. I always thought that Herm and I were, too, but now I am starting to wonder if I just persuaded myself that I understood him."

"I don't know if men and women ever understand each other, Kate. But you are right that Mik and I are a fine match—like two halves of a whole."

"Yes, that's it. I noticed how you always stand on his right side, as if you need to be on that side and never on the other. Will you tell me what that is about?"

"Gisela didn't tell you? I am surprised, and rather pleased at her discretion." Marguerida took a deep breath. "Shortly after I returned to Darkover, I was forced to make a journey into the overworld, to destroy what remained of Ashara Alton, and when I did, I pulled the keystone from a tower she had made there, and it . . . imprinted itself on my left hand. And then, later, Mikhail and I went into the past, and when we returned, he had the ring of Varzil the Good, which he wears on his right hand. This has given us a particular ability to combine our matrix energies together, to do certain workings that I can't describe to you."

"The Overworld? Is that the realm of the gods or something?"

"Not that I know of. It is a place and not a place at the same time, and even though I have been there a few times, I still don't even begin to understand it. And if the gods are there, no one has reported it."

"Marguerida, tell me the truth. There is something more going on here than taking Regis' body to this *rhu fead*. I can feel the tension in the mounted men, and in everyone else, including you. It feels like you are expecting a storm or something."

"If I had never told you that you possessed a degree of empathy, you never would have gotten so sensitive, would you?"

"Probably not. What is it?"

"We have received some information that the forces of the Federation may try to attack the funeral train after we leave Carcosa."

"I thought you expected an attack on Comyn Castle."

"That too."

"I see. And Hermes left the castle and went to this Carcosa village because he had heard of the plot?"

"Yes." Marguerida was uncomfortable now, for keeping the truth from Katherine for so many days, and more, from her own reluctance to put the other woman into danger. Perhaps she could be persuaded to remain behind in the town.

"Well, that explains a great deal. No wonder Herm didn't tell me anything. I would have thought about it certainly, and who knows who might have caught my worrying. I confess that I never thought how difficult it might be to keep a secret in a world full of telepaths. It is better that I didn't know." She paused and frowned. "Gisela didn't know about this either, did she?"

"No, she didn't, because at the time we were not sure that her father was not mixed up in the entire stupid mess." Thinking of *Dom* Damon, Marguerida spoke with more feeling than she intended, letting her damped-down fury expose itself.

"And now?"

"Now we know that *Dom* Damon was not conspiring with Lyle Belfontaine, which is a great relief, because having another enemy in our midst is more than . . ."

"My father-in-law does not seem to be to be a very able plotter, Marguerida. He just seems like an ignorant man who hits women when he does not get his way." She paused and looked ahead, at the men riding ahead of her, finally fixing her gaze on Francisco Ridenow. "That man in the green-and-gold tunic there wants watching, if you ask me. I'm sure I was introduced to him, but for some reason I can't recall his name—only that he is a person who makes me very uncomfortable!"

Marguerida's eyes widened at this comment. How had Kate, without real *laran*, discerned that *Dom* Francisco was a potential threat? And how was she going to persuade the woman to undergo testing? "Why him in particular."

"Something about the way he sets his shoulders, and how he keeps looking at Mikhail with . . . rancor."

Marguerida nodded in agreement and grimaced a little. "Yes, that is close to the mark. *Dom* Francisco imagines that he could possess my husband's matrix and use it, that it rightly belongs to him because it was his ancestor's."

"But when Giz explained to me a bit about the matrices, she said they were keyed to individuals. Hermes wears this pouch around his neck, and always has, but until she told me, I never had any idea what was in it. I just knew that it was something I should not touch or pry into. I thought it was some sort of amulet, like those my people wear to keep the ghosts away. So, how can Francisco think he can use Mikhail's, if he knows that matrices are fixed on a person? For that matter, if what Gisela told me is accurate, how can Mikhail have one that belonged to this other person, this Varzil fellow?"

"When Varzil passed his matrix on to Mikhail, he managed to incorporate Mikhail's own starstone into it—don't ask me how! I saw it with my own eyes and I still don't understand it! It was as near to magic as anything I have ever seen."

"What would happen if Francisco got hold of the thing?"

"I don't know, but I think it would probably kill both him and Mikhail."

"Does Francisco know that?"

"Yes, but he doesn't believe it, Kate."

When the party drew into the courtyard of the Crowing Cock just after midday, Marguerida was very glad to dismount and stretch her legs. She hadn't ridden for any length of time in several years, and she found she was rather stiff. The insides of her thighs ached and she yearned for a hot bath, a long massage, and a clean bed to sleep on. More, she wished that she did not have to ride farther that day.

The yard was much too small to take in the entire funeral train, so most of the wagons and carriages pulled up outside the walls separating the inn from the street. Despite this, by the time the funeral wagon had been drawn inside, and the members of the Comyn and their Guards entered, the courtyard was crammed. Grooms rushed forward into the bustle and took the reins of the horses as their riders dismounted, and the ostlers were shouting at one another as they attempted to manage the near chaos.

Marguerida started toward the entrance and noticed there were black marks on the cobblestones beneath her feet. A faint smell of burning seemed to hang in the air, muted by the recent rain, but still noticeable. She was momentarily distracted by this and was caught unawares when a pair of arms excitedly encircled her waist.

"Mother!"

She turned in the embrace and looked down at her eldest child, still a few inches shorter than she was. His dark hair was unbound, as he preferred it, and his eyes shone with pleasure, as if he were as glad to see her as she was to see him. He looked none the worse for his adventures, and there was a new air of confidence about him she had not seen before. "Nico! You scamp!" Marguerida could not bring herself to scold him more than this, even though she had rehearsed a number of pungent sentences beforehand. A vast weight of anxiety lifted from her, and her heart felt ready to burst with delight. She let herself clutch him hard, pressing him against her chest, feeling the bones in his shoulders beneath his shirt and tunic.

"It was your own fault," he answered, after giving her a quick kiss on the cheek.

"*My* fault—how did you arrive at this remarkable conclusion?"

"If you had not told me I was dull and never gave you a moment's worry, I might not have decided to go off on my own."

Marguerida followed this entirely specious line of reasoning with amusement. She was so glad to have Domenic safe beside her that she would have agreed with almost anything. "Yes, I suppose I should be grateful that you did not decide to try to circle Comyn Castle along the rooftops."

Nico laughed at this. "I might have, but I have no head for heights." Then he drew away a little, as if anxious about something, and she noticed a rather scruffy-looking girl standing uneasily behind him. "I would like to present my friend Illona Rider, Mother. She has lived with the Travelers all her life, and can tell you all about them." His tone combined a kind of pride and wariness at the same time.

For a moment Marguerida was a little puzzled as to what to make of this, and then she extended her right hand. "How do you do? I am Marguerida Alton-Hastur, and I am glad to meet any friend of my son's."

The girl looked at the offered hand for a moment, as if it were a snake, then took it gingerly and shook it briefly. To Marguerida's eye, she seemed underfed and unprepossessing. Her wiry red hair stood out wildly from her skull, escaping from the wooden clasp at the back of her skinny neck, and her green eyes were too large for the thin face. The cloak she was wearing smelled of smoke and ash, and beneath it, the garments she wore seemed to have been made for a larger person. She gazed at

Marguerida with a combination of fear and defiance that was disquieting, then lowered her eyes to the seared stones.

"I don't know nearly as much as Domenic thinks," Illona muttered gruffly, shuffling her feet under her.

"Well, whatever you know would interest me. I have been very curious about the Travelers since I saw their wagons for the first time sixteen years ago, and while my friend Erald has told me a few things, he is too obsessed with his music to pay attention to interesting details." Who was this girl? Their brief physical contact had startled her, because she could sense the presence of *laran* in her rather strongly. And why, Marguerida wondered, was she wearing Nico's old cloak, while he stood out in the chilly day in his tunic and shirtsleeves?

"Do you mean Erald the Balladeer? He went with us three summers ago, and I could not make heads or tails out of him," Illona answered, relaxing slightly. "He hardly ate and never seemed to sleep, but only sat around plunking away at his instruments like a madman."

"Yes, that's him," Marguerida answered, glad to find some common ground with her son's new friend.

Someone came up behind her, and Marguerida recognized the familiar imprint of Dyan Ardais in her mind. He stepped beside her and looked at Domenic. "You look none the worse for your adventure, Nico." He smiled at the young man in a friendly way, and then at his companion. Marguerida saw his eyes widen with surprise.

Does she remind you of someone, Dom *Dyan?*

Of all the . . . who is this, Nico?

The girl beside me is called Illona Rider, but it is my belief that you might have known her mother. There was a stern quality in the boy's mental tone.

Dyan shifted from foot to foot and stared at the girl, who looked back at him rather fiercely. Marguerida wondered if she was overhearing the unspoken conversation, but from the expression on her face, decided she was not, quite deliberately. Illona was consciously keeping herself from overhearing anything by concentrating on the rabbithorns in a nearby enclosure. And what the devil was Nico up to? *I did know a woman once, with hair like that. . . .*

Then I suspect Illona is your nedestra, Dom *Dyan.* Nico's words sounded accusing, and Dyan turned red with embarrassment. *She was found as a baby, in the ruins of a village that had been raided by bandits, and was saved from death by the Travelers. It was up in Ardais country, and she seems to have the Alton Gift, untrained but there, as near as I can tell, which made me think of your own father, you see.* Domenic was relentless now, and Marguerida could sense his steadfastness, his affection for this rather unprepossing girl, and his odd loyalty to her.

Perhaps. She is certainly the image of . . . Eduina MacGarret. But that doesn't mean . . .

At least you can remember her name, among so many. Domenic gazed at Dyan, who at thirty-seven was still unmarried, and scandalously re-knowned in the Comyn for the number of his illegitimate offspring.

Marguerida wanted to laugh at the situation, but she knew she had to put a stop to it. *Nico!*

I'm sorry, Mother, but I . . .

Yes, son. I understand. But this is neither the time nor the place for . . . a reunion. Does your little friend have any idea . . . ?

I don't think so—she can overhear a lot, even without a matrix, but she has learned how to block rather effectively. And she would happily leave her laran by the side of the road, if she could. She has been very upset, discovering that she has it, and if I hadn't distracted her by teaching her to read these past couple of days, I think she would have gone to pieces from grief and sheer terror.

So that is why you wanted the book—I have been racking my brains since I got your letter. Is she a good student?

Very. She is smart and fast. And I liked teaching her.

I am glad of that.

"Let's get inside, out of the wind," Nico said, looking less fierce now. Dyan Ardais was still standing there, looking uneasy and embarrassed, as if he did not know quite what to do next. Marguerida remembered their first meeting, years before, when he had come into her bedroom while she was recovering from her first episode of threshold sickness. His mother had sent him there to suggest that he might be a suitable spouse for her, and he had been awkward and miserable. In retrospect, it was still a funny experience, but Dyan had never been entirely at ease with women of his own class, and preferred the company of farmers' daughters to those of the Comyn. He must have a dozen children up in the Kilghards by now, acknowledged only by generous gifts to the mothers. She suspected that the only reason he was embarrassed now was because

Nico had found out about another one. And what would this girl think of the whole thing, when it was explained to her?

"That sounds like a good idea—you must be cold without your cloak, son."

"Not really. Come along, Mother. Evan MacHaworth has a meal waiting, and I am sure you must be hungry after your ride." He glanced over Marguerida's shoulder and grinned. "I guess *Domna* Katherine is not going to kill Herm after all."

Marguerida turned and looked behind her. Hermes Aldaran stood and lifted his hands to help Kate down from the saddle. When she did not move, he put his hands around her slender waist and swung her down beside him. The man's face was pale in the watery sunlight, and there was a ruddyness in Katherine's cheeks which might be anger or some tenderer emotion. "Gisela said I should box your ears," she heard Katherine tell him in a strangled voice.

"That is the least I deserve," her husband answered, sounding not at all contrite. "You are the most beautiful sight I have seen in days."

"Save your charm for someone who wants it, Hermes-Gabriel Aldaran. I am not ready to forgive you yet."

"I did not expect you to be, but I had hoped my letter . . ."

"Your letter does not get you off the hook."

Apparently unaware of the interested gazes of several people, Herm considered his next words. Then, in Terran, he said, " 'Fie, fie, unknit that threatening unkind brow.' "

"Hermes, that is my line, not yours," Katherine answered in the same language, torn between amusement and despair in dealing with her unrepentant spouse.

"True—then, 'Why, there's a wench! Come on, and kiss me, Kate.' "

"Oh, you are impossible!" Then, in front of the bemused view of the Comyn, only a few of whom had understood what they had said, she grabbed his ears, pulled him toward her, and gave him a firm buss on the mouth. Kate drew away, looking a little breathless and pink with pleasure. "Now, be good, and I might forgive you in a few years."

This was too much for several in the crowd, and there was muffled laughter, which made both Herm and Kate look around and realize they were being watched. The woman turned quite red, but Herm just made a deep bow to the audience. Then Robert Aldaran stepped out of the throng and clasped his brother strongly.

"You haven't changed much, *bredu*, except you have lost your hair and your waistline." Herm chortled and thumped Robert across the shoulders.

Marguerida turned away from this reunion and told her son, "Food sounds very inviting. Where is Rafaella?"

"She is doing a bit of spying—I wanted to go with her, but Uncle Hermes said I could not." Nico paused, then shrugged. "Actually, what he said was that if I was not here to meet you, Katherine would not have to murder him because you probably would instead. And since I am very fond of him . . ."

Marguerida had to laugh at this. "He was right. I have been extremely anxious to see you, and to know with my own eyes that you had not come to harm. The slow pace of the funeral train has nearly driven me mad." She put one hand on Nico's shoulder and the other on the girl's and started toward the door of the inn. Dyan Ardais trailed along beside her, watching the girl with an unreadable expression on his face.

She seems like a very nice mother, and not at all like the stories about her. But she is probably just pretending. I wonder what it is like to have a real mother? She likely makes Nico go to bed early, and wash behind his ears. I hope she doesn't bewitch me, as she did to her husband.

Marguerida caught these quiet musings unwillingly, and raised her eyebrows at the last. Was that what the common folk said about her? It had not occurred to her that she might be a subject of gossip until now, and she found it extremely unpleasant. If only they had not immured themselves in Comyn Castle for all these years, letting the imaginations of the populace run wild with who knows what! Well, they would just have to remedy that another day! She forced the problem out of her mind, away from the future and back into the present.

Mikhail was coming toward them, with Donal close behind him. He grinned broadly at the sight of his son and Domenic slipped from her grasp and stepped forward to meet his father. She watched as her husband's blond head bent a little downward and Nico's dark one looked up. "I am so glad to see you safe, Domenic."

"Herm made sure I came to no harm, Father." Something more passed between them, some unspoken words, and Marguerida saw her son's rather serious face brighten.

Glancing over her shoulder, Marguerida watched Herm and Katherine again, wondering what was passing between them. It would have been easy to snoop, but she held her curiosity in check. She saw Kate shake a gloved forefinger in her husband's face, and Hermes bow his head a little, so his bare scalp gleamed in the soft light. He looked so much like a naughty boy being scolded that she had to turn away quickly to hide the laughter that bubbled up involuntarily.

They entered the warm inn, and the smell of food swept around them. A smiling man came bustling from the rear of the building, wiping his hands on a white apron. He bowed and greeted them like old friends, not strangers, and turned to lead them into the dining room. The tables were laid with what were clearly the best linens, and the scene was so ordinary that she could hardly believe that after this meal, they were going to ride deliberately into an ambush.

She was going to worry herself into a fit if she didn't stop thinking about it, Marguerida told herself firmly as she took off her cloak. She hung it on a peg, and the girl, Illona, did the same. She wondered why the girl was wearing her son's cloak and frowned over the small mystery. Then she found herself thinking like an interferring mother, like Lady Javanne, concerned that her son had fallen in love with this scrawny girl who could not, no matter who her father was, be a proper consort for the future ruler of Darkover. She was stunned at herself for a second. When had she turned into such a snob?

Illona seemed to sense something of her thoughts, and turned very red, making the freckles on her pert nose stand out. "All my things were burned up in the wagon, and Domenic lent me his cloak, *domna*, and one of MacHaworth's daughters let me wear some of her things," she said, trying to sound calm and not succeeding very well.

"Burned up? When was this?" Marguerida was suddenly furious, her pleasure of a moment before gone. She realized that her father and husband, with the very best intentions in the world, had not told her everything that had happened in Carcosa. She glanced at Mikhail, and he had the grace to look uncomfortable. *Forgive me, caria—you had a great many other things to worry about, and I could not bear to add to it.*

Dammit, Mik!

The girl flinched, catching the edge of her anger and mistaking its direction. She began to shiver all over. "Three nights ago, when we did this play that made . . . it was terrible. The people got upset, and they attacked our wagons, and my aunt Loret was killed, and . . . don't be angry with me!" Tears began to course down Illona's face, as if she had been holding back for days, and could no longer control herself.

Marguerida did not respond at once. She was aware that there had been some sort of ruckus, and she now understood the marks on the cobblestones and the slight smell of ash outside. She even knew that several people had died and others had been injured. She had not really cared, because all that had mattered to her was that her son was safe. Until that moment, the whole thing had been rather abstract and distant. Now she felt the full force of the event, and saw the human face of the tragedy. Her heart ached for this child who had lost the only family she had ever known. Dyan Ardais, if he was Illona's father, as seemed very likely, would not be able to step into the void left by the death of Loret. He had never taken the least interest in any of his numerous offspring, and she did not think he was going to start now.

Marguerida reached out and took Illona into her arms, and let the girl sob into her chest. "No one is angry at you, dear child." She stroked the coarse hair gently. All the emotions the girl had held in check flooded through her, a bundle of terrors and experiences that shocked her. It was a great muddle of memory and feeling, all held together by the fear of what would happen to her now.

After several minutes, Illona's weeping began to subside, and she hiccupped a few times. Marguerida dug into her beltpouch and produced a serviceable handkerchief. The girl took it, wiped her eyes, and blew her nose fiercely. She started to hand back the soiled cloth, then turned red. "I really messed up your nice hanky," she muttered, hunching her shoulders and trying to make herself very small.

"That is what they are for," Marguerida answered calmly. "It will get washed and be as good as new." She reached out, without really thinking, and patted the wan face, as she would have done with her daughter or Alanna Alar. Illona flinched. "I am not going to hurt you, child."

"They say your hands are . . ."

"Oh, that. Only one hand," she answered, lifting the left one, "and only when I will it to be dangerous. You are perfectly safe, I promise."

When she had held Illona, she had felt the fear coursing beneath the natural grief. The girl was like a half-wild animal, unlike anyone Marguerida had ever encountered before, and her *laran* seemed very powerful, if completely untrained. She knew, from that contact, that the young woman was terrified of going into a Tower, that she believed the *leroni* did unspeakable things there. She looked into the sharp face, rather grubby from weeping, and wondered what she was going to do with her. Then she chided herself for assuming she was going to do anything whatever—it was not her responsibility at all.

Let Dyan see to her. A quick glance at the Ardais man made her realize immediately what a stupid notion that was. And somehow she could not imagine Lady Marilla being able to handle this particular girl. Marguerida sighed. She really did not need another foster-child, but she knew, almost as if she had experienced the Aldaran Gift once more, that she was probably going to have one.

"Nico told me you were nice," the girl said gruffly, "but I just thought he was speaking as a son. I didn't really believe him. But, maybe you are, and you won't seal me up in a room and make me . . ."

Marguerida waited for her to complete her sentence, and then realized that the girl could not bring herself to say the words that rested in her mind. "No one is going to shut you up anywhere."

Oddly, this seemed to satisfy Illona, for her taut shoulders relaxed slightly, and she sniffed into the hanky again. Then her vivid green glance darted around the room, until it found Domenic, now standing between his father and Herm Aldaran in front of the fireplace, and something of a smile began to play across her generous lips. Kate was standing behind Herm, her face relaxed at last, and Robert Aldaran and Donal were just a step away from the group, the paxman vigilant and the man reflective.

Marguerida followed her look, and studied the tableau. After a moment she realized there was something strained in the set of Mikhail's shoulders, and knew that something was disturbing him.

Mik, what's the matter?

I am having a bout of envy, caria. *Look at Nico! See how he looks at Herm, and tell me I have nothing to feel jealous of.*

Yes, dearest. I see it now. He left us a boy, and now he is really a man, and he regards Herm with the sort of intimacy you have never had with him. You would have to be inhuman not to feel wretched.

That is it, I suppose. I feel I just missed something very important in my son's life—something I should have been present for.

And how many of your important passages did Dom *Gabriel miss because of Regis?*

There is that, damn you. Don't you understand that you are not supposed to point out unpleasant things to me when I am upset? There was an undertone of humor in the thought.

Yes, I do, but as your mother so often points out, I am not a suitable wife.

Well, she can't witness this event, and for that I am very grateful. And he is safe and strong, and filled with a confidence I doubted I would ever find in him, so I guess I should be pleased. Later perhaps.

Marguerida held back a laugh at her husband's expense. She felt, for a moment, lighthearted. She had her firstborn back, and he seemed none the worse for whatever adventures he had had. If only they were not riding into the jaws of an ambush in a few hours, she would have been entirely content. But they were, and her momentary pleasure left her, and all the worries flooded back again.

She sat down on a long bench beside one of the tables and gestured to Illona to sit beside her. The girl did, just as *Dom* Gabriel, who had been riding, to his fury, in one of the carriages, stamped into the room. His leg no longer allowed him to ride on horseback for any length of time, and he resented the infirmity enormously. Marguerida saw him take in the group before the fireplace in a quick glance, and then he came and sat down next to her. There was something very solid and comforting in his presence these days, and she was glad that the old man was on her side, as well as that he was so long reconciled with Mikhail.

"Stop your fretting, Marguerida. It won't do a drop of good, and will just tire you out," Dom Gabriel told her sternly. Then he smiled, his eyes almost disappearing in the wrinkles of his face. "Now, introduce me to this young woman, will you."

Marguerida had almost forgotten about Illona for a moment, and realized that the girl was a little overwhelmed by so many noble strangers. "Certainly—Illona, this is my father-in-law, *Dom* Gabriel Lanart. *Dom* Gabriel, this is Illona Rider, a friend of Nico's."

"Illona—that's a pretty name. Here, come sit beside me, girl. I am a little deaf these days, and I want you to tell me all about yourself." The older man smiled genially, and to Marguerida's surprise, the young woman grinned back at him.

She could sense Illona's fear start to recede, as if she found *Dom* Gabriel unthreatening. Well, he was very good with Yllana and with Rafael's daughter. She slid off the bench, circled around, and sat down on his other side, still clutching the soiled handkerchief in her hands. It took her a moment to realize that the girl was relieved to put a little distance between herself and Marguerida. She sighed. Her life had been so much simpler when she was just Ivor Davidson's faithful assistant, and she spent an indulgent moment thinking of that part of her past.

Then serving boys started to bring out platters of food, and she found her mouth watering. She had worked up quite an appetite, in spite of her worries, and *Dom* Gabriel was right. Marguerida swung her long legs over the bench, reached for a tankard of ale, and grinned fiercely. There was nothing she could do about the future except meet it—but not just yet.

24

Lew Alton paced back and forth in the entry hall of Comyn Castle, his boots ringing on the stonework. For the first time in many years, he wished he had a large glass of firewine, or were already drunk. He still occasionally drank wine, but he had not experienced such a strong desire for it in a long time. He was annoyed at his body for betraying his weakness to him, but pleased with himself for recognizing the signals of his own unease. Later, when it was over, perhaps he would indulge himself. He knew better than to try to work in a circle with his senses muddled by alcohol.

For the first time in centuries, perhaps since it had been constructed, Comyn Castle was nearly empty. It was an eerie feeling, the great pile of white stone no longer crammed with the energy of the nearly thousand people who usually inhabited it. Instead of the familiar minds of his many kinsmen, there was a circle of *leroni* from Arilinn, plus Rafe Scott, who had chosen to remain there instead of following the funeral procession to the *rhu fead*. Most of the servants had been given instructions to slip away as the funeral train departed, and the children had left right after the ceremony the previous day. Getting the children to a safe haven was, in his opinion, the most nervewracking part of the plan, and he had not been able to relax until he had received word of their safe arrival.

All he could do now was wait and wonder what would happen—if it did not drive him completely insane first! There were so many variables that no one could possibly anticipate, and Lew hoped they had covered the most important ones. Surely the spies of the Federation in Thendara had noticed *something*, even though every effort had been made to present the appearance of normality. Or perhaps Lyle Belfontaine was overconfident—it would be consistent with his character. Arrogant little man.

The mental stillness of the place was really getting on his nerves, and Lew made a conscious effort to calm himself. He would need to be in control when he joined the circle, when Belfontaine attacked, if he did. He would not permit himself to think about his daughter, riding into the jaws of danger, where he could not protect her. A bitter laugh rose in his throat. Marguerida had been looking after herself quite well for years now, and she had all the protection she needed in her husband. The Alton Gift, which he possessed, combined with Rafe's knowledge, was needed to make their part of the plan work, as Marguerida and Mikhail were needed for the attack on the train. It was rather late in the day to start having second thoughts. He sighed and ran the fingers of his remaining hand through his hair. The logic of their plan was perfect, but his mind still gnawed at it, looking for flaws.

The entry was very cold, and he was only going to wear himself out, with his pacing. Lew thought about Marguerida as he had last seen her, mounting her horse. Her skin had been pale in the flickering lights of the torches in the Stable Court, and her fine hair had curled around her brow in the damp morning air. There was nothing he could do for her now, so he might as well stop worrying. It had been blowing up for rain, and she was probably going to get wet. He hoped that was the worst she would suffer.

The castle was spooky, almost tomblike without its usual background noises—the random and inescapable thoughts of maids and servants bustling about at their duties. At that moment, he would even have welcomed the brittle and quarrelsome mental echoes of Javanne Hastur—a thought that brought a smile to his face. She had gone to Arilinn the previous day, too exhausted from the funeral to make more than a feeble protest. He felt his mood shift as he thought of Javanne. During the funeral the reality of her brother's death had finally hit her, and all of her anger and bravado had collapsed into sorrow. Her strength seemed to desert her like a puff of smoke, and when he had last seen her, she had to lean on her husband's arm just to walk.

It had been a tumultuous few days, and he found his thoughts going to Cisco Ridenow. He had not often encountered that dour man, with his pale hair and eyes like blue ice, since he had been appointed, against centuries of tradition, as head of the Guards. He found himself remembering how Cisco had entered the Crystal Chamber, taken in the shards of glass scattered around the perimeter of the room, the assorted weapons flung carelessly on the floor. His expression had been unreadable, his mind shuttered, but he had eyed each person seated around the table with caution, as if he were evaluating their military value and was not terribly impressed by what he found. He had listened intently, without surprise of any kind. And when he had spoken at last, the room had gone silent. "If they actually intend to attack the funeral train, then it seems likely that they will also attempt to occupy Comyn Castle—which we must prevent, obviously." He had glanced around at Lew, Mikhail, and Danilo, daring them to contradict him. When no one raised any objection, Cisco, never one to waste words, had gone on. "I have considered this possibility for some time, and I have a plan."

Mikhail had nodded, concealing any surprise. "Good. Tell us what you need." Where a moment before, there had been tension, a mood of calm now seemed to encompass the table. Whatever disagreements had existed in the past were forgotten for the present.

Cisco had spoken in short sentences, chopping off his words, and Lew realized that he had seriously underestimated the deviousness of the commander. The scheme he unfolded was a clever combination of military and *laran* talents. For someone with no actual experience in the field of combat, Cisco had a grasp of tactics worthy of the strategies of one who had fought a hundred campaigns. It was a daring and innovative scheme, and Lew had felt a deep admiration for the man.

The fact that the entire plan depended on a series of illusions was both pleasing and terrifying. First there was the illusion that all of the Castle Guards had left, and that the castle itself was nearly uninhabited. The City Guards were assigned to stay out of sight, adding to the impression that no attack was expected. And, knowing how easily baited Lyle Belfontaine was, Lew believed he would walk into the trap, that it would be just too tempting to forgo. And if he didn't, that would be fine as well.

Lew found himself remembering the exchange between Cisco and Marguerida when the man had hesitated at last. "I do not know what we can do against energy weapons, and I confess this has worried me for some days now."

"*Dom* Cisco, are you familiar with the original construction of Comyn Castle?"

"I do not quite follow you, *Domna*."

She gestured to the ruined telepathic dampers, gleaming in the light from the high windows. "When the castle was constructed, or at least when it was begun, it was very different than it is today."

"And how do you know this?"

"I still possess the memories of Ashara Alton who was, in many ways, the architect of this building. There are passages that have been closed up for years. Actually, there could almost be said to be two castles, one within the skin of the other. You could hide a thousand men in those corridors, if you had them and knew their locations. And there is more."

Cisco's eyes gleamed. "You have my undivided attention, *Domna* Marguerida." The others in the Comyn Council were equally interested, and even as weary as they were, they had leaned forward, bristling with curiosity.

Lew remembered the heightened color in Marguerida's cheeks as she went on. "I know that most of you think that Ashara placed much of her power in the Old Tower. But, she was a wary old bird; she loved control, and most of all, she wanted to keep herself secure. So she constructed this maze of a building, but the most devious and clever thing she did was to hide a number of large matrices at all the entrances."

"What the devil are you talking about?" That was from Francisco Ridenow, who was observing the interchange between his son and Marguerida with visible unease.

"The matrices are inactive at present, and they are well concealed behind the stonework." She lifted her left hand from the table. "I can bring them into life quite easily."

"And why have you never mentioned this remarkable fact until this moment?" Javanne demanded, her voice hoarse and weary.

"There was no need."

"And why has no one other than yourself been aware of these matrices?" Lady Marilla was not hostile, just curious and rather confused.

"I believe that Valenta Elhalyn is aware of them, and has been since she was a little girl. And I suspect that Regis knew of their existence as well."

"Nonsense. He would have mentioned it if he had known," snapped Javanne. "More, what use would they be against off-world weapons?"

"There is more than one way to skin a cat, Javanne," Marguerida had answered serenely, refusing to be baited. "And none of them are pleasant for the cat. What is the one thing that all humans hold in common?"

"I am too tired for stupid riddles, girl!"

"Of course you are, Javanne. I apologize." The older woman had looked shocked at this. Marguerida had taken a deep breath and gone on. "We are all of us, regardless of sex or position, possessed of fears, which, at times, can ride our minds like banshees." She had looked around the table then. "Most of the disagreements we have had in this room come from our fears, our thoughts of the terrible things that *might* happen. And what is a matrix except a device for amplifying thought? Our foes are just as fearful as we are, and by activating the guarding matrices at the entrances, we can enlarge the fears of our enemies, whatever they might be, can we not?"

"How?" Cisco was rubbing his callused hands together and looking almost gleeful now.

"The *leroni* will be coming into Thendara from Arilinn for the ceremony tomorrow. If they do not return there, but remain here, they can create a working circle, and wreck havoc on the minds of anyone who is stupid enough or foolish enough to try to attack Comyn Castle. No one is likely to fire a blaster when the ghost of his great grandmother is standing before him."

Cisco had nodded. "I see what you intend. But it will need someone with the Alton Gift to direct it, will it not?"

"I believe that I can do that," Lew had heard himself say. Everyone had stared at him for a moment, and a sense of hope had begun to come from the exhausted minds around the table. "In fact, I have been wanting to drive Lyle Belfontaine crazy for years!"

He paused in his pacing for a moment and looked up. He had walked through that entrance hundreds of times in his life, and he had never known or suspected that a large starstone had been hidden above the lintel. Until it had been activated, it had been invisible to him, and to anyone else. Lew suspected that Regis had known about the hidden defenses, at some deep level. As a living matrix, it was difficult to imagine he had not. But, like Marguerida, he had never seen fit to mention it to anyone. With good reason, he decided, since they could be used against some outside enemy, but in the wrong hands, they could have been turned against the inhabitants of the castle itself.

They were as ready as they could be now, with a hundred Guardsmen secreted in a hidden passage that ran from the barracks to an opening in the wall of the castle about fifty feet away from where he now stood, and the circle of *leroni* from Arilinn. Part of Lew hoped that Belfontaine would not attack the castle, but would stay behind the walls of HQ. His strength was less than it had been a few days before, because the City Guards had arrested a number of his men for brawling and locked them up in the old John Reade Orphanage. But another part of him rather wished that Belfontaine would attack, so he could pay off some old scores.

Enough. He had to calm himself, even if it killed him. Lew stomped out of the entry and into the reception room to one side. There was a fire roaring on the hearth, and a circle of chairs had been placed in front of it. Half were occupied by the men and women who had come from Arilinn, while the rest of them were standing or walking to and fro, as restless as he was himself. He gazed in amazement at one older woman who was placidly knitting by the fire, as if nothing was more important than keeping her stitches uniform.

"Stop fussing, Lew," Valenta said quietly, appearing beside him without warning, trying to match her short stride to his longer one. He had begun to pace again without noticing it. At twenty-eight the beauty she had possessed as a child had blossomed into its fullness. Her dark hair was braided and coiled around her head, and her skin shone with health. The rosebud mouth was poised as if at the start of a smile, and her dark eyes sparkled with her usual mischief, despite the tension all around them. When she put a hand on his forearm gently with the butterfly touch of the telepath, he could feel the power that radiated from her.

She was young enough to be his grandchild, but Lew found it impossible not to confide in her, as if she were a contemporary. "I can't help it, Val. I want to be here, but I want to be on the road at the same time, and I keep hoping all this effort will be in vain—that nothing will happen."

Val shook her head. "Well, of course that would be very nice, but you know as well as I do that something is going to happen. You don't have to have the Aldaran Gift for that. Why, even those without *laran* know something is up—the merchants have shuttered their businesses and the streets are nearly empty. More, I sense a clutter of energies advancing toward us, so I suggest you stop fretting and get ready to smash them like bugs."

"Bloodthirsty wench," he said fondly, aware now of the movement of minds toward the castle. He felt a flood of relief. The waiting was over, and now all they had to do was find out if their plan would work.

"Nonsense! With a little luck not a drop of blood will be spilled, and if it is, it will not be Darkovan blood." Valenta grinned, displaying perfect teeth, but sounding almost disappointed.

"Do you think our plan will work? I know it is rather late to be having second thoughts, Val, but can we really frighten a bunch of trained fighters with a few illusions and shadows?"

"They are just men, Lew, and all men and women are afraid of the darkness inside them. All we have to do is wake it up. Oh, they may have superior technology, but they do not know what we have, and that is our advantage." She gave a brief nod. "And with those trap matrices to increase the power of their imaginations, they will likely surrender without a shot being fired."

"You are probably right, and I am just being a worrier."

"Yes, yes, I know. At your age, you should be sitting by the fire, reading a book and smoking your pipe."

Lew glared at her, horrified at the image she presented. "That is not what I meant." Then he realized she was teasing him, and made himself smile back at her.

Rafe Scott walked into the room just then, his eyes narrowed with concentration. "Our roof spotters report about seventy Terrans marching toward the castle, dressed in Federation uniform. At least they are not disguising themselves, so we don't have to pretend we don't know who is coming to call."

"Seventy? That is fewer than I assumed. Armaments?"

"Standard issue side arms, battle helmets, combat suits, and two small energy cannon seems to be the extent of their armament."

"Cannon?"

"Yes, but don't worry. I remember the things being in Ordinance when I was still at HQ, and to the best of my knowledge, they have not been tested in at least a decade. They are probably more for show than for use, since I think that Belfontaine does not expect any real resistance."

"Is the City Guard in position?"

Rafe nodded. "They are behind the enemy, and out of sight. Belfontaine should have thought to cover his back, but he was always a headstrong fellow. If the troops try to retreat, they can be contained for a time, as long as they don't start shooting."

"When do you want to begin our work?" Val asked softly.

"We should probably start preparing now, but I would like them to get almost to the front door before we actually attack them," Lew answered, beginning to enjoy himself in spite of his persistent fears. At last he would have something concrete to do!

"That close?" She sounded a little doubtful.

"They have brought nothing which can breach these walls, Val, and I think that Belfontaine really expects an immediate surrender. All the cutbacks the Federation has imposed have left them without much in the way of advanced weaponry, and what they have is nearly obsolete, although on Darkover it is still pretty powerful." Rafe was so calm when he spoke that both of them were comforted.

"I wonder what Belfontaine's excuse for attacking the castle is going to be," Lew mused. "Is he with them, or has he stayed behind in the safety of HQ."

Rafe gave a muffled snort. "I saw him from the roof, strutting like a banty cock, all tarted out in a combat suit adorned with ribbons he never earned." He gestured to a longviewer hanging around his neck, an instrument he had requisitioned at HQ years before and had not returned when he retired. He often brought it to the castle and took the children up to the roof for the pleasure of being able to see all the way across Thendara. Lew could sense the amusement in Rafe's mind, and realized that he had his own scores to settle with Belfontaine.

Now Lew could sense the press of minds approaching through the nearly deserted streets, Belfontaine's among them. He exuded confidence even at this distance, not to mention a certain righteousness of purpose. His men did not entirely share his mood, however, and he noticed doubt here and there, little quivers of unease that he knew the waiting *leroni* would use to advantage.

This was not a strategy that Lew would ever have conceived, for it was an empath's plan, and he had never thought of that particular *laran* as something that could be used offensively. But Val was right—everyone had fears and terrors that could be roused with the right stimulus. His own did not require any help, and he cursed his imagination silently, then forced himself to stop.

"Let us begin." Val made a small gesture, and everyone took their places in the circle of high-backed chairs except the two women who were to be monitors. The old woman who had been knitting pushed her work into a bag and shoved it beneath her seat, then began to pull her matrix stone from beneath her soft robe. Lew found her movements very peaceful, and felt his own spirits begin to settle down.

Val moved to the chair in the center of the circle, sitting tidily. There was no sound except the crackle of the fire and the faint rustle of silk being removed, as gleaming matrix stones were revealed. One of the monitors tossed something into the hearth, and a pleasant smell started to waft around the room.

After several minutes Lew could sense the atmosphere in the chamber begin to shift, a coalescing of thought and energy, focused on Valenta. He had not worked in a circle in years, except for a couple of practice runs earlier in the day, and it felt unfamiliar yet right at the same time. And, really, he had nothing to do except use the Alton Gift to channel all this wonderful energy into the large matrices above the entrance. His breathing deepened, and he felt himself become enmeshed in the circle, without strain, as if he had been doing it every day for ages. Now they would see if matrix science could outdo the technological "advantage" of the Terranan. He chuckled deep in his chest. It really was an elegant plan, and if they got out of this in one piece, he was going to raise several cups to Cisco Ridenow's health.

Lyle Belfontaine strode along a narrow street, ignoring the raw day and the faint feeling of unease in the back of his mind. He was not worried about capturing Comyn Castle, for he was sure the servants that were left in the huge building would not try to stop him. It was the other, the assault along the road, that concerned him. He had sent orders for the attack the night before, and he knew that the forces from the Aldaran Domain had left there. He had had a lot of trouble with Commander Shen, who was in charge of the Federation troops in the Hellers. He was old-line military, from some family that had been serving the Federation for generations, and he had protested Lyle's orders. Some nonsense about attacking civilians without provocation. Belfontaine had insisted that the funeral train was harboring dangerous enemies of the Federation—namely Hermes Aldaran, but others as well—and Shen had finally, if reluctantly, agreed. With any luck at all, Shen and his honor would not survive. It was only a pity he could not reach Vancof and tell the scrawny assassin to make sure of that, but the shortbeam was not responding. How dare Shen question his orders!

It had taken several frustrating hours of transmissions back and forth before Shen had obeyed, and Lyle had wondered if the entire plan would fall apart from the failure of the technology they depended on. Cottman's star was going through one of its periods of sunspot activity, and that had interfered with the proper functioning of their equipment. And he wasn't worried about the actual attack on the funeral train—it would either work or it would not. No—it was the trail of transmissions which disturbed him more than a little—the evidence that could hang him if things went awry. But it was worth the risk, to pay back these stupid and stubborn people for refusing to join the Federation. They had brought this on themselves!

And there was always the possibility that the Federation would never know what he was about to do—that they would not come back to remove the personnel from HQ at all. When Granfell had made that suggestion a few days before, he had dismissed it. But now, as the silence from the relay station continued, Belfontaine was not so sure. Perhaps they would be abandoned. Well, if they were, he would have the planet in his own control.

There would be no one to challenge his authority. Granfell would be dead, if Vancof followed his orders, and so would anyone else who might dare to oppose him. Really, he should be more grateful to Miles, for coming up with the idea in the first place. A shame the man was not to be trusted. But he could not have a second-in-command who might be a traitor, could he?

Belfontaine had not been in this section of Thendara very often, for he rarely left the comfortable confines of the base. He looked at the buildings on either side of the street—wide for Cottman IV but narrow by the standards of any civilized city—their high stone walls looming above him. He saw the painted signs that hung out from the shops, and noticed that the shutters were drawn in. It did seem rather quiet for midday—the streets seemed almost empty of the normal traffic, and if anyone was alarmed by the sight of several squads of armed men marching along this avenue, there was no indication of it. Perhaps this was a day of mourning, after yesterday's funeral. He almost regretted that he had not attacked then, but he had had no idea that there would be such an event, one so public and vulnerable. He had not had time to organize an assault, and it was probably for the best. Less than a hundred men against the populace of Thendara and the Guard units were not odds that appealed to him.

Belfontaine's few spies had assured him that the funeral train had left that morning with everyone from the castle, including the Guardsmen, accompanying it. So why was he increasingly anxious? Could he trust his agents? What if someone had anticipated his attack, and made it appear that the castle was a ripe plum just waiting to be plucked? No, there was no one that clever, was there?

Ahead, he saw the gleaming white walls of Comyn Castle and his worries began to slip away. How he hated the building, which represented his failure to bring Cottman to heel for the Federation! It was payback time, and he felt exultation swell in his chest.

Then his previous anxiety returned. He almost felt as if the building were watching him, observing his march somehow. It was an eerie sensation, and Belfontaine realized his nerves were not as steady as he had previously thought. He almost wished that it were not empty, that he would have the opportunity to slaughter its obstinate, arrogant inhabitants. What victory was there in seizing an empty palace? A sour taste filled his mouth, and he knew that he would never have dared to attack Comyn Castle unless it was unguarded. This honest insight rattled him badly, and he gritted his teeth. He had to get a grip on himself!

He glanced at the readouts on his visor, little specks of light that encoded information, showing him the position of his men. It calmed him to see that, and the momentary self-awareness of fear faded away. He liked the smell of the helm, and the sense of command it gave him. With it, he could direct his men instantly, and also have a view of any opposition. Not that he expected any. The Castle Guards had gone with the funeral train, and he had arranged for trouble in the Horse Market to draw the City Guards to the other side of Thendara. So why did this litany of certainty fail to reassure him?

It was too quiet—that was what was getting on his nerves! There should be people in the streets, even if it was a day of mourning. He swallowed the foul taste in his mouth.

It was actually better this way, Belfontaine told himself almost desperately now. Dead civilians tended to arouse the interest of Boards of Inquiry, and if he could manage a bloodless coup, it would be to his advantage. He wished he knew more about the actual layout of the Castle. He had tried to find out, during the years, and he knew that by repute it was a regular warren of corridors and rooms, large enough to hide a thousand men. Except that even if one combined all the City and Castle Guards, they did not number that many.

There was something uncanny about the white building ahead of him. Was that someone on the roof? No, just a shadow. But he looked at the surrounding buildings, at the rooflines of the nearest ones, trying to see if there were any watchers there. Supposedly, his combat helm should have indicated the presence of anyone, the heat of their bodies making a signal, but the local stone seemed to block that function. Typical— whenever you really needed them, machines let you down. It was some kind of law, wasn't it?

Quelling his rising anxiety, Lyle Belfontaine advanced, his boots and those of his company making a steady beat against the cobblestones of the avenue. It was a regular, rhythmic sound, and it began to steady his nerves. He knew that men going into combat were often nervous, and decided that he must be experiencing that. It was nothing to be concerned over.

Now he stood at the bottom of two flights of wide stairs, leading up to the main doors of Comyn Castle. For a moment he stood and gazed at the great carved doors, allowing himself the pleasure of anticipating their destruction. He barked a command into his helm, and two squads started to move up the stairs. It was all going just as he had planned, and he let himself grin behind his visor.

He was admiring their efficient progress, the splendid way they moved together as the squads advanced up the first flight of stairs. Then the men seemed to hesitate, and he saw one man bat his helm with a gauntleted hand, as if trying to get the mechanism to function correctly.

Before he could wonder what was happening, he felt an itch begin to crawl across his scalp beneath the helmet. It seemed to have a lot of legs—some sort of insect. How could the damn thing have gotten under his helm? And he could not get at it without taking the accursed thing off! He shook his head to one side, trying to dislodge whatever it was, and felt the itching increase. It seemed like several large crawly things were on his scalp, and his skin began to roughen in the warmth of the combat suit. Visions of centipedes began to rise in his mind, the sort that were common on Lein III. Perhaps the suits had become infested with some local insect, and the heat of his body had roused them. He held back a shudder and tried to concentrate on the readouts again.

Something was wrong! Where a minute before he could place every one of the eighteen soldiers on the steps without actually looking at anything except the dots of colored light in his display, now eight of them were gone! Simply vanished! Stupid machinery! The things were supposed to be foolproof, but of course they would go off-line just when they were most needed. Damn the Federation for giving him old equipment, years out of date! He shook the helm with both hands—there must be a loose connection. His attempt to fix things did not improve matters at all.

A thin, wailing sound came over the comlink, nearly deafening Belfontaine as the scream pierced his eardrums for several seconds before bubbling into silence. Then all the displays in his helm burst into life, leaving dazzling spots dancing before his aching eyes. There were shouts all around him, penetrating the thick insulation of the helm. A sputter of light surged again, and then the helm went dead. The nasty stink of burning insulation rose in his nose, and he tried to pull the thing off without disengaging the toggles that held it to his combat suit. Smoke began to cloud the visor as he scrabbled to release the clasps that held the helm in place.

After what felt like an eternity, but was actually only a few seconds, Belfontaine managed to get his gloved fingers around the toggles and undo them. He pulled his helmet off and gasped for air. The cold wind chilled his skin, but it felt wonderful for a moment. His eyes teared with the combination of smoke and wind, and he blinked to clear them.

A scene of chaos met his burning eyes. He stared in astonishment as the eighteen men who had reached the landing between the two flights of stairs screamed and tore at their helms and protective garments. He watched expensive helmets being smashed against stones, and saw one man ram his fingers into his own eyes. Several others turned and started to run down the stairs toward him.

"Stop!" His command was borne away on the wind, and it had no effect. A trooper dashed past him, discarding his weapons as he ran, screaming lustily. The eyes of the man seemed glazed and vacant, and a line of spittle drooled from the gaping mouth. Belfontaine reached out to restrain him, but the man just pushed him away, knocking him down so hard that all the air left his lungs.

The combat suit protected him, but Belfontaine could feel the impact of the fall. Dazed, he watched the troopers still on the landing dance around, pulling off their suits, screaming and vomiting. Then he turned and looked behind him, to find that the rest of his small force had gone mad as well.

He tottered to his feet, desperately trying to regain his own control. The suit suddenly felt too hot, and remembering how his helm had shorted out, he looked down to see if there were any telltale wisps of smoke. It became hotter and hotter, until it was intolerable, although he could see nothing wrong. *Get out of the suit!*

Belfontaine pulled at the closures, and felt the suit slip down his body, puddling around his knees and leaving him in his thermal under-suit. The brisk wind cooled his overheated body quickly, and he tried to understand what was happening.

You always were worthless, Lyle. You were a failure from the day you were born! He heard the words and knew the voice, even as his mind rejected them. Then he saw the speaker standing in front of him, his tall and powerful father, sneering at him and making him feel smaller than he was. The vision was transparent at first, but then it solidified and began to move closer. Reflexively, he lifted his arm to deflect the blow he anticipated, now totally unaware of the actions of his troopers around him.

He cowered before the image of his father, trying to make his voice work, to say anything that would keep him safe. But his throat was closed with terror, and he felt his bowels loosen. The smell wafted upward, and Belfontaine trembled with shame.

Then, as suddenly as it had appeared, the vision of his father vanished, and he could see that there were men sitting on the landing, sobbing or screaming. He turned to look at the rest of his troopers, and saw that most of them were in retreat. And worse, riding toward them, was a company of City Guards. Were they insane, to ride against energy weapons? Then he saw that none of his soldiers were even reaching for their blasters—they were too busy jumping around and trying to get out of their suits. This damn planet was driving them crazy!

Before he could quite grasp this new development, he heard another sound, of stone sliding over stone, and turned toward the noise. An opening had appeared in the wall of the castle, to one side of the great doors, and the Castle Guards he had been assured were gone poured out.

Belfontaine reached to his side, where a blaster should have been, and felt his fingers brush against the weave of his thermal undergarment. He leaned down to the discarded combat suit which lay around his ankles, trying to find the weapon.

Hello, little man.

The words boomed in his mind, echoing like cannons, familiar and not at the same time. It was too much, and for the first time in his life, Lyle Belfontaine fainted.

When consciousness returned, Belfontaine found himself lying on a long couch, his battle gear gone. There was a pleasant fire in a huge maw of stone, and the smell of Cottman balsam drifted out from it. He lay in his fouled thermals, dazed and bewildered.

There was a faint rustle of fabric, and he turned his head in the direction of the sound. A dark-haired woman in a jewel-red garment came into view. It fell in soft folds around her slender form as she walked toward him, a soft veil fluttering from the top of her head. "Feeling better?"

He stared at her, for a moment incapable of comprehending the question. Belfontaine's command of the local language had never been very good, and in his present muddled condition, it abandoned him entirely for a few seconds. Then he understood and nodded, sitting up so quickly that his head swam. She was small, no taller than he was, and young enough to be his daughter, but clad only in his soiled thermals, he felt helpless and vulnerable. And disgusting—he stank of sweat, fear, and worse.

The sound of boots on stone came in from behind the couch, and Belfontaine turned around to see who it was. Lew Alton, grinning like a fiend, appeared. If he had not lost his weapons, he would have blasted the hateful man right then.

"You have always wanted to see the inside of Comyn Castle, haven't you, Lyle, and now you have achieved your ambition," Alton said gravely. "Would you care for a glass of wine?"

For a moment this barefaced effrontery robbed Belfontaine of the power of speech. Then he snarled, "What are you doing here? I thought you left with . . . and what did you *do* to me and my men?"

"I did not do anything to you, little man. All your troubles you have brought on yourself. Now, about the wine. I am going to have some, and I suggest you do the same." Lew walked to a small table and poured two glasses. Then he looked at the silent woman. "Would you like some, too, Val?"

"Yes, I believe I would," she answered. Alton poured another, then picked one up and handed it to her. He placed the remaining glasses on a small tray and moved toward Belfontaine.

Little man. That was what he had heard just before he . . . no, he did not want to think about that. Belfontaine was sure he had heard Lew's voice, but not in the air. There was a different resonance. He must have shouted over some sort of device, some primitive thing, an ancient loud-speaker probably. He had only thought he heard the words in his mind. The whole thing must have been an illusion due to his agitated state.

The smugness of the man was infuriating. There had to be a way to penetrate Lew Alton's arrogant triumph. But he felt so weak, confused and mortified that it was hard to muster up enough strength to focus his mind. It was as if all his emotions except fear, had faded into shadows. Yes, he was most definitely afraid, but he was damned if he was going to let it show.

He took the offered glass, forcing his sluggish mind to work. There had to be a reasonable explanation for all this. There was no way a bunch of backwater primitives could have defeated trained troops so easily. He sipped a little of the wine and racked his brain.

The combat suits had been sabotaged in some manner—that must be it! Some of the native personnel must have done it, though he could not imagine how. And now he was a prisoner. It had never occurred to him that he might fail, and he remembered how his father had appeared and called him worthless. It was all impossible! The silence in the room weighed on him.

"I thought you were with the funeral train," he muttered, hating the whine in his own voice, and still trying to find some sense in the whole mess. The train! How much time had passed? He could not tell, and there was no clock that he could see. The train had left at daybreak, and he had waited for several hours before he began his assault. He shuddered at his realization of the failure of it. By now the ambush should have taken place, and no one but he knew that most of the members of the Comyn Council were likely dead. The troops from the Hellers would not be wearing Federation combat suits, so they would be immune to this unexpected treachery. Yes, he could definitely salvage something.

Belfontaine bit his lower lip. He longed to announce what he knew, to wipe the smug expression off Alton's scarred and wrinkled face, to tell him that his daughter was dead! But he must not waste his advantage so cheaply. Let him think he had the upper hand for a time. The wine was rather good, and it seemed to be clearing his mind slowly.

"I am sure you did, but since I expected you to come calling, I decided to be a good host and await you."

"You . . . expected . . . me?" The wine turned to vinegar in his mouth.

"Of course. You convinced yourself that Comyn Castle would be an easy target. You have always underestimated us, Lyle. It is your fatal flaw."

"Fatal? What are you going to do to me?"

"Why, you will be my guest for a time." Lew Alton's face was solemn, but there was a light in the Comyn lord's eyes that made Belfontaine uneasy." And later, I am going to turn you over to the Federation—always assuming they come back for you—and let them deal with you. Of course, when my son-in-law returns, he may have some other ideas—nothing too terribly barbaric, I assure you."

That was too much! He could not stand it a second longer. "You will have to wait a long time, then, because he is not coming back! He's dead, and so is everyone else in that party!"

Alton appeared unmoved, not the least bit afraid. "Now, now, Lyle. It would have been much wiser not to have admitted knowledge of that. Much wiser."

Belfontaine felt the blood drain from his face. His ears rang, and he felt nauseous. With a great effort he swallowed the saliva that filled his mouth and screamed, "You stupid bastard—your daughter is dead!"

To his fury and amazement, Lew Alton did not react except to appear mildly amused. "No, little man, she most definitely is not!"

25

The carriage rattled along, and Domenic shifted back and forth on his bench. He was riding with his back to the driver, and the forward movement of the vehicle threatened to unseat him. Across from him, Herm and Katherine were silent, each lost in their own thoughts. It did not take *laran* to be able to tell they had much to talk about, and Domenic wished he had gone in the carriage with Illona and his grandfather Gabriel, so they could have the privacy they clearly needed.

"Please, it's clear you have much to discuss," he finally told them, unable to endure their tense silence any longer. "If you can pretend I'm not here, I'll try my best not to listen." Then he turned and looked through the window, watching the thighs of the Guardsman who was riding beside the vehicle.

Herm gave a sort of grunt, a sound Domenic was now very familiar with. "I wish it were that easy, nephew."

Katherine turned and studied her husband. "It *is* that easy, except that you don't want to talk to me—you just want to charm me into forgetting the past few days. Domenic is not the problem, Herm. *You are.*"

"What has gotten into you, Kate? I said I was sorry!" *I go away for a*

446

*few days and when I see her again, she seems like a different person—one I
don't know at all.*

"Sorry is not enough, and you know it!" She paused, seeming to
gather her resolve and perhaps her nerve, and then went on. "Why are
you such a *runaway?*"

"*What?*" Herm turned a deep shade of red, as if her words had hit
some mark that shamed him.

"Well, aren't you? Don't you try to sidestep getting close to anyone,
even me? I don't know why I didn't realize it before. No, that's not true.
I did know it, and it was one of the reasons I married you—the more fool
I."

"You are going to have to explain that, Katherine, because I am completely lost."

"I know it sounds ironic, but it seems that I never understood myself
until I came to Darkover—why I am uncomfortable with most people. I
married you, Hermes-Gabriel Aldaran, partly because I was so comfortable with you—and now that I'm here I've realized that the reason that I
was more at ease with you than with other people is that you are remote!
Oh, you are sweet and loving and utterly devoted, but there is a part of
you that is always held back. That part made me feel unthreatened, but
now things are so different! If we are going to mend this marriage, you
have to change!"

Domenic wished he could stop his ears—he was trying not to listen—
but he was fascinated at the same time. Was this the sort of thing his
parents said to each other when they were alone? It must be, since he
knew both Mikhail and Marguerida were very strong and stubborn people, and they could not have managed their years of marriage without
some sort of argument. It gave him a new and not entirely pleasant insight
into the relationship between the two most important people in his life.

"Remote?" Herm sounded peevish, and almost childish now.

"Yes, and withholding, too! Or do you believe that this 'hale fellow
well met' you pretend to be is the real Hermes?"

The man squirmed and knitted his fingers together. Then he swallowed hard and replied, "I avoid introspection whenever possible."

"Then you had better stop avoiding it, or else I am going to . . . well,
I'm not sure. Perhaps I will join the Painters Guild and leave you. Or let
your brother support me for the rest of my years. Even though you have
exiled me to this strange world, I am not without options!"

"You are asking me to change who I am. I don't know if that is realistic. I don't know if I can."

"I want you to try. I will not be shut out again, nor abandoned, Herm. You should get that through your thick Aldaran head right now!"

"It isn't enough that I love you?"

"Not nearly, *cario*." The term of endearment did not take the sting out of her demand, and Domenic held back a smile, lowering his head a little so his mouth was concealed. He realized he was learning something important about being an adult, although he could not quite understand it yet.

"What do you want of me, Kate?" He seemed humble now, sincere and a bit afraid.

"I want you to grow up! No more games and schemes, and no more secrets, at least not from me!"

Herm looked downcast for a minute, and Nico tensed, waiting for his response. "I don't know who I am without my plots and schemes, Katherine."

"Then it is about time you started finding out."

The man gave a great sigh. "Do you know how much I hate it when you are right?"

"Yes." Kate reached over and put her hand on his interlocked fingers. "If I did not love you so much, I would not be bothering, you know."

"What did I ever do to deserve you?" He bowed his head.

Katherine leaned over and kissed his shiny pate. "You were born under some lucky star, I suppose," she murmured.

Domenic yawned, not from tiredness, but to release the tension in his jaw. It was amazing—they had both been very angry at each other just a few minutes before, and now it was over, for the moment. He suspected that the matter was not completely settled, that Kate would have to chide her husband again and again. But peace had been restored, and he felt he had learned a lesson. He wished he could ask his mother about it, but that would mean revealing what had passed between his uncle and Katherine, and he would not do that. After chewing over it mentally for several seconds, Domenic let it go and he turned his attention outward. He scanned the minds of the Guardsmen riding beside the carriage, and then reached for those more distant ones he knew waited beyond.

* * *

At the head of the slow-moving train Mikhail and Marguerida rode side by side. They were both tense and alert, and around them, the mood of the Guards was grim. The sound of hooves, the jingle of bridles, and the occasional snort of mount or bray of mule were the only noises which punctuated an increasingly oppressive silence. Marguerida swallowed in a dry throat, the taste of one of MacHaworth's excellent fowl pies lingering in her mouth, and hummed a scale. Mikhail glanced at her when he heard the tones, smiling just a little.

The midday meal had been chaotic, noisy and almost fevered, as if everyone realized that it might be their last, and was determined to make the most of it. She was relieved to have Domenic back, and was glad she had persuaded him to ride in one of the carriages instead of on horseback. It was not much protection, but at least he would be out of sight during the actual fighting. She hoped she was right. It was easier to worry about her son than to think about what awaited them up the road.

Rafaella had been able to give them a clear idea of exactly where the ambush would most likely come. She and the rest of her Renunciates had been doing a good deal of quiet spying since the previous evening, and at least they had a fair idea of the number and location of the enemy. What they did not know, and what worried Marguerida and Mikhail most, was what sort of weaponry they would be facing. Rafi said that the men were dressed in Darkovan clothing, and seemed to have cudgels and short swords. But Marguerida was unable to completely convince herself that the Federation forces would not try to use their superior weaponry against the funeral train.

She took a deep breath and drew her mind into a less stressful channel. Marguerida knew she had to conserve her energies for the attack, that she would need all her wits about her, and if she started imagining blaster bolts, she would be exhausted by the time they reached their foes. Instead, she turned her thoughts to Illona Rider, who might or might not be a child of Dyan Ardais.

It was clear from the way Dyan had behaved that he was reluctant to acknowledge the girl. Marguerida had never completely understood him, after all it was no shame to father *nedestro* children, and all Darkovan children were so very precious! He should have rejoiced to know that another child of his lived! Something would have to be done about Illona, whether or not Dyan acknowledged her. She sighed. Fostering was the obvious answer, but she was not sure she wanted to take on another adolescent herself. Alanna was enough trouble already, and she had the suspicion that her difficult charge would not be pleased to have a rival for the affections of those around her. More, Marguerida was fairly certain that Nico would be caught between the two girls.

She remembered what people had said to her so long ago: "An untrained telepath is a danger to herself and everyone around her."

The girl needed training, too. And she did not doubt that Domenic was correct in his guess that Illona had the Alton Gift. Marguerida had felt the girl's nascent *laran*, and it was enough like her own to make her believe her son. But she did not think that Arilinn would be a very friendly place for a Traveler child, and she suspected that after a few rebuffs from the other students there, Illona would simply run away. No, she must either foster the girl herself or send her someplace like Tramontana. And fretting about it now was not doing her any good at all.

Against her better judgement, Marguerida turned her mind back to the present. Had they thought though all the possibilities? Could they protect enough of their own people with the combined energies of her matrix and Mikhail's to halt the attack? They had tried to test the limits of their powers, and knew that it could stop an arrow easily. It had been a nerve-racking experience for them, and even more so for the hapless Guardsman who was asked to aim his bow toward them. But whether it would be able to stop a blaster was another matter entirely. It was really a shame that the Command Voice was such a limited resource, that it did not reach beyond a hundred feet with any reliability. They had decided not to risk that, since it would affect friend and foe alike, leaving those outside its influence free to do as they wished.

Marguerida shifted in the saddle, turned, and looked behind her. She found Francisco Ridenow riding a few lengths back, and remembered that Kate had told her to keep an eye on him. Then she turned ahead again, and strained her distance sense to its utmost. She had done this several times already, but this time she was rewarded with the faint glimmer of mental energies about a mile beyond. It was still too far for her to distinguish individual minds, or to discover anything really useful from them.

You are doing fine, caria.

Thank you for the reassurance. I feel like I am going to explode at any moment.

Well, you do resemble a kettle about to come to the boil—but a fine kettle, indeed.

I never thought that being likened to a pot would seem so . . . loving!

They rode in companionable silence for a few minutes, each lost in their own thoughts.

Mother!

Yes, Nico.

I can hear that Vancof now—he's not with the rest, but is in a thicket where he can see us coming. A lookout, I guess. And he seems a bit surprised at our numbers, and is starting to worry. He's trying to decide whether to retreat and tell the main party, or stay where he is. Well, he really wants a drink, and he is very worried, mostly about his own skin. He's wishing that he had run off days ago, that he wasn't under orders, that Granfell was dead—a lot of jumbled thoughts. Hmm . . . I am getting the impression that there is some sort of division.

Division?

He's remembering some argument last night, between Granfell and the head of the soldiers from the Hellers, Commander Shen. It is not really clear, but I think that maybe this Shen was brought down here with orders he doesn't like, or that maybe he doesn't like the whole situation. Sorry I am not able to be clearer, but Vancof's mind is not very focused. Part of him wants to be anywhere else but where he is, but the rest needs to find out what is going to happen. It is as if he is paralyzed with indecision and curiosity at the same time.

Well, perhaps Shen is more honorable than Granfell and does not think that attacking civilians is right.

It is something about the nature of the orders they received, I think. Maybe this Shen fellow just doesn't want to get caught doing something the Federation would punish him for. I wish I could tell you better.

You have already done a great deal, Nico. Thank you, my little spy.

Marguerida cleared her throat, annoyed by how taut her muscles were, and told Mikhail and Danilo Syrtis-Ardais, who was riding on her right, what she had just learned. She felt buttressed by the two men, as well as by the comforting bulks of the Guardsmen riding around them. "That is useful to know," was Danilo's only comment.

"I would give a great deal to learn exactly what the nature of the orders was, if this mess ever gets sorted out."

"What do you mean, Mik?" It was such a relief to speak, to let her tension express itself, however minimally.

"Who gave these orders? Was it Granfell or Belfontaine?"

"Why does that matter?"

"I think that Mikhail means that if Granfell is in charge, then Belfontaine can say he knew nothing about this, but if he gave the orders, and it ever becomes public, the Federation is going to be in a real situation." Danilo spoke very slowly, as if he were puzzling it out even as he spoke.

"I don't see that it matters, one way or the other, if the Federation is leaving Darkover anyhow." Marguerida spoke sharply.

"Perhaps. But what if they do not? It is going to be difficult to explain either way—not to mention our part in things."

Marguerida shrugged, trying to keep herself from being drawn into new worries. "They have given us the perfect reason—the funeral train was attacked by bandits, and they were slain."

"I hope so. But we have to consider that the Federation might change its mind, and decide that we somehow provoked them."

"Stop. We cannot start second guessing now, Mikhail," Danilo said crisply. "Let's just get through this alive, and worry about the outcome afterward."

Donal, who was riding on Mikhail's left, gave a little bark of unexpected laughter. "You mean 'Kill them all and let the gods sort it out'?" he asked.

"Something like that," Danilo replied, looking a little embarrassed by this blunt pronouncement.

The nearest Guardsmen suddenly grinned, as if they rather liked the sentiment the young paxman had expressed. Faint chuckles rose from tense throats, and the grim mood lifted for a moment. Everyone seemed to take a breath, as if their lungs were aching for air, before settling back into vigilance.

Mikhail gave Donal a look of mixed approval and apprehension and shifted in his saddle. Then he turned his eyes toward his wife. *This all feels so unreal, as if we were . . .*

In some old poem, beloved? 'Into the Valley of Death rode the Six Hundred . . .'

That's it! I could not put my finger on it, and it has been driving me frantic.

This is not a poem, and we are not *riding into the Valley of Death, my* cario. *This is very real. And people will die this day, not the least poetically.* Marguerida could feel the sternness of her thoughts, and the conflict beneath them.

How . . .?

I had a brief flash and saw bodies, but whose I cannot say, except that neither yours nor Nico's were amongst them.

And you?

I hardly think I could have seen what little I did without knowing of my own death, Mikhail. Marguerida refused to let herself think about the possibility that she might have been dead in her own vision and never have known it. That was too frightening.

Now they were within a quarter mile of the waiting enemy, although there was nothing except the silence of the birds to suggest anything unusual. They could see no figures in the trees ahead, nor any movement. But Marguerida could pick up the tension of the ambushers, even if she could not sort them out individually. Here and there were a few focused thoughts—from seasoned veterans, she suspected. Was this Shen among them, and could she discover him?

And what might she do if she did? She turned over several ideas in her own mind, wondering if she could use the Alton Gift at this distance on someone she had never encountered in her life. She rather doubted it would be effective, and it probably would not stop the attack. There did not seem to be any way out of their peril, and she knew she should just stop looking for other avenues.

At last she faced herself, and looked fiercely at the real problem with their plan. It had seemed perfectly fine back in the Crystal Chamber, but her husband was going to use his incredible powers in a way he never had before—he was a healer, and now he intended to be a destroyer. She shuddered suddenly. She did not want to kill anyone, and neither did Mikhail!

Part of her wanted to relieve him of the terrible responsibility, to take it on her own shoulders. But she knew she must not, that they must share the outcome together. Mikhail would never be able to forgive her if she tried to protect him now. She had to let him do this thing which ran against the grain, against everything he had stood for since he received Varzil's ring. Her own powers could do a great deal of damage, but it was Mikhail's that would ultimately decide the day. He was the ruler of Darkover now, and that meant she had to let him do what was needed, for anything else would unman him.

This was, she thought wryly, a fine time to be having second thoughts. Marguerida examined her sudden spate of ethical considerations, chided herself for not thinking of them earlier, and decided that she would just have to live with the consequences. Donal was right. Let the gods sort it out. The only problem—there never seemed to be any around when they were needed.

Then, with a flash of insight, she knew that Mikhail was experiencing his own struggle, too. If it was hard for her, how much more difficult must it be for him? Neither of them were at all bloodthirsty, and the idea of killing the men still secreted among the trees, even if they were enemies, was morally repugnant. But she would do the deed, and suffer the consequences of conscience another day.

Still, it was hard. Marguerida forced herself to accept things as they were, rather than as she wished they might be, and finally felt herself let go of her reluctance. Her doubts remained, gnawing at the back of her mind, but she shushed them sternly, and turned her attention back to the small wooded draw where the enemy waited. She sensed alertness, fear, excitement, and after several moments, something else. What was it?

Hesitation, she decided at last, from one mind among so many. Was this Commander Shen? In view of the little information Domenic had given her, it seemed a likely conjecture. Marguerida had the impulse to try to influence that faint but discernible emotion, to nudge this unknown person into a peaceable direction. It would have been a delicate thing to manage with someone she knew well, and nearly impossible with a stranger, but she was tempted. If only she could speak to this person, she could use the Command Voice. Surely it would be better for the enemy to withdraw without engaging—lives could be saved.

The opportunity passed. She felt the stranger quell his doubts, harden his resolve, and determine to give the order. "They are going to attack, Mik," she said quietly.

"Was there ever any doubt of it?" His voice was thick with tension.

"Yes, for a few moments, there was."

"Damn!"

"I know. But somehow we will come out of it. . . ."

"This is going to change everything—I can feel that now!" *And the worst part is, I think Varzil foresaw this. It was more than just getting the ring*

away from Ashara when he died—he said that it had to exist now for the
future of Darkover! I wish it were not so. I will not be the same person after
today, and I do not know if I can live with that . . . but I must.

Marguerida glanced at her husband for a moment, wondering what
he meant. And then she knew, had always known, but had concealed it
from herself, to protect herself from the pain this day would bring her
husband and herself. This was their destiny, hers and Mikhail's. It gave
her a terrible feeling of helplessness, as if she had never had a choice.
Fate had put a finger on her life, and the best she could do was try to
survive it. Since that day, years before, when she had returned to Darkover, had set her foot down on the tarmac of the spaceport and crossed
from the Terran Sector into Thendara, she had been preparing for this
moment in time. And Mikhail too. That she could accept, although it cost
her, but there were others involved, and she experienced a flash of fury
that her strange destiny must include them. There was nothing fair about
it, she decided, and then ruthlessly closed her mind to further rumination.

Dirck Vancof lowered the longviewer and wiped a bead of moisture
from his brow. In spite of the cold breeze blowing across the rise he had
chosen to sight from, he was sweating like a pig. His guts were knotted,
and his head pounded. He shook his head. The train was much better
guarded than he had expected, and he had a sinking sensation, one he
knew all too well. He never should have gotten involved with Granfell's
insane plan.

Then, almost magically, everything became completely clear to him.
If he stayed where he was, he was going to get killed. He was torn with
indecision for a moment—should he just take off into the woods and
fields beyond? The idea of spending the rest of his life on this chilly hell
of a planet was vile. Worse, without the Travelers to conceal him, he had
few resources. Yes, he could pass for a native, but he was sick and tired
of Darkover, and had been for five years now.

A slow grin began to grow. He turned and started down the hill,
toward the encampment where the techs had set up their equipment. He
knew what he had to do now, and it was so obvious and so simple that
he could hardly believe it had taken him so long to think of it. To hell
with all of them, Granfell and Belfontaine—he was going to take care of
Mother Vancof's little boy.

Halfway down the hill, he saw Miles Granfell climbing toward him, and he smiled to himself. The fool had no idea that Belfontaine had ordered him to kill Granfell, and the man was going to make it easy. His miserable luck was changing at last.

"I was coming to get you," Granfell told him as he drew near. With a nod, Vancof moved down the hill a few feet more, and then, without a wasted movement, he plunged a knife into Granfell's throat, using the incline of the slope to compensate for the other man's greater height. He glimpsed a flicker of surprise in the gray eyes, and there was a spasm of movement from his hands. A bubbling gurgle came from the gaping mouth as blood gushed from the wound and spilled down onto his garment. Then Granfell's knees buckled, and he went down, sliding down the hill until his body encountered a tree.

Vancof walked over to the corpse, bent down to make certain the bastard was really dead, and yanked out the knife. He wiped the blade on Granfell's tunic, and kicked the dead man's torso for good measure. Then he strolled away, whistling under his breath.

A few minutes later he reached the encampment and looked around casually, as if he did not have a care in the world. Most of the troops were already in position, and the only people he saw were a few techs waiting for something to happen. They paid no attention when he strolled toward the two heavy flyers that had ferried them down from the Hellers the night before.

He entered the unguarded door of the closest one, pressed the button to close it behind him, and walked toward the controls. It took no more than a few seconds to sit down and punch the controls into life— the machine was easy to operate and he had flown them before. The engine hummed as he set the coordinates for the spaceport in Thendara.

Vancof heard a dull thump against the closed door of the vehicle, and, very faintly, a shout. Then the flyer lifted effortlessly off the ground and he was aloft, soaring over the trees. He had a last glimpse of the encampment, and of the funeral train stretched along the road. For a second he thought he saw something explode on the road, and wondered what was happening. He gave a shrug and sped away into the air.

Marguerida heard Danilo exclaim beside her. She saw he was pointing into the sky and she saw the shimmering outline of a flyer for a moment, rising above the trees. Almost before she had time to wonder if they were going to be assaulted from above, she heard the howl of voices, and a group of men burst out of the trees ahead of her. They were dressed in Darkovan clothing, muted brown or green tunics, their faces concealed under scarves. They charged into the foremost Guardsmen, swinging thick sticks at the legs of the horses.

But the Guards did not lose control. Instead, they pulled their mounts together, using them as both a defense and an offense. The horses reared and kicked out at the attackers, and at the same time their large bodies protected their riders for a few moments. The Guardsmen began to wield their swords and spears efficiently, cutting at heads and shoulders. There was the twang of bowstrings, and a flight of arrows arced into the trees. From the cries, several found their marks.

Clever, she thought, as she yanked her hand free of her riding glove, then pulled the silken mitt beneath it away. It was almost exactly what real bandits would have done, if they were on foot against men on horses. Behind her she could hear shouting, as the drivers of the wagons and carriages pulled their vehicles into defensive positions around the horse-drawn hearse which bore the body of Regis Hastur and the coaches containing the noncombatants. At the rear of the train, the doors of several carriages opened, and the men who had hidden within them, waiting for just this moment, bolted out.

A second rush of attackers surged from beneath the trees, and she could hear the shrieking of frightened horses. Marguerida extended her hand, palm upward, rejecting the panic that threatened to seize her, and saw Mikhail's ungloved hand steady above it. As her matrix grounded and supported his, there was no doubt, no hesitation, nothing but a sureness of purpose that calmed her instantly and filled her with an almost euphoric bond of unity as they began to build the wonderful cone of power that only they could create between them.

Light burst from the gleaming jewel on Mikhail's hand, rising up toward the clouded sky, surrounding her, then widening into a globe of shimmering energy that would protect them, the body of Regis, and those in the guarded coaches. Marguerida slipped into the sensation of completeness that was the joining of her power with that of Mikhail, all the love that they had given one another over the years poured into a single certainty.

She caught fragments of thought as if from a great distance, but the terror within them barely reached her. It was just a jumble of energy, and Marguerida saw it as a whirl of colors, sickly yellows and greens.

The thick sticks fell to the ground, and swords were cast down. The Guardsmen seized the moment and charged the momentarily paralyzed men, and slew a few before stubby metal objects appeared from beneath the muffling garments. There was a bright flash from one then, and a Guardsman fell back with a large hole in his chest. His horse reared and kicked at the attacker, and there was another blast, catching the mount in the muzzle. It fell on the enemy as it died, its weight pinning the man to the earth, while he screamed with fury.

Mikhail drove his thoughts through his matrix, drawing on Marguerida's supportive energy. A broad beam of light snapped from the blinding facets, wove out from the protective bubble, and fanned across the oncoming fighters. Guardsmen yanked their horses aside, for Mikhail's weapon could not distinguish friend from foe, and they had been forewarned. It flickered into the cluster of now firing troopers like lightning, searing the men so quickly they could not think to escape its scorching touch.

Everything seemed to slow to a crawl, and all Marguerida could do was endure the hideous vision that opened before her eyes. The dull metal weapons disintegrated, and then the men who held them seemed to . . . fall to pieces. Mikhail had reversed his healing ability, and now he was undoing the very sinews of the enemy. Blood flowed from every bodily orifice, as torsos collapsed in on themselves, the ground was a river of blood as men turned to ghouls then to corpses in a matter of moments.

There was confusion everywhere now, with the Guardsmen desperately scrambling to get out of the reach of Mikhail's deadly energy, and those who remained of the first attackers running blindly in every direction. The men who had only started to emerge from the cover of the trees were caught unprepared, and had no time to save themselves. The baleful light from Mikhail's hand spread across the thicket, blasting everything it touched. The conifers went up like torches, and the smell of burned flesh mingled with the hot tree resin, as the ground turned from red to black with bloody ash. Those few more fortunate foes who were beyond the range of this destruction were being ridden down by the Guardsmen.

Fire began to leap from tree to tree now, the rich sap of the evergreens feeding its hunger, adding to the confusion. Now Marguerida could clearly hear screams of pain and fear, and they made her sick. But she did not waver, and neither did Mikhail. Instead, she sensed him guide his horse to one side, and she turned with him, so that his destruction began to work its way down the side of the road toward the back of the train. She tried not to think of the rear of the caravan, where there was no protection for the fighters and the Renunciates. She knew that there were people back there who were dying in the service of the Hasturs. Swords were little use against blasters, but she felt them bravely fighting on regardless.

The sound of the battle began to change, and, as if from a great distance, Marguerida realized that what remained of the enemy had only one thought in its communal awareness—*get away!* Neither she nor Mikhail had imagined how terrifying the manifestation of their power would be to the Federation troops. She heard the occasional sizzle of blaster fire, here and there, between the burning trees, but even as she listened, it became less frequent.

The battle at the front of the train was over almost before it began. A few more were caught in the continuing energy of Mikhail's matrix. Those who escaped it were hacked down by the guardsmen, or were trapped by the fire. She could hear their mental chorus of despair and disbelief as they perished. These men were stunned by the turn of events, humbled even as they died.

From within the smoke and flames Marguerida saw a mounted man, riding toward the fight, his face still concealed. She sensed his mind, his purpose, and worse, his fatality. It was only for a moment, and she wondered if he would turn away. Instead, he rode directly into the glare of Mikhail's destruction, raising a gloved hand in a kind of salute as he turned to ash. There was a last thought, strong enough to penetrate her senses even in the chaos. *At least an honorable death.*

Mikhail moved his hand slightly, and the protective shield around them started to diminish. Marguerida felt the withdrawal of energy, the painful loss of the tremendous intimacy that they had shared during the brief battle, and then only her own weariness. She closed her eyes, focused on clearing her channels, and slowly felt the exhaustion drop away, to be replaced by ravenous hunger of a sort she had not experienced in years. Then, before she was prepared for it, the shock and grief struck her. So many good men had died in the short minutes of the battle, and more were going to.

Without a word, she pushed aside the emotion, and saw that Mikhail was dismounting, followed by Donal, who was ghastly pale. Two Guardsmen protested this action, but Mikhail was already walking toward the slumped bodies of those who had been outside the circle of his protection. He bent over a fallen Guard, then knelt on the ground beside him, while Donal hovered at his back, vigilant even in his slowly diminishing terror.

The movement of a horse alongside her as she began to swing out of the saddle to join Mikhail seemed perfectly normal, and Marguerida barely noticed it. Then she realized that Francisco Ridenow was riding toward Mikhail, lifting his sword, a look of hatred on his pale face. Donal started to turn at the sound of hooves behind him, but not quickly enough. In a second he was down on the ground, trying to avoid being trampled.

Before she could move, or even try to use the Command Voice to stop Francisco's attack, Marguerida saw another movement from the corner of her eye. Rafael Hastur's horse thundered forward and he brought the hilt of his sword down on the head of the Ridenow lord so hard there was an audible crack. The man swayed in his saddle, clutching at the pommel with his free hand, then swung around to bring the blade of his sword down on the neck of Rafael's horse, missing the rider's knee by a few inches. The horse shied and screamed, beginning to fall.

Donal scrambled to his feet, his face dripping blood. She saw the young paxman brush his eyes clean, and then he drove his sword into Francisco's thigh, screaming, "You traitorous bastard!"

Then a half dozen Guardsmen surrounded *Dom* Francisco, and one of them knocked him out of the saddle. He lay unconscious, blood spilling from his leg, and Donal, furious and swaying, raised his weapon to finish what he had begun.

"No!" The word sprang from Marguerida's mouth without thought.

Donal hesitated, and one of the Guardsmen dismounted quickly and bent over the fallen lord. He looked up at her. "You want him alive, *domna*, or should we let him bleed to death?"

Mikhail pushed between Donal and the Guardsman, his face grim and pale. He studied Francisco for a moment, then knelt down beside him. Without a word, he placed his hand above the wound, the light glittering from the facets of his ring in the red light from the fire behind him. Within the space of a few seconds the bleeding had begun to slow. "I want him alive," he told the Guard. "Death is too easy an escape."

"If you say so, *vai dom*, if you say so." The Guard seemed disappointed.

Marguerida looked down at Francisco, and the entire scene became surreal, as if she could not really grasp what had just happened. Kate had been right. As she tried to grapple with her inner confusion, she felt an agitation bloom at the edge of her mind. It was faint at first, and then it penetrated the cloudiness within her. She turned and stared toward the back of the funeral train, toward the carriages, and felt her heart tighten terribly. She could see movement, the rush of fighters back and forth, punctuated by the occasional wild flare of blaster fire. A clutch of fear seized her guts, twisting them.

Domenic! Mikhail's head snapped toward her, and then she started to run through the milling horses and men, past the great flat wagon where the body of Regis Hastur lay in his coffin. A broad chest rose before her eyes, clad in the blue of the Hastur Guards, and she pushed her right hand into it and shoved with all her weight. Despite his greater heft, the man went down on his bottom into the dirt, making a noise as the air was knocked out of him. Behind her, she could sense Mikhail following, and several others trying to make certain he was safe.

Her mouth was dry, and her blood was hammering in her veins so loudly she barely heard the shouts around her. All she could think of was to get to her son as quickly as possible.

By the time she reached the carriage, she was gasping for breath. The door was open, and a pair of legs hung down to the ground. Marguerida moved around the door and peered inside. Domenic looked back at her, his eyes very wide and his face a sickly white. In his hand there was a short dagger, smeared with blood. The torso and head of a man lay sprawled at Nico's knees, a wound in his thick neck. Katherine was shrunk back into the far corner and Herm was trying to staunch a flow of blood from his left shoulder.

"He didn't think a boy was any danger," Nico muttered dazedly, and then vomited up the excellent lunch he had eaten an hour or so before onto the bloody floorboards. The dagger slipped from his fingers and Marguerida swept him into her arms, hugging him fiercely.

Katherine slid across the bench toward her husband. With a sharp movement, she yanked the undersleeve from her chemise, pulling like a madwoman until the stitches gave way. She dragged the torn sleeve out from beneath her tunic and tied it above the wound as fast and tightly as she could, swearing and crying at the same time. Herm was only half conscious, but he kept muttering that he was all right.

Marguerida swallowed hard, assured herself quickly that her son had come to no physical harm, and crawled onto the back of the dead man, her knees pressing against the still warm flesh beneath the clothes. "Here, let me help, Kate."

"What can you do?" shrilled the other woman, appealing to her with stricken eyes.

"You would be surprised," she answered, calmness claiming her so suddenly she wondered where her fear had gone. The makeshift tourniquet had slowed the flow of blood, but Herm's arm was a gory, terrible sight. "Get out of my way!"

Katherine stared at her for a moment, looked as if she would not move, then drew back. Marguerida leaned toward Herm, lifted her still bare left hand, and closed her eyes. By Aldones, she was tired! It felt like an eternity before she could locate the vessels that had been damaged. The cut had missed the artery by no more than a breath, but the wound was bleeding badly.

"What are you doing?" Kate shouted, frightened and furious at the same time.

"Let her be," Domenic yelled back, then spewed again.

"It is all right, Kate," came Mikhail's voice from behind Marguerida. She knew he was standing at the open door of the carriage now, and she felt his weariness as well as her own.

Marguerida tried to close her mind to the sounds around her, the braying of the frenzied mules, the shouts of Guardsmen and Renunciates. That was easier that shutting out Katherine's panic, Nico's horror, and her husband's concern. It seemed to take forever, but at last she managed to focus on nothing but Hermes-Gabriel Aldaran, and for a time, she was isolated with him. She lifted her matrixed palm and moved it across the severed flesh, cauterizing the wound. Momentarily she felt herself falter, and then felt Mikhail support her until she had the strength to complete the task at hand. It would need to be cleansed and sutured, but for now she had stopped the bleeding.

Marguerida finally realized she was kneeling on a corpse, and she drew herself onto the bench beside her son. Her face was covered with sweat, and her hands were trembling. She drew her sleeve across her brow, and caught a whiff of her own fear-charged sweat and the blood on her hands. She wrinkled her nose in disgust. Katherine was staring at her, her own hands covered with Herm's blood, her skin a shade of white

Marguerida had never seen before. "He will be all right, Kate, until a healer can clean him up," she managed to croak.

She was too tired to move, but the noisome atmosphere of the carriage was nearly unbearable. She wanted to get out of the carriage more than anything, but her body refused to move. Then Marguerida saw a pair of strong hands grasp the heels of the dead man still lying on the floorboards, covered with vomit and blood. They yanked hard, and the corpse began to move away. There was a dull, sickening sound as the body hit the earth, and she felt her gorge rise. She swallowed hard, forcing her lunch to stay in her belly, as the door on the opposite side of the carriage was pulled open.

She saw a Guardsman and one of the Renunciates there, eyes anxious. She heard the sound of the dead body being dragged aside, and then Mikhail leaned inside. Herm groaned and opened his eyes slowly. He tried to lean forward and gave a gasp of pain. Katherine leaned forward and put her bloodied hands under his arms, supporting him as much as she could.

"Get him out and bring a stretcher," Mikhail ordered the Guard on the other side of the vehicle. "Lady Katherine, you might get down now, so it will be easier to reach Herm." When she did not move, he spoke more sharply. "Ease him back onto the bench and get out!"

She stared at him dumbfounded, and then she slowly moved her husband against the seat and clambered down. "I am never going to get into a carriage again! Never!" Then she started sobbing.

The carriage rocked as the Guardsman climbed in, and the Renunciate reached over and took Herm's upper body. It took only a few seconds to remove him from the close quarters, but it seemed a very long time to Marguerida, still sitting on the bench, too tired to stir.

"Don't worry, Mother. That's Danila, and Aunt Rafi says she is a good healer." Domenic gave a rather hysterical laugh. "She's been wanting to get her hands on Uncle Herm for days now. Come on. Let's get out, too. Here, I'll help you."

A hand grasped hers, and then a slender arm encircled her waist. Marguerida smelled her son's flesh as he pulled her against him, the filthy odor of his breath so near her face nearly oversetting her again. Beneath that the scents of fear and sweat were mingled with woodsmoke and the faintest hint of mountain lavender in the fabric of his clothing. For the first time in her life, she leaned on her firstborn and allowed him to help her to her feet. He was safe, and that was all that really mattered.

Once they were out of the carriage, Domenic did not release his hold on her, but kept his arm around her, as if he knew she would collapse if he let go. Then Mikhail swept both of them into his arms, and she leaned her head against his broad shoulder. The three of them stood there, surrounded by armed men, and the cries of the injured. Something was missing, and after a moment of flogging her tired brain, Marguerida realized that the sound of blaster fire was gone.

Reluctantly, Mikhail released her. "How did that man get into the carriage?" he demanded, his voice angry but sure.

"He broke through our ranks and then fell to the ground, *vai dom*. We . . . I thought he was dead, and there was so much going on. . . ."

"I see," Mikhail answered, unconsciously mimicking a tone that Regis had used when he was displeased. He glanced around at the bodies of both Terranan and Darkovans that were scattered across the ground. "He was a bit cleverer than his friends. Are you all right now, *caria*?" There was a curt quality to his voice, one she had never heard him use before, and she gave him a sharp look. Then she realized that he was holding himself together by will alone, and that he needed her to be strong.

"Yes, Mik, I am better now." She lied, and knew it. He probably knew it as well, but he just nodded and gave her a firm squeeze on the shoulder. Nico was still beside her, his arm around her waist, and she looked into his face. It was the same familiar one she knew so well, but he was not the same person who had greeted her a few hours before in Carcosa. The boy was gone forever. Now he was a man. She felt grief, a stab of loss, for a moment, and wished she could call back the innocent child she loved. But it was too late for that.

The sky overhead went dark, and Marguerida looked up, to find the sun shadowed by great black clouds. The wind quickened, gusting around them, fanning the flames on the hillside. Something darker than the clouds came out of the sky, a jagged mass of movement. Carrion crows, a flock of hundreds of the birds, swooped down from the heavens, drawn by the smell of blood and death from who knew where. One, bolder than the rest, hopped down onto the body of the man that Nico had killed and darted a sharp beak into the soft flesh of the face.

Then the storm hit, and rain began to sweep across the devastation on the road and the hillside beyond it. The wind drove the rain against her skin, and she was drenched almost at once. It moved quickly, the wind pushing the torrent forward in a steady line, a downpour that lasted a mercifully brief time before beginning to slacken off. It soaked the burning trees, the dead and the living, washed the blood from the ground, and then scudded away to the east, leaving behind only a few sporadic showers. The fires were out, and a good thing they were, for the survivors had no stamina left to battle a raging forest fire.

"Father, there are still some people up at the top of the hill."

Mikhail nodded, rain dripping off his face. He turned around and found his brother Rafael and Donal at his back, soaked and silent as shadows. "Rafael, will you take charge of rounding up the survivors? Your Terran is good enough to manage, I think. Get them sorted out as fast as you can. We'll send them back to Thendara with the wounded."

"Why don't we just leave them to die of lung fever?" Rafael Lanart-Hastur was only half jesting. "No, I suppose that would be barbaric."

"There is still a flyer up there, and if they gather their wits, they can escape," Nico told his uncle.

"I saw a flyer leave just before the fighting started," Marguerida said, her voice almost as rough as the caw of the carrion crows that were trying to get at the bodies of the dead.

"That was Vancof, Mother. I caught his thoughts as he took off—he killed Granfell and left for HQ." Nico shuddered. "What a horrid mind he has."

Rafael turned and signaled to some of the Guards, then walked away and started up the ruined hillside. The rain had put out the fires, and there were dozens of bodies visible now. Marguerida watched them, remote and unfeeling for a moment.

Marguerida! The sharp intrusion of Lew Alton was like a slap in the face. *Are you all right?*

I wish people would stop asking me that! No, but I am alive, and so are Mikhail and Domenic.

That is very good to know, daughter. If anything had happened . . .

A great many things happened. Father, but I am too tired to tell you right now. She tried to order her brain into rational thought. *There will be several carriages of captives and wounded coming into Thendara later. Including Francisco—he tried to kill Mikhail, the damn fool!*

He what? No, don't tell me. It will keep. I will see to everything at this end, child. Be safe and come back to me as soon as you can.

I will, Farther. If this nightmare ever ends.

Marguerida felt the contact with her father terminate, and turned to her husband. She reached out and slipped her unmatrixed hand through his arm. They stood, shoulder to shoulder in the drizzling rain, silent and lost in their separate thoughts. At last he turned and looked into her face, and she saw a peculiar light in his eyes that had never been there before.

"I never imagined how terrible battle could be," he said gruffly, as if he was almost ashamed of his feelings. "And I will never forgive the Federation for this cowardly attack."

Marguerida shook her head. "It wasn't the Federation, Mik. It was a few men with more ambition than good sense. And speaking of cowardly attacks, let's not forget *Dom* Francisco."

He groaned softly, and tears began to trickle from the corners of his eyes. "I can't bear to think about that betrayal right now!" He swallowed several times, trying to bring himself to speak, as if he could not stand to be silent but had no words. At last he managed, "I never thought I would use my powers . . . the way I did. I turned men into dead things, bare of any dignity. And other men, good men I have known for much of my life, died to keep me alive. I don't know if I can live with what I did, Marguerida."

"Mik . . ."

Having begun, Mikhail could not stop the anguished words. "I never really understood why Regis feared me, why my own mother and those others . . . now I do. And it is breaking my heart. I never should have brought . . ."

Marguerida understood, but she knew that she could not let her husband continue in this way. Later, they would both sort out the pain within them, but not now! "Stop it! You did what had to be done, Mikhail."

"Did I? Did I really? Are you sure I was not just trying to prove myself or some other. . . ."

"Mikhail Hastur—you are a good man and you will make a fine ruler for Darkover, but not if you tear yourself to pieces over things that it is too late to change."

"Donal was right in the end." The tears had stopped slipping down his cheeks and he seemed calmer.

Marguerida stared at her husband, bewildered and trying to make sense of his words, her mind confused by his sudden change of mood. "What?"

"Kill them all and let the gods sort it out," came the voice of the young paxman, still standing nearby. Domenic cast a look of admiration at his kinsman and the start of a grin played across his face.

Mikhail's shoulders slumped for a second, and then he straightened his spine and looked almost serene, as if he had passed through some inner conflict. "None of us will ever forget this day," he whispered. "As long as I am alive, I will remember what I did and why—but it hurts, *caria.*" *I am heartsick and tired, but I must not hesitate. I have a world to protect, and I swear that I will do so, no matter how great the cost. I only pray that I am not taking on more than I can endure.*

26

The following day dawned chill and cheerless. After a silent breakfast of hot porridge and fried cakes, the much diminished funeral train set out from Halstad. The little village about six miles beyond the site of the battle had been stunned at the incursion of almost two hundred people the night before, and it had been almost amusing to watch them scurry around, attempting to provide accommodations for so many. The inn had only three sleeping rooms in it, and lacked many of the other amenities of the Crowing Cock, including the bathing room. Instead, Halstad used a communal facility for the entire village. Far into the night the weary travelers had taken their turns, washing away the stench of sweat, ash and blood from their bodies, while the dazed villagers brought loads of firewood to keep the tubs warm.

It had been a numb evening, punctuated by brief attempts at conversation which trailed off in mid-sentence, as if the speakers could not recall what they intended to say. *Dom* Gabriel had drawn Domenic to his side, and kept him close, with Illona always near him. The safety of his other grandfather had begun to ease the roil of his emotions, to release the horror of killing a man. Domenic was sure it should not bother him as much as it did—the man had been an enemy and a stranger. But, it did, and after an hour, he had decided that his feelings were probably natural rather than morbid. Slaying another was not a casual act. He thought of Vancof, who had killed the nameless fellow in Carcosa, then Granfell just before the battle, without, it seemed, the least hesitation. It likely did not bother the man's conscience at all. No, it was better to sorrow over the dead soldier than to pretend it had not mattered.

Domenic was aware that he was not alone in his confused emotions, for everyone around him was experiencing something very similar. His father was the worst, wracking himself with a kind of savage guilt that made the young man cringe each time he caught the edge of his thoughts. He had killed one person, but Mikhail had slain dozens. How much more terrible it must be for him!

Sleep had helped, crowded into a wide bed with Dani, Danilo, *Dom* Gabriel and Uncle Rafael. Illona had gone with Rafaella, to sleep with the Renunciates in their tents, and he suspected she was glad to be out of doors rather than within the crowded inn. Mercifully, he had not dreamed of the dead soldier, or if he had, he did not remember it.

But Domenic was hardly refreshed as he rode beside his mother, on a better horse than the one Herm had brought him at the start of their sad adventure. He was already missing his new uncle, who had gone back to Thendara with the rest of the wounded, the captured techs and surviving soldiers. He was still unsettled, and although his mood was not as bleak as the previous night, Nico could sense the inner darkness lurking in the corners of his mind, waiting to emerge. It would take a great deal more than food, rest, and dry clothes to ease the impact of a blade thrust into living flesh.

The road curved to the west now, and beside it there were huge stands of trees, hardwoods and conifers. He breathed in the scents of the woodland, and tried to listen to the calls of the birds or the rustling of small animals. Instead, all he could hear was the rough sound of the air in his lungs, and the subtle groan of the world. He wanted to get off his horse, put his feet on the ground, and fall into a trance with the incredible murmur of the earth—to forget everything that had happened to him since he had sneaked out of Comyn Castle.

Part of him was very glad he had discovered the plot against his father, but another portion of his mind sincerely wished he had continued to be a dutiful son and stayed home. Domenic knew he had done well, had kept his head in a tricky situation. He had saved his father's life, and he was now a man. Still, he felt miserable inside, and it was not just because he had killed a man. The night before he had assumed it was only that, but as he looked at the trees, he realized that there was a great deal more bothering him than murder.

But what? A niggle of thought was trying to force itself up from the depths of his mind, and after a minute, Domenic realized he was trying very hard to avoid it—that he was pushing whatever it was down with as much energy as he could muster. What thought could cause him such anguish?

Then, as if he had surrendered by merely asking himself the question, realization blossomed in his mind. He did not want the future which lay ahead of him—to return to Thendara, to live in Comyn Castle, and prepare to wait out the decades until he assumed his father's position. As deeply as he loved his parents, the idea of spending every day with them for what felt like an eternity was unbearable. But, he had to do his duty, didn't he?

It was more than a sudden rebellion. He had been trying for months to find some way out of the prison that Comyn Castle had come to be. Ever since he had begun hearing the voice of the world, he had wanted to be in another place, somewhere very quiet perhaps, without the constant bickering of the only home he had ever known. But Mikhail would never permit him to go away, would he?

His chest ached, and Domenic noticed that he was holding his breath. He released his lungs and drew the sweet, clean air into him, almost gasping. Marguerida gave him an inquiring look but did not speak. Instead she waited for him, as she often did, to tell her what was the matter.

His mind raced, trying to find some starting point, so he would not sound like a whining child. Instead, his thoughts dashed off in what felt like several unrelated directions, leaving him more confused than he had ever been in his life. What was he doing—what was he supposed to do? Duty warred with desire, making the previous day's battle seem unimportant by comparison. And then he *knew*, as if the doubts had never existed, that his future was his own to choose. Domenic went from uncertainty to sureness between two breaths, and the oppressive weight that had plagued him vanished as if it had never been.

He had to discover why he could hear the heart of the world burning, why his *laran* was so different from anyone else's. It was so simple—why hadn't he understood sooner? It did not matter that he was the heir, that he had duties and obligations to his father. He was possessed by a greater duty, to the entire planet.

An astonishing bubble of laughter rose in his chest. What vanity! He was only a boy, really, and he had no business even thinking about abandoning his obligations for a hut in the woods. That was ridiculous! And yet . . . and yet. . . .

No, not a woodland retreat, not for him. He would not last out the winter on his own, and he knew it. But there must be somewhere he could find to sort out all the muddle in his mind and heart, where he would not always be yearning for his tempestuous cousin Alanna and subject to the fury of his grandmother. But where?

Nico frowned for a second. Then his brow cleared, and once again the answer was obvious. There was a place where he could study and contemplate, and he was annoyed that it had not occurred to him sooner. He would go to Neskaya, for surely, if anyone could help him puzzle out this mystery, it must be Istvana Ridenow. But how was he going to get his mother to agree to such a plan? She was so glad to have him safely back, her first and most beloved child, and she would resist another separation with all the will she possessed. And his father would as well, he suspected.

Domenic glanced at her, and found she was still waiting for him to speak, that her golden eyes were watching him tenderly. He saw the lines along her mouth, her sorrow and tension, her grief at Regis' passing, and at the deaths of both the Darkovans and the Terranan the previous day. He marked the stubborn line of her jaw, and felt himself hesitate again. She was a loyal ally and a fearsome opponent. But he had to try to convince her, and it must be now. It would not wait for a more convenient moment, or another time. He took a long, deep calming breath.

Mother, I am not going back to Thendara.

What? Don't be silly, Nico—what are you talking about! Haven't you had enough excitement for the moment? She seemed a bit surprised by his announcement, and underneath it there was a sense of irritation. He felt dismissed, a child speaking childish things, and it angered him a little. He gritted his teeth and forced himself to restrain his mild anger—he would *make* her listen and understand!

It is not a matter of excitement, because I think the last few days will last me for a lifetime. But I can't go back to Comyn Castle and be shut in again.

Nico, no one is going to shut you in. That was Regis' way, and it is not your father's. What has gotten into you?

Mother, you just don't understand!

Of course I don't—mothers never understand. I remember telling Dio that she didn't, but I think now she just knew better than I did what was best for me, Domenic. Things are much too unsettled for now for you to start traipsing around Darkover. The mental tone was patient and indulgent at the same time.

I have no intention of traipsing anywhere. What I want is to go to Neskaya and study with Istvana. Aunt Rafi and some of her sisters can guide me there, right after we bury Uncle Regis. And I will take Illona with me, because she must get some training, and she is not going to cooperate with people she does not know. She trusts me, I think, and will come along with me. That was an idea that popped into his mind without warning, and all he could say about it was that it felt right.

Hold your horses, young man! If you want to study with Istvana, we can have her return . . . but you can just put any idea of gallivanting off out of . . .

Mother, I will not go back to Thendara!

Nico, I am much too tired to have this discussion right now. I don't know why you are—

This is not a discussion—it is a demand. And if you refuse to let me do what I feel I must, then I will just run away at the first opportunity. He wasn't certain of this, but it sounded like a good threat.

Yes, I suppose you might try to do that. She turned away and her shoulders slumped a little. *And you might even succeed. Why, Nico, why?*

I must have some peace and quiet! I cannot endure another day of endless bickering and petty jealousies. Domenic could feel his control slipping away, his fear and anger destroying his discipline. At the same time, the murmur in the heart of the world begin to resound in his mind's ear, familiar and almost comforting. The volume seemed to increase, and for a brief moment he was aware of nothing but the creaks and groans of the planet. Peace and quiet might be an impossible goal, but he was sure that if he didn't discover why and how he heard these things, and soon, he would cease to function. He was not even certain that Neskaya was the best place to go, but Istvana was reknowned for her innovative techniques, and he trusted her. It was the only idea he could come up with at the moment.

Why should you be spared what the rest of us have to endure, son? Be reasonable. We have to settle a great many things, and you will be needed at your father's side. Next spring, perhaps, if you still feel the same way, or the year after. This is not the best time.

Mother, if I wait for a best time, I will be in my dotage! There is never going to be a good time for me to do what I know I must do, and I am not going to argue about it. If you and Father will not let me do this, then I will take off on my own! And likely break my neck in a mountain pass or something equally fatal!

Marguerida turned and glared at him. *Aren't you being rather dramatic?*

Domenic was enraged by this remark, and his heart pounded in his chest. Sweat popped out from his forehead, in spite of the chill of the day, and he had to force himself not to start to shake. He had to make her see! Without considering the consequences, he deepened the rapport with his mother, and allowed the steady roar ringing in his mind to reach her. Unprepared, Marguerida gasped and swayed in her saddle, then clutched her forehead, dropping the reins against the horse's neck.

He reached out and grasped her arm before she could fall, while he pulled back the surge of energy, a mixture of anger and the noise of the world. It was almost too much for him, trying to master so many diverse things at once, and he was ashamed of himself for losing control. Mikhail turned and reached out to steady his wife from the other side, looking puzzled and concerned.

"What is it, *caria?*"

"Nothing. Nothing. Just a slight giddiness. I am fine." She plucked up the reins again, righted herself firmly in the saddle, and gave Domenic a look that would have turned him to stone only a few weeks before. *What the hell did you do? What was that . . .?*

I am not absolutely sure what it is, Mother. But if I don't find out, I'll lose my mind.

Marguerida bent her head and fell into a silent reverie. At last she announced with an air of resignation, *I know that sound, although I only heard it once before, and much more distantly.*

You know what it is? He was amazed, and vastly relieved at the same time. How could she know?

Yes, I do. It is the heart of the world, seething and roaring. Oh, Nico! I touched it once, long ago, before you were even conceived, and only for a moment, although it felt like much longer. Do you hear it all the time?

Mostly. Sometimes it is fainter than now, but it seems to have been getting louder lately. I was afraid to tell you, that you would think I was insane.

Is this what has been disturbing you? I just thought it was your feelings for Alanna . . . I feel rather foolish, son. Her mind seemed to clear, as if she was discarding everything irrelevant in a rush of concentration, holding back a tendril of fear that tried to claim her.

You mean that you misjudged me? Well, I do have feelings for Alanna, and they do nearly drive me mad, but I am sane enough to understand the difference between a hopeless desire and what is possible. Being near her makes it harder, because I have to commit so much energy to keeping my lusts in order that I have less to use for . . . this heart of the world stuff. I have loved Alanna since I was a child, but I have always known that no matter how I felt, she could never be anything except a beloved sister and cousin. More, I understand that having been raised with her, my feelings might not be exactly what I imagine them to be—simply because I haven't met very many girls who were not my relatives. I need to be away from Alanna, for her sake and mine, and I must be away from Grandmother Javanne and all the rest of them, too!

You are much wiser than I suspected, son, and that makes me feel very old, Nico. And inadequate. I feel as if I have missed several important things, that I was not paying you sufficient attention. Arilinn will not do?

No. I don't think so. Istvana has known me since I was in diapers, Mother, and there is no one I can imagine who is better equipped to help me learn about this part of myself. Even Valenta Elhalyn does not have the experience to guide me, and there is no one else at Arilinn that I can think of who might be able to understand what this new . . . new Gift is. I might be able to move mountains, although I surely hope that is not the case.

Goodness! That hadn't even crossed my mind! A new Gift. Yes, I can see now. We can't have you cracking the foundation stones of Arilinn, can we?

That is not nearly as funny as you think it is, Mother!

Now, Nico, after all these years, you must know that my first response to any crisis is to make jokes. How severe you can be. I think I do not know who you are anymore, which is a terrible admission for a mother to have to make. Very well. We will send you to Neskaya, although I doubt that Istvana will thank me for it, and you can take Illona with you. I was foreseeing trying to foster her, and to be entirely honest, I was not looking forward to it.

Domenic felt her organize her thoughts with an abruptness that was rather startling to observe. Had she always been so ruthless? Probably—he was her child, and he had never really thought about all the decisions she must have made over the decades, the adult choices that he was only now starting to understand, and he knew she must have always possessed this keenness of mind and spirit. *And will you explain it to Father?*

Hmm . . . I am tempted to make you do that yourself, but Mikhail has so many other things on his mind at present that he would not listen as well as he might. Yes, I will tell him. It is going to break his heart a little, son, for he feels he has lost you already to Hermes, and to lose you again to Istvana will be a hard blow.

Lost me to Uncle Herm?

I'll explain it to you another time, Nico. Now, let me have some quiet, so I can marshal my arguments.

Yes, Mother—and thank you!

You are a good son, Domenic—the best. I would do anything for you except what . . . you have just asked of me. I would rather give you a moon than let you . . . Marguerida gave a gusty sigh and he saw that she was blinking tears away fiercely. His father's was not the only heart that looked to be rent, and for a moment, he wished he had not chosen the course he had. Then the feeling passed, and he rode on, at ease for the first time in months.

The strange pink grass that grew around the *rhu fead* shimmered with dew, and the large yew trees that stood like sentinals nearby rustled in the wind. Beyond the grass, Domenic could see the shifting coils of Lake Hali, where he had gestated in his mother's womb, for the first time in his life. It was eerie, and the people standing beneath the solemn trees and on the ever-rosy grass were uncomfortable.

The long wagon which had carried Regis' bier from Thendara had been rolled close to the building itself, a modest structure of stone on which no moss gathered nor ivy twined. Between the tall yews and the shrine there were a number of mounds, also covered with the remarkable pink grass. Close to the building, they had sunk down into the earth, while those farther away were more prominent. No gravestones stood at the head of the mounds, but these were the graves of the Hasturs, centuries of rulers immured in earthy anonymity.

At the far end of the row of mounds, one stood out, barely sunken yet. Even though no one had told her, Marguerida knew this was the resting place of Danvan Hastur, the grandfather of Regis, dead for nearly half a century. Beside it, the earth had been opened, and there was a deep hole, waiting for the most recent arrival. She had an eerie feeling, looking at the unmarked burial places, knowing that Mikhail would one day be laid there to become part of the mystery that was Hali.

She trembled, remembering how near he had come to joining his uncle beneath the grass. In all the hectic activity on the road, Marguerida had managed to put the traitorous attack of Francisco Ridenow out of her mind, but now it returned, playing in her mind's eye like a terrible dream. True, not a hair of her husband's head had been touched, but the nearness of death made her think of what might have happened. And he had spared the man's life, which was right and merciful, but was going to create a difficult problem in the future. Clearly *Dom* Francisco could not be allowed to continue as head of the Ridenow Domain—Cisco would take his place—but then what?

Marguerida forced herself to stop trying to find the future—it would manifest itself no matter what she did or thought. Instead, she turned her attention back to her surroundings. Guardsmen stood on the rosy grass arrayed in a long rank on either side of the coffin. The wind rustled the yews, making a pleasant sound, and somewhere a bird sang a haunting melody. Everything seemed very still, as if time itself was waiting.

She watched Mikhail, his eyes red with weeping, grasp the handle on one side of the coffin at the front while Danilo Syrtis-Ardais took the other. Behind them, Donal Alar and *Dom* Danilo Hastur lifted the back, and together, the four men moved away from the wagon toward the open grave. The wind shifted, and the scent of Lake Hali drifted across the ancient site, cooling her cheeks and bringing back memories of another time.

Marguerida watched the white-clad Servants of Aldones follow them. They were the same men who had officiated at the public ceremony two days before, and she knew they had left Thendara as soon as their duties were done, and had returned to Hali well ahead of the funeral train, without encountering any troubles. She envied them the quiet of their journey.

When the pallbearers reached the freshly dug grave, they shifted their stances slightly. Bracing their feet against the soft ground, they carefully lowered the coffin into the hole. She could see their muscles straining as they hefted their weighty burden. Then they knelt and bowed their heads as the Servants moved forward.

The first Servant advanced, a young man scarcely older than Domenic. He bore a silver basin in one hand and a bunch of flowers in the other. Solemnly he dipped the heads of the flowers into the water and flicked glistening drops over the coffin.

"In the name of Evanda I bless you, bright mother who brought you to birth and smiled on your deeds. May they live always in the springtime of our memories."

The oldest of the remaining Servants followed him, casting handfuls of sand. It made a sweet rattling sound as it struck the wood of the casket. "In the name of Zandru, He who limits life and binds the days, I claim your bones. Earth to earth and dust to dust you shall remain . . ." A shiver passed through the mourners at these words, for few spoke that name lightly except in curses. The crowd shifted from foot to foot, and then the third Servant began his approach. He raised a censer, swinging the open-work copper vessel so that smoke billowed over the grave, mingling with the scent from the lake. The sharpness of the smoke stung her eyes, but she barely noticed.

"In the name of Avarra I receive you, for She is the Harvester. In Her dark womb you shall lie, and be transformed."

There was a long silence then, as the smoke wafted over the coffin. In the shadow of the yews, it seemed very dark now, as if the sun were hidden in clouds. The color of the vapor issuing from the censer was almost black against the dimness of the light.

Then, suddenly, there was a bright flash, and a lantern was opened. The brightness that shone forth was eye-searing, and the darkness around the grave receded. "In the Name of Aldones I exalt you!" The fourth Servant's voice rang out triumphantly. "Son of the Son of Light, your spirit shall illuminate the way for those who follow you!"

He stepped back, head bowed. A sigh went through the crowd as everyone realized it was finished, that there were no more words to be spoken. It was so brief and so simple, and yet, what more needed to be said? The emotions expressed were formal and conventional, but deeply meaningful—replete with the history of centuries of tradition. Marguerida felt the release that the words had given, and felt something within her let go at last. She put an arm around Domenic's shoulders and wiped the tears from her cheeks.

"I am going to miss him," she said very softly.

"Me, too. And nothing is ever going to be the same again, is it?"

She laughed slightly then, and tugged at the locks of his hair gently. "Nothing is ever the same, Domenic, no matter how much we wish it will be."

EPILOGUE

Days had passed, then weeks. Autumn had faded and winter had begun to grip Darkover. On an icy morning Marguerida and Mikhail stood on the parapets of Comyn Castle, on a space cleared of the most recent snow. Cold lingered in the swept stones, penetrating into her boots and up under the many flannel petticoats she wore. She barely noticed the discomfort as she drew her heavy cloak more closely around her. Thendara lay beneath them, in a blanket of white, glistening in the sullen light of the sun behind the clouds, but she had no eyes for the city.

Marguerida strained her eyes toward the complex that lay at the limits of her unaided sight. She could just make out the ugly square buildings of HQ, where the Federation had maintained a presence for a hundred years. The large sweeps of tarmac around the structures were covered with snow, and if there were people moving there, they were too far away to be seen except with a farviewer. The only one they had was being quite unfairly hogged by Rory, who was as excited as if this were a glorious occasion, not a difficult complex event. The damn boy was irrepressible.

Nothing was happening yet, and Marguerida let her attention lapse. She thought about what had happened since they returned to Thendara

479

more than forty days before, caught between relief that it was finally over and sorrow at the cost of lives. She was tired to her bones, and depressed as well. Food and rest had restored her body, but her spirit—and Mikhail's—remained despondent. Marguerida could only hope that with the final departure of the Federation, they could begin to return to their normal selves. She knew in her heart that they would not ever be as they had been; that what they had done together on the Old North Road would always be with them, as inescapable as the deaths they had caused.

It had demanded all the discipline they had acquired to endure the days that had followed their return to the city. Instead of a triumphant celebration of victory, there were a myriad of problems to be faced. *Dom* Francisco was healing from his injuries, and Comyn Council had yet to decide just how he would pay for his treachery against Mikhail. There was no question in their minds that he must give up his seat on the Council in favor of his son Cisco, but whether he should be executed or allowed to live remained an issue of lively debate for the future.

They had dealt with the few survivors of the battle on the road, ten techs and half a dozen soldiers, as kindly as they could. She shivered with something more than cold at that memory, for it had violated her standards of ethical behavior more than a little. She and her father had used the Alton Gift in a way that repelled them, to tamper with the memories of the techs and soldiers, so that while they remembered the general events of the fight on the Old North Road, they had no recollection of anything remarkable occurring. No memory of the globe of light that had smote their compatriots so mercilessly remained when they were finished with their vile task. Lew had shaken his head and muttered, "The things I have done for Darkover," and gotten terribly drunk for the first time in years.

The hapless Planetary Administrator, Emmet Grayson, had stepped into the breach left by the capture of Lyle Belfontaine, expressing outrage at the attack on Comyn Castle and exerting himself to make the best of a bad situation. From him they learned that Dirck Vancof had not succeeded in his attempt to escape. When he had put the flyer down on the landing field and stepped out, dressed in native clothing, he had been mistaken for a Darkovan and shot before anyone bothered to ask questions. Marguerida suspected that his well-deserved execution had saved Grayson a great deal of further embarrassment, and wondered to herself if the shooting might not have been more deliberate than accidental.

Then for three weeks after their return, there had been no word from the Federation. The continued silence from the Regional Relay Station had nearly driven Grayson to distraction. When the Administrator had finally received a message, years had dropped from his face. After that, it had only been a matter of helping him organize their departure. Now, all they had to do was wait.

A distant booming sound brought her back to the present with a start, and then there was a bright flare of light. A Big Ship plummeted downward, sending billows of moisture up into the air as the heat of it vaporized the snow on the tarmac. It was a glorious sight, the flare of the landing jets and the smooth black hull of the ship standing out starkly against the whiteness behind it.

When the vapor began to settle, Marguerida could see heavy vehicles start across the field. They rolled over the now snowless tarmac, and she thought she could see ramps being lowered. It was very hard to be sure at this distance. The first carrier reached the ramp and started up, into the belly of the ship, the rest following. It was rather a letdown after all the anticipation. Grayson had organized everything ably, and in half an hour, the last carrier was loaded aboard. Marguerida could not help but wonder what awaited the men and women leaving Darkover. Grayson had let slip a few things about the present state of the Federation that suggested there was a civil war going on in parts of that far-flung comglomeration of planets, that worlds had rebelled against Premier Nagy and the Expansionist forces. She suspected they were lucky that they were being taken away at all, but she knew her information was spotty at best.

The ramps vanished back into the black hull, and for several minutes there was no activity to be seen. The sky was darkening and a few snowflakes began to fall as the little group waited. Then a blaze surrounded the Big Ship for a moment, and it ascended as swiftly as it had come down, lifting away as if it weighed nothing instead of tons and tons. Like a sword of light it rose until it pierced the clouds and was gone from view.

No one spoke for several seconds. "Well, that's the last of them," Roderick announced cheerfully.

Marguerida looked at her redheaded younger son, glad to see that even the most momentous events did not disturb his constant enthusiasm for everything. At least she still had him to cluck over, now that Domenic was with Istvana Ridenow in Neskaya.

"I doubt that, Rory," Mikhail said as sternly as he could, infected by his younger son's high spirits in spite of himself.

"But didn't we throw them out?" the boy persisted.

"Not really—there were complex reasons for their leaving; but that does not mean they will stay away forever, son."

"Father, I think you are being very gloomy. You have been like that ever since you came back. I am sure they are gone for good."

Mikhail looked at Marguerida over Roderick's head, quirking his eyebrows a little. She understood the unasked question, and wished she had an answer. She had no sudden vision of the future, nor had she been plagued by any since their return. It did not mean anything—the Federation or some other force might return after she was dead. It was not a comforting thought, that she and Mikhail might have to leave the problem to their children.

Marguerida turned and started back toward the doorway into the warmth of the castle. "I hope you are right, Roderick," she said.

"Of course I am. Why would they leave if they were only going to turn around and come back?"

"I don't know—but just remember than the Federation has the ability to return if they choose, and we cannot assume anything."

"Oh. Well, I hope they don't, because they are bad people, like that Belfontaine man."

"Not all of them are bad, Rory," Mikhail insisted, then shrugged at the impossibility of explaining the complexities of interstellar politics to a thirteen-year-old.

"And if they do, you can just . . ."

"No, Roderick!"

"But, Father ! Why not? Or is this one of those things I'll understand when I am older again? I am so sick of . . ."

"Yes, Rory," Marguerida interceded. "You are very tired of being told you don't understand. And I am pretty sick of hearing you complain about it. Now let's get something to eat."

She felt Mikhail just behind her, and turned to him, slipping into his arms and feeling the coldness of his cheek against hers. Then, without word or thought, they both looked back, through the open door, at the abandoned buildings on the other side of the city. "What do you really think, *caria*?"

"That this is not the end, that it is not finished."

"Why?"

"I think that as long as there is the technology to travel between the stars, there will always be the chance of visitors, Mik. And if the little we learned from Grayson is accurate, and the Federation itself is coming to pieces, it will not remain in bits forever."

"You sound like your father."

"I know. Someday, someone will come to Darkover from the stars again—it is as inevitable as snow in winter. But that is for another day, another year." She leaned against his shoulder and rested her head. Marguerida could sense the dark tone of his thoughts, and wished she knew some way to brighten his mood. But only time, she knew, would cure what ailed her husband and herself.

He reached a hand out and shut the door to the roof. They turned and started for the stairs, hand in hand, shoulder to shoulder. At last he said, "And we will meet that day when it comes, and not a second before."